Dark Shadows Series

Five Steps Ahead

Ten Seconds Too Late

Against The Clock

FIVE STEPS AHEAD

Samantha Baca

Content Warning:

This book contains language and storylines that may be bothersome for some readers and is intended for a mature audience. Violence and sexual scenes may be shown in detail as well. The reader is encouraged to reach out to the author directly (authorsamanthabaca@gmail.com) if they would like to further discuss the content warning(s) for this book.
Warnings for Five Steps Ahead:

Stalking

Violence

Murder

Sexual content

<u>One</u>
Hannah

Drip. Drip. Drip. The sound of leaking water filled the empty room that smelled of mildew from the dampness in the air. My head hung against my chest as I tried to lift it, the weight of it unbearable. Slowly I forced my head backwards and took a moment to rest as I opened my eyes and looked around. The room was dimly lit with concrete floors and windowless concrete walls with nothing around me other than the wooden chair I had been bound to with rope. I tried to pull at the restraints as the thick rope bit at my skin without giving.

I listened for the sound of the dripping water but couldn't hear it anymore. Did that mean that someone was there with me? My body trembled as I strained to hear any sounds that might tell me where I was or who was there. As I slowly tilted my head forward my eye caught a glimpse of something shimmering on the floor from the dim light that barely hung from the ceiling. I leaned forward as far as the rope would allow as I tried to see what it was. As my head dipped forward toward the ground, I heard the familiar dripping sound once more as I felt something wet trickle down my face. Beneath my chair was a puddle of blood. My blood.

<u>Two</u>

Hannah
21 Days Ago

"Do you want another cup of coffee, Han?" My mother peered at me over the top of the coffee carafe she held up as she awaited my answer.

"I'm good, thanks, mom." I shuffled the papers together that I had been working on for my final project and shoved them in the binder with the other items that I needed to complete before the weekend was over. I sighed as I unplugged my laptop and stuffed it in my backpack along with the binder before zipping it shut.

"Are you off already? I feel like you just got here." Disappointment crossed her face as she noticed my belongings packed up as I tucked my chair back under the wobbly kitchen table that she refused to get rid of. It had been in our family long before I was born and it was needless to say that it was literally on its last leg.

"I have to meet up with my group for our final presentation next week, then I need to finish the three term papers I have due. There's a lot to get done. I'm sorry, mom." I gently reached over and touched her arm before sliding on my backpack and bouncing it against my back as I tried to shift the contents inside to balance the weight. Once situated, I pulled my beanie on and adjusted it so my hair wouldn't be a mess later when I took it off. My hair was thick and full, and always a magnet for attracting static cling, especially with beanies, but it was too cold outside not to wear one.

"You work yourself so hard, I just don't want you to burn yourself out." She sighed as she smiled up at me, sympathy reflecting from her emerald green eyes that I was blessed to get from her. "I'm proud of your drive and ambition, I really am. My baby girl is going to do big things with her life."

I smiled back at her warm smile and leaned in to kiss her cheek. It killed me that I couldn't spend more time with her, even though we both knew that it would happen when I decided to go to school in the city. One of the hardest decisions I ever had to make in the 19 years I had been alive was leaving home right after my father died, and abandoning my mother so I could go to the college that I prayed for years to get accepted to.

The train ride back to the city was relatively quiet as people moved around me over the duration of the 2 hours it took before it reached my stop. I listened as the automated voice announced the next stop and put my notebook and pen back in my backpack as I stood up to get off on the next exit. I was thankful to have had the time on the train to work on one of my term papers but still felt overwhelmed with how much work I needed to get done over the next three weeks.

The ground was snow packed from the recent storm that had moved in while I was at my mom's and I was thankful that it cushioned the slippery ice beneath. Trekking through New York City in the winter was a skill that I hadn't fully developed just yet and never understood the women who would breeze past me in bad weather without losing their footing. Granted I had always been a clumsy person so I couldn't blame it ALL on the weather.

I walked the few blocks to the coffee shop where I was meeting my group and slipped inside the door as a couple was heading out. The wind had started to pick up and I was anxious to get inside and let my body warm up for a few minutes before I had to dive into another school project. I'd learned that the majority of the professors preferred group projects which was a big change compared to high school. I wasn't a fan of working in groups and hated that I was socially awkward. But then again, wasn't your freshman year in college supposed to be all about social awkwardness?

The coffee shop was busy with people at every table and a line that wound its way to the door. I pulled off the brown knit beanie and let my silky brown hair fall down to the center of my back. A wave from the back of the room caught my eye as I made my way to the back table where my group was already sitting. I smiled as I made my way over and stopped in the corner to pull off my backpack and jacket before sitting down to join them.

"Hey, Hannah." Amber pulled a seat around from behind her for me to sit.

"Thanks." I smiled as I slid into the hard metal chair and scooted myself up to the table. Our group was small, only five of us, which helped keep my anxiety down. Amber and I had all of the same classes together, which I was thankful for, so we spent a lot of time together. I looked around the table, noticing that we were still waiting for Joel. I sighed a breath of relief that I wasn't the last one who had kept everyone waiting.

"How was your mom?" Amber asked quietly as the other two from our group talked about a project they were working on for another class.

"She's good. It was nice to see her but this weekend just felt like it went by so fast. I don't feel like I even saw her much while I was there, we were both so busy." I rubbed my hands together while I worked to warm myself up from the brutal cold I had just been in.

"Is she still working at the diner?"

"Yeah. And now she started a second job working at a coffee shop in the morning. She's literally working 10-12 hours a day between both jobs. I wish I could help her with the bills but I can barely afford things here." My chest rose and fell with the heaviness of the burden that I knew my mom had taken on after my dad died. He didn't have life insurance and they were barely getting by when he first got sick. Things just kept getting worse as the months went on with medical bills piling up and my mom having to miss work to be with my dad.

My heart pulled in my chest and I blinked rapidly to force away the tears that threatened to spill over. I missed my dad more than I could have ever imagined I would have. When we found out that he was terminally ill we tried to brace ourselves for what it really meant but no one told me that I would have to learn to live with a heart that was missing a huge piece of it.

Amber offered a sympathetic smile as she patted my hand. Joel made his way over to the table as he squeezed in between the tables and spun a chair around backward before plopping himself into it. He grinned as he tugged off the Yankees beanie that was plastered to his head. He was always late and honestly, I was surprised that he had even bothered to show up.

The hours went by quickly and I glanced up to look around the coffee shop as I noticed it was almost 7:00. I still had a ton of studying to do and had this overwhelming feeling that I would always be behind in this class after struggling through it all semester. Amber looked over and studied my face as I sorted through the notes I had taken and highlighted a few things that I would need to study before the final exam.

"You okay?" Her voice was gentle as she nodded to the notepad that was almost covered in yellow highlighter.

"Yeah, I'm just trying to wrap my head around everything for the final exam. Professor Wright pulled me aside last week and warned me that I needed to do well on the final exam or I might not pass the class." I let out a heavy sigh as I remembered our conversation as I was leaving class.

"Do you have a quick minute, Hannah?"

"Sure."

"I'll make this quick and to the point. I know that it's your first year in college and things feel different than high school, but things move quickly here and it's very easy to go under before you even realize you're in trouble. My advice is to find a study group or a mentor on campus and get the help that you need so you do well in my class. Right now, I don't see you passing unless you really push yourself to learn the material."

"You'll do just fine, Hannah. You're a smart girl." Amber

smiled reassuringly. I wasn't the type of person who had ever been in a study group but I had decided to take his advice and luckily, Amber invited me to join the one that she was in. There was so much more work involved and it made me wonder if I was actually putting in the right amount of effort on my own once I saw how much effort these study sessions required.

I shook my head to try to clear away some of the frustration and get in the right mind set for the somewhat blind date I had agreed to meet here after we were done. I didn't date often and I would usually prefer to go home and freshen up and get ready before a date but with my busy schedule these days there just wasn't any time for that. Amber had talked me into getting on Single2Mingle which was supposed to be a more modern dating website that focused on building a relationship from a friendship. I hadn't been in the city very long before the school semester started so I hadn't made any friends. Amber thought the app would be great for helping me make friends and possibly find a hook up or two.

Amber's eyes locked onto mine as I scanned the room for the guy I was supposed to be meeting. I watched as she wiggled her eyebrows and subtly nodded behind me. Slowly I turned my head as I looked over my shoulder to see a guy sitting at a table a few feet away from us. His head was down as he looked at his phone, his sandy blonde hair falling across his forehead. I couldn't see his face but the black leather jacket fit his body in a way that I could see the definition of his muscles beneath it. A wave of giddiness flowed through me as I waited for him to look up so I could see if I recognized his face.

I felt my phone buzz on the table and looked down to find a message alert on the screen. Excitement coursed through me as I hoped it was my date telling me he was there and to look behind me. I still hadn't gotten a look at the guy's face but part of me hoped it was him.

Disappointment hit me as I read the message that he was running late. I looked at Amber and shook my head no. She gave a half smile as she packed her things into her backpack and stood to leave as she waited for someone to pass by so she could get out. The rest of the group had started to pack up their things and were leaving as well as I rifled through my purse to find my makeup bag. Since he was running late, I had a few minutes to try to freshen up.

I quickly applied a light peach colored lip gloss and added a quick touch of powder to freshen up my makeup. My finger ran under my eyelashes as I attempted to wipe away a rogue eyelash when I felt dark brown eyes watching me in the mirror. My eyes made contact with his and for a moment I got lost in his look. There was a pull that I had never felt before and part of me wanted to go over and talk to him and forget about the date that I was actually waiting for.

"Hannah?" A deep male voice startled me as I jumped in my seat and slammed the compact shut. My hand went to my chest as I looked up at the guy standing in front of me. Tall, husky build, wavy jet-black hair, and a letterman jacket that barely fit the width of his body. He looked exactly like his online picture.

"That's me." I stood up to shake his hand as he pulled me into a bear hug and almost knocked the breath out of me.

"Of course it is, beautiful green eyes and brown hair, with a sexy little body- just like in your profile picture," he whispered in my ear, still holding me in a tight grip.

Out of the corner of my eye I saw the guy behind us lower his head as he tried to stifle a laugh. I waited until he let me out of his embrace before sitting back down and waiting for him to take his seat. He stood behind a chair with his hands on the back of it as he looked at me expectedly.

"Everything okay?" I asked as I looked at him with confusion. He created a nervousness inside of me that I couldn't put my finger on. Maybe it was his over the top aggressive greeting or the fact that he was reluctant to sit down like a normal person.

"Yeah, aren't we going to go get coffee?" He nodded to the line that still wrapped around the tables and was now outside the door.

"Um, yeah, we can do that. I just don't want to lose this table since it's so busy in here." I watched as he looked around, completely oblivious to the number of people there until I mentioned it.

"Oh. Wow. Yeah, one of us should stay and hold the table then I guess." He waited as he watched me to see if I was going to offer to go get the coffee for us. Now I wasn't one of those women who believed that men had to pay for everything and do everything for women, but I did expect a LITTLE bit of romance. A small gesture of some sort. For Pete's sake, it was a $4 coffee, not a steak and lobster dinner. I waited in my seat as I thought about ways to end the date so we didn't have to decide who was going to go get the coffee when I saw him shrug his shoulders and look at me.

"Alright, I'll go stand in the line. Do you want just regular coffee or do you want something fancy?"

"Regular coffee is fine, thank you." I replied through somewhat clenched teeth. This was the worst start of a date I had ever been on and I was kicking myself for listening to Amber when she encouraged me to give him a chance.

"Cool, I'll just tell them I'm with my grandma. They always give old people free coffee." He patted the back of the chair as he walked off and stood at the back of the line.

I slumped back in my chair and tapped my fingers along the table as I contemplated ways to escape without being noticed which was downright impossible given there was only the one entrance at the front, where he was standing, and the emergency exit in the back which would sound off an alarm if I opened the door. I could just see the headline now:

College student flees coffee shop using emergency exit to get away from cheap date!

The line moved quickly as I continued to think of ways to get out of this awful date when I felt someone watching me. Out of the corner of my eye I could swear that the guy behind me was still watching me but as I slowly turned my head in his direction his eyes were glued to his phone while he slowly lifted his coffee cup to his lips. I must be desperate if I thought he was watching me when he was really just there to drink his coffee and look at whatever held his attention on his phone.

A few minutes passed by as Chet made his way back to the table with our drinks. If ever there was anyone clumsier than me, it had to be Chet. He stumbled over the leg of a chair as he tried to maneuver through the packed maze and sat the drinks down on the table with so much force that the coffee in my cup sloshed around and spilled from the closed to-go lid.

"So, Chet, tell me something about yourself." I popped the top off of the coffee and wiped the cup down with a napkin. Deep breaths, I reminded myself as I flicked the sweetener packets he had brought with him before tearing them open and pouring them in as I waited for an answer.

"What do you want to know?" He wrapped his mouth around the plastic straw and pulled a large drink of his frozen coffee through before reaching up and grabbing his head.

"Ahhhh…brain freeze!"

I had to try to control myself as I fought to roll my eyes for fear that they would get stuck in the back of my head. I continued to stir my coffee while I waited for him to recover from the trauma he was suffering at the hands of a $15 drink that was mostly ice. A few minutes passed by with him grunting and holding his head and with each minute my interest in continuing the date faded.

"Woah. Talk about a headache. That one is gonna linger for a bit." He pushed the drink to the side as if its presence offended him.

"Okay, something about myself…ummm…I don't know? What do you want to know? "His face wore the same pouty look that I had seen every time someone asked a child what they learned in school that day. This was definitely not turning out to be a good date.

"Do you have any hobbies? Any extracurricular activities?" I tried to feign interest as I brought the cup to my lips and took a sip of the hot fluid that was already ten times better than this date.

"I don't really do much. School. Play football. Hook up with girls." He smiled after he said the last sentence and looked at me. "A LOT of girls, if you know what I mean."

I couldn't tell if my eyes actually got stuck in the back of my head or if they just felt like they were. How had I ended up on this date? Why hadn't I said no? Then I remembered that I agreed to it because there weren't any other guys wanting to meet me and I had started to feel a little desperate. I looked away, disgusted with myself for still sitting here with this idiot, when I saw him open the dating app on his phone and swipe right. Seriously? He was accepting another date while sitting in front of me? I took a deep breath as I drank the last of my coffee and sat it down on the table.

"Wow. That's great. Really great." I slid my cell phone across the table and tucked it into my pocket. "I'll be right back, I'm going to use the restroom." I stood up before he could say anything and discreetly picked up my backpack as I made my way through the few tables at the back and made my way into the bathroom. It was small but had 3 stalls and two sinks along the vanity with a full-length mirror. Suddenly I didn't feel well and bent over as I splashed my face with cold water.

The room started spinning as my body fought to stay standing. I tried to hold on to the counter as my mind scrambled to make sense of what was happening. I was fine until a few minutes ago. Until I drank the coffee. Panic filled me as I tried to figure out what to do before it was too late. I tried to will myself to reach down and dig my cell phone out of my pocket but I knew that if I let go of the counter, I would fall. My legs felt like they were weighted down and unable to move. Quickly it spread through the rest of my body until I had no choice but to let go as everything turned black around me.

Three

Max
20 Days Ago

"Ma, I don't have time to track her down right now. I'm at work." I ran my hand through my hair in frustration as I stood over my desk, listening to my mom carry on about my youngest sister. "I get it, she's mad and she left. She'll be back, you know that."

I shifted my weight as my mom started rambling on in Italian about Elena and their fight over Elena's new boyfriend that my mom already despised. It wasn't anything new. Elena was the baby of the family and dad always let her get away with everything, much to the frustration of my mom. After seven children, six of them girls, my dad found it was better not to fight about much when it came to Italian American women. Couldn't say that I blamed him.

"Ma, listen, I really have to go. I'll come by later and check on things. Okay?" I grabbed my cell phone off the desk to see Elena's name on the screen. "No ma, I can't just put a warrant out for his arrest because you don't like the guy." I slid my finger over the button to answer my cell phone as I tried to end the call with my mom. "Yeah, okay, I'll see you tonight. Love you too, ma."

I let out a deep breath as I lifted the phone to my ear, waiting to hear my sister's high pitched shriek that she always had when she was upset.

"Hey Leni." I started to pull the phone from my ear in anticipation when I noticed how quiet it was on the other line. A shiver ran down my spine as my gut told me something was wrong.

"Help me." Her voice was a soft whisper but there was no doubt that it was Elena.

"What's wrong?" I sat in my chair and pulled myself into the desk as I unlocked my computer and pulled up the cell phone tracking screen. I could hear faint movements in the background as she stayed silent.

"Leni, where are you?" I asked quietly to make sure whoever she was with didn't hear me.

"I don't know. It's dark. And cold." Her voice was so quiet that each word almost broke off before she could get it out.

"Try to look around and see if anything looks familiar or if you see anything that you can tell me about." I coaxed her as I entered her phone number in the tracking system and waited as it tried to locate it.

"Who's there with you?" I probed as I stared at the spinning circle as the system continued to try to locate her. My years in law enforcement taught me that if it didn't pop up within a few seconds, it wasn't going to pop up. My mom hated

that I went into law enforcement at the tender age of 21 and even 8 years later, she didn't hate it any less.

"I think I'm by myself now." I could hear the fear in her voice and every part of me wished I could figure out where she was and go and save her. "I'm scared Max."

"It's gonna be okay. We're gonna work through this together." I reached for a pen and the notepad on the corner of my desk so I could take down as many notes as possible when I saw the pop-up window confirm no trace was found on her phone. My anger started to rise as quickly as my anxiety as I tried to get out of my own head and think through things like the detective I was supposed to be.

"Are you able to walk around?"

"Yeah."

"Okay, that's good. Do you see any windows? Any light coming through from outside?"

"There aren't any windows. Just a light hanging from the ceiling." Her voice was still low and I wondered if she thought someone was there.

"Keep walking, tell me what you see as you walk."

"There's nothing, Max. It's concrete walls and a concrete floor."

My mind tried desperately to remember when my mom had said that Elena took off so I could try to figure out how much time had passed and narrow down a possible location. It sounded like she was in an abandoned warehouse but there were a ton in our neighborhood so that didn't help much.

"Do you see any-"

"Shhhh!"

I froze as I tried to listen to what was happening as she urgently shushed me before the phone went eerily quiet. Something had startled her and freaked her out and I needed to know what it was. I waited patiently with my ear pressed as hard as possible to the phone.

"No! No! Please! Don't!" I could hear commotion as Elena begged in the background and my stomach clenched as I listened to her. My jaw tightened while my knuckles turned white as my grip on the phone increased. There was a loud sound that I couldn't make out followed by footsteps. I prayed that it was Elena coming back to the phone and that she had fought off whoever was there. I held my breath as I waited for her voice when I heard someone pick up the phone.

"Wrong number." A low voice growled into the phone before it was disconnected.

"Son of a bitch!" I slammed my phone down on my desk as those around me looked up, startled. My body was on edge as adrenaline forced its way through me. I ran a hand down my face over the scruff of my jaw as I tried to calm myself down. There was no way I could just sit there when my baby sister was missing and in trouble. I grabbed my things before I checked out for the day with my team and made my way to my mom's. I hoped she had the answers that I was looking for.

I had been at my parents' house for an hour and felt frustrated that it had taken so long for everyone to sit down and just listen so I didn't have to keep repeating myself. By now all 5 of my sisters and my parents were sitting at the table as they listened to what I had been trying to tell them.

"That's all that I know, so if you have any information about where she's been, who she's been hanging out with or talking to, or what time she left last night - now is the time to tell me." I looked around the dining room table. Time was ticking and I needed them to focus before we lost more valuable time. Every second mattered at this point.

My mom sat at the table with her hands folded in front of her while my dad gently rubbed her shoulders. I knew this was hard for her and that the amount of guilt she had from their fight was blocking her ability to remember anything that had happened before then. There was mumbling around me as my sisters talked quietly in small groups, working to get the information that I had asked for. There were plans to meet up with neighbors and check in with her friends to see if anyone had talked to her but I knew that still wasn't going to get me the information that I needed.

I continued to watch my phone for any calls or messages from Elena but it had been silent ever since our call had been disconnected. My department had started working on the case and still hadn't been able to get an exact location on her cell phone. I knew they were working every angle they had but it didn't help the helpless feeling that continued to eat at me. My head was pounding from the stress of the day, the intensity getting worse from the constant noise in the room. I needed to get away from everything for a few minutes and just clear my head. Allow my instincts to take over. I wandered through the house as everyone stayed focused on their conversations in the kitchen and made my way up to Elena's room.

My parents' house was small for the number of people that lived in it over the years. Growing up we always shared bedrooms until I reached the preteen years and my dad insisted that I needed my own space. They had converted the attic into a room for me and the 6 girls split the two bedrooms while my parents slept in the smaller room of the 3-bedroom house. Over the years as my sisters grew up and started their own lives, they moved out and everyone would shift accordingly. Elena and the 2 younger girls were the last 3 to still live at home and Elena had decided to take the attic so she could have her own space once she started her freshman year of college.

I climbed the ladder that led to the attic and looked around the small space that had once been my sacred space. Clothes were tossed about the back of the chair that sat in front of the makeshift desk holding her laptop. There was a pile of papers and notepads to the left and an empty coffee mug to the right of the computer. Other than that, it was pretty clean. I sat on the edge of the bed as I quickly flicked through the papers, hoping to find something that might be helpful.

Notes from her psychology classes and a to do list for her upcoming finals made up the pile as I sat them back down where I found them. I let out a frustrated sigh as I picked up her laptop and opened it, surprised that she didn't have it set up to require a password to get into it. I had nagged her for years about making sure she had a password to make sure no one could get in, and for once I was thankful that she hadn't listened.

The screen glowed brightly at me as I looked at the login page to her school email account. She had logged out of it but hadn't closed the window. I looked around and found a few other open windows as well, all of them school related with search results related to psychology. I was about to close the laptop when I looked down and saw a chat text box in the bottom right corner of the screen.

I moved the mouse over and clicked on the button to enlarge it to full screen as I scrolled up to the top of the messages. Along the top was a banner for an online dating website, a new one that I wasn't familiar with. I personally hadn't used any online dating websites but I knew that a few of my sisters had used them. I leaned back against the wall as I pulled out my phone to get a few pictures of the screen in case I needed it later for the investigation.

My sister's user name was shown as EROM31802 with a picture of her from her senior trip to DC last year as her profile picture. There was a lengthy conversation between her and a user named 5StepsAhead that started last night around 10:30. There wasn't a profile picture for the other account so I assumed it was a guy, though I didn't know why she would be talking to a guy that didn't have a profile picture. Had I not taught her anything?

I scrolled through the messages after taking down the information I needed and felt disappointed when there wasn't much in the conversation that was helpful. A lot of basic questions about how school was going and if they were ready for winter break. Maybe this was someone from one of her classes? But why would she be talking to them on a dating website? Why not email or text? From the tone of the messages it didn't seem like she knew this person very well, but I could be wrong. I was almost to the end when I saw a message from Elena, complaining about the fight with my mom. 5StepsAhead had been quick to respond to her, offering comfort as he confirmed she didn't deserve to be controlled by anyone anymore, she was a strong independent woman. Elena responded with a winking emoji followed by a few heart emojis as the guy continued to compliment her. My heart started to race as I continued to read their conversation and dropped once I read the last few messages.

5StepsAhead: Why don't I meet you for a cup of coffee so we can talk? Maybe I can cheer you up?

EROM31802: I don't know, it's getting kind of late. I don't know if anything is still open.

5StepsAhead: There's a coffeehouse right there on the corner of Union and Second street. They stay open 24 hours. I can meet you there in 15 minutes.

EROM31802: Okay, I'm on my way.

I took a picture of the screen with the date and time stamp that showed 10:47 last night and forwarded it to my partner as I closed the laptop and put it back where I found it. She had left to meet someone from an online dating app and I had no idea if she actually knew this person already or not. I wouldn't imagine that she was the kind of person to go meet a random stranger that late at night but Elena was always the most unpredictable out of all of my sisters. I sighed as I left her room the way I found it and was about to make my way back to the office to work through the new information I found when I got a call to head to the hospital to talk to a college student who had been given a date rape drug at a coffee house last night. I was about to protest and tell them to find someone else to do it when I heard the tone in my partners voice as she added that the victim had met the guy through an online dating website. My stomach churned as I made my way to the hospital to see if there was any connection to my sister.

<u>Four</u>
Hannah
20 Days Ago

I woke up to a pounding headache as I looked around to find the machine that was making the god-awful beeping noise. My mind was foggy as I had no idea why I was in the hospital. I looked down and found an IV in my wrist and a hospital band with my information on it. Why was I in the hospital? How did I get here? I felt my anxiety rise as I started to freak out. My breathing quickened as I struggled to take a deep breath which caused another alarm to start beeping.

A few minutes later a nurse walked in and smiled as she went to the cluster of machines next to me and looked at the screens.

"How are you feeling? Any pain?" Her voice was calm though there was concern in her eyes as she looked me over.

"Why am I in here?" My voice was shaky as I held onto the side bed rail and looked up at her.

"You were brought in last night. You passed out in the bathroom of a coffee shop and a woman found you and called 911."

I stayed silent as I tried to figure out why she was giving me the look she was giving me. It felt like she was waiting for me to confess to something but I had no idea what. I didn't remember much after meeting Chet last night but I did remember getting up and going to the bathroom because the date was going so poorly.

"Is there anyone that I can call for you?" She pressed a few buttons on the monitors as she made notes on a small piece of paper she had pulled out of the pocket of her scrubs.

"My friend, Amber. Her phone number is in my cell phone." I looked around and realized that I had no idea where my personal belongings had gone and whether I even had a cell phone anymore. The nurse walked over to a closet and opened the door to pull out my backpack and the clothes I had been wearing last night. She sat both piles on the foot of the bed as I patted the pockets of my jeans for the cell phone. I was relieved when I felt something hard and reached in and pulled out my phone.

"I can go ahead and call her." I offered as I held up my phone.

"Sounds good." She gathered my belongings and put them back into the closet before walking out and closing the door.

I pulled up Amber's name in my contacts and was about to press send when I heard a knock on the door. The door opened and I had to blink twice, not trusting my eyes when I saw the most drop dead gorgeous man walk in. The olive colored skin. The strong jaw line that framed his perfect face and full lips. The golden brown eyes that studied me as if I was an animal in the wild. He looked like he could be a model, rocking the tousled hair look and making jeans and a gray T-shirt look beyond sexy. My heart skipped a beat as he came closer.

"I'm Max, NYPD." He approached the side of my bed with caution as he lifted his shirt for me to see the badge that was attached to his belt. A sliver of well-defined muscles greeted me as I smiled back at him.

"How are you feeling this morning, Hannah?" He pulled out the stool that had been slid under the sink and sat on it as he studied me. I felt nervous that I still didn't remember what had happened last night and now all of a sudden I had NYPD visiting me in the hospital.

"I have a terrible headache and I'm still not sure what's going on or why I'm here."

"Well, hopefully we can help each other figure that out." He let out a deep breath as he looked down at the file he held in front of him. "Can you tell me what you do remember about yesterday?"

"I can try. Where do you want me to start?"

"Let's start with the morning. Then just walk me through your day. People you saw. People you spoke to. Anyone that you had contact with."

"I started the day at my mom's house. She lives in Hudson. I took the train back into town around 1 and got back a little after 3. I met with a group from school at Java Jazz Coffee Shop around 3:30 and then met a date around 7:15 at the same coffee shop. We didn't spend that much time together, maybe 30-45 minutes? Then I excused myself to use the restroom and I don't remember anything after that." My hands trembled as I felt embarrassed that I didn't know what happened after that. My eyes looked up from under my eyelashes as I watched him write down what I had told him.

"Can you tell me about the guy you were meeting?" His tone was soft, like the tone you used when you had bad news to give someone.

"His name was Chet. I met him through an online dating app. We didn't talk much so I didn't know much about him other than he went to NYU, like me."

"What dating app was it?"

"It's called Single2Mingle."

"Would you be able to pull up his online dating profile for me?"

"Sure." I reached for my phone that was sitting in my lap and unlocked it. Once I had his profile pulled up, I handed the phone to Max and watched as he wrote down some more information.

"I apologize, but why exactly are you here?" I asked, hoping it didn't sound as rude as I was worried it did after I had already said it. He smiled as he closed the file and clicked his pen before sliding it into his back pocket.

"After you were brought in unresponsive last night, they did some blood work to try to figure out what happened. The blood work showed you had Rohypnol in your system." He looked at me with one eyebrow raised as the blood drained from my face.

"Oh no…no no no no. I don't do drugs! I can barely afford ramen noodles!" I held my hands up in defense as I realized that they thought I came in passed out last night because I was on drugs. And now NYPD was there, ready to take me in for drug use. I lowered my hands and shook my head as I started to cry.

"Hannah, I'm not sure that you understand." His voice was sympathetic as I looked at him through blurry tears.

"You think I'm a drug addict." I sobbed as I tried to get my words out. "And now…now you're here to arrest me." I lowered my head into my hands as I cried harder.

"You're not under arrest." He took a deep breath as he rolled the stool closer to the bed and folded his hands on top of the file folder.

"I'm not?" My face was red and splotchy as I looked around for a tissue to wipe my nose with before snot ran down my face. Between the two of us, I was not the attractive one at this point.

"You're not." He smiled a tight smile. "I'm here because we have a missing person case that also deals with someone who she met through the same online dating website."

"A missing person? Did they meet up with Chet also?" Confusion was setting in as none of this was making any sense.

"We don't know yet. But given that you had a date rape drug in your system while on a date with someone you met from the same website, we want to look into every possibility."

"Date rape drug?" My eyes grew big as I now understood what he was getting at. No wonder I couldn't remember what had happened.

"It's usually slipped into a drink. The victim rarely knows it's there until it's too late and already in their system. Can you tell me what all you had to drink last night and if Chet had access to your drink?"

"Coffee. I had already been there with my study group but had been drinking from my water bottle. He offered coffee and had been the one to wait in line and get it."

"Were you able to see him the entire time?"

"I wasn't watching." I let out a breath of frustration. Not with the questions but with myself for being so stupid.

"Did he have access to your drink?"

"Yes."

"Are you willing to file a police report and give us a statement about what happened?"

"Yes."

A nurse walked in as he stood up and scooted the stool back under the sink.

"Thank you for your time today. An officer will be by shortly to have you complete the paperwork and to take your statement, but if you need anything in the meantime, here's my card. If you remember anything that might be helpful- call my cell." He extended a business card to me as I reached up and took it.

My mind was still trying to process everything that had just happened. The missing girl. The date rape drug. Things could have been so much worse than they were so I tried to stay focused on the fact that nothing else could possibly go wrong. Just as I was about to pick up my phone to call

Amber, I saw a voicemail alert on my phone. I didn't feel it vibrate and the number on the call log showed as restricted.

I pressed the play button as I held the phone to my ear and listened.

Hannah, this is Claire at Ferguson and Wales. We've been waiting for you to show up for work today, however since you still have not arrived and it is 3 hours past your start time, we are accepting your no call no show resignation. Please call me to set up a time to come in to collect your personal belongings and final check.

My stomach dropped as I listened to the voicemail again. Okay, so I was wrong. Things could get a lot worse.

Five

Max

17 Days Ago

The bar was quiet for a Thursday evening as I waited for Trevor to meet me. He had been my best friend since we were in elementary school and felt like the brother I never had. When I first told him that Elena was missing 3 days ago, he hit the ground running and stopped everything he was doing to help me find her. I hadn't slept since her disappearance, and there had been no leads, which made it worse. There didn't seem to be a link between the guy she met online and the one that Hannah had met. Frustration continued to eat away at me.

The door opened and the afternoon sunlight filtered through the dingy dive bar as Trevor gave a quick nod to acknowledge Jon, the bartender, before making his way to the high-top table where I was sitting. This was our go to spot and we had been coming here so long that Jon no longer bothered asking what we were drinking, he just brought our usual and kept them coming until we nodded that we were finished.

"What's up, man?" Trevor gave a quick pat to my back before sliding out of his black leather jacket and hanging it on the back of his chair as he sat down. He had perfect features that drove women crazy and made me think he should be featured on the cover of some cheesy romance novel. His eyes scanned the room as he smiled at me and ran a hand through his already tousled hair as some blonde in the corner lowered her head and blushed.

I gave him the same look I had been giving him for years when I would catch him flirting with a girl who was barely legal.

"What?" He laughed as he leaned back for Jon to sit his beer in front of him. "I can't help it if she finds me attractive." His smile spread across his face as he looked past me to make eye contact with her.

"One of these days you're gonna be calling me to come bail you out of jail and I'm gonna say- I told you so!" I laughed as he took a drink of his beer, pretending he didn't hear what I said.

"So any news on Leni?" His eyes met mine and I could see the anguish mirrored in his that I felt in mine.

"Nothing. They're coming up empty with every lead. Since I can't work the case because she's my sister, I feel even more out of the loop. And it doesn't help that my mom is up my ass, calling fifty times a day to see if I've heard anything." I lowered my head as I spun my empty beer bottle around on the worn-out cardboard coaster. I wasn't sure what the purpose was for the coaster given that the table was in worse shape.

"I've been asking around the coffee shop and the other businesses close by. No one remembers anything." He sighed and took another swig. "Anything come from the online dating stuff? Were you guys able to get any information from the profile?"

"Very little. It wasn't the same guy that met up with the other victim. Apparently, a lot of people use this app in that neighborhood and meet up at that coffee shop. We're still looking into it though."

"What about her cell phone? Was Mindy able to track it after all?" There was a desperation in his voice that I could relate to. It was the same desperation that had clung to me like a wet T-shirt for the past 3 days. Mindy was my partner and had taken the lead on this case for me. We had been working together for the last 2 years and she had met my family several times, attending a few of my sisters' high school graduations so this felt personal to her as well.

"The last place they were able to accurately trace the call was a few blocks north of the coffee shop. There are a lot of businesses in that area and Elena described a vacant warehouse type of building, which there aren't any in that area. So, we still have no idea how far away she is from where her phone was tracked to." I ran my hand down the thick scruff of my jaw from the beard that had voluntarily decided to sprout when I didn't make time to shave this week.

I felt my phone vibrate on the table and looked down, praying that it was Elena or at least an update on her. I unlocked the screen to find a text message from an unknown number.

Unknown: Hi, Detective Romano, this is Hannah. We met at the hospital. I wanted to see if you had a few minutes to talk? I think someone might be stalking me. Strange things have been happening since I got home from the hospital and I don't know how else to explain it.

I felt Trevor's eyes on me as I reread the text again. I shook my head no quickly to confirm that it wasn't about Elena as my fingers started to reply.

Max: Hannah, are you safe where you are? I'm on my way to meet you, confirm the address where you'll be and I'll head your way now.

I waited as I saw the dots bounce across the screen as she typed. A message popped up confirming that she was safe and that she was in her apartment. I looked over the address and knew where it was.

"Hey, I gotta go. The girl from the hospital thinks someone might be stalking her so I need to go check it out." I slid a twenty dollar bill onto the table and tucked it under my beer as Trevor finished his drink.

"Want me to go with you?"

"Sure, let's get going. She's a couple blocks away, I told her I was on my way." We walked toward the exit and waved at Jon on our way out. The sun had started to set which made the temperature outside feel twenty degrees colder than it actually was. I pulled my black beanie down further on my head as I shoved my hands into my overcoat for warmth. Trevor and I walked in silence the short distance to Hannah's apartment. As we stood outside her door I thought about sending her a message to let her know that Trevor was with me but then decided it wasn't official police business so it shouldn't be an issue.

A few seconds later her door swung open and her eyes were wide, a fear on her face that I didn't remember seeing at the hospital. The tension from her jolted me to move my hand to my gun, unsure of what the real threat was.

"Hannah, are you okay?" I asked cautiously as I tried to peer around her to look into the apartment for any sign of a threat.

"Um, yeah. I think so?" Her voice was low as her dark green eyes scanned the empty hallway behind us. I met Trevor's eyes as he subtly shrugged, as he quickly scanned the hallway, not seeing anything odd on the way up to her apartment either.

"Do you mind if we come in?" I kept my voice calm and looked directly at her as I tried to get her to make eye contact. Once she did, I saw the tension in her shoulders ease some as she stepped back and held the door open for us.

"This is my friend Trevor," I nodded behind me as we stepped into the small space of her studio apartment. "We were meeting for a drink when I got your text. I hope you don't mind him coming along."

"Not at all," she mumbled as she closed the door and stood by the kitchen counter. I didn't know what had happened before we got there but whatever it was had her spooked.

"Are you sure everything is okay?" I probed. "Your message said that you thought someone might be stalking you?"

"Yeah. It's been a few days and things have just been weird since I got home from the hospital." She sighed as she looked over at us as we stayed standing by the door. "You can sit if you want to." She nodded to the couch that lined the wall with a window behind it.

To the right of the couch was a bed and a dresser, to the left was the kitchen with a small island that had 2 barstools. There was no room for a kitchen table or chairs, the full-size refrigerator taking up the majority of the room in the small kitchen. I looked around, taking it all in and found a door along the wall that was closed. My guess was that it was the bathroom, a very small one at that.

"Can you tell me about what has been happening?" I pulled a pen and a small notepad from the inside pocket of my coat and sat on the couch as Trevor sat next to me.

"It started out as little things. Things that were just odd but could have been from me being too tired or stressed with finals. When I first got back from the hospital, I had put my backpack on the floor by the door, it's where I always put it. After I took a shower, I came in here and it was on the floor by the couch. The next day, on Tuesday, I went to my work to give them a doctor's note from the hospital to try to get my job back and when I got back, the window was open. That's when I started to get freaked out. I NEVER open that window. For one- it's really old and I worry that it would break if I did open it. And two, it's like 18 degrees outside- there's no reason to open it." She took a deep breath as she walked to a barstool and sat down. Her hair was pulled up into a messy knot on her head, a few short strands of brown hair falling loosely around her face. It reminded me of Elena and how she wore her long brown hair in a similar knot on her head as well. My chest hurt at the thought so I tried to redirect my thoughts and focus on the information she was giving me.

"After I closed the window, I looked through the apartment and obviously didn't find anyone. I mean, it's pretty small- where would anyone hide?" She expanded her arms out as she showed the size of the room. "I'm on the top floor, it's not like anyone is coming and going on the fire escape without drawing attention from the apartments below. So, I checked the locks again, made sure the door and window were secured, and took a shower. After my shower I realized that I needed to do laundry so I gathered everything up and went to the laundry mat down the block. I came home and put away my clean laundry before I left to meet my group for a study session. When I got back, there was a black lacy bra and matching thong laying on my bed." Her eyes looked past us at the bed as I watched the color drain from her face.

"Does anyone besides you have a key to the apartment?" I asked as I finished writing down the last note about the lingerie.

"No, just my mom. But she lives 2 hours away and wouldn't have any reason to do any of this."

"Is there anything else that has happened since Tuesday?"

"Yesterday I had my first day back at work and when I got home the door was unlocked. Not open. Just unlocked. I looked around and nothing was missing so I don't think someone broke in to steal from me. I checked the apartment again and didn't find anyone. I ended up pushing the coffee table against the door so I would hear it if anyone tried to open it last night while I slept."

Her eyes looked tired and now I could see why. I hadn't been able to sleep knowing that my sister was missing and she wasn't getting any sleep because someone seemed to be getting in her apartment and messing with her head.

"And then today..." Her voice trailed off as she looked at the counter beside her. "There was this note under my door when I got home from work this evening. That's when I decided to text you."

She picked up a white envelope and handed it to me. I sat the notepad and pen on the coffee table in front me as I took the envelope and pulled out a single piece of paper that had been ripped out of a textbook. It was clear it had been ripped by the jagged lines and the uneven shape. In black marker were the words:

You should be careful who you meet online.

I lowered the note and looked over at Hannah as I laid the note on the coffee table for Trevor to read. He knew better than to touch it as it was now evidence.

"Do you know who would have sent this to you?" I asked as I nodded at the letter. She shook her head no as she got down from the barstool and walked over to her backpack. I watched as she sat it on the island and pulled a textbook out. She walked over to us and opened it to a page that had been torn and was missing a chunk in the same exact shape as the note sitting on the coffee table in front of me.

"No, but they tore the page out of my textbook." She sighed heavily. "I hadn't even made it to that yet. Bastard."

I had to bite the inside of my cheek to keep from laughing as I saw the faint smile pull at the corners of her mouth. I was happy to see that she hadn't completely lost her sense of humor but wouldn't blame her if she had. All of this was creepy as hell. Something about her smile pulled me in and made me want to see more of it.

"I can write you a note for your professor if needed, we will need to take this into evidence." I offered a gentle smile as she laid the textbook on the table in front of me and took her seat on the barstool again.

"The really creepy thing, the one that bothers me the most, is what had happened right before you got here." Her eyes met mine and I waited anxiously for her to go on. I arched an eyebrow as she subtly nodded her head and continued.

"I was using the restroom," she looked over at the closed door, "and as I was about to flush, I heard the front door slam closed." She pulled her lower lip through her teeth nervously as she watched for our reaction. It made sense now why she had acted the way she did when we first got there.

"May I?" I looked toward the bathroom for permission to look inside as she nodded yes. I got up and made my way the short distance to the closed door and pulled it open. It was a small space, as I had guessed from the width that her door sunk in from the outside wall. There was a small shower to the left, a toilet in the middle, and a sink with very small counter space on the right. I took a step inside and pulled back the shower curtain to confirm there was no one there, granted she had already said she heard someone leave, not come in.

I backed out of the bathroom and closed the door as I had found it as I heard Trevor and Hannah talking about online dating. I picked up my notepad and made a few additional notes while I listened to their conversation. Trevor had this natural ability to ask the right questions to get people to really open up and it had always frustrated me that he never wanted to go into law enforcement with me. He would have been great at it. Instead he managed a local gym and was a personal trainer, which he was also great at as well.

"Have you met any other guys from the dating website?" Trevor asked Hannah as I looked up to wait for her answer.

"Not on this one, no. I had just started this one recently and didn't put a ton of effort into it because I've been so busy with school and work. I used a couple of other apps before this but it's been a few months since I've been on a date with any of them." She looked over at me as her cheeks flushed and I wondered why she would be embarrassed about admitting that in front of me. It's not like I was one to talk. I couldn't even remember the last date I had been on.

"If you can, make a list of everyone that you've recently had contact with, on all apps. Any message requests, and hook up requests- anyone who you may have declined to respond to. Once you have that list, we can look it over and see if we can narrow down who this might be." Trevor explained as he looked at me with a smug smirk.

"I can probably do that for you now. Chet is really the only guy I've talked to in over 4 months. That was part of the reason I said yes. I wasn't getting any other requests so I figured I shouldn't be picky and just give him a chance. Maybe he's mad because he thought I walked out on our date after I passed out in the bathroom and never came back?" She looked between us as if one of us would have the answer.

"It definitely could be him. Guys do stupid stuff when they take a blow to the ego. We'll pick him up and see what we can find out." I clicked my pen and slid it into the inside pocket of my coat along with the notepad and Hannah's note. "Do you feel safe to stay here tonight or do you have somewhere else you can stay?"

"I actually asked my friend Amber to come stay with me.

She still lives at home and needs a break so she's going to stay for a few days."

"Sounds like a good plan. Remember to call me if anything happens, I live close by and can get here quickly." I smiled warmly as Trevor stood up and we walked to the door.

"Thank you, I will." She held the door open as we stepped into the hallway and smiled again. "Will I get an update on what happens with Chet?"

"As soon as I have more information, I'll touch base with you to get you an update."

"Thank you, I really do appreciate your help. It was nice to meet you, Trevor."

"You too." He smiled as he turned away, lowering his head so I couldn't see his face as we heard the door shut behind us. I listened closely to make sure I heard the locks before we walked down the hallway to the stairs.

"What's that look for?" I asked as we started down the stairs, shoulder to shoulder.

"You know she's barely legal, right?"

His smirk got under my skin as I knew what he was getting at. Was she hot? Fuck yeah. Was I interested? Probably. Was I going to act on anything? Not while my baby sister was still missing and some psychopath was stalking Hannah. It was definitely going to make it harder to work on her case when I felt such a strong electricity between us.

"You read it wrong. I'm not interested in her. I'm just doing my job." I side eyed him as we continued down another flight of stairs.

"Is that so?" He chuckled. "I've never known you to go to someone's house when you're not on the clock to help with something that a service aide could do."

"She had my card, I told her to use it. I'm still technically working her case with the date rape drug."

"Yeah and she sure used it alright. She could hardly keep her eyes off of you and you know it."

"Whatever."

Was that true? Was she interested in me as well? I felt myself getting excited at the thought and quickly shook it away.

"Is that why you had to keep adjusting yourself while we were sitting on the couch? Or was it cause I'm just so desirable, you couldn't help yourself?" He bumped his shoulder against mine as we reached the final stair and opened the door into the cold chill of winter.

I rolled my eyes at him as I had nothing to say to that. Did she physically impact me while I sat so close to her? More than I would ever be willing to admit. We walked the short distance to the subway and said goodbye as he headed home and I headed to the office to update the information I had from Hannah and to put in the request to bring Chet in for questioning.

<u>Six</u>

Hannah
16 Days Ago

"How did you sleep?" I asked Amber as she slowly sat up on the couch and stretched her arms up over her head.

"Good for the most part." She rolled her head a few times as she stretched some more and I knew the old worn-out couch had left her feeling stiff like it had done to me the few times I had fallen asleep on it.

"I told you, you should've slept in my bed with me. There was more than enough room." I walked into the kitchen and filled the coffee pot with water, desperate for that first sip to wake me up. We had been up late last night talking but even after we fell asleep I was restless the majority of the night, feeling like someone was watching me.

I tried to push everything out of my mind and just focus on finishing my last few classes but I couldn't shake the idea that someone was actively going through stuff in my apartment. At first I thought I was just crazy, then I thought maybe I had a random homeless person who had figured out how to get in, but after I got the note yesterday I knew it was Chet.

It was my own fault for not finding out more about the guy before agreeing to go on a date with him, but even then, how was I supposed to know that he would become this obsessed weirdo and stalk me? We definitely didn't click when we first met each other but I didn't pick up the vibe that he thought it was going all that well either. I imagined he thought of me as the girl you take in the bathroom stall for a quickie, not the girl you take home to mother. If I was so disposable then why was he going to these efforts to mess with me and stalk me?

The last few drops of coffee trickled into the pot before I poured two cups and made my way over to sit next to Amber on the couch. The snow had started to come down hard this morning which left a chill by the window. We sipped our coffee in silence as we watched the snow fall peacefully outside.

"Did you sleep better last night?" Amber asked as she took a sip of coffee and sat her cup down on the coffee table.

"A little, but I was still restless. I had this really uneasy feeling that someone was watching me." A shiver ran through me as I remembered being extremely anxious and freaking myself out throughout the night.

"It was me. I was watching you," Amber joked as she wiggled her eyebrows at me. I rolled my eyes as I tried to keep from laughing so I didn't spew coffee at her.

"So that's why you didn't want to share the bed? I get it, you're one of those girls who likes to watch people. What's that called? A voyeur?" I winked as I saw the flush in her cheeks from my teasing.

"You know it!" She giggled as she pulled her legs up underneath her and turned to face me head on. "But seriously though, I kinda had that same feeling, like someone was in the room, watching us." Her tone was serious, all joking gone as she watched for my reaction.

I didn't know what to say. I didn't want to think that someone had gotten in again last night, while both Amber and I were in the room. How would they have even gotten in? Before I played around with the idea that maybe I was such a heavy sleeper that I didn't hear them, but last night I heard every time Amber got up to get a drink of water or to use the bathroom. Maybe it was just our minds playing tricks on us and forcing us to believe that someone had been watching us because we were so fixated on everything that had been happening.

"I'm sorry, I know that having me stay here was supposed to be helpful and make you feel safer. I wasn't trying to freak you out." She reached over and touched my leg gently. "I shouldn't have said anything."

"No, it's okay. You don't need to be sorry." I looked around the room as I toyed with the idea of calling in sick for work today. It wasn't really that far of a stretch given that I had this constant headache and nausea for almost a week. As much as I didn't want to go in, I knew that I needed to since I had already been fired once this week and barely got my job back. Reluctantly I sighed as I stood up and sat my empty coffee mug on the table by Amber's mug that was still more than half full. Either she was slow at drinking her coffee this morning, or there was so much anxiety pushing through me that I had drank mine in record time.

"I'm gonna jump in the shower and get ready for work. There's food in the kitchen if you want to help yourself to breakfast."

"Thanks, I'll see what I can find to cook for us before you go."

I smiled as I walked over and pulled out clothes to wear from my dresser and headed into the bathroom. I closed the door but didn't lock it in case Amber needed anything, which sounded silly and overly paranoid.

Once the water warmed up, I took a quick shower and let myself enjoy the hot water as it ran down my face for a few minutes at the end. The pipes squealed as I turned the water off with one hand while reaching behind the shower curtain to grab my towel from the hook where I always kept it with the other. My fingers scraped along the bare wall as I kept patting, trying to find the towel. Cold metal found my fingers as I felt the empty hook. I pulled the shower curtain back, expecting to find the towel in a puddle on the floor but it wasn't there. I looked around the small space of the bathroom and found it neatly folded and piled on top of my clothes on the bathroom sink.

My stomach sunk as I pulled the shower curtain around me in an effort to cover myself while I stepped forward and reached over to lock the bathroom door. My fingers trembled as I fumbled with the lock before turning it successfully. I let the shower curtain fall as I quickly grabbed the towel from underneath my clothes and wrapped it around me. A nagging feeling inside told me that something was wrong. I had put my clothes in the same spot I put them every time I took a shower, how did they end up on top of the towel that was hanging by the shower when I first got in?

I quickly dried myself and slipped on the yoga pants and sweatshirt I had been wearing earlier as I struggled to hear what was going on in the apartment. Everything sounded quiet, no sounds of Amber being attacked which was where my mind was currently going.

I kicked the towel to the side as I slowly unlocked the bathroom door and stepped into the open space of the apartment. The room was eerily quiet. The front door looked like it was still shut and I could smell food cooking on the stove but there was no sign of Amber. I slowly took a few steps toward the kitchen as I smelled the food starting to burn when out of the corner of my eye I saw something dripping off the coffee table.

My eyes followed the trail of coffee that was slowly trickling from the puddle on the table into the new puddle that had started on the floor, the coffee mug laying on its side by the coaster it had been sitting on. A shiver ripped through my body as my eyes slowly moved up, the sheer curtains blowing gently from the outside breeze that was sending an icy chill through the room. I stepped around the puddle of coffee and kneeled on the couch as I pulled the curtains back and looked out the open window. Amber's body laid lifeless on a fresh blanket of snow as the blood pooled around her. I covered my mouth as I began to scream, the sound muffled by the pounding in my head as my heart threatened to explode.

Seven

Max

16 Days Ago

"Hannah, can you walk me through what happened this morning?" I sat on the edge of the coffee table and looked at her as she watched the forensics team move around us, collecting as much evidence as they could. The call came in from a neighbor reporting a suspicious person running from the back alley, no one knew at the time that it was actually a murder. Hannah remained shut down and didn't respond to any of my questions. I wasn't sure that she even knew I was there. Her eyes were red and puffy as she held a trembling hand up to her mouth and rocked back and forth on the couch. My instincts shouted to grab her and hold her, to comfort her and make her feel better, but I knew I couldn't. I looked around for the detective who was taking over this portion of the investigation and waved him over.

"Are you done with her?" I asked as I nodded at Hannah.

"Just about. We may have more questions for her but we won't really know any more until forensics finishes up." He tugged at the brim of his hat and looked sympathetically at Hannah.

"Well, if it's all the same to you, I'd like to get her out of here." I pulled a business card from inside my overcoat pocket and handed it to him. "She'll be in my custody if you need anything else. My cell is on 24/7."

"You got it, Detective." He slid the card in his back pocket as his attention was drawn away by another officer calling him.

I looked around to see what she might need since she wouldn't be able to come back to the apartment for a while. I grabbed her cell phone from the coffee table and tucked it in my pocket as I made my way to the door and grabbed her backpack. She was still rocking back and forth on the couch so I didn't bother asking permission before opening her bag and looking inside. The front pocket had her keys and a small canister of mace. The middle pocket had a phone charger and a couple of protein bars, a beanie, some gloves, and her metro card. The back pocket had her books and notebooks for school. I zipped it up and walked to the bed as I looked around for a suitcase or duffel bag for her clothes.

I gently tossed her backpack on the bed as I leaned down and felt around under the bed. I was relieved when I saw a small suitcase tucked in the corner under the bed by the nightstand. I pulled it out and shook it a few times to clear the dust from it before standing it upright and unzipping it. I had no idea what clothes to pack for her and it felt slightly inappropriate to be going through her personal belongings but she wasn't in any position to pack her stuff herself so I didn't really have a choice. There was a likelihood that her apartment would be off limits for a few days to a week while they continued to work the crime scene below. The murder was one thing but with the added report of having someone stalking her, they would be sure to scour every inch of her apartment.

I pulled open the first drawer of her dresser and breathed a silent sigh of relief when I found pajamas and sweats. I grabbed a few pair of sweatpants and tucked them into the suitcase along with the NYU sweatshirt she was wearing last night when I saw her. I quickly went through the rest of the drawers, working my way down one side then up the other. I knew the last drawer had her most personal belongings and my palm started to sweat as I looked over at her before pulling it open. Inside were rows of neatly folded bras and panties, arranged by color. I tried not to overthink anything as I grabbed random garments and forced myself not to picture her wearing any of them. I was about to grab a handful of panties when I felt a piece of paper under my fingertips. I reached down and pulled out a small folded note that was tucked inside a pair of black lace boy short panties.

Thought of you when I bought these, can't wait to see you in them.

My eyes darted over to Hannah as I held the note in my hand. I looked back down at the note and found that it was written in black marker, matching the note she had shown me last night. The writing was block like in style, each letter crisp and clean. It almost looked like it was typed out and printed, the penmanship consistent and fluid. There were a few spots that there was a slight bleed from the ink and my guess was that they had used a fine point permanent marker. I slid the note into my pocket as I zipped the suitcase shut and walked over to the detective I had been talking to as I nodded my head for him to step to the side.

"I need these ran through forensics ASAP." I said quiet enough for only him to hear as I handed him the pair of underwear. His eyebrow arched as he looked at the sexy pair of underwear in his gloved hand.

"I've been working this case and we believe she's being stalked by a guy that she met from an online dating site. She was found in a bathroom, passed out, Rohypnol in her system when she was admitted to the hospital. She's been finding notes and I just found one tucked inside of those." I looked down at his hand as he reached for an evidence bag and dropped them inside.

"I'll let you know as soon as we have something."

"Thanks, I appreciate it." I turned and walked the short distance to gather the suitcase and backpack from the bed as I made my way over to Hannah.

"Hey, let's get you out of here, okay?" I smiled warmly as I reached my hand out to her to help her up. Her eyes met mine, filled with tears, as she grabbed my hand and allowed me to help her up. I was relieved that she was able to acknowledge that I was there, but the sadness in her eyes nearly broke my heart. I had seen sadness plenty of times in my career but had always been able to keep people at an arm's distance so it didn't impact me. This was different. This felt more personal. Maybe it was because my sister was still missing and no one had heard from her in days, or maybe it was because I could see the goodness and the purity in Hannah's eyes and someone like her didn't deserve to have to go through this.

My apartment was only a few blocks away and thankfully the weather had cleared most of the traffic which made it a quick trip. Once we were inside, I sat her belongings down on the bistro table that was tucked in the corner, behind the couch. The living room and kitchen were basically one fluid room with nothing separating them other than a small island that jetted off of the counter by the sink that sat below the small window. There was a stove next to the fridge that shared the same wall as the bedroom and bathroom on the other side. I had been in this apartment since I first left home at 17 and at one time, had shared it with Trevor. Before I graduated and became an officer, rent was impossible to pay on my own.

I watched as Hannah lingered in the doorway, not at all aware that she was somewhere else. I needed her to talk to me and walk me through what had happened but I knew that as long as she was in shock, I wasn't going to be able to get anything out of her. I gently led her to the couch with my hand on her lower back and helped her to sit. My phone vibrated against the thick denim of my jeans as I walked into the kitchen to get her a glass of water. I reached in and pulled it out, sliding the button to answer it.

"Romano," I said as I held the glass under the water dispenser in the fridge and filled it.

"Detective Romano, this is officer Stamos. We were able to locate the suspect you asked us to bring in, Chet Johnson." Her voice didn't sound too pleasant and I wondered if she was just trying to be professional or if that was just her natural, unenthusiastic personality.

"Okay, great. Can you please let my partner know? She'll be in to question him. Just keep him in holding until then."

"I'm sorry, I can't do that."

I sat the glass down on the kitchen counter as I watched Hannah look absently at the tv across from her.

"And why the hell not?" There had better be a damn good reason why I was being told that we couldn't hold this asshole for questioning when he was now a murder suspect.

I would talk to whoever I needed to talk to if it meant we talked to this guy now.

"Because, he's dead. With all due respect, sir, we found his body an hour ago."

What the fuck? I ran a hand down my face and closed my eyes as I shook my head.

"Cause of death?"

"It's still to be determined but it appears to have been blunt force trauma. There are several bruises as well as puncture wounds. Possible strangulation. We don't really know yet."

"You know all of this and he barely died an hour ago?" I questioned; it didn't add up. How did he sneak into Hannah's apartment, murder her best friend, then was beaten to death himself less than a few hours later?

"Sorry, we found his body an hour ago. He appears to have died several days ago. I would guess close to 5 or 6 days based on the decomposition."

"Get him to the morgue and I want an update as soon as possible. Have them rush the autopsy. I want a cause of death and time of death as soon as possible."

"Yes sir."

I hung up the phone and slammed it down on the counter as I looked up at Hannah. She didn't even flinch from the sound. Sitting in front of me was a woman who was in more danger than she could even know and it was now my job to try to save her while I continued to look for my missing sister. I opened the cabinet next to me and grabbed the bottle of antacid as I threw a handful in my mouth and started making calls to my team with the update.

<u>Eight</u>

Adam

16 Days Ago

I rolled my eyes as I watched the overweight rent a cop scurry around the dead body as if it was going to change the outcome of the situation. Little did they know he had been dead almost a week so it was a little too late to be worrying about him now. I leaned back against the cold brick wall of the abandoned building behind me and took a deep drag off my cigarette as I watched the shit show continue to unfold.

The problem was that this was all completely avoidable, yet no one was smart enough to see that. I was the kind of guy that went after the things that I wanted. There wasn't anything that I wanted that I couldn't have. Sure, sometimes there was a struggle and some push back. But in the end, I always got what I wanted. Even if I had to get rid of the things that threatened to stand in my way.

I pushed off the brick wall and tossed the cigarette to the ground before stomping it out with the heel of my steel toed boot. It was a short distance to the abandoned building that held the last girl who said no to me. While everyone was still fixated on the dead frat guy, I didn't want to risk them hearing the obnoxious screams that threatened to undo everything that still needed to be done.

58

<u>Nine</u>
Hannah
16 Days Ago

They say that the first time you experience the death of someone who is close to you, that you learn what death really is. You learn how to go through the grieving process, how to work through each of the 7 stages of grief. That you grow from it. You learn to value and appreciate life more and your relationships with others. What they don't tell you is that each time you see a dead body, it imprints itself on your memory. A permanent reminder of what you've lost.

I didn't know anyone when I first moved to the city. I was scared and alone and desperate to prove to myself that I could do it. That I could live in a big city that would swallow me whole the first opportunity it had. And it almost did. Then I met Amber and things felt easier. More balanced. Calmer. Happier. She became my best friend and I felt like she was the sister I always wished for growing up as an only child.

Her life was beautiful and she was the symbol of happiness. She was popular without being stuck up. Nice without having people walk all over her. Strong and determined. And thanks to me, her life was cut short. She would never have her fairytale romance that she had dreamt about since she was a little girl. She wouldn't have tiny fingers wrapped around hers with little voices calling her mommy. A tear rolled down my cheek, my hand absentmindedly wiped it away, the ache from the raw skin burning at the touch.

Max sat across from me in an oversized leather recliner and rocked gently as his fingers moved quickly across his cell phone. He was trying to work through the details of everything that had happened this morning but I could see the stress etched on his face, the worry beneath his brow, as he became more distracted by whoever he was talking to on his phone.

We had gone over the details several times, each time an attempt for me to remember something else that might be helpful. What more could I say? We were talking on the couch, drinking coffee, then I went to take a shower and someone murdered my best friend and threw her out the window of my apartment as if she was nothing more than the trash that littered the sidewalks below.

My head ached as I shifted my position on the couch and pulled my knees closer to my chest. My cell phone screen lit up with a new email alert and I instinctively reached for it, worried about the lectures I had missed today that would be guaranteed to show up on the final exams in a few weeks. I slid my finger across the screen and pulled up the email from Joel to our group. There was a quick note about sending the lecture notes from the classes we missed and a joke about our late-night partying that must've been the reason to keep us out of class today.

I let out a shaky breath as I wiped another tear away and sat the phone down on the couch beside me. Max's eyes caught mine as he looked up from his phone, noticing the new tears. I shook my head no as I pulled the blanket up closer to my chest and tried to bury myself in it.

My mind raced as I thought about how I was going to tell those in our group about what happened to Amber. Sure, they weren't as close to her as I was but they still spent the past 14 weeks getting to know her. I felt my chest tighten as I thought about everyone that would soon be finding out, a reminder of how I felt when my mom told me that my dad had died. The difference was that we knew it was coming. I was able to try to brace myself for the inevitable. This was the complete opposite. There was no bracing yourself for something like this.

"Everything okay?" Max's voice was low and even as he studied me from across the room, his phone now sitting on the end table next to him.

"Yeah, it was an email from my study group. They were sending the lecture notes from the classes that I missed today."

"You're welcome to use my computer to print them if you want to. I know you have finals coming up and probably need hard copies." His eyes looked tired and I heard the empathy in his voice as he tried to sound reassuring while knowing that finals were the last thing on my mind right now. We were in that awkward moment of not knowing what else to talk about while trying to avoid talking about what was really on our minds.

"Thank you, that would be great." I smiled as I pulled the blanket off of me, eager to get up and do something other than sit on the couch and obsess over Amber. Even though I knew I would be a total wreck, I regretted not going in to work today and worried that their sympathy would only last so long before they let me go again. At least I would have had a distraction from everything that had happened if I would have just gone in. It was too late now.

He walked me down a short hall to the bedroom and pointed to a small wooden table against the wall that housed a computer and printer that barely fit the length of the table. I pulled out the metal folding chair and sat down as I waited for him to finish typing in the password to unlock the computer. As he pressed enter the screen changed and a picture of him surrounded by a handful of girls and two older people greeted me. I looked up at him in question as I hadn't expected a family picture to be his wallpaper.

"I'm the oldest of 7 children, only boy." He smiled as he folded his arms across his chest and leaned back against the wall, one foot crossed over the other.

"Your poor dad," I joked as I studied the picture. The girls were all young looking and aside from a few, all looked like they could be the same age. Each girl had dark hair and dark eyes, but there was one who stuck out to me the most. She looked familiar and I couldn't put my finger on how or where I knew her from. Her eyes were slightly lighter than the others, more of a hazel color than brown. I continued to study the picture when I felt Max's eyes on me.

"That's my baby sister, Elena." He started to smile and I noticed that it faded as quickly as it started. He looked away and I wondered what the story was.

"She looks really familiar." I turned my head slowly back to the screen and studied her features. She was smiling but it was one of those smiles that didn't fully reach the eyes. It was more of a forced smile, one that you give when someone is taking your picture. Not a real smile. There was a look on her face that made me feel uneasy. It almost felt like she was silently asking for help. From what, I had no idea. So many of us have our own personal demons that no one ever knows about.

"She went to NYU and was studying Psychology. Maybe you guys had a class together?"

"Elena? What's her last name?" I pulled my brows together as I tried to remember if the name sounded familiar but I was drawing a blank.

"Romano." He shifted his weight and turned slightly on the wall to look directly at me with his arms still crossed over his chest. The last name sounded familiar but I still couldn't picture her as Elena. The softness of her voice filtered through my mind as I remembered her from my intro to psychology class. She had made a joke on the first day when we did the mandatory self-introductions that she was just like Joey's family on *Friends*- Italian American family with 6 girls and 1 boy.

"Leni? Does she go by Leni?" I asked as I looked up at him and saw a shift in his posture when I mentioned her name.

"It's been her nickname since she was a baby." He smiled sadly as a private thought made its way through his mind. "I gave it to her."

"It's a cute nickname." I smiled. "She's in my Intro to Psychology class." I felt satisfied now that I knew where I recognized her from but something about the way Max reacted to her tugged at my heart. Something was wrong, I could feel it.

"Wait, did you say she *went* to NYU? Did she recently decide to stop going?" I was trying to remember the last time I had seen her in class. The class wasn't that big so it should have been easy to notice if someone was no longer in it but then again, I was hardly ever focused on who was showing up for class unless they were in my group. Max's face fell and a paleness washed over his olive toned skin as he looked down at the floor.

"She's missing." He slowly lifted his eyes to meet mine as his shoulders slumped after having said the words out loud. I brought a hand to my mouth as I took in the information. It all made sense now. His reaction to her picture, the added stress I've seen weighing him down today, the somberness to his tone when we discussed what happened to Amber. My mind struggled to try to process what he had said, too many questions fighting to be asked first.

"How long has she been missing?"

"Since Monday." He ran a hand through his hair and let out a deep breath as he pushed off the wall and sat on the edge of the bed across from me. The room was decent sized for a New York apartment but the confined space between the bed and the desk meant that we were even more in each other's space. I could feel the heat from his body as his leg slightly brushed against mine as he sat down. The smell of his shampoo lingered in the air making it hard to breathe anything other than his scent.

"Technically since Sunday night but I didn't know about it until Monday morning when she called." His eyes filled with tears and I saw his jaw clench as he fought back the emotions he was feeling. "She called me for help and I still haven't been able to find her."

I could hear the anger and frustration in his voice as he

sat up taller and squared his shoulders. I didn't have any siblings so I didn't know what it was like to have someone to look after and take care of, but I imagined that him being the older brother meant that he was feeling a huge amount of guilt right now for feeling like he couldn't protect her. He was trying to be strong and not show his emotion but I could see right through the tough guy act. I saw the sensitive, caring man who needed someone to tell him that it would be okay. I wondered if he had anyone who would do that for him.

In the family photo he was in the center with the girls spread out on both sides of him and in front of him with his parents behind him. It portrayed as him being the center of the family, the one who held everything together. I reached forward and placed my hand on his knee, feeling him tense beneath my touch as his eyes wildly looked into mine, unsure of what I was doing.

"I'm really sorry about your sister, Max." I smiled as I maintained eye contact, almost a challenge for him to let down his guard with me. I didn't know him aside from the detective who was helping me with my own problems but something told me that he needed a friend right now as much as I did. Someone to just be there and say that everything would be okay.

I felt his body start to relax beneath my hand as he placed his hand on top of mine. I sucked in a breath and held it as I waited for him to push my hand away but was relieved when he gently squeezed it before holding it. It was surprisingly soft, the warmth of it comforting.

"I'm really sorry about your friend."

The tears started rolling down my face before I could try to stop them. Tears for Amber. Tears for myself. Tears for Max. They fell together in a perfect blend of sadness and loss as I felt him move his hand from mine and gently pull me over to the bed next to him. I sat beside him as he pulled me close to him and held me as I cried. I felt his chest shake and refrained from looking up as I knew that his tears had started to join mine. He needed this embrace as much as I did.

We spent the evening in the living room trying to forget the morning and everything else that was currently plaguing us but found it nearly impossible. His mind was still on trying to find something on his sister and mine was refusing to focus on the notes I had printed that Joel had sent. I tossed my highlighter on the coffee table and leaned back against the couch as I stretched my legs out in front of me. I had been sitting on the floor for hours and my body was starting to protest. I was about to get up when I heard a knock on the door, Max looking at me in question.

"Don't ask me, I don't live here." I joked as he laughed and walked to the door. I could tell that he wasn't expecting anyone which made it even more unsettling that someone was showing up unannounced at his door when his sister was still missing. I've seen plenty of shows where the police show up unannounced to tell you someone died. I lifted myself from the floor and my stomach tightened as I waited for him to open the door.

"I brought beer and pizza," Trevor announced as he walked in holding a pizza box and a 6 pack of beer. His eyes went wide when he saw me, first looking at me then looking at Max with a smirk on his face as he walked in and sat them on the island.

"Hey Hannah, nice to see you again." He side-eyed Max as he looked back at me with a huge grin. "Didn't expect to see you here. Am I interrupting something?"

"Hannah is staying with me for a little bit." Max closed the door and folded his arms over his chest as he looked at Trevor and waited for his response. I watched as Max's jaw tightened as he had some unspoken showdown with Trevor. Trevor looked like he was trying to figure it out but I knew that he was about to lose whatever game he thought they were playing.

"Is that so?" Trevor turned to look at me and I felt Max's gaze turn my way as well.

"Yup. It's true." I pulled at the bottom of my oversized NYU sweatshirt and anxiously chewed my bottom lip as the two of them continued to watch me. There was a thick tension in the air and I waited for someone to give in and say something to break it.

"Someone broke into my apartment again and murdered my best friend, then threw her out the window of my apartment, so I'm kinda staying here for a little bit until it's safe to go back." I shrugged my shoulders and took in a deep breath to replenish the one I had used to get all of that information out in one long winded sentence.

Trevor's eyes shot up as Max's face relaxed before they exchanged a look between them. I plopped myself down on the couch and pulled my legs up underneath me, trying to curl into a tiny ball under my sweatshirt.

"God, Hannah, I had no idea. I'm so sorry." Trevor came and sat on the other end of the couch and gently patted my leg. I had just met him last night and yet he was one of the most sincere and caring people I had met since moving to the city.

"Thank you." I smiled as he continued to pat my leg, thankful for the comfort he was offering. Max grabbed the beer and pizza from the island and sat it on the coffee table as I moved my stuff out of the way. He opened the pizza box and nodded for me to take a slice. I wasn't used to being the center of attention and it definitely felt strange being it with two very attractive men. I reached in and grabbed a slice then retreated back to my corner of the couch as I watched them get their slices. Max got up and went to the kitchen, bringing napkins and a bottle opener back with him. I reached out and took a napkin as I stuffed another bite of pizza in my mouth. I hadn't realized how hungry I was, especially given that I hadn't eaten all day.

Max opened a beer and handed it to Trevor before opening another and extending it to me. I froze and didn't know what to do. I didn't want to be rude and decline his offer but I also didn't want to get caught drinking underage in the presence of law enforcement. I quickly chewed my bite and blotted my mouth with my napkin as I tried to swallow as quickly as possible.

"I um, I can't." I could feel the heat creeping up my neck as I felt the embarrassment wash over me. If we were anywhere else and he was anyone other than the detective that was helping me, I would have accepted the drink in a heartbeat. I felt like such a prissy good girl for having to say no, but I didn't want him to think that I was reckless and irresponsible.

"You don't drink?" Trevor asked sincerely without the judgement I had expected to hear.

"I'm not 21. Yet." My face felt like it was on fire and suddenly I wished I was anywhere but there.

I saw a smirk cross Trevor's face as he took a bite of pizza and watched Max's reaction to the news. Max had to have some idea of how old I was if I was in the same class as his sister, right? I could see the slightest blush on his face as his shoulders tightened and he avoided Trevor's look.

"Hannah, it's fine. You should have a beer with us." He nodded to it as he continued to hold it out to me. My eyes searched his face, waiting for the punch line or for him to deceive me and arrest me once I took the bait. I looked to Trevor who looked at me with a smile that said he knew something that I didn't. He raised his eyebrows as if challenging me to take it as he slowly brought his bottle to his lips and took a sip.

"I promise, I'm not going to arrest you or turn you in for underage drinking." He sat the beer in front of me then took his place on the floor by the recliner again. "I have 6 sisters, the youngest is 18. I know that none of them waited until they were 21 to start drinking. I don't expect that you're waiting either."

Reluctantly I reached forward and grabbed the beer from the table as I smiled at Max who gave me a subtle nod as he took a sip.

"So, just how old are you, Hannah?" Trevor rested the beer bottle on his thigh and settled against the couch, waiting on my answer.

"I just turned 19 a few weeks ago." I took a sip and closed my eyes as the cold liquid made its way down my throat. I hardly ever drank and knew that it wouldn't take much for me to get buzzed. Part of me wanted the beer to take hold and help me forget what had happened but part of me knew that I couldn't allow that to happen.

"Still just a babe," Trevor said as he looked at Max over the top of his beer bottle as he took another drink.

"How old are you?" I looked at him with the smirkiest look I could manage, unaware of whatever was going on between the two of them.

"How old do you think I am?"

"27? 28?" I tried to do quick math so I didn't sound stupid but I had no clue how old you had to be to make detective. I was hoping my wild guess worked in my favor.

"We're both 29." He pointed a finger back and forth between him and Max, though there was no one else there for me to be confused about who the 'we' might be.

I took another drink as I sunk lower into the couch, allowing the pizza to digest and the beer to take its hold on me.

"Is that too old?" Trevor asked as he watched me.

"Too old? For what? Like life in general?" I was confused on why he would ask me that then I saw the blush on Max's face again and it clicked. I heard Trevor chuckle as he finished his beer and sat it on the table next to the almost empty pizza box.

"Want another?" Max asked him as he reached to grab him another bottle.

"I don't know? Am I too old for another one, Hannah?" His laughter was contagious as I rolled my eyes and watched him take the beer from Max. I didn't bother responding as I knew I had already labeled myself as the geeky little girl who wasn't very bright and didn't bother to take any risks. Of all of the first impressions I could make, this was the one that I screwed up the easiest.

The night went on with us finishing off the pizza and talking over beers. Laughter floated around the room as they told stories about their wild days growing up together and even though my mind constantly stayed focused on what had happened to Amber, I was thankful for a small break to feel something other than grief.

Ten

Max

13 Days Ago

I've had plenty of girlfriends throughout my life yet none of them have ever made me feel the way I've felt having Hannah stay with me. It was completely unexpected and honestly I never imagined that I would be taking her back to my place after her best friend was murdered, but that was exactly what had happened.

There was something about Hannah that made me want to protect her, and not just in a - it's my job- kind of way. I wanted to protect her as much as I wanted to protect my own family. Maybe it was because she was the same age as my baby sister, who was still missing, or maybe it was because I felt like she was an innocent naive girl that needed someone to look out for her.

We had talked about Leni and for the first time since she went missing, I actually broke down and cried. I was so frustrated and disappointed in myself for letting Hannah see that side of me but as hard as I fought to hold it in, she fought even harder for me to let her be there for me. Someone who was going through a loss of her own, that same day no less, took the time to hold my hand and comfort me. I've never known anyone like that in my entire life. I have always been the one to hold things together and to be there for everyone else, I never knew what it felt like to have someone be there for me.

When I first met Hannah I pegged her as this wild, reckless, college girl who got herself into the same situations as my sister and never saw her as the mature, responsible person she really was. It was almost like she didn't know how to be wild or reckless. Something told me that there was a lot in life that Hannah hadn't yet experienced and that piqued my curiosity in the worst way.

The weekend flew by with Hannah trying to force herself to study and get through the last few term papers she had due while I worked on trying to find new leads on Elena's case. It was driving me crazy that I wasn't allowed to work her case, and even more so when I couldn't get updates from my team.

Trevor had been by a few times to bring food and coffee for us after I failed to realize that I needed to go grocery shopping. Hannah never complained about the food options and half the time I had to remind her that she needed to eat something. I knew that no matter how hard she tried to throw herself into her studies she wasn't able to get out of her own head or to stop thinking about what happened. She would sit on the couch or the floor and be so consumed with whatever she was reading, pushing her reading glasses back up her nose as they would slide off. It was adorable. I found that she had quite a few little quirks about her that made me want to memorize every little thing that she did. I found myself wanting to know more about her and then hating myself for it when I knew that there could never be anything between us. I wasn't a relationship kind of guy and she deserved much more than a random hookup.

The walk across campus was cold as the wind started to pick up, forcing us to walk faster. Over the weekend I had been reassigned to work Hannah's case and nothing else, which meant that I was to keep her in my sights at all times until we caught the person who was stalking her and had murdered her best friend. That meant that not only was she still going to live with me, but she was going to have me escort her to work and school until we felt there wasn't a direct threat against her. I worried that she would feel like she was being treated like a child but she surprised me with how easy going her attitude was with everything. Almost like she liked my company.

Warmth greeted us as I pulled open the heavy door to the old building and held it open for Hannah. The heater was on full blast, warming the hallway that reminded me of high school. There were classrooms lining both sides of the long narrow hallway which felt oddly quiet for the end of the semester. I looked around and found a few classes that were filled with students but most of them were empty.

I followed as she made her way to the only room that had its door propped open. The room was small and set up lecture style with all of the desks facing toward a desk and whiteboard at the front of the room. Hannah lowered her head as she walked in, a few students already in their seats while the professor stood behind his desk. I knew it would be hard for her to show up to classes that she had with Amber, having to answer questions from her classmates about where she was.

The professor took notice of me as I walked in with Hannah, taking my place along the back wall while she took her seat and started pulling out the items she needed from her backpack. He looked to be in his mid-thirties to early forties, muscular build from what I could see from his button-down shirt and fitted jeans. I imagined this was the image girls fantasized about when they thought about hot professor types and a fury of jealousy flowed through me as I wondered if Hannah was one of those girls.

I gave a tight smile as he continued to watch me out of the corner of his eye while he wrote out a list of topics on the whiteboard. A few more students shuffled in and took their seats until there were only a few empty seats left. I watched Hannah chew nervously on the end of her pen while she stared at the empty seat next to her and knew that it had to be Amber's seat. I wanted to go to her and comfort her but now wasn't the time or the place. The professor walked over and squatted down beside Hannah as the rest of the students started to fill their seats. I kept my head down as I tried to avoid being any more of a distraction for her than I already was.

"Good morning, Hannah. I just wanted to check in and see how things were going with the study group?" His voice was low with an empathetic tone to it.

"Good morning. It's going well. I feel like I'm more prepared for the final exam." She let out a shaky breath as she forced a smile. "Or at least I hope I am."

"I'm sure you'll do just fine. Your last assignment reflected the progress you've been making, but maybe try to squeeze

in an extra study session or two before the final if it makes you more comfortable."

"Thanks, I'll try to do that." She let out a soft laugh as she tucked a strand of hair behind her ear as he stood up and walked to the front of the class to start the lecture.

I felt my phone vibrate in my pocket as the room grew quiet, heads down as hands worked quickly to write down the notes as he spoke. I unlocked my phone and found a text message from Mindy confirming that she had the autopsy report on Chet as well as some updates from forensics about Hannah's case. There was a back door to the classroom which allowed me to sneak out of the room to call her without disrupting the class. I slowly closed the door, waiting until I heard the click, before sitting down on the bench that lined the wall in between the doors of Hannah's class. I knew Hannah was safe and she wasn't going to be able to leave the room without me seeing her so I didn't have to hover over her right now. I held my phone to my ear and waited for Mindy to answer.

"Hey, how's college treating you?" She joked as she answered the phone, knowing where I would be since Hannah had a full schedule of classes today.

"Good, I think I'm ready to pledge a frat and make really bad decisions," I teased back, thankful to have a lighthearted conversation with Mindy, even though I knew it would be changing in a matter of seconds. She laughed and I could hear the change in her tone when there was nothing else to joke about.

"So, what's the news?" I asked as I looked down the empty hallway.

"The autopsy shows that Chet died a week ago today. Blunt force trauma to the head, several broken ribs, a punctured lung, and a fractured skull. He would have bled out from the head wound if he hadn't been strangled to death first. It was a very violent death and unfortunately they weren't able to recover anything that could be used for DNA testing."

She let out a deep breath and I knew that it was about to get worse.

"We also got a trace on Elena's phone and were able to follow it to an empty warehouse a couple blocks away from the coffee shop she had met the online guy at."

My heart started racing, I couldn't believe there was finally a break in the case. I wanted to be ecstatic that we had a location to go off of but Mindy's voice said it all. If there was good news, she would have started with- Max, we found her! But she didn't. She saved the bad news so she could wait just a little bit longer to break my heart.

"Where did they find the body?" I swallowed hard, trying to force the bile back down.

"In a warehouse. The body isn't recognizable, we're still waiting for confirmation. But Max, they found her cell phone next to the body." The last words came out as a whisper. My head dropped as Mindy continued to talk, her words floating in the air around me but never actually making it to me. I sucked in a deep breath as I stood up and walked outside, welcoming the harsh chill in the air as it prickled the back of my neck. My breathing was ragged as I slammed my fist into the brick wall, leaving a trail of blood along the way.

I was too late.

Eleven

Hannah
11 Days Ago

"Is there anything I can help with?" I asked Amber's mom as I followed her into the kitchen with an empty tray of food. It felt weird being there when it was supposed to be a small gathering of Amber's family to remember her, but her parents had insisted that I come and I didn't have the heart to say no. The funeral had been that morning followed by the wake at her parents' house. Both were emotionally draining as I relived that morning over and over. To sit with her family and hear them tell stories about how wonderful she was felt like a dagger was jabbed into my heart over and over as I sat there knowing that her death was my fault. I was the reason that they were sharing stories and crying weeks before Christmas.

"I've got it honey, thank you." She smiled up at me with a smile that never met her eyes. There were bags under them that confirmed she hadn't slept in days mixed with the puffiness from crying. Still, she had a motherly look, one of love, as she came over and placed her hand over mine and smiled at me.

"My Amber sure was lucky to have such a wonderful best friend. I'm so happy she had you in her life, dear."

I wanted to tell her not to say nice things, to take back the adoring look she was giving me and replace it with the hatred she should feel for me because it's what I deserved. My lip trembled and I fought desperately to hold the tears back. This woman didn't deserve to have to comfort me when I was to blame for what happened. My hand trembled beneath hers and I forced myself to look away.

Warm arms pulled me and wrapped me in a hug as she gently rubbed my back. Unable to hold it in any longer a sob escaped my throat as the tears spilled over, staining the navy-blue satin shirt she was wearing. I was embarrassed that I was falling apart in front of her mom but I also felt comforted for the first time since everything had happened in a way that no one else could comfort me. The way only a mother could. I desperately wished to have my own mother there with me, to hold me and tell me everything was going to be alright, but that would mean that I had to tell her what had happened. I couldn't bear to add any additional stress to her life, she was already struggling to keep herself afloat and didn't need anything in addition to worry about. Besides, there wasn't anything she could do anyways. I was still staying with Max and that was the best protection I could have right now.

I felt her hug me tighter as my sobbing continued, a week's worth of stress finally dissipating. Quietly she whispered there, there, over and over, my body responding to her calmness. I slowly pulled back and quickly tried to wipe my tears away with the back of my hand even though it was evident I had been crying. She smiled sympathetically and my heart broke all over again for her.

"I'm so sorry about what happened to Amber," I blurted out before I could think about what I was saying. "It was all my fault, if she wouldn't have come stayed with me, she wouldn't —— she wouldn't——" The words caught in my throat as I struggled to get them out while sobbing again. I felt a hand on my lower back and knew it was Max as my body shook from the weight of my grief.

"Hannah, look at me, dear." Her voice was gentle, her eyes waiting patiently for mine to find hers through the blurriness of the tears. I looked at her and tried to take deep breaths to get my breathing back to normal.

"Hannah, you didn't do any of this. This wasn't your fault. We all know that it wasn't your fault, none of us blame you for what happened to her."

"But..," I stammered as she held up her hand for me to stop.

"No, I repeat, it's not your fault." She pulled out a chair from the small dining table and sat down as she nodded toward the other chair for me to sit in. I pulled it out and sat down, waiting for her to continue.

"Amber went to stay with you because she loved you and she wanted to make sure you were okay. She had told me about what was happening and assured me that she was going to keep you safe. No one could have predicted what would have happened honey, not a single one of us." Her voice got quiet as she finished her sentence, her attention focused elsewhere.

"I was actually on the phone with her right before it happened." She looked up at Max and I felt his weight shift behind me as this was news to both of us. "She had called me when you were in the shower and told me that she felt like someone had been watching you guys. She tried to stay awake to catch them but she never saw anyone. I remember hearing her get the pan out and her telling me that she was going to make breakfast before you left for work, then all of a sudden her voice sounded further away and I could tell she was talking to someone."

"Did you hear what they were saying?" Max asked as he pulled a notepad from his coat pocket and patted his other pocket until he found a pen.

"I couldn't hear it very well but I know that she asked what they were doing there so it seemed like she knew the person. I didn't hear much after that but it sounded like there was struggling and things were kind of muffled. A few seconds later a man's voice came on the line and said 'wrong number' and hung up." She trembled and looked up at Max as he wrote the information down.

"Are you sure that's what they said?" he asked with his brows pulled together, the pen hovering over the notepad.

"Yes, it was definitely 'wrong number'. I remember it because I thought it was odd he would say that when she had called me, even though he probably didn't know who had called who, let alone that I was her mother."

Max's face was pale as he stared down at the notepad before writing the information down. Something had changed in him when she told him about the phone call and I wondered if he was mad that his team didn't think to check her phone records since this seemed to be important information.

"Thank you, ma'am, for the information. I appreciate it. It's very helpful." He put the pen and notepad back into the pocket and looked down at me with a serious expression that I hadn't seen from him before.

"Hannah, I need to get some information back to my team so I need to go in for a bit. Do you want me to have an officer come meet you here and escort you back home when you're ready?"

"No it's okay, I can go with you now." I smiled and reached out to hold Amber's mom's hand as we both stood up. "Thank you for including me today, I really appreciate it and again, I'm very sorry for your loss."

We said our goodbyes to Amber's family then made our way to the station so Max could work on whatever it was he needed to do. He was strangely quiet and it was eating at me that I didn't know what had happened that could be upsetting him this much.

The snow crunched beneath our boots as we walked in silence, the weather surprisingly calm yet freezing as usual. I shoved my hands into my coat pockets in an effort not to reach out and grab his hand that was so close to mine that I could feel the heat of his body through his leather gloves.

"Is everything okay?" I asked as we walked up the steps to his office and waited for him to punch in the code to open the door. He glanced at me as we waited for it to beep, his hand on my lower back, guiding me in once the door opened.

"She said that it was a man's voice and he told her it was the wrong number." He nearly sprinted down the hallway of offices while I quickened my pace to try to keep up.

"Yeah, and?"

"When I was on the phone with Elena, some guy came on the line and said 'wrong number', then hung up on me. It can't be that big of a coincidence, right?" His eyes were wild as they searched mine to tell him he was right.

"I don't think I would call it a coincidence." I wasn't sure where he was going with his train of thought but the fact that there was a connection to his sister who was taken and then murdered and my best friend who was just murdered made my blood run cold. I ran my hands up and down my arms as a shiver ran through me.

"So what does this mean? What's next?" I asked even though I knew it probably sounded stupid.

"I want to look at the information my team has collected on Elena so far and see what other leads they might have had. Then maybe I can start trying to find a connection and we can nail this guy."

I watched as he walked into an office with two desks across from each other, a large whiteboard with a cork board on each side of it took up the wall in between their desks. I looked at the whiteboard and noticed a few things scribbled on it with arrows pointing to additional information and a few pictures taped in between. Max stood in front of the wall as he frantically searched back and forth, running a hand through his hair in frustration.

"What's wrong?" I asked as I stood beside him.

"It's gone." His voice was low and angry.

"What is?"

"Elena's case. All of the information I had gathered for them and sent to them- it's gone. It should be up here as an active case and it's fucking gone!" His voice boomed as I saw his fist clenched, ready to punch something. I flinched at the bandage that was already wrapped around his fist from when he hit the wall when he first got the news about Elena. I reached up and put a hand on his shoulder to try to calm him down and felt him immediately pull away from me. Embarrassed I pulled my hand back down and tucked it in my pocket, stepping further away from him to give him distance while I tried to pretend like I wasn't embarrassed by his rejection of my touch.

"She's not even in the ground yet for fucks sake! How could they do this?" He turned to look at me as he pointed at the wall, anger and disgust written on his face. "The case isn't closed until we have the killer and they're already moving on as if she didn't matter!"

I could see his chest rise and fall with each breath he struggled to take and wished there was something that I could do for him. If I had Trevor's number, I would call him and ask him to come but I didn't. I stood helplessly in the corner as he turned his attention back to the whiteboard. The office was small and sitting on the desk beside me was a framed photo of a pretty blonde woman and a man who had his arms wrapped around her as they shared a kiss. My guess was that it was his partners' desk from what he had told me, though I didn't know what she looked like. The desk was organized though there were stacks of files lining most of it. Off to the side on the top of two piles of files were two black folders with a post it note on top that read:

Romano

Myers

My heart sank when I saw Amber's last name on the post it note, a reminder that they both had shared the same unfortunate fate. I wondered if the black folders meant that the victims were deceased. Max was at his desk looking through a small pile of papers when I saw him look over at me.

"There are files over here that say Romano and Myers, are those what you're looking for?" I asked as I nodded at the edge of the desk where they sat.

Max stalked across the room as his eyes darted around to find the files in the piles that I was referring to then stopped dead in his tracks when he saw the black folders. His hand shakily reached out and grabbed them from the pile as he pulled the post it note off.

"What does black mean?" My voice was quiet as I wasn't sure what his mood was at this point.

"It means the case is dead. It'll be filed as a cold case because they weren't able to solve it." His eyes found mine and his shoulders slumped as I took in his words.

"But Amber hasn't even been gone a week, how can they say the case is closed? And you haven't gotten the report back yet on Elena, they haven't even confirmed it was her." I immediately felt the anger and frustration that I had seen on him when he saw the board had been cleared of their cases, meaning no one was going to work on them anymore.

"I know. Let's take these and get out of here." He shoved the files inside his leather coat and zipped it up as we made our way out of the office and back to his apartment.

Twelve

Max
11 Days Ago

I had been a total dick and I hated myself for it. Hannah wasn't someone that I ever wanted to hurt but I saw the look on her face when she tried to comfort me and I pulled away from her touch. There wasn't anything I could do to change what had already been done but I still felt like shit for what happened and didn't know how to bring it up. We had been back at the apartment for a few hours and had started writing out everything we knew so far between Elena's case, Amber's death, and the stalking that had been happening with Hannah. We were looking for any possible connection but at this point we were drawing blanks and I knew we needed to take a break and eat something since we hadn't eaten since the wake this morning.

It was after seven when the Chinese food was delivered and my stomach growled in anticipation of it. We cleared the table and sat on the couch as we ate, neither of us speaking as we shoveled food into our mouths. I felt bad that I had been so distracted that I hadn't bothered to take care of feeding either of us, especially since Hannah had been through so much in one day with the funeral and finding out that they had already closed the case on Amber's murder. I was thankful that Hannah had taken some time to talk with her mom on the phone before the food got there, even though she had mentioned that she still wasn't going to tell her what was going on. She seemed to be a little more relaxed after their conversation which helped me to relax as well.

We finished our meal in silence as a movie played on the tv for background noise. Now was the time to try to talk to Hannah and apologize for earlier but I didn't know what to say or how to say it. Being the coward that I am, I got up and went to the kitchen for the bottle of wine that was still sitting in my fridge that I hadn't bothered to open after my last date went south. I opened the bottle and poured two glasses, bringing it back and setting it on the coffee table as I handed a glass to Hannah. She eyed it suspiciously as she reached out and took it.

"I'm not sure you're really that good of a cop if you keep giving underage girls alcohol." She raised an eyebrow as she took a sip. I watched the way her mouth moved as she drank the wine, the slight lick of her lips as her body relaxed with the first taste.

"Technically I'm a detective. That means I'm just supposed to solve cases, not worry about intoxicated minors." I winked as I took a sip and watched her fight the smile that threatened to take over as she took another sip and focused on the tv.

"I'm really sorry about earlier." I took a deep breath and waited until I had her full attention before continuing. "I wasn't trying to be rude when I pulled away from you."

A slight shade of red crept up her chest and neck as she took another drink, her grip on the stem of the glass firmer as she avoided looking directly at me. Her hair was pulled up into a messy knot on her head again, giving me a perfect view as the blush lingered on her fair skin.

"It's not a big deal." She shrugged her shoulders and shook her head as she turned back to face the tv. I hated that she felt this way about it and I hated even more that I was starting to feel something for her and wanted to feel her touch again.

"Hannah, it is a big deal. I didn't mean to hurt your feelings."

"You didn't."

"I think I did."

"You must be wrong." Another long sip of wine as she continued to avoid looking at me, her glass almost empty. The way she purposely avoided me reminded me of Elena and her fiery temper.

"Then why won't you look at me?" I probed as I sat my glass down.

"I'm watching this movie."

"Yeah? What's it about?" I smirked knowing that she hadn't been watching it and by the look on her face right now, she had no idea what movie it was.

"It's about this guy who works at a hotel and his family gets to live there." She turned toward me, her jaw jutted out with the most adorable, sassy look on her face. I chuckled much to her irritation.

"Is that so?" I asked as I turned slightly against the couch to face her.

"Yes, he was given the hotel to look after during the quiet season and he's living there with his family. He's going to teach his son about managing a hotel."

"Have you seen it before?" I already knew the answer but asked anyways.

"Obviously, it's like a classic." She rolled her eyes for dramatic effect as she finished the last sip of wine and sat the glass on the coffee table. Against better judgement I leaned forward and refilled both glasses as she leaned back and pulled her knees up to her chest.

"Does it have a happy ending?" My smile spread across my face and there wasn't a damn thing I could do to stop it.

"It sure does." Her matter of a fact attitude made it even more hilarious that she was trying to bluff about knowing the movie.

"Should I be worried that you think it's a happy ending when he goes crazy and tries to kill his family?" I raised my eyebrows as her head whipped toward me with shock on her face.

"That doesn't happen," she scoffed while eyeing me suspiciously.

"Watch and see." I pointed to the tv and watched her reaction as the famous *Here's Johnny* scene played out, her eyes wide with horror that she was caught. She looked over at me as she chewed her bottom lip back and forth between her teeth.

"Well, who's to define what a happy ending should look like anyways?"

"Is that your psychology approach to being wrong?"

"Shut up!" She reached over and pushed my chest playfully as I caught her hand and pulled her into me. Her breathing hitched as her mouth was inches from mine, the smell of the wine sweet on her breath. Slowly I ran my hand behind her head and waited, unsure of whether to kiss her. Everything inside of me wanted it but I knew that I shouldn't go for it. She was too young and more importantly, I was supposed to be protecting her, not making out with her.

Her eyes closed and her lips parted slightly as she let my hand hold her close to me.

"Hannah..." I breathed, fighting everything that told me this was a really bad idea. "I don't want to take advantage of you." I swallowed hard as I tried to force myself to let go of her. She was just a baby and who knew if she would still want to kiss me if she wasn't buzzed from the wine and emotionally vulnerable with everything going on. I owed it to her to do the right thing. Her eyes fluttered open as she pulled back a little and tilted her head to look at me.

"Why would you feel like you were taking advantage of me?" Confusion etched her face along with the disappointment I had seen earlier.

"Because you've been drinking and you've been through a lot recently. A lot today." I ran a hand down my face, the stubble on my jawline prickly beneath my fingers. "I don't want to take advantage of the situation."

"Max, I'm not some young, stupid kid. I'm fully capable of making my own decisions and knowing what I want."

"What do you want?"

"You."

Her voice was direct as she looked me in the eye. There was something different in her that I had never seen before. A passion that I was curious to explore combined with a maturity that I had been doubtful of. I watched as she turned and straddled me, taking my face in her hands before leaning down and gently kissing me. Her lips were soft against mine, the taste of wine mixing with the taste of her. I closed my eyes and allowed myself to enjoy the moment, knowing it would be over before I was ready for it to end.

Her fingers made their way through my hair as she deepened the kiss, her tongue gently making its way into my mouth. I felt her body shift as she sank lower against me and leaned in, her breasts pressed firmly against my chest. Her kiss became more urgent as she slowly rocked her hips against me and for a moment, I felt what it might feel like if she were riding me. I tried to push the thought out of my head while trying to keep my erection from protruding through my jeans. As if knowing my dilemma, I watched as she pulled back and broke the kiss, biting her lip as she pushed herself down lower, directly on top of my throbbing dick. She reached down and started to lift her sweater up when I gripped her wrists to stop her. She pulled back as if I had slapped her and studied my face as she tried to figure out what had happened.

"We can't do this Hannah." I blew out a breath and leaned my head back against the couch, her sexy body still straddling me.

"Why not?" There was an irritation to her voice as she scowled down at me.

"Because, it's not right. Because I'm way older than you. Because I'm supposed to be protecting you. Because I just can't take advantage of you, Hannah." I worked my jaw back and forth in frustration. "There's too much at stake here and I don't want you to get hurt."

"Okay." She pursed her lips as she rolled off of me and stood up beside me. She looked around before spotting her backpack and walked over to grab it.

"What are you doing?" I asked as she slung the bag over her shoulder and stuffed her cell phone into her pocket. She grabbed her coat from the recliner and hung it over her arm as she walked to the door. I jumped up and stood in front of it before she could open it.

"I'm leaving," she snapped and I could tell that she was pissed. I didn't blame her, I knew I shouldn't have let things get that far, but I also couldn't let her leave.

"Hannah, I know you're mad and I'm sorry. I didn't mean to lead you on and I'm not trying to make you feel unwanted or rejected. Please stay," I pleaded as I begged her to stay.

"Look, I've stayed long enough. Nothing else has happened, I think it's time I go." She blew out a breath and looked past me to the door. "If you don't mind?" She looked pointedly at me until I moved from the door and let her pass.

"Hannah. Please?"

I closed my eyes as the door slammed shut knowing that it wouldn't do any good to follow her at this point. I picked up my phone and called Mindy. Regardless of how pissed I was

with how they were handling my sister's case, I still needed
her to get someone to watch over Hannah since we hadn't
figured out who was stalking her. It was going to be a long
night.

Thirteen

Hannah

8 Days Ago

I hadn't spoken to Max since Wednesday after I left his apartment, all calls forwarded to voicemail and text messages had been ignored. The minute I walked out his door I was instantly filled with regret. Regret for allowing myself to think he was interested in me and making a move on him. Regret for allowing myself to think that a real friendship was developing between us and that I could feel safe with him. And most importantly, regret for leaving and going back to my apartment where I was reminded of Amber and felt the most vulnerable. I didn't know anyone else in the city well enough to ask to stay with them and I hadn't worked as many hours this week so I couldn't afford a hotel room. The only choices were to stay with Max and be constantly reminded of his rejection or to stay by myself and pray that the rookie looking cop posted outside my door was enough to keep me safe.

I hadn't noticed anything unusual in my apartment since I had come back and every time I left to go to class or work, there was an officer waiting outside my door. It was oddly reassuring that I wasn't really alone but unsettling that my every move was being watched. The sun peaked through the sheer curtains, casting a warm glow across the hard wood floors as the sun made a rare appearance. Today was supposed to be a break from the weather which was nice except that it didn't really matter for me since it was Saturday and I didn't have anywhere to go.

I pushed the blankets back and sat up, stretching to relieve some of the pain I had from sleeping on Max's couch. Sitting on the coffee table were piles of text books and notebooks with a handful of highlighters and pens next to them, waiting for me to dive in and start studying for finals. I took a deep breath and let it out, dread flooding through me as I thought about trying to study. I hadn't been able to study for over a week and today didn't feel like it was going to be any different. Reluctantly I slid my feet down into my slippers and got out of bed. I grabbed a hair tie from my nightstand and twisted my hair into a bun on the top of my head.

My feet padded lightly across the floor as I made my way to the coffee pot when I noticed something under the door. I slowly walked over and bent down, a dark red liquid slowly pooling in from the hallway. My body tensed as I stood up and looked around, the bathroom door still closed. Slowly I walked over and pulled it open, turning to look inside. Holding a breath, I grabbed the shower curtain and yanked it to the side, my heartbeat pulsing in my ear. I brought a hand to my chest and leaned against the wall as I dropped the curtain, relieved no one was behind it.

As I made my way back into the room, I swiped my cell phone from my night stand and unlocked it. I didn't know who I should call since I didn't know what was actually happening. Was my mind playing tricks on me and making me think something bad had happened? Was I just seeing things that weren't really there? Maybe the cop, I still couldn't remember his name, had spilled a soda and that's what was coming in?

I slowly walked back to the door and looked down at the puddle that had grown dramatically bigger in the few minutes I had been gone. The liquid was too thick to be soda. Deep down in my gut I knew that it was blood. Problem was, I didn't know whose blood it was. I tried to stand on my toes and peek through the peephole without touching the blood which was rather hard given that it had pooled under the door. Taking another deep breath, I slowly moved to the side and opened the door. A loud thud rang through my apartment as the cop who had been sitting in the chair outside my apartment fell into the room and landed lifelessly on the floor.

I brought a hand to my mouth to stifle a scream as I jumped back, tears flooding my eyes. My fingers rapidly found Max's name in my contacts and pressed send. I waited for him to answer as I stood trembling over the dead cop, each second feeling like an hour had passed. After the sixth ring the call went to voicemail and my frustration started to build. I felt open and vulnerable as the person who was assigned to protect me laid dead in my apartment. And my guess was that it had just happened or someone would have freaked out and there would have been commotion in the hallway. I hung up and pressed the button to call again, shifting my weight from side to side while chewing my fingernail.

"Hannah, I'm so glad you called me back." His voice sounded groggy like he had just woken up.

"He's dead! Max, he's dead!" I nearly shouted into the phone as my panic continued to rise, my eyes constantly searching the hallway for any signs of movement. What if whoever did this was still outside?

"Who's dead?" His tone was sharp and more focused as I heard movement on the other end.

"The cop, the one outside my apartment. He's dead and he's in my apartment. And he's dead, Max. Dead!" I knew I was borderline hysterical and he could hear it in my voice but as I continued to stare at the dead body everything around me felt like it was closing in.

"I'm on my way."

I could hear the sound of his keys followed by the sound of a door slamming and heavy footsteps.

"Stay on the phone with me, okay Hannah?"

"Okay," I whispered as I clutched the phone to my ear and paced back and forth. The pool of blood had gotten even larger and I had to take a few steps back to avoid stepping in it. As I walked backwards, I felt the smooth wood of the coffee table as I bumped into it, almost knocking myself over. I sighed as I turned to focus on getting myself to the couch without tripping over something else when I looked down and found a note on the couch cushion.

"Oh my God," I mumbled, forgetting that Max was still on the phone.

"What's wrong Hannah?" He sounded winded as if he was running and trying to talk at the same time.

"There's a note on my couch."

"What does it say?"

"Some people shouldn't sleep on the job."

"What?"

"That's all it says- 'some people shouldn't sleep on the job.' There's nothing else."

"Okay, I'll be there in just a second. I'm down at the front door now." I heard a click as he hung up and continued to stare at the note in my hand.

A few minutes later Max's head appeared in my doorway as he spoke into his cell phone, his eyes landing on me as soon as he stepped inside.

"Are you okay?" He reached down and rolled the body over, feeling for a pulse while he studied me. I could see the tension in his body as he stood up and ran a hand down his face as he took in what had happened. I didn't know if he knew the cop but I had to imagine that it was hard to see one of your own down regardless. A few minutes later I heard heavy footsteps coming down the hall followed by cops making their way into the apartment and talking to Max. I leaned back against the couch and closed my eyes, trying to remember a happy time in my life that didn't involve death or fear.

Eventually Max was able to break away while the other officers took over the scene. He sat beside me in silence as I continued to sit with my head resting against the couch, my eyes clenched shut.

"I know that you don't want to stay with me anymore, and I respect that, but you won't be able to stay here for a while since it's an active crime scene." His voice was gentle but I could hear pain behind his words as they lingered on the topic I had refused to talk to him about since I left that night. "Is there anyone that I can call for you that you can stay with?"

"I don't have anyone. Amber was my only friend and she's dead." I opened my eyes and turned to look at him as tears filled my eyes. "Honestly, I would go back home to stay with my mom if I didn't have finals next week, but I'm kinda scared that I have some sort of curse on me that people who come within a 50-yard radius of me end up dying. You might want to move further away." I closed my eyes and leaned my head back again feeling defeated by life in general.

"Would you consider staying with me again? Please?" I felt his hand reach out and hold mine, the warmth comforting.

"I don't think that's a good idea."

"Why not?"

I looked at him and raised an eyebrow, my expression doing the talking for me.

"Hannah, you haven't given me a chance to explain what happened."

"I know what happened," I snapped, cutting him off before he could offer some overly recited explanation about how it wasn't me, it's him. I hated that I was acting this way with him but honestly, it felt better to keep him as far away as possible. If he was far away then I wouldn't feel the pain each time he rejected me.

"No, Hannah, you don't. And quite frankly, you're being real immature by refusing to listen."

My eyes flew open as I stared at him, disbelief that he had the nerve to call me immature. I saw a smirk start to cross his face as he tried to hide it, knowing that he had said the right thing to get my attention. I knew there was a pretty big age gap between us and secretly wondered if that was his only hang up about being with me. I had spent plenty of time at work and in class trying to figure out whether I had misread everything between us. Was he really not interested in me? It sure didn't seem to be the problem when I sat on his lap and could feel the promise of a good time underneath me. A promise that quickly grew the longer I sat there.

"Fine. Talk." I sat up and turned toward him as I crossed my arms over my chest and glared at him. I was furious for him thinking that I was too immature but I didn't want to give him any more credibility by acting like a child right now and throwing a fit. I tried to relax my posture enough to show that I was still angry but not overly angry like a child who didn't get what they wanted. I needed him to take me seriously and treat me like an adult. I'd struggled all my life with everyone treating me like a child and now I was out on my own, an adult, and needed to be treated like one.

"Right here? Right now?" He quirked his brow as he looked over at the crime scene a short distance away from us and looked back at me. In that moment I felt like the child he thought I was. Someone so caught up and focused on their own hurt feelings that I didn't even pay attention to what was going on around me. I felt the blush creep up my neck as I relaxed my arms and turned away from him.

"Why don't we go back to my place? We can talk and then figure out the plan for where you're going to stay?" He offered as he stood up and looked down at me.

"Fine. But I don't plan to ever come back to this apartment so I want to pack up a few things first if that's okay?"

"That should be fine, I'll check in with the other officers and make sure there's nothing they need you to leave. How much stuff do you have?"

"Not much, I left most of my stuff at home and really just brought the essentials with me like clothes and stuff for the apartment." I shrugged as I looked around, comfortable with leaving more than half of the stuff here if it meant I never had to come back to this haunted apartment again.

"Go pack up your clothes and the stuff you need and I'll help you in a few minutes." He smiled and walked over to the other officers as I stood and reached beside the couch for my backpack. I started loading the books and stuff from the coffee table into my backpack when I remembered the note that I hadn't given to Max yet. I tucked it into my backpack along with the other stuff and made my way back to my dresser to pack up the little bit of clothes I had. A framed picture of me with my mom and dad before he got sick sat on my nightstand, my one personal item I had brought with me to make it feel more like home. I wrapped a thick sweater around it and placed it in the suitcase I had just brought back from Max's.

I sat on the edge of the bed with my suitcase almost ripping at the seams, over filled with clothes and my favorite blanket. My backpack sat on the bed beside me and for a moment I was depressed with just how little stuff I actually had in my life that meant anything to me. People always had stories about sentimental items and things that were given to them by a close relative but I had none of that. Max shook the officer's hand and walked toward me, eyeing the suitcase and backpack next to me.

"Is that all?" He looked around as if I had somewhere to hide additional luggage that he hadn't seen.

"Yup." I patted the suitcase and felt a sense of sadness wash over me as I had no idea where my life was going at this point. In just a few weeks everything went from calm and easy to chaotic and scary. I knew that Chet wasn't responsible for any of this after Max told me that he died shortly after our date, but it really felt like everything in my life was going well before I met him. I stood up and slung the backpack over my shoulder as he pulled the handle up on my rolling suitcase and followed him out of the apartment and away from the place I had hoped to call home.

<u>Fourteen</u>

Adam
7 Days Ago

Roses are red
Violets are blue
You don't see me
As I stand over you

My hand reaches out
To brush a strand of your hair
In the still of the night
You're completely unaware

I'll continue to watch you
Until you notice me
Things are more complicated
Than they really need to be

You've given me no choice
Than to go on this path
You think you've found new love
But I know it won't last

You can try to run
You can try to hide
I'll always be in the darkness
My time I'll gladly bide

Lurking in the shadows
Knowing your every step
I'll do whatever to make you mine
I'll go to any depth

Rest your pretty mind and
Cast away your fears
Pretend you're safe with the cop around
But remember, I'm always near

Fifteen

Max

7 Days Ago

My phone buzzed against my thigh, waking me up. Hannah and I had been up late the night before which led to me getting a late start Sunday morning. While I had hoped to talk to her and clear the air about what happened last time, she avoided me every time I brought it up. I was thankful to have her agree to stay with me and left it at that. I groaned as I rolled off of my stomach and fished my phone out of my pocket. Mindy's name flashed across the screen creating an irritation that I wasn't ready to deal with this early in the day. I silenced the call and rolled over, setting the phone on my night stand.

Thirty seconds later I watched the phone vibrate across my nightstand as Mindy called again. I could try to keep ignoring the calls and put my phone on silence but I worked with her long enough to know by the 3rd call she would give up and come over. Weighing my options, I ran my finger across the button to answer the call, given that it felt like the better option against having to see her.

"Yeah," I grunted into the phone without a single ounce of pleasantness.

"Nice to talk to you too." I could tell she was trying to test the waters by lightening the mood but I wasn't in the mood for it. I glanced over at the black folders sitting on my desk and clenched my jaw. I heard a deep breath on the other line and knew that she knew what my current temperament was.

"Okay, I get it, you're mad."

I rolled my eyes. I was about to hang up the call when she started to speak again and caught my attention.

"I know you have the files, and I know that you're pissed off that the cases were closed. I get it, I was furious as well. But Max, we have an update from the autopsy and they confirmed that it wasn't Elena's body."

I froze as I tried to process what she said. It wasn't Elena's body. That meant she might still be alive.

"Whose body was it?"

"They confirmed through dental records that it was another young girl, similar build and looks. Her family has been contacted and they are waiting for them to identify the body. There was a small tattoo on her ankle that they are hoping the family will recognize so they can confirm the identity."

"Did she know Elena? Was there any connection?"

"We don't know at this point. Just thought that I would tell you that it wasn't Elena which means her case is still open." I could hear the relief in her voice that matched my own.

"Thanks for the update." I was ready to hang up and be done with the call but something told me that I shouldn't be so hard on Mindy. If Elena was still alive, I needed all of the help I could get to try to find her.

"That also means I'm going to need the files back. Can I expect you to bring them by the office tomorrow or do you want me to come get them?"

"I can drop them off. I'll be out with Hannah tomorrow anyways, it's her last week of classes this week."

"How are things going with her staying with you? I heard about what happened yesterday, we're still trying to talk with the other neighbors to see if anyone heard or saw anything that can help us catch this bastard."

"Things are fine, she's trying to keep it together this week and focus on school but I really don't know how she does it. I don't think I would even know what day it was if I had been through everything she went through this past week."

"She's definitely had more than her fair share." Mindy let out a soft sigh and I could hear movement as she moved the phone to her other ear. "So, Jack said that he thinks we need to bring you back on the case. How do you feel about that? I know you're still looking after Hannah but we can see about getting another officer to take over."

"So they can have the same fate as the last one? I don't think so."

"I know, but we need you focused on this case if we have any hope of cracking it. You've seen how successful we've been without you." There was a pause as she waited for me to say something snarky. "Don't make me beg."

"I'll see what I can do. I really don't want to leave Hannah on her own but then again, I don't really trust anyone to keep her safe." I blew out a breath knowing this was going to bite me in the ass before I even said it.

"Well, there is one person."

"Who's that?"

"Trevor."

"You really think Trevor is the best person for this?" she asked cautiously. She had only met him a handful of times and he hit on her each time.

"We're basically the same person, so yeah, I trust him."

"If you think it will work." Her voice trailed off with doubt.

"Trust me, he's not going to hit on her." Annoyance flowed through me as I pictured the idea of him flirting with Hannah. What got me even worse was the idea of Hannah welcoming it.

"The only girls Trevor avoids hitting on are the girls you-" I could hear the palm of her hand smack her head on the other line. "Max, you fell for this girl? Already?"

"It's not like that."

"Except that it is. I can hear it in your voice."

I rolled my eyes as I got out of bed and adjusted my T-shirt. She was right and we both knew it. The problem was that I was still refusing to believe it myself.

"I gotta go. I'll be in touch tomorrow and let you know what time I'll be in the office. Thanks for the update on Elena, keep me posted if anything else comes up."

"Will do." She sighed as she hung up. My shoulders felt tense and while I would love to blame it on sleeping wrong or the built up stress from Elena, I knew that it was the tension between Hannah and I that was causing it.

I put my phone in my pocket and walked down the hall into the living room to find Hannah sitting on the floor at the coffee table with books spread out around her. Her brown hair was pulled up into a messy pile on top of her head with a few pencils holding it all together. She tapped the pen in her hand against her knee as she focused on the page in front of her, frustration etched on her face. I leaned against the wall and took her in as I tried to figure out how to start our day that would be better than how we ended our night.

She looked up, surprise written on her face as she noticed me standing there. She pulled the white cord that hung by her neck causing two earbuds to fall into her lap.

"Sorry if I woke you up, I was trying to be quiet." She reached down and turned the music off on her phone before unplugging the earbuds and wrapping them up into a neat ball before tossing them into her backpack.

"You didn't wake me, I got a call from Mindy with an update on Elena's case."

"I thought it was closed?" She moved her books from the coffee table back into her backpack except for one which she held on her lap after she climbed up and got comfortable on the couch.

"It was, but they confirmed the body wasn't Elena's. They are waiting on a positive ID from the family but they are pretty sure they know who it is."

"So what does that mean now? Do they know where she might be?" There was a hopefulness to her voice and I wanted to be as hopeful as she was that we would find my sister alive.

"Starting tomorrow I'll be going back to the office and working on the case." I waited for her response to this news before going on. Her face dropped and I waited for her to ask me not to go in, to stay with her and keep protecting her.

"I'm sure they'll be happy to have you back on the case. More heads are always better than one." She smiled and looked down at the book in her lap, her fingers slowly skimming the edge as she hesitated on opening it. It felt like now was the time to try to clear the air and talk about the other night. I needed things to be easier between us without all of this built up tension.

"Hannah, I really want to talk to you." I walked over, closing the distance between us as I sat on the other end of the couch and faced her. She folded her hands on top of the book and turned to look at me. Her eyes looked fiercely green and for a moment I thought I might get lost in their depths.

"Okay." She was short but the attitude that had been there the last few days had gone away. I held out hope that this would go well.

"I am so sorry for the other night. I didn't mean to hurt your feelings." My eyes searched hers, desperately looking for a sign of how she really felt about it. I might have stopped things between us the other night but now I felt like my heart was on the line and on the verge of being rejected.

"You didn't." She swallowed hard and I knew it was a lie.

"You know, this conversation will go so much better if we don't lie to each other." I tried to sound as playful as possible even though it was true.

"I'm not lying." A blush crept up her cheeks as she fidgeted in her seat. Lie number two. I raised an eyebrow in response which was immediately met with a blush that covered her neck and chest as her eyes darted away from mine.

"You know you're cute when you get caught lying."

I was taking a gamble and putting myself out there. If she felt the way I thought she felt about me then this should be easy and turn into a fun, flirty game. If I was misreading her then this would no doubt end with me being some weird, creepy, older guy preying on an innocent young girl. I prayed for the first option as I waited for her response. Part of me wanted her to want me as much as I wanted her, but I also knew that what we would both want out of this wasn't going to be the same and she would end up getting hurt. I hated myself for that but I found that I couldn't stop myself around Hannah. There was something that drew me to her and I felt like I needed her as much as I needed air to breathe.

"You don't know me well enough to know when I'm lying." She tilted her face slightly to look at me, still refusing to give me her full attention.

"I'm a detective, it's my job to read people." I grinned as I shifted in my seat and stared at her.

"Well then, you must not be very good at your job." Her tone was definitely flirty as she looked at me from over her shoulder.

"Alright, then let's make this fun, shall we? I will tell you everything that makes me believe you're lying and if I'm right, you have to scoot closer to me. If I'm wrong then you can move further away from me. Deal?" Excitement flooded through me as I thought about getting closer to her.

"Fine. I hope you like to lose. And I hope your neighbor has plenty of room for me in their apartment because that's how bad you're gonna lose." She smirked and my body immediately reacted to it. I was about to break every rule in the book, and for once, I didn't care. Maybe rules were meant to be broken.

"Alright, first sign that you're lying," I rubbed my hands together dramatically as if that would help.

"You swallowed hard when you said I didn't hurt your feelings."

She froze and I knew I had her as I watched her body get rigid.

"That wasn't a lie, you didn't hurt my feelings." She swallowed hard again and I had to fight to stifle a laugh.

"Your body is betraying you." I warned. She looked at me pointedly and scooted a fraction of an inch closer to me. My grin grew and spread across my face as I knew how hard this was really going to be.

"Sign two that you lied to me was the blush that crept up your face, not once, but twice."

"That wasn't a blush, it got hot in here." She folded her arms across her chest.

"Well, in that case, I could always open the window and let some fresh air in here if that's the problem?" I pointed to the window and raised my eyebrows in question. I watched as she shivered at the thought and chuckled.

"I'm fine now, thank you."

"Good, that's good. I would hate to point out how you shivered in response to the window being open, yet you still have that blush that creeps up your chest and throat, all the way to your cheeks." I pointed in her direction for her effect.

"I don't blush."

She was stubborn, I had to give her that.

"Oh really? Okay, so then what is this?" I lightly reached over and ran my finger along the trail of skin that was slightly pink, her body reacting to my touch. She rolled her eyes and scooted toward me.

"Third sign you're lying to me is the lack of eye contact. You'll look anywhere to avoid looking at me."

Her shoulders squared as she turned to look at me, a defiant look on her face as she refused to scoot any closer to me. There was a small gap between us which felt too big. I wanted her closer. I wanted to hold her and touch her and feel her body against mine.

"Well, that fixes one lie," I joked as I adjusted on the couch, closing some of the space between us. Her body reacted and

I desperately wanted to reach out and touch her to see what else her body would do when I touched her.

"You think you know everything, don't you?" There was an edginess to her tone as she watched my body as if I might pounce on her.

"Not everything, but I do know a lot about people and body language. It helps to know when people are lying or when their body is saying something their mind won't allow them to." I let my gaze travel leisurely over her body, noticing everything her body was saying that she was trying so hard to fight. Like the way her knee was slightly angled toward me or her hand that had moved closer to mine on the couch. The way her breathing had changed the closer I got to her. Or the way her nipples hardened beneath the T-shirt she was wearing with the tight black yoga pants that I was eager to rip off of her.

"Okay, so what exactly is my body language saying?" She tilted her head to the side and her eyes tried to make eye contact as they fought the urge to roam my body. I could tell that she was as curious about this chemistry between us as I was but she was scared to explore it.

"Your body language is saying that it wants me. The way your legs are slightly spread toward me, eager for me to feel how turned on you are. Your breathing has gotten more rapid the closer we sit to each other. And you tilt your head in a way that leaves your neck exposed, an easy path for my tongue to run down it."

Her eyes grew hooded as she listened to the words I said, her attention focused on me instead of avoiding me. She looked up at me and our eyes locked on each other, desire evident on both of our faces. My hand fought the urge to reach out and pull her into me as she subtly licked her lips.

"Hannah, I wanted to be with you the other night, more than you could know. Which given that you were sitting on my dick, I'm sure you knew." I saw a blush creep up her face as she lowered her eyes, casting a quick glance at my crotch before looking at the floor.

"I only said no because I didn't feel right letting anything happen between us. I'm supposed to be protecting you, not hitting on you. And given how much you've been through recently, I didn't want you acting on impulse because you were upset. I needed to know that if we had met under any other circumstances, you would still want me. I couldn't risk taking advantage of you."

Her posture changed and became more relaxed as she stared down at her bare feet on the rug. Slowly I reached over and lifted her chin up so I could look at her.

"Don't think for a second that it was because I didn't want you or that I don't find you attractive. You're one of the sexiest girls I've met and it's taking a whole lot of self-control to keep my hands off of you." I let out a nervous laugh and waited for her to say something. Anything. Her silence was killing me as I laid it all out on the line.

"I think that even if I hadn't met you under the same circumstances, I would still be incredibly attracted to you." She scooted closer and I could feel the heat from her body close to mine. "So attracted that I would be lying if I said that I wasn't turned on sitting this close to you. You're not the only one fighting urges right now." She worked her bottom lip between her teeth and watched me.

I reached across and wrapped my hand around the back of her head as my lips gently kissed hers. Her hands wrapped around the back of my neck as she deepened the kiss, pulling me toward her until she was laying on her back, my body on top of hers. The kiss was hungry and greedy as we fought to catch our breath, lust too much for us to fight it. My hand roamed down her neck, across her shoulder, and over her breast as she arched her back in response. I could feel how ready her body was for me and worked quickly to strip her of her shirt. Her chest heaved as she worked to pull my shirt up and over my head, stopping to run her fingers down my stomach before reaching for the drawstring of my sweats.

It was so arousing to see that she wanted this as much as I did, my erection bulging beneath the thick fabric of the sweat pants. I wanted her naked beneath me, I wanted to lick every inch of her while memorizing every detail I could of her body. My hands trembled with desire as I reached down and pulled at the top of her yoga pants, pulling them down her long legs, along with her panties. Laying beneath me on the couch was the most beautiful girl wearing nothing but a black lacy bra. I took a step back and stared at her as I licked my lips and tried to adjust myself. Hannah's eyes grew wide as she took in my size, desire heavy in her eyes. I worked my pants and boxers down and let them fall to the floor as I stood naked in front of her.

She swallowed hard and licked her lips as she spread her legs in invitation. I wanted to be inside of her already but I was more focused on making sure I took care of her. Slowly I kneeled down on the floor and gently pushed her knees apart, my shoulders holding them in place as my mouth began devouring her. Within minutes I found the rhythm she liked and worked my tongue around her as she came undone, calling my name while wrapping her fingers in my hair. She looked absolutely stunning as she came and I knew it was a face I wanted to see over and over again. I slowly scooted her away from the edge of the couch and made my way inside of her, feeling her tighten around me as I chased my own sweet release.

Sixteen

Hannah
7 Days Ago

Sunday afternoon rolled by without us noticing as we had spent the majority of the morning making love. My body still felt the after effects of our love making marathon and I wasn't sure how I was going to sit all day the next day in class as the soreness was starting to build. To say that he was well endowed would be a huge understatement. Max had left twenty minutes ago to grab us lunch while I tried to get my attention back to studying with no luck. Frustrated, I tossed the highlighter to the floor beside me and laid my head back against the couch cushion, memories of Max taking his time with me overriding anything I had just read. There was a knock on the door and I stilled, unsure of whether or not I should open it. It wasn't my apartment and Max wasn't there to tell me what to do. I contemplated my decision as another knock came, louder this time.

I stood up and opened the door to a young kid holding a small bouquet of flowers between his gloved hands. He extended the bouquet to me, lifting it higher toward my hands when I didn't reach out to take it.

"I think you might have the wrong apartment." I looked questioningly at him and waited for him to confirm who the delivery was for, even though I didn't actually know any of

Max's neighbors. It wasn't like I was going to be much help by saying, 'oh yeah, Ms. Jackson, she's two doors down.'

"Apartment 702. Says right here on the card." He plucked it from the pick that was holding it and flipped it around so I could see for myself. Printed in black ink was my name and Max's address. I reached out with a trembling hand and took the small vase, wondering who would be sending me flowers here. No one knew I was staying with him. I watched as he walked down the hallway and waited for the elevator before going back inside and closing the door. Just for safe measure I slid the deadbolt into place and locked the door.

I sat the vase down on the island and looked at the card that was still in my hand when I heard Max's key in the door. I walked over quickly and unlocked the deadbolt as Max smiled on the other side, a bag with take-out boxes filled to the top in one hand and a tray with two coffee cups in the other. His smiled faded as soon as he saw my expression and looked around the room. He came in and I closed and locked the door behind him.

"What's wrong?" He sat the bag of food down on the island next to the flowers and looked at them before looking up at me. For a quick second I prayed that it was some weird but romantic thing that Max did while he was out and that the flowers were from him. The voices in my head laughed hysterically as my hand started to sweat around the card I was still holding in between my fingers.

"Who are the flowers from?"

"I don't know. Someone just delivered them." I showed the card toward him as he walked over and took it from me.

"Did you open the card yet?" His eyes searched mine though I didn't know what he was looking for. I shook my head no and waited for him to open it for me. He flipped it over and read the name and address on the front before looking back at me.

"Does anyone know that you're staying here?"

I shook my head again and knew that was my confirmation that the flowers weren't some cute romantic gesture from Max.

"Do you want to open it? Or do you want me to?"

"Can you please?" My stomach churned as I waited for him to read it out loud. His finger ran under the seal on the back and pulled a thin card out. His brows furrowed as he read the card, my anxiety worsening as I waited. He looked over at me then down at the card again. A quick shake of his head before he began reading.

You don't know what you've done
A fire you've done started
Someday you'll have to make your peace
With the recently departed

I tried to warn you
About playing by the rules
A girl like you is never happy
I refuse to be your fool

Your time is coming
The clock is ticking

No one can save you
Your blood will be dripping

I felt the color drain from my face as his words filled the air around me, smothering me like a wet blanket. He flipped the card over and looked at the envelope it came in. I already knew that there wasn't any information about where it came from or who sent it. We both knew who it was, only we had no idea who it actually was. I ran my hands up and down my arms in an effort to get rid of the chill that covered my entire body.

"Are you okay?" He sat the card and envelope on the island and wrapped me in a hug. I felt safe with him and in that moment, I didn't want to be anywhere else other than in his arms. His apartment had felt like a safe place until now. Now everything in my life had been tainted by whoever it was that had become obsessed with me.

"Yeah, I'm fine," I lied. My stomach grumbled loudly and Max let out a soft chuckle.

"Why don't we sit down and eat before everything gets cold." He smiled warmly as he let go of me and walked over to the bag with our food. I stared at the flowers, a small bouquet of beautiful assorted flowers and felt sad that something so beautiful had been used for something so ugly. A hand reached out in front of me with a coffee cup and I snapped back to reality, smiling as I took the cup from Max. I grabbed his and took them over to the coffee table as he followed me with the food.

We sat and ate in silence with the tv on for background noise. I didn't want to talk about the flowers or the eerily creepy message that had been sent with them. I didn't want to talk about how someone found me at Max's apartment and how I no longer had a safe place to stay because this person always seemed to know where I was. I didn't want to talk about school and the stress of how I felt I was going to fail every class my first semester at NYU and lose my scholarship. I didn't want to talk, period.

After lunch we relaxed on the couch for a bit as I laid in his lap and he responded to several emails and text messages on his phone. I knew he was working on Elena's case and now the added details of mine. I wanted to force him to forget about everything and just be in the moment with me but I knew that wasn't possible. His high energy flowed through him and into me as I laid on him, making me feel more anxious than I already was. I needed to get up and do something to take my mind off of everything.

"I'm gonna go take a shower." I leaned up and kissed his cheek then made my way down the hall and into the bathroom. I stripped down and waited for the water to get hot before stepping in the walk-in shower. The water rained down on me peacefully as I laid my back against the cold tile wall and let myself cry. Slowly I slid down the tile until I was sitting on the floor with my knees pulled into my chest, warm water soothing my skin. I lowered my head and sobbed as I thought about everything that had happened over the past few weeks. Losing my dad had been one of the hardest and most trying times in my life, but this felt like it might be even worse. I felt helpless knowing that it wouldn't be long before whoever was stalking me would finally make their move. I heard a soft knock on the door before it slowly opened.

"Just checking on you, are you okay?" Max's voice was filled with concern but I couldn't catch my breath between sobs to answer him. The truth was that I wasn't okay; not even a little bit. I tried to catch my breath as I heard light footsteps approach the shower, the curtain pulled back as his eyes filled with sadness when they found me. He leaned in and turned the water off before reaching down and picking me up. I didn't care that I was naked or wet, I just let him carry me to his bed and wrap me in a blanket as he curled up next to me on the bed and held me. Slowly my breathing calmed and I felt my body relax against his as I drifted off to sleep.

I woke up a few hours later to an empty bed. It was embarrassing that Max had seen my meltdown and I felt even more like a child who had to be cared for. I got up and realized that my clean clothes were still in my suitcase in the living room. Reluctant to waltz in there naked, I decided to raid Max's closet and threw on a pair of sweatpants and a T-shirt that looked soft and worn out. I stopped to look in the mirror and noticed the puffiness in my eyes along with a small hickey on my neck. My hand reached up to touch it as I thought about Max's mouth on mine, kissing my neck as he thrust inside of me. The hickey was the result of his third orgasm. My hair was still wet in spots so I combed through it quickly and tossed it up in a messy bun on my head using a pen I found on his desk. I knew he wasn't expecting me to come out there dressed like a beauty queen but I didn't want to look like a complete slob either.

As I walked down the hall into the living room I heard him talking and stopped short when I saw Trevor sitting on the couch. Suddenly I felt very on display wearing Max's clothes and no underwear as they both looked at me, Max's face lit up with a smile.

"Hey Hannah," Trevor called over his shoulder as he turned his attention back to the tv.

"Hey." I looked at my suitcase in the corner and saw the clothes I was wearing earlier neatly folded on top leaving me no option to escape into the bathroom and put a bra on. Self-consciously I folded my arms across my chest and went and sat in my usual spot on the couch.

Spread out on the coffee table were sheets of paper with circles and arrows pointing in every direction. I leaned closer and found that it was all information related to my stalker and the little bit of information that Max had on Elena. I looked up at him as I leaned back on the couch and waited for him to tell me what was going on.

"We're trying to piece everything together." He nodded at the table as if that explained everything. I looked over at Trevor and he smiled though it didn't reach his eyes which made me wonder if he was called over to help solve this as a result of the card I got earlier. His eyes shifted and found the hickey on my neck, a smirk spreading across his face as he turned to look at Max with one eyebrow raised. I felt my cheeks flush, desperate to take the attention off of what had happened with Max and I earlier. I didn't bother looking to see what Max's reaction was, that would just make it worse. The fact that Trevor knew Max and I had done something was bad enough, I couldn't handle it if Max was going to gloat about it.

I slid off the couch onto my knees and leaned over the coffee table as I read the information they had linked to each bubble. There was a bubble for Elena, one for Amber, and the one in the middle was for me. My stomach soured as I acknowledged that they knew as well as I did that I was at the center of all of this. It seemed there was a connection between Elena missing and me, but I had yet to figure it out. I looked at my bubble and read each of the arrows with information on them. The notes I received. The cop that was murdered. My underwear drawer, which had been messed with not once, but twice. For all I knew this psychopath could be running around wearing a pair of them and I wouldn't even know it. I hadn't noticed that there was a new pair of underwear in my drawer with a note, would I really notice if a pair was missing?

I studied the information regarding the notes and each one had details about it being written in marker. I had never paid attention to that but then again, I hadn't paid much attention to the notes in general. Something was nagging at me just below the surface and I felt desperate to find it.

"Do you still have all of the notes that I've received?" I looked up at Max, hoping he still had them with him since he hadn't been in to the office.

"Yeah, let me go get them." He walked down the hall to the bedroom and came back with a Ziplock bag filled with the notes. He handed it to me and I laid each one out on the coffee table in the order in which I received them, including the one that came today.

Each note was a different size but each one was written on a page from a textbook. I didn't remember having any pages missing from my textbook other than the very first note but yet these still looked familiar. Each one had either a header or page number which seemed odd to me until I realized it was a clue. Instinctively I reached over and grabbed my backpack, flipping through the textbooks inside until I found my Introduction to Psychology book. Quickly I flipped the pages until I found the one that had been ripped. I placed the first note against it and found it matched perfectly.

I looked at the second note and saw a page number on the bottom. Going off of instincts I flipped through the same textbook until I found that page number. I studied the note and compared it to the same page of the textbook, the text the exact same. A shiver ran down my spine as I found the other note matched as well. I looked up at Max and Trevor as they leaned forward and studied me, waiting for me to confirm what I had found.

"All of these notes were written on pages torn out of this Intro to Psychology textbook," I held it up for them to see, "the only problem is that my book only has one page that is missing. That means these were torn out of someone else's book." There was a look of understanding followed by a look of confusion on their faces as they didn't make the same connection that I did.

"I had both Amber and Elena in the Intro to Psychology class." I let out a deep breath as my hand trembled holding the text book. Max leaned back in the recliner and closed his eyes as he ran a hand down his face.

"So you think the person that's stalking you also knew Amber and Elena?" Trevor asked as Max continued to rub his face.

"I do. That seems to be the strongest link, we were all in that class together and now one of us is missing, one is dead, and one is being stalked. I would say this is the path we need to look at."

Trevor and I talked amongst ourselves as Max called Mindy with the update. They decided it was best to keep working through the progress we were making which meant Mindy was on her way over to Max's apartment. I wasn't sure how I felt about meeting the woman who had decided that my best friend's case should be closed when the killer was still on the prowl.

I went through the notes I had collected for that class and didn't find anything that would be helpful, even though I had no idea what I was searching for. A handful of graded papers were sitting on the coffee table as I thumbed through papers from another binder when Max walked by and stopped abruptly in front of me.

"What class are those from?" He pointed to the stack of graded papers and looked across the coffee table as Mindy and Trevor shifted their attention to us.

"Um, I think these are all from the Intro class. Why?" I looked up at him as something crossed his face and he picked up the top paper and laid it next to one of the notes.

"The ink on this paper looks like the same on the notes- a fine point black marker. See?" He held up them up side by side for us to look. While they were both black markers, I didn't notice anything else that looked familiar.

"Let me see." Mindy extended her hand and Max passed them over to her. "It does look like the same type of pen but the curve and slant of the writing don't match. See how they slant their A in the note but it's not slanted here on the paper?" She leaned down and laid them on the coffee table to show us.

My mind was slowing down as it felt like we had spent hours going over the same thing, over and over again. I gently rubbed my temples as Mindy said goodbye and left. I was thankful for the break and hoped this meant that Trevor would leave as well so I could try to get some rest. A yawn took over and I fought the urge to curl up on the floor and sleep where I was. Max closed the door behind Mindy and slid the deadbolt into place before coming and sitting next to me on the couch.

"You ready for bed?" he asked as he laid his hand on my knee. I glanced over to see if Trevor had noticed but he was too consumed by something on his phone to pay attention as he rocked slowly in the recliner.

"Yeah, I have a long day tomorrow with classes so I better get to bed soon."

"How about you sleep in my bed with me tonight so I can make sure you're safe?"

I looked pointedly at him then looked at Trevor, pleading with my eyes for him to stop so Trevor wouldn't know we had hooked up. I saw the smirk on his face as he looked over at Trevor who still had his head down looking at his phone.

"Don't worry, I already know you guys are hooking up." He didn't bother looking up as he kept texting. I reached over and smacked Max's chest with my hand as he caught it and held onto it.

"You told him?" I whispered accusingly.

"He didn't have to. I could tell the moment I saw him. He's not all stiff and rigid like he was. Plus, there's the hickey on your neck." He looked up and smiled as he slid his phone into his pocket. I leaned back against the couch and closed my eyes while I prayed the couch would swallow me whole and spare me from this utter humiliation.

"It's not a big deal, is it?" Max leaned back against the couch next to me and spoke softly as I peered at him from the corner of my eye. I blew out a deep breath. It didn't really matter but I felt totally self-conscious that Trevor knew what had happened. Especially since Max and I hadn't even talked about it ourselves yet. Were we in a relationship? Was it just a one-night stand? I had no idea but the way he was looking at me and touching me made me feel like maybe it was more than that to him.

"I don't think it matters at this point." I sighed and stood up. "I'm heading to bed. And I'm taking your side because it's more comfortable." I raised my eyebrows and smirked at him as I started toward the hallway.

"Goodnight, Trevor," I called over my shoulder.

"Goodnight, Hannah. See you in the morning."

I stopped dead in my tracks and turned around, knowing there was something going on that I didn't know about.

"Why am I seeing you in the morning?"

"He's actually staying the night." Max swallowed hard and waited for my reaction before continuing. "Then he's going with you to all of your classes tomorrow." He smiled the cheesiest smile I had ever seen for half a second I couldn't be mad at him.

"Okay, walk me through it. Why is he going to my classes with me?"

"Hannah, whoever is stalking you found you here. They don't seem to care that you're staying with a cop so I don't trust them to not do something stupid. Trevor is staying here so he can help me protect you. And he's going with you to your classes to make sure you're safe." He let out a breath. "I can't take any chances Hannah. My sister is missing and that kills me. I can't stand the thought of something happening to you too."

"Fine." I sighed and looked over at Trevor who was watching the exchange between Max and I with the same interest someone does with watching a fight on Jerry Springer. "But we're stopping for donuts and coffee on the way in the morning." I turned and pointed to Trevor.

"You got it." He smiled and I saw Max relax as I walked down the hall and climbed into bed, leaving the day behind me as I drifted off to a place filled with memories of my dad.

Seventeen

Hannah
6 Days Ago

"That's your breakfast? A sugar filled glazed donut and vanilla latte?" Trevor eyed the donut in my hand as he flicked a packet of Splenda into his black coffee and put the lid back on.

"Hey, sugar keeps me going so I can make it through finals this week. I don't remember half of what I've studied and my only other option would be to start doing speed, and Lord knows, I can't afford a drug habit right now." I smiled as I took the latte from the barista and walked behind Trevor as we made our way out of the packed coffee shop. It was busy 24/7 with college students getting their fix for early morning classes or late-night cram sessions.

I slowly sipped my coffee in between bites as we walked across campus. It was another cold morning and I couldn't wait for the semester to be over. My bank account couldn't wait either given that I had taken this week off to focus on school. I took another big sip of coffee to try to warm myself up, pushing the impending financial crisis out of my head. I had plenty to worry about including new housing options on top of everything else. My recent phone call with my mom had ended with her asking if I needed to borrow money. That's when I knew I was in over my head- when my mom who is barely making ends meet, starts asking if I need money. My lungs filled with air as I took a deep breath and forced it out slowly and steadily.

"So, what's the deal with you and Max?" Trevor caught me mid sip, forcing me to turn away from him to keep from spraying coffee in his face. Of all of the things we could talk about to fill the silence, this was what he wanted to focus on?

"What do you mean?" I wiped my mouth with the back of my gloved hand and looked at him, hoping he would be clearer on what he was really asking before I embarrassed myself with divulging too much information. I had been obsessing over that same question.

"Are you guys just hooking up? Or are you wanting a relationship?" His eyes searched mine as if there was a secret answer that he was looking for that he didn't trust me to say out loud.

"We haven't really talked about it, things kind of just happened yesterday. I took a nap then next thing I know, you're living with us and asking about it as we walk to the final exam that I'm bound to fail." I veered off to the trash can and tossed in the dirty napkin from my donut and the empty coffee cup. When I looked back at Trevor, he was smiling but it wasn't a warm smile. I licked my lips as I tried to brace myself for a conversation I wasn't ready to have.

"You seem like a really nice girl, Hannah. I don't want you to get hurt, so you should probably talk to Max about what this is before things go any further. Just my advice- don't set your heart on a relationship. He's not that kind of guy."

His words were direct and carried a punch that knocked the wind out me. I didn't know what to say to that so I walked past him through the double doors that he held open, and made my way to the lecture hall. I could hear his footsteps as he trailed beside me, a few steps back, and wondered why he felt the need to warn me about Max. More importantly, I wondered why he said that Max wasn't the kind of guy to be in a relationship. While I had secretly wondered about it myself, I wasn't ready to hear the actual truth.

The room was already filling up, the rows toward the front of the class already taken by a handful of students that I knew from their obsessive Q&A sessions at the end of every lecture. I made my way a few rows back from where they were sitting and took a seat at the end of the row so I didn't have to climb over anyone once I was finished. Trevor sat next to me and studied the room, his phone in hand as he sent text messages every few minutes. My guess was that they were to Max since my phone had been quiet the moment Trevor and I left, yet Trevor's phone hadn't stopped. I could tell that Max felt uneasy this morning about leaving and going back to work. He asked me about my schedule so many times that at one point I gave up and just text it to him so he would have it. It boggled my mind how he could be so concerned with me and where I was going or what I was doing, yet he didn't care enough to want to be in a relationship. Or was that just Trevor talking? I shook my head in frustration and tried to clear my head and focus.

My backpack was light today with only a few notebooks and pencils, which felt weird. I was so used to lugging everything around with me that I felt almost naked not having a heavy backpack full of books. I had purposely left them at Max's apartment to try to keep my nerves calm so I didn't freak out and try to cram a bunch of studying in while I waited for the final exam. As I tapped my pencil on the folding table of my chair, I instantly regretted not having my books so I could study. I watched as the room continued to fill with anxious bodies, all of us waiting on the professor, which according to Trevor's phone, was now 9 minutes late.

A few minutes later the doors at the front of the room flew open and Professor Wright walked in, offering a small wave as everyone watched him. Within minutes he had his briefcase open and was giving the directions for how to complete the final exam as he walked up each row and handed out a stack of tests to be passed down the row. By the time he got to me he was winded and his face was redder than usual. I reached for the stack of papers at the same time he lost his grip on them and they went flying around me. I bent down to pick them up and almost collided with his head, a nervous laugh escaping my throat.

"Sorry," I whispered as I grabbed what I could and sat up right.

"No big deal." He smiled and reached beneath the empty chair in front of me to grab the last few tests. As he turned to walk to the row behind me, I noticed something caught his step and looked down as he wiggled his foot, his black boot stuck in something on the floor. A quick shake of his leg and it was free, allowing him to continue on his was as he passed out the remaining tests. I took the test on top and passed the others to Trevor to pass to the rest of the row. My hands trembled as my anxiety spiked, worried about whether I was ready for this exam.

Professor Wright made his way back down to the front of the room and stood in front of his desk as he announced the start of the final exam which would have 10 minutes added to the end due to him being late. I was about to write my name on the top of it when I noticed Trevor looking at the exam with an odd look on his face. He leaned closer and reached across to rub his finger along the corner. A small red dot smeared into a bigger red blob, confusion on my face as I watched him. He looked at me and mouthed the words 'are you bleeding'?

I looked down at my hands and didn't see any cuts or scratches then pulled up the sleeves of my sweater, not finding anything either. I shook my head no and followed his eyes as they shifted toward Professor Wright who had his back turned to the class and was quickly wiping something off the sleeve of his black overcoat with a tissue from the box on the desk. He pulled his arm across him as he wiped along the back side of his forearm, up to his elbow, studying the fabric carefully. From where I was sitting I could see a tear in the coat as he pulled it tight against his arm as he worked to clean it.

Looking satisfied he took the tissue he was using and wadded it up, tossing it in the trash can before turning around and checking on the class. Trevor and I exchanged a look as we watched the tissue covered in bright red fall into the wastebasket. As I looked down at my test with the red stain staring back at me, I wondered what had happened that made him so frenzied when he came in. He was usually calm and collected, today it looked like he had gotten into some sort of altercation before class. I lowered my head, closed my eyes, and said a quick prayer before starting the final.

An hour later I walked up to his desk and extended a shaky hand as I handed in the exam that would determine my fate in the class. He looked up and smiled warmly as he took the test from me, quickly flipping through the pages to make sure I had completed all of them.

"Have a good break, Hannah."

"Thank you." My voice was soft to keep from disrupting the rest of the class as they continued working on their test but I still couldn't stop thinking about the blood on his jacket earlier.

"Um, Professor, are you okay today?"

I really hoped I wasn't overstepping but his behavior had me concerned.

"Yeah, I'm okay. Why do you ask?" He tilted his head to the side as he sat my exam face down in the pile on his desk.

"I noticed that you were bleeding earlier. Some of it had gotten on my test." I smiled nervously and watched as a faint blush crept up his face.

"Oh, yeah, that. I'm so embarrassed. I was trying to help a kid chase down their dog that got away and as I reached for the leash, the dog ran away and I fell into a chain link fence. Turns out I'm not as graceful as I thought." He chuckled softly, the corners of his eyes wrinkling in response.

"Well, I'm sorry that you have battle wounds, but I personally would have appreciated the gesture." I smiled at him as I saw Trevor waiting for me by the door. "Have a relaxing break, maybe I'll see you next semester." I shifted my backpack and returned his smile before heading off to meet Trevor.

We walked out into the cold air and I took a deep breath, thankful that one final was done. The day felt long and I was relieved to be done with 2/3 of my final exams by the time Trevor and I caught the train back to Max's apartment. My mind was tired and I didn't want to think about anything school related for the rest of the day. We lucked out and found 2 seats toward the back as people shuffled around us with each stop. We were two stops away when I noticed Trevor get up and looked down at me.

"You ready?" There was a different tone to his voice, like he was putting on a show for someone. Confused I looked around quickly and didn't notice anyone that looked suspicious.

"The stop is still two stops away," I said quiet enough for him to hear but not loud enough for anyone else to pay attention.

"We have a stop to make along the way." He spoke sternly as he side-eyed a guy sitting across from us, a few seats down. The guy was wearing a hoodie pulled low over his face, making it hard to see him.

"Okay." I stood up and let Trevor take my hand as we waited for the door to open. As people started to push around me, I felt Trevor's strong hand guide me out and to the side, away from everyone. He pulled me close to him and from the angle we were at, it looked like we were in an intimate embrace. I stilled as I smelled the musky scent of his aftershave and noticed the stubble on his jawline. My body was tense, though I tried to look relaxed, as I waited for whatever it was he was doing. He lowered his head and tilted it toward me as he shielded my face with his.

"What's going on?" I whispered as I watched him intently watching someone close to us. He glanced at me before raising his arm and leaned against the metal beam above my head. It was freezing on the platform as the train whirled past us, the crowd thinning out with it.

"Stay still and try not to move."

I froze in place, nervously waiting to know what had him so spooked.

"The guy in the hoodie followed us from campus and he was taking pictures of you on his cell phone while we were on the train."

His words shot a chill through me as I thought about someone watching me and taking pictures of me without me having any clue. I was thankful that he was there. Obviously, I sucked at protecting myself, case in point. His body relaxed against me as his hand wrapped around my waist and pulled me closer to him. I sucked in a deep breath as I tried to remember that he was doing something other than hitting on me.

"I want to see how he reacts to seeing you with another guy."

"He's still there?" I felt stupid for asking. Why else would we still be in this intimate embrace if he wasn't.

"He's leaning against the other wall, on his cell phone. We'll leave in a few, if he follows then I know he's following you."

"Just tell me what you need me to do," I whispered even though no one else was close enough to hear me.

"I'm going to pretend to kiss you, then we'll hug and you'll walk away. Go to the 7th street station and take the train the rest of the way. From there go straight to Max's apartment, don't make any other stops along the way."

I looked up at him with fear in my eyes, there was no way he would be putting me out there as bait. Was there?

"I'll be right behind you. If this is the guy Hannah, we need to catch him and this may be the best way to do it."

I sucked in a deep breath and tried to reassure myself that I could do this. All I had to do was walk to Max's apartment. And survive.

"Okay." I let out the breath I had been holding as I turned into Trevor and wrapped my arms around him. I twisted our bodies slightly to make it a clear view where the guy in the hoodie stood. If we were going to put on a show, might as well go all in. We needed this to work. I leaned forward and tilted my head, resting my lips gently on Trevor's. I could feel his body's initial reaction to it and wrapped my hands behind his head to keep him from pulling back. His body gave in and I felt as he pushed me against the column and kissed me deeper, knowing we were both putting on the best show we could. As he pulled away, I wrapped him in a hug and leaned close to his ear.

"Make it count," I whispered as I pulled away and let my hand linger in his, looking adoringly over my shoulder like I imagined lovers did. Or at least that's what I'd seen in the movies.

I turned around and let Trevor drift out of sight as I wrapped my coat tighter around me and adjusted my backpack on my back. I took the stairs quickly and tried to use my peripheral vision to see if I could see anyone next to me wearing a hoodie. Who was I kidding? It was winter in New York. Everyone was wearing hoodies or overcoats which made it feel like an uncomfortable Where's Waldo puzzle. Except that Waldo was a mysterious stalker who liked to kill people in their downtime.

The streets were busy as I tried to stay focused on getting to the next station and not on who was around me. I pulled the zipper up higher on my coat and tried to tuck my head inside as I pulled the drawstring on the hood tighter around my head. If I could try to conserve as much heat as possible, maybe it wouldn't feel so bone chilling cold.

I was a few streets over when the crowd started to thin out, people going their separate ways. A tingle shot through me as I thought about whether the guy in the hoodie was near. Would he make his move out in the open like this? I tried to calm the fears that coursed through my mind as I reassured myself that Trevor was close by. I had no idea where, but I prayed he still had eyes on me.

The crosswalk sign lit up, encouraging me to go about my way when I felt someone next to me slightly bump my shoulder. I rubbed my hands together as I tried to get my mind to tell my feet to keep moving. From the corner of my eye I saw a black hoodie and my stomach dropped. Was it the same guy in the same black hoodie that Trevor was worried about or was it some weird coincidence that someone else in a black hoodie would bump into me? My mind tried to focus as I moved one foot in front of the other, crossing the street and continuing down the stairs to the train. My legs trembled as I swiped my metro card and pushed through the turnstile heading to the platform to wait for the next train.

The cold chill made my skin feel on high alert as I found a solid concrete wall to stand in front of, helping to ease my anxiety. I slowly looked around for a sign of Trevor or the guy in the hoodie and didn't find either. My stomach sank at the thought of going to the apartment by myself and turned sour at the thought that something could have happened to Trevor. I listened as the train approached and looked around once more before making my way through the crowd of people pushing their way around me. I held onto the handrail above me as the train pulled forward, still no sign of Trevor.

Eighteen

Max

6 Days Ago

"What do you mean you LOST her?" I barked into my cell phone.

"I'm sorry, Max. I thought this guy was following her and I needed to see if it was the guy who's been stalking her. I planned to meet up with her at the 7th street station but she walked faster than I anticipated and somehow got lost in the crowd." Trevor blew out a loud breath and I could hear the frustration in his voice.

"Have you checked my apartment?"

"Yeah, she's not there."

"How long ago did this happen?"

"If she got on the train that she should have gotten on, then she should have made it to your apartment twenty minutes ago. Easily."

"Did you follow the guy in the hoodie?" I tapped my foot impatiently as I tried to think of what the next step should be. I needed to find Hannah and I needed to find her now.

"I watched him walk up next to her at a crosswalk but he didn't make contact with her. They stood next to each other then went separate ways when they crossed. She was my priority, not him."

"So you're telling me that you lost her for nothing?"

"I feel bad enough already, just tell me where to look for her and I'll go there."

"Check her apartment, that's the only other place I can think of. I'll try calling her." I hung up the phone and paced behind my desk as I dialed her number and waited for her to answer. After the eighth ring I got her voicemail. I could feel my blood pressure rise as I hit redial and continued to pace along to the ringing tone in my ear. No answer. I looked at my watch and grunted knowing that she should have easily made it back to my apartment by now.

I ran a hand through my hair as I tried to think of other places she could have gone but I couldn't imagine that she would purposely tell Trevor that she was going directly to my apartment then go somewhere else. That wasn't like Hannah. Something was wrong.

Irritated, I hung up the phone and slammed it down on my desk. Mindy looked at me out of the corner of her eye with an eyebrow raised at the loud distraction. Staying in the office wasn't going to do any good if I couldn't concentrate and I definitely wasn't going to be able to until I knew where Hannah was. I grabbed my leather jacket off the back of my chair and flung it on, grabbing my cell phone and pressing send again as I held the phone to my ear and made my way to the 7th street station.

I walked the entire platform looking for any clues as I waited for the next train that would take me to the station that Hannah should have gotten off at to go to my apartment. I was out of ideas so I decided to retrace her steps and see if anything gave me a sign of where she could be. Trevor had called to confirm that she wasn't at her apartment and that the crime scene had already been cleared. While that was good news that Hannah could go home, I was reluctant to tell her because I wasn't ready for her to leave.

The train was nearly empty which gave me the opportunity to sit and think for a minute as I waited for my stop. There had to be something that Trevor and I were missing. Something that would lead Hannah astray. The train slowed to a jerky stop, forcing me to keep going. I walked the path that I imagined Hannah would have taken and looked down each dark alley for any signs she might have been taken down one. As morbid as it seemed, the detective in me knew it was a possibility.

As I got closer to my apartment, I felt tense and couldn't shake the feeling that I was missing something. Where could she be? Her apartment wasn't far from mine and there wasn't much in between other than apartments and a few restaurants and shops. Then it hit me, the only other place she could be that we hadn't thought of was the coffee shop that she went to all the time to meet up with her group from school. I turned on my heel and jogged down the block, hopeful that I would be right.

The coffee shop was packed 24/7 with a constant line out the door and today it was no exception. I pushed my way inside and ignored the looks and snide comments from those that thought I was trying to cut in line. Quickly my eyes scanned the room searching for Hannah, praying that my instincts were right and that she would be here.

I had almost given up when I looked around the entire room with no sign of her before spotting a table at the very back by the bathroom. Sitting by herself at the table, Hannah looked out the window and cried as she clutched her jacket tight around her. I let out a deep breath as I pushed through the overly crowded tables and made my way to her.

"Hannah, what are you doing here?" I kneeled beside her, her green eyes filled with tears as her fingers trembled above her lip as she tried to wipe them away.

"Are you okay?"

She nodded yes and then looked out the window again. I followed her eyes as she stared vacantly at the people passing by.

"What's going on? You were supposed to meet Trevor back at my apartment." My voice was gentle as I struggled to figure out what had happened and why she was so upset.

She wiped her eyes with the back of her hand and reached into the napkin dispenser for another napkin to blow her nose. She took a rugged deep breath and turned to look at me. I smiled warmly as I pulled the chair out next to me and sat beside her.

"While I was on the train, I reached into my pocket and found a note." She sucked in a few breaths, the effects of crying making it hard for her to get her words out easily.

"There was a note in your pocket?" I was confused and prayed that it wasn't like the notes she had been receiving from the stalker. Maybe it was a note from Amber that she forgot was in there and seeing it made her want to come back to where they used to hang out. She nodded yes and reached down into her pocket to pull out the note.

"It wasn't there before I went to class and I haven't taken my coat off all day so I don't know how it got there. But it was there." She looked out the window while I read the note.

If you want to know who killed your friend

Go to the spot you used to meet

Don't talk to the cop

Or I'll hang the pig by his feet

Real classy. I shook my head and fought the urge to crumple the note, knowing that it would have to be added to the other notes that were being collected as evidence. So that's why she didn't tell us she was coming here and wasn't answering her phone.

"What happened when you got here?" I asked quietly while my blood felt like it was boiling. She continued to stare out the window as she started talking.

"I got here and didn't know what I was looking for. I scanned the entire room, looking for something- anything that would tell me what the note was about. All of the tables were empty except for this one. Sitting across from it was a guy wearing a hoodie." She looked directly at me. "The guy that Trevor was worried about."

A chill ran through me as I thought about her alone by herself with this psychopath.

"What did he say?" I asked through gritted teeth, furious that Trevor had put her in this position to begin with.

"That I was being followed. Not by him, by someone else and that he wanted to warn me."

I studied her face to look for a reaction to this but she was emotionless as she kept talking as if she was reciting the weather forecast for the next week.

"He didn't have any information, other than that. But Max, he knew Elena." Her eyes met mine and I froze.

"What do you mean that he knew Elena? What did he say?" My heartbeat was racing as I waited for her to tell me everything this guy knew about my sister.

"They had just started dating a few weeks before she went missing. She was supposed to meet him that night but she never showed up." I watched as she swallowed hard as she looked down and folded her hands in her lap.

"The night she went missing."

I leaned back against the cold metal of the chair and closed my eyes as I rubbed my temples. My head felt like it was going to explode.

"Did he say anything more? Did you get his name? Is he still here?" My questions came out as rapid fire as I searched the room for a guy who I had no idea what he looked like.

"He didn't say anything more than that. I didn't get his name, he was in a hurry to leave. He seemed scared and anxious, but I don't know why."

"So why would he leave you a note to come here then not tell you anything other than someone was following you and that he knew Elena?" The frustration was getting to me and came out in my tone, causing Hannah to flinch at the anger in my voice.

"He didn't leave me the note. I don't know who did. He risked talking to me to tell me to be careful. He kept looking over his shoulder like someone was watching him." She took a deep breath before continuing. "Can't say that I remember what it feels like to NOT feel like someone is watching me."

I smiled as I reached over and patted her hand. There was part of me that was relieved that she was okay but a bigger part of me that was disappointed that there was yet another dead end. I would give anything to find the sick bastard and put an end to all of this, to bring Elena home safe and keep Hannah out of harm's way.

"I'm sorry, Hannah, I know how hard things have been for you." I blew out a breath and instantly kicked myself for saying it. How could I possibly know just how hard things have been for her? I wasn't the one who was living this nightmare that she was stuck in and I hated that I sounded so insincere. "Well, I don't actually know because I'm not the one who's going through everything, but I can imagine." I ran a hand down the scruff on my face and looked around the coffee shop. Someone had left her a note to meet them here so there was a slight chance they had shown up though the likelihood of them showing their face now was pretty slim. Based on the last few notes, whoever was watching her was also now watching me and knew that I was in law enforcement. It got under my skin as I sat there next to her, feeling like we were being hunted. "I don't think that whoever wrote that note is going to show up." I nodded at the paper sitting between us on the table.

"Yeah, me neither." She took a deep breath and swiped it off the table before stuffing it back in her coat pocket.

"You want to get out of here? Head home?"

"I don't even have a home anymore, but yeah, let's get going. This place just reminds me of Amber and I can't handle it anymore." She stood up and pulled her backpack from beside her and slid it onto her back. It broke my heart that she felt she didn't have anywhere to call home and part of me wanted to tell her that she could actually go back to her apartment whenever she was ready.

"Actually-" My throat was instantly dry as I choked on the words that fought to get out. Her eyes watched me with concern as my coughing fit continued.

"Are you okay?" She gently touched my arm as I turned away to avoid coughing in her face. I knew I needed to tell her she could be free of staying with me but my body seemed to be standing in the way of being able to do so.

"Yeah, dry throat," I croaked in between coughs.

"Want me to grab you some water?" She offered as she glanced up at the line that wound out the door and around the corner. I shook my head no as I headed into the men's bathroom and turned on the faucet. I leaned forward and cupped my hand under the water as I took big gulps of water, hoping to stop the cough.

I came out of the bathroom to find Hannah exactly where I left her, her arms folded across her chest as she looked at me with concern.

"Are you sure you're okay?"

"Yeah, I'm fine. Let's get going." I placed my hand on her lower back as I guided her out of the packed coffee shop, the weight of my decision not to tell her about her apartment sitting heavily on my shoulders.

Nineteen

Hannah
4 Days Ago

"Do you want the last slice of pizza?" I called down the hall to Max who was in the bedroom trying to find a file for Elena's case. He had spent the majority of the day on the phone with Mindy or screening calls from his mom and sisters. It was over two weeks since Elena had gone missing and each day that passed seemed to increase the number of times per day that his mom called for an update. I could see the toll it was taking on him to not have an answer for his family each time they called.

"Nope, go for it!" he yelled back, rummaging through the mess he had made earlier. An anonymous tip had come in yesterday that someone had spotted Elena working at a night club that was known for human trafficking and Max had been obsessed with trying to get a lead that actually went somewhere. His team had immediately investigated the tip and scanned all of the surveillance video from the club and the neighboring businesses which all confirmed there was no sign of Elena. But the fact that someone had called in about her had everyone feeling anxious.

Max had been pretty restless last night and the few times that I had woken up he was in the living room plotting out the timeline and every tip they had received. Trevor had been around and was trying to be helpful but at one point he took a step back and warned me to let Max do his thing. Apparently when he got this fixated on something, there was no stopping him. The tension in the apartment was thick and we still had yet to talk about what was going on between us. It didn't take much for me to see that Trevor was right about Max not being a relationship type of guy, he was showing me that on his own. He didn't touch me or even spend time with me the last few days as things got more intense with the case.

Today was my last day of finals and I was desperate to try to make something feel like it was normal again so I suggested that we order a pizza and veg out. So far, I had eaten by myself while watching reruns of *The Big Bang Theory* while Max shuffled about distracted. While it wasn't my ideal way to spend time together, I gave in and realized that Trevor was right, I needed to let Max do whatever Max was going to do. I celebrated the small victory of getting him to agree to take a plate of pizza with him to the bedroom. Whether he ate it or not, I had no clue.

I was starting to feel restless as the night continued on and I had nothing else to distract myself from my own thoughts. Max's anxiety was like a wet blanket that was smothering the apartment which made the idea of going back to my own apartment seem very appealing. A room haunted by dead bodies or a place that wasn't home and filled with tension? Hmm, tough decision.

I shifted on the couch and grabbed the remote as I flipped through the channels on tv before giving up and putting it back on the same channel. My mind was busy and I needed a distraction. I could try to call my mom but it was already getting late and she was either working a night shift or sleeping before her early morning shift. Instinctively I opened my text messages and started typing a message to Amber when grief flooded through me and I remembered that I couldn't talk to her either. I closed my eyes and took a few deep breaths, working to calm myself as I heard Max's footsteps coming down the hallway.

"Hey, you okay?" He paused at the couch and looked down at me as I slowly opened my eyes and smiled.

"I'm feeling restless and anxious." I sat up straight and turned to look at him. He had a pile of papers in his hands and looked ready to do more work. My heart sank a little, desperate for any human interaction that would get me out of this funk. As if sensing my predicament, he sat the papers down on the coffee table and grabbed his coat off the back of the chair where he had tossed it earlier.

"Get your jacket." He nodded to the corner of the living room where my few personal belongings had started to accumulate.

"Why? Where are we going?" I asked as I reached over and grabbed my jacket.

"Out for some fresh air. I think we both need a break from this apartment." He sighed as he slid into his jacket and waited for me to zip mine up.

"Do I need to change?" I looked down at my worn-out jeans and the faded Yankees T-shirt I was wearing. I didn't know where he planned to go but I wanted to make sure I was warm enough and dressed okay.

"Nope, you're fine." He smiled as he walked to the front

door and held it open for me.

We walked in silence for a few blocks before heading into a cozy diner that was tucked away on a side street. It was nice and warm inside with classic memorabilia adorned along the walls and a jukebox sitting in the corner by the waitress podium. A Beach Boy's song played softly throughout the room as a waitress wearing a poodle skirt and roller skates headed our way with a handful of menus.

"Just two?" she asked as she slowed down and grabbed onto the side of the podium to stop herself.

"Yes, please." Max smiled at me as we followed her to a booth in the back of the diner and watched as she skated off, nearly colliding with another waitress on roller skates. I stifled a giggle as I pictured how many times a day they must run into each other and envisioned it turning into a roller derby type atmosphere during their busy hours.

"What's so funny?" Max smirked as his eyes glistened, waiting for my response.

"I was just picturing this turning into roller derby when it gets really busy." I giggled as his gaze shifted to watch as another waitress almost ran into a table before catching herself and stopping.

"Yeah, I'm wondering if the skates are something new. None of them seem well coordinated to handle the skates." He chuckled as he looked down at the menu. I left mine sitting to the side of me since I was still full from the pizza I had pretty much singlehandedly eaten by myself not that long ago.

"I figured maybe we could get dessert? They have the best milkshakes and their peach cobbler is ridiculously good."

He peered over his menu and smiled. There was something about the way that he smiled at me, so flirty, that just sent chills throughout my body. We hadn't talked much about the other night when we had slept together and so much had been happening since then that kept it from happening again. While I technically slept in his bed every night, we weren't anywhere near sleeping together. I remembered Trevor's advice the other day about not getting too close, Max doesn't do commitment. Maybe that was all that it was. A quick hookup and nothing else.

Part of me wanted to believe that there was something more between us. That he felt the chemistry as much as I did. That he was constantly as turned on by me as I was by him. Maybe it was all in my head. I shook my head to try to get rid of the thought as I felt his eyes land on mine.

"Everything okay?" His eyebrow arched.

"Yeah, I was just thinking."

"I can tell. Want to talk about it?" He sat his menu down and leaned back against the booth, watching me.

"Na, it was just silly thoughts." I lied as I tried to lift my menu higher to hide the heat from the blush that I felt creeping up my chest.

"What do you know? I happen to like silly." He reached forward and gently lowered my menu, his gaze quickly finding the blush that I knew he was looking for. I watched as he subtly licked his lips before looking back up at me, a smug look on his face. Just as he was about to say something else a woman came flying toward our table, almost slamming into it before bracing herself against the wall next to us.

"Sorry about that," she muttered as she blew a stray piece of curly red hair out of her face and pulled a pen out of the pocket of the apron tied around her waist. "I'm Wanda, what can I get you guys to drink?" She looked back and forth between us as her pen hovered over a folded-up piece of paper that had scribbled writing covering the majority of it. Max nodded towards me as he pretended to cough to hide the laugh that threatened to burst through. I chewed my bottom lip as I avoided looking at him, knowing that if I did I would lose it and be in hysterics.

"Hi," I cleared my throat to get rid of the laugh that still lingered, "I'll have the cherry cheesecake milkshake please. And a side of fries." I smiled as she jotted my order down and looked to Max.

"I'll have the same." He smiled but looked away as quickly as he could as she tucked the pen back into the apron pocket and used the table to turn herself around. She had to be in her fifties or sixties and it was apparent that she was not good at roller skating.

"Be out with those shortly," she huffed as she pushed off the table and rolled away.

Max and I looked at each other and erupted in laughter as she left. I couldn't remember the last time that I had laughed that hard but the more he laughed, the harder I laughed. Then the inevitable happened and I laughed so hard that I snorted, which of course made Max laugh even harder.

A few minutes later our laughter started to subside and we caught our breath. It was the distraction that I had been needing. For a moment I stopped to think about how much my life had changed in just a few weeks and panic started to course through me as I realized that I no longer had a normal. There wasn't the safety or familiarity of anything that was normal. The only constant in my life right now was Max and I wasn't sure how much longer I would have him. The easy answer was as long as someone was still stalking me and killing people, then Max would still be there. But what happened when it was all over? Where would we stand at that point?

The mood shifted between us as the waitress came rolling back to our table with two glasses of ice water. She sat them down in front of us and tossed a few straws next to them on the table.

"There's an issue with the machine for the milkshakes but they're working on getting it fixed. Might be a little bit of a wait. Did you want me to cancel them and get you something else?"

Max looked at me and raised his eyebrows for my input. I shrugged and waited for him to take the lead.

"We're not in a hurry." He looked to me as he said it and I nodded my head in agreement, "We'll go ahead and wait for them to fix it."

"Okie dokie." She smiled and rolled off again, leaving us to the awkward silence that had started to fill the space between us before she got there.

"What's on your mind?" Max peeled back the wrapper and stuck the straw in his water, twirling it around as he waited for my answer. I watched the ice cubes as they were shuffled about in the water, dancing around each other helplessly, and realized that it was symbolic of my own life.

"I don't have a normal," I blurted out as he watched me closely, still stirring the cubes around in his water with the straw.

"Care to elaborate?" His voice was gentle though I could hear a playfulness to it.

"In general. In life. I don't have anything that's normal. I don't have anything that is comforting. When things start to feel chaotic, I don't have anything to cling to, to try to ground myself. Everything is so out of the norm for me right now that it's actually become the norm to not have a norm. Does that even make sense?" My voice was rising with my anxiety and I quickly scanned the diner to make sure I hadn't caused a scene.

"It makes sense, I totally get it. Different situation, but I've been in your place before where your whole world feels like it's been shifted and nothing is the same." A sadness washed across his face as he looked down and let go of the straw.

"When I really look back, things haven't been normal since before my dad got sick. When he got sick, everything changed and nothing ever went back to normal. Then he died. Then I left for college. And now everything else that happened. I don't even know what normal is anymore."

"How old were you when he got sick?"

"It was my junior year in high school. I quit hanging out with my friends and quit softball so I could help my mom take care of him. I skipped most school functions so I could help out and be there for him. I promised myself that I would make my senior year the year that I did all of the things you're supposed to do and make it the best year ever. But then he got worse and I hardly did anything but go to class then go home to help out with my dad. I worked a part time job to try to help with the bills so that gave me even less time for school or friends." I let out a ragged breath as I thought back to how sick he really was. "By the time prom and graduation rolled around, we didn't know how much longer we would have with him so I missed both. I got my diploma but I didn't walk with my friends or hear the motivational speeches that are supposed to prepare you for the real world. He died a week after that." A tear slid down my face and I quickly tried to wipe it away with the back of my hand before he noticed.

"That's really tough, I'm so sorry Hannah."

"It's okay, it's life. Like you said, you know what it feels like to have your world shifted." I smiled and hoped that it would leave an opening for him to elaborate on his comment earlier and share something personal about himself after I just unloaded my life story on him.

"Yeah, life definitely isn't fair sometimes." He shifted uncomfortably in his seat and I could tell that whatever it was, he didn't want to talk about it. There was something in me that wanted to know. If there wasn't that much time left to spend with him, I wanted to make the most of what I had left. For once I wanted to be able to say that I actually tried to make something work, that I wasn't always a victim to the success of my relationships with others.

"So what happened?" I probed.

He sighed and looked at me like he was debating whether or not to tell me. He knocked his knuckles against the table as he looked away, working his jaw the way he does when something stresses him.

"Love happened." His eyes met mine and I saw a pain hidden behind the amber color of his eyes beneath the fluorescent lights. I waited for him to continue but when he looked away, I knew I would have to keep pushing. Just as I was about to ask him about it the waitress appeared at our table with a plate of mozzarella sticks and a bowl of marinara sauce.

"These are on the house since it's taking so long to get that machine fixed." She sat the plate down between us and rubbed her hands down the front of her apron. "My shift is over but another waitress will be by soon with those shakes. Just wave her down if you need anything before then." She smiled and rolled away.

I reached down and picked up a mozzarella stick, breaking it in half to let the steam out as I played around with ideas of how to get him to talk.

"So what happened with love?" I asked softly as I pretended to be distracted by the oozing cheese as I held it above my mouth and took a bite. It was piping hot and I immediately regretted not thinking this through before I tried to pretend to be cool.

"I was engaged. She left me on our wedding day. Stood me up at the altar. Had her sister tell me that she couldn't marry me because she was in love with someone else." He paused and looked up at me. "She was in love with my cousin and was pregnant with his child."

I felt the mozzarella stick fall from my fingers as it landed on the table in front of me, my mouth hanging open as I stared at Max.

"What?!" It was a stupid answer but all that I could manage to get out. Things like this didn't happen in real life. These were the kinds of things you saw on soap operas where people were paid to be terrible human beings.

"Are you serious?" I asked without realizing how rude it

might come across.

"Unfortunately." He ran a hand through his hair and tilted his head to look at me. "That's why I don't do relationships anymore."

His words felt like they reached across the table and slapped me, the sting of them as I realized that this was the conversation that we needed to have but had been avoiding. I watched as he nervously ran his finger along the rim of glass, watching me as he waited for my response.

"I get it, it's hard to trust people when you've been hurt." I tried to keep my answer simple and generic. Keep all emotion out of it. Don't confess any secret feelings of hope for a happily ever after with him.

"Look, Hannah-" he started and I knew where he was going with it. My palms started sweating as I shifted in my seat and looked down to avoid looking at him.

"I get it, Max. We don't have to talk about what happened. It was a one-time thing," I snapped as I picked up another mozzarella stick and shoved it in my mouth. I was far from hungry but felt desperate to be unable to talk to him. Maybe he would get the hint and do the same. While I had really needed a distraction, now I was anxious to have any conversation other than this one.

"Hannah, it wasn't like that." His voiced pleaded with me to look at him so I did. Big mistake. His eyes were soft as they searched my face and for a moment, I wanted to accept the comfort they offered.

"Like what? A one-night stand?" I could feel myself getting defensive and tried to keep it under control. He closed his mouth and clenched his jaw as he leaned forward and played with the empty straw wrapper.

"Because it's not like we've slept with each other since then. We don't call each other boyfriend or girlfriend. We don't say I love you." I was starting to ramble and knew I needed to get to the point. "It's simple. We slept together and that was it. You're protecting me until we find whoever is responsible for everything, then we'll go our separate ways. I don't have any other expectations. Trust me, Trevor warned me right away that you weren't a commitment type of guy. I got the message, loud and clear." I shoved the rest of the mozzarella stick in my mouth and looked away. My pulse was racing and my face was flushed as I prayed that I would be given one moment of peace and not choke on the damn mozzarella stick after having the guts to tell Max how I felt. Only I didn't really tell him how I felt. I told him what I thought he wanted to hear.

"Wait? When did Trevor tell you that I wasn't a commitment kind of guy?" He leaned forward and I could hear the change in his tone. I didn't want to get into the conversation that I had with Trevor, even though it was short, I didn't want Max to know that we had talked about him. It was a little too late now. I grabbed the glass of water in front of me and made myself busy as I sucked down as much water as I could to keep from having to talk to him.

Out of the corner of my eye I saw someone rolling toward us with a tray loaded with milkshakes and two baskets of fries.

"Hey guys, sorry about the wait." She placed the shakes on the table in front of us then sat the baskets of fries in between. She turned to look at Max as she sat his in front of him and I saw panic in his eyes.

"Max!" she exclaimed as she pulled the tray to the side and reached out to squeeze his shoulder. "Oh my God! I can't believe it's you!"

He looked like he had just seen a ghost as he pulled away from her touch and looked up at me.

"Hey Adrianna." There was no friendliness to his tone and the look he gave her made my blood run cold.

"How are you?" she asked cautiously while sneaking a peek of me out of the corner of her eye. I could tell she was trying to figure out if I was his girlfriend.

"You're really going to ask that?" He shot a look at her that made her straighten her posture as she licked her lips.

"I see that you're still mad about the past but I really think we should sit down sometime and talk." She pulled her shoulders back and looked at him like a mother would a child that she was trying to teach a life lesson.

Max let out a laugh that sounded maniacal and I worried for a minute that he would turn into the guy from The Shining. I still couldn't get that movie out of my head. Everything felt like it was playing out in slow motion as I watched them, not knowing what was actually happening.

"Mad that you left me on our wedding day or mad that you got pregnant by my cousin- which one am I supposed to be over by now?"

My stomach sank as I realized who this woman was. I looked up and took in her features as I tried to picture how anyone could do to Max what she did. She was stunningly beautiful with black hair that was pulled up into a messy bun with a few side swept bangs. Her olive colored skin was flawless which allowed her to be beautiful without wearing much makeup. The red lipstick went perfectly with her uniform and she looked like the classic pinup models you saw in hotrod magazines.

She had the perfect shape with big boobs, small waist, and wide hips with a well-rounded ass. Instantly I knew that I would never be the type of girl that would be with a guy like Max. She was the type of girl that ended up with guys like him. The beautifully attractive always found each other.

My stomach churned as I continued to sit there uncomfortably as they talked, obviously for the first time since they were supposed to get married. I had no idea how long ago it was but Max seemed to be pretty hung up on it still which made sense why he didn't want a relationship. I thought about how to escape and leave without them knowing but as soon as I scooted toward the edge of the booth to get up, she took a step toward me and blocked me. I watched as she coyly looked down and smirked. I didn't like her for what she did to Max, but now I hated her for being such a bitch.

"Max, it was in the past. Can't we be adults and sit down and talk?" She reached over and ran her hand across his fingers on the table. "We have a lot to catch up on."

I wanted to throw up from the over the top show she was putting on. This wasn't my business and I had no intention of siting through anymore.

"I'm going to go and let you guys catch up." I shot him a look that told him I was done and grabbed my phone from the table. I scooted to the edge of the booth where she was standing and raised an eyebrow at her while giving her my best 'don't fuck with me' face. She chuckled as she rolled to the side enough so I could get out.

"Hannah, I'll walk you home." Max scooted to get up when I looked over my shoulder and gave him a cold stare.

"Don't bother." I walked outside and welcomed the bitter cold as I shivered from the flood of emotions that were racing through me.

Twenty

Max

3 Days Ago

Last night definitely didn't go as planned when I offered to take Hannah out for a much-needed distraction. The thought of us together in a relationship had been constantly nagging at me since the moment we slept together. I had feelings for Hannah, whether I wanted to or not, but I had no idea what to do with them. Honestly, I wished I could just go back to sleeping with random women and not having to try to figure out this whole relationship thing.

I was relieved when I got home that Hannah was there, laying on the couch. She pretended to be asleep when I came in twenty minutes after she got there, but I figured if she wanted space, I needed to give it to her. I knew she was mad and I couldn't blame her. We literally went from having a conversation about our relationship and her feeling like I didn't want to be with her to running into my ex fiancé and having so much tension in the room it could have smothered someone.

The walk from the diner back to my apartment was short and I desperately tried to get away from Adriana so I could catch up with Hannah. The last thing I had wanted was for her to walk the streets by herself at night when there's a psycho out there watching her. My focus was on Hannah regardless of how hard Adrianna tried to break it. I knew the moment she saw Hannah that she was jealous. The side-eyed looks she gave her didn't get past me either. She was the same jealous, insecure person she was when I was with her. Every attempt I made to get up to go after Hannah was met with a stronger attempt from Adrianna to get me to stay.

The over the top flirting that went ignored. The running her hand up my arm while pushing her leg against my side so I could tell she wasn't wearing panties. The not so quiet whisper of how she wasn't wearing panties. And when all of that went unnoticed, she resorted to fake crying and went on to tell me how her life fell apart in the three years since I last saw her.

She carried on about how my cousin left her and she lost the baby shortly after. No one loved her and she was seen as a cheater so people didn't respect her anymore. She lost her plush job and had to take this job waiting tables just to get by. The more she went on and complained about the petty things in her life that were a direct result of the poor decisions she made, the more I wanted to be with Hannah.

I tried to sleep but knowing that she was sleeping on the couch instead of in my bed really got under my skin. Maybe it was because I felt like I was supposed to protect her and couldn't if she wasn't next to me? Or maybe it was because I felt like I didn't want to be apart from her. Around 2:30 this morning I gave up and made my way to the living room so I could at least be in the same room as her. At some point I must have fallen asleep because I barely heard it when she slid the deadbolt and opened the door, looking over her shoulder as she tried to sneak out with her suitcase handle in one hand and her backpack slowly sliding down her back.

"Where are you going?" My voice was groggy as I rubbed my eyes and sat up straight in the chair.

"I am going to go look for a hotel to stay in for a few days while I look for an apartment." Her head was down while one foot lingered outside the door. I could tell she wanted to leave and never look back. But something held her there and I couldn't let this moment pass by.

"Hannah, can we please talk about last night?" I walked over and held the top of the door to try to keep her from closing it and walking out on me forever.

Her eyes looked away from mine as she fidgeted with the zipper of her coat while she thought about what I was asking of her.

"Please, Hannah. Just let me talk and explain what happened. If you're still wanting to leave after that I'll help you find somewhere to stay."

"Fine," she whispered as she tucked a strand of hair behind her ear and stepped back inside the apartment just enough for me to close the door.

"Do you want to sit?" I offered as I nodded toward the couch. Her standing there, ready to leave, was making me anxious and I felt like I was going to lose the nerve to tell her how I felt.

"I'm fine here."

One thing about her was when she was mad, she was really mad. I took a deep breath and swallowed hard as I rubbed my hands down the front of my sweats. I had six Italian sisters, I could handle this.

"Okay," another deep breath, "Hannah, I'm so sorry about last night. Nothing went how I had hoped it would and my only intention was to get you out of the apartment for a little bit and celebrate that you were done with finals." I let out the breath I had been holding as I rushed through the sentence. "Everything was a disaster and it was all my fault."

She stayed quiet while I talked, continuing to look anywhere but at me.

"Hannah, will you please talk to me? I know you're upset but this would be a whole lot easier if I knew why." I reached for her hand which was quickly pulled away so I couldn't touch her.

I blew out a frustrated breath as I ran my hands through my hair and shook my head. This woman just might be the death of me. I've never had to work this hard to get a girl to not be mad at me and I grew up in a house full of nothing but women!

"First of all, it would be a whole lot easier to talk to you if you were actually dressed." She looked at me then glanced at my bare chest before looking away. "Can you do something with that? Like, cover it up already." She pointed at my chest as a blush crept up her neck before she looked away.

"So my body bothers you now?" I asked with a smirk as I looked around for something to put on.

"Yes. Now cover your ridiculous abs and toned chest or I'm going to leave and we won't talk at all." She had turned fully around and was facing the wall while I had to hold in my laughter. I didn't dare tell her how adorable she was unless I wanted that wicked mean girl to come back. I found a shirt behind the couch and pulled it over my head as she was turning back around.

"Better?" I raised an eyebrow, challenging her to meet my eyes.

"Yes." She was still blushing and I was relieved that even when she was super pissed off at me, she still found me attractive.

"Now can we talk?"

"You know we don't have to do this, right?" she asked as if I was supposed to have some idea of what she was talking about.

"Do what?"

"Talk," she sighed, "I think we said everything we needed to say last night."

"I don't think we did."

"Max, you don't want a relationship, you made that clear. And then you ran into your ex-fiancé and I could see the tension between you two. That relationship isn't over and you deserve the chance to go after the person you love."

She didn't get it, she completely misread everything last night. I didn't want to be with Adrianna. Even if Hannah wasn't in the picture, I still wouldn't want to be with Adrianna. I learned the hard way the type of person that she is and that wasn't the kind of person that I wanted to be with.

"Hannah, I don't want to be with Adrianna. Not by any means. I could never forgive her for what she did to me and what she put me through. People like that don't ever change. And when I said I wasn't ready for a relationship, I meant right now. Or at least I thought I did? I really like you Hannah and I care about you. What does that mean in terms of a relationship? I have no idea. But you weren't just some random one-night stand for me. I've never felt that way about what happened between us." I took a step toward her and gently touched her arm. This time she didn't pull away.

"I think I still need to stay somewhere else for a few days. Clear my head." She refused to look at me as my hand fell from her arm. I sucked in a deep breath hoping it would replace some of the air that had just been knocked out of me. Even with everything I told her, she still wanted to leave.

"Okay," I sighed, "If you need space, I'll give it to you."

"Thank you. I'll let you know where I'll be staying as soon as I find something affordable." She turned toward the door and I knew I had to tell her that she could go back to her apartment.

"Your apartment is actually ready now if you wanted to go back there." I looked away to avoid having her see the guilt on my face for not telling her sooner.

"When did you find out that it was ready?" Her tone changed and I knew she was upset, again.

"A few days ago. Trevor went by to see if you were there when you didn't come back to my apartment and he told me the crime scene was cleared. Mindy called that night to confirm."

"So you've known for a few days that I could go back and you didn't tell me?"

I gulped as I looked down.

"I was trying to keep you safe."

"That wasn't your decision to make. I'm a grown woman, Max, I can make that decision for myself."

"Hannah, I'm sorry that I didn't tell you. But even if I

had, would you really have gone back to stay there, given everything that's happened there? You said you didn't have anything that made you feel safe, yet you're walking away from it."

"I'm supposed to feel safe here?! With someone who's been lying to me and leading me on?!" Her voice rose and I knew I wasn't going to like what came next.

"I wasn't trying to lead you on."

"Well, you didn't do a good job of not leading me on, now did you?" Her eyebrows shot up in question as she waited for my answer.

I closed my eyes and pinched the bridge of my nose as I thought of what to say next. She was right, I hadn't been trying to not lead her on. We were both walking down the same path toward a relationship except at some point I took a detour and didn't tell her.

"Exactly my point," she snapped as she shifted the weight of her backpack and pulled up the handle of her suitcase, "I'm going to go back to the only place that I can call home right now because even with all of the death and unhappy memories of that place, it still feels better than being here with you. If you can't be honest with yourself, how can I ever expect you to be honest with me?"

She turned toward the door at the same time a loud knock came from the other side. She looked at me with confusion on her face, both knowing that it wasn't Trevor because he was out of town on business.

I walked over and opened the door to a woman covered in blood and bruises. My heart stopped and my stomach sank when I looked closer and recognized the battered face in front of me.

"Elena."

Twenty One

Hanna

3 Days Ago

I watched with my jaw hanging open as Max reached out and grabbed Elena before she fell to the floor. She looked weak and I barely recognized her as the girl from my class. Her black hair was matted to her head from the dried blood that looked to have been there for weeks. Her face and body were dirty and covered in cuts and bruises. The jeans she wore had tears in them with blood stains underneath. Whatever she had been through, it looked like she had just barely survived it.

I moved out of the way as Max brought her in and laid her on the couch. He was talking frantically to her, asking her to wake up and stay with him as he checked for a pulse while looking for the sources of injury. Adrenaline pushed through me as I watched, trying to figure out how to help.

"What can I do?" I asked as he spoke to her in Italian.

"Call 911, ask for an ambulance!" he called over his shoulder while keeping his attention on his sister.

I called and requested the ambulance and asked if they could get Mindy over here as well. Within minutes the apartment was filled with people shuffling about so I took it as my cue to leave. I walked the short distance to my apartment, constantly looking over my shoulder. It felt weird to be walking to my apartment and suddenly I realized just how scared I was to be by myself. And I was 100% by myself. Amber was dead. Max was busy with Elena. Trevor was out of town. There was no one left. No one to protect me. No one to keep me company.

As I took the few steps up to the entrance of my apartment building, I felt footsteps right behind me. I moved slightly to the right. They moved slightly to the right. I was almost in front of the elevators when I felt them stop directly behind me. My blood pressure skyrocketed as my heart beat wildly in my chest. Slowly I turned to look over my shoulder as the bell dinged to the elevator. Out of the corner of my eye I couldn't see anyone behind me. The doors to the elevator slowly opened with no one inside the cart. I was about to take a step when I saw a hand come out from behind me. I spun around as my hand flew to my chest in fear.

Standing at least three feet below me was a little boy, maybe four or five years old. There was a huge smirk on his face as he slyly waved, right before a frantic woman came barreling through the outside doors looking for him.

"Frankie! I told you not to run off like that!" she scolded as she reached down and grabbed his arm to pull him back to her, "I'm so sorry if he scared you, his older brother has been teaching him how to sneak up on people and he hasn't learned not to do it to strangers yet." She let out a heavy breath as she pulled him in front of her, tucked underneath her very swollen pregnant stomach. "As you can tell, I can't quite keep up with his speed these days." She laughed nervously.

"It's fine, really," I said as I took a step toward the elevator as the doors closed before I could get on. I pushed the button for the elevator to return as I watched the mom escort her son out of the building and hold his hand so he couldn't get away from her again.

I took a few deep breaths to try to calm myself as I waited for the elevator to return. In a way I was happy to have space from Max so I could clear my head, and so he could deal with things with Elena, but it also felt really unnerving being back at my apartment.

The bell dinged and this time a man and woman got out and walked past me as I took their place on the elevator. I waited anxiously for it to reach my floor as I played with keys in my pocket. Just a few more seconds and I would be back to the place that I swore I would never come back to.

The doors opened, forcing me to make a decision. Go back to the place that haunted me or make a run for it and never come back. I felt like I had been doing nothing but running for a long time and it was exhausting. If I wanted to be able to root myself then I had to start somewhere. Why not just make amends with my past, deal with my demons, and take control of my life? I pulled my shoulders back as I stepped off the elevator and walked down the hall.

The key shook against the lock as my hands trembled trying to unlock the door. I took a deep breath and tried to focus. It wasn't that hard. Just a key in a lock. No big deal. Except that the key was about to open a door that I didn't know what it held inside. I knew I wanted to move forward with my life but that meant I had to deal with things too. Was I strong enough?

"Need help?" A man's voice to my side startled me, forcing

the key out of my hand and to the floor. I watched as Trevor bent down and picked up the key, unlocking the door for me.

"I thought you were out of town?" My mind felt like this was a dream, there was no way that Trevor was really there, helping me and keeping me from having to do this on my own.

"I was, I got back early." He shrugged as he held the door open for me to go inside. I pulled my suitcase and stepped inside, looking around unsure of what to expect.

The apartment was freshly cleaned, no sign of any of the recent tragedies that had taken place. The flooring had been replaced and new curtains were hung in front of the new window that had been updated from the makeshift one they had put up after Amber's death. The door closed behind me as Trevor stood next to me, taking it all in.

"You sure you want to stay here?" His voice was gentle and sincere with a hint of concern. I knew he had talked to Max.

"Yeah, it's better than the alternative right now." I tilted my head to look at him.

"I'm not the best at relationship advice and I shouldn't have said what I said about Max not being that type. Sorry I overstepped."

We stayed standing next to each other, staring at the couch as if we were glued to the floor and couldn't move. I was afraid that if I did, the conversation would stop and I wouldn't be able to say what I needed to say.

"You didn't overstep. You just told me the truth, and honestly, it helped. If you hadn't told me that he wasn't a relationship kind of guy, I would be sitting here, waiting for him to change his mind and want to be with me."

"What makes you think he doesn't want to be with you?"

"He told me at the diner that he doesn't do relationships. Then I saw how he was with his ex. I'll never be her so how could it ever work between us? It was bound to end, one way or another."

"You are nothing like Adrianna. Absolutely nothing about you is the same as her." The way he said it with such conviction made my heart hurt. I knew that I could never be her. And if I could never be her, then I could never have Max. I swallowed hard to try to force the lump in my throat back down.

"I know I'm not her. She's gorgeous and confident. And who knows, maybe she's actually nice?" I shrugged trying to get the weight of the world off my shoulders.

"Do you really think that you're not as good as her? Is that what this is about?" He folded his arms across his chest and turned to look at me. My palms started to sweat as I wanted to run and hide to avoid the intensity of the look he was giving me.

"I don't know," I muttered as I looked down and played with the handle of my suitcase.

"Hannah, you're 10 times the woman Adrianna is. Sure, she's good looking and men trip over their dicks trying to get to her, but you have more than that."

I had to bite the inside of my cheek to keep from laughing at the absurd and very detailed description he used to confirm that men wanted Adrianna.

"She's shallow and goes from guy to guy until she gets bored or she finds someone else who has something she wants. She's lucky that she's good looking because that's all she has going for her."

I breathed a sigh of relief and looked up at him. He was such a great person, it was no wonder that Max considered him a brother.

"Thank you, that's sweet of you to say."

"It's the truth. At one point, she even hit on me. But then again, who wouldn't?" He playfully nudged my shoulder with his.

"I'm sure Max took that well!" I joked then blushed when I remembered that Trevor and I had kissed the other day. I wondered if he had told Max about it. I knew I hadn't. Not that I purposely kept it from him, it just didn't cross my mind because it was so insignificant and I forgot about it.

"He was pretty pissed about it. With her. Not me." He rocked back on his heels and smiled. "I've always been the good friend that he can trust."

"Oh great, and here I am, the girl that kisses his best friend!" I palm smacked myself in the forehead and wished it would at least knock some sense into me.

"Na, he knew why we did it."

"He knows?!"

"Of course. Hannah, that was an innocent kiss but I still wouldn't keep that from him."

I lowered my head in shame and knew that I should have thought to tell Max about the kiss. What if he thought I was the same as Adrianna now? I kissed his best friend and didn't bother to tell him.

"It wasn't a big deal and he knew that Hannah. He wasn't

upset about it. He didn't ask me questions about how it happened or who initiated it. He agreed that it worked for what we were trying to do."

I looked up at him cautiously.

"Give Max time, he's going through a lot right now and honestly, I don't think he even knows which way is up at this point. He may not be ready for a relationship, but he cares about you Hannah. I can see it in how he watches you and how protective he is over you."

"Did he send you here to talk to me?"

"Actually no. I called and he told me about Elena. I was headed over there to see her and try to help when he started freaking out that you had left. I told him to stay with Elena and I would come check on you. So, here I am." He held his arms out for proof.

"Have you heard any more on Elena? Is she okay?" For a moment I had gotten so consumed in my own world that I had completely forgotten about what had happened.

"I got a text from Max a few minutes ago. They are at the hospital. Her injuries were pretty bad and she's now in a coma. Max is staying there until they know more."

"Oh my god!" I covered my mouth with my hand as I took in the news. "Was she able to tell him anything about where she had been or who had taken her?"

"When I talked to him earlier, he told me that she had whispered 'five steps' but that she lost consciousness before she could finish. He's not sure what it means but I'm supposed to help him remember so we can look into it."

"That's weird. Maybe she was only 5 steps from home?" I pondered as my brain focused on trying to solve a riddle I knew nothing about.

"Could be. I'm planning to go back to his apartment later and go through the files to see if there's anything in the notes about it. Maybe there's an abandoned building close by that we didn't think of or maybe a house that we missed. Who knows, it's a pretty open clue, if it's even supposed to be a clue."

"Well, if you need help, just let me know."

"Thanks. You sure you're going to be okay here? I can stay if you want me to."

"Thank you, I appreciate the offer but I'll be okay. I would rather that you help Max with Elena. Will you keep me posted if they hear anything else about her?"

"Of course."

He smiled and gave me a hug before walking out the door and leaving me to the silence of the empty room.

Twenty Two

Adam
3 Days Ago

Roses are red
Violets are blue
It won't be too long now
Before I come for you

I have to be careful
And plan my next step
The last girl got away
Which means there's more to prep

I can't risk anyone seeing
What I'm about to do
I stood right next to you
And you didn't have a clue

Time will go quickly
Then we'll be together
Bound to each other for eternity

Like two birds of a feather

My fingers are itching
To reach out and touch you
I'll have to settle on pleasuring myself
No one else will do

You may not think you know me
You'd say we've never met
I've always been close by
Now I'm five steps ahead

Twenty Three

Max

3 Days Ago

"No, ma, they don't have any updates on her." I blew out a frustrated breath as I leaned back against the uncomfortable metal chair in the ER waiting room and listened as my mom continued to ask a million questions about Elena. They were all ready to get in the car and drive over the second they heard she was in the hospital, but luckily I was able to keep them at bay for now until she was awake. I just couldn't deal with that chaos on top of everything else right now.

"Look ma, I gotta go. I'll call as soon as I have any information, you don't have to come down here."

A man wearing scrubs and a lab coat came through the double doors wearing a look of defeat on his face. Panic filled me as I waited to see which family he was there to deliver bad news to. My mom was still mumbling in the background about lasagna or spaghetti and did I want my sister to bring me something to eat but I couldn't focus.

"Gotta go, love you, bye." I slid the button to end the call knowing that I would hear about it later. Mindy and Trevor were sitting a few seats over talking quietly when they saw the doctor approach and stopped.

"Sandoval family?" he called out as his tired eyes scanned the room.

I stood up and laced my fingers behind my head as I paced the short distance between the waiting room and the vending machines along the wall. Off in the distance a woman sobbed as the doctor assured her that they had done everything they could. My stomach was in a knot as I waited for someone to give us an update on Elena.

Before we got to the hospital she had lost consciousness right as she was trying to tell me something. Five steps was all that she was able to get out. Since then she had been slipping in and out of consciousness and at one point they thought she had slipped into a coma. Things have been unstable and unpredictable since then. We were waiting for them to finish running tests and labs, and hopefully in that time, Elena would regain consciousness and stay awake. The last few hours felt like days that were starting to blur together and it wasn't even noon yet.

Trevor had gone by my apartment after checking in on Hannah and making sure she was situated in her apartment. It killed me that she left earlier in the middle of everything else, especially given how the conversation between us had ended. She wanted space and though I was reluctant to want to give it to her, I found that I didn't have a choice now that Elena was found. Still, it didn't keep her off my mind. Thoughts of her constantly floated through my mind as I pictured her curled up on the couch in her baggy sweater watching tv, or sitting on the floor with her hair a mess on her head while she pushed her reading glasses back up her nose. While she probably needed new glasses, it was so adorable that I couldn't imagine not watching her chase them around.

"I'm going to go grab some coffee, can I bring you guys a cup?" Mindy asked as she stood up and picked up her wallet from the seat next to her.

"That would be great, thank you." I smiled as she walked away and took her empty seat by Trevor. There was a small table that was pushed up against the wall that had scattered magazines on it before Trevor took it over and laid out the papers from the file he brought from my apartment with Elena's case. He was deep in thought as he read through some of the initial notes that were taken. I sat back and closed my eyes, taking a moment to relax while I could.

"Hey, do you know what happened to the other notes you had? The stuff you wrote down when you were at your mom's?"

I looked over at him and scanned the table for the piece of paper I had used that day.

"It should be in the file. It's smaller, it was from my notepad."

"I can't find it anywhere." Trevor moved stacks of paper around and lifted the pile to look underneath as he grumbled under his breath.

"It has to be in there somewhere. I'll help you look." I reached over to grab a stack of papers when a note caught my eye. Trevor's eyes followed mine as I picked it up and read it. There was a print out of Elena's phone records leading up to when she was taken and for a few days after she was taken. My blood started to boil as I gripped the paper tighter, my knuckles turning white.

"Here you go, one cream, two sugar." Mindy held out a to-go cup of coffee in front of me as I pulled back and looked up at her with fury in my eyes.

"A simple thank you would suffice," She muttered as she sat the cups of coffee down between Trevor and I, and took a seat across from us. She leaned back and crossed her legs as she took a slow sip out of her cup.

"Why the fuck didn't you tell me they were tracing Elena's phone after she went missing? You said they weren't able to track it." My words were heavy, anger laced through each one.

"Because they weren't able to trace it right away. By the time they tracked it, she wasn't there anymore." She let out a sigh as her shoulders slumped.

"How do you know she wasn't there? Did you look everywhere? Check for hidden places that she could have been kept?"

"Max, the day we got the trace on her phone was the day that we found her phone next to the other body. The forensic team scoured that place and didn't find any sign of her. You know as well as I do that she was likely moved long before they ever tracked her phone."

"You still should have told me. I should have been informed of every little detail. God damn it!" I slammed my fist on the table almost knocking over the cups of coffee. Mindy flinched in response.

"Max, you can be mad all you want. I know that this is your sister and I feel for you, I really do. But you DO NOT get to sit there and act like we didn't do our jobs. I have worked tirelessly on this case, Max. I've spent more nights at the office, sleeping at my desk because it's the middle of the night, only to wake up obsessed with solving this case. How dare you sit there and come after me for not doing something! You don't have any idea the number of hours we have spent working this case. If anyone's been more invested, it's me!" Mindy stood up and stalked off, the sound of her boots fading in the distance.

I felt like shit for what just happened. Everything was starting to take its toll on me and I was lashing out at everyone it seemed like. I worked the muscle in my jaw trying to relieve some tension as I looked over at Trevor who was watching me while sipping his coffee.

"I'll apologize when she cools down," I muttered.

"I didn't say anything."

"You didn't have to. I see the look in your eyes." I tried to watch my tone before Trevor and I got into it next.

"Things are tense, I get it. Let's focus on what we need to and worry about the rest later. Okay?"

That was why this guy was my best friend. We balanced each other out and as always, he was being my voice of reason and forcing me to be logical because that's what was needed right now.

"Alright. What do you got?" I picked up the cup of coffee and took a drink as I looked at the papers in front of us.

"Unfortunately, not much. I've gone through and looked at all of the places that she had gone before she went missing and looked at what is near them in a five-foot radius. I'm not coming up with anything." He let out a deep breath and tossed his empty cup into the trash can behind him.

"So then I focused on the coffee house that she was supposed to meet that date at. There's a ton of stuff in that area, but five feet doesn't get you anywhere that would make sense. I started looking at 5 blocks and 5 miles," he tossed the papers down and leaned back in defeat, "I don't know, I think we're jumping down a rabbit hole with this whole five-foot thing."

"Why are you so focused on five feet?" My curiosity was peaked as I tried to figure out his logic and where he got five feet from.

"You told me earlier that the only thing she was able to say was 'five feet'." He looked at me with confusion on his face and suddenly it clicked in my head. I had totally blocked out what Elena had said to me which was why I had told Trevor right away so he could remember.

"Shit! I totally forgot about that!" I leaned forward and pushed the papers around as I looked through what he had on top.

"I was trying to go back to your original notes about everywhere she had gone before she went missing but I can't find them."

"That's odd. I can always call my sisters and see if they remember. Did you look at houses by my parents? Maybe it was someone at one of the neighbors? A neighbor could be five feet away." My mind was racing as I tried to think about what neighbors we had talked to and which ones we hadn't.

"Did you talk to all of the neighbors?" Trevor asked as his excitement started to build with mine.

"No, the girls only talked to a few. But it should be easy to get a team out there to do a quick interview and see if anyone seems suspicious enough to justify doing a search of their property to see if that's where she was being held."

"Romano Family?" A nurse appeared in the hallway and my heart stopped. She didn't make any efforts to come into the waiting area which meant she wasn't planning to talk to us out here like they did everyone else. My pulse quickened as I looked at Trevor.

"Go on, I'll talk to Mindy and give her the update so we can get this going."

I nodded and walked off to join the nurse as I tried to brace myself for what she was about to tell me.

Twenty Four

Hannah

3 Days Ago

An old 90's hip hop song floated through the apartment as I finished wiping down the counters with disinfectant wipes. Even though I knew the apartment had been thoroughly clean, I couldn't stop myself from going through and cleaning everything again. I tried to convince myself that it was the best way to feel like I was making a fresh start when deep down I knew that it was really just a way to keep myself busy so I wouldn't be alone with my thoughts.

I had called my mom earlier and caught her in between jobs so we had a little bit of time to talk and catch up. It felt odd not knowing what to talk to her about since I couldn't exactly be honest and tell her everything that was really going on. So I did what I did best and pretended everything was fine while shifting the focus away from me. My mom hinted that she had made a new friend and after thirty minutes I got her to confess that it was a boyfriend. I was surprised that she hadn't mentioned it sooner, but then again who was I to talk, given the secrets I was keeping. There was a mix of emotions that came with the news but I was pleasantly surprised when happiness overrode the anger and resentment that I had expected to feel.

It was after seven when I finished cleaning the apartment and decided to quit for the day. Trevor hadn't given me any updates on Elena and I felt awkward texting Max for an update. My mind was foggy where Max was concerned and I didn't want to complicate things any more than they were. As much as I tried, I could not get my mind off of Max. The way he made me feel when we were together. The random jokes he would tell when I found myself getting a little bit too stressed out with studying. How he would pick some place for dinner and then order a handful of items, hoping that I would like them when I was too distracted to pick for myself.

I played around with the idea of Max not being interested in me because honestly, it felt a lot better than to try to trick myself into believing that he was interested. It was confusing to say the least and I started to wonder if my lack of experience with relationships had tainted my view of what a real relationship should look like. The only one that I ever really saw growing up was my parents and they had a really great relationship. I wouldn't say perfect, because obviously I saw them fight about plenty of things, but for the most part it was damn near perfect. My dad constantly went out of his way to make my mom happy and she did the same. They were always so wrapped up and focused on whether they were making each other happy that I don't think they ever stopped to make sure they were actually happy themselves. I didn't doubt that they were happy, not by any means. But I did use their relationship to compare what I had with Max and felt confused when I saw some of the same things from their relationship overlapping in ours. If we even had one. I needed another distraction but this time I knew it was going to take more than some fresh air and a milkshake that I didn't even get to drink.

My stomach growled at the same time a knock on my door alerted me to my food delivery. I was starving and didn't have the energy to go buy actual food. I tipped the kid the few bucks that I had on me and took the bag of Chinese food as he walked away. The smell filled the apartment, replacing the overwhelming disinfectant and cleaning products I had been using. I locked the door and slid the deadbolt in place before heading to the couch with my food.

I turned the tv up loud to continue watching the Friends marathon I had been watching. It was cheesy comedy and it made me feel less alone as the sound of laughter filled the room. There was only so much silence I could take before my mind started to get the better of me.

I stuffed the last bite of egg roll in my mouth and sat the empty cartons on the table, leaning back to allow my stomach the space it needed to expand with the massive amount of food I'd just shoved in. It was hot. It was delicious. And it was just the right amount to send me into a nice food induced sleep coma.

Three hours later I woke up to the tv still playing episodes of Friends as I looked around for my phone to check the time. It was almost eleven and I was feeling pretty disappointed that I didn't have an update from Trevor or Max on Elena. My heart sank when I acknowledged what it really meant. If I had any questions about where I stood with Max, this just confirmed it. Important enough to make a show out of trying to talk me out of leaving but not important enough to give me an update on something important in his life.

As weird as it may sound, the apartment felt different as it did earlier now that it was night. Earlier I was a little anxious being back in the apartment but I was able to work through it. There were frequent pep talks to myself about how I could do it, I was a strong woman. But now that it was night the anxiety was even stronger and I felt even more restless than I did before. It must all be in my head, my subconscious playing tricks on me. I had learned about the power of the brain in my psychology classes so it wasn't that far-fetched that it would be messing with me.

I sighed as I got up and took my empty containers to the trash. It felt good to move around even though I knew I should technically be trying to fall back asleep. Who was I kidding? I knew there wasn't any chance that I was actually going to get sleep tonight. I opened the fridge out of habit, looking for something to snack on. Knowing that it was empty I started to close it when I glanced down and saw the bottle of champagne that Amber had given me right after midterms. We had been spending most of our time together and she wanted to celebrate the end of the semester by popping open a bottle and letting go of all of our stress from finals.

Tears rolled down my face as my hand trembled and reached out for the bottle. I debated whether to leave it in there forever or to open it and drink it. What would Amber have wanted? That was a stupid question. If I knew her, she would be mad that I let a good bottle go to waste just because she wasn't here. Amber was always focused on celebrating life, not waiting to live it. I wiped the tears from my face with the back of my hand and pulled the bottle out.

A few minutes later I popped the cork, scaring the shit out of myself from the sound as liquid came fizzing out of the top. Thankfully I was smart enough to open it by the sink to avoid a complete mess. I cleaned up the small spill on the counter and wiped down the bottle before taking it with me to the couch. Who needed a glass when you were drinking for one?

The marathon on tv had ended and of course, there wasn't much else on regular tv at midnight on a Thursday night. I tossed the remote next to me, taking another drink from the bottle, and grabbed my phone. Facebook proved to be a combination of boring and depressing as all of my friends shared celebration photos of being done with the semester, their cute and cuddly Christmas photos with their boyfriends, or the random drunk picture from partying too hard. Irritated that I didn't have anything remotely happy to share, I closed the app and scrolled through my phone for something else to entertain myself with.

There weren't too many apps on my phone so I scrolled through them fairly quickly before landing on the dating app. My finger hovered over the option to delete the app when I remembered why I had it in the first place. Amber. She had encouraged me to get it so I could start meeting people and make new friends. When I questioned the ability to make friends through a dating app she assured me that there were a lot of really great guys on there and that I didn't have to sleep with all of them, I could have standards and just be friends with them if the chemistry wasn't there. She always knew how to make a joke out of things so I wouldn't take it too seriously.

I adjusted on the couch and pulled my legs up under me before taking another drink of champagne and setting the half empty bottle on the coffee table. I was already feeling buzzed and didn't want to end up drunk and alone in my apartment tonight. I opened the app and scrolled through the few notifications I had waiting for me since the last time I had used it, which had been right after Chet. There were a few guys who had waved and a handful of unread messages.

I went to the unread messages and clicked the oldest message first. It was from almost two weeks ago and didn't have a profile picture. The message was short and generic.

ShyGuy247: Hi, I would like to get to know you.

I pressed the delete button and went to the next message. This account had a profile picture of greased up abs and no head. Just abs that looked like they were taken from a Magic Mike movie poster. I didn't have to read the message to know what it was going to say but I read it anyways.

BigToni187: Hey mami, hit me up if you want a taste of big papi from NYC baby.

I forced myself to swallow hard as I felt the champagne trying to make its way back up. Yuck! Seriously, this is what guys thought girls wanted to hear? I moved along to the next message and noticed all of the remaining messages were from the same person. They didn't have a profile picture either and it kind of creeped me out that they had been consistently emailing me for almost two weeks with no response back.

I sat up straight and opened the first message.

5StepsAhead: I find that women who study psychology tend to be more educated and highly intelligent, would you agree?

While I had expected a typical email about how lonely they were or how pretty I was, I was surprised that they didn't comment on either of that. They had actually read through my profile and saw that I was going to school and studying psychology. Curiosity took over as I opened the next message.

5StepsAhead: One of the hardest things about online dating is finding people who aren't there for the right reasons. Men who just want a quick hookup. Women who are looking for free fancy dates. It's rare to find someone who is on here for the right reasons, which brings me to ask, what are you looking for?

I was strangely impressed with the conversation and found myself wanting to talk to whoever this person was and answer their questions. I found myself feeling giddy as I opened the next message that was sent a little over a week ago.

5StepsAhead: I hope that I'm not being a bother, I've seen that you haven't been active recently or read my other emails so I assume you've been busy with school. I find myself drawn to wanting to talk to you and hope that you don't find this creepy or odd. Just say the word and I'll stop messaging you, though I hope you might be interested in talking to me when you're not busy.

I chewed my lip nervously as I debated whether to respond. Before deciding too quickly, I decided to read the last message that was sent yesterday.

5StepsAhead: I wanted to make one final attempt to try to sway you to talk to me. I really hope that you'll give me a chance, I have a feeling we would have a lot to talk about and maybe even be friends if nothing else.

The last sentence stayed with me after I read it and Amber's words rang through my mind about using the app to make new friends. If for nothing else, I could always say that I did it for Amber. It's not like I was agreeing to go on a date with the guy, I could just send a few emails and see what happened. There was no harm in that.

Then why did I feel guilty about Max? It wasn't like we were dating, he had made that pretty clear. And I hadn't heard from him in over 12 hours so maybe I should consider meeting this guy. I started feeling nervous as I thought about what to write when a new message popped up in my inbox from him.

5StepsAhead: Either you're taking a break from cramming for a final tomorrow or you're up late celebrating that finals are over. For your sake, I hope it's the latter.

A smile crossed my face as I began to type.

Me: I actually had my last final yesterday and am trying to figure out how to spend all of my new found freedom and downtime. You're up late as well, should I ask the same?

5StepsAhead: Congratulations! Here's to hoping you find a productive, yet relaxing way to spend your time. My last class wrapped up this morning and I am up late because I just sent in the last items that were needed for me to finish the semester.

Me: Congratulations to you as well. How do you plan to spend your new free time?

5StepsAhead: Unfortunately I'm pretty tied up with a project that didn't quite go as planned so I'm having to take care of a few things before I'll be able to enjoy my time.

Me: That's too bad, I hope it gets resolved soon.

5StepsAhead: It will, I can see the end in sight. Should only take a few more days for things to calm down, then I can pick up where I left off.

Me: I'll send positive vibes your way.

5StepsAhead: Thanks, that's super nice of you.

Me: You're welcome.

I didn't know what else to say and the conversation felt like it hit a dead end. Maybe it wasn't going to be as exciting as I had imagined. A yawn forced its way out and I considered wrapping it up and attempting to get some sleep. Right as I was about to send a message to say goodnight, a new email popped up.

5StepsAhead: Do you think I could take you out for a cup of coffee sometime? Go celebrate the end of the semester?

My mind raced with what to say to that. Did I want to meet him? It was just coffee, there wasn't really any harm in that, was there? Although my last coffee date with Chet didn't end so well. I was so confused and didn't want to make the wrong decision. Part of me wanted to make Amber proud and go for it, but the other part of me felt like it was way too soon to start dating. But then again, he had only asked to meet for coffee and his email did say maybe we could be friends. I closed my eyes and tried to think past the fuzz the champagne had created in my head.

Me: I don't know, I don't even know your name...

A few seconds later a new message popped up.

5StepsAhead: It's Adam.

Me: I guess coffee would be a good way to celebrate. Did you have a day in mind?

5StepsAhead: I'm tied up with that problem that came up for a few days, can you do Sunday?

Me: Sure, Sunday is fine. Did you have a place in mind?

5StepsAhead: How about Java Jazz on Union and Second? Is that close to you? If not, we can find somewhere in the middle.

My stomach dropped when I saw the name of the coffee shop and wondered if this was all a sign from Amber to go for it. How else would one explain drinking the bottle of champagne that she left on the same night that I start talking to guy who wants to be friends AND who wants to meet at the coffee shop that Amber and I used to go to. I wasn't about to mess with fate.

Me: That works for me. Just let me know what time on Sunday and I can meet you there.

5StepsAhead: I look forward to meeting you. I'm going to call it a night. Goodnight, sweet dreams, Hannah.

Me: Goodnight, Adam.

I closed out the app and yawned again feeling a mixture of nervous and excited about Sunday. I tried to figure out why I was feeling nervous when everything seemed like it was working out the way it should but something still felt off to me. Then I realized that I had no idea what he looked like and we didn't bother to exchange phone numbers. I had to remind myself that it was just a quick cup of coffee in a crowded place, nothing could really go wrong there, could it?

Twenty Five

Adam

3 Days Ago

The one that got away.

We all have one. Someone that was vital to something that was important to us. Someone who could make things better for us. Someone that we wanted to spend our lives with.

How she got away- I had no clue. But thanks to her I had fresh cuts from the glass she tried to stab me with before breaking free and running away. This wasn't the first time she had attacked me. Just earlier that week she had ripped a hole in my jacket and cut my arm, making me late for class. She was a feisty one, and that's what I loved the most about her. Even if she wasn't THE one.

She had delusions of wanting to leave and claiming that she didn't want to be there. I tried to understand the pleas she tried to get out from behind the bandana I had to gag her with but they just didn't make sense to me. We were meant to be together. Why would she want to leave? Every time she denied our love, it made me even angrier.

I tried to show her how much I loved her but she couldn't be trusted. If I gave an inch, she took a foot. If I untied her from the chair, she swung it at me. If I undid the gag, she would scream at the top of her lungs. If I tried to touch her she would jerk away and give me the dirtiest looks.

The hospital had been more than frustrating, refusing to let me see her unless I confirmed my relationship to her. Just as I was about to proudly confess that she was my girlfriend, the stupid cop showed up and refused to leave her room. His timing was impeccable. A nurse asked about the cuts on my arm and face, making too many mental notes about what I looked like, before offering to have a doctor take a look. That was my cue to leave and now thanks to Elena's antics, I was forced to lay low for a few days.

It was hard to accept that I had to let Elena go but how do you keep someone who keeps fighting so hard to get away from you? It felt like she didn't appreciate any of the things I was trying to do for her.

I was pleasantly surprised when Hannah answered one of my emails tonight, I was beginning to get frustrated with her as well. I'd spent weeks trying to get to her but people kept getting in the way and leaving messes that I had to take care of. She was a beautiful, intelligent girl, and I took notice of her in class the very first day. She looked so nervous in her oversized NYU hoodie as she had to keep sliding her glasses back up her nose as she tried to take notes during the lecture. She was focused and over the course of the semester, I found she had a lot of little quirks that were sweet and innocent, just like I imagined she would be. Chewing on her pens. Pulling her brows together in a frown when she was reading something that was complicated. I could tell she was interested too with the attention she gave me and how much she soaked up the words that I said. It was such a turn on to see how she responded so easily to me.

She agreed to meet me for coffee on Sunday and I thought it was only fitting to meet at the coffee house that we had been going to together for months. Maybe we didn't actually get to sit down and drink coffee together, but I was always there, always watching, nonetheless. I just needed a few more days to let the wounds heal before I took Hannah as my own. I could tell that she wasn't going to fight me the way Elena had. She looked like the kind of girl that liked to be controlled and I was happy to be that guy for her.

We were going to be happy together. I just knew it.

Twenty Six

Max

2 Days Ago

Beep. Beep. Beep. The machines hooked up to Elena blended together to form a numbing orchestra of sadness as she lay lifeless in the bed with tubes down her throat to keep her alive. The night had been long but I refused to leave her side as she fought as hard as she could before they eventually had to intervene. Early this morning I had to finally convince my family to go home and get some rest and I would let them know as soon as she was awake.

I rubbed my eyes as the sun started to filter through the window into the dark room. My body was exhausted but I couldn't stand the idea of something happening to her while I was sleeping so I drank my weight in coffee and stayed up to watch over her. I checked my phone, hopeful for a call or text from Hannah, yet disappointed when there was nothing.

I wanted to reach out to her yesterday to see how she was doing, but when I wasn't overthinking my decision to give her space, I was busy with stuff with Elena. Trevor had stayed with me the majority of the day and eventually left around ten last night, stopping to check on Hannah's apartment on his way back to mine to look for the missing notes we still couldn't find. He agreed not to bother her, just make sure everything looked okay.

My stomach had been in knots since she left my apartment yesterday morning and it was killing me not being able to talk to her. I wanted to finish our conversation and make sure she knew how I really felt about her but I didn't get the chance before my world exploded around me. Hell, I wasn't sure if I even knew how I felt but I still found myself wanting to talk to her about feelings that I hadn't bothered to sort out. Being with Hannah felt so different than being with Adrianna. Adrianna was a constant battle, it always felt forced. When people say you have to work to make a relationship work- I honestly believed that with Adrianna. But with Hannah, it never felt like work. I wanted to make her happy. I wanted to be around her. I wanted to soak up every smile she offered and drown in the sound of her laughter.

A nurse came in and smiled as she checked the monitors and made some notes on her clipboard.

"Any changes?" I asked quietly even though I knew the answer.

"Nothing significant." She sighed as she continued to write before looking up at me. "But right now, we're happy that she's maintaining. Hopefully her body will be able to rest and heal a little bit. The more rest she gets, the stronger she will be, and the easier her recovery will be."

I let out a breath as I leaned back against the worn-out leather chair and closed my eyes. It was a waiting game and we knew that, but it didn't make it any easier. I felt helpless which was a feeling I despised. There weren't many things in life that had ever made me feel the way I felt when I looked down at my baby sister, hardly recognizable. I silently said another prayer for a full and quick recovery, desperate to be able to talk to her and find out who did this to her.

My phone buzzed on the table beside Elena's bed as a text message came through. I felt excited for a quick moment that it was Hannah, but that quickly disappeared when I saw Trevor's name on the screen.

Trevor: Give me a call when you have a chance. I think I've found something that might be helpful.

I could feel the energy flowing through me as I pressed send and waited for him to answer, my fingers drumming along the table beside me.

"Hey, I wasn't sure if you were awake yet."

"Yeah, I didn't sleep last night so I've been up for a while now." I chuckled and smiled when I heard the faint laughter on his end. I looked to the side to check on Elena, careful not to be too loud even though she wasn't awake. I was hopeful that she was just sleeping and that she would be waking up and giving us all hell again really soon.

"I found the notes that we were looking for, the ones you had originally taken at your mom's house."

"Where were they?" It had been eating away at me that they were the only ones that were missing and they should have been with everything else in her file.

"On the floor behind the desk. They must have fallen or slipped through the crack behind the desk."

"I did have things spread out across the desk the other day so that makes sense. What did you find?" Anxiety was starting to build as I waited for Trevor to just get to the point and tell me what he found.

"You're never going to believe this- do you remember the

guy Elena was going to meet up with from the online dating site?"

"Yeah...." I held my breath and waited as I tried to remember everything I could about the conversation she had with the guy. Nothing really bothered me about their conversation other than he didn't have a profile picture and I wasn't sure if she even really knew the guy.

"Guess what his user name is for his profile?"

I racked my brain trying to remember what it could have been when all of a sudden it clicked and my stomach dropped. I looked down at Elena and let out a heavy breath.

"Five steps ahead."

"Bingo."

Twenty Seven

Hannah
2 Days Ago

I pulled my hair up into a messy bun on top of my head and stared at my features in the mirror. Maybe I needed a new look? I seemed to live life the easy way these days and never bothered to actually wear my hair down anymore, let alone take the time to dry and curl it. I used to love spending hours getting ready, even if I had no wear to go. I sighed when I realized just how bad of a funk I was really in. I had never drastically changed anything about my look and wondered if now was the time to just go for it. I closed my eyes and tried to imagine myself with jet black hair instead of the light golden brown that everyone always complimented. It had always suited me and my fair complexion but black would make my green eyes really stand out. I played around with the idea as I pulled on my hoodie and grabbed my cell phone and keys before heading out for a quick run.

I wasn't much of a runner and never had been but today I decided it was a great day to start. I needed something new in my life, something to change who I was and propel me in a new direction far from where life had currently taken me. I started increasing my pace as I walked toward the park, trying to get my heartbeat up before I attempted to run like

I knew what I was doing. It was early in the morning for me but the city never sleeps so there were already quite a few people out walking and running. I pulled to the side of the path and stopped to stretch as I looked around and found that not a single person had even noticed me. That's one thing I was learning to love about living in a big city- you could be as invisible as you wanted because the majority of the time no one noticed you anyways.

I took a deep breath as I stood up right and looked at the path directly in front of me. There were a few people walking ahead of me and a handful of people hanging out in the grassy area beside me but other than that it wasn't too populated. Giving it everything I had, I pushed off and started running, not giving a damn about my insecurities or what anyone around me might be thinking about me.

It took a few minutes for my body to adjust as I struggled to catch my breath and had to slow down a little. For being so young I was apparently out of shape and needed to start slower than I thought. I slowed my pace to a comfortable jog and smiled when my body found a rhythm.

The weather was perfect for my impromptu run with a rare sunny sky and no snow or wind. It was a few weeks away from Christmas and there was another major storm expected to hit in a few days. I focused my breathing on inhaling deeply and felt alive and invigorated each time the cold air filled my lungs.

I was totally in the zone, unaware of anyone around me as my footsteps pounded against the pavement, creating a peaceful tune. Out of the corner of my eye I saw someone jogging next to me and tried to quicken my pace to put some distance between us. I didn't want to be obvious or rude and look directly at the person beside me so I kept my eyes forward and focused on my breathing as I ran harder.

The only problem was that the faster I went, the faster they went. They were constantly in line with me, running right beside me. Not having much of a choice I slowed down and moved over to the side to let the people behind me keep running. I was bent over at the waist, trying to catch my breath, when I noticed they stopped and pulled over too.

"What the hell is your problem?" I demanded as I straightened up, still trying to catch my breath. I had heard from Amber plenty of times about the dangers of running by yourself in the park and right now I was seriously kicking myself for not being more prepared. Why hadn't I thought to bring mace or some sort of weapon with me? Maybe I wasn't ready to be on my own in the big city after all.

"You're still not a morning person, are you?" Trevor teased as he took in the sight of me struggling to catch my breath.

"What are you doing here?" I made my way over to an empty bench and sat down, feeling it shift as Trevor sat beside me.

"Like you, I was going for a run."

"Are you following me?" I was irritated and part of me felt angry and hostile that he had found a way to taint my attempt at something new in my life. In reality, I think I was angrier that he caught me attempting to run and not being very successful at it given that he wasn't winded at all and I was pretty sure I was going to need an oxygen mask soon.

"I should be asking you the same." He leaned back against the bench and lifted a bottle of water to his lips, taking a long drink while watching me.

"Why would I be following you?" I eyed his water as my throat burned and wished I would have thought to bring a bottle of water with me. It was obvious who was the experienced runner between the two of us, even if his lean and sculpted body didn't give it away.

"I come running here every morning, and this is the path that I start on. Today is the first time I've ever seen you here running." His eyes danced wildly as they looked into mine and I could tell he was enjoying this. "So why are you stalking me, Hannah?"

I tried desperately to fight the smile that pulled at my lips and looked away in frustration. Just when I thought there wasn't anyone as charming out there as Max, along comes his best friend.

"I wanted to do something different. I'm in a funk." I shrugged and looked off in the distance.

"I get it. I've done crazy things trying to get out of a funk before." His tone was sympathetic and for a moment I imagined this might be what it felt like to have a sibling. That special kind of love where someone genuinely cares for you without wanting anything in return.

"I don't want to sound bossy but can I give you a piece of advice?" He looked at me out of the corner of his eye, making me nervous about what I might be lectured on.

"Sure." The initial irritation and frustration had subsided and I was thankful to be able to sit and talk with him for a few minutes.

"This park isn't always the safest place for women to run by themselves, even during the day. You might want to look at getting some mace, or if you want, I can let you know when I'm coming and we can run together."

My heart melted at the offer to run with him knowing that he was just doing it to be nice. I'm sure he runs way faster than what I'm able to do so I didn't want to take him up on the offer and hinder his workout. But I still felt important and that was a big boost to my currently deflated ego.

"Thank you, I'll look into getting some mace." I smiled as I rolled my eyes, knowing I had already given myself the same lecture a few minutes ago when I thought he could be some sex crazed predator after an imposter runner in the park.

"Sounds good. Just don't try to use it on me, got it?" He joked and I found myself laughing along with him.

"I wouldn't dare! Plus I'm sure you could outrun me anyways and get away before I got you."

"I don't know, you're pretty fast. You really picked up speed when you were trying to get past me."

"I was mad and irritated that someone was in my space." I laughed and remembered how focused I was on running and not at all worried about who was beside me.

"Well, remind me not to get on your bad side again." He playfully nudged me with his elbow as an awkward silence fell between us, the elephant in the room finally making its appearance.

"So, how's Elena?" My voice was low as I stared at the family having a morning picnic on the grass across from us.

"She still hasn't woken up yet. It's just a waiting game at this point."

"I'm sorry." I desperately wanted to ask about Max and see how he was doing but I didn't. I hadn't heard from him once since I left and deep down, I knew that it was my cue to walk away. Keep it as a clean break, don't muddy the waters. Forget the fact that my heart felt shattered into a mess of tiny pieces from all of the recent loss. Just move on.

"Me too." He sighed heavily and I could tell this was hard for him too. "But we think we have a lead and are looking into the guy from that online dating app, the one she was meeting the night she disappeared."

There was hope in his voice which made me smile.

"That's good. Hopefully it points you guys in the right direction."

I remembered Max telling me that she had met someone from the same online dating site that I had met Chet on and felt guilty about my upcoming date. I chewed my lip nervously as I looked away, hoping Trevor wouldn't notice it.

"What's wrong?" He leaned forward and turned toward me, invading my personal space.

"It's nothing." I was pretty sure my lip was going to look like it had been inflated with Botox from the amount of swelling I could feel building from chewing on it so much.

"Hannah." The tone in his voice got my attention and I found myself turning to look at him.

"Really, it's nothing."

"If there's something that you remember or that you know about the online dating site that could help us- I need you to tell me. I know that you're mad at Max, and I get it, but this isn't about him right now. It's about Elena. She's like a sister to me, Hannah." He reached out and held my hands as he pleaded.

"No, it's nothing like that. I promise."

I took a shaky breath and tried to figure out how to get around telling him that I had a date. He let go of my hands and watched me cautiously as he tried to figure out what was wrong with me. I was a terrible liar and knew that I didn't have much of a chance getting away without telling him.

"Is there something going on with you? Something with the guy who's been stalking you?"

I felt my face flush and looked away, my foot tapping uncontrollably. This felt like it was quickly getting out of control but I couldn't tell him that I had a date with another guy when I just barely stopped talking to his best friend a day ago. If Max had any questions about how I felt about him, this would confirm every doubt that he ever had. Not even a week after we stopped talking and I was already meeting someone I didn't know from the same dating app that his sister used when she went missing. If he didn't care about me as a girlfriend, I knew that it would still piss him off nonetheless.

"Hannah, I swear- I'm about to lose my mind. Just tell me what's going on. If not, I'm two seconds away from throwing you over my shoulder and locking you in my apartment until you tell me."

I licked my lips while my heart beat wildly in my chest. I pulled at the hem of my pullover hoodie and looked down.

"I have a date on Sunday."

There. That was it. The secret was out. I saw the surprise in his eyes as he processed the words and struggled with why it was so hard for me to tell him.

"Okay." He nodded and looked off in the distance, still processing.

"I didn't want to tell you because I didn't want you to think that I was the kind of girl to run from guy to guy." I watched him as I tried to explain, nothing but silence on his end.

"Max meant a lot to me. I've been really hurt that I haven't heard from him since I left but I get it. There's a lot going on and it's easier if we just have a clean break from each other. Whatever we were- we just break it off and go our separate ways."

"Hannah, I'm not judging you for going on a date."

"Okay." I straightened my posture and leaned back against the bench unsure of what he was going to say, if anything at all.

"Just promise me that you'll be careful, okay?" There was something in his voice that pulled at my heart, a worry of some sort that he hadn't spoken.

"I will. I know you're overprotective because Elena met someone from the same dating site but I promise, I'm getting to know the guy first." I smiled to reassure him then questioned if it was him that I was trying to reassure, or myself. In all honesty, I didn't know anything about him other than his name was Adam and he went to school. A shiver ran up my spine and I wondered if I was crazy for going on the date after all.

"That's not what I'm worried about." He looked at me and his eyes were soft as if they pitied me.

"I'm worried about you, Hannah."

"Why?"

"Because I think you're reaching a breaking point. You've been through a lot in a short period of time and you haven't really processed any of it. I've seen it too many times where people get pushed too far and they become so desperate to escape that they become reckless."

"So because I'm meeting someone for coffee, I'm being reckless?" I could feel myself becoming defensive as I thought about his words. I knew that I was in a rut but I wouldn't call it a downward spiral like he was insinuating.

"That's not what I meant, Hannah. You mentioned that you went running today because you're in a rut and needed something new. You're meeting someone you don't know for coffee when someone has been actively stalking you and you're not at all worried about it. So yeah, it makes me worried about you. You're not acting like yourself."

"Maybe I'm tired of being myself. Had that ever occurred to you? Maybe I'm tired of being the girl that is so boring and predictable that no one notices her. Maybe I want to actually live life for once and feel the thrill of doing something new!" I was practically shouting and knew that I had reached a new breaking point. But not the one he talked about.

"Look, I appreciate you wanting to look out for me but I'm good. And if you don't mind, I need to get going. I have places to go and things to do."

I didn't wait for him to say anything as I jogged off and made my way to the nearest store to grab some scissors and hair color before going back to my apartment.

Twenty Eight

Max

2 Days Ago

The battery icon on my laptop turned red as I continued my search through the online dating site, trying to figure out who 5StepsAhead was. I had created a fake dating profile and used a photo of Mindy- with her permission, to try to lure the guy in to talk to me. Unfortunately he was either smarter than I thought or dumber than I gave him credit for.

The notifications showed that he had opened and read the emails I had sent to him but there was no response. I tried one last time and had to put a lot of thought into how a woman would talk to a guy on an online dating site. I was clueless but knew that I had to get it right and make it seem like Mindy was really interested in him or it would fall through.

After several attempts with no luck, Mindy literally stepped in and took over my laptop, emailing the guy to tell him how impressed she was with the new book he was reading, and how he couldn't possibly be THAT smart AND good looking! I rolled my eyes as she walked Trevor and I through each response before he ended their conversation by telling her that he enjoyed their conversation but he wasn't looking for anything. After probing a little bit more he admitted that he had a date on Sunday and was interested in where it would go so he wasn't interested in meeting anyone else at this time.

It had now become my newest obsession to find out who he was meeting before Sunday, and if possible, where they were meeting. Trevor had been working with one of his friends who was an IT genius to try to get him to hack in and find out the location of this guy but that was proving to be impossible as well.

It was almost four in the afternoon and my body was feeling the impact of sitting at a makeshift table in the uncomfortable chair I had been in since last night. I sighed as I pushed the tray away and plugged in the laptop, allowing it to charge while I took a break. Mindy, Trevor and I had been working non-stop since this morning and I needed to stretch and get some blood flowing through my body. I was desperate for some fresh air and a view of anything other than the yellow tinted cream colored walls I had been staring at.

"Want to go downstairs and grab something to eat?" Trevor offered as if sensing my irritability.

I looked over at Elena, the urge to say yes overruled by the guilt of leaving her in case she woke up.

"I'll stay with Elena," Mindy offered, taking my seat by her bed. "Go get something to eat, stretch your legs, and get some fresh air. I'll call you if anything changes."

"Thanks, I appreciate it."

I knew that I could take my mom or sisters up on the offer to come and sit with Elena but I couldn't afford the distraction right now. My dad was doing a great job of keeping them distracted and had insisted that they spend time cleaning the house to get ready for Elena to come home. My mom was desperate to have her back home and didn't bother to object as she worked to deep clean the entire house. My dad was a smart man, I had to give him that.

Trevor and I took the stairs instead of waiting for the elevator. It felt good to be up and moving, my body sore from being sedentary for so long.

"Anything you feel like?" Trevor asked as we walked outside and headed toward the food trucks that were lined up.

"Burger sounds good, you?"

"I can do a burger." He smiled and something felt odd about it. It was the kind of smile he had when he knew something that he didn't want me to know.

"You seem off, what's up?" I asked as we got in line and waited.

"Nothing." He avoided eye contact and I knew it wasn't nothing. It was something. And it was something that I needed to know.

"Is it about Elena or Hannah?" I raised my eyebrow and waited for him to come clean.

"Hannah."

I watched as he kept his attention on the line in front of us instead of looking at me.

"What's going on with Hannah?" This time I put my hand on his shoulder and turned him so he had no choice but to look at me. He blew out a breath before sighing and making eye contact.

"I'm worried about her."

"Why? Has she received more notes? Did something happen at her apartment?" The worst thoughts I could think were flooding my brain, guilt for being with Elena instead of watching over Hannah taking over. I clenched my fist at my side while I waited for the bad news.

"No, she's fine. I think, I mean I don't know for sure."

"What does that mean? Why are you worried about her?" We moved forward and I waited anxiously for him to get on with it and tell me.

"I ran into her this morning while running."

"Hannah was running? I didn't know she runs." I shook my head at the thought and realized I didn't know as much about her personal life as I thought I did.

"She doesn't. She decided to start this morning because she's trying something new."

"Okay..." I was unsure of where he was going with this.

"She got really defensive, Max. About a lot of things. I think she's being reckless as a way to try to cope with everything that has happened."

"I don't know that running is really a cry for help," I offered, looking at the menu as we were next in line. I felt relieved that it wasn't as big of a deal as he had made it out to be.

"She has a date on Sunday. With some guy she met on that online dating site."

My head jerked toward him. There was no way that Hannah was going on a date with someone she didn't know. She wasn't that kind of girl, she had told me herself when she talked to me about her date with Chet. Was she just telling

Trevor that to see if it would hurt me?

"Are you sure?" I asked between clenched teeth. "Maybe she just said that so you would tell me and I would get jealous?"

"That's the thing- I had to pry it out of her. She didn't just voluntarily tell me that she was going on a date. She wouldn't have told me if I hadn't pried it out of her."

I felt like the wind had been knocked out of me as I approached the order window with a sudden lack of appetite.

"What can I get you?" The guy asked from the window as he impatiently waited for my order.

"Burger and fries," I muttered as I processed what Trevor had just told me.

"Everything on it okay?"

"Yeah, whatever." I waved absently as I walked off in a daze, leaving Trevor to place his order. I sat down on the metal bench and hung my head as I thought about Hannah going on a date with another man. The thought of it made me physically sick. If she was ready and willing to date someone else that quickly then that had to mean that she wasn't that interested in what we had to begin with. Feelings of being with Adrianna filled my mind and I found myself comparing the two to each other. Both were beautiful and both had stolen my heart before giving theirs to someone else.

Twenty Nine

Hannah

1 Day Ago

It felt weird looking at myself in the mirror and seeing short, jet-black hair. Yesterday was the first day that I had decided to focus on being the new Hannah, the one who was adventurous and free spirited. After my conversation with Trevor I had never felt more excited to walk away from the old Hannah and find out who the new Hannah was.

He had said he was concerned about my reckless behavior but I didn't feel it was reckless at all. If I wanted to change who I was then that was all the approval that I needed. I had lived my life for so long being worried about what everyone else thought and seeking other's approval, never bothering to worry about my own.

A quick trip to the store and I had everything I needed to update my look. Gone was the predictable Hannah with the normal hair color. Here to stay was the new Hannah with a cute short bob of black hair that really made my eyes stand out. A couple of YouTube videos and half a bottle of champagne later and I was a new woman!

I had spent the morning getting groceries and picked up a few new outfits to try on for my date tomorrow. I liked the idea of spending the day playing around with my hair and makeup while trying on different outfits, especially since I had nothing else to do with myself on a Saturday. Lately my weekends had been consumed with studying but now that all of that was over, I could finally let loose and enjoy my downtime.

By noon my stomach was growling so I threw together a quick sandwich and sat down to eat while checking my email. There was a new one from Adam, asking me to meet him tomorrow at 11:00 in the morning at Java Jazz. I ate my sandwich while I thought about my response and played around with the idea of cancelling. It irked me that I was being so predictable so I confirmed I would meet him there at 11 and pressed send. There was no backing out now.

I went back to trying on outfits and seeing how they looked with my new hair and makeup, completely oblivious to the time. A knock on my door caught my attention and butterflies filled my belly as I wondered if it was Max. I sat the short dress down on the bed and walked over to the door, waiting to see if they were going to knock again before opening it. Really I was just trying to get the courage to open it in case it was Max. A few seconds later and there was another knock. Instead of peeking through the peephole like a normal person, I latched on to the excitement of not knowing who it was and opened the door.

"Wow." His voice was low as he leaned against the doorway and shoved his hands into his pockets.

"Wow what?" I asked as I pulled the door in, blocking him from coming in.

"You look different." His eyes studied my hair and face before traveling down my body and forcing the heat up my skin as I blushed.

"That was the goal." I nervously ran a hand through my newly short hair and looked at him. "What do you want, Max?"

"Can we talk for a few?" He stood upright and looked past me into the apartment.

"I think we've said all we've needed to the other day." I leaned against the door to make the opening even smaller.

"You might have, but I definitely wasn't finished." He stepped closer and I felt the buzz of his body next to mine.

"I don't think there's anything else we need to talk about." I protested as I tried to keep my position.

"Well then, you can just listen." He smiled coyly as he stepped further into my space and stepped inside. His body gently grazed mine as I felt his hand slide across my waist as he passed by.

I closed my eyes and shut the door. My nerves were on edge as I tried to figure out what he wanted and why he was there. I had wanted to talk to him days ago but now that he was here, I couldn't remember what I wanted to talk about.

I turned to face Max and found him looking at the dress on the bed next to the other outfits that I had picked out for my date tomorrow. His brow was furrowed as he looked at each one, all skimpy outfits compared to what I usually wear. On the floor by the bed were a few pairs of thin heeled, strappy high heels to go with the outfits. He bent down and picked one up, holding it in the air by the stem of the shoe.

"Is this for your date tomorrow?" He eyed me cautiously as his jaw clenched. I licked my lips and swallowed hard.

"How did you hear about that?" I asked, knowing that he had talked to Trevor.

"Let's just say that I know things."

"You talked to Trevor."

"I did, he's worried about you. Told me that you weren't acting like yourself. I decided to come see for myself." He sat the shoe down where he found it and looked back at me. I felt nervous and uncomfortable as he looked me over, taking the few steps across the room to close the gap between us as he ran a hand through my hair. I closed my eyes and held my breath as I felt his touch that I had been desperate to feel for days.

"I can see what he means."

His words were simple but they felt like they cut through me with a knife. There was a condescending tone that started to eat away at me.

"Yeah, well, I wasn't looking for approval. Maybe you need to go." I squared my shoulders and stepped back.

"Is that what you want, Hannah?" His voice was low and raspy. My body felt alive next to his and I knew exactly what I wanted.

"Yes," I whispered, both of us knowing that I was lying.

"Look me in the eye and tell me, Hannah. Tell me that you want me to walk out that door and never come back. Say it and I'll do it." He watched me as he waited for my reaction.

My body turned slightly toward his as it felt the pull that I couldn't deny. I wanted to reach out and touch him. Kiss him. My fingers trembled by my side as they itched to grab him and pull him towards me. I looked up and licked my lips without thinking about it. No matter how hard I tried to control it, my body would always find a way to his.

"That's what I thought." He quickly reached out and grabbed me, pulling me in and wrapping his arms around me as his mouth crashed down over mine. I lifted my hands up and ran my fingers through his hair, clawing my way to bring him closer to me. He grasped down and lifted my butt as I wrapped my legs around him, feeling him walk over to the bed. The kiss broke for a quick second as he leaned over and pushed the outfits off the bed before laying me down on it.

There was a hunger in his eyes and I wanted him to devour me. I watched as he pulled his shirt over his head in one swift movement, revealing his rock hard abs and beautifully chiseled chest. He was seriously what girls dreamed of when they thought of the perfect man with the perfect body. His eyes looked me up and down as he unbuttoned his jeans and slid them down. Stepping out of them he leaned down on the bed, his erection trapped beneath his boxers, and pulled me closer to him.

"Were you planning to wear this on your date tomorrow?" he asked as his finger ran down the front of my lacy black button down tube top and hovered over the top of my denim skirt.

"Yes," I whispered as his hand slid down the front of my skirt and over my panties.

"Do you have any idea of what that does to me?" he grunted as his fingers pushed my panties to the side and slowly slipped a finger inside. I arched my back as I let out a moan as his finger easily glided back and forth. There was so much I needed to say to him but right now, I didn't want to talk, I just wanted him to keep touching me the way he was and help me get the release that I needed. I felt him pull the top of my tube top down with his teeth, freeing my breasts in the process. He groaned under his breath as he pulled a nipple into his mouth and sucked hard. My hands grabbed his hair and pulled him closer to me as my pelvis started to grind against his hand.

"I don't want anyone to see you like this, Hannah. Just me." He was breathless as he shot the words out in between the slow torture he was inflicting on my nipples as he went back and forth, sucking on both. His fingers dipped further inside causing me to want more. "Fuck, you're so wet, baby," he growled close to my ear.

"I want you, Max," I panted. "Now, Max, now!" I was getting closer, the friction on my clit the right pace to send me over the edge as I imagined his thick cock filling me again.

"Do you want me more than you want the guy you were planning to wear this for? Huh, Hannah? Do you?" There was a possessiveness to his voice as he said it, turning me on even further. I liked the jealousy in his voice.

"I want you more than anyone," I whimpered in his ear. I was getting closer and needed him to get me there. I adjusted my position beneath him to force his hand to rub against my clit as his fingers moved inside me. The friction felt wonderful as I rocked back and forth against his hand, building the pressure I needed.

Suddenly he stopped and my eyes flashed open to look at him.

"Frustrating, isn't it?" He was propped up, hovering over me as he watched for my reaction.

"It is." I blew out a frustrated breath, feeling my orgasm

slipping away as my chest heaved up and down.

"Now take your physical frustration and imagine what it feels like to be me. To see the girl I'm crazy about wearing this sexy fucking outfit to go on a date with another man because she refuses to hear me when I tell her how crazy I am about her. That's frustrating, Hannah."

My shoulders slumped as my body relaxed beneath him and I took in his words. Suddenly I didn't have any desire to go on the date tomorrow. I wanted this man right here in front of me. The one who was making the effort to show me how much he cared about me.

"I'm sorry." I let out a deep breath and looked him in the eyes.

"I'm gonna need more clarification. Is this just an apology so I'll finish getting you off?" He chuckled as he rolled over and laid next to me.

"No," I reached over and swatted at his chest, "I'm sorry for not listening when you were trying to talk to me and for making you jealous."

He grabbed my hand and laced his fingers between mine.

"You certainly know how to drive me crazy," he joked, a small laugh filling the room.

"Same here." I looked up and studied his face. "I wasn't trying to make you jealous, I was just trying to figure out how to move on with my life. How to get over you."

I lowered my eyes as he leaned in and kissed my forehead. While I wanted to go back to the hot, passionate road we were heading down just a few minutes ago, I was perfectly content just being in his arms. It felt right.

"Well, I'm happy to drive you crazy again...if you know what I mean?" His voice got lower as he rolled over on top of me and made his way planting kisses down my neck as his hands slid my skirt up to my hips. Firm hands grabbed my ass and my back arched, inviting him in to where I needed him.

There was an urgency to the way he moved as he freed himself from his boxers and slid my panties to the side before entering me. I gasped at the sudden contact and dug my nails in his back as he rocked back and forth inside me. There was no slow, gentle love making tonight. It was quick, and rough, and delicious as he took his time to give me my release before getting his.

An hour later I rolled over and felt his arms wrap tighter around me as he held onto me in his sleep. We had talked for a bit after we made love but eventually we both gave in and fell asleep, which was easy given neither of us had slept the night before. He had given me updates on Elena and where they were at with everything but it was quick and we didn't get into too much detail.

Around 11:30 we woke up to his phone ringing. I looked at him as I turned the light on, my stomach clenching as I waited for the bad news. No one ever called in the middle of the night with good news. He reached over and grabbed his cell phone, sliding the button to answer it.

"What's up?" he asked as he mouthed Trevor's name to let me know who was calling. I waited on pins and needles, waiting to find out what he was calling for.

"Are you serious?! Okay, I'll be right there." He hung up and quickly rolled out of bed, grabbing his clothes from the floor and getting dressed as he looked around for his shoes.

"What is it? What's happening?"

"Elena is awake." He smiled as he leaned in and gave me a kiss before rushing off to the door. He stopped to look at me before he opened the door.

"Go! Go!" I waved him off, excited for him that she was finally awake. "Update me later, just get over there and see your sister." I smiled and watched as the door closed behind him.

Thirty

Max

6 Hours Ago

The night had been long and the only way I was keeping track was with the hourly check-ins the nurses did on Elena. A new set of nurses came in as our regular nurses checked out for the day, confirming it was seven in the morning and the shift change was happening. I took a break to let Elena get situated with the new nurses and ran downstairs to get us breakfast. My family was already on their way down to the hospital so it was about to get even more crowded. The line at the food truck was moving quickly as I saw Trevor heading toward the entrance to the hospital. I waved and flagged him down before he went inside.

"Hey, how's Elena doing?" he asked as he clapped a hand on my shoulder.

"She's good. I'm hoping to talk with her this morning, she was still pretty out of it last night. But then again, my mom and sisters are coming so who knows how much talking we will get in." I chuckled as Trevor smiled, knowing that it was true. "Thankfully she stayed awake so that was a good sign that she should be on the road to recovery." I smiled as I took the cups of coffee from the girl in the food truck and handed them to Trevor as I waited for the last cup of coffee and our burritos.

By the time we got back up to Elena the nurses were leaving her room followed by a doctor. I was disappointed that we had missed the doctor but they hadn't told us that he was expected to go by for an update. I quickened my pace and caught up with him right as he made his way to the nurse's station.

"Hey, doc. I was wondering if you could give me an update on my sister, Elena Romano?" I stood back to give him some space so it didn't feel like I was being too aggressive. He peered over the thick bifocal lenses and looked me up and down before looking back at her file.

"Who did you say you were?" His voice was as raspy as someone who had smoked 10 cartons of cigarettes a day for the last forty years.

"Her brother. Max." I waited for him to acknowledge my relationship to her, surely the nurses had told him that I had been there with her since she was admitted.

"Your sister is doing well, considering everything she went through. We'll do some more tests and scans this morning to make sure there's nothing that we missed, but she should be able to be discharged by this evening or early tomorrow morning." He was vague and it was getting to me in the worst way.

"Is there any news on what had happened? Did you get the results back on her other tests?"

"Look, I have to get to the next patient in my rounds. If you want the full update, have your brother fill you in."

I stared at him confused.

"I'm sorry, who?"

"Your brother."

"I don't have a brother."

"Okay, then Elena's other brother. He was just here, I updated him on everything. Left maybe 10 minutes ago." He tapped his pen on the countertop and nodded toward the clock before grabbing another file and walking off.

Chills ran down my spine as I looked at Trevor and he looked at me. Who the fuck had been there, pretending to be Elena's brother? As if on cue, we both ran into Elena's room and pulled the curtain back. I was relieved to find it was just Elena in the room, no one else.

"What the hell?!" She held her hand to her chest as she looked at Trevor and I with fear in her eyes as we startled her.

"Was someone in here recently?" I asked as I looked around. Trevor pushed past me and checked the bathroom while I waited for an answer.

"Um, yeah. The doctor. The nurses. The person who brought me a tray of food." She nodded at the tray beside her. "You saw most of them before you left."

Trevor and I exchanged a look as I sat down next to her.

"Max, you're scaring me. What's going on?"

"I asked the doctor for an update before coming in here and he was really vague. When I asked for more information he told me that I needed to get the updates from Elena's brother. The one he had just talked to 10 minutes before I got there."

Her hand went to her mouth as the color drained from her face.

"He knows that I'm here," she whispered as her eyes filled with tears.

"Did anyone look or act suspicious that was in your room?"

"No, but I was really busy with talking to the nurses. The only person that came in that wasn't a nurse was the person who brought my tray, but they were still wearing scrubs so I figured they worked here. They were the only one who didn't talk to me."

"Have you checked your food tray?" Trevor asked right as the door opened and a bubbly woman came in holding a food tray in her hand.

Trevor and I watched as she approached the bed and noticed the food tray next to Elena. She looked down at the covered lid and stepped outside before coming back in.

"Can we help you?" I asked.

"I have a food tray to deliver but it looks like someone else already delivered one." She nodded toward Elena. "I thought maybe I had the wrong room but it says it's for 704 and this is 704." She shrugged as she held the food tray in front of her and waited.

"Well then, I guess she gets two today," I joked nervously, curious to see what was going on. "You can go ahead and set that one down over there if you don't mind?"

She smiled at me as she left it on the open counter space by the sink and walked out of the room. Elena looked confused as she looked back and forth between the two trays.

"Why would they bring me two food trays?" she asked innocently.

"My guess is that they didn't," I said as I looked at the food tray sitting next to her. I looked at Trevor, feeling nervous about seeing what was really under the lid. He gave a slight nod of agreement as I slowly reached down and lifted the lid.

Sitting on the plate was a bologna and cheese sandwich with a note attached to a toothpick stuck in the sandwich. I pulled the toothpick out and slid the paper down. I unfolded the paper which was a piece of paper torn out of a text book. As I unfolded it, I saw the familiar black ink from the marker used in the notes to Hannah. I cleared my throat as I read it out loud.

Roses are red

Violets are blue

You thought you could leave me

But I found you

I tried to build us a life

Where we could live together

You threw it all away

You severed the tether

I wanted to love you

And only make you happy

You wanted to defy me

Each time you attacked me

Everything I did

I did it for us

I say it was in the name of love
You say it was lust

I thought I was what you wanted
Everything you said you'd need
People tried to warn you not to talk to strangers
Their advice you did not heed

Maybe next time you'll learn your lesson
Of random strangers you shouldn't bed
Even though you got away I'll always be 5StepsAhead

My stomach soured as I read the note and saw the same patterns as the notes Hannah had been receiving. When I was done I looked at Elena who had tears running down her face.

"Elena, do you know who wrote this?" I asked as I held the note in the air. "Do you know who took you?"

She shook her head no as she violently sobbed. I went to her side and leaned next to the bed and held her as she cried. Her body felt small and fragile compared to mine as I focused on being gentle so I didn't hurt her.

"I don't know who it is. He never let me see his face, he always had it covered."

"Did you recognize his voice?"

"It always sounded familiar but I couldn't figure out why." She continued to sob as her breathing changed in response to her crying.

"Does this note mean anything to you?" I asked, feeling her cry against me again, unable to answer me.

"Leni, what is it about the note that keeps getting to you?" While I could imagine the whole thing would bother anyone because it was creepy as fuck, I knew my sister well enough to know that something in specific was triggering this reaction.

"It's okay, you can tell me. You're safe now," I whispered as I gently rubbed her back.

"The guy that I was meeting before he took me, his profile name was 5StepsAhead."

She cried even harder after she said it.

"Shh, it's okay. We're looking for him, not to worry." I tried to reassure her.

"What do you mean?" She wiped her tears away and looked up at me.

"When you first went missing, I went through stuff in your room and saw your conversation with him. Then when you came to my apartment the other day, you whispered 'five steps' before you passed out."

"I was so stupid to meet up with him. I didn't even know what he looked like." She let out a ragged breath.

"Can you walk me through what happened?" I asked, thankful for the natural progression into the conversation.

"I'll do my best, most of it is kind of fuzzy. There's a big chunk that is completely missing." She took a deep breath and then looked at Trevor and I.

"I was really upset about the fight that I had with mom, she was all over me about the guy I was seeing, even though she hadn't even met him. When this guy offered to meet up for coffee, I decided to go because I was so mad at mom and wanted to spite her. If she thought I was some cheap tramp who just went out with anyone then I would show her just how many guys I could date at once. I went to the Java Jazz coffee shop that he suggested and waited for him. I was pretty sure I had been stood up when this kid brought me a drink that I hadn't ordered. He said that he had been asked to bring it to me as an apology for making me wait, that the guy I was waiting for was on his way. I didn't think anything of it and it was delivered by someone wearing the same aprons they wear, so I drank it. Not even thirty minutes later I started to feel weird and got up to go home. I don't remember anything after that."

I swallowed hard as I stood watching her with my arms crossed against my chest, jaw clenched. It made sense now why she didn't know where she had been taken- she was drugged before he took her.

"Later, when I woke up, I was in this abandoned warehouse. I wasn't restrained at all, just left to sleep on the cold floor. That's when I called you. Not long after, I heard someone come in the room and that's when he found me on my cell and took it away from me. He was wearing a mask and said that he couldn't let me see him yet. That it wasn't time." She looked down at her hands before continuing.

"The first few days were the hardest because I didn't know what he wanted. He just kept mumbling about how he had to prepare, she was coming soon. One was for practice, the other was for keeps. He would bring in different things each time he came back and would be gone for long periods of time. The stuff he brought was weird- like canned goods, bottled water, and picture frames. But each frame was empty at first." A few deep breaths to steady herself then she continued with her story.

"I fought every chance I got that first week, or however long it was. It felt like forever. There weren't any windows so it was hard to tell if it was day or night. Shortly after he took me there, he tied me to a chair so I couldn't try to escape. He bound my hands and feet. Whenever he got close enough I would try to reach out and grab his knife or knock him down but he caught on quickly and would say, nope, she's not ready yet. Can't bring my love in until this one is in line. It was so weird and it felt really uncomfortable. I don't know who he was talking about but he constantly referred to them as his love."

I reached into my pocket and pulled out the pen and notepad that I always kept on me and jotted down the new information. Elena waited while I wrote and started again when I nodded for her to continue.

"Soon he started bringing pictures in and added them to the empty frames. It was all the same girl- long dark brown hair, really pretty girl. He would tell me how soon our family would be complete, we just had to wait until I was ready. So then it occurred to me that if I wanted to get past this guy, I had to play his game. Instead of constantly fighting him, I had to be interested in him. So I slowly started to act like I was interested in him. I stopped fighting whenever he would touch me and I acted like I liked it. He would tell me how I was doing such a great job and that he was staying five steps ahead. A few days before I escaped I thought I had a chance so I took it. Unfortunately, it wasn't a well thought out plan. He had brought in a new picture frame and I 'accidentally' broke it, keeping a piece of glass tucked inside my pants. As he was getting ready to go to class, he went to give me a goodbye hug- it had become our ritual- and I reached out and tried to stab him. The problem was that I missed and tore the arm of his jacket, cutting his arm in the process."

I shifted my position and looked up at Trevor who was listening with the same intensity as I had, and looked even more pissed off.

"When I cut him, that was when he finally went crazy. He kept screaming about why I didn't love him, why I didn't want to be with him. His anger turned to rage in a split second and that's when he attacked me. At one point I pretended to be unconscious so he would leave me alone. As part of my punishment he withheld food and water for several days, forcing me to eat moldy bologna sandwiches if I got hungry enough. I realized that if I wanted to live, I had to play the part again. He was starting to get obsessed with whoever this other girl was, adding several photos a day and building a shrine for her. I slowly started showing remorse for what I did and tried to play up the loving wife that he insisted I needed to be. The night I left we were having dinner, a celebration of my good behavior the past few days, so I was allowed to sit at the wooden patio table with him without having to be tied to the chair." Her shoulders rose and fell with the deep breath she took before she went on with the story.

"I had complete freedom of my hands and feet but I felt completely weak from not eating in days and was dehydrated. I think that was the only reason he didn't restrain me- he knew how weak I was already, I wasn't much of a threat. He poured us wine and went to check on something from his phone before joining me for dinner. As he sat down I reached over and smashed the wine bottle against the concrete wall and used the sharp point as my weapon. I held it out and swung at him every time he reached for me as I backed myself out the same path I had seen him coming and going. I tripped and started to fall when he reached out to grab me, my only opportunity to be free. I let myself fall as I felt him crush me as he fell on top of me, the sharp point of the wine bottle piercing his shoulder. I knew it wasn't enough to kill him but it was enough to immobilize him for a few. That's when I took off running and didn't stop."

She exhaled loudly as she shifted her position in the bed and laid back.

"Would you be able to describe the building you were in?" Trevor asked from the other side of me.

"I didn't see it until I left but then I was so focused on staying ahead of him that I didn't bother to look around or to look for any landmarks that would show where I was."

"I'm really proud of you, Leni." I smiled as I took in everything she had told me and wondered what additional information she might be able to give us about the guy if we asked the right questions.

We ate our breakfast and drank our coffee in silence as Trevor and I took in everything Leni had told us. A few minutes after she had finished telling us, my family came in her room, making the small space even tinier. I was thankful that for whatever reason, they were late today, and that I had a chance to talk to Elena before they got there. I don't know how much I would have been able to get from her with my mom sitting beside her, criticizing everything she did and asking her why she would meet up with a guy she didn't know. I knew my mom and sister well enough to know that not much was going to change from the fight they had before she went missing.

Once it was after 10, I texted Hannah to say good morning and see how she was doing. Since she wasn't an early riser I wanted to give her time to get up and get some coffee in her before I approached the topic of whether she was still planning on going on that date. After hearing what Leni told me, I would never feel comfortable with anyone doing online dating. It made my stomach hurt not knowing what Hannah's plans were.

Thirty One

Hannah
1 Hour Ago

I was pleasantly surprised to wake up to a text message from Max this morning. I sat up in bed to read it, soreness from the night before reminding me that he really was there and that it hadn't been just a dream. After the 3rd time our bodies were fully satisfied and depleted. I sent him a text back wishing him a good morning and stumbled out of bed to go make some coffee so I could get my day started. It was after 10 and I still hadn't decided whether to cancel my date or not but I knew I needed to make a decision quickly. It would be rude not to let someone know that I wasn't planning on showing up.

The coffee trickled down into the pot as the heavenly aroma filled the air. I took a cup with me over to the couch and sat down as I opened my laptop and waited for it to finish running some updates. I sipped my coffee while I waited, knowing that it would take a while for them to finish since my computer was so ancient. Ten minutes later the screen changed and a picture of me with my parents as my screensaver greeted me. I sat my cup down on the coffee table and picked up my cell phone to find a text message from Max, asking what my plans for the day were.

I chewed my bottom lip as I struggled with what to do, even though deep down I knew what I wanted to do. I wanted to cancel my date and spend the day talking to Max, or even better, be with him. But I felt guilty for not following through with my date because it might be what Amber had wanted. I took a deep breath and tried to clear my head. If I wanted to start a new life, I had to stop focusing on what Amber would want from me. She wasn't here to see it so it shouldn't matter as much as I was letting it.

I opened the dating site and went to my messages with Adam, clicking on the most recent email confirming our date at 11. It was 10:25 so there should still be plenty of time for him to see the message before getting there. I typed a quick message, apologizing for the last minute notice but I would be unable to meet him after all. I clicked the send button and leaned back against the couch, satisfied with my decision. A few seconds later a notification popped up with an error message. I clicked it open and it showed undeliverable due to a profile that no longer existed. Frowning, I closed out the notification and clicked on Adam's profile. Another error message- this user no longer exists.

Irritation lingered around for a few minutes when I realized that I was apparently the one who was going to be stood up since he had already deleted his account before we even met. Guess it was for the best anyways. I signed out of the site and closed my laptop, sitting it on the coffee table. I picked up my coffee cup and took a drink as I settled back against the couch and contemplated whether to call or text Max. I knew I should text since he might be busy with Elena and unable to talk, but the selfish side of me longed to hear his voice. As if reading my mind, a text came through from Max, asking if I was okay since I hadn't texted him back yet. I smiled as my fingers moved across my phone to reply.

Me: Sorry, I had to take care of something. No plans today. You?

I watched as the dots danced across the screen as he was typing.

Max: No plans here, either. Spending time with Elena before she gets bombarded with questions from Mindy and the team. My family just left now so she'll get a small break before she has to tell the story again. They hope to discharge her this evening.

Me: That all sounds like great news. I'm happy to hear it.

Max: So, are you going?

My eyebrows pulled together as I read his message. Go where?

Me: Where am I supposed to be going?

Max: The date.

Oh. I rolled my eyes at my own forgetfulness as I totally spaced it out already and forgot that Max knew about the date.

Me: I cancelled it, but I'm pretty sure I would have been stood up anyways.

Max: Why do you say that?

Me: I emailed him to cancel and he had already deleted his profile.

Max: That's weird.

Me: Yeah, I guess. But at least I didn't have to be the one to cancel.

Max: True. Where were you supposed to meet? Please tell me he wasn't picking you up at your apartment.

Me: No, we were meeting at Java Jazz by my apartment.

Max: Was that your idea?

Me: Nope. It was his idea.

Max: Something doesn't feel right with this. Did you give him any of your personal information?

Me: I didn't give him any information about myself.

I thought back to our conversations just to make sure, nothing popped into my mind that I could remember that was personal other than I had just finished finals. We didn't even exchange phone numbers. Then it hit me that he had called me by my name yet I never told him what it was. A chill shot through me as I thought about how stupid I had been to agree to go on the date in the first place. My phone buzzed in my hand as Max's name showed on the caller ID.

"Hey."

"Hannah, does this guy know anything about you? Where you live? What you look like?" He sounded anxious which had me worried.

"We didn't talk about any of that, Max. I mean he knows what I look like because of my user profile picture, but he doesn't know where I live."

"Do you know what he looks like?"

"He doesn't have a profile picture." I sighed and knew what was coming.

"Hannah- " My name came out as a breath as I heard him sigh on the other line. "You agreed to meet a guy that you don't know, and don't even know what he looks like?"

"I know his name." I offered, hoping that it would give me a little more sympathy that I wasn't completely stupid.

"What's his name?"

"Adam."

"Adam what?"

I could hear the irritation in his voice and knew Detective Max was about to come through soon.

"I don't know, I didn't ask."

"Did you tell him your name?"

"No......" I stalled as I tried to think of how to tell him that he knew my name.

"But?"

"But he knew my name anyways."

"How did he know your name?"

"I don't know, Max! I drank half a bottle of champagne, I was exhausted and feeling sad- I didn't ask that many questions!"

"Okay, okay, I'm sorry."

I could hear voices in the background and he sounded distracted by whoever it was.

"You sound busy, I can let you go." I offered as I was ready to end this conversation.

"It's fine, it's the hospital police. They're here to talk about the security footage from this morning."

"Why? What happened?"

"A guy was here, asking about Elena. He pretended to be her brother to get information from the doctor about her." He pulled the phone away from his mouth as he spoke to someone else before coming back on the line. "Whoever it was got into Elena's room and left her a note inside of the food tray that looked like it was from the hospital. We're trying to see if we can get a good picture of who the guy is."

"Do you think it's the guy who took her?"

"I think it's a really good possibility. The note he left had some specific things that only she would know about from being held captive with him. But Hannah, the notes look identical to the ones you were getting. They are written on pages torn from a text book and are in black ink from a marker."

I shivered as my body was covered in goosebumps.

"Does she know who it is?" My voice was shaky with fear.

"She doesn't. She never saw his face, he wore a mask the entire time."

"Hannah, I have to ask- what was the profile name of the guy you were supposed to meet?" His voice was laced with tension that now matched my own.

"Five steps ahead," I whispered as I tried to connect the dots.

"Fuck!"

The boom in his voice startled me, causing me to jump in my seat. I got up and carried the coffee mug to the kitchen counter.

"Hannah, you're not safe there. I'm on my way to get you. Don't leave before I get there and keep your phone on. Don't hang up, whatever you do. Okay?!"

"Okay," I stammered as I tried to put the pieces together. Something was wrong. Very, very wrong.

Thirty Two

Adam

20 Minutes Ago

Do you know what the most frustrating thing in the world is? When someone agrees to do something then changes their mind at last minute. It was my BIGGEST pet peeve and made me see red every time it happened. Elena had said she would love me and promised to stay with me forever, then she attacked me and left. She was constantly just within my reach but her two little bodyguards at the hospital kept getting in my way. I wasn't so much concerned with having her back. Why beg someone to want to be with you? But regardless, she still needed to pay for what she did. And there was a hefty price tag on it.

For a little bit I had considered forgiving her debt because I was so excited about where things were going with Hannah. But then I found her flirting with the guy in the park, the same one who kept getting in my way with Elena. Shortly after that, I watched her try on and buy slutty clothes to go with the trampy new haircut and color. I was livid when she decided to change her hair without asking me first. She needed to follow the rules before she found herself in the same position as Amber and where Elena was headed.

I considered myself a very patient and disciplined man except for when you made me angry. And lately, I was angry a lot. So much so that I felt blinded by the anger. But everything would soon change, I could just feel it. All of my hard work and sacrifice would finally pay off.

Now we were in a moment of truth, a moment to determine Hannah's fate. She had spent the night with the cop, tsk tsk tsk. I could already tell that he had gotten in her head and would convince her not to meet me so I deleted my profile before she could try to cancel. She was confused, I could tell. But if she just let me between her legs as easily as she let him, she wouldn't be confused about anything. She would enjoy it, just like I did every time I pretended it was her hand working me over as I jerked myself off under the table in class.

I didn't have much time to waste thinking about all of the things she had already done. I had to get going if my plan was still going to work. It was almost 11, time for our date.

Thirty Three

Max

15 Minutes Ago

"He's going after Hannah- it's the same fucking guy!" I whispered loudly to Trevor as I tucked my gun in the back of my jeans. "Stay with Leni and don't let anyone in here. If they force her to be discharged, take her to your apartment and wait for me there."

I practically ran out of the room and down the hall while Hannah waited quietly on the other line. A few people yelled curse words at me as I flew by but I kept going. I had to get to her and I knew the clock was ticking.

"You still there?" I huffed into the phone as I ran out the front doors and into the crowded area by the food trucks as I darted in between people and made my way to the street. I could try to hail a cab and pray that there were no delays getting to Hannah's, or I could keep running the 5 blocks until I got to her. I checked my watch, ten minutes until eleven.

I wasn't sure if or when this guy was coming for her but something in my gut screamed for me to go get her. I shook my head and took off running down the street, deciding that I couldn't risk getting stuck sitting in a cab somewhere.

"I'm here. Are you okay?" Her voice was filled with concern.

"Yeah, I'm just running. Don't hang up, I'm coming to you." I panted as I kept running.

It felt like it was going to take hours to get to her at this rate, my body toying with the idea of giving up on me. I stopped for a quick second to catch my breath and looked down at my watch. Eleven on the dot. I could hear background noise at Hannah's and pushed the phone against my ear to try to hear what was happening.

"Wow, you got here quick," She said directly into the phone as I heard her turning the locks on the door. There was an easiness to her voice now, the sound of relief. My heart dropped as I heard the door open.

"Hannah! Don't open the door, it's not me!" I screamed into the phone, knowing it was too late. I started running, as fast as I could, as I kept the phone pressed against my ear. I heard a loud thump and stopped in my tracks. My pulse was racing as I waited to hear Hannah's voice again. There was movement on the other side and I prayed that maybe she just dropped her phone. A few seconds later I heard the door click shut and a male's voice came on the line.

"Wrong number."

Thirty Four

Hannah

Drip. Drip. Drip. The sound of leaking water filled the empty room that smelled of mildew from the dampness in the air. My head hung against my chest as I tried to lift it, the weight of it unbearable. Slowly I forced my head backwards and allowed a moment to rest as I blinked open my eyes and looked around. The room was dimly lit with concrete floors and windowless concrete walls with nothing around me other than the wooden chair I had been bound to with rope. I tried to pull at the restraints as the thick rope bit at my skin without giving.

I listened for the sound of the dripping water but couldn't hear it anymore. Did that mean that someone was there with me? My body trembled as I strained to hear any sounds that might tell me where I was or who was there. As I slowly tilted my head forward my eye caught a glimpse of something shimmering on the floor from the dim light that barely hung from the ceiling. I leaned forward as far as the rope would allow as I tried to see what it was. As my head dipped forward toward the ground, I heard the familiar dripping sound once more as I felt something wet trickle down my face. Beneath my chair was a puddle of blood. My blood.

My head was killing me and I assumed that it was from whatever injury I had that had caused so much bleeding. I didn't know how much time had passed by or where I had been taken. It was dark and the concrete made the entire room feel cold, sending a shiver through my body. My eyes adjusted to the darkness as I looked around.

A few minutes later I heard footsteps approaching and my body went rigid as I waited for whatever was about to happen. A man wearing the same mask as the person who was at my door stood in front of me and looked at me as they tilted their head. He reached out and touched the spot on my head where it was bleeding. I jerked back away from his touch, his fist clenching in response.

"You know, if you hadn't been such a naughty girl, this wouldn't have had to happen this way." His voice was quiet and almost sounded familiar though I didn't know why. I stayed silent as I watched him like a caged animal, focusing on every little move he made.

"I've been working hard to build us a nice home, would you like a tour?"

I didn't answer as there were no possible words that I could use to respond to that. Who the hell was this guy and why did he think he was building us a home?

"I'm going to untie you- you can be a good girl- can't you?" He tilted his head in question as he held a pocket knife in the air, waiting for my confirmation before cutting the rope. I felt the tension give as the first rope was cut, then the second. He bent down and cut the ropes around my feet, leaving me completely free. Part of me wanted to take off and run but from the way this guy was built, I knew he would catch me before I made it two steps. The last thing I wanted to do was provoke this guy.

He reached out his hand for me to take as I eyed it cautiously. I saw his jaw clench from under the mask and stuck my hand out for him to take it. As I looked around, I noticed the room was rather big with 5 different entry points. Each door lead to a hallway that went to God knew where. It felt like an impossible maze to try to figure out. I was ready to get this over with and took a step forward when he reached an arm in front of me to stop me.

"Not so fast. Close your eyes, it's a surprise." His voice had a sing song tone to it which made me feel even more uneasy as I closed my eyes and allowed him to lead me out of the room. I tried to count the steps I had taken before we got to the next place but lost track after he pushed me forward and I stumbled before his hand steadied me. A few minutes later we stopped and I listened as I heard his steps fade away from me.

"Okay, now you can look." His voice was cheerful, giving me the creeps, as he walked back toward me.

I let my eyes adjust to the lighting in the new room as I slowly looked around me. Off to the side was a wooden patio table that had been set with plates and wine glasses, a lit candle in the middle. I stared at it with curiosity as I tried to figure out what was behind it. It appeared to be some sort of shrine set up with picture frames of different shapes and sizes, similar to what you would see at a memorial site for someone who had died.

I felt his eyes on me as I looked at the picture frames before turning away.

"Don't be shy, you can go look at them. You'll like them, trust me."

I looked at him wearily as I slowly walked over to the area with the picture frames and found that there were upwards of 100 frames. Each one had a picture of me. My jaw dropped as I stared on in disbelief.

Me in class. Me at the library. Me at the coffee shop. Me with Amber. Me on my date with Chet. Me in my apartment watching tv. Me in the shower. My stomach churned as I kept looking at the series of photos until I got to the most recent ones.

Me with Max. At my apartment and his. Photos of me after Amber died. Photos of me at her funeral. Photos of me jogging with Trevor.

I lifted a trembling finger and held it to my lips as I looked at the photos of Max and I from last night. My black hair wound tightly in his hand as my head leaned back while I rode him. My bare breasts on full display. I felt like I was going to throw up. Whoever this person was, they had been obsessed with me for months. And I had been completely oblivious all along.

Thirty Five
Max

I was out of breath as I flew up the last few steps to Hannah's apartment and burst through the door that was left slightly open. My hands were steady as they held onto my gun, my eyes quickly scanning the apartment for any sign of Hannah. I cleared the apartment in seconds, confirming that no one else was there.

"Son of a bitch!" I slammed my hand down on the counter and closed my eyes. She was gone and I had no fucking idea where she could be. My phone rang and for a second I prayed that it was the asshole who took her, calling to negotiate a deal. The problem was he didn't take her as a hostage so he could get what he wanted. He took her because she was what he wanted.

"Romano," I growled into the phone as I ran a hand down my face and looked around for anything that looked out of place.

"Hey, it's Mindy. My phone died so I'm using the one in Elena's room."

"What's up?" I felt irritated and frustrated, the last thing I wanted to do was talk on the phone. I wanted to be chasing this asshole down and get Hannah back but I had no fucking idea where to start.

"Trevor caught me up on everything. Where's Hannah?"

"Gone. I was too late." I quickly explained my phone call with Hannah as I was headed over and the moment when she opened the door. I also confirmed that it was the same guy who took Elena based on the notes and the consistent use of 'wrong number' when he hung up Elena's phone, Amber's phone, and now Hannah's.

"I started having them track Hannah's cell phone the second Trevor told me what was going on, just to be on the safe side. But..." Her voice trailed off and I knew what she was reluctant to say as I spotted Hannah's phone on the floor behind the door.

"But you can't because it hasn't left her apartment. I know, I'm looking at it." I let out a sigh as I walked over and picked it up.

"I'm sorry, Max. But we did find that the guy has a tattoo that Elena was able to describe for us."

"What kind of tattoo?"

"She said that it looked like a Y with a capital I in the middle of it. I did some searches on my phone and she confirmed the image. It's the Greek symbol for psychology, Psi."

Something about what she said clicked in my head and I closed my eyes to try to focus on why that sounded so familiar.

"Where was the tattoo?" I asked as a memory floated around in my head, just out of reach.

"His forearm. She saw it a couple of times when his sleeves were rolled up. It's the only thing we have so far that tells us who this guy is. We're going to go off of that lead and see where it gets us."

"Don't bother."

"Why not?" Her voice sounded worried.

"Because I know who it is." I grabbed Hannah's cell phone and made my way to my office in record time.

Thirty Six

Adam

My hand hurt and again and I was pissed that I was forced to have to do what I did. I wanted to spend the night with Hannah, getting her settled into our new home but then for whatever reason, she fought me on it. She ruined everything. She led me on. Led me to believe that she was the one I was destined to be with. The perfect woman who was content sitting in the shadows, not needing attention. The quiet one who never spoke up for herself, who was a natural submissive. The one who was going to save herself for me. For something special.

I don't know what happened to that Hannah. She started changing and I made every effort to rid her life of the negative impacts. Her blind date at the coffee house- he was just planning to sleep with her and forget about her. I saw him put the drug in her drink. Not going to lie, I was kind of disappointed in myself for not thinking about it first. But he had to go. I had to get rid of him so he couldn't corrupt Hannah.

And then her so called "best friend". Man, she was a piece of work. She never put any effort in with her school work and I could tell that Hannah carried her on all of the group projects. I knew she was the one who was encouraging

Hannah to date lots of guys and have fun and that just wasn't okay. So I got rid of that problem too.

But then Hannah got involved with the cop. Not just any cop. Turned out it was the brother of the girl who was going to be Hannah's new best friend. See, I wasn't a total monster. I knew that Hannah would be sad without a best friend to talk to and have girly moments with, so I had Elena lined up for her. She was another quiet girl in class, always focused on her studies and never paid attention to the boys in class.

Then I found that both Elena and Hannah were both on the same dating website and that made me furious. I started talking to Elena first, just to test the waters. I had been watching her for a while so I already knew how slutty she actually was. But it didn't matter to me, she wasn't Hannah. As long as Hannah wasn't sleeping around, everything would be okay.

Except I found that Hannah was fucking the cop. And not the sweet, romantic love making that I had pictured when I thought of her and I together. No, it was the dirty stuff that I watched on porn to jack off to at night before I started my collection of photos.

Things could have been easier. A lot less messy. No blood. No bodies to try to clean up. If only she would have listened.

Thirty Seven

Hannah

I opened my eyes to a pitch black room and wondered if I had actually even opened my eyes. One was swollen shut, dried blood pulling at the skin as I forced it open. Instinctively I tried to reach up to touch it but found that my hands were once again bound to a chair. The air was thick with a dampness that irritated my throat, making it hard to swallow. Or perhaps it was dry and raw from screaming for help earlier as I took a few blows to my head.

The room was quiet and I couldn't tell if I was alone or if someone was with me. It was too dark to see anything in the room which gave me intense anxiety. I took a deep breath and closed my eyes while I waited for whatever this was, to be over. A vision of my dad floated around in front of me and I relaxed at the thought that I would soon be with him.

Thirty Eight

Max

"Get me everything you can on this guy." I looked around the small office that Mindy and I shared as my team stared at me as I filled them in on what I knew. "I want it NOW!" I slammed my fist on the desk and watched as everyone scattered about.

It had been three hours since Hannah was taken and every minute that passed by felt like a dagger to my heart. Seeing what he did to Elena left me on edge every second that Hannah was with him. I walked over to the whiteboard and looked at the information that I had collected and taped to the board over the last hour. Elena had been discharged shortly after I left and insisted on coming to help out. She looked exhausted as she sat behind my desk, Trevor standing behind her.

"I still can't believe it's him," she said as she walked over to stand next to me and looked at his picture that I had printed from the school's webpage.

"Me neither. But it all makes sense now, in a way." I sighed and stared back at the picture of the guy that I had been in the same room with, never knowing he was the person responsible for everything with Elena and Hannah.

His picture reminded me of a high school yearbook picture as he smiled in front of a blue back drop, his brown hair and dark brown eyes complimented by the color. Professor Adam Wright had been teaching at NYU for three years and this semester Elena and Hannah had several classes together with him. The connection to everything had finally been pieced together but not before Amber lost her life and Elena barely escaped with hers. My throat felt dry as I tried to swallow and not think about what Hannah's fate would be.

I knew the moment Mindy described the tattoo on his forearm that it was him. Something drew me to his tattoo the day I went to class with Elena and saw it. There was something about him that day that I couldn't put my finger on. At first I just assumed that he was some stuffy pompous professor that was irritated that someone was in his lecture that wasn't enrolled but now I understood what the real issue was.

Looking back it felt like all of the clues were there all along, I just missed them. Maybe that was just how it was with this case, maybe it was a little more obscure than usual. Or maybe I was so distracted by Hannah that I had turned into a shitty detective and completely ignored the signs as they stared me in the face.

The notes that were written to Hannah had all come from a textbook, which she confirmed was one of her psychology textbooks. From a class that she had with Adam. The other notes were taken from the same textbook, just not from Hannah's. Hannah said from the very start that she had classes with Elena and Amber yet I didn't think of the fact that the notes could have been from one of their textbooks. One was missing and one was dead- that should've been on my radar. And the black ink used on each note was similar to that of the marker I saw him writing with during the few minutes I was in the class.

I was beyond frustrated and disgusted with myself for not catching these things earlier. My body was sore and achy, the tension starting to build. I went to my desk to grab a handful of Tylenol when I saw Elena walk closer to the board and study Hannah's picture. My heart hurt that I even had to put her picture up there. That she had gone from someone I had just seen and made love to 24 hours ago to someone that was missing and possibly dead. I shook my head as I forced myself to swallow the pills, trying to shake away the thought.

"Is this the girl that's missing? The one you're dating?" Elena pointed at Hannah and looked back at me. I watched as Trevor shrugged, knowing he had filled her in on my relationship with Hannah.

"Yeah, that's Hannah."

"She looks familiar." She turned back and stayed staring at the photo as she tilted her head.

"You guys had a couple of classes together, that's probably why you recognize her." I walked over and stood next to her, staring at Hannah's picture.

"No, that's not it..." She was lost deep in thought so I stayed quiet to let her think.

A few minutes passed by in total silence before Elena gasped and startled me.

"She's the girl!" She covered her mouth with her hands as her eyes went wide with fear.

"What girl?"

"The girl from the photos." She turned back to look at Hannah, the color draining from her face. "There were so many photos."

"What are you talking about? What photos?"

"He had this shrine with like a hundred picture frames, each one had a picture of her. He talked about her all the time, it was really creepy." She shivered at the memory.

"Why didn't you say something before when you knew it was Hannah?" My eyes searched hers wildly, wondering if having this information sooner would have made any difference in where we were with finding them.

"Because he never called her Hannah. I didn't know that was her name. He only ever called her his love."

I struggled to swallow the bile that threatened to make its way up from my stomach.

Thirty Nine

Adam

WHO THE FUCK DID SHE THINK SHE WAS? I WAS NOT SOMEONE TO FUCK WITH. YOU DON'T SAY NO TO ME! I AM THE FUCKING KING. THE ALPHA. THE OMEGA. I AM THE RULER OF MY WORLD.

I swung hard, feeling the energy flow through me the way it did every time I felt human bones splinter beneath my fist. The soft tissue tearing beneath the skin and turning a shade darker than my soul. The beautiful sound as they screamed out in pain. It was such a thrill and I loved the power and control I had over them when they watched me with fear in their eyes.

She quickly lost consciousness and I couldn't take it any longer. I stood in front of her and unzipped my pants while her head laid back against the chair, blood dripping down her face. I leaned forward and wiped the blood off as I pulled my dick out. I grabbed it with the hand covered in blood and watched it get harder with each stroke until it was covered in blood. I pumped harder and harder as I looked at her lifeless body in front of me, feeling the orgasm shoot out of me and all over her bloody clothes.

My body jerked as my dick fell limp in my hand. The fogginess that had taken over started to lift as I looked down and saw the blood stain on my hand and dick. I looked in front of me at Hannah and my heart sank, what had I done?

Forty
Hannah

"Good morning, Hannah. Do you want some breakfast?"

I woke up, unsure of where I was as I looked around. There was a small amount of light that filtered into the room from a skylight directly above me. It was different than the room I was originally held in when I first got here, but I still had no idea where I was. I looked to my right where the voice had come from and expected to see the guy in the mask. Instead my heart dropped when I realized who was there, talking to me.

"Professor Wright? What are you doing here?" I was confused and suddenly I wondered if I had been released and he had found me and taken me somewhere safe. He smiled as he poured orange juice into a glass and brought it over to me. I noticed a cut on his hand with a thin white towel wrapped around it.

"We can't stay here, we have to go!" Tension filled my voice as I looked around for any sign of the guy in the mask.

"We're not safe! I have to get to Max, he can help us!"

I looked at him as a dark smile slowly spread across his face, sending chills through my body. As he stepped to the side I looked behind him and saw the picture frame with the photo of Max and I from the other night sitting on top of the wooden table. Slowly my eyes made their way up to his and the smile on his face started to fade.

"We won't be calling him. Not to worry, you're very safe where you are." He sat the juice down beside me when I refused to reach out and take the glass. "If you would've been a good girl when I tried to talk to you last night, you would know that."

He took a few steps away from me and lit a cigarette as he leaned up against the brick wall, his jeans soiled with blood stains. He was wearing a button down shirt like he wore to class and had the sleeves rolled up, showcasing the definition in his arms. My mind was still spinning as I tried to put everything together on how the man who I sat in front of every other day in class was the same man who had brought me here and attacked me last night. He watched me as he pulled a few drags from the cigarette.

I looked away and focused on the picture on the table. It was separated from the shrine and I blushed as I realized that it was the topless picture of me with Max. My cheeks heated as I remembered us being together and now how violated I felt that someone else had been watching. Just what else had he seen?

His eyes shifted to mine and he turned his head to look at the picture as he pushed off from the wall and stomped on the cigarette to put it out. He walked over and picked the picture up and looked at it as he ran a hand across his jaw like he was upset about something in the picture.

"Do you see this picture, Hannah?" He turned it toward me as he stepped closer, a look of anger in his eyes. I nodded my head yes, afraid to speak.

"Who is this girl?" His voice was steady with an icy edge to it as he grit his teeth. I looked at him but said nothing as my breathing quickened.

"I said, who is it?!" he shouted in my face, causing me to flinch. A brief flashback of last night floated through my mind as I remembered the back of his hand coming toward me and causing the same reaction before the sharp sting of the contact blinded me.

"It's me," I whispered.

"No Hannah, that's not you." He shook his head and walked off still holding onto the picture frame.

I let out a shaky breath as I quickly looked around and tried to find a door or a window, anything that could help me get the hell out of here. Nothing. A few minutes later I heard heavy footsteps as he made his way back into the room. The worry lines above his brow were thick as he walked over and stood right in front of me, holding a picture frame in each hand for me to look at.

"This- this isn't you, Hannah." He held up the picture of me with Max and shook it in the air. "THIS is you. This is the Hannah that I know." A small smile graced his lips as he looked adoringly at the picture. I leaned slightly forward, trying to get a better look at the picture without getting too close to him.

In the picture my hair was long and pulled over my shoulder, one hand twirling a piece of it around my finger while I looked down at my text book. In the background were tables and chairs from the cafe I used to go to with my study group. I don't remember much from this picture but I can tell that it was from the beginning of the semester by the way I'm dressed and how uncertain and nervous I looked in it. My eyes traveled away from the picture and to his face as I silently questioned how many other photos he had of me when I didn't know he was there. The thought sent chills through my body.

"Do you remember her?" He tilted his head to the side and looked at the picture as if that was going to give me some insight into what I should be saying.

"I do. I remember this timid looking girl who showed up for my class, looking scared and afraid as she picked a seat toward the back of the room. I could tell that you wanted to blend in and not be seen. But you were far too beautiful for that. So I moved you to the front, closer to me. And that was the best thing I ever did, Hannah. We got to know each other so well, don't you think?"

I didn't feel like I knew him at all. The professor I thought he was, was a completely different person than who was standing before me now. I swallowed hard, the bruises around my throat reminding me of what he was capable of.

"But this Hannah-" he held up the other photo, "I don't know who she is." He shook his head again and walked over to the tables and sat down the picture frames. He slowly made his way back to where I was as if he was stalking me. Waiting for me to try to make a run for it so he could have the thrill of a chase. I stayed put, barely moving with each shallow breath I took.

"So you tell me, who do you think she is?" His eyes danced wildly while waiting for my answer. A tear fell down my cheek as I chewed my lip nervously. I knew better than to speak. There was no right answer and being silent was as much of a wrong answer as trying to actually answer his question.

"You know what I think? I think she got mixed up with the wrong people and they led her down the wrong path. But it's okay. You know why?"

I shook my head no nervously.

"It's okay because you're young and naive. You don't know better. And thankfully for you, you have someone like me to help guide you." He smiled as he took a seat on the hard concrete floor across from where I was sitting. He crossed his legs and rested his hands in between and for a moment, I saw a vulnerable child in the way he looked.

"You see, Hannah, I've been taking care of things for you for a while now. Not with a thank you or even an acknowledgement on your part. But like I said, you're young and still learning. It takes some people longer than others." He winked and gave me a smile that under any other circumstances, would have been a welcomed gesture.

"When you first started coming to my classes wearing skirts and heels, I'll be honest- I thought you were trying to impress the other guys in class. But then you would put on your sexy reading glasses and participate in the lecture and I knew it was all for me. And I loved every fucking minute of it. I can't tell you how many times I would wait for you to cross or uncross your legs so I could try to get a glimpse of your panties. That was hot as hell! And then I realized that it wasn't just me who was attracted to you, you felt the same for me. Why else would you wear short skirts and silk blouses that showed how hard your nipples were when you took off you jacket? Girls your age don't dress that way for school. But I get it, you were trying to show me how mature you are so I wouldn't be worried about our age difference."

The way his eyes lit up as he talked about me made my stomach sour. I had to force myself to focus on a beam of light against the back wall to keep myself from throwing up. I hated the days that work had flowed into school and I had no choice but to run from one to the other, which meant I had to be dressed for work. Early on in the semester it was an almost daily thing but eventually I figured out a better system and Maggie worked to make sure I got out on time so I wasn't late for my evening classes. I never once paid attention that he was checking me out in class and waiting to see if I was wearing panties or not.

"You were a big tease but I'll admit, that was part of the excitement for me with this little game you started to play where you would show off for me, thinking that I wasn't paying attention. Hell, I have voyeuristic fantasies too so I get it. But then something changed and you started showing off for other guys. And that pissed me off. Then you would show up to class and you were all eyes on me again. The perfect little school girl, so eager for the professor to teach you what he knows. So the only thing I could put together was that Amber was the bad influence. She had to be dealt with." He shrugged his shoulders nonchalantly.

I closed my eyes at the memory of her, sadness overcoming me as I struggled to keep from crying.

"Then, on top of that, you started making bad decisions, Hannah. The online dating app. The date with that frat guy. None of those were you. You were better than that." He reached over and gently placed a hand on my arm, my body going rigid at the touch. A flash of anger quickly crossed his face but retreated as he pulled his hand away.

"I can't blame you for everything, like I said, you're young and don't know better. Like you didn't know that the frat guy had ulterior motives for your date. I was there that day, Hannah, at the coffee shop. I was so nervous and excited at the same time because I had planned to come over and talk to you. To ask you out on a date. You were warming up to me so much in class, I could just feel the chemistry between us. But then your date showed up and I watched as he slipped something in your drink before he gave it to you. I didn't want to have to step in, I wanted to see what you would do on your own. And I was so proud of you for walking away and going to the bathroom. You didn't let him win and get what he wanted." He took a moment to let out a sigh as he watched me until I made eye contact with him.

"You were better than that and I made him pay for what he tried to do. I saved you, Hannah, and I've been doing nothing but that ever since. I saved you from the frat guy. I saved you from Amber. I saved you from the rent a cop at your apartment who was busy watching porn on his phone than protecting you. Which was silly that he was supposed to protect you because in reality, I was already doing that!" He let out a laugh that quickly got louder and bordered on hysterical.

"And then you kept going downhill. You started flirting with the cop and I figured you did it to tease me, to make me jealous. I knew you were getting my notes, I saw each time you found them. But the cop, he was a bigger problem and not as easy to handle. I thought maybe you just wanted to test me, give me a real challenge so you could make sure I was capable of always taking care of you." His voice got quieter as his fists clenched near his sides.

"But then you fucked him. You cut your hair and changed the color so you could look like all of the other little whores that parade around this town, pretending their pussy is too good for me. You turned into someone I don't know Hannah and now I have to figure out what to do with you."

My hand trembled as I slowly reached up to wipe the tears away that were falling down my face. There was so much to process with everything he had just told me but if there was anything that was certain- it was that I was never leaving this room.

<u>Forty One</u>
Max

"Where are we with the information I asked for?" I shouted through my office knowing it would filter out into the surrounding offices to the team that was supposed to be finding out everything they could on this fucking asshole who took Hannah.

"We're working on it!" A voice shouted back, immediately getting under my skin.

"Work harder! I need something on this guy NOW!" My pulse beat in my ears as my blood pressure skyrocketed. I glanced down at my phone to see a text message from my sister of Elena sleeping. Even though I knew she wasn't at risk because this fuck face had Hannah, I still felt the need to know where she was at all times. That's the thing when someone you love goes missing- it changes something inside of you to never trust anyone or anything again. I slammed my cell phone down on my desk in frustration from our progress as Mindy eyed me from across the room.

"Breaking your phone isn't going to solve anything," she muttered from under her breath.

"Excuse me?" My emotions were on edge as I challenged her to say it to my face.

"Look, Max," she pushed away from her desk and stood to

face me with arms crossed over her chest, "I know that this is frustrating and you feel helpless- but don't be a dick to everyone or you're going to find out just how helpless they can be. We're all working on this, as a team. Trust the process."

I looked at her as I worked my jaw back and forth, the anger compounding. It had already been 24 hours since she went missing and we all knew that the more time that went by, the less likely it was to have a positive outcome. I laced my fingers behind my head and turned to face the whiteboard that had been set up with Hannah's case. Every little thing we had was already a dead end.

A vibrating noise came from my desk and I walked over to see Hannah's phone ringing. My heart sank when I saw the words 'mom' on the caller ID. I wanted to answer and talk to her, to let her know that everything would be alright, but I couldn't do that because I didn't know if everything would actually be alright. I pressed the ignore button and turned my attention back to the whiteboard when I heard Trevor walk in and say hi to Mindy. There was no need to turn around and say hi, we both knew he wasn't there for a social call. He stood next to me and we both stared at the wall in silence. No one needed an explanation of why he was there, he had made it very clear that Hannah was now as much a part of his family as Elena, and he wasn't stopping until she was found.

A few minutes later an overweight college looking kid came flying into my office, huffing and puffing.

"We got a trace! We got a trace!" His face was red from running as he wiped the sweat from his brow with his arm. Mindy came around from behind her desk and took the printout he held in his hand.

"Are you positive this is it?"

"Yeah, we searched every record we could find. He's not using burner phones so this is definitely his phone. It's linked to his name and the billing address matches his address." There was excitement in his eyes as he talked and looked around the room for someone to join in.

"Where does it show he's at?" I asked as I stepped closer and looked at the printout that Mindy held between us for me to look at.

"That's the problem, it's a very faint trace. It keeps pinging in an area full of abandoned warehouses so we don't have an exact location. But we have it pinned down to a five mile radius." He beamed with pride as Trevor and I glanced at each other.

"I want that location sent to me now, and get a team out there to secure every building. No one goes in or out of that area without being cleared by me first. Get the perimeter set up immediately, then we'll start moving in." I felt energized as I waited for the coordinates to be sent to my phone. Within seconds I had them as I grabbed my keys from the desk and took off with Trevor beside me.

Just as we were about to take the exit that would lead us to the location, a thought occurred to me and I veered off and took a detour. It wasn't the best decision but in the heat of the moment I felt like we could use all of the help we could get. I called my sister and had her wake Elena up, asking her to meet me outside in a few minutes. As I pulled up Elena was waiting outside with my other sister, Adelina. I kept my foot heavy on the brake as both girls climbed into the back seat as I waited impatiently for the click of their seatbelts before speeding off and making my way to the warehouses.

"What exactly is going on?" Adelina asked as she leaned forward between the front seats and looked back and forth between Trevor and I.

"They found a trace on a cell phone and we think we have the location."

"So, why do you need Leni if you already know where it's at?"

I loved that as the oldest of the girls she was just as protective as I was. She was always like their second mom, stepping in to steer them in the right direction when needed without overstepping her role as their older sister.

"Because they can't get an exact location. There are several warehouses and they can trace it within a five mile radius, but that's it. I'm hoping that something- anything- might look familiar to Leni and she might be able to point us in the right direction so we can narrow it down and find the warehouse she's actually in."

"I don't know how much help I'll be, I told you that I didn't really pay attention to much when I left. I just ran." Leni's voice was quiet in the backseat as Adelina leaned back and pulled her into her side to hug her.

"I know, Leni. It's okay if you don't remember anything. I just thought if there was the possibility that you did remember something once you were here, maybe it could help us." I smiled at her in the rear view mirror as I slowed the car and pulled to a stop in front of a gated in parking lot. I looked down at my phone and confirmed it was the right location as Trevor and I looked at each other. The gate had several locks on it, proving to be a challenge to actually get inside, let alone anywhere near the warehouses.

I sighed as I slowly crept forward, looking around for any signs of entry on any side of the massive property. This was an abandoned area right outside of town and these buildings all looked the same. I slowly went around the block and kept looking for another entrance. Just as I was about to keep driving forward I heard Elena gasp from the back seat and cover her mouth with her hands.

"What's wrong?" I slammed on the brake and whipped around to look at her.

"That building, across the street with the bell on top of it, I used to hear a bell in the mornings around sunrise."

I strained to lean forward and found the bell that she was talking about which gave me comfort that we were at least in the right area, even though I still had no idea what building Hannah was in. Then a thought occurred to me, how if everything was fenced in, did Elena get out?

"Leni, how did you get out of here if everything is fenced in? Did you jump the fence?"

"No, there wasn't a fence where I came out. It opened up into a field and that actually led to a main street a couple of blocks away. That's where I found someone to give me a ride to your apartment."

I looked around and leaned against the steering wheel, frustration getting the better of me. For miles and miles there was nothing but fence and no open field. And according to my phone's GPS, there wasn't a main street anywhere near here. I laid my head on the steering wheel and sighed as I realized we had been led down another rabbit hole.

Forty Two

Hannah

The room felt like what I would imagine a solitary confinement prison cell felt like. Solid concrete walls. Solid concrete floors. No windows, just a dingy light that hung from a rusted chain above me. The room was barely big enough for the wooden table and chair that he put in here before he locked the door and left.

My mind was still trying to process through everything that had happened and just how long he had actually been watching me for. I felt so stupid for not noticing anything. My mom always told me that I was way too trusting of people and that I had to learn not to walk with my head in the clouds. It appeared she was right.

I sat down at the table and looked at the handful of picture frames in front of me that had been left behind so I could figure out which girl I wanted to be. It was a timeline of when I first started at NYU until now. Even I was a little surprised by my own transformation. A quiet, meek, shy girl that was forced to adjust to life in the big city. I sighed as I picked up a recent photo of Max and I, thankful that this one had me fully clothed.

I tried to think back to who I was back then compared to who I was now. It didn't feel like I was that different, but deep down I knew that I was. And honestly, he was right. It was Amber that had changed me. She forced me to be confident and to go after what I wanted. She had warned me that nice girls like me would get swallowed up in this city if we didn't stand up for ourselves so I took her advice and slowly, I started to find out who I wanted to be.

So much of my adolescent years were focused on taking care of everyone else that I didn't really think about myself. I wasn't upset about the experiences I had missed because I felt needed by my family. And that was a good feeling. It made me feel like an adult.

But then when I got here and started college, I realized just how much of a kid I really was. I hadn't become an adult by any means. I was so naive that I didn't know what it meant to take care of myself on my own. Then Amber showed up and showed me how to be more responsible and how people my age should act.

Sure there were plenty of new experiences that I had in college when everyone else was having them in high school, but I found that unless you openly talked about it- no one knew you hadn't done it. Just like Max had no idea that I was still a virgin when we had sex. I had learned enough to know that if I had told him, he never would have gone through with it.

I didn't regret it, not even a little bit. I cared deeply for him and wanted him to be my first. The way he looked at me and how he treated me, it just felt right. And given that he never said anything about it, it didn't seem like he knew that I had no idea what I was doing. I was thankful that Amber had talked me into going on birth control right away, another way she taught me responsibility.

The pictures stared back at me as I leaned back in the chair and allowed myself a few moments to just let my mind wonder. It wasn't like I had anywhere to go or anything to do. Adam- it felt so weird to call him anything other than Professor Wright- had left and I had no idea where he went or when he was coming back.

I was still confident that I was not leaving the confinement of this room anytime soon, let alone leave this building. The only thing left to do if I wanted to stay alive was to figure out what game he was playing and how to play my hand.

Forty Three
Max

"There's no easy entry point. If I ram the gate like I want to, it'll be loud enough to give us away." I held my phone in front of me while I talked on speakerphone to Mindy. We had circled the property a few times, not finding any way in or out that wasn't locked and no sign of an empty field.

"Okay, I'll send the rest of the team further out and see if we can create a larger perimeter." Mindy sighed on the other end.

I drummed my fingers anxiously on the steering wheel while I waited for Mindy to confirm what our other options were after checking in with the team. Glancing in the rearview mirror I caught a glimpse of Elena asleep on Adelina's shoulder as she moved her fingers quickly across her phone before her eyes looked up and met mine.

"Just sending Gia an update so mom will stop calling Leni's phone every few minutes. She's super paranoid that she's going to go missing again, even though she knows that she's with us." She rolled her eyes and went back to texting.

"Hold on, we've got something." Mindy called out to someone else, bringing my attention back to her.

"What?"

"His phone is moving. Like he's actively moving right now. Son of a bitch!"

"Where?" I looked around and started the car, ready to go but no idea where.

"Let me zoom in really quick. He must have stepped into a good cell phone range and it finally picked up the exact location."

I chewed the inside of my cheek as I waited, each second feeling like an hour.

"Right there! He's 2 blocks over heading south on Broadbent."

I looked down at my phone and switched the screen to bring up the GPS location at the same time Trevor opened his and typed in the address. After zooming in a few times I found the street and realized it was 4 blocks away. I put the car in drive and sped off in the direction, determined to catch this prick.

"I'm on it-" I started before I was interrupted by Trevor.

"No one should approach him- I repeat NO ONE should approach him." He spoke loudly to make sure Mindy could hear him clearly from where he was sitting.

"And why the fuck not?" My nostrils flared as I turned to look at him, the car jolting to a stop. In the rear view mirror I saw Leni's eyes open as she sat up and looked around.

"Because, just because we know where he is, doesn't mean that we have any idea where Hannah is. What if he came by here to clean up another mess and he's keeping her somewhere else? We can't jump on this right away Max, you know better than that."

I slammed my hands on the steering wheel and looked out the window. He was right.

"Max, we'll follow him and I promise, we will NOT lose him. I'll keep you updated on where he is. Right now your only job is searching those buildings while he's gone and trying to find Hannah. If he has another place he's hiding, we'll find it."

I hung up the phone and continued driving, slowly, towards Broadbent. Adrenaline was coursing through me as I looked around, wondering if Hannah was even in one of these buildings or if he had purposely led us here to fuck with us.

As the car crept forward, I heard Elena shift in the backseat as she rolled down the back window.

"What are you doing?" I asked as I watched her in the mirror.

"I recognize that smell." She leaned her head out further, taking in a deep breath.

"What smell?" Trevor asked as he looked back at her.

"It's sweet, like a pastry."

I looked around and off in the distance I saw the sign for a local cereal manufacturer.

"There's a cereal plant up ahead." I nodded and pointed in the direction.

"Where do you recognize it from?" Trevor asked with curiosity.

"I smelled it when I ran, but I was pretty out of it and delirious so I thought I was just hallucinating that I was running to a happy place that smelled delicious."

I slowed the car to a stop at a light at Broadbent and leaned forward against the steering wheel. If Elena had smelled the cereal when she left then she had to be in this area since we didn't smell it until we got closer to Broadbent, which was also the street Mindy tracked Adam on. My gut told me that we were almost to wherever Hannah was being held but I still couldn't see an opening to any of the buildings.

Just as I was about to consider ramming one with my car, I pulled forward and sharply inhaled when off to my left was a hidden path that led back to a few abandoned warehouses. Along the unpaved road that led back to them was an empty field. I breathed a sigh of relief as I sped off toward the warehouses, praying that I wasn't too late.

Forty Four

Adam

I had no choice but to leave. To just walk away and hope that she would come back around and be the woman I needed her to be. Being in the same room with her, I could tell she was different. How could I have missed how far gone she really was over the last few weeks? I had been trying to work as quickly as I could to save her from that cop but things kept getting in the way, things I had to take care of. If only I could have gotten to her sooner…

I took my time walking the few blocks over to the gas station knowing that I was being watched. Honestly, I was surprised that no one had approached me yet, even as I lingered around inside the store, picking snacks that I had no intention of eating. But I knew their game and their angle was that no one would approach me until they knew where Hannah was. They would be careful and try to hide in the shadows, hoping I would screw up and somehow lead them back to her. The problem was that they would never find Hannah. That's what happens when you constantly stay five steps ahead.

Forty Five

Max

The car skid to a stop in front of four abandoned and run down warehouses, that honestly, didn't look like they were in any condition for anyone to enter. I put it in park and got out as I quickly looked around, trying to narrow down which one Hannah might be in. Each one looked identical which wasn't helpful at all.

I put Elena in charge of staying on the phone with Mindy so we knew where Adam was at all times, and apparently he was in no hurry whatsoever as he lingered on the chip aisle, contemplating which flavor of Pringles he wanted before putting them all back. It was odd behavior, to not be paranoid and looking over your shoulder when you're holding someone hostage which lead me to believe that he knew he was being watched and was putting on a show. That also meant that I had a short window to try to find Hannah before he got bored and came back.

The warehouses sat in a square with a small courtyard in between them, a dried up fountain in the center. I looked around and found the field that Elena had talked about and narrowed my choices down to the two buildings that were right next to it. She mentioned that she took off and immediately went into the field so it seemed unlikely that she would have been in one of the other buildings.

I ran a hand down the scruff of my face as I looked at the two buildings, trying to justify why I would pick one and not the other. If I screwed this up, it was someone else's life that was at stake. Trevor looked over and watched me before looking at the same buildings.

"What are you thinking?"

"I'm thinking it's one of these two." I pointed at the two buildings as Trevor nodded in agreement.

"How about I take that one and you take the other? We'll do a quick sweep and see what we can find."

I liked the idea of being able to cover more ground but it made me nervous having Elena and Adelina with us. I couldn't be focused inside the building while being worried about them out here by themselves and I felt a heavy burden allowing Trevor to go inside knowing that he was another innocent life I was putting at risk. It wasn't like he was law enforcement and this was just part of the job.

"I like that idea but I don't think we should leave them." I nodded subtly at the girls.

"We can split up." Elena offered, stepping forward. "I can come with you and Ade can go with Trevor. Then you won't have to worry about us and we'll have more eyes inside."

She shrugged as she waited for my response. I blew out a heavy breath knowing that we didn't have any other options and we were wasting even more time standing out here talking about it when we could be inside looking for Hannah.

"Okay, that's fine with me."

Trevor and I exchanged a look and nodded before we walked in separate directions to the building we were going to check. Elena hung up with Mindy after giving her the update on what we were doing, and Mindy agreed to call the moment Adam started heading back this way so we weren't surprised.

I walked around the building and hoped that something would trigger a memory for Elena, confirming that we had the right one. She looked around but shook her head no in response to my raised eyebrows knowing what I was asking her. We made our way to the back side of the building that led directly out to the field and found a door. I pulled the handle, praying that he would be a complete idiot and it would be unlocked. I grunted as I kicked the door in frustration. It was a steel door with a handful of locks and chains wrapped around the handle. By the time I got someone out here to cut the locks and blow the door down, it would be too late.

"Max, look." Elena nodded to an area toward the end of the building that had boards nailed where a window would be. Hope pushed through me as I ran over and looked at the board. It was relatively thin, the wood starting to decay. I glanced beside me to make sure Elena was out of the way before leaning back and kicking the board, watching with satisfaction as it broke free leaving a small opening into the building.

I pulled off my jacket and used it to sweep some of the debris out of the way before helping Elena in. I climbed in after her, giving it a second for my eyes to adjust to the darkness inside. It was eerily creepy as the cold cement sent a chill through my body. After a few seconds my eyes had adjusted to the darkness and I found Elena looking around.

"Anything look familiar?" I asked, hopeful that something would at least feel familiar. She shook her head no as we started walking down the narrow hallway that led to an open room shaped like a pentagon. Each wall had a hallway that led somewhere else making this the creepiest maze I had ever been in.

"I've been in this room," Elena whispered, walking ahead of me. "I barely saw it but I remember looking around to try to find a way out and feeling overwhelmed with so many options, not knowing where any of them actually went."

"Well, I guess we just pick one and start there."

We took a few steps and went down the next hallway that led to an empty room with a blanket and pillow. Off to the side was a memorial looking display with assorted picture frames. I was about to walk over to look at them when Elena grabbed my arm and pulled me back. Her face had gone pale in the dimness of the room, sadness filling her eyes.

"I don't think you want to go over there." She kept her voice low while her eyes pleaded with me.

"Why not?" I glanced back over my shoulder and looked at the set up. Chills ran up my spine as I thought about how much this reminded me of a sacrificial scene in a cheesy horror movie.

"Let's just keep looking for Hannah." Her grip on my arm got tighter and part of me wanted to listen to her, to heed her advice, but the Italian part of me was too stubborn. I quickly slipped out of her grip and made my way over to the photos.

Sitting in front of me were pictures of random girls that I had never seen before. All of them in this room. All of them in pain. All of them terrified. My eyes scrolled through quickly, looking for the one of Hannah when I stumbled upon the one of Elena. My stomach dropped as I picked it up and looked at it, not fully prepared for what I was about to see.

In the picture her mouth was gagged with a bandana, hands bound behind her while she sat tied to a chair. I took a deep breath and shook my head, the chair catching my eye in the process. Not even 10 feet away from me sat the chair that my sister was bound to as she was tortured. I looked back down at the photo, at the look in my sister's eye, and that's all it took to get me running.

I heard Elena running behind me, sniffling as she cried, never slowing down as we ran into the next room. Then the next. Before I knew it we had made it through every room with no sign of Hannah. I stopped for a minute and bent over to catch my breath when I saw Elena pull out her phone and read a text message.

"Mindy sent a message 20 minutes ago but I just got it now."

"What's it say?" I was still out of breath while I waited for the update, hoping that they went ahead and just picked him up and took him in.

"He's here."

<u>Forty Six</u>

Hannah

Regret. Regret is what kills the living when we're forced to deal with the death of someone that we love. Regret that we didn't see them more often. Regret that we didn't talk about the things that were most important to us. Regret that we didn't say I love you as often as we should have. Regret that I never told my mother what was going on and now I would likely die without her even knowing that I was missing.

I stared at the beam of light on the wall above me, getting lost in my thoughts of all of the things I should have done differently. My mom was my best friend and I thought I could protect her by keeping this from her, but in reality I was hurting her more because she would never know what really happened. I took a deep breath and let it out as I felt my irritability rise each minute I was stuck in there.

It was hard to know just how long it had been because there were no clocks, no phones, no windows to know if it was day or night. Maybe this was all part of the plan. Maybe he was going to let me sit in here until I died and rotted. My body would be forced to shut down when it no longer had what it needed to survive, which honestly would be a better death compared to the brutal attack I had already been through.

I looked around for what felt like the millionth time, searching for any possible way out. There was a small vent above me that I could try to get to if I stood on the table and jumped, but given that I'm bigger than a rat, I wouldn't actually fit in the small pipe.

"Hannnnaaaahhhhh!"

My attention was immediately pulled to a faint voice calling my name. Calling like they were looking for me. I waited a few minutes and heard it again. I shook my head, convinced that I must be going crazy and hearing things when I heard it again.

"I'm in here!" I shouted back, desperate for whoever it was to hear me. My voice echoed off the concrete walls and I realized that the only way anyone would hear me was if my voice was loud enough to force through the vent and carry out into whatever room they were in.

This was it, my only option. I climbed up on the table and shouted as loud as I could, continuing to shout until my voice broke. My throat was dry but I kept forcing it, reaching on my tiptoes to try to get as close as I could get.

"I'm in here! Help me! Please! Help!" I screamed, praying they would come find me before it was too late. I startled as the door jerked open, Adam's eyes furious as he saw me on the table. His hand was trembling as I watched his body react to the anger. This was the same way he looked at me before he snapped last time.

"You should be careful who you ask for help." He taunted as he came over and kicked the table out from underneath me.

<u>Forty Seven</u>

Adam

Imagine my surprise when I got back and found Hannah acting like a lunatic, standing on the table, screaming out for someone to come help her. I'm not usually one to judge but in this case I would strongly recommend that she have a full psych evaluation to deal with her hallucinations.

I watched as she fell from the table, fear in her eyes as common sense came back to her. Maybe she wasn't as stupid as I thought. Maybe she was trainable. I smiled with satisfaction as she cowered beneath me, watching me like I owned her. Which I did.

The board in the back that was covering the window had been kicked in so I knew that one of the filthy pigs had been in here while I was gone. If they knew what was good for them, they would make sure they left. Putting your nose in other people's business wasn't something that I took lightly. It infuriated me. I looked at Hannah, so scared and desperate for love, and realized that maybe this was a good time to show her what I was capable of. To show her just how much I loved her by getting rid of those who didn't.

Forty Eight
Max

I slowly crept along the wall, reaching a hand behind me to guide Elena. We barely had a heads up that Adam was back before we heard the door open and found a place to hide. I sent Trevor a text as soon as we had the update and prayed that they would get out unnoticed. Granted none of us were getting out unnoticed since my fucking car was sitting outside in the parking lot, but at least he didn't know where we were inside. We had tried to call out to Hannah as loud as we could before he came in, and for a moment I could swear I heard her call out in response.

My nerves were on high alert as we slowly made our way down the hall, unsure of where he was. I quickly ran my hand over my back, making sure my gun was still there. Not that I've ever had an issue with not having my gun where I couldn't find it, I've just never needed it while playing a game of cat and mouse with a freaking psychopath.

I could hear faint voices and stopped, pulling Elena in behind me. My head strained to the right to try to hear better. If I could figure out exactly where they were, it would give me the advantage. My pulse was racing as I waited, desperate to hear Hannah's voice. A huge part of me now wished that I didn't have Elena with me, feeling like shit for putting her in danger, once again. I prayed that Mindy and her team were on their way, setting up a perimeter to make sure this asshole had nowhere to go if he decided to leave. One way or another, this was ending here and now. I took a deep breath and slowly inched along the wall in the direction of the voices.

It was a bold and risky move as we entered the open room, knowing that there was nowhere to hide. I had to make a quick decision about which hallway I thought led to where Adam and Hannah were. As I was about to decide, I found myself face to face with Adam as he walked into the room, dragging Hannah in by her hair.

My eyes went wide with terror as I looked at her and the bruises covering her body, dried blood in her hair. Her head was pulled down, preventing her from being able to see me. My heart sank and I wanted to rush over and grab her, get her away from him and the evil look on his face. I've met a lot of really bad people in my career but I've never been face to face with the devil. Until now.

I gently pulled Elena behind me as I reached back and drew my gun, pointing it directly at his head.

"Let her go!" I stared deep into his eyes, watching as they danced wildly with excitement. "Now!"

My voice echoed through the room, Hannah's body flinching at the sound. Adam watched me with wonder before titling his head back and laughing. It wasn't just any laugh, it was the blood curdling laugh you hear in your nightmares as you desperately try to wake up.

I kept my hand steady as I watched him, glancing down to check on Hannah. Her body looked limp and for a gut wrenching moment I feared I was too late. I had to remind myself that I had seen her move, she had responded to my voice. She wasn't dead.

"Do you really think that she wants you to save her?" He laughed harder and reached into his back pocket to pull out a knife. "She doesn't need saving from me," he paused for a moment as he held the knife in the air and watched Elena as she shifted behind me, "I'm saving her from YOU." He pointed the knife directly at me.

"And it looks like you brought back my other friend, sweet Elena." His voice was laced with sarcasm and disdain as he acknowledged her. I wanted to pull the trigger and be done with this psycho but I couldn't do anything until I was sure that Hannah was okay. Right now I couldn't risk her being that close to him with the knife. One quick movement and he could stab her as I pull the trigger.

I bit my lip as I watched, waiting for a fraction of second where Hannah was safe so I could make my move. There was no budging. As if sensing what I was thinking he pulled hard on her hair, forcing her closer to him. I watched as she started to fall before he yanked her up by her throat. Fury ran through me as I felt helpless, forced to do nothing but watch.

"Why does she need saving from me?" I asked through gritted teeth, hoping to get him talking so I could distract him away from her.

"Don't you see? You're the problem." He waved the knife in the air as he looked from her to me. "She was a sweet girl, the perfect woman to marry and keep as a wife until she met you. Then you had to stand in the way and poison her with your lies and lead her into temptation."

"I've never lied to Hannah. I care about her, just like you do. We both want to make sure she doesn't get hurt." I tried to remember everything I could from the hostage negotiation courses they required us to take but all I could really think was bullshit, bullshit, bullshit.

"So you've told Hannah everything? You told her about Antonio?"

Hannah looked up at me, Adam's hands still wound tightly in her hair. I had no clue how he knew about Antonio. I watched as Hannah looked at me, waiting for me to respond.

"So you haven't told her about Antonio..." He looked down at Hannah and forced her face up to his with the end of the knife pushing her chin toward him. "It seems that Mr. Righteous over here hasn't been all that honest with you, Hannah. It seems even he has some ugly skeletons lurking in his closet."

I waited for him to put the knife down, to move it anywhere other than underneath her chin. My blood pressure was soaring as I watched, helplessly.

"You see, Hannah, I did a little bit of research on him when I found out that he couldn't leave you alone. After some digging, it seems he has quite the temper." He slowly slid the knife down to her throat. "It seems that your little lover boy over here was once engaged, did you know that?" He looked at her and waited for her to shake her head yes. His eyes turned toward me and I could see the hatred in them as he continued.

"Did you know that his fiancé left him for his cousin?" He asked the question to Hannah while watching me the entire time. Hannah already knew this, it wasn't like he was telling her something she didn't know.

"And when he found out, he went a little crazy. Beat his

cousin so bad it left him in a coma. Almost killed him. As for the fiancé, well, she sported a black eye for a few days that went well with the bruises around her throat." He gave me a look like he just played the winning hand in a poker game. I swallowed hard as I watched Hannah process the information. She knew about Adrianna leaving me for my cousin, but I had never told her the rest. Very few people knew the rest. It's why I didn't do relationships and never wanted another one.

I watched as Hannah's eyes grew wide before looking at me with horror. I swallowed hard to try to keep the bile down. This wasn't anything that I ever wanted her to find out, and definitely not like this.

"Is that the kind of guy that you want, Hannah?" He pressed the knife to her throat, pushing the tip harder against her skin until she shook her head no. My fingers itched to pull the trigger, this was pure hell.

"It looks like she's on the receiving end under your hand as well." I nodded to the bruises on her skin and winced at the black eye that I could see better now that her head wasn't being forced down.

"I didn't do this to Hannah!" His voice was high as if he was shocked that I would suggest such a thing.

"Hannah did this to herself. She was the one who couldn't listen or follow directions. Poor decisions have consequences, you know that." He looked at me sympathetically. "I love Hannah, I would never hurt her."

This guy was out of his fucking mind. I was debating on what to do next. Hannah was my biggest priority but I had yet to find a way to get her away from this guy while keeping both her and Elena safe. Off in the distance I saw a shadow move along the wall and held my breath as I waited to see who it was. As far as I knew, Adam was working alone, but I've also been wrong before. Now wasn't the time or place to be gambling on the unknown.

A few painstakingly long seconds passed by and I saw Trevor creep along the side of the wall that opened into the room behind Adam. His hands were steady as he kept his aim on Adam, acknowledging me with a nod. I turned my head slightly while keeping my eyes on Adam and whispered to Elena.

"Run, now. Go back the way we came and run fast. Do NOT come back here. GO!" I made sure she understood the tone of my voice as I saw Trevor move slightly to the side. His aim on Adam was better than mine and I was thankful that Adam hadn't noticed Trevor. With Elena out of harm's way it made it easier for us to try to get to Hannah.

Elena darted out behind me and took off running, just like I asked her to. Anger flashed across Adam's face and instinctively, he jolted forward to chase after her, letting go of Hannah. In an instant, Trevor ran across the room and grabbed Hannah, pushing her behind him as he turned and angled his body toward Adam. With his gun aimed at his chest while I kept mine at his head, we outnumbered him two to one and he just lost his only bargaining chip.

"So what's it gonna be? Are we doing this the hard way or the easy way?" I asked, taking a few steady steps toward him. While putting a bullet in his head would give me pure satisfaction, I was easily content with taking him in and seeing to it that he served a life sentence behind bars.

"You don't get it... you just don't understand what you've done." He ran his hands through his hair and pulled it as he looked back and forth between Trevor and I. I knew this look. I'd seen it too many times in my life to know that he was about to lose it and this wasn't going to end well for him.

"Why don't we go down to the station and you can fill us in?" I took another step forward as he started to pace back and forth.

"I can't go to the station. I can't go anywhere. You're screwing everything up. We're running out of time."

"Look, I have no idea what you're talking about, but you're really getting on my last nerve." Another step closer. My finger itched as I started to close the distance between us.

"No!" he shouted, startling all of us. Quickly he reached back and pulled out a gun from his jeans and pointed it back and forth between Trevor and I. Out of the corner of my eye I watched Trevor put one hand behind him as he tried to keep Hannah shielded, the other hand steady as he kept his aim.

"Hannah belongs with me. She always has, she always will. She's my soulmate and without her- neither of us deserve to live. She gets me, she's nice to me. She wrote a beautiful essay about what she went through when she lost her dad and it was like we went through the same thing when I lost my mom. Only, she loved her dad. I hated my mom. But when you kill someone, you have to feel somewhat bad about it. What kind of monster would you be if you didn't? I didn't want to hate my mom. I didn't want to kill her. But things happen and you have to move on. Hannah, she's just like how my mom was. So I'm gonna need you to get out of the way and release her before I have to kill you too."

The look on his face changed and I saw a side of him that I hadn't seen before. It was like something snapped and the nervous, anxious Adam that was rambling on a minute ago was replaced by a stone cold version who had absolutely no issue with killing Trevor and I to get to Hannah. I felt my hand start to sweat as I glanced at Trevor to make sure he was still shielding Hannah.

"Like I said, you need to get the FUCK away from her." Adam turned to face Trevor, gun tilted sideways as he took two aggressive steps toward him. I watched Trevor take a step backwards with Hannah right behind him. Everything felt like it happened in slow motion as I watched Hannah stumble to the side as Trevor took another step backwards with her, Adam leaning to the side and aiming his gun directly at her head. The gunshot echoed through the room as I heard the body drop to the floor, a pool of blood quickly forming around it.

Trevor turned around in time to catch Hannah, steadying her as I rushed over to Adam, kicking the gun away from his hand before reaching down to check for a pulse. I looked up to see Hannah cuddled into Trevor's side, eyes wide with terror. I shook my head to Trevor and stood up, walking as quickly as I could to get to Hannah. I pulled her into my arms and wrapped her in a hug, never wanting to let go of her again. Off in the distance I could hear Trevor on the phone, calling Mindy with the update and to confirm it was okay to send the team in.

I escorted Hannah outside, still tucked under my arm as we passed a slew of uniformed cops rushing to the scene. Outside the sky was overcast and gloomy as another winter storm was quickly approaching. My heart filled with joy when I found Elena and Adelina in the backseat of my car while Trevor leaned against the hood, waiting for Hannah and I to be done with questioning. Nothing felt better in my life than knowing the people who I loved and cared about were safe and that the psychopath who was responsible for everything was dead and rotting in hell.

Forty Nine

Hannah

"How do you feel?" Max asked as I slowly opened my eyes and looked around the room, remembering that I was in the hospital.

"A little sore," I croaked, my voice hoarse from screaming earlier. My hand reached up and touched my throat as I winced in pain from trying to talk.

Max gave me a sympathetic smile and handed me a Styrofoam cup filled with ice water. I took a long, slow drink, enjoying the comfort the ice created as the cold water made its way down my throat. I pulled back, indicating that I had enough as Max sat the cup down on the tray beside my bed. I glanced out the window and noticed the sun trying to push through the overcast sky.

It was early in the morning according to the clock on the wall but I had no idea what day it was. Being locked up in the warehouse with Adam felt like it was months when I knew that it was only maybe days at most. It's amazing how being held captive and tortured plays with your mind and creates delusions of reality. I took a deep breath and shook my head as I tried to get the image of Adam lying dead on the floor out of my mind. When I first heard the gunshot I didn't know where it came from and it felt like it took forever to know who had been shot. Trevor had pushed me back behind him when the body hit the floor and for a second my heart stopped beating, thinking that it was Max.

"I know that you can't really talk, which works out really well for me." Max scooted his chair closer to me and rubbed his hands down the front of his jeans nervously.

"I haven't been completely honest with you and I apologize for that. I didn't want to tell you about Adrianna before but now I think it's only fair for you to know why I didn't want to be in a relationship."

His shoulders rose and fell as he sucked in a breath and reached over to hold my hands.

"What Adam said, about me hurting Adrianna, that wasn't true. I never laid a hand on her, Hannah, I swear. I didn't tell you about what had happened because I didn't want to bring that part of my life out in the open again. I've worked really hard at pushing it away, and that's where it needed to stay."

I watched as he fidgeted in his chair, obviously uncomfortable with having to talk to me about this. My stomach dropped when Adam told me about Max attacking Adrianna and for a moment, I actually questioned whether it was true. Maybe Max really was a violent person and that's why he had pushed me away from the start.

"After things ended with me and Adrianna, I went my own way. I threw myself into work and I vowed to never see her or my cousin again. I was done with them. Then one day, Adrianna showed up at my apartment with a black eye and marks around her throat where someone had tried to choke her. I wouldn't put it past her to do it to herself for attention but I could tell by where the marks were at on her throat that she wasn't physically able to do that."

He squeezed my hands tighter and I smiled, hoping to encourage him to keep telling me what had happened.

"She told me that Antonio had attacked her after she told him that she was pregnant with his baby. He didn't want to be a father and we all knew that. I was pissed that he had hurt her, so I went to his house and confronted him. Long story short, he denied it all and laughed when he thought I would believe Adrianna over him. She stood behind me, cowering while he made fun of her and called her a whore. And, I kinda lost it. I punched him so hard that he lost his balance and fell backwards into the solid wood coffee table. The impact of the fall caused brain damage and that's what put him in a coma. I was wrong for hitting him, but I never attacked either of them, Hannah. It's important to me that you know that. I would never hurt anyone like that."

His eyes started to fill with tears as I squeezed his hands before reaching up and wiping a tear from his face. It melted my heart to see him so open and vulnerable in front of me. I wanted to reach over and wrap my arms around him and never let go. This man had the biggest heart and would do anything for those he loved. I had no doubt in my mind that this now included me.

Fifty

Hannah

I sat by the window in my apartment and watched the snow fall outside as I waited for Max to get off of work. My work had closed early due to the weather and gave us the full day off for Christmas Eve, instead of the half-day they had originally promised. I wasn't sure what to do with my unexpected free time. It was the first time in my life that I was going to spend Christmas without my mom and that made my heart ache in ways I couldn't describe. I had made sure to send her gifts out yesterday, hoping they would make it in time for Christmas. Things had been crazy after I got out of the hospital and I totally spaced getting them shipped before the storm hit.

Max had been staying with me a few nights a week while I stayed with him the other nights. Neither of us wanted to be apart from each other but there still seemed to be some uncertainty in the air on whether we were ready to be exclusive. I knew I was but I didn't know where Max's head was at. Things had been busy on his side as well with his family and spending more time with them now that Elena was back. The whole situation was horrible and really shook all of us, but in the end it also brought Max's family closer together after they felt the impact of almost losing part of their family.

I tried hard not to be, but I was insanely jealous of Max's relationship with his family and how close they were. Sure, I was really close with my mom but I didn't make it up to see her that often anymore and we both seemed to fall into a new norm of it being okay. I missed her dearly but part of me knew that I still had to figure out who I was and what I wanted in life, which meant that I needed to give this a try, regardless of how much I wanted to call it quits and run back home to her.

My mood had been sour the last couple of days as I struggled to find things to put me in the holiday spirit and take my mind off of missing my mom and Amber. Max sent a text that he was on his way and that he had a surprise for me. I sat my phone down on the couch next to me and pulled the heavy knit blanket up over me as I laid my head on the pillow behind me and continued to watch the snow fall.

Twenty minutes later I heard a knock at the door and got up to let Max in. When I opened the door my jaw dropped as I saw my mom standing in front of me with her arms stretched wide and a suitcase by her feet. Right behind her was Max with a huge smile on his face.

"Merry Christmas!" She smiled and stepped forward, pulling me into a hug as the tears started to roll down my cheeks. I hugged her even tighter as I started to sob. Quickly she pulled back and held onto my arms as she looked at me, concern etched on her face.

"Han, what's wrong?"

"I missed you so much!" I started to cry even harder, unable to believe that my mom was in my apartment and that I wasn't going to spend Christmas without her.

She grabbed me and pulled me into another hug as we scooted to the side for Max to come in and sit her luggage down by the door. He gave us some space as he went to the kitchen and started a pot of coffee, smiling at me when I looked over at him.

"How did you get here?" I asked as I wiped my tears with the back of my hand and looked at my mom to make sure she was really there.

"The train," She teased then looked over at Max. I let out a laugh and walked with her over to the couch and sat down.

"Max actually reached out to me and asked if I could come in for Christmas. He said that my girl was having a hard time right now and could use some holiday cheer." She leaned back against the couch and gave Max a warm smile from across the room.

"Wait- how did you get in touch with my mom?" I leaned forward and waited for an answer.

"I had your phone and she had called the first day that you went missing. I kept her information in case I needed it." He swallowed hard and a silence fell over the room as the topic we all wanted to avoid talking about just came up.

I had called my mom from the hospital and told her everything that had happened over the last few months with Amber, Elena, Adam and the kidnapping. She was thankful that I was okay, but obviously disappointed that I hadn't told her what was going on sooner. In the end she was as supportive as she's always been and I regretted that I hadn't told her anything before then.

"So you brought my mom here for Christmas?"

"I knew how much it would mean to you and that you were feeling pretty down not spending it with her." He filled three cups of coffee and brought them over, sitting them on the coffee table between us as he stood next to me and placed a hand on my shoulder.

"I can't believe you did that." I looked up at him and ran my hand up his arm. My heart felt like it might combust with the amount of love I felt at that moment.

"I would do anything to make you happy, Hannah."

My mom's eyes filled with tears while she discreetly tried to wipe them away.

"I would do anything to make you happy too, Max." I smiled back at him warmly and watched as he looked to my mom before looking back at me.

Slowly he moved around to in front of me and got down on one knee. I let out a gasp as I watched him, nervous and uneasy as he cleared his throat before reaching into his pocket and pulling out a diamond ring.

"Max," I whispered. What was he doing? The man who swore he didn't want to get married was kneeling before me, holding the most beautiful symbol of love while my mom sat beside us, sniffling as she wiped the tears as they ran down her face.

"Hannah, I've made a lot of mistakes in my life. I've done a lot of things that I'm not proud of. I swore that I never wanted to be in another serious relationship, that marriage wasn't in the cards for me." He let out a shaky breath as his hand slightly trembled. "But when I thought I was going to lose you, when I saw what that monster did to you, I knew that I never wanted to live another day without you. I don't know what the future holds. I don't know what obstacles we'll face. But I know that I want to live each uncertain moment beside you. You've stolen a piece of me that I didn't know was still inside of me."

He reached up and held the ring up to me.

"Hannah, will you make me the happiest man in the world and be my wife?" His eyes looked at me with hope.

I covered my mouth with my hand as I looked back and forth between him and my mom, not believing what was happening.

"Max, are you sure?" There was so much doubt in me that this was what he really wanted. Were we ready for this?

"I've never been surer of anything in my life. Please don't leave me hanging down here forever." He let out a soft laugh as he shifted his weight.

I licked my lips as a huge smile spread across my face, leaning down and grabbing his face to plant a kiss on his lips.

"Yes, Max, I will marry you!" I squealed as I felt him stand up, wrapping me in his arms and swinging me around as I giggled.

"You had me worried there for a minute," he teased as he sat me down and slid the ring on my finger before bringing my hand to his mouth and kissing it.

"Well, I have to keep you on your toes." I winked playfully before sliding out of his arms to sit next to my mom, showing her the beautiful ring. My heart felt overwhelmingly full as I sat between the two people I loved most in the world, excited for what the future would bring.

TEN SECONDS TOO LATE

Samantha Baca

Content Warning:

This book contains language and storylines that may be bothersome for some readers and is intended for a mature audience. Violence and sexual scenes may be shown in detail as well. The reader is encouraged to reach out to the author directly (authorsamanthabaca@gmail.com) if they would like to further discuss the content warning(s) for this book. Warnings for Ten Seconds Too Late:

Graphic violence

Sexual content

Suicide— mention of, not shown in detail,

and not with a main character

Domestic violence- mention of, not shown in detail,

and not with a main character

Mental health and depression

<u>One</u>
Elena

I chewed my nail as I clutched my glass of wine to my chest, unable to pry my eyes away from the TV as the woman desperately tried to run after the man who had taken her child. She was determined, but I could already tell that he was faster and stronger than her. That's how it always played out. No matter how strong the woman is, there's always a predator that will overtake her. My stomach soured as I thought back to when I had been kidnapped and held captive. I wasn't sure that I would ever escape; each day that passed made it less likely.

A knock on the door startled me, and I flung my arms in the air, sloshing the wine out of the glass. I gasped and set it down on the coffee table before I got up to grab a towel from the kitchen. I patted my arms and chest dry and then tossed the towel in the sink when there was another knock.

I looked through the peephole, my heart still racing from the movie. Whoever was there had their face turned away from me, keeping me from seeing who they were. I was about to walk away and grab my phone when they turned around, and I finally saw their face. Letting out a shaky breath, I turned the lock and slid the deadbolt to open the door.

"Hey, I thought you had to work late?" I stepped to the side and waited for him to come in. Instead, he lingered at the door with his hands shoved into his pockets, his jaw locked in place.

"Are you okay?" I asked, feeling as if something was wrong.

"Fine."

I pulled my head back slightly and tilted it to the side. Something was *definitely* different about him.

"Have you been drinking?"

"What's it to you if I have been?" His words weren't slurred, but the smell of whiskey was heavy on his breath.

"I'm just a little worried about you. You don't seem like yourself."

"Maybe I'm not."

"Did I do something?" I asked, narrowing my eyes in confusion. This wasn't like him and my skin prickled at the realization.

"I don't know. Did you?"

"What's with the games?" I asked, starting to grow impatient and frustrated. I put my hand on my hip and raised a brow. "If something's wrong, then just tell me. Otherwise, I don't know why you're acting this way." I was acting braver than I felt.

"Does it scare you?"

The icy tone in his voice was more jarring than his actual words.

"No," I said slowly. "You don't scare me."

He paused for a moment, studying me with cold, calculating, dark eyes. Something shifted between us, and I felt the icy chill radiating off of him.

"Are you sure?"

Suddenly, my instincts kicked in, and I took a step back, away from him as he stepped toward me. My heart was racing as panic forced its way through my veins, sending me back into the darkness I felt when I was held captive last year.

I grabbed the side of the door, slamming it shut when he reached out and caught it. His hand wrapped tightly around the wood as he held it. His eyes locked onto mine, forcing a wave of fear to crawl up my spine. I took another step back, desperate to get away from him. He was inside my apartment now, the door still open.

"You're breathing fast. Eyes are dilated. I would bet that your palms are sweaty. Fear is coursing through your body right now, and you're trying to decide whether or not to trust *me* or your instincts that are telling you to *run*."

"Why are you doing this?" I whispered. He knew what I had been through; why would he think this was funny?

"So, which is it, *Elena*?" My name rolled off of his tongue in a way I'd never heard before. "Do you trust me, or are you going to run?"

"Stop it!" I demanded, my fists shaking at my sides. "Just go! Get out of my apartment! We're done." I pulled my shoulders back and tilted my chin up as my body trembled.

"Actually," he laughed, shutting the door. "We're just getting started."

I watched in horror as he slid the deadbolt in place, knowing that no one would be able to get in if needed. My head was spinning, and my body screamed for me to get the hell out of there and call for help, but it was too late.

<u>Two</u>
Elena
14 Days Ago

"Are you nervous about Max and Hannah coming over for dinner?" Trevor asked, sliding his hand across my waist as his chest pressed firmly against my back.

I had been jittery all day—or more like all week—and couldn't explain it. Half of my family was worried that I was stressed out about the one-year anniversary of my kidnapping, while the other half were convinced that I was just overwhelmed with trying to decide whether or not to go back to school in January. I had taken two semesters off and hadn't figured out if it was a temporary break or a permanent one. Finding out that one of your professors was secretly obsessed with their students and kidnapping them would make anyone question whether they really wanted to go back.

The joy of having a big family was that no one was ever in complete agreement, which led to plenty of arguments over who was right without forcing me to have to sit down and actually talk about it with any of them. It's not like they would understand anyway.I knew that the likelihood of encountering another "Adam"—or Professor Wright as I had known him–was slim, but that didn't mean that it was impossible. It was New York City, and stranger things had happened.

"Maybe," I admitted, looking up at him as I rested my head against his chest.

Trevor and I had been secretly dating for a while now, and tonight was the night that we were finally going to tell my brother, Max, and his fiancé, Hannah. This would be nerve-wracking for anyone with an overprotective brother, but it was even more so with an overprotective brother who was a cop and just so happened to be best friends with my new boyfriend. Yeah, this wasn't going to be awkward at all.

I tried to force the thoughts about what could possibly go wrong out of my head before they got there. The last thing I needed was to look like I was more of a mess than I already was. Maybe it was the pressure of letting my family into my personal life, or perhaps it was the fear of what my brother would think when he found out. Either way, my nerves were shot, and I suddenly wished I was old enough to drink a beer without my brother scolding me.

When Trevor and I first started dating, there was this insane chemistry between us that had us practically climbing each other every chance we got. It was passion-filled with trust and this sense of knowing that I could be myself with him without worrying that he would judge me. He knew what I went through when Adam took me and had been there with me every step of the way in my recovery since then, which made it feel weird that I hadn't been able to bring myself to tell him—or anyone—about the odd stuff that had been happening. It wasn't anything extreme, just little things that seemed to mess with my head, and the last thing that I needed right now was for everyone to overreact and try to wrap me in a protective bubble. Again.

I tried to chalk it all up to living on my own for the first time in my life. Plenty of my friends had mentioned how they didn't like being alone, so they found roommates to keep them company. Maybe that was all that this was? I just needed a roommate.

But then again, it felt like I already had one and didn't know who they were. Who else would turn the TV on while I was asleep in the middle of the night or leave the stove on while I was in the shower?

"It'll be fine," he assured me, running his hands up and down my arms. I felt a shiver slip through me as he wrapped his arms tighter around me. Instantly, I felt myself relax into his touch, feeling the comfort he always provided me without even trying.

"What if Max is pissed off when he finds out?" I asked, biting my lip.

"Then he's pissed off." He spun me around and shrugged, locking his arms together around my lower back with his fingers laced together right above my ass.

"He's my brother. And your best friend," I countered. "And a cop!"

"Do you think he's going to arrest me for dating his sister?" he chuckled, the dimples in his cheeks setting in with his beautiful smile.

"It's Max," I sighed. "I wouldn't put anything past him."

The doorbell rang, and I felt my palms start to sweat again.

"Well, it looks like we're about to find out," Trevor said, pulling me in for a quick kiss before he rushed off to answer the door.

I nervously ran a hand down my sweaterdress, wondering

if I looked too dressed up. Was he going to assume that this was a double date? It technically was, but I wasn't sure that I was ready for him to know about us just yet.

"Hey, Hannah, come on in," Trevor said, his voice carrying into the living room. I waited anxiously, listening as I heard them by the front door, hanging up their coats.

"Dinner smells delicious," Hannah commented, coming around the corner. Her eyes lit up when she saw me. "Hey, Elena! I'm so happy you're here!"

And just like that, the stress and anxiety that had been building up quickly evaporated when she pulled me into a hug. Hannah had been dating my brother for almost a year, but it felt like she and I had been sisters forever. Which was a genuine compliment, given that I had five real sisters who I was close to as well.

Hannah had been kidnapped by Adam shortly after I had escaped, and luckily, my brother was able to find her before anything terrible had happened. It created a bond between us that no one else could understand, and for that, I was thankful. Hannah could relate to a lot of things that I felt and was the barrier that I needed with my brother when he got to be too overbearing.

"You look so pretty," she cooed, stepping back but holding onto my arms as she took in my outfit. I smiled sheepishly, thankful for the distraction from the look my big brother was giving me from the entryway.

"Don't worry about him," she whispered. "He was grumpy before we got here. He'll be fine after we eat."

"I don't know about that," I muttered between my teeth as I

walked over to say hi to him.

Trevor had slipped into the kitchen while we were talking and announced that dinner was ready before Max could start questioning why I was there. We sat down at the table, and I made sure that I was tucked between Hannah and Trevor, so Max was directly across from me. I wasn't scared of my brother, but I also had no idea how this would go.

"Alright, dig in," Trevor said proudly, setting a basket of breadsticks on the table between the pan of lasagna and the bowl of salad.

We served ourselves while he poured glasses of water and wine, then sat down. I smiled at him the way I always did, then felt Max's eyes on me and looked away.

"So, Hannah, how's school this semester? Are you almost done?" Trevor asked, guiding the conversation to a safe topic.

"It's good, but I've decided to shift majors." She kept her eyes on Trevor, but I noticed the way her hand gripped the fork tightly as Max's jaw twitched.

"Oh? To what?"

"Forensic science."

I felt my eyebrows pull up in surprise and tried to force my expression to return back to normal before she noticed.

Trevor raised his wine glass and continued to give her his full attention as he took a sip.

"What made you decide to switch from psychology–if you don't mind me asking?"

I loved that he wasn't judgmental like my brother. I could already see the disapproval etched on his face and the tension in his body as he clasped his hands together tightly in front of him on the table.

"Well," Hannah paused. She took a deep breath and glanced at Max. "After what happened last year, I decided that psychology wasn't for me. At first, I thought that it would help if I could understand *why* Adam did what he did, but I've realized that I'm not ready to open that box yet. Instead, I'm redirecting my studies to the area that I'm currently obsessed with, much to *someone's* dismay."

"You're obsessed with forensic science?" I asked quietly, wondering if she had been thinking about the same things that had been stuck in my head for the past year.

She nodded and took a bite of lasagna. She took a drink of water and then looked over at Max again. His face was stoic as he waited for her to go on, not bothering to touch his food.

"For whatever reason, I can't wrap my head around the idea that Adam died. I know that I was there when it happened and that, technically, I saw his body, but my brain has hidden so many of those details for me that it feels like none of it really happened. That *maybe* there's a chance that he didn't really die. For all I know, he's still out there. Just waiting to come back and do it again."

"Hannah, we've been through this," Max sighed, reaching over and gently resting his hand on her arm. "He's dead. He cannot and will not hurt you ever again."

He looked up and locked eyes with me for a moment before adding, "*Either* of you."

My stomach somersaulted as I tried to force the images out of my head. The dark room. The photo shrine. The walls that felt like they were constantly closing in. The blood.

I shivered involuntarily and picked up my fork. My fingers trembled as I forced myself to cut a piece of lasagna and take a bite without drawing any attention to myself. I felt Trevor's hand slide over to gently squeeze my knee and let out the breath I was holding before I took a bite.

"Yes, I know," she shrugged. "But I can't force my mind to accept what it doesn't want to. I know that we've been to his gravesite, but how do I know that it's not some sort of setup? What if it's the body of another person that he killed? What if he faked his own death?"

Max started to say something but clamped his jaw shut and pulled his hand back in frustration.

"I get it," I said to Hannah, ignoring the looks from Trevor and Max. "I often worry that he's not really dead and that he's coming back for me too. It's hard to relax and not feel like you constantly have to protect yourself. It's exhausting on so many levels."

"Thank you," she replied sincerely. "No one else gets it."

"I know."

My therapist and I had been over it countless times, and she knew my triggers before I even noticed them. If someone started to get too close to me, I would put up a wall and force them out. It had happened several times with Trevor and me in the last few weeks. Natalie assured me that it was likely the stress of remembering when I was taken last year and everything that happened after that. She even asked for

Trevor to join us for an extra session so she could speak to both of us and help him understand how he could support me. We talked in great detail about the physical things that could trigger me—like walking up behind me without me noticing, dark rooms, touching my throat, or using any pet names.

We continued with dinner after Trevor graciously changed the subject again to something less stressful. After he and Max finished complaining about the Yankees and other sports-related stuff, I knew that it was getting to the time that we needed to share our news with them. That's what this dinner was for, after all.

"I'll clean up," I offered, getting up from the table and grabbing my plate. I reached over for Trevor's when he reached out and grabbed my hand, stopping me. He set my plate down on his and pulled me onto his lap.

"Leave it; the dishes can wait," he said softly.

I felt the heat quickly spread through my body, flushing my olive-toned skin. My hair was pulled up, which gave everyone a clear view of the blush that was creeping up my neck and onto my cheeks.

I glanced at Max and noticed his brows pulled together as he stared at us.

"Elena and I have something that we wanted to share with you guys." Trevor's hand planted firmly on my knee to keep it from bouncing. "We've been dating for a few months and have decided that it's time everyone knows that we're in a relationship."

"How long is 'a few months'?" Max asked without hesitation.

"Since June."

"June?"

Trevor nodded, keeping his attention on Max while Hannah and I stayed quiet.

"Six months, and you didn't think to say anything before now?" Max cocked his head to the side and narrowed his eyes.

"Elena wanted to wait."

"For what?"

"To make sure you didn't arrest me for dating her."

I was going to kill him for making fun of me, but after Max tilted his head back and laughed, I felt better that Trevor had successfully eliminated some of the tension that was mounting around us.

"I wouldn't arrest you," he teased. "But that doesn't mean that I won't break a bone or two if you hurt her."

"Max!" I scolded, pursing my lips the same way our mother does when she's embarrassed by something we've said.

"What? I don't care if it's Trevor or some other guy—I will break some bones if anyone hurts you."

Except Adam.

That wasn't a fair thought, but I couldn't keep it out of my head. Had Hannah not been taken right after I escaped, I don't know what Max would have done to Adam if he ever found him. But part of me believed that the only reason he killed him *was* because of Hannah.

"Well, I don't see anyone needing any broken bones anytime soon," I joked, wrapping my arms around Trevor's neck. It felt good to have Max know about our relationship, but I dreaded that I still had to tell my parents and sisters about it. Being one of seven kids made it hard to do something without the entire family knowing.

Three
Trevor
12 Days Ago

"So, you survived dinner with Max," Roman chuckled as I walked into the office Monday morning.

"Yeah, it wasn't as hard as I thought it would be. I think Elena was more stressed out about it than I was. But then again, she's just overwhelmed with a lot right now, to begin with."

I set my coffee and bagel down on my desk and pulled off my jacket. Roman and I shared an office with desks across the room from each other and a large window between us. It wasn't the best view since it looked out to the alley behind the gym, but at least it let in some natural light.

"What's going on with Elena?" he asked, leaning back in his chair and propping his feet up on the desk. That was the nice thing about where we worked—it wasn't a professional setting with stuffy suits and ties. It was tennis shoes and workout gear mixed with loud noises and men talking shit while they worked out.

"Honestly, I don't know." I ran a hand through my hair, remembering that I needed to get it cut soon. "She's been really stressed out the past few weeks, and her therapist thinks that there are some underlying feelings that she never dealt with after her attack. It's coming up on a year since it happened, and she thinks that maybe the holidays have triggered her memories of stuff that she had repressed."

"I can relate to that," he sighed.

Roman was officially retired after serving in the Marines as a sniper, and we had had several deep conversations about PTSD and the long-lasting impacts his career has had on his life.

"I don't know what to do for her to make things better. She shuts down anytime we talk about what happened, and I get it. I don't like to talk about it either because I get so mad that I can't see straight. But I feel like she's heading in this downward spiral, and I can't catch her fast enough."

"Have you tried talking to Max about it? Maybe he can talk to her?"

"I haven't been able to before now. He would have asked why I knew so much about his sister and probably would have kicked my ass if he found out that way."

Roman tipped his head back and laughed.

"I would pay to see that."

"Shit," I laughed. "Just because he's a cop doesn't mean that I can't take him."

Laughter filled the room as another voice joined in.

"Oh really? Care to make a wager on that?" Max asked, leaning against the door frame with his arms crossed over his leather jacket. He raised an eyebrow and looked between us.

"I don't think you can afford it," I poked. "Not with the big wedding that Hannah has planned."

He winced and ran a hand down his face.

"She's killing me with the small details," he whined. "I don't care whether the rose petals are pure white or white with little purple veins in them, yet she's upset that I'm not helping her. I helped with the big decisions, like where to have it and what kind of food we should have."

"Didn't she veto you on both?" Roman asked, his fingers tapping together as his hands formed a steeple.

"She sure did." He pushed off of the wall and shook his head. "I don't see why we couldn't do it in my parent's backyard and have a barbeque."

"Because it's a wedding and not a retirement party, you old grump." I laughed and rolled my eyes.

"Well, thankfully, Elena is going by later today to help Hannah with the tiny details that I'm apparently incapable of handling."

She hadn't mentioned anything about it to me, but I wasn't going to bring that up. We weren't at the point that she had to check in with me before she went anywhere or did anything, but I thought that we had at least gotten to the point of sharing the little details of our days with each other. Or at least I had.

"So, since the girls will be hanging out and planning for hours, do you want to meet up and grab a beer after work?"

"Sure," I said, taking a sip of my coffee. "I'll meet you at seven."

He said goodbye and then left, leaving Roman and me to start our workday. The hours flew by, and before I knew it, it was lunch, and I still hadn't heard from Elena. I pulled out my cell phone and sent her a quick text, asking how her day was going.

Two hours later, I still hadn't heard anything from her, and I started to worry. It wasn't like her to avoid me, and I felt the anxiety begin to build that something was wrong and she wasn't okay. I called it a day early and left Roman to close up while I headed to her apartment.

I tried calling her a handful of times, but each one went to voicemail. My pulse was racing as I climbed three flights of stairs, not bothering to wait for the elevator. By the time I got to her floor, I was in full fight or flight mode and barreling to her door. I knocked several times and waited.

After the fifth time of knocking so loud that one of her neighbors opened their door to see what all of the commotion was about, I decided to call Max and ask him to get a key from her landlord to do a welfare check. I just prayed that he got there in time.

<u>F</u>our
Elena
12 Days Ago

I was singing along to Ariana Grande when my front door flew open, and Trevor and Max rushed in. I screamed and clutched the towel around my body, still wet from the shower I had just taken.

"What the hell are you doing?!"

"We came to check on you," Trevor exclaimed, his face showing the stress he was under while Max crept through my apartment in full cop mode, checking for any intruders.

"Why didn't you call?" I raised my brows, as well as my voice, and waited for my heart to find its way back into my chest after they scared the living shit out of me.

"I did. I've been calling and texting you for hours. I stood outside knocking until your neighbor threatened to call the police. Finally, I called your brother and asked him to get a key from the manager so we could check on you."

"I haven't had a single call or text from you all day," I said, rubbing my temples while pinching the top of my towel against my body with my elbows.

Trevor looked at me as if I was crazy before slowly pulling

his phone out of his pocket and showing me the messages he had sent and the calls he had made.

"That's weird," I muttered, walking over to the charger on the end table where my phone was plugged in. I picked it up and pressed the home button, but the screen was black. "It's dead."

It didn't make any sense that it was dead when I had been charging it for over an hour.

Trevor bent down and checked the charger, reaching behind the table to where it was plugged in. He wiggled it loose and then pulled it out. The wires by the plug were completely exposed and frayed.

"This is your charger?" he asked, holding it up in the air.

I reached over and took it from him, looking at the damage.

"It's brand new," I whispered. "I just bought it because my other one stopped working."

"Are you sure this isn't the old one?" he suggested, placing a hand on my shoulder.

"No, I purposely threw that one away. I just bought this one. The package is still on the cou..." I turned to look behind us, and my jaw dropped when I saw the charger still sitting on the counter in the brand new packaging that hadn't been opened.

He reached over and grabbed it, checking the box that it was still sealed inside of.

"I swear—I opened it and changed it before I plugged my phone in."

"It's okay, things happen. I'm just glad that we figured it out before this one started a fire. How long has the wire been exposed like that?"

I shook my head in frustration, knowing that he wasn't going to believe me.

"It's never been like that until now."

His eyes narrowed as he studied me. He was so insanely good-looking that I wanted to wash the worry off of his face and replace it with the smile that lit up his dark chestnut eyes. The eyes that used to look at me with adoration and not concern that I had lost my mind.

"Well, why don't I get the new one plugged in for you while I'm here," he offered, avoiding what I had said. He pulled the table out, holding the lamp steady with one hand while he maneuvered with the other. "Have you eaten today?" he asked over his shoulder as he opened the package and pulled the other charger out.

Why did everyone always assume that strange things happened to me because I was hungry? It wasn't like I got super delirious with low blood sugar and did things that I couldn't remember, yet it seemed to be the fix-all as far as they were concerned. *Elena's a little off today? Give her a Snickers–she'll be fine.*

I hadn't bothered to answer him when Max came out of the guest bedroom and spotted Trevor messing with the charger. Trevor glanced at him over his shoulder and then put the table back where it belonged.

"Her charger was bad, so her phone died," he explained.

Max walked over and looked at the one still in my hand, his

brows furrowed.

"That's the one you've been using? That could have started a fire, Elena," he scolded.

I closed my eyes and slowly forced out the breath that was holding all of the sarcastic things that I wanted to say.

Trevor and Max talked for a few minutes while I stood there, uninterested in their conversation. It was happening more and more lately, the lack of interest in anything. Natalie assured me that it was normal to feel some depression as the memories tried to resurface, but this felt like something else.

I was finally living on my own, and for once, I had never felt more alone than I did now.

Five
Trevor
12 Days Ago

I spun the bottlecap on the table, waiting for Max to finish his phone call. Jon came by and set another round of beers on the table, clearing the empty ones as he walked away.

Max and I had been coming to this bar since it first opened, and Jon had been one of the best bartenders I had ever met. He took the time to get to know people, and he was by far one of the most genuine and kind-hearted men around.

"Get me the update as soon as you have it," Max said, ending his call and putting his phone down on the table. He picked up his beer and took a long drink, the stress of his day being washed away.

"Everything okay?" I asked, not wanting to dive into the conversation I knew we were about to have.

"Yeah," he muttered. "No. I don't know. We had a lead on the guy that's been terrorizing the college, but it looks like it's turning into another dead end."

"Sorry. That sucks."

We sat quietly for a few minutes, drinking our beer and avoiding the elephant in the room. I glanced down at my phone, checking to see if there were any new messages from Elena. Nothing.

Hannah agreed to let Max know as soon as Elena showed up at their apartment and update him again when she left. As far as I knew, they were hanging out and talking about what color to have the toilet water for the wedding. Who knew what kind of details they were getting into.

"So," he said evenly. "Should I be worried about Elena living on her own?"

I knew what he was really asking, and I didn't have an answer for him.

"Honestly, I don't know."

"That cord could have set her apartment on fire."

"I know," I breathed out, feeling the stress from this afternoon still sitting on my shoulders.

"Do you think that it's just her being young and not knowing these things, or do you think that there's something else going on that we need to be worried about?"

I leaned back in my chair, picking at the label that was starting to peel off the bottle. Elena and I had been dating for months, and I had noticed that she was beginning to act differently lately, but I had no idea whether this was a simple accident or if we did need to worry.

It scared the shit out of me when I couldn't get ahold of her. My mind had started to scatter to every worst possible situation that it could come up with. Once I saw that she was okay, I was relieved until I found the charger cable frayed with the wires exposed.

Plenty of people used and abused their electronics, so it wasn't a total surprise that her charger was in bad shape, and that's why she bought a new one. The problem was with *how* she reacted to it. She was surprised to see it; I could tell by the look on her face.

"I think she's a very smart girl and is more than capable of being on her own." I kept my eyes locked on the bottle, avoiding looking at him so he didn't call me on the bullshit that was laced in my words. I believed every word I said; I just didn't trust them right now. Something was going on with her, and I was determined to figure it out.

"But…"

I looked up at him, frustrated that he called me on it.

"But I think something else is going on, and I don't know what it is."

"I know that things are *different* now that you guys are dating," Max said, looking around the room before he continued. "But I need you to know that you can always come to me if something is wrong. She's my baby sister—"

"I know she is," I interrupted, suddenly feeling defensive.

"AND you're my best friend," he continued. "Whatever happens between you guys is your business, but it won't change things between us unless you really fuck up. Then I'll kick your ass, and we'll see about being friends."

He winked, and I felt some of the tension lift from my shoulders.

"You know that I love her, man. I always have. It's just a different type of love now."

"I know," he smiled. "She loves you too."

I felt the smile pull up at my lips, hearing him say it.

"How do *you* know that? She hasn't even told *me*."

"I could tell by how nervous she was at dinner. She wouldn't care what I thought if you guys were just fooling around."

I felt my phone vibrate on the table and looked down to find a text message from her. I sent back a quick reply, asking her to let me know when she got home and if she felt like company.

"Is she heading home?" Max asked, looking at his phone.

"Yeah, did Hannah text you too?"

He nodded with a smile.

"She's a good woman," I said, changing the subject.

"That she is."

"How's she doing with everything?"

"I wish I knew." He shook his head in frustration and spun his empty beer bottle on the table. Jon glanced over and pointed at us before Max shook his head, declining another.

"I'm a detective. I'm supposed to be able to read people, and I can't figure her out. She says that she's fine and that it doesn't bother her that it's coming up on a year since everything happened, but I don't think that it's true."

"Why not?"

"Because so much happened last year. How could she not be upset about it? Her best friend was killed. She was kidnapped and tortured by her own professor. She witnessed his death. We got engaged and moved in together. There's been a lot to cram into a year, and I can't imagine that she's not reminded of these things, just like Elena. I feel like I'm just waiting for both of them to have a breakdown, and I don't know when it's coming."

"Maybe it's not?" I suggested. Hannah had been open about her feelings since everything happened and talked about her best friend, Amber, often. I hadn't noticed the depression or anxiety in her that I had seen over the past few weeks with Elena, but a lot of that probably had to do with their situations and how different they were. Elena had been held a lot longer than Hannah and had tried to escape several times before she was successful. Hannah was found quickly after she was taken and didn't endure the same trauma that Elena did.

"I hope so," Max sighed, digging into his wallet for a couple of bills.

"Don't worry about it. This one is on me," I said, reaching into mine. I tossed down enough to cover our bill, as well as a generous tip for Jon.

"Thanks for meeting up tonight. I better get home before Hannah has the entire wedding planned without me," he joked. "Or better yet, maybe I should stay out a little while longer?"

I tipped my head back and laughed.

"I would rush home if I were you. She's probably ordering a pink vest and polka-dot bowtie for you as we speak."

His eyes widened with mock surprise.

"Are you heading over to Elena's?"

I picked up my phone and opened the new message from her.

"No," I shook my head. "She said she has a headache and is going to bed. I'll check on her in a little bit to see how she's doing."

"Do you want me to stop by on my way home?" he offered, slipping into his leather jacket.

I hated not knowing if she was okay or not, but even more, I hated the sudden overprotective feeling that was consuming me.

"Yeah, if you don't mind?"

"I'll text you in a bit," he said, clapping my shoulder before he took off.

It was after nine by the time we left, but I was too wound up to go home and wait around to see if she was okay. Instead, I went to work and decided to burn off some energy there.

<u>Six</u>
Elena
10 Days Ago

"No, ma," I groaned into the phone. "I don't need to come stay the night; I'm fine."

"The power is out, and you're by yourself in the dark. Don't be silly, Elena. Just come home, and I'll make you dinner."

My stomach growled at the thought, and I wondered how desperate was I for company and whether a homemade meal was enough to get me over there. It was the middle of the week, and I had already run out of the groceries I had bought on Sunday while I was out with Trevor. Where all of the food went, I had no idea. I didn't remember eating half of what was missing, but the extra curve in my ass suggested that maybe I had.

"I have an early day tomorrow. I'm just going to read a book and then go to bed."

"How are you going to read in the dark?" she countered, calling me out on my lie.

"I have an app on my phone. That's how I read all of my books."

"So you're going to drain the battery on your phone to read

a book? What if there's an emergency, and then you can't call for help because your phone is dead?"

Ugh. She had a point.

"Just come have dinner with us, Leni. I'm making risotto, your favorite."

I looked outside at the dark, cloudy sky. It was cold with the promise of another snowstorm coming soon, but if anything was going to lure me out in this weather, it was my mother's risotto.

"Fine," I grumbled. "I'll be there in thirty minutes."

I hung up and sent a quick message to Trevor, letting him know that I would be at my parent's house for a while. He had been overly anxious lately and suddenly needed to know where I was at all times. I didn't know if it was because of the phone charger incident the other day or if Max was more in his ear now that he knew about us. Either way, I could feel him hovering, and it was spiking my anxiety even further.

There was no need to get ready, but I still made sure to run a comb through my hair and take it out of the messy ponytail it had been in since I got home from work. The last thing that I needed was my mom worrying about whether or not I could handle living on my own and working a full-time job. I knew the circles under my eyes would already concern her; I didn't want to add fuel to the fire by looking too tired to take care of myself.

I pulled on my NYU hoodie and shoved my phone into the pocket before grabbing my backpack and flinging it onto my shoulder. Luckily I had an extra charger that I kept in it so I could make sure to charge my phone at my parent's house just in case the power wasn't restored by the time I got home.

The streets were quieter than usual, likely due to the weather getting worse. I walked quickly, making my way to the subway as I tried to escape the bitter cold. Once I got on the train, I found a seat in the back and sat down. There was an older man across from me, reading a newspaper, and a mother on the other side of the train, peeling back a banana for her toddler. It wasn't overly crowded, yet I felt the uncomfortable feeling of someone watching me.

I tried to shift my focus after I couldn't find the source of the perceived threat I was feeling. The speaker announced the next stop, and I stood up, ready to get off. I held onto the bar above me as I walked down the aisle and waited by the door. The train jerked to a stop, and the doors slid open.

Just as I stepped onto the platform, I felt a heated gaze burning into the side of my head. I turned and looked over my shoulder as the doors pinched shut behind me. Sitting a few seats over from the door was a man wearing a hoodie. He looked up right as the train started to pull forward, and I saw Trevor's unmistakable face.

By the time I got to my parent's house, my blood was boiling. I knew that things between Trevor and I felt a little strained lately, but I couldn't believe that he had sunk to the level of spying on me. Didn't he trust me? I had told him where I was going, so there shouldn't have been a reason to follow me.

I opened the door and walked in, a soft smile pushing across my face at how comfortable it felt to be home, the immediate feeling of being safe and protected. I knew that it would be different to live by myself, but I hadn't expected the level of fear that came along with it. Whether or not that was normal for people living alone for the first time, who knew. I didn't have anyone I could ask without having them immediately judge me and try to talk me out of it. As far as they were concerned, I was still the helpless victim who needed to be protected. And I was tired of it.

<u>Seven</u>

Elena

9 Days Ago

"Okay, so walk me through what happened," Natalie said softly, leaning back in her chair.

I was sitting across from her, my foot tapping anxiously on the imported foreign rug that matched the eclectic décor in her office as I tried to force my thoughts to come out more calmly than what I had felt.

Last night I got a text message back from Trevor while I was at my parent's house, thanking me for letting him know that I had gotten there alright. He claimed that he was stuck at work, trying to put together some marketing material to draw in more clients for the new year. I stared at his message for so long that I thought that my phone would burst into flames from the fire that was roaring inside of me. It was one thing to follow me but another for him to lie about it and act like he didn't see me catch him at the end.

"It's Trevor," I said angrily through gritted teeth. "He followed me last night."

She lowered her head until her glasses slipped down to the end of her nose, and she looked over them to see me. A single eyebrow arched, and I knew that she was as shocked by this information as I had been.

"The power was out in my neighborhood last night, so I decided to go to my parent's house for dinner. I texted Trevor to let him know that I was heading over there so he wouldn't be worried about me since we both know he's been a little overprotective since the charger incident." I paused and forced out a frustrated breath, pressing my feet flat against the floor so I would stop moving. "I kept feeling like someone was watching me on the train. It was this eerie feeling that I couldn't shake. I looked around several times and didn't see anything odd, so I tried to ignore it. When I stepped off of the train, I looked over my shoulder and saw him."

I shook my head as the anger started fueling the fire inside me that I hadn't been able to put out since it happened. When I called to schedule a last-minute appointment with Natalie this morning, she had gone out of her way to squeeze me in on her lunch break. Not that she was actually taking one with the sushi still sitting untouched on her desk, getting dangerously close to going bad.

"What did he do?"

I let out a maniac laugh and instantly regretted it. I was *this* close to feeling like I was about to lose my shit—which was why I was sitting in my therapist's office when I should have been at work.

"He just stared at me. Sat there and acted like it was nothing."

Natalie pushed her glasses back up her face and turned to her computer, typing something before she returned her attention to me.

I glanced at the clock hanging on the wall behind her and knew that we only had ten minutes before her next appointment would be here.

"Have you asked him about it?" she asked, swiveling her chair to face me.

"Nope," I shook my head. "I've been too pissed off to talk to him. He texted me back after I got to my parent's house and thanked me for letting him know I was there. Lied about being stuck at work."

"Did you respond to it?"

"No."

She leaned back in her chair and folded her hands in her lap.

"Why do you think he followed you?"

"I have no idea," I blew out. "I'm tired of everyone hovering over me, worrying that I'm some fragile baby that they have to take care of."

She offered a sympathetic smile but said nothing. We had been doing this long enough that we didn't need to go into those details anymore. She knew how I felt about the constant attention that my family gave me and how I struggled to get past my frustration that they didn't trust me to take care of myself. And maybe it was for a good reason. I had been reckless when Adam took me, and they all knew that. Sure, people make mistakes and learn from them all the time, but mine almost killed me. I guess I could see where they were coming from on some level, but that still didn't make what Trevor did okay.

"I think the best approach would be to sit down with Trevor

and ask him about it. Be upfront and honest. It won't do either of you any favors if you're not."

"What if I can't get past my anger with him?" I asked, worried that I would let it get the best of me and ruin the best thing that had ever happened to me.

"Then you need to let him know that you're angry. It's not your job to shield him from your emotions, Elena. It's your job to share them openly with him. If you feel that he did something wrong, then it's your responsibility to tell him. He may disagree, and he may not understand your feelings, but that's for him to sort through and process—not you."

She spun around to answer her phone, letting her receptionist know that she would be out in a moment.

"Relationships take work, and you owe it to yourself to give this one a chance. If you don't, you'll never know what it might have been. Go home, take a nice bath, and try to relax. When you're feeling calmer, reach out to Trevor and find time to talk to him. In-person, Elena. Not text. Face to face where you can see his emotions, and he can feel yours."

I sighed and stood up, knowing that she was right. I hadn't come here looking for her to fix things between Trevor and me, but I felt better knowing that I had been able to get some of my anger out before I talked to him.

"Thanks for squeezing me in at the last minute," I said, glancing down at her uneaten lunch. "I owe you sushi next time."

"No, you don't," she laughed and picked it up. "I actually didn't bring anything else to eat today and forgot that I had this in the fridge. I was about to eat it when I noticed the expiration date passed a few days ago. I didn't want to interrupt you by leaving to go throw it away.”

“Well, I’m glad that you didn’t eat bad sushi,” I said, scrunching my face in disgust. I unzipped my purse and grabbed a granola bar out of the side pocket. “Here, this isn’t lunch, but it’ll hopefully hold you over until you can grab some real food.”

She smiled and took it, the kindness in her eyes lighting up her face the way it always did.

“Thank you, Elena. I appreciate it.”

“See you on Monday,” I said nervously, hoping that I could wait that long to see her again. Something about being here and talking to her was calming, which was another thing that I deeply missed these days.

“If you need anything before then, you know how to reach me,” she assured me as I walked through the door.

Once I got to my apartment, I went inside and locked the door, making sure both locks were in place. It was an obsessive habit that I had started since I moved in, but lately, it felt like I constantly kept forgetting whether or not I had locked the door. Natalie assured me that stress could cause problems with remembering stuff, which wouldn’t be a big deal if it wasn’t something as important as making sure the door was locked and that I was safe inside.

Taking her up on her advice, I made my way to the bathroom and started a bath. Soaking in a hot bubble bath sounded wonderful, and the smell of lavender was sure to soothe me. While the tub was filling, I went to grab the book I was reading and my phone, just in case anyone needed me.

I got back to the bathroom and set everything down as

I stripped my clothes off and stepped in. The water was borderline too hot, but once I sat down, the heat started to melt my stress away.

My phone chimed, alerting me to a new text message.

Trevor: Hey, I feel like we haven't seen each other much lately. Can we get together soon and talk?

I was about to text him back and ask why he had been following me when I remembered Natalie's advice— *in person, Elena. Not text. Face to face where you can see his emotions, and he can feel yours.*

I worked my jaw back and forth in frustration, ready to get past this hiccup and move on. I loved Trevor—even if I hadn't verbally admitted that to him yet—and didn't want this to end over something stupid. Maybe he had a good explanation for why he had been following me?

I fought the urge to open the door to a conversation via text message and simply replied *Okay*.

I put my phone on the edge of the tub and lowered my shoulders into the water as I closed my eyes and tried to remember a time when I didn't feel so overwhelmed and stressed.

<u>Eight</u>

Trevor

9 Days Ago

"Christmas is two weeks away. Have you figured out what you're getting for Elena?" Roman asked as he rounded his desk and sat down, bringing his coffee cup to his lips.

I sighed and tossed my pen onto my desk. It was hopeless. Everything was so frustrating and confusing between us right now that I had no idea what to get her.

"I'm going shopping with Max later. I'm sure I'll find something while we're out," I mumbled, cracking my neck.

"Are you guys fighting?" He eyed me cautiously before turning to his computer to check his email.

"Not fighting. Things are just—I don't know—weird between us."

"How so?"

I blew out a breath and leaned back in my padded rolling office chair, resting my feet on my desk.

"She's so distant with me all of a sudden. Like I did something wrong, but she won't tell me what it is."

He chuckled under his breath and shook his head while he

scanned his inbox.

"So then apologize."

"For what?"

"Whatever you did wrong."

"But I didn't do anything wrong."

"Then she wouldn't have any reason to be mad at you, now would she?"

I narrowed my eyes and stared at him, hoping I would develop some sort of superpower that would drill a light into the side of his head, and I could see what he was really thinking. Roman was a man of few words, but unfortunately, he was usually right.

"So what you're saying is that I should apologize and hope that she gives in and tells me what I did wrong in the first place?"

He pointed a finger at me and winked.

"Bingo. Admit that you know that she's upset with you and that you're sorry for whatever you did, but that you want a chance to talk about it so you can avoid upsetting her in the future."

"And that's supposed to work?" I tried to keep the doubt out of my voice, but it didn't work. Elena was the youngest of seven kids—six girls, with Max being the only boy. She came from a large Italian family that lived in the Bronx. I knew better than to think that I would get off easy if I really did do something to piss her off. I had seen her angry plenty of times watching her grow up, and I've always been thankful that I was never on the receiving end.

"You won't know unless you try, now, will you?" He laughed and pushed away from his desk, letting his chair roll back to the wall. "I've got a new client coming in at eleven, so I'll be up front if you need me."

"Sounds good," I said, offering him a half-assed wave as he left. It reminded me that I needed to start bringing in more clients if we were going to keep the momentum going and finish the year as strong as we had started. I made a quick note to reach out to past clients and talk to them about their goals for the new year. Thankfully, being a personal trainer meant that I saw an increase in business every January with the handful of health and wellness resolutions made.

I picked up my phone and checked for a text from Elena. She was supposed to be at work today but had called in—again—complaining of another headache. I had asked Max about it and if she had a history of chronic headaches or if this was something new. He couldn't remember her having them growing up, so I had been worried that maybe something was making her sick in her new apartment. My mind had been fixated on as many different toxins as possible before Max assured me that she was probably just stressed and needed to rest for a few days.

I sent her a quick text and set my phone down, determined to get some of the billing done that I needed to send out before the end of the month. My attention had been so scattered that I was weeks behind what I needed to have done already. While I could stay late and wrap things up, I found that I was more worried about getting home so I could try to spend some time with Elena—when she was actually in the mood to see me these days.

I thought about what Roman had said and decided it

couldn't hurt to apologize to her, even though I had no idea what I would be apologizing for. I've never known her to be a vindictive person who held a grudge, so this felt odd to me. Elena was the type of woman to get mad and make sure you knew it, then she was over it. She didn't draw things out for the sake of getting attention, yet that's what this felt like—her drawing something out without bothering to let me in on what had happened.

A few hours later, I decided that I had made a decent dent in my workload and checked in with Roman before I left. Elena still hadn't returned my texts, and I didn't want to call her if she wasn't feeling well. However, that didn't stop me from making a quick stop at the store to grab a few things to cheer her up.

With a dozen roses in one hand and a bag full of chocolates in the other, I made my way to her apartment, feeling the giddiness that I usually felt when I came to see her. I waited patiently for the elevator and stepped aside to let an elderly couple off before I walked in and pushed the button. Right as the door was closing, I saw Elena walk past me, smiling as she looked up lovingly at the guy next to her. My eyes scanned them quickly before the door closed, my stomach knotting as I saw her fingers laced between his. The dark hoodie he was wearing covered his face, so I couldn't see who it was, but I suddenly had my answer to why she wasn't returning my texts.

Nine
Elena
8 Days Ago

I curled up next to Trevor and tucked my feet underneath me as we watched some action movie that he had picked. I wasn't in the mood for the fast-paced fight scenes, but they seemed to have him occupied as we watched it in silence. Not that I enjoyed talking during a movie, but it felt like we hardly talked at all these days. If anything, at least it still felt comforting to have him physically next to me.

My thoughts were scattered as my mind wandered from the handful of to-do lists that I had. I still had Christmas shopping that I needed to finish, but thankfully my sister, Adelina, needed to finish hers as well, so we were planning to tackle it together tomorrow. Christmas was still two weeks away, and I had the entire weekend to make a dent in my list.

I was lost in thought about what to get Trevor for Christmas when I felt his hand move up from my knee to my thigh. I turned my head to look at him, recognizing the look in his eyes. The movie hadn't ended yet, but without looking at the TV, I could hear the couple having sex. He licked his lips and shifted next to me, drawing me closer as his finger lifted under my chin to tilt my head back as his lips found mine.

The tension in my body started to evaporate as his hand slid up my thigh and around to my ass, pulling me over to sit on top of him. A moan escaped my lips as I lowered myself on top of him and felt his already hard cock beneath me. He deepened the kiss, grabbing my ass more firmly as if he needed to be inside of me as badly as I wanted him. The nice thing about how new our relationship was, was that it didn't take much to get us in the mood for each other.

I slowly pulled away, breaking the kiss as his brow furrowed in frustration. I chewed my bottom lip playfully as I lifted my shirt up and over my head, revealing a new black lace bra that pushed my breasts up and made them look fuller. I had bought it on a whim the other day with the hope of reigniting the spark that had started to fizzle over the past few days.

I waited for him to comment on it, but either he was super horny and didn't notice, or he simply didn't care. I felt the sting of disappointment as my excitement deflated inside of me.

I blew out a frustrated breath, trying to get out of my head and back in the moment when I felt his hands reach up and slide across my back as his fingers worked the clasp on the back. A few seconds later, the bra was being slid off of my body before his eager mouth quickly covered me in kisses and pulled a hardened nipple into his mouth.

My eyes fluttered close as I ran my fingers through his hair, feeling the ache grow between my legs the harder he sucked. Just when it would start to feel like too much, he would release one and move on to the other, capturing it between his teeth before beginning his delicious torture that was slowly pushing me to the edge.

I reached down and ran my hand along this thick cock, loving that he had worn joggers, so I had easier access. He growled against my chest as I rubbed him harder, desperate to feel him.

"Fuck," he groaned, pulling away and making a popping sound as he released my nipple.

In one quick movement, he grabbed me by my waist and flipped me onto my back at the other end of the couch. I laughed and adjusted the pillow under my head as he watched me while pulling my leggings and panties off. Once I was fully naked, I let my legs fall to the side, giving him the view that I knew he loved.

His eyes immediately focused on the Christmas tree landing strip I had done a few days ago. I smiled as he looked up and locked eyes with me.

"Well, that's festive," he said, his voice thick. "I think it's time we see what's under the tree."

"I think it needs a present or two," I joked, enjoying the light-hearted, flirty change to our evening.

"Well, lucky for you, I'm in a giving mood." He dropped his sweats, taking his briefs with them as his erection sprang free. I watched with hungry eyes as his hand wrapped around it, stroking it up and down as he took the few steps toward me and kneeled in front of the couch. His strong hands gripped my thighs as he scooted me over and leaned forward, swiping his tongue along my slit.

I gasped and closed my eyes, savoring the warmth of his mouth as he parted me with his fingers and continued to lick his way across my folds and up to my clit. One of many things that Trevor did well was getting me off quickly with oral sex. His tongue was as magical as a unicorn and earned him *many* compliments in the first few months when we decided to cross the line of him being my brother's best friend and, therefore, off-limits.

My spine started to tingle as my back arched, my desperation to have him get me off starting to take over. I dug my nails into his shoulders, right on the cusp of a mind-blowing orgasm when he pulled away.

My eyes shot open as I stared at him in disbelief. He leaned back and wiped the corners of his mouth while having the nerve to smile at me like he didn't just rob me of one of the best highs of my life.

"What's wrong?" I asked, trying to force the frustration out of my voice as I popped up on my elbows.

He shrugged and licked his lips as he crawled up onto the couch, hovering over me.

"I wasn't ready to exchange gifts yet," he teased playfully before leaning in to nip the bottom of my ear.

"Trust me," he said softly, "you're gonna come when I'm ready for you to."

Before I had the chance to reply, his mouth was on mine, kissing me tenderly as his hands roamed slowly across my body. I felt the prickle of goosebumps left in his wake. As mad as I was a few minutes ago, that anger was quickly replaced with need as his fingers started rubbing my clit again, bringing me back to where I had been before he stopped. I arched my back and spread my legs as far as I could, allowing him the access he needed.

"Please, Trevor," I begged. "I'm so fucking close."

I felt his muscles tense around me before he reached down and guided his cock to my entrance. I was wet and ready for him, but I still wanted that orgasm. He pulled his fingers away and slid inside, thrusting hard as I stretched around him. Usually, he went slowly since he was so well endowed, but tonight was different.

I cried out as he pushed further, the sensation both wonderful and overwhelming at the same time. Before I had time to adjust to him, I could feel him rocking deeper as his hands roamed my body and up to my face. I opened my eyes, searching his while our bodies synced together, finding the perfect rhythm. I closed my eyes and lifted my hips, meeting him as he pumped faster. I knew that he would be close by the way he was breathing.

His hand curled up as his thumb gently grazed my jaw. I tilted my head back, panicking for a moment when I felt his hand trail down to my neck. It was one of my triggers, and he knew it, so I didn't know why he was suddenly touching me there. My eyes shot open as my body stiffened in response.

"Trevor," I warned, reminding him that I couldn't stand to have anyone's hands around my throat.

Instead of pulling away, his fingers tightened harder around my throat, quickly cutting off my air supply as his other hand worked between my legs and started rubbing my clit. My senses were in overdrive as I fought the anxiety that was creeping up my spine, along with the teasing sensation of a possible orgasm.

The harder he thrust, the quicker the pad of his thumb

worked against my sensitive nub, and the tighter his grip was around my throat. Just when I was sure that I would pass out, I felt the first spasm in my pussy as his hand dropped away from my neck. His finger kept the pressure that I needed as I came undone under his touch, my body bucking as the most intense orgasm ripped through me. A few seconds later, I felt him release inside of me.

My head was spinning over what had just happened. I waited for him to pull out before I scooted up the couch, grabbed the throw blanket from the back, and wrapped it around myself. I watched him with curious eyes as he rolled over and sat on the other side of the couch.

I gently raised my fingers and touched the spots where he had held me, wondering if I was going to have bruises. I couldn't tell if I was more upset that he had done that, to begin with, without talking to me, or if I was more ashamed that I had one of the most incredible orgasms of my life from it.

"I should get going," he said, bending down to collect his pants from the floor.

"It's Friday night," I replied, feeling as stupid as it sounded. "You always spend the night on Friday."

"I know," he huffed as he slid his joggers up his legs. "But I have stuff to do, so I need to go."

Something felt off with him, but I couldn't figure out what. He finished dressing and pulled his cell phone out of his pocket a few minutes before mine vibrated on the table. I picked it up and found a new text message from him.

Trevor: How are you?

My brows pulled together as I read it, wondering if this was his way of trying to talk about what had just happened. My anger started to flare as I set my phone down in my lap, still naked except for the blanket that I pulled tighter around my body.

"Why are you texting me when you're standing right there?" I asked, irritated.

He laughed softly and kept his head down as he continued to do something on his phone.

I rolled my eyes and reached for the remote. The movie had already ended, and since I was now spending the night by myself, I could pick a chick flick instead of the action ones he had insisted that we watched.

A few minutes later, he had his stuff and was out the door. I put my sweats on and curled up on the couch, ready to start a movie, when I heard my phone vibrate again. I unlocked the screen and opened the new message from Trevor.

Trevor: We need to talk. Dinner tomorrow night? I'll cook at my place.

I clicked out of the text without answering it. I felt dizzy from the game he was playing and still wasn't in the mood to deal with it. If he wanted to talk, he could have stayed and done so. It wasn't like we hadn't had tough conversations in the short time we had been together. For whatever reason, something had changed between us, and I wasn't sure what it was. Ever since we came clean to Max that we were dating, he had started to act different, and I wasn't sure that I was a big fan of it. While I understood that it was hard for him to cross that line with his best friend's litter sister, it hadn't seemed to bother him until now. Maybe Max was getting into his head and making him nervous? He had a way of doing that.

I was about to set my phone down so I could start the movie when I noticed a notification icon on the main screen. I clicked it, remembering that the new cameras I had set up earlier were programmed to alert me whenever there was movement. I had totally forgotten to turn them off before Trevor got here, which meant they had been recording the entire time. I opened the app and watched the video that it had saved. I fast-forwarded, my fingers trembling the closer it got to the part where we had sex.

A few minutes later, I stopped pushing the button and let the video play out on the screen. I watched as he hovered over me, his hand snaking around my throat as a look of horror etched onto my face. I wanted to look away, but part of me needed to keep watching. A few seconds later, he was plowing into me as my face contorted into a mix of pleasure and anguish as I climaxed.

I closed the app and set my phone on the table. Maybe the cameras weren't such a good idea after all.

<u>Ten</u>

Trevor

7 Days Ago

"Any word from Elena?" Roman asked as he walked into the office. It wasn't unusual for us to come into the office on the weekend, but we tried to keep it to as minimal as possible. This time of year, it was almost a guarantee that we would be working weekends as we got ready for the rush of new clients that we would be getting in a few weeks after the new year started.

"No," I sighed, leaning back in my chair and tossing a stress ball into the air before catching it. It was almost flat at this point, not having done much for my stress as I squeezed the life out of it.

"When did you talk to her last?"

He pulled out his chair and sat behind his desk as he pushed the mouse across the mousepad to wake his computer up.

"I sent her a text last night asking her to come over for dinner tonight so we could talk."

Roman turned his head slightly and looked at me, one eyebrow quirked.

"A text?"

I shrugged, feeling the weight of the problem as it sat squarely on my shoulders. I rolled them a few times, hoping to release some of the tension.

"It's the only way I get her to talk to me these days. And even that is rare."

"Are you going to ask her about the other guy?" Roman asked, shifting in his chair before he spun around to face me.

"I have to," I laughed. "Right?"

Now it was his turn to shrug.

"Did you guys ever say that you were exclusive?"

I pulled in a deep breath, feeling my chest rise and fall as I slowly let it out.

"I didn't think that we needed to."

He laughed and tried to keep the humor off his face but failed.

"What's so funny about that?" I asked grumpily.

"Don't get so mad," he said lightly. "It's just that you're thirty and dating someone who is nineteen. You can't just automatically assume that Elena is on the same page as you are if you guys haven't discussed it."

I crumpled up a piece of paper and tossed it across the room into the basketball hoop above the trashcan. He was right, I just hated to admit it.

"Either way, we need to talk. About the other guy. About us." I paused for a moment, trying to force down the nausea that had been threatening me all morning. "I'm not sure if she even wants to be with me anymore. Maybe it's just the weight of the stress that she's been under with everything this year or the trauma she's still dealing with from being kidnapped. Something has changed, and I'm determined to figure out what it is, even if it means that we don't stay together."

Roman offered a sympathetic smile before we both got busy with the work that needed to be done. A few hours later, I still hadn't heard from Elena, so I assumed she wasn't interested in coming over for dinner. I got a text from Max, asking if I could swing by for a few to help him with something for the wedding.

I decided to call it a day early, knowing that my mind was too consumed with everything else to be able to concentrate on work. I arrived at Max's apartment an hour later, smiling when I saw Hannah spread out on the floor with an absurd amount of fabric swatches scattered around her.

"Oh good, you're here!" she squealed and got up to hug me. "We need your help."

"Okay," I laughed as I shrugged out of my coat and hung it by the door. "What can I do?"

"You should have run when you had the chance," Max joked and clapped his hand on my shoulder before closing the door and heading to sit down in the living room. His apartment was a decent size for New York City but still small enough to feel overwhelmed by the amount of stuff spread out in the room.

"You said you needed help, so I came," I laughed, shrugging helplessly as I followed Hannah over to the couch.

"We're having trouble picking the color for the groomsmen to wear," Hannah explained as she sat down and picked up a handful of swatches.

"Don't we just match whatever the girls are wearing?"

"That's a possibility," she answered, her brow furrowed. "But Max seems to think that the guys won't want to wear hot-pink vests or ties."

"Well," I laughed, sitting down and picking up a handful of options so I didn't smush them. "I would agree with that. Pink really isn't my color, let alone *hot pink.*"

"That's why we need something that will go with it and pull it all together." She leaned back against the cushion and blew a strand of hair out of her face.

"And I'm the best you could find to help with this?" I wrinkled my nose at the same time that I heard a knock on the door.

"Don't worry," she assured me as she hopped up and ran over to the door. "I called for backup!"

She opened the door, and a frantic-looking Elena walked in. My heart started racing as I took her in, the look of panic on her face as she scanned the room around her as if she was looking for something. Or rather *someone.*

"Elena, what's wrong?" I asked, standing up and turning to face her. Her eyes danced wildly as they found mine.

Max jumped up, rushing over to where she was. Soon, we were all hovering around her, waiting for her to answer us and tell us what had happened.

"Nothing," she said nervously. "I'm fine."

"You don't look fine," I replied quickly, earning a glare from her. I bit down on my tongue to keep from saying anything else that would further upset her.

"I am."

I took a few steps back, giving her some space as Hannah helped her out of her jacket and hung it by the door next to mine.

"What's going on, Elena?" Max asked, legs planted firmly with his arms folded across his chest.

"Calm down; you don't have to go into cop mode," she said with an eye roll. "I said that I'm fine."

"Do you want some tea?" Hannah offered, changing the subject and leading Elena into the kitchen by her elbow.

Even though the space was small, and we could still hear and see them, it felt like there was enough privacy for Max and me to have a quick talk without her hearing.

"Do you know what's going on?" he asked quietly, standing beside me as we continued to watch them in the kitchen.

I shook my head, frustrated that, for once, I had no idea what was going on in her life. How had things changed so drastically between us in just a few days?

"Something's got her rattled," Max commented under his breath. "Maybe she'll talk to you later when you guys are by yourselves, without her big brother hanging over her shoulder."

I snorted and then turned my head to look at him.

"I doubt it."

"Why?"

"Because I'm not sure that there's anything for us to talk about anymore."

I could feel my anger starting to build as I balled my hands into fists and then released them.

"What's going on? Did something happen between you guys?"

"I don't have any fucking idea," I breathed out quietly. "She's been mad at me for who knows what, and when I went over to talk to her the other night, I saw her leaving with some other guy."

Max turned his attention back to his sister and narrowed his eyes.

"What the fuck?" he muttered. "That doesn't sound like her."

"Well, it was. I asked her to come over tonight for dinner so we could talk, and she still hasn't responded to me. So, I guess that makes it really clear where we stand."

A few minutes later, the kettle whistled as Hannah got the tea ready for Elena. They joined us in the living room, and Hannah did her best to get everyone focused on the task of finding matching colors for the wedding party. While I tried to be a team player by offering suggestions and putting different swatches together, I was distracted by Elena constantly being on her phone.

By the time we were done, Hannah was beaming, and Max was relieved that he didn't have to look at any more fabric swatches. I pulled on my coat and was getting ready to ask

Elena about dinner when I saw her checking her phone again.

"Thanks for all of your help, you guys," Hannah said as she walked us to the door.

"No problem," Elena said, still looking down at her phone. "I have to go, but I'll talk to you later."

It was unclear who she was talking to since she didn't bother to make eye contact with anyone before she opened the door and bolted out.

"What was that about?" Hannah asked, looking between Max and me.

"I have no fucking clue," I muttered as I leaned in to hug her.

Max gave me a nod as I left, and I knew that it meant he would call me later when Hannah was busy, and we could talk. As I walked out of their apartment and made my way to the subway, I couldn't shake the feeling that something wasn't right.

<u>Eleven</u>

Elena

6 Days Ago

I woke up with a pounding headache that refused to go away by the time I was supposed to head over to my parent's house for Sunday dinner. I had called my mom and explained that I wasn't feeling well, rushing her off of the phone before she peppered me with questions about what was going on. To say that she was overly concerned about me these days would be an understatement. I had more people up my ass than a frequent flyer at a proctologist's office.

I had no idea what time it was as the day dragged on, my head still throbbing with an intensity that made me nauseous and cranky. When a text message from Trevor came through, asking if we could get together to talk, I promptly ignored it and put my phone on Do Not Disturb while I laid down to take a nap. While I doubted that it would get rid of the headache, at least I wouldn't have to be awake and conscious to deal with it.

The dark clouds outside blocked any traces of sunlight from my room, creating a welcoming environment for me to rest. I laid down and pulled the crocheted blanket that my grandma had made me up to my chin, shivering against the cold chill in the room. I had already turned the heater up several times, yet it felt like it was barely sixty degrees. The last thing I needed right now was a heavy electric bill from blasting the heater when I had missed almost a week of work and would have to find a way to make up those hours. Being on my own was already proving to be a lot harder than I had imagined.

My body finally started to relax into the softness of the mattress as sleep threatened to take over. As my eyes fluttered closed, I saw the shadow of someone walk past my bedroom. My heart jumped out of my chest as I flung the blanket off of me and sat up. I tried to listen carefully for sounds of movement but couldn't hear anything past the blood pulsing in my ears.

I stood up on shaky legs and kept my eyes on the door, looking for a sign of the intruder. My hand reached down between my bed and the nightstand, searching for the baseball bat that I always keep next to me. I fumbled around for a few more minutes, frustrated that I couldn't find it. Finally, I gave up, trusting that I could scream loud enough for a neighbor to come help me if needed—not that it had helped any when I screamed the night that Adam took me.

The panic and reminders of that night rushed through me, sending chills up my spine as I walked through the door and down the short hallway to the living room. I desperately wanted to turn around and look behind me to make sure no one was there, but I had seen enough horror movies to know that it was a rookie mistake. Always keep your eyes open and be alert to all of your surroundings.

I stepped into the living room, quickly scanning the space between it and the kitchen. Everything looked the same as

I had left it not that long ago with no signs of anyone else being here but me. I took a few cautious steps toward the kitchen after determining that the curtains were too flat against the wall for anyone to be hiding behind them. My breathing was shallow as if I was too afraid to let on that I was in the room. Or maybe it was just that I was paralyzed by fear and had forgotten how to breathe.

Everything in the room was quiet and calm as I looked around, feeling crazy for thinking I had seen someone. As I let out the breath that I had been holding, I heard the sound of a lock clicking in place as the front door shut.

Twelve

Trevor

6 Days Ago

Sundays were supposed to be my day to relax and unwind before starting a new week, but today I was anything but relaxed. The past few days with Elena had really gotten under my skin and left me questioning everything between us.

I had racked my brain trying to figure out what had gone wrong between us but kept coming up empty. Nothing had seemed to trigger anything serious, yet here we were, possibly at the end of a relationship that had just started.

The only thing that I could link back to when I started noticing the change was that it all began to unravel after we had come clean to Max about our relationship. He seemed cool with it—surprisingly—but that didn't mean that Elena was still fine with everything. I had known her the majority of her life since Max and I became best friends at an early age. I also knew how close she was to her family and how important her brother's opinion was to her.

But was that really enough to drive her away and into the arms of another man? Or was Roman right that she was just young and didn't know how to be in a committed relationship? Better yet, maybe it was the fact that we hadn't sat down and discussed what we wanted from this when it started. I was crazy about her and couldn't imagine being with anyone else, but that didn't mean she was on the same page. Which should have been obvious since I saw her holding hands with someone else a few nights ago.

I shook my head as if to clear the frustration that was forcing its way through my head again. It was like trying to solve a Rubik's cube—impossible unless you were some sort of child genius, which I wasn't.

Bending down, I picked up the stack of laundry I had just finished folding and took it to the bedroom to put it away. I wanted to pick up my phone and call her, but I knew that she would be at her parent's house for family dinner and didn't want to interrupt her time there. Not like she would answer anyway, given that my text from earlier still went unanswered.

I went to the kitchen, pulled out a packaged salad that I had picked up earlier, and pulled the cover off of it. My fork hovered in the air as I tried to force myself to pierce a piece of chicken and enjoy my meal. Instead, I set it down and picked up my phone, shooting off a text message to Max before I could talk myself out of it.

Me: How's Elena tonight?

Before I could set my phone down, I watched the dots bounce across the screen as he replied.

Max: No idea. She didn't show up for dinner.

Me: Why not?

Max: Headache.

Me: Again?

Max: Same thing I said.

I blew out a heavy breath as I scrubbed a hand down my face.

Me: Are you going to check on her?

Max: Heading that way now.

I set my phone down and pushed my salad away from me. I didn't have to ask Max to update me once he knew if she was okay; I knew that he would as soon as he knew. It was the waiting part that was going to kill me.

Thirteen
Elena
6 Days Ago

My heart was still racing as I whipped open the door and looked down the hall, trying to find whoever had just been in my apartment. The only thing that I saw before the elevator door closed was a dark hoodie that looked a lot like Trevor's. I bent over and tried to catch my breath after running down the hall, the mix of adrenaline and fear pushing my nausea up my throat.

If I thought that my headache was bad before, it was ten times worse now. I stood up and made my way back to my apartment, checking over my shoulder every few steps just to make sure that whoever it was didn't somehow make their way back up to my apartment.

Part of me wanted to be the superhero you see in movies that dashes down the stairs and makes it to the elevator right as the doors slide open, and you see who's inside. I contemplated the idea for half a second until I realized that I would likely die from exertion before I even made it to the second floor. Pasta and heavy carbs had become my lifestyle lately, and the extra pounds they added to my ass would only make it that much harder to run after someone.

I went inside and locked the door, my fingers trembling as I slid the chain into place. I stepped back and stared at it, daring someone to try to come in again.

My breathing was finally starting to return to normal when my phone vibrated across the counter, whipping my attention from the door to it. I rolled my eyes at my reaction, knowing that there was nothing to be afraid of. It was simply a text, and most likely, it was from Trevor.

I picked up my phone and slid my finger across the screen to unlock it.

Max: I'm on my way up. Open the door.

I sighed heavily as I typed out my response.

Me: Have you ever heard of saying please?

Max: Open the door.

I set my phone on the counter and walked to the door, looking through the peephole to make sure he was actually there. Once I saw his head moving from side to side, scanning the area, I slid the chain and then reached down to unlock the door.

"Hey," I said, trying not to sound too breathy. I leaned my arm against the door as casually as I could.

He narrowed his eyes and came inside, his shoulders tense and rigid as he walked around in full cop mode. I waited for him to finish whatever he was looking for so he could get on with why he was there.

"What's going on, Elena?" he asked, running a hand through his hair before turning to look at me.

"Nothing." I shrugged and then wrapped my arms around myself, trying to get warm again.

"Why's it so cold in here?"

"I don't know," I confessed. "I turned the heater up earlier, but it doesn't seem to stay warm, and I can't afford to keep cranking it up right now."

He walked over to the thermostat on the wall and leaned forward to read the tiny numbers.

"It's set to sixty-two, Elena. It needs to be at least sixty-eight for it to stay warm." He reached up and pressed the buttons until he was satisfied with the new temperature. "I'll give you money for the bill."

I rolled my eyes and shook my head.

"Seriously, Elena, you can get sick from keeping your apartment that cold. It's not going to change your electric bill that much to keep it a little warmer in here."

"I know that," I scoffed, frustrated because I knew that there was no way that I had left it at sixty-two.

"Then why do you have it turned down so low?"

"I didn't!" I cried out, my emotions getting the better of me. This was too much—all of it was just too much for me to handle right now.

"Then why was it set that low? Is your heater broken?" He stepped closer to me, putting a hand on my shoulder as I trembled.

"I don't know. It doesn't seem to be."

"So then *you* set it to that temperature?"

I could hear the confusion in his voice.

"No," I snapped, hating that we were about to have this conversation.

"Then who did?"

"The hell if I know! Probably the same person that I caught leaving my apartment a few minutes ago."

He pulled his hand away and immediately reached behind his back for his gun. He didn't actually pull it out, but I could tell that it was a natural reaction for him.

"Someone was in your apartment?"

His eyebrows were raised so high they didn't look like they were still attached to his forehead.

I nodded, unable to say anything more.

"Why didn't you call me? Which way did they go?"

He was standing right in front of me, the smell of garlic fresh on his breath from dinner at my parent's house.

"I saw someone in the elevator as the door closed. I didn't get there in time to see their face or anything else."

"Was it a man? A woman? How tall were they? What were they wearing?"

He was going a mile a minute and sending my blood pressure even further through the roof.

"Seriously, Max—you have to calm down with the whole cop thing. You're going to give me an embolism here in a few if you don't stop rapid-firing questions at me."

I felt the air change around us as he took a step back and

turned around, trying to get it together. I knew this was as hard for him as it was for me, given the whole kidnapping thing last year.

"I will try to stop asking so many questions at one time, but I need you to sit down and walk me through *every single detail* of what happened. It's very important, Elena."

I nodded and followed him over to the couch. The heater kicked on, the sound startling me for a second until I was comforted by the warmth that was floating between us.

"Start from the beginning," he instructed as he sat down across from me and pulled out the notepad and pen that he always kept in his coat pocket.

"I don't even know where to start," I laughed, feeling as crazy as everything was about to sound. "Strange things have been happening for a week or so now, and this just adds to all of that."

"Like what?"

I pulled in a deep breath and slowly let it out. Natalie had taught me to focus on my breathing when I needed to calm myself. It used to work, but now it was getting harder and harder to find any peace.

"Like the phone charger incident. Waking up to find the TV turned on in the middle of the night when I know that I had turned it off. Finding the stove turned on when I get out of the shower." I paused for a moment and inhaled again. Once I was ready, I continued. "Today, I've had a terrible headache—so bad that I can barely stand to be awake. I called mom to let her know that I wasn't coming to dinner, then turned up the heater and went to my room to lay down.

I was freezing, so I curled up with the blanket that Nonna made me and laid down. As I was starting to fall asleep, I saw someone walk past my door. I got up and looked around the apartment, trying to convince myself that I had dreamt it until I was in the kitchen and the front door closed."

Max's knuckles were white from how tight he gripped the pen as he wrote the details down.

"What happened after that?" he asked, his voice softer than I had anticipated.

"I went after them. I looked down the hallway to see if I could find which direction they had gone. Then I heard the elevator ding and rushed off that way. I barely got there as the door was closing. I didn't see anything other than they were wearing a dark hoodie."

I wanted to add a snide comment about how it looked a lot like the one that I had seen Trevor wearing a lot lately, but the last thing that I needed was to fill Max's head with worry that his best friend was messing with his baby sister.

Deep down, I wanted to believe that it *wasn't* Trevor, but the person that I saw did look a lot like him with his build and the way he walked. It wasn't likely, but then again, it wasn't impossible. He had been acting strange lately, so there was no telling what he may or may not do.

Max finished writing, then set his pen and notepad on his thigh and leaned forward, resting his arms on his knees.

"Is there something else going on, Elena? Something that you're not telling me?"

I shook my head and frowned, unsure of what he was trying to insinuate.

"I can't help you if I don't know the truth about what's going on. That means I need to know everything, even the stuff you may feel ashamed to tell me. I'm your big brother, Elena. There's nothing that you could ever do that would make me love you any less or think bad of you. You can trust me."

"I've told you everything, Max. I don't know what it is that you think you know, but if you can just spit it out already, that would be great."

I pulled my legs up under me, still trying to get warm even with the heater blasting around us. One thing was for certain—the damn thing wasn't broken by any means.

He leaned back and sighed, running a hand down the scruff on his jaw.

"I know, Elena."

"Know what?" I lifted my hands in the air, thoroughly confused.

"About the other guy that you've been seeing."

My jaw dropped before I could stop it, the tension behind my eyes starting to build again.

"What the hell are you talking about?"

"Let's not play games, Elena. Trevor saw you with someone else. He's been trying to talk to you about it, but you keep avoiding him and acting distant with him."

My mind was going a mile a minute, trying to piece together the story he had just told me. None of it was true, and why Trevor would tell him such a thing was beyond me. Maybe I wasn't wrong about him after all, and he was making up stories to keep Max from finding out what he was really up to. If that was the case, two could play this game.

"Are you kidding me right now?" I asked, pure disgust attached to every word. "If anyone has been distant, it's been him. Not only that, but he hasn't been himself in so long that I'm not sure I even know who he is anymore."

"That's funny," Max laughed sarcastically. "He said the same thing about you."

"And you believe him?"

"I don't know what to believe because you won't talk to me. You won't tell me what's going on. All I have is what he tells me and that he's worried about you. We all are."

"Why bother talking to you? You guys didn't even believe me about the charger. Why would I tell you anything else? Just so you can turn around and make it look like I'm crazy?"

Max blew out a frustrated breath and looked at me, his eyes softer and his tone more sincere.

"No one thinks that you're crazy. We're just worried about you."

"You keep saying that," I snorted.

"Because it's true."

"Then why is Trevor acting the way he is?" I blurted out, knowing that Max likely had no idea what I was talking about. It wasn't like Trevor was going to talk to him about trying to choke his sister out during sex, even though he knew it was a hard limit for her. Either way, something had changed with him, and I was dying to know what it was.

"Acting worried?" he asked, tilting his head to the side.

"No, not worried." I stopped for a moment to think about how I would describe him instead.

"Distant. Cocky. Inconsiderate." I shrugged my shoulders and added, "Weird."

"I don't know, Elena," he said warily, and I could tell that he didn't want to get into the details of our relationship. "I think you guys definitely need to sit down and talk, though."

"That's the problem—he never wants to talk while he's here. He sends me texts while he's standing right next to me, then leaves and sends me another one to ask me to get together for dinner so we can talk. It's weird, and I just don't have the time or energy for these games."

Max frowned, and I could tell that he knew this didn't sound like Trevor either. Good, at least someone else thought it was odd and not just me.

"I don't know what to say," he sighed, lifting his hips to pull his cell phone out of his pocket. "He's texting me now to see how you're doing. He's been worried about you all night. Maybe take the first step and call him this time? I'm sure it's not easy for him to approach you after seeing you with someone else."

"Yeah, maybe," I said, even though I didn't mean it. I needed to figure out what was going on with Trevor and find out why he was making up these stories before I fought with Max about it.

"Well, I need to get back to mom's to pick up Hannah. Are you going to be alright?"

I nodded and pushed up off of the couch to walk him out.

"Be sure to keep that baseball bat by the door, just in case you need it," he said over his shoulder to me.

"I would if I could find it," I muttered, rubbing a hand along the band of tense muscles in my neck.

"You mean that one?" Max asked, nodding to the kitchen counter where it was lying next to a stack of mail that hadn't been there earlier.

My heart dropped as I stared at it, wondering when it was put there. Obviously, sometime before the intruder ran out of my apartment, but it was more jarring not knowing how long they had been there, to begin with, especially since I was home all day and apparently not alone.

"Oh yeah," I said dismissively as I shook my head. "I forgot that I put it there earlier."

Max gave me one final look-over before opening the door and stepping into the hallway.

"Keep the door locked and call me if you need anything. I can be here in a few minutes."

"Will do," I said as I forced a smile and closed it behind him.

I quickly locked both locks and slid the coffee table over to block the door, just for good measure. Then I walked over to the counter and moved the baseball bat to the side as I looked at the stack of mail that had been sitting underneath it. As I picked it up and sorted through it, a picture fell to the floor. I bent down and picked it up, wondering who the beautiful girl was with so much sadness in her eyes.

<u>Fourteen</u>

Trevor

5 Days Ago

I tapped my fingers anxiously on the table, rattling my coffee cup as I waited for Max to show up. He had sent a quick text last night that said that Elena was fine and that we should talk in the morning. We decided to meet at the café on the corner, but he had yet to show up.

I glanced down at my watch, checking the time as the seconds ticked by. The waitress glanced in my direction, looking to see if I was ready to order. I shook my head no and continued to stare out the window, waiting for him to get there.

Obviously, Elena was safe—otherwise, Max wouldn't have left her apartment last night. The part that got me and had me up in arms was that he wanted to talk to me. I didn't know if it was the tone of his text—was that even a thing? This morning it definitely felt like a thing. Or if it felt like the dreaded, *we need to talk* conversation that everyone hated in relationships. As much as I had been trying to push the thought out of my head all night and this morning, I couldn't help but wonder if Elena had sent Max here to break up with me.

Ten minutes later, I felt like my heart was going to explode out of my chest. Thankfully, Max showed up at that moment, and the look on his face looked like he was about to put me out of my misery.

I leaned back against the worn-out booth and blew out a breath. *Here it comes.*

"Hey," Max said as he slid out of his jacket and into the booth opposite of me. "Sorry I'm late. Hannah wasn't feeling well this morning."

"Is she okay?" I asked, my voice scratchier than I expected. I sipped my coffee, hoping that it would help.

"I hope so." He tossed his gloves on the table and then set his phone down, checking for any new notifications. "She's not sure if she caught a stomach bug or if she has food poisoning, but she's been throwing up since last night."

"That sucks," I mumbled, too distracted by what he was going to say about Elena to be able to focus on anything else right now.

"Yeah, her mom is coming to stay with us in a few days, so I hope she's better by then."

I nodded and looked around, counting down the seconds until my life would explode around me. Okay—so maybe that was a little dramatic, but the thought of losing Elena pulled at my heart in a way that I had never felt before, and I honestly wasn't sure that I would survive losing her.

"Anyway, the reason why I asked you to meet me this morning..." he started, his voice tapering off as the waitress walked by.

"Thank fuck," I mumbled, relieved that he was finally going to get to it. I felt my jaw tense when the waitress turned around and noticed him sitting there, choosing that moment to take our order.

A few painstakingly long minutes later, I ordered food I had no plans of eating and leaned forward to make sure I heard every word out of Max's mouth.

"Alright, where was I?" he asked, looking as frazzled as I felt.

"Elena," I blurted out impatiently. "If you're here to break up with me for her, please just do it already and put me out of my misery."

Max let his head fall back as a laugh tumbled out of his mouth.

"You're kidding me, right?" he joked, the corners of his lips still tugging up as he tried to be serious.

I pinned him with a look as I locked my hands together in front of me on the table.

"She didn't send me here to break up with you," he confirmed with an eye roll. "And even if she did, I would have said no and made you two work your own shit out."

"Good to know," I mumbled, feeling somewhat relieved.

"I'm here because I'm worried about her. When I went to check on her, she was panicked and said that someone had been in her apartment."

My heart chose that moment to explode out of my chest as I stared dumbly at him, unable to speak.

"What the fuck?" I finally asked, trying to get my thoughts together. "Why didn't you tell me last night? I could have gone over there and stayed with her. Or had her stay with me. Did you check her apartment? Have any leads on who it was or what they wanted?"

My mind was going a mile a minute, the questions spewing out faster than fireworks on the Fourth of July.

"Calm down," Max said sternly, looking around to make sure I hadn't drawn attention to us. "*That's* why I wanted to talk to you in person. I didn't want you freaking out and rushing over to her apartment and making things worse."

"Worse?" My eyebrows shot up my forehead. "How would I make it worse?"

"By doing what you're doing right now. I know that you love her and that you want to protect her, but you can't freak out every time something happens to her."

"And why the fuck not?"

"Because she needs us to back off and let her live her life without keeping her in a bubble. She has to be able to experience things—the good and the bad—without us constantly intervening and rescuing her before she has a chance to figure it out herself."

"You're starting to sound like Elena," I muttered, trying to force my shoulders to relax a bit.

"That's because those are her words—not mine. Trust me; there's nothing that I would love more than to wrap her in a bubble and protect her from this ugly world that we live in, but it's not fair to her. She deserves to have a life and not constantly live in fear after what Adam did to her."

"But someone broke into her apartment. How are you not upset and freaked out about that?"

Max leaned back as the waitress slid his plate in front of him. Once she was gone, he picked up his fork and studied his plate before answering.

"I was. When I first got there and she told me that she had seen someone in her apartment—it took everything that I had in me not to throw her over my shoulder and lock her in my apartment, so I could watch over her. I yelled at her—which I instantly felt bad about—for not calling me the second that it happened, but then when she explained everything, I realized that she did everything that I would have told her to do if she had called me."

"So what now? We just let someone sneak around her apartment and do nothing?" I questioned.

"I couldn't find any evidence that anyone had been there. I checked the doors and windows, no signs of forced entry. So unless someone had a key, I don't know how they would have gotten in. She said that she was starting to fall asleep when she saw them, that it woke her up, and she went looking for them."

"Did she at least take a weapon with her?"

"She couldn't find the baseball bat that she keeps by her bed. She said that she went through the living room and kitchen and didn't see anything that looked out of place, but then she heard the door close, and that's when she followed them into the hallway."

I pushed a breath of air out as steadily as I could, the tension in my shoulders starting to build again.

"Someone was getting into the elevator as she caught up with them, but she couldn't see who it was."

"Do you think that she made it up?" I asked, hating the doubt in my voice.

He shook his head and took a bite of his eggs. After he finished chewing, he wiped his mouth and said, "No, I don't think that she made it up. But, I do think that the lack of sleep and stress that she's been under might have made her think that she saw something that she didn't."

"So you're not worried that there's an actual threat to her," I said slowly, starting to put everything together. "You're worried that she's about to have the breakdown that we've all been trying to avoid."

He nodded and pushed his plate to the side before setting his fork on top.

"She's going to fall, and she's going to fall hard. I need you there to catch her before she hits rock bottom."

I scrubbed a hand down my face, feeling the weight of what he was asking me to do.

Fifteen

Elena

5 Days Ago

I sat outside the door to Natalie's office, waiting for her to come in. Usually, her receptionist was here to let the clients in, but it seemed no one was running on time this morning. Guess that was a Monday morning for you.

I hadn't slept last night and spent the majority of the night staring at the door in my bedroom, waiting to see someone walk by again. Finally, around three in the morning, I gave up and went to lay on the couch, convinced that I would sleep better out there. Instead, I heard the sirens and sounds of the city, which were a reminder that there was crime happening all around me and that I would likely never feel safe again.

My phone said it was 8:25, which meant that Natalie was almost half an hour late for our meeting. I chewed the inside of my cheek nervously, wondering if she had stood me up or worse—if something had happened to her. I was about to stand up and leave when I heard heels clicking on the tile floor in the hallway that leads to her office.

She rounded the corner with her head down, her fingers flying rapidly across her phone. Before I could say anything to let her know that I was there, she looked up and jumped, bringing her hand to her chest as her phone went flying to the floor next to me.

"Elena!" she exclaimed, her eyes still wide with surprise. "What are you doing here?"

I stood up and dusted off my pants, pulling my brows together in confusion. I grabbed her phone and handed it to her.

"I'm here for my appointment?"

Now it was her turn to look confused.

"But it's not until this afternoon." She unlocked her phone and pulled up her calendar to confirm. "See," she said, turning it toward me. "Your appointment is today at 4:30."

I leaned in and looked at the screen, seeing my name in bold, right at the bottom as the last appointment of the day.

"You changed my appointment?" I asked, feeling stupid for showing up early. Had they called and confirmed that it was going to change?

"No," she said softly. "You changed it two weeks ago and asked for an afternoon spot instead of morning, so you didn't have to miss work."

"I did?"

She nodded and regarded me cautiously as she waited for the pieces to fall into place in my head. Unfortunately, they didn't.

"I don't remember doing that," I muttered. "Sorry, I'll leave and come back this afternoon."

Natalie reached into her purse and pulled out her keys. After unlocking the office door, she stepped to the side and waited for me to go in.

"You don't have to see me right now," I said, feeling bad for derailing her day.

"I don't have an appointment until ten this morning."

"Is that why Abby isn't here yet?"

"Yeah, she wasn't feeling well, so I told her to come in later if she felt like it. It's a slow day for me today, so I can manage on my own if she's not better."

I took a deep breath and looked around the small waiting room that I had sat in a few times a week for the past year. I had always found it calming, and it was one of the reasons that I hadn't turned and ran in the opposite direction the moment I first agreed to come. Max had insisted that I do a handful of sessions before I could give up, and after I met Natalie, I decided that I wasn't ready to stop.

"Are you going in late to work today?" Natalie asked, pulling me out of my thoughts. She unlocked her office door, and I followed her inside.

I chewed my lip nervously before answering.

"I actually called in."

Her head whipped up in surprise. She tried to keep her expression neutral—it was what she did best as a therapist, but even I saw the concern on her face.

As quickly as it appeared, it disappeared, and she pulled her shoulders back and sat down in her chair. I sat where I always sat and crossed my legs, hoping to shield myself from her judgment somehow.

"You seem to be missing a lot of work these days," she noted. "Are they okay with that?"

"I'm not sure," I admitted. "They haven't said anything so far, but I doubt that they're considering giving me a promotion or raise any time soon."

"Do you want to talk about work?" she asked, turning on her computer and moving her mouse around once the monitor lit up.

"Not really," I laughed, still feeling nervous.

"How about some coffee or tea?" she offered, pushing away from her desk. She walked over to the station that she had set up in the corner of the room.

"Tea would be great," I said. "Decaf if you have it."

She nodded and inserted the k-cup into the Keurig before turning and studying me as she leaned against the wall and waited for it to brew.

"You look tired," she said passively as if making a general note to add to her files after I left.

"I am," I laughed, too tired to try to hide it.

"Still not sleeping well?"

"I had another *incident*," I said, my voice dropping on the last word.

She turned to finish the tea and inserted another k-cup into the machine as she started her coffee in the travel mug that she had brought with her.

"What happened?" she asked over her shoulder as she added honey and stirred.

This wasn't the first time we'd chatted over tea, so it wasn't any surprise that she remembered how I liked it.

"I saw someone in my apartment."

She whipped around, knocking over the bottle of honey in the process.

"Are you okay? Did you call the police?" Her voice rose an octave with her concern.

"I didn't have time to. By the time I followed them to the elevator and went back inside, Max was already on his way up to my apartment."

"Did he know that someone had been there?" she asked, brows furrowed as she handed me the cup of tea. I carefully took it from her and set it on the coaster by the edge of her desk.

"No, he was just coming by on his own. I told him about it, though."

"What did he say?"

She finished stirring the sugar and creamer into her coffee, put the lid on, and joined me at the desk again. I went over everything that had happened—the missing baseball bat, the door closing as someone left, and the fact that my *detective* brother hadn't seemed concerned that anything strange had happened since there were no signs of anyone breaking and entering. She nodded and took notes but didn't have much to say about any of it, which made me feel even more uneasy. *Why was no one worried about this?*

"Did you get a chance to talk to Trevor?" she asked casually as she finished jotting something down on her notepad. She looked up and waited for my answer.

I swallowed hard, trying to decide whether or not I wanted to tell her what had happened.

"I um, tried to," I said nervously.

"What happened?"

"He texted me on Thursday and asked if we could get together to talk. I remembered what you said about talking to him in person, so I was short with my text back and said, *okay*. He came over Friday, but he was acting different, and I just assumed that he was mad at me for being short with him, or maybe he was acting that way because he knew that I had caught him following me on the subway. I don't know."

I paused and looked away, remembering the way his hand had felt around my throat. I could feel myself beginning to panic again as my breathing increased and my heart started racing.

"Elena, it's okay to talk to me. This is your safe space," Natalie said calmly. "Take a few deep breaths if you need to, and then try to tell me what happened that's bothering you."

I did as she suggested, pulling deep lungfuls of air in and slowly releasing them back out. She knew my triggers and could tell that something had happened.

Once I felt calmer, I told her about him choking me during sex and felt the blush creep up my neck as I admitted that I had an orgasm from it. I knew that people talked to her about all sorts of things, but I couldn't imagine their sex lives were part of it. Surprisingly she remained unaffected and didn't seem bothered in the least as she talked to me about how this is a kink for many people and that the decreased oxygen can make an orgasm more intense. Even though I didn't feel better about Trevor doing it, I did feel better that I had told someone else, and they hadn't judged me for it.

"When it happened, how did you feel?" she asked before clarifying, "with Trevor—did you feel safe? Did you feel like you could trust him?"

I sat back in the chair and thought about it for a moment. My spine tingled the same way it had that night when he first got there, and I realized that I had my answer. I hadn't felt safe with him that night, and that was a huge red flag for me now that I was aware of it.

<u>Sixteen</u>

Trevor

4 Days Ago

"Alright, one more set, and then we're done," I said as I watched my new client raise the bar above her head, her arms trembling slightly with the weight of it. I kept my eye on her, my stance ready to move if she needed help.

A few minutes later, she was finished, and I was done for the day. I cleaned up and made my way back to the office, finding Roman sitting at his desk with a frown on his face as he stared at his computer.

"What's wrong?" I asked, tossing my phone on my desk as I grabbed my bottle of water to refill it.

"These numbers aren't adding up. With all of the new clients that we've been booking, we should have more coming in next month than what it's showing."

I frowned and walked over to stand behind him as I stood over his shoulder and looked at the spreadsheet he was studying.

"That doesn't make sense," I muttered, running a hand down my face. I had spent hours the past few nights trying to get everything updated to get caught up before the end of the year.

"Did you forget to add the sign-ups from last week's promotion?" he asked, looking over his shoulder at me.

"No, they should all be in there. Everything should be there," I said frustratedly.

"Well, something has to be missing."

"Nothing is missing!" I yelled, my voice rattling off the walls as Roman pulled back and looked at me.

I stepped away and pushed a hand through my hair.

"What's going on?" Max asked as he walked into the room, looking between Roman and me.

"Nothing," I bit out, still feeling the anger and irritation building inside of me.

He looked from me to Roman, waiting for him to answer.

"I said it was nothing," I snarled, walking to my desk and slamming the water bottle down.

"It doesn't look like nothing," Max said evenly, shoving his hands into his pockets.

"Whatever," I muttered, swiping my phone from the desk and pushing past him as I walked out.

"I thought we were going to grab dinner?" he called out as I left.

I knew that I owed him more of an explanation, but right now, I couldn't find one to give him. My head was a mess because of everything with Elena, and I knew that deep down, if the spreadsheet was wrong, then that meant that I had done something to screw it up. The last thing that I needed right now was more work on top of what I already needed to finish.

It was after six on Tuesday, and there were only nine days left until Christmas, which meant that I needed to finish my shopping. I had been putting it off, distracted with everything else, and putting in more hours at work than I had ever had to do before. It felt like no matter how hard I tried to get caught up, nothing worked.

I stopped by a food cart, grabbed a quick bite, and then made my way to the store. Not that I had planned on going to the shop where Elena worked, yet I somehow found myself there, wandering the aisles as I hoped that I might run into her.

I had a basket filled with bubble bath and soaking products that I had no idea if my mom would like, but it wasn't like I pictured Roman or Max while shopping for this stuff. I had to make it look like I was there for a reason—without looking like a desperate stalker trying to find time to see my girlfriend and make sure that she was okay.

Plus, I still needed to buy for my mom, and last I knew, she was into this girly stuff. I picked up a lavender ball-looking thing and brought it to my nose as my eyes scanned the store, hoping to catch sight of her. I was still walking with it pressed to my nose as I rounded the corner and ran right into her.

A pile of stuff went flying into the air and fell to the floor around us as she whipped around and looked at me. Her dark hair was pulled tight into a bun on top of her head, showing off the necklace I had bought her last month for her birthday. It warmed my heart to see her wearing it, especially given how hard things had been between us lately.

"I'm so sorry," I said as I tossed the ball into my basket

before setting it down to help her clean up the mess. She bent down, her jeans pulling tight across her ass as she did, and scooped a handful of packets together before setting them on the shelf beside her.

"What are you doing here?" she asked, not bothering to look up at me as we continued to find the ones that had flown further away. I grabbed the few that I had spotted a couple of feet away and handed them to her.

"I needed to finish up some Christmas shopping," I said, reaching down to pick up my basket.

She leaned forward and looked inside, eyeing the contents before looking back up at me.

"Max is more of a citrus kind of guy," she replied, the corners of her lips tugging up slightly at her joke.

"I was thinking about some of this for my mom," I laughed.

She furrowed her brow and reached inside, moving things around to get a better look.

"Your mom doesn't have a tub, so it's going to be hard for her to use some of that."

I swallowed hard and tried to look away before the blush crept up my neck and covered my face.

"Honestly, I have no idea what half of this stuff is. But I'm super behind on finishing my shopping, and this seemed like a good idea before I started."

She smiled, and for the first time in what felt like forever, it felt natural.

"Here, let me see your basket." She extended her hand and

waited for me to pass it to her. Once she had it situated on the shelf beside her, she pulled some stuff out and left the other in the basket. "There, that should work better. I have a couple of new face masks that I was just putting out—before someone scared the shit out of me—that she would probably like as well."

I nodded toward the basket and winked as I replied, "you're the expert, whatever you think she'll like."

A satisfied grin pulled tight across her face as she added a few of the packets to the cart and grabbed the other stuff that she had pulled out.

"I can put those things back," I offered, not wanting to make more work for her.

"It's okay; it's my job."

I followed her through the aisles as she put everything back where it went, and I tagged along like some lost, lonely puppy.

"I'm surprised to see you are working so late," I said, trying to keep the conversation going.

She looked over her shoulder at me with an expression that I couldn't quite read.

"I'm actually working a double shift today. I've missed a lot of work and needed to make up some of my hours, so I can afford to pay rent."

"I can help if you need it," I offered, a little too eagerly.

"Thank you, but no." She turned and faced me, her shoulders squared the way she gets when she's feeling defensive.

"I don't mind," I added more softly.

"I know, and I appreciate it. But I have to learn how to do these things on my own. I can't constantly have everyone saving me all the time. I missed a few days of work, and now I need to make up those hours. My boss was pretty flexible and let me use some of my sick time as well, so that should help."

I avoided saying what I wanted to say and went with, "That's great; it sounds like you've really got a hold on what you need to do."

Inside I was screaming, begging for her to let me help. Before she moved out and got her own apartment, I had offered for her to live with me. It wasn't that we didn't think we would end up living together at some point in the future; Elena had said no because she wanted to know that she could do it on her own first. I knew this was important to her, and I owed her the respect to support her as she did it.

"Yeah, I'm tired, but soon I'll be caught up on my hours and back to my regular schedule. Thankfully we're busy with the holidays, so they were able to let me squeeze in the extra hours."

"Sounds like everything is working out favorably for you." I felt awkward, not knowing what else to say. This was the most I had gotten to talk to her in days—weeks? Who knew at this point. It felt like the days were melting together, and I had no idea what was happening anymore.

"I get off at seven," she said, looking up at me under her dark lashes as she reached over and fixed the bottles of nail polish on the rack. "Do you want to grab a bite to eat?"

My heart started racing the way it used to when we first started dating.

"I would love to."

"Perfect," she smiled. "I need to get back up front and finish unloading the last few boxes of stock that came in. I'll meet you by the door at seven, and if you still need ideas for what to get me, there's this new apple-pear line that came in that is *to die for*. Megan is working that section right now and can help you pick out some stuff … you know, just in case you need it."

She winked and walked off, tossing me a flirty smile over her shoulder as she disappeared out of sight. I went in search of Megan and found the items that Elena had mentioned. While Megan had suggested a few things that could be used together, I decided to buy the entire collection, as well as the plum-apricot one that she said Elena had been in love with as well.

A couple of hundred dollars later, I stood by the door with bags full of presents as I waited for Elena. People bustled past me as they came in from the bitter cold, ready to get some shopping of their own done before they moved on to the next store. That's what Christmas in the city was like—mindless wandering from store to store until your wallet was empty, your arms were sore from the weight of the bags, and your head felt like it would explode from the overstimulation.

Right at 7:02, I felt Elena walk up beside me as I tucked my phone into my pocket and reached out to hug her. It felt weird like I wasn't sure if this was something that we did anymore. When she didn't pull away, and I felt her body relax against mine, I held her a little tighter and felt thankful that maybe—just maybe—things were starting to get back to normal between us. Max warned me that Elena was spiraling toward a nervous breakdown, but the woman standing next to me looked like she didn't have a care in the world.

Seventeen

Elena

4 Days Ago

I leaned back into the recliner and watched as Trevor moved about in the kitchen, getting the paper plates and napkins before bringing the pizza into the living room. It felt good to be in his apartment again, and I was already feeling like myself again with him.

When he showed up at my work, I was surprised and didn't know how I would feel about it. Things had been so off with us lately, and I was still struggling to find a way to talk to him about what had happened Friday night. It seemed like every time I tried to start a conversation with him, he would start talking about something else or avoid me.

"Are you ready to eat?" he asked as he balanced everything and then set it down on the coffee table.

I scooted off of the chair and slid down to the floor, rubbing my hands together as I waited for him to open the lid to the pizza box.

"I am sooo ready," I said, drooling as the rich aroma filled the room. I reached in and pulled out a slice before scooting over and leaning against the couch while Trevor fixed his plate.

The pizza was delicious—just like it always was— but tonight it tasted better than ever. Maybe I was just overly hungry, but it felt like there was this insatiable appetite inside of me that could devour the whole damn thing by the time Trevor took his first bite.

My stomach growled as I chewed and swallowed, desperate for more. I didn't bother trying to make small talk—there was time for that later. Right now, it was pizza time.

I finished my slice and licked my fingers, not wanting to waste it by wiping it off on a napkin. I reached in and pulled another piece free, looking sheepishly at Trevor before retreating to my spot on the floor, where I huddled against the couch and went back to eating.

Trevor chuckled and leaned back against the other couch, sitting opposite me on the floor. He took a bite and then wiped his face with the napkin while he chewed.

"What's so funny?" I asked between bites.

"Nothing," he laughed. "I just forgot how cute you are when you're hungry."

I smiled and then leaned forward, watching him as I grabbed another slice. I knew that I would probably regret eating this much later, but right now, it felt like what my body needed– Trevor and heavy tomato sauce-covered carbs.

"I was starving," I giggled, finally covering my mouth with the napkin while I talked. I might not have wanted to waste any food by wiping it away, but I was still a lady. Well, sort of.

"Well, there's plenty, so eat up."

I smiled and finished my slice, debating whether or not to

have another. After Trevor finished his and grabbed one more, I felt my stomach start to protest and knew that I was done. I climbed up onto the couch and pulled the blanket hanging over the back of it over me. I felt more comfortable in his apartment than I did anywhere else. Sometimes I kicked myself for being stubborn and not considering moving in with him instead of getting my own place. Sure it's good to be on your own and know that you can do it, but I wasn't sure that the loneliness and discomfort were really anything to brag about.

After Trevor finished eating, he took the box and our trash to the kitchen, then came back and joined me on the couch. I sat up and waited for him to get comfortable before I laid down again, resting my head on his lap. He turned the TV on and flipped through the channels until he gave up and settled on some cooking show.

Neither of us was really into it, but I rolled onto my side and pretended to watch it while I tried to think about how to start the conversation with him that we needed to have. The longer I waited, the more it felt like maybe we would be okay if I didn't bother. Perhaps it was just a little misunderstanding? Both of us had been stressed and overwhelmed with things lately, so it was possible that we just had a couple of off days.

I smiled as I felt his fingers run lightly up and down my side, the way he always did when we cuddled like this together. His touch was always soft and gentle, teasing me with the things that I knew he could do with those fingers. I shifted again, this time making my boobs pop up more in the new bra that I was wearing—the one he didn't seem to notice the other night. I brought my leg forward and twisted my back some, giving him a better view of my ass as his hand slid down and palmed it.

I let out a small gasp as his fingers slid down the crack of my ass and toward the ache that was beginning to build. It had only been a few days, but I already needed him again, my body humming with anticipation of what was about to come.

I rolled onto my back, allowing his hand to move with me as it trailed across my hip and then lingered over my pussy. I looked up at him and chewed my bottom lip. He shifted beneath me, and I could tell that he was getting as worked up as I was.

He locked eyes with me as he flicked the button on my jeans open and pulled the zipper down. I wiggled my hips, allowing him to move them down my body before he tossed them to the floor. He repositioned his hand and pushed the lace of my g-string panties to the side as his fingers slid over my slit.

I opened my legs wider, allowing him more access as I closed my eyes and covered his hand with mine. I needed him inside of me, touching me and teasing me until I came apart. He slowly trailed his finger over my skin, leaving goosebumps in its wake as he delayed my pleasure. I waited a few seconds for him to get to it, but when he didn't, I bumped his hand out of the way and replaced it with my own.

I heard him exhale heavily as he pulled my panties down further, exposing myself to him even more. I dipped a finger inside and moaned before I rubbed it up and along my clit. I knew he was watching me masturbate, even with my eyes closed, but I didn't care. I wanted to get off, and knowing that he was watching, turned me on more than I would have thought.

Wanting to give him a show, I pulled my hand out and then reached down and removed my panties, tossing them to the floor with my pants. Next, I reached up and pulled my shirt up and over my head, adding it to the pile on the floor. I laid back down on his lap, licking my lips as I watched his eyes follow my hand back to my pussy.

My fingers trailed along the Christmas tree landing strip, remembering how much he liked it last time before they were eagerly making their way inside again. I rubbed my clit hard and fast, watching him as I worked myself over. A few seconds later, my hips were bucking off of the couch as my orgasm ripped through me.

Once I was done, Trevor gently nudged me to sit up. When I did, he stood and stripped down, tossing his clothes to the floor with mine. I watched as his dick sprung free, his erection long and hard as it touched his stomach. He gripped it with one hand and slowly stroked it as I watched.

"That's mine," I said, my voice raspy and filled with desire.

I laid down where I had been before and pulled him down to me, so he had no choice but to lay on top of me as his cock slid into my mouth and down my throat. I opened my legs, giving him a place to rest when I felt his tongue lick my slit. I moaned, still sensitive from the orgasm I had a few minutes ago.

I hollowed out my cheeks as I sucked, taking him deeper as I stroked what didn't fit in my mouth with my hand. His tongue was busy licking up my juices as he mercilessly sucked my clit and built me up for another mind-blowing orgasm.

The closer I got, the harder and faster I sucked. I knew that he was close too, but at the last minute, he pulled out. Before I could object, I felt his mouth tight against my pussy as he flicked his tongue rapidly against my sensitive nub, forcing me to climax. I came on his face, my thighs shaking as they tightened around his head.

He laughed and pulled away, gently wiping his mouth as his hard as a rock dick teased me.

"You should have come in my mouth," I said, reaching for him to finish him off.

"I wanted to come in your pussy instead," he whispered, getting up to pick up his pants from the floor.

I knew that he was getting a condom, and as much as I loved that we were safe with each other, I wanted him here and now. I was on the pill, and it wasn't like we hadn't skipped using one the last time we did this.

"We don't need it," I said breathlessly, grabbing his hand and pulling him back to the couch. He raised a brow but sat down and watched as I slid on top of him.

I closed my eyes and moaned as he filled me, stretching me with his thick cock.

"I like the new bra," he said as he reached behind me to unclasp it.

"Thanks," I breathed, not bothering to tell him he had seen it last time.

He flung it across the room and leaned forward, pulling a

hardened nipple into his mouth while he gently pinched the other one between his fingers. I rode him harder, grinding my pelvis against his and squeezing as tight as I could with each thrust.

The harder he sucked my nipples, the more I felt the ache building inside again. This would definitely set a new record with the number of orgasms I had in one day. I wasn't sure if someone could die from too many orgasms, but I was about to find out.

I felt him drop his hands and grab my hips, guiding me as I rode him the way he needed me to. I closed my eyes and kept the rhythm as I felt him come inside me.

His hands released their grip and gently wrapped around my waist, pulling me into him as he held me. And just like that, it felt like we were back to where we had once started.

<u>Eighteen</u>
Elena
3 Days Ago

I headed home from the coffee shop, my legs wobbly and shaky as I pulled my coat tighter around me to fend off the bitter cold. It was late, and I knew better than to meet someone that I didn't know by myself, but I had been mad at my mom and wanted to prove a point.

I tried to stay upright and not fall to the ground the way my body wanted to. I still had such a long way to go, I couldn't give up now. But something was wrong. Something was very, very wrong. I could feel it in my bones, or rather from the numbness that was slowly creeping over my body and forcing me into a deep sleep that I didn't want.

My eyes fluttered shut, the heaviness of whatever was running through my blood too strong to fight. If this was death, it wasn't as bad as I thought it would be.

I could hear faint footsteps walking around me, someone muttering close by but not close enough for me to hear what they were saying. I tried desperately to wake up, to open my eyes and see where I was.

I knew that I wasn't safe—I was very far from safety. I could feel it in my bones. But there was also nothing that I could do about it. I was paralyzed and frozen in this hell, unable to protect myself or fend off the grabby hands that kept reaching out to touch me.

Finally, the room went silent, and the footsteps stopped. I didn't want to allow myself to rest, but my body needed it. I felt weak and knew that I needed my full strength before I tried to do anything to get myself out of this situation.

I laid there—wherever it was—for what felt like forever before my eyes slowly opened, and I took a look around. It was hard to see where I was because it was so dark. The room was cold and empty. Nothing but concrete around me. The walls. The floors. Everything was concrete.

I sat up and felt around in my pockets as I continued to look around for anyone who might be there with me. I found my phone and quickly found my brother's name. I waited nervously, chewing my nails as I looked around.

I was about to give up when he finally answered the phone.

"Hey, Leni," he answered, my heart skipping a beat, knowing that he would come find me now that I had him on the phone. I was still weak and unsure of whether I was alone or not.

"Help me," I whispered.

"What's wrong?" he asked, the concern registering in his voice.

I couldn't answer–my voice was stuck in my throat. A noise off in the distance had caught my attention and made me fearful that someone was there with me and would hear me before I could tell Max to come get me.

"*Leni, where are you?*" *he pressed.*

"*I don't know. It's dark. And cold.*" *I kept my voice low as I continued to scan the area around me for any signs of movement.*

"*Try to look around and see if anything looks familiar or if you see anything that you can tell me about.*"

I looked around, hoping to find something helpful. There was nothing. I knew that I had to give him more information than that, but I had nothing to give him.

"*Who's there with you?*" *he asked.*

"*I think I'm by myself now,*" *I said shakily.* "*I'm scared, Max.*"

"*It's gonna be okay,*" *he assured me.* "*We're gonna work through this together.*"

I waited patiently for him to tell me what to do. If anyone could save me, it was my big brother.

"*Are you able to walk around?*"

"*Yeah,*" *I answered. I wasn't sure that my legs had built up the strength they needed to do so, but I also wasn't tied to anything.*

"*Okay, that's good. Do you see any windows? Any light coming through from outside?*"

I looked around even though I already knew the answer.

"*There aren't any windows. Just a light hanging from the ceiling.*" *I stared at it, hating that the old rusty thing that was barely hanging by a thread was the only light that I had available to me.*

"Keep walking; tell me what you see as you walk," he instructed.

I didn't want to tell him that I was too weak to go far, so I tried anyway. I took a few steps and looked around. There was nothing but concrete for what felt like miles.

"There's nothing, Max. It's concrete walls and a concrete floor."

"Do you see any—"

I heard footsteps heading my way and panicked.

"Shhh!" I whispered loudly into the phone.

Whoever it was, came at me quickly, grabbing the phone and pulling it from my hand.

"No! No! Please! Don't!" I begged as they pried my fingers off of it.

The tears started rolling down my face as I heard them say "wrong number" before hanging up. My one chance at freedom was gone.

"You stupid bitch!" a low voice growled before reaching behind and grabbing me by the ponytail. My head jerked back as they tightened their grip on me.

I tried to lift my arms to fight them off when I felt a hand close around my throat, cutting off my air supply. Fingers dug deeper into my flesh, squeezing painfully as I gasped for a breath.

I reached up and clawed at them, desperately trying to make contact with whoever it was. I squirmed and tried to get out of the death grip they had me in. The more I moved, the harder they pressed. In a moment of desperation, I threw my head back, making contact with theirs.

A muttered curse word was all that I heard before they reached up and covered my mouth, making it even harder to breathe.

I tried to suck in a breath but couldn't.

My lungs burned.

My head felt dizzy.

Just one breath, that was all that I needed.

I tried to pull in oxygen through my nose, but the smell of blood was too much for me to handle. It must have been from where I had headbutted them.

The seconds ticked by loudly in my ear as I counted down until I was out of time.

I tried again to take a breath, the fingers wrapped around my mouth so tightly that it felt like my jaw would break.

If I could just get a little bit of oxygen, I might have a chance.

I felt my body start to go numb. My legs shook and trembled as they lost their strength. I could feel my body sinking to the ground as I succumbed to my death.

"Elena, wake up."

I felt fingers on my arm, shaking gently but with urgency.

"Elena, come on, baby, I need you to wake up."

I tried to focus on the voice, the comfort of safety that felt so close yet so far away.

I was so weak, unable to move or open my eyes. I wanted to wake up and see Trevor, to know that I was safe, but I couldn't. I was locked in the dark dungeon of my nightmares, the place that took part of my soul every time I visited it.

A few seconds later—hell, maybe it was minutes or hours, who knew at this point—I felt a cold washcloth on my chest.

"Take a deep breath, Elena. Listen to my voice, you're safe."

I felt the darkness start to lift, the heaviness on my body suddenly gone. I shot up on the bed, panting as I looked around, sucking in as much oxygen as I could.

Trevor was sitting beside me, concern etched across his brow. The washrag sat beside him where it felt when I jolted up.

"You're okay," he said softly and calmly. "Just take a deep breath and focus on my voice."

I tried to do as he instructed as I wildly searched the room, looking for Adam. I knew that he wasn't there, but that never stopped me from searching for him. My breathing was still erratic as I pulled in as many breaths as possible, afraid that I would be deprived of them again.

My body was trembling as I sat in bed, trying to regain control. I hated having these attacks and hated even more that a year later, they hadn't gotten any better. Even though I had stayed at Trevor's apartment more times than I had stayed at my own, it still felt foreign and strange to me right now.

"Look around and tell me five things that you see," Trevor

offered.

I felt silly every time we did this, but it actually helped.

"When you're ready," he added as he climbed up the bed to sit next to me. He gave me plenty of space without touching me as he leaned back against the padded headboard.

I sucked in a deep breath and held it before I slowly pushed it out. My pulse was still racing, and my fingers trembled against my thighs as I sat there, trying to force my mind to focus on the room around me.

"Water bottle, picture frame, television, phone, and blanket." I kept my eyes focused ahead of me and didn't turn to look at him. I knew that he was there if I needed him, but right now, I needed to concentrate on my breathing and getting the oxygen back into my lungs.

"Tell me four things you can touch."

His voice was calming, and it felt like we had done this a thousand times. Maybe we had? I lost track a while ago.

I took another breath, this one more jagged than the last. I dug my fingers into the blanket as I tried to push the anxiety down. It was just a dream, that was all.

My voice trembled as I answered, "The bed, the rug, the curtains, and you."

I heard a low chuckle and felt myself relax a little bit. Not enough to release my death grip on the blanket, but enough to allow me to take a deeper breath in.

"Now, tell me three things that you can hear."

I looked around the room, keeping my head still while my

body worked on getting back to normal. Besides the blood pulsing past my ears, I couldn't hear much.

I watched as the TV on the dresser in front of me turned on, the volume bar at the bottom changing as Trevor turned it up.

My lips twitched as a smile started to pull across my face. If there was ever a reason to love Trevor, it was his constant support with whatever I was going through.

"The TV, the radio, and the rain outside," I answered, letting my eyes wander over to the window that was splattered with raindrops.

"You're doing great," he said, shifting beside me as he crossed his ankle over the other in front of him. "Let's keep going. Two things that you can smell."

My shoulders relaxed some as I took a deep breath, this time feeling the air fill my lungs fully before I slowly let it out. I glanced over at the bag of stuff from the store he had bought earlier and smiled.

"Lotion and body wash."

"That's cheating," he laughed, knowing that I was referring to the items in the bag.

I shrugged, feeling relieved that my body was finally starting to regulate itself.

"Alright, last one," he said soothingly. "One thing you can taste."

I turned to look at him over my shoulder and grinned.

"You."

He chewed on his bottom lip and smiled back at me.

"You already used that one."

I rolled my eyes and slid back on the bed, leaning into his shoulder as I gently nudged him.

"What can I say? You're something I like to touch and taste."

He lifted his arm and pulled me into his side before planting a kiss on the top of my head.

"Right back at you," he replied.

"Thank you," I sighed, thankful for the ease of the breath that floated so effortlessly through me.

"You don't need to thank me."

I sat quietly next to him, focusing on nothing but how I felt beside him. Relaxed. Comfortable. Safe.

"That one didn't last as long as the others," I commented, knowing that he was fully aware of how long my panic attacks could last.

"Have you been having them again lately?" he asked as he gently rubbed his fingers up and down my arm.

I shook my head, partly lying to him. It wasn't panic *attacks* that I was having, but more so staying in a constant state of panic. It was like one huge attack that never ended, and I had no idea what to do about it.

"I know that everyone is just waiting for me to have one and fall apart," I admitted, tucking my chin into his chest to hide my face. "And honestly, I feel like I'm waiting for the same thing."

"It's okay if it happens, Elena. We're all here to help you through it."

I waited a few minutes and thought about what to say before answering.

"I'm afraid that if I fall apart, no one will ever be able to put me back together again. I'm tired of being the broken girl that everyone always has to worry about."

He squeezed me tighter against his body as the tears fell down my face. It felt good to confess this to him, almost as if a weight had been lifted.

"You will never be that girl, Elena. I promise you."

"How do you know," I asked, tilting my head up to look at him. "What if these panic attacks never stop? What if I can't ever move past what happened with Adam? I'm not the same person I was before it happened, and I'm scared of who I might turn into."

He looked down at me with sadness in his eyes.

"I've seen the people that break. You're not one of them." He looked away before saying anything more. "It's late. We should get some sleep."

I nodded and wondered what he was hiding. There was more to what he had said, and I was determined to find out what it was.

Nineteen

Trevor

3 Days Ago

I woke up at five, having slept off and on after waking up around three to help Elena with her panic attack. She was still sleeping soundly in the bed beside me, her breathing even and gentle, which was a relief compared to what it had been earlier.

I moved around the room quietly to keep from waking her up. It was Thursday morning, and I had a pile of work stacked up on my desk, waiting for me to get to it. I sent Roman a quick text message to let him know that I would be in late this morning. While I hated missing work and staying later tonight, it was more important to make sure she was okay this morning.

Elena had been having panic attacks since her kidnapping, but they had started to die off a few months ago. We all had hoped that they were finally going away and that her therapy sessions were helping her to process and work through what had happened. If I could give her anything in the world, it would be to relieve her of the demons that continued to haunt her.

Watching her struggle last night was hard. In the six months that we had been dating, Elena had had several nightmares, but none of them were at the level or intensity of what she had last night. She was gasping in her sleep, pushing away and swatting at me as I tried to wake her up. I could feel the panic radiating off her, and every second that passed before she woke up sent my anxiety further through the roof.

I wasn't even sure if I would be able to pull her out of her attack with our usual methods, but it was all I had at the time. Her panic attack not only affected her, but it also triggered memories that I had worked tirelessly to bury deep beneath the layers of grief.

When she asked how I knew that she wouldn't always be the broken girl that no one could fix, I didn't want to tell her how I could promise her such a thing. I didn't want to tell her that I had known that girl or that I had tried to save that girl but couldn't. Losing Natasha was a pain that I had never been able to dull, and I carried the weight of her death around with me as if I was the one who had pulled the trigger that night.

I shook my head to clear the image from my mind and walked to the kitchen to start a pot of coffee. I wasn't sure what Elena's plans were for the day, but I couldn't imagine that they didn't involve coffee. Once the coffee was started, I headed into the living room to sit down and answer a few emails. I turned on my laptop and waited for it to start up.

As I waited, a new text message from Max came through.

Max: How are things going with Elena?

I scrubbed a hand down my face and reread the message, wondering how to respond. Did I tell him that we had a great night together before she had one of the worst panic attacks I had ever seen? Did I mention that she confessed that she was worried she was heading toward a breakdown and feared that she would never recover from it? It was hard to know how much to tell him and how much to keep to myself at this point.

Me: She's fine. Sleeping.

It didn't take long until I saw the dots bounce across the screen as he replied.

Max: Have you asked her about the other guy?

I blew out a frustrated breath and set my phone down. I knew that I needed to talk to her about it—mainly because everyone was down my throat telling me to talk to her about it. Between Roman and Max, I wasn't sure who was more annoying with their constant requests for updates on it.

I had planned to ask Elena about him, but every time I tried to bring it up, something would distract us, or it just felt like it wasn't the right time because we were fighting. It didn't help that I hadn't seen her much lately and refused to have that conversation through text messages.

Everyone seemed to think that I was fine because I wasn't losing my shit over it. What they didn't know was that I had been livid when I saw her with someone else. So much so that I had to spend the next day patching up the hole in the wall where I had punched my fist through it after I got home. I'd spent time burning off some of my anger at the gym, but even that wasn't enough.

I heard my phone ding again and picked it up to find a text message from Roman.

Roman: I'll get started on the reports, and we can talk

about them when you get here.

I worked my jaw back and forth, remembering the mess I had made and hadn't had a chance to fix. Instead of talking to him about it yesterday, I stormed off and spent the night with Elena. Apparently, my priorities were getting mixed up along with everything else in my life these days.

I sent Roman a text message back before responding to Max.

Me: No, not yet.

Max: You need to talk to her.

Me: I'm aware.

I didn't have time to get into everything through text messages this morning and wanted to change the subject before getting myself worked up and angry again. *If* I decided to talk to her about it this morning, I didn't want to be heated before we even started.

Max: I just want you guys to figure this out and be happy.

You and me both.

An hour later, I was on my third cup of coffee and starting a new pot when Elena walked out of my bedroom. Her hair was a wild mess on the top of her head as she rubbed at her eyes. She was wearing one of my t-shirts with nothing underneath.

"Good morning," I said, trying to keep the thickness out of my voice as I tried to swallow. She stretched, raising her arms above her head as the shirt rode up and barely covered her.

"Morning," she sighed, leaning side to side as she pulled her body in ways that made me want to ravage her.

I cleared my throat and lifted my mug to my lips, allowing the hot liquid to burn my lips as I forced myself to look away.

"Shouldn't you be heading to work?" she asked as she sauntered toward the coffee pot and filled her cup.

"I'm going in late today," I said as I pressed send on my email before exiting it and turning off my computer. I put it on the coffee table and walked over to join her.

"You don't have to babysit me," she muttered before taking a sip of coffee.

I walked behind and snaked my arm around her waist before I leaned in to whisper in her ear.

"No one is babysitting you. I just wanted to make sure you were okay this morning."

She looked up at me over the rim of her mug as she eyed me suspiciously.

"What do you have on your agenda today?" I asked, changing the subject.

"I have work at eleven."

"Are you working late again tonight?" I tried to keep the concern out of my voice, but I hated her working late nights, especially when she had to go home by herself.

She finished taking another drink before setting her mug on the counter.

"I'll be closing, yes."

I heard the sharp tone in her words, but it was the way she narrowed her eyes at me and held her hand on her hip that let me know that she wasn't in the mood to have this argument. Again.

I sighed and leaned back against the counter, folding my arms over my chest.

"I just hate you going home late to an empty apartment."

"I know, you've told me."

"You can stay here with me if you want," I offered, hoping that she would finally reconsider.

"I can't just live here, Trevor," she groaned and shook her head.

"Why not?"

I had been asking Elena to move in with me before she ever signed the lease on her apartment. We didn't fight about much—until recently—but this was the one thing that always seemed to divide us.

"Because I'm not ready to live with you. I love spending time with you here, but I also like having my own space and being independent. You know how big of a deal this is to me."

I pushed off of the counter and walked to her, pulling her into my chest.

She didn't fight me as I held her against me and rubbed my hands up and down her back.

"I'm not pushing you, it was just an offer. I know that you're working later hours for the holidays, and sometimes it's scary going to an empty apartment that late at night."

She laughed against my chest then looked up at me.

"Since when are you scared of anything?"

I swallowed and tried to push away the memories of how terrified I was when she went missing. It was a pain that I had never felt before—not even with Natasha—and never wanted to feel again.

"We all have our weaknesses, Elena."

I watched the same curious look cross her face and pulled away before she could ask me about it.

"We better get ready, or neither of us is going to make it to work today." I reached down and swatted her bare ass, loving the sound as it echoed around us.

She jumped and turned to look at me, a mischievous grin on her face.

"You're going to kill me with all of this sex lately," she giggled, walking over and running her hand along the front of my sweats.

"Last night was a fun night," I agreed, vividly remembering her body trembling against my tongue as her orgasm ripped through her.

"I think we've had more sex this week than in the six months that we've been together."

She laughed and patted me on the chest before walking off to my bedroom. I followed after her, confused by her statement.

"We've had more sex than that," I countered, furrowing my

brow. "Twice in one night isn't a new record for us."

"No," she laughed, "but some of the other stuff you've done recently is definitely new and unexpected."

I watched a blush creep up her neck before it kissed her cheeks. She turned and looked away, seeming embarrassed by something.

Now I was really confused because last night was the first time we had been together since before everything started happening. Maybe she was confusing her sexcapades with the other guy instead of me? The thought sent fire through my veins as I balled my hands into fists at my side.

"What are you talking about?" I bit out with more anger than I had intended.

She pulled her head back and gave me a strange look.

"You know what I'm talking about, Trevor." She sat down on the edge of the bed and crossed her arms. "I know that we've been avoiding talking about it, but I think it's time that we just clear the air about it and move forward."

I swallowed hard, my Adam's apple pushing tightly in my throat. So that was how we were going to approach this thing with the other guy—like it wasn't a big deal?

"Well, I've been waiting to talk to you about it but haven't found the right time." I worked my jaw back and forth, waiting for her to respond.

"It's funny because I've been waiting to talk to you about it, but every time I do, you seem to change the topic or find some way to distract me, so we can't."

My brow wrinkled in confusion.

"Are you messing with me right now?" I asked.

"Messing with you? Why would I be messing with you? If anyone has been messing with anyone, it's been *you* messing with *me*."

I leaned against the wall and ran a hand down my face.

"What in the world are you talking about, Elena? We've hardly seen each other in—I don't even know how long now. Since the charger incident at your apartment? How could I possibly be messing with you?"

She tilted her head back and laughed. Not just a sarcastic laugh, but a manic laugh that started to worry me that she really was about to lose it.

"I don't know why I expected anything different," she muttered, shaking her head. "Fits in with everything else you've been doing lately."

"That *I've* been doing? You're the one who's been seeing someone else, Elena! And you didn't even bother to talk to me about it. Maybe all of the sex you think we've been having was really you with this other guy!" My voice boomed through the room, causing her to flinch in response.

"What the hell are you talking about? I haven't been seeing anyone but you."

I arched a brow and stared at her, unable to believe that she was sitting right in front of me, lying to me.

"I saw you, Elena," I said firmly through gritted teeth.

"When?"

"Last week. You seemed mad at me after the charger

incident at your house and wouldn't talk to me through text. I decided to bring you flowers to apologize for whatever I had done wrong, and as I was getting in the elevator, I saw you leaving with another guy."

Her face went blank as she stared at me.

"I haven't been with another guy, Trevor. And you know that."

I shook my head, trying to force some of the frustration out.

"Are you calling me a liar?" I asked. "Because I know what I saw, Elena."

"I don't know what you are," she said sternly as she stood up and took a few steps away from me. "But I know that this isn't the only weird thing that you've been doing lately, and I'm over these games."

"What else have I done?" I questioned, throwing my hands up in the air.

"What haven't you done?" she scoffed. "It's like you're determined to make me look crazy. Like you're purposely doing things to make me think that I'm losing my mind. You're the one forcing me into these breakdowns that I keep having, and I don't know why. What's in it for you, Trevor? Do you need to be the hero again and save the day? Does your ego need that much boosting that you would risk my sanity to get it?"

I pushed off of the wall and took a step toward her before I saw the panic flash through her eyes. I stopped and pointed at her.

"You know that I would *never* do anything like that. Why in the world would you ever say that?"

"Because you're driving me crazy, Trevor. *Literally crazy*! You text me when we're standing right next to each other. You act like you have no idea what I'm talking about, even when we just talked about it the other day. And then the whole choking incident—that was too far, Trevor, and you knew it."

The color drained from my face as I watched her start to lose it in front of me. Was this the breakdown that Max was worried she would have?

"What choking incident?" I asked, worried about what she was going to say. Was she making this shit up, or did she really believe it had happened?

She put her hand on her hip and stared at me with one brow arched.

"You know what I'm talking about."

"I can guarantee you that I don't."

She rolled her eyes and looked around the room as if she was searching for the answer. Finally, she focused on me again and looked me in the eye with a look of satisfaction on her face.

"Alright, then I'll show you. I have it on video."

Things were unraveling faster than I could try to hold them together.

"You have what on video?"

"Us having sex on Friday night and you choking me until right before I came."

I felt a chill run down my spine as my head was

overwhelmed with questions that I needed to ask but didn't know where to start.

"Let's go," I said, stepping aside so she could leave the room.

"Where?" she asked, her anger still radiating through the room.

"To see that video."

<u>Twenty</u>
Elena
3 Days Ago

The trip to my apartment was quick but felt like forever, given how tense things were between us. Neither of us bothered to talk, our anger too heavy to deal with at the moment. I tapped my fingers impatiently on the rail in the elevator, waiting for it to hurry up and get to my floor. Once the doors opened, I pushed off and walked out, not bothering to check where Trevor was behind me. Even though I could see his nostrils flare, I could still sense his overprotectiveness radiating off of him.

Once the door was open, I stepped inside and held it, so it didn't slam in his face. I looked around quickly, making sure nothing was out of place. No matter how hard I tried, I still couldn't shake the feeling that someone was constantly coming and going when I wasn't looking.

I heard the door shut behind me and glanced over my shoulder at Trevor. His eyes scanned the room, likely looking for where I had hidden the camera. It gave me a slight sense of satisfaction that he hadn't easily found it, which meant that whoever had been coming and going hadn't found it either. It also meant that he hadn't seen it the other night when we had sex—the night he was acting like never happened.

I was about to walk over to the bookshelf next to the TV when something on the counter caught my eye. I walked over and found an envelope sitting on top of the mail that I hadn't brought up myself. There wasn't anything written on it, just a plain-white, blank envelope.

"So, where is the camera?" Trevor asked, pulling me away from the mysterious object that felt more ominous the longer I stared at it.

I snapped my attention over to him and raised a brow. His impatience was making me feel more irritable than I was already feeling. I walked over to the bookshelf and pulled the textbook out that was hiding the camera. I had taken the time to cut the smallest hole in the bottom of the spine to make sure no one easily spotted it.

When I picked up the book, my heart dropped to the floor. I ran my fingers along the spine that was perfectly intact. I looked at the bookshelf again, double-checking to make sure I hadn't picked up the wrong book. I leaned in and slowly scanned each book, desperate to find the one with the camera.

"Is everything okay?" he asked as he walked over and stood beside me, looking at the book in my hand.

"No," I muttered. "Everything is not okay."

I felt like the world was spinning out of control around me. How had this happened? Had he spotted the camera and snuck into my apartment to get rid of it just to make me look crazy? Aside from Max, Trevor was the only other person who had a key to my apartment, which was given to both of them shortly after the phone charger incident. Before that, no one had access to my place, and I felt a lot safer back then.

"What did you do with it?" I asked, pushing the book back on the bookshelf and placing my hands on my hips.

"Excuse me?" He pulled his head back in shock.

"The camera, Trevor. What did you do with it?"

He stepped back and worked his jaw back and forth. His blue eyes darkened as he looked around helplessly.

"I have no idea what you're talking about, Elena."

My body was heating up with anger as I took a step toward him. I pushed a finger into his chest as I narrowed my eyes and stared at him.

"Stop it with these games. I don't know what you think this is—but I'm not interested in it. Just tell me where the camera is or leave."

Trevor's hand reached up and gently wrapped around my wrist as I continued to poke him. His eyes softened as he looked past me to the coffee table.

"That camera?" he asked, nodding to the box.

I pulled my hand away and spun around. There was no fucking way that this was happening. How did the camera get back in the box, and who the hell had put it on the coffee table? I slowly walked over and picked it up, examining the seal that was still intact on the outside of the box.

"You've got to be kidding me," I muttered as I continued to move the box around, looking for any spots where it might have been opened. The problem was that I clearly remembered taking it out of the package and then throwing everything in the trash once I had it set up. And how on earth did the book get fixed?

"Maybe you thought you had done it but hadn't gotten around to it yet?" Trevor offered, the anger in his voice now replaced with sympathy.

"No!" I shouted, sitting the box back down on the coffee table and turning to look at him. "Trevor, I'm not crazy. I had that camera set up. I watched the video after we had sex—I saw the whole thing."

His brow arched, and I couldn't tell if the smirk that threatened to cross his face was because he thought I was going out of my mind or because he was judging me for making a sex tape and then watching it.

"I didn't watch it because I was being a pervert," I sighed, pushing past the thought. "I watched it because I had seen a notification that there was movement, and I wanted to see what it had picked up."

My mind was going a mile a minute as everything started to fall into place. If the camera was up and had caught Trevor and me having sex, why hadn't I got the notification when someone was in my apartment? Come to think of it– I hadn't gotten any notifications since the sex incident.

I pulled out my phone and unlocked the screen before flipping through to find the app for the camera. I chewed my lip anxiously as I flipped between the two main screens, knowing that I had put it on the first page, right next to my social media icons. I went to my settings and scrolled through the list of apps, my stomach knotting when it wasn't there anymore.

I sat on the edge of the couch and went to the app store, typing in the name of the program. It pulled up the app, and a few minutes later, it was downloading again. Once it was complete, I entered my log-in information and pressed enter. I glanced up at Trevor, knowing that if I couldn't prove that I had the camera set up when we had sex, then he would think he won whatever this was between us.

I looked down at my phone, frowning when it popped up with an error message. I entered my information again and waited for another error message. I tried to reset my password and let out a grunt of frustration when the new message confirmed there was no account on file with that email address.

I sat my phone down on the couch next to me and leaned back, shaking my head in irritation.

"It's okay, we'll figure this out," Trevor said gently as he sat down on the other end of the couch.

I could feel my anxiety building again and knew that I needed to get a handle on this before I felt like it was out of my control.

"I think that you should go," I said sternly with my arms folded across my chest. I didn't bother to look at him, knowing that if I did, I might get lost in the eyes that used to make me feel comfortable and safe.

I watched as his shoulders rose and fell in defeat.

"Elena," he begged. "Please, let's talk about this."

I got up and walked to the door, holding it open for him.

"There's nothing to talk about. I need space, and I need you to leave. I'm not the girl who needs saving anymore, Trevor, so you're going to have to find her somewhere else."

A few seconds passed before he pushed his hands into his thighs and stood up. He shook his head as he walked past me and slipped out the door without saying another word. Once he was gone, I locked and slid down it.

Something was going on, and it was up to me to figure out what it was.

Twenty-One
Trevor
3 Days Ago

"Again, I'm sorry for missing that," I apologized to Roman as we looked over the spreadsheets together.

I stood up and clapped him on the shoulder before I headed back over to my desk. It was a little after three in the afternoon, but it felt like it had been days with how long this day had dragged on after I left Elena's apartment.

I wanted to text her and see how she was doing, but I knew she would reach out to me when she was ready. Unfortunately, I didn't know when that would be. It could be an hour from now. A few weeks. Months. Hell, it could be a year with Elena depending on how mad she was.

Deciding to get caught up on work, I made a fresh pot of coffee and planted my ass in my chair, ignoring anything and everything so I could focus. By six, Roman was packing up to leave for the night when Max strolled in.

"Hey, wanna go grab a beer?" he asked as he leaned against the doorway.

"Can't," I mumbled as I continued to stare at the spreadsheet on my computer. "Another time."

"What's with him?" Max asked Roman as if I wasn't still in the room.

"Don't know. He's been that way all day," Roman answered.

"Did something happen with Elena?" Max asked.

I tried to ignore the question and pretended to be working when I felt their heavy gazes burning holes into my head. I blew out a loud, annoyed breath and pushed the keyboard away from me as I leaned back against my chair.

"She wants space, so I'm giving it to her." I folded my hands across my stomach as I raised my brow at them.

Roman set his stuff down on his desk, no longer in a hurry to go anywhere.

"What does that mean?" Max asked, walking closer to my desk. "What happened?"

"Honestly?" I questioned, not sure that he wanted to hear this any more than I wanted to say it. He nodded, and I let my shoulders fall with the breath that I let out. "I think she's having that mental breakdown that we've all been worried about."

"Is she okay?" Roman asked with genuine concern in his voice.

"I don't know," I admitted. "Things were fine yesterday, then she had a panic attack in the middle of the night."

"Nightmare?" Max inquired.

I pursed my lips and then rubbed them together.

"Yeah, worse than any of the other ones I've seen her have before. I couldn't get her to wake up, and when she finally did, she was gasping for air."

"Was it about Adam?"

I nodded and lowered my eyes.

"Panic attacks are hard," Roman said softly. "Try to give her some time to work through it. It may seem like it's easy to move past it once it's over but trust me when I say that the aftereffects of one can stay with you longer than you'd think."

"That's the thing– it's not just the panic attack. Everything just spiraled out of control after that."

"Like what?" Max asked, sitting in the empty chair in the corner of the room.

 "She started accusing me of random things—things that didn't make any sense. She claimed that we had slept together recently, and I thought maybe she was mistaking it for the other guy—so I asked her about him. She got really angry and defensive, claiming that I had tried to choke her during an orgasm," I swallowed hard and looked away from Max as I said it, "and that she had video to prove it."

"She recorded you guys having sex?" Roman asked, his brows shooting up on his forehead.

"No," I shook my head. "At least I don't think she meant to on purpose."

I took a deep breath and backtracked what I was trying to say.

"She claimed that she had the cameras already up, and they caught us having sex. She was going to prove to me that this had happened, but when we got to her apartment so she could show me, the camera wasn't there."

"Like someone took it?" Max questioned.

I leaned forward in my chair and rested my elbows on my desk, rolling my head around my neck a few times to relieve some of the tension that was quickly building.

"No one took it because she never installed it. The camera was still sealed in the box, sitting on her coffee table."

"Did she remember leaving it there once she saw it?" There was a hope in Max's voice that I felt bad for ruining when I said no.

"She got really angry with me and told me to leave. I don't remember her exact words, but she keeps telling me that she's not some girl that needs to be saved. The scary thing is that she's convinced that I'm doing these things to her to make her look crazy so I can turn around and save her. Some sort of ego boost or something, according to her."

"Are you?" Max asked, his jaw tight as he held his hands together in front of him.

I pushed a hand through my hair then glared at him.

"Are you seriously fucking asking me that right now?" I bit out.

"It's a fair question," he replied sternly. "Something is happening, and a lot of it seems to fall back on you."

"What's happening is your sister's life is falling apart right in front of us, and instead of trying to help her, you're standing there pointing fingers as if I would ever do a damn thing to hurt her. The fact that you don't know me better than that says a lot about our friendship."

"I'm her big brother and a detective—it's my job to look at every possibility—"

"Then get the hell out of my office and go do your job."

I met his glare as the tension thickened in the room between us. Max muttered something under his breath before he stood up and walked out.

Roman gave me a nod before picking up his stuff and following behind him, leaving me alone to my misery and silence.

Twenty-Two

Elena

2 Days Ago

I sat nervously outside Natalie's office, waiting for her to finish with her client. I had gotten here early, determined to be focused when I saw her instead of the chaos that I felt bubbling around inside of me.

It was a week until Christmas, and I still hadn't finished any of my shopping. Who could when their whole world felt like it had been turned upside down?

Between the fight with Trevor yesterday and the moldy bologna that was waiting for me in the fridge when I got home from work, I couldn't concentrate on anything other than figuring out what was going on. I had accused Trevor of doing stuff to mess with me so he could look like the hero and save the day, but now I wasn't so sure that I was that far off from the truth.

Out of everything in my fridge that could have been placed in the middle of the empty shelf, waiting for me to find it, was moldy bologna sitting on a plate. Very few people knew that Adam had forced me to eat it when he was punishing me while I was being held against my will. The only people I had shared that information with were Trevor, Max, and Hannah.

Call me crazy—oh wait, he already did—but out of the three of them, he was starting to look more like the culprit after all.

Ten minutes later, I sat against the wall and watched as a woman walked out of Natalie's office, blotting her eyes with a tissue as she headed toward the door. I forced myself to relax as Abby sat at her desk; her eyes narrowed at the computer screen as she reached her hand out to answer the phone that was ringing beside her.

"Yes," she said quietly, glancing up to look at me before looking away. "Okay. Yes. Will do."

I felt my heart sink to my stomach when she turned and looked at me, folding her hands in front of her on her desk.

"I'm sorry, Elena, Natalie will have to reschedule. She's had something come up."

I swallowed hard, pushing my emotions to the back of my throat as my blood pressure started to rise.

"Did she say what it was?" I asked, my voice hoarse and scratchy.

"Unfortunately, that's not information that I can discuss. However, if you'd like, I can see what she has available next week?"

"Next week," I repeated numbly. There was no way that I could go that long without talking to her.

She nodded and tried to smile sympathetically.

"Don't bother," I mumbled under my breath before grabbing my purse from the chair beside me and getting up.

"Elena..." she called out as I stormed out of the office,

letting the door slam behind me.

My heart was racing as I rushed down the stairs, not bothering to wait for the elevator. It felt like the walls were closing in around me, the air thick as I tried to take in a breath.

Just a few more steps, that's all you have to go before you're outside and can take a deep breath.

I pushed my legs to move faster, nearly tripping on the last few steps, forcing me out into the lobby with a force that drew the attention of the few people who were in there.

I tucked my chin to my chest and hurried out, avoiding the curious glances of the onlookers around me. Once outside, I took a step out of the way and leaned against the wall, sucking in as much air as I could while my legs trembled beneath me.

My whole body was on high alert, ready to run again if needed. It wasn't unusual for me to go into this mode when my anxiety spiraled out of control, but for once, the tingle that traveled up my spine told me that I had a reason to run.

I looked around, surveilling the area as I searched for any possible threats. It was a silly thing to do given that this was New York City, and even the rapists and murderers blended in easily with the tourists and business people rushing to wherever they needed to go.

I pushed off the wall and turned to head to the subway when I hit a solid wall of muscle. Strong arms wrapped around me, holding me steady as I slowly looked up, wondering who I had just barreled into.

Roman looked down at me with concern etched on his face.

His brows pulled down, making his brown eyes look darker

in the shade of the skyscraper beside us. I tried to steady my breathing but couldn't.

"Are you okay?" he asked, his hands still holding me upright as my legs threatened to give out on me at that moment.

"Yeah, I'm fine," I replied, knowing that I was lying through my teeth. Whether he knew it or not, that was another question. I had met Roman a handful of times with Trevor, but this was the first time we had ever talked by ourselves.

He didn't say anything, just continued to stare at me as his eyes searched for whatever he was looking for.

"I um, better get going." I tucked a strand of hair behind my ear and stepped back. I avoided eye contact for fear of what he must be thinking about me right now.

Had Trevor been talking to him about me? Did he know about all of the crazy things that had been happening? Even worse—did he think that I was crazy? I definitely wasn't making a good impression at the moment as I jittered around more anxious than a drug addict trying to pass a drug test in front of a cop.

When he continued to stare in silence, I pulled my lips into a thin line, trying to force a smile to appear before I stepped to the side to walk away.

I got half of a step past him when I felt him grab my arm and stop me.

"Are you sure you're fine?" he asked, his voice tenser than before.

"Yeah," I nodded as enthusiastically as I could. "Just late for work."

It was as if I couldn't stop lying. They were flying out of my mouth quicker than I could stop them. I had the day off and planned to go home and catch up on sleep if my mind would let me.

I gently pulled out of his grip and gave him a tight smile before shoving my hands in my pockets and walking away. Once I was a few blocks past him, I let out the rugged breath that I had been holding and made my way to the subway. While I had been expecting something creepy to happen on my way home, I was pleasantly surprised by the noneventful trip back.

Maybe I was going to be able to get that sleep after all.

I got off the elevator and walked down the hall that led to my apartment, wondering who the guy in the leather jacket on the other side was. He didn't look familiar, but he had his head down, looking at his phone as I approached.

Since he didn't seem at all aware that I was there, I slid past him, unlocked the door, and slipped inside before closing it quickly behind me. I flipped the locks into place and tossed my purse on the counter as I kicked my shoes off and toed them over to the corner.

I headed to the bathroom, allowing my eyes to close for a brief moment as a yawn forced its way through my overly exhausted body. When I opened them, I gasped and clutched my hand to my chest as I jumped back a step.

"Max!" I yelled, still holding my chest as if I was afraid my heart would leap right out of my body. "What the hell are you doing here?!"

His fingers moved swiftly across his phone before he locked it and tucked it into the pocket of his jeans. He leaned casually against the door as if he hadn't just scared the soul out of my body. I wasn't sure if this was what people meant by an out-of-body experience, but it sure as hell felt like one to me.

I raised an eyebrow while I waited for him to answer me.

"I came to check on you."

His voice was even– nothing in his tone to give me any more information than that.

"You could have called," I replied sternly.

"I did," he said, nodding to my phone sticking out of the jacket of my hoodie. "You didn't answer."

I pulled my phone out and found two missed calls from him.

"So that automatically means that you just show up and let yourself into my apartment?"

"I don't play around when it comes to your safety."

I rolled my eyes and snorted.

"How long are you going to hold that against me?" he asked, folding his arms tighter across his chest.

"What?"

"Not saving you in time with Adam."

My heart leaped into my throat, proving again that it had no idea where in my body it was really supposed to be.

This wasn't something that we had talked about before. In fact, aside from Natalie, I hadn't talked to anyone about the feelings that I harbored against Max when it came to my kidnapping. It wasn't like it was his fault, yet I had this anger that lingered around every time I thought about how I had him on the phone, and yet he still couldn't find me. He was always my superhero when I was growing up, but I learned the hard way that his powers only worked with make-belief play.

"I don't know what you're talking about," I said as another lie spewed out of my mouth.

I turned around and walked over to the couch as he followed me. Pretending that I wasn't bothered by the conversation, I reached for the remote and turned on the TV.

"Stop with the bullshit, Elena," he snapped, plopping down in the chair across from me. "We can keep pretending that you don't hate me for what happened, or we can talk about it and work through it."

"There's nothing to talk about," I replied with my eyes still laser-focused on the TV.

"Yes, there is," he pushed.

I could feel the tension building between us from the words we refused to speak.

"You can easily see that I'm safe," I said, changing the subject while still avoiding eye contact.

"You don't have to stay. I'm sure Hannah needs you at home."

"You're as stubborn as Ma," he grumbled as he leaned back and worked his jaw.

My eyes darted over to his, the anger radiating off of me.

"What did you just say?"

He leaned forward and rested his arms on his knees.

"I said that you're as stubborn as Ma," he repeated.

"Wow," I blew out, shaking my head in disbelief. "I can't believe that you went there."

"Well, someone had to tell you the truth."

I narrowed my eyes and gave him the silent treatment.

After a few minutes, he blew out an irritated breath and stood up.

"Alright, fine. If you don't want to talk, I won't make you. But someday, you're going to have to face the demons that haunt you, Elena. And that means talking to me about the anger and resentment you have for me over Adam."

I bit the inside of my cheek to try to force the tears from stinging my eyes.

"I would have come for you right then and there, Leni. If I would have known where you were, I would have come for you. There wasn't a damn thing in the world that could have kept me from getting there. We did *everything* that we could to find you. Every damn thing."

His shoulders rose and fell as he turned to walk away. He stopped in his tracks and looked down at the coffee table, spotting the picture sitting on top of it.

Something about the way his fingers trembled as he reached down to pick it up sent a chill through me. He held it up to his face and covered his mouth with his other hand. Max had always been the strong, rugged brother who didn't show his emotions often, so his reaction to the photo caught me completely off guard.

"Where did you get this?" he asked as he kept staring at it.

I paused for a moment, not sure of what to say. *It was left for me in my apartment by whoever keeps sneaking in to fuck with me?*

When I still hadn't answered a few minutes later, he turned around to face me and looked directly at me when he asked, "Where did you get this picture, Elena?"

There was a warning in his tone.

"It was left in my apartment."

"By who?"

"I don't know?" I shrugged, telling the truth for once today.

He went back to staring at the picture, ignoring everything around him. His phone started ringing, but he didn't make any effort to pull it out of his pocket and answer it.

"Who is she?" I asked, leaning forward on the couch as I waited nervously for the answer.

"Natasha." Her name rolled off of his lips in a whisper that I could barely hear.

I waited for him to go on, having never heard of her before now. It was evident that she was important to him, or he wouldn't have had that reaction to her photo.

His phone started ringing again, this time pulling him out of his trance enough for him to check it but not answer it.

"Who is Natasha?"

He sat down, sitting the photo on his knee as if he was afraid to lose it.

"She was Trevor's sister."

"Was?" I questioned, feeling a chill wrap around me.

"She died ten years ago."

My stomach sank with sadness as I leaned back against the couch.

"I didn't know that he had a sibling," I admitted, instantly feeling bad that I hadn't known this about him. We had known each other for years and had been dating for six months—you would think that I would know if he had any siblings—dead or alive.

"He had two," he said sadly. "Triplets. One girl and two boys."

My head was spinning as I tried to process this information. Why had he never mentioned anything about his family before? I knew that his dad left when he was a kid and that his mom was always a single mother, never bothering to remarry, but you would think that he would talk about his siblings, especially being a triplet.

"Where's his brother?"

I knew better than to ask the questions that I didn't really want the answers to, but deep inside, I needed to know. The man that I thought I knew better than anyone was quickly turning into someone that I didn't know at all.

Max's face fell even more when he closed his eyes and shook his head.

"Hunter died a few years ago."

"What?" I whispered, covering my mouth in shock.

How could there be so much death and sadness in one family?

"Car accident."

"What happened to his sister?" I asked quietly, ashamed that my curiosity was getting the best of me.

"She killed herself." He pulled in a heavy breath and slowly let it out. "She used to have terrible panic attacks that Trevor would try to help her with. In the end, it was just too much for her, and she couldn't take it anymore. She was convinced that someone was stalking her and trying to make her look crazy."

He stopped talking and looked up at me as if he knew that his words had triggered my own feelings of being crazy lately. But if anything, everything suddenly made sense. I closed my eyes and pinched the bridge of my nose.

"That's what he was referring to," I said as the puzzle all finally clicked into place.

"What who was referring to?" Max asked, confused.

"Trevor," I sighed. "I had a panic attack while I was at his apartment the other night. I told him that I was afraid of becoming someone I didn't know—someone who couldn't be saved. He told me that he's seen people that break and that I wasn't one of them."

"Her death was hard for everyone, but Trevor took it the hardest. He had it ingrained in his mind that he had to be the one to save her. When he couldn't, he took that to heart and never forgave himself for it."

My heart broke for Trevor as I felt the weight of the grief that he continued to carry around with him.

Max's phone rang again, interrupting our conversation. He pulled it out and sighed before looking up at me.

"It's Hannah; she's still sick. I need to go by and check on her."

"Okay," I nodded as I got up and walked with him to the door.

He shoved his phone back into his pocket and grabbed his coat that had been hanging on the coat rack.

"Did Trevor ever figure out what was happening to her?" I blurted out before I could think it through.

Max furrowed his brow as he shrugged into his coat.

"What do you mean?"

"You said that she thought someone was stalking her and trying to make her look crazy. Did Trevor ever figure out who was doing it?"

His face fell as he looked down at the floor before raising his eyes to meet mine.

"She was convinced that it was him."

Twenty-Three

Trevor

2 Days Ago

"Cheers to Thirsty Thursday!" The blond girl with fake boobs pushed up to her chin yelled as she slammed her shot glass into the girl beside her, laughing hysterically as the alcohol sloshed all over them.

I rolled my eyes and lifted my beer to my lips, trying to tune them and their obnoxious behavior out. It had already been a long day, and I was ready to call it quits. Had Max not sent me a text, asking me to meet up, I would have already been home and probably in bed. I glanced down at my watch, grimacing at the thought given that it was barely after six-thirty.

Jon shook his head at the girls as he wiped down a glass with a towel before sitting it on the shelf behind the bar. A few minutes later, the front door opened and the light filtered in from outside, nearly blinding me in the dimly lit room. Max made his way over and gave Jon a quick nod before taking off his jacket and sitting down on the barstool across the table from me.

I took another sip, not bothering to say anything. It wasn't like we weren't going to talk about what had happened yesterday. I just wasn't ready to deal with it yet. I had a massive headache that had controlled most of my day, not to mention the stress of trying to get things ready for Christmas since it was right around the corner. Even though I wasn't huge on doing anything big for the holiday, I knew that it was important to my mom, and that was reason enough to make it a big deal for me.

Jon came over and dropped off Max's beer before walking over and tending to the drunk girls in the corner.

"Have they been here long?" Max asked with a nod in their direction as he lifted the bottle to his lips and took a drink.

"Long enough to be celebrating *Thirsty Thursday*," I muttered.

I could see the wheels turning in his head as he tried to shift from cop mode to friend mode.

"They're probably just burning off some steam from finals. You know that Jon wouldn't serve minors, and he's seen so many fake IDs that no one even bothers trying to use them here anymore," I commented, saving Max from the hassle of trying to solve a problem that we didn't need right now.

He shrugged as if he didn't care and took another drink before turning his attention back to me.

"How's Hannah?" I asked casually.

I hated the tension that lingered between us, covering us in a blanket of awkwardness that wasn't natural. If we had beef with each other, we'd always just deal with it and move on. But, now that it involved Elena, it felt like neither of us knew how to navigate the new territory.

"She's on the mend, finally keeping food down," he replied as he set his bottle down on the table in front of me. "Is that who you really wanted to ask about?" He gave me a pointed look as he read my mind.

I let my head hang, feeling the ache in my neck and shoulders from the stress that wouldn't leave no matter how hard I tried.

"How is she?" I finally asked, looking up at him.

He waited before answering, making me squirm with anticipation. There hadn't been a moment since I walked out of her apartment that I hadn't thought about her. The fact that she had asked for space from me had shattered whatever was left of my broken heart. It would be stupid to say that it had ever been whole when I had given it to her, to begin with.

"She's fine," he answered, his eyes wandering back over to the group of girls that were pouting and sticking their bottom lip out at Jon as he cut them off.

"That's all you're going to give me?" I asked with a sarcastic laugh tied in.

"If you want to know more, you should ask her yourself."

"She told me to give her space. She's made it real clear that she wants nothing to do with me right now."

"Maybe it's because you left a picture of a girl in her apartment and didn't bother to tell her who it was?"

I pulled my head back and furrowed my brow.

"What the hell are you talking about?"

He narrowed his eyes at me as his jaw tightened.

"You know what the hell I'm talking about. That was a dick move, Trevor."

"Are you kidding me right now?"

I caught Jon's eye as he walked past and nodded to my beer, asking for another. It was obvious that I was going to need more to get through whatever this was with Max.

He tilted his head to the side as he studied me.

"She was right about not needing to be saved– you know that, right?" he asked with a stern tone.

"You're not making any sense right now," I muttered, scrubbing a hand over the stubble that had popped up over my jaw the past few days.

"She's not Natasha, Trevor. So you can stop all of the bullshit. I know that it's coming up on the tenth anniversary since she died, but there's no reason to bring Elena into this. If you need to see a therapist and work through your unresolved grief, so be it. But leave my sister the fuck out of it. It's not fair to her, especially after everything she's already been through, and you of all people should know that."

He stood up and pulled out his wallet before tossing a twenty-dollar bill on the table.

"Seriously—what the fuck are you talking about?" I asked as my head spun.

"You left a picture of Natasha in her apartment. You've been obsessed about Elena needing help and trying to save her. I should have seen it before," he sighed as he ran a hand through his hair. "But now that I know what's going on, I'm here to put a stop to it. Leave my sister out of your bullshit. I won't tell you again."

He tapped his knuckles on the table, then turned around and left. Jon gave me a puzzled look as he set my beer down in front of me.

"Is he coming back?" he asked.

I shook my head and picked up my beer, not bothering to explain because that would mean that I had some sort of idea of what the fuck had just happened.

Twenty-Four

Elena

2 Days Ago

I woke up feeling more rested than I had in days, though my dreams were enough to make me not want to sleep again. Shortly after Max left, I laid down and willed myself to sleep. Finally, after however many hours, I fell asleep. I was in such a deep sleep that I hadn't heard my phone ring seven times or the notifications from the numerous voicemails that my mother had left me, checking on me and trying to confirm what my plans were for Christmas Eve.

It was the first year that I didn't live at home during the holidays, and she was struggling with trying to keep some of the traditions alive. It wasn't like she hadn't gone through this with my other sisters as they started leaving the house, but it felt like it was a lot different since I was the baby. A few of my sisters still lived there, so there was no reason that she couldn't keep the tradition alive with them, but that was a fight to have with her another day.

I rolled out of bed and set my phone down on the nightstand. Trevor hadn't called or texted me, which left me feeling a little disappointed, even though I had been the one to tell him that I wanted space. Of course, that didn't mean that I hadn't hoped that he would ignore me and still try to get a hold of me. I mean, come on, is fighting for the person that you love too much to ask for?

The clock on the wall confirmed that it was a little after eight and that I had slept the majority of the day away. It was great that I had caught up on the rest that I needed, but it also sucked because that meant that I would be up late tonight and had to get up early for work tomorrow.

I decided to take a shower before rummaging through the kitchen to find something to eat. My mind was still fuzzy as I tried to process everything Max had told me when he was here earlier. I walked absentmindedly to my dresser and grabbed clean underwear before pulling a hoodie and some yoga pants out of my closet.

The hot water was soothing, helping me relax as I tried to unwind from the past few weeks. I was confident that I would still be anxious until I talked to Natalie, but for some reason, talking to Max earlier had helped to calm me down. Maybe it was because I felt like I finally had some of the answers that I had been looking for with Trevor. Even as confusing as everything was, it felt like it was all starting to make sense.

I now understood why he was so good at helping me through my panic attacks but would never have guessed that it was because he used to do it for his sister. Knowing the guilt that he carried over her suicide made me realize that he was feeling desperate as he watched me struggle with my own anxiety. He must have been worried that I was going down the same path that she had, and the fear of history repeating itself would make anyone do something crazy. Even if that meant stalking your current girlfriend and making her look insane, just so you could swoop in and feel like you saved her.

I stayed under the hot water for a few more minutes before I reluctantly turned it off and grabbed the towel off of the hook beside the shower. I quickly wrapped it around me and pulled my hair into another one while I dried off. The heat seemed to be fluctuating in the apartment again, but it was likely due to the storm that was coming in. Unfortunately, it seemed like we weren't going to get any breaks with the weather before Christmas with bitter cold storms, one on top of another.

I pulled the curtain back and stepped out of the shower before looking around for the clothes I had brought in. The towel started slipping down my body, so I tucked the corner in tighter and bent down, spotting them on the floor under the toilet. They must have fallen off when I grabbed the towel.

I got dressed and hung the towel up on the hook by the door, and headed to the kitchen to find something to eat. It was a silly thing to do, given that I already knew that I didn't have anything decent to eat. I could always go over to my mom's house and raid her fridge, but it was getting late, and I didn't want to scare her if I showed up randomly, looking for food.

Closing the fridge, I gave up and grabbed my keys and phone so I could go grab something close by. As I walked into the hallway and locked the door, I spotted the same guy from this morning sitting outside the door across the hall from me. It seemed strange that he was still there, but it didn't bother me enough to ask him about it. It wasn't like he was hanging out around my door or trying to get into my apartment.

Ignoring the nagging feeling that I should be more worried about who was hanging around my apartment, I got in the elevator and pressed the button to go down to the lobby. The doors opened a few minutes later, and I headed down the street to the deli on the corner.

It was freezing outside, and I instantly regretted not bundling up in something warmer before I left. My hoodie was warm but not thick enough to shield me from the wind as it whipped past me. I pushed my way inside the store and let the door slam behind me.

The deli was quiet, with just a few people inside. I grabbed a sandwich from the refrigerated section then browsed the chip aisle for something to go with it. As I walked up to the front, I browsed the wine selection, wishing that I wasn't fighting with Trevor right now so he could buy me another bottle. It's not like it was a secret with Max, but he also wasn't likely to buy his underage sister alcohol. Trevor, on the other hand, didn't mind buying a bottle or two here and there that we would share when he came over.

I waited in line behind a mom and her two kids as they rang up their groceries and paid. It reminded me a lot of my childhood, going to run errands with my mom while my dad was busy working two jobs so she could stay home to take care of us.

Once it was my turn, I headed to the counter and laid my items down. The cashier mumbled something along the lines of hello as she started ringing me up. I glanced around and grabbed a few candy bars before sliding them over with my stuff at the last minute. She waited for me to swipe my card, then tucked my receipt in the paper bag before rolling it closed and handing it to me. I offered a smile before walking away, but it was missed as she focused on the next customer behind me.

The walk back to my apartment was painful as I fought against the weather. I was a few feet away from the door to the lobby when I saw a man in a dark hoodie walk out. Before they could turn around, I caught a glimpse of their face. My heart skipped a beat as I picked up my pace.

"Trevor?" I called out loud enough to notice him stop for a split second before pulling the hood over his head and walking off in the other direction.

I ran after him, pissed that he was acting as if he hadn't heard me call out his name. I dodged a few people who muttered curse words at me along the way, but by the time I got to where he had been, he was gone.

I got in the elevator and headed up to my apartment. When I got there, the man in the leather jacket was no longer there, and my apartment door was wide open.

Twenty-Five

Trevor

1 Day Ago

"So, what brings you in to see me today?" Natalie asked as she subtly tilted her head to the side and leaned back in her leather office chair.

I looked around the room, suddenly feeling like it was smaller than the last time when I was here with Elena. I hadn't planned on calling and begging for an appointment this morning, but I was thankful when they had a last-minute cancellation a few minutes before, and Natalie agreed to squeeze me in.

"I'm sorry, I don't really know how to start," I admitted, fidgeting in my seat across from her.

"Take your time," she said calmly, not bothering to turn her attention to the ding that sounded from her computer with a notification.

I rubbed my hands together and tried to get my heart to slow down.

"I'm sure you're wondering why I'm here without Elena," I laughed. "I doubt you ever expected to see *me* as a patient."

"I'm always open to new patients."

I blew out a shaky breath, wondering if it was a mistake to

come here.

"Does she talk about me?" I blurted out. I knew I didn't have to clarify who I was asking about. Hell, I knew that I shouldn't even ask in the first place, but part of me needed to know how much Elena had told her recently and whether Natalie was already judging me based on that.

"I'm not at liberty to discuss other patients."

I nodded, confirming that I knew that, yet it didn't stop me from pressing for more information.

"Has she seemed okay lately? I know you can't give me any details, but I just need to know if she's okay."

Natalie crossed her legs under the table and shifted in her seat as she continued to watch me.

"What makes you think that she's not okay?"

"I don't know..." I laughed. "Everything."

I knew that I sounded like I was losing my shit, and at that moment, I was.

"If you're concerned about her safety, then I suggest that you notify the proper authorities."

I continued to nod and folded my hands together in front of me as I stared at the floor. Why had I thought this would be a good idea?

"Why don't you tell me why you're really here, Trevor," she probed gently. "I can tell that something is bothering you. You wouldn't have called to schedule an appointment with me if not."

I forced myself to lean back in the chair, hoping that it

would keep me from jumping up and pacing the room.

She waited patiently for me to get my thoughts together.

"I think I'm losing my mind," I blurted out.

She reached forward and picked up her coffee mug, bringing it to her lips to take a sip before she set it back down.

"That must be a hard feeling to process and deal with."

I pulled my lips into a thin line and took a deep breath.

"Has anything happened recently that might be responsible for that feeling?"

"I'm sure you already know what's been happening from what Elena's been telling you."

"Why don't you tell me your side of it," she said, redirecting me.

I knew that no matter how hard I tried, she wasn't going to give me any insight into her sessions with Elena.

"Things have been different for a few weeks. Elena has seemed overly stressed, and as you know, we've all been worried that the anniversary of her kidnapping might be hard for her. She started acting weird, and we grew distant with each other for about a week or so—I can't remember how long. Anyway, she and I had dinner together the other night, and she mentioned some things that she insisted had happened between us, but I don't remember any of them. When I questioned her about it, she got really defensive and told me that she needed space."

"What kind of things?" Natalie asked.

I leaned my head back against the top of the chair and stared at the ceiling for a few minutes while I tried to remember everything she had accused me of.

"Some of them were random little things. Like me texting her when we were together. Or me following her on the subway when she was heading to her mom's house. But the one that got me the most was when she said that we had been intimate together and that I had tried to choke her."

I felt the color drain from my face as I swallowed down the bile that was starting to rise.

"I couldn't believe it when she told me about it, but she was so pissed off at me for not believing her that she insisted she could prove it because it was recorded on the camera that she had put up in her apartment. When we got there, the camera was still in the package, sitting on the coffee table. When I tried to talk to her about it, she freaked out and said that I was doing things to make her look crazy so I could be the hero and save her."

Natalie reached for her pen and jotted something down on a notepad before looking back at me.

"That is a lot to process, and I can understand the stress that you must be feeling. Have you talked to Elena since then?"

I shook my head and looked away.

"We both know Elena's past and why she would make a comment about needing to be saved. What I'm curious about is why *you* tensed when you said it. Your shoulders scrunched up, and you winced, which makes me feel like this might be part of the reason that you're feeling the way you are."

And there it was—the topic I had subconsciously been

hoping to avoid.

"Max went by her apartment yesterday and found a picture of my sister, Natasha. He didn't say how it got there, but he was pissed off about it."

"Did he say why he was upset?"

"He thinks that I'm doing things to Elena to make her feel crazy so I can save her."

She furrowed her brow and studied me for a moment.

"I'm not making the connection," she admitted.

"Max thinks that I'm trying to find a way to save Elena because I couldn't save Natasha. When we were growing up, she used to have terrible anxiety attacks that I would try to help her with. I do the same thing now for Elena."

"Why do you feel like you couldn't save Natasha?"

"She committed suicide. It was all my fault."

"I see," Natalie said quietly as she wrote more down on the notepad. "Why do you feel that it was your fault?"

"I used to have psychogenic blackouts when I was younger. I wouldn't remember anything that happened during them. Natasha started having her panic attacks around the same time and started to be afraid of me. Eventually, the blackouts stopped, and she and I got really close—she finally trusted me enough to let me help her with the anxiety attacks. Right before she died, her attacks started getting bad again—like really, really bad. I tried to help her, but she would freak out and yell at me not to come near her. No matter how hard I tried, she was convinced that I was trying to hurt her, not help her."

Natalie sat in silence for a few minutes while I blinked rapidly, trying to force the tears away before they could come out.

Finally, she spoke, her voice soft and gentle.

"When people take their own lives, it's never anyone else's fault. I understand that it feels like you failed her by not being able to save her."

My stomach churned as I sat up straight in the chair and looked her in the eye.

"What if it's happening again? What if I'm doing the same thing to Elena that my own sister accused me of?"

"What's that?"

"Tormenting her to the point of wanting to kill herself."

Natalie's eyes widened despite her attempt to keep the horror off of her face.

Twenty-Six

Elena

1 Day Ago

"What time is it?" I asked as I rolled over on the couch and glared at Max as his fingers flew furiously over the keyboard on his laptop.

"Early," he muttered without looking up at me. "Go back to sleep."

I flung the blanket off of me and swung my legs off the couch as I sat up.

"It's kinda hard to sleep when you're typing a mile a minute."

"I have work to catch up on," he said evenly as he stared at the screen.

Max had been at my apartment since I called him last night when I found the door open. It wasn't any surprise that he would rush right over, however, I hadn't expected him to pack up and move in. Or at least that's what it had felt like.

I got up and walked into the kitchen to start a pot of coffee when his phone rang.

"Romano," he answered, holding the phone between his ear and shoulder. "Okay, send me the video."

He pulled his phone away and set it on the edge of the chair beside him as he kept typing.

"What video?" I asked, not bothering to hide the fact that I had been eavesdropping.

"The one of your apartment. The site had crashed last night, so they weren't able to pull it until this morning."

The coffee pot was mid-air as I poured the water in when I stopped and stared at him.

"You have video on my apartment?"

"Yeah," he replied, still not focusing on me.

"Max!" I yelled angrily, forcing him to look over in my direction. "You put me under surveillance?"

"I needed to make sure you were safe." He closed his laptop and set it on the coffee table before getting up to join me in the kitchen.

"You should have told me."

"You would have told me not to do it."

I raised my eyebrows at him to confirm that he was correct with that assumption.

"Look, it's not a big deal. I have one camera set up outside to see who comes and goes."

"Is that the only one?" I questioned with my hand planted firmly on my hip.

He looked down and inhaled heavily.

"Max."

"There's one in your living room as well."

I picked up the towel that was hanging by the sink and

swatted him with it.

"Are you kidding me?! That is such a violation of my privacy! And I'm pretty sure it's illegal!"

"I was worried about you. I didn't know how else to make sure you were safe other than moving in with you, and Hannah told me that I couldn't do that."

"What if I walk around my apartment naked? Did you ever think about that?"

His face flushed an unflattering shade of red as embarrassment spread across it.

"I'm sorry," he said sheepishly. "I honestly never thought of you doing that until now, and it's not something that I ever want to think about again."

I narrowed my eyes at him and stepped closer, pushing my finger into his chest.

"What if Trevor and I were having sex in the living room, Max? I bet that's not something that you want to see either."

I paused for a moment and then smacked his arm.

"You're not even the one monitoring the video, are you?"

He shook his head.

"So who is the creep who has been watching me, Max?"

"He's a new guy. His name is Lucas."

I stepped away, needing distance from him as I tried to remember everything I had been doing in the living room the past few days. Had I done anything embarrassing?

Then I remembered the random stranger that had suddenly

been hanging out by my apartment.

"Is he tall and skinny, wears a leather jacket?" I asked through gritted teeth.

"So you saw him," he said, shaking his head in disbelief.

"He's been hanging out in the hallway directly across from my apartment."

He tilted his head back and closed his eyes.

"Fucking rookie."

"Well, maybe you shouldn't trust people you don't know to spy on your little sister and invade her privacy."

Max's computer dinged from the coffee table, and we both turned to look at it.

"That's the video," he commented before walking away to check it.

I followed and stood next to him so I could see over his shoulder. The video was short but showed a perfect picture of Trevor inside my apartment, coming from my bedroom with something tucked under his arm.

I leaned in to get a better view but couldn't tell what it was.

A few seconds later, another video popped up, showing the door from the hallway. We watched as Trevor walked out, not bothering to pull the door closed behind him. The guy who had been in the hallway wasn't there anymore. Trevor walked down the hallway and stood in front of the elevator while he waited for it. He turned to the side to check behind him, giving us the perfect view of what was in his hand.

I gasped and covered my mouth as I asked, "Is that my

blanket from Nonna?"

Max's shoulders tensed as he slammed the screen shut.

"I'm going to fucking kill him."

Twenty-Seven

Trevor

1 Day Ago

After I left Natalie's office, I hadn't bothered to go to work. Instead, I texted Roman and let him know that I wasn't feeling well and would catch up on stuff this weekend. I locked myself in my apartment, trying to force the terrible thoughts out of my head that had managed to manifest and fester after talking to Natalie.

I had replayed everything that Elena had told me over and over in my head, trying to put the missing pieces of the puzzle together. If what she was saying was true, that meant that she wasn't the one we needed to be worried about. I knew that this day might someday come, but I hadn't stopped to think about what it would mean when it happened.

After Natasha died, I had sworn to myself that if I started having the blackouts again, I would leave and walk away so I didn't hurt anyone and make them suffer the way she did. The thought of no longer having Elena in my life was enough to burn a hole in my heart and make me wish that it had been me all those years ago instead of Natasha.

I was lying on the couch, trying to shut out the world, when I heard a knock on my door. I growled under my breath and willed whoever it was to go away. I wasn't in the mood to talk to anyone right now. Well, other than Elena. I would give anything to talk to her and fix things between us. The only problem was that I wasn't sure whether things were still fixable. I couldn't ask her to love me when I knew the power that I had to hurt her.

I closed my eyes and tried to focus on my breathing when I heard another knock. I muttered a curse word under my breath as I got up to answer the door. I flung it open, surprised to see Roman standing on the other side with a drink tray holding two cups of coffee and a brown paper bag from my favorite bagel shop.

The look on his face was one that I had seen a handful of times, and I knew that no matter what I said, he wasn't going to leave. I opened the door further and stepped to the side to let him in before closing it behind us.

"You didn't have to come by," I said grumpily as I resumed my spot on the couch. Roman quirked a brow at me as if that was the stupidest thing he had ever heard and set everything on the counter while he took his jacket off. A few minutes later, he was shoving a cup of coffee at me as he tossed the bag of bagels on the coffee table.

"Thank you," I smiled as I took the cup, forcing it to last longer than a few seconds. When had my life become so hard that it was nearly impossible to smile?

Roman sat down and looked around as he sipped his coffee.

"Eat your bagel," he instructed with a nod toward the bag.

"You're so demanding," I mumbled, reaching forward to pick it up.

"You get grumpy when you're hungry, and given that we're

going to have a talk that you don't want to have, I don't need you any pissier than you already are. So eat."

I rolled my eyes and took a bite, closing them for a brief second as the savory seasonings of the Everything bagel rolled over my tongue. It wasn't often that I ate a lot of carbs, but Everything bagels were my weakness.

Roman reached in and grabbed the other bagel. We ate in silence and finished our coffee before I got up to clean the mess. It wasn't that it bothered me to leave it sitting there on the coffee table; I just knew that I wasn't going to want to hear whatever Roman had come all the way over here to tell me.

Was he coming to scold me about my outburst the other day? Maybe it was to lecture me about being a better boyfriend to Elena? Or it could be about how shitty of a friend I've been to Max. The options were endless, and honestly, I already knew they were all true. It was hard to believe how much my life felt like it had unraveled in just a few weeks. It was like I blinked, and then everything was different, and I hated that.

I washed my hands, further stalling, then made my way back to the couch when there was nothing else that I could do to delay talking with him. I was a grown man, so I could always just tell him to fuck off and kick him out of my apartment, but I respected Roman too much to do that. He was a great friend, and if he was here, it meant that this was important to him. *I* was important to him.

I sat down and tried to force my rigid body to relax against the soft cushion while he looked calm and overly collected in his button-down shirt and dark denim jeans. The guys at the gym always joked that we were brothers from another mother because we were similar in so many ways—other than how we looked. Roman was tall, dark, and handsome and always dressed to impress. On the other hand, I was lighter-skinned, average height, decent looking, and usually lived in joggers and a t-shirt when I was at work—which lately was always.

He leaned into the side of the chair and studied me.

"I don't know what's going on with you," he admitted with a shake of his head, "but I'm worried about you."

I scrubbed a hand down my face and sighed.

"There's nothing to worry about," I lied.

"Bullshit."

I crossed my ankle over my knee and played with my shoelace to avoid meeting his eyes.

"It's nothing."

Roman leaned forward and rested his elbows on his knees.

"You're a terrible liar."

"What do you want me to say? That I fucked everything up? That I'm a shitty boyfriend and an even more terrible best friend? I'm well aware of how much I've screwed things up, and I'm going to fix them. Don't worry."

"Fix them how?"

"The only way that I can." I looked up and met his eyes. "By leaving."

Roman tilted his head back and let out a loud laugh which

irritated me more than it should. He thought this was funny? My life was literally crumbling around me, and he found it comical.

"Leaving," he repeated. "Because running away from your problems is really going to solve them?"

"With all due respect, you don't know shit about my problems. Trust me—leaving is the only way that I can fix this. It'll be better for everyone once I'm gone."

"Better for who? The girl who loves you and will be devasted when you ghost her? The best friend who has been there for you through some of life's hardest moments? Your mom, who has lost *every single person* she's ever loved? Me—your business partner who needs you to get your head out of your ass so we don't go under before the new year can even start?"

I raised a brow at him and pulled my mouth into a thin line.

"Business partner? When did that happen?"

"Today." He sighed dramatically and then added, "After I get done saving you from your damn self. You'll see how much you need me and offer me the position because you'll realize that you can't do this without me anymore."

I nodded and tried to keep the grin off of my face as he pretended to flick a piece of lint off his shoulder—*cocky bastard.*

"As much as I appreciate your concern, you have no idea what's going on. I'm not the man that everyone thinks I am. Elena might love me now, but she won't when she finds out who I really am. When she learns about the monster that lives inside of me, waiting to prey on someone as perfect as she is, she'll run and never look back if she's smart."

"How so?"

Flashbacks of Natasha trembling on her bed, crouched in the corner with a blanket tucked under her chin as she tried to protect herself with it flooded my brain. There was no other way out of this than to just admit the truth—I was a monster and didn't deserve to be loved by the people who had once trusted me.

"There are things about my past—things that I'm not proud of. It's part of who I am, and I can't change it, even if I wanted to. I don't want to hurt Elena, but that doesn't mean that I won't."

"We all have a past, Trevor. If anyone understands living with things that they regret, it's me. I've done things that no one should ever know about because it will haunt them and push them to the brink of insanity. If you're a monster, then that makes me one too."

"It's different, Roman. You did those things for our country, to protect us from people who wanted to harm us. You aren't a monster for that. You're a hero."

Roman chuckled and ran his thumb down the thin goatee that covered his face before locking eyes with me.

"I've taken people's lives from a mile away. They never saw it coming as the bullet ripped through their body, claiming their last breath. I hid in the darkness, lurking in the shadows as I planned my next kill. I waited for the perfect moment to end their life—not to spare them from the pain of death but to make sure that they felt *every agonizing moment* of it. I didn't afford them the comfort of quick and easy—I made it brutal and tortured them until the very last moment as I tried to make them feel an ounce of the pain they inflicted on their victims. Now tell me how you're a bigger monster than me."

The anger in his voice echoed off of the walls as his fists turned white from clenching them so tightly. He didn't talk much about his time as a sniper, and I knew that it was because it wasn't something that he enjoyed reliving. Some guys talked about their glory days or would brag about their sharpshooter skills, but not Roman. Those memories were enough to drive anyone to the depths of darkness that you could never come back from.

"My sister took her own life because she was being tortured and tormented by me. I have no memories of it because I used to have these blackouts. The only thing that I knew was what she or my brother would tell me had happened. My mother was a single mom who was working three jobs to try to support us, so she couldn't stop to get me the help that I needed, even if she wanted to. They stopped for a while, and I started to get close to Natasha. For a short time, she trusted me again. Then out of the blue, she started fearing me again. The next thing I knew, she put a bullet through her head and left a note that she would finally be free from me."

I pinched the bridge of my nose and forced my eyes closed as I tried to push the tears away. Reliving the guilt and grief of my childhood was too hard to deal with, which was why I constantly kept it locked up and buried as far below the surface as I could.

"Does Max know about your sister?" Roman asked, his voice lacking any of the judgment I had expected.

"Yeah, he was there when I found her. He tried to do CPR, but it was too late. She was already gone."

"So he knows about what happened with her and hasn't considered you a monster all these years—hell, he's even okay with you dating his sister. Why would you suddenly be a monster now if you weren't before? What's changed?"

That was the question that had been haunting me all day.

"I worry that I'm blacking out again and that Elena's been telling the truth about all of the things that she said I was doing. The things that I don't remember."

He inhaled heavily, his shoulders lifting then falling as he processed what I was really saying.

"I didn't mean to hurt my sister, Roman. I would have given anything to save her, and yet I'm the reason that she's dead. There's no way that I could live with myself if anything happened to Elena. She's been through enough already."

"I saw her yesterday," he blurted out randomly. "Elena," he clarified a few seconds later when the look on my face showed how confused I was.

"Where?"

"A couple of blocks away from work. I was heading there, and she came flying out of this building, looking frightened as she struggled to catch her breath. I asked if she was okay, and she said yes, but I could see on her face that she wasn't."

My heart ached, knowing exactly what he had seen. I hated that I hadn't talked to her lately and didn't know where she was coming from or why she was so upset. I wanted to pick up my phone and call her, just to make sure that she was okay, but I knew that I couldn't do that anymore. Those days were over.

"I was going to let her go on her way, then decided at the last minute to follow her, just to make sure she was really alright."

"Did she see you?" I asked, instantly pulled into the story.

He shook his head and frowned. "I live in the shadows, remember?"

I rolled my eyes and then nodded for him to continue.

"I followed her to her apartment and found something interesting."

He sat there with a smug smile, killing me with anticipation.

"What did you find?"

While part of me hoped that he would say that he had seen me there, another part of me cringed at the thought that this was all really happening. My mind still hadn't wrapped around everything at this point, and I found myself still clinging to the tiniest ounce of hope that there was another explanation for everything so I didn't have to say goodbye to Elena.

"Aside from the rookie cop posted up outside of her apartment and the cameras in the hallway, someone was in her apartment."

My heart leaped out of my chest as I leaned forward to hang onto every word. *Was it me? Please don't let me have hurt her.*

"Turns out that Max was in her apartment while she was gone. She hadn't even noticed the guy outside—I mean, if she did, she didn't seem to put together that he was assigned to watch her. I could hear her yelling at Max for scaring her, but she still didn't realize that she was being watched."

I let out the breath that I had been holding and tried to calm down.

"Did she know about the cameras outside?"

"No. I don't think so. Max didn't tell her about the cop either. He kept everything from her. She was more concerned with finding out about Natasha."

I pulled my head back in surprise and frowned.

"How did Natasha come up?"

"When Max was leaving, he found a picture of her and asked her where she got it. She said that someone left it for her and then asked him who it was. He told her the story but didn't go into too many details."

I swallowed hard, trying to push past the lump in my throat. She knew. She knew that I was a monster and what I had done. If I hadn't lost her before, I definitely would lose her now.

"What did she say?" I asked nervously. I wanted to ask *how* she got the picture of Natasha, but I was pretty sure that I already knew the answer when I looked over at the empty frame sitting on top of the mantel with the other frames. *How had I not noticed that it was missing?*

"That she finally understood what you meant about her not being the broken girl that couldn't be saved."

A single tear slid down my cheek as quickly as my thumb brushed it away.

"She wasn't afraid of you, Trevor. She *empathized* with you."

"Why are you telling me this?"

"Because you deserve to know the truth. You deserve so much more than you allow yourself to have. We all make mistakes, but that doesn't mean that we have to spend the rest of our lives paying for them."

I leaned forward and covered my face with my hands as the tears burned my skin with the grief they carried with them.

"I don't know what's happening with you and Elena," he continued as I tried to pull myself together. "But I do know that she's not afraid of you. Pissed off at you–probably–but not scared. I also know that Max cares about you, and even if he is ready to beat your ass right now, he wouldn't do anything to lose your friendship."

"I think it's too late for that," I laughed as I picked up my phone and read the text message that had just come in from him. "He's heading over here to talk to me."

"Well, whatever it is, I'm sure you guys will work it out."

"You don't know Max," I joked, suddenly feeling lighter than I had felt before he got here.

"Na, but my buddy Mike and I have been through some rough shit, and we always come out better than we were before."

"You have a friend who puts up with your crazy ass?" I asked, faking disbelief.

"Yup. We've been friends since first grade."

"That's a long time," I whistled. "Is he an only child? Is that why he bonded to you because he didn't have any siblings to harass him? Was he desperate for a friend?"

"Funny," he replied sarcastically. "He's the oldest of three kids, has two younger sisters."

"Well, take my advice—don't date either of them." I didn't bother laughing because I knew that sentence had more truth laced in it than I wanted to admit.

"No fucking way," he laughed. "He's in the FBI and works in the witness protection program. His job is *literally* to make people disappear."

I covered my mouth with my fist as a laugh erupted out of it. The thought of Roman being afraid of his friend was the comedic relief that I needed today.

"It's nice to see you finally laugh again," he commented as he stood up. "I'm here if you need anything, but do me a favor and fix things, so I don't have to. Talk to Elena, talk to Max. Fix your shit and get back to work because I'm not going to be partners with whoever this crazy version of you is." He twirled his finger in the air between us and then left.

While talking to Roman had helped lift some of the weight off of my shoulders, I still couldn't help but feel like everything around me was still getting ready to crumble.

Twenty-Eight

Elena

8 Hours Ago

Saturdays were supposed to be relaxing, but I had felt on edge ever since Max left my apartment yesterday. He went to talk with Trevor but hadn't bothered to give me any updates on what happened other than that it was *handled*. Whatever that was supposed to mean.

I threw a few slices of leftover pizza from last night into the microwave and waited for it to heat up. Today was going to be a stress-free day if I could help it. I had already taken a quick shower but didn't bother putting on anything other than my comfortable tights and a worn-out hoodie so I could lounge all day and do nothing.

My sisters had all taken turns calling and texting to see how I was doing and if I needed anything. Word got around fast in my family, and the drama was at an all-time high as they gossiped about the fight between Max and Trevor and— more importantly—who won. I hated feeling so out of the loop with everything, so I ignored most of the messages after confirming that I was fine and didn't know whether or not Trevor had a broken jaw. If they wanted to know, they could ask Max. That should keep him busy for a while.

The microwave dinged, so I took out my plate and headed over to the couch. I grabbed the blanket from the back and wrapped it around me as I got situated and turned on the TV. I wasn't in the mood for mindless TV, but I also didn't want the heartache of watching couples in love, so that ruled out any romcoms or chick flicks. The last thing I wanted to see was someone else getting their happily ever after when mine now felt so far out of reach.

I kept flicking through the channels until I landed on a true-crime show. My gut reaction was always to find something else to watch after what had happened to me, but suddenly I felt the need to push through and force myself to watch it. I used to love watching these shows before I was kidnapped and hadn't realized that I was still allowing Adam to have that power over me by not watching them anymore.

A commercial played as I took a small bite and chewed while my other hand was firmly wrapped around the remote in case I needed to change the channel. It was pushing boundaries and forcing me to take a step outside of the comfort zone that I had created right after everything that had happened. The one that forced me to be so constrained in this tiny bubble that even the tiniest thing could pop it. I was done living my life that way, and now was the time to change it.

I took another bite and accidentally bit my tongue when the show started, and an image of a house covered in crime scene tape filled the screen. My stomach twisted in knots as I tried to swallow the bite, my throat suddenly dry. I couldn't pry my eyes away from the TV as I reached over and picked up the glass of water from the coffee table.

A woman was narrating as they moved from the outside

of the house to the living room that had bloodstains across the walls and covering the floor. I turned my head away instinctively and shut my eyes, feeling my heart pound against my chest.

My eyes fluttered open, trying to adjust to the darkness around me with the only bit of light floating in through the crack in the wall beside me. My mouth felt swollen, and as I moved my tongue around, I could taste the bitterness of the blood on it. I tried to push myself up and felt my hand slip on something wet on the concrete beneath me. I rolled over and ran my finger in the liquid before lifting it to the dim light. Blood. I was lying in a puddle of blood, and I didn't know if it was mine or if it was from where I had cut him.

I felt my anxiety beginning to build and took a few slow, deep breaths in. I knew that I was in control of this and could change the channel if I wanted to. I was *not* the victim on TV. I was no longer the victim to anyone.

I opened my eyes and looked at the TV, relieved when I saw that it was a commercial again. It felt like I was torturing myself by doing this, but at the same time, I was tired of sharing my life with the demons that continued to haunt them. If I could learn to move past that trauma and accept it, then I would be more prepared to deal with it, so I could live a life where I wasn't constantly afraid of everything.

I finished eating one slice of pizza and lifted the other to take a bite when I heard my phone on the coffee table ding with a notification. I set the slice back on the plate and reached over to it.

Trevor: There will never be enough ways to tell you how sorry I am. I never meant to hurt you, and I will go to

my grave with the weight of knowing that I did.

I held my breath as I reread the text message. My fingers brushed across my lips to keep from instantly replying to his message and telling him that I forgive him and that we could work through whatever this thing was between us.

Instead, I exited the text message and set my phone back on the coffee table before wiping the tear away from my eye. I picked up my pizza and focused my attention on the show that had returned.

I knew that I needed to deal with things with Trevor but now wasn't the time. My heart wasn't ready for the trauma that was heading my way.

Twenty-Nine

Trevor

7 Hours Ago

My fingers flew quickly across the keyboard as I entered in the data from the reports that Roman had left on my desk. It was already after one in the afternoon, and I had what felt like eight shots of espresso to get me to this point. I had no idea how much I really had when the barista cut me off after six—who the hell cuts someone off of shots of espresso? Anyway—that hadn't stopped me from popping into the convenience store across the street to pick up a few energy drinks before making it into the office.

It was quiet for a Saturday with a few guys working out when I got here but quickly picked up a few hours later. I was thankful for the energy boost to help me crank out the work we needed to get caught up on before the end of the year. It was five days until Christmas, and my goal was to have everything wrapped up at work so I could take that week until New Year's off to spend time with my mom.

After losing both of my siblings, I knew that the holidays were always hard on her, but it was especially hard when Natasha decided to kill herself on Christmas Eve. Growing up, we always spent the days leading up to Christmas playing board games and drinking hot chocolate. My mom would nearly work herself to death by picking up extra hours to make sure she had enough money to get each of us something special for Christmas, while my dad was usually drunk and passed out in his chair by the tree.

He never cared about the holidays, and I don't think I ever saw him give my mom a gift for Christmas or her birthday. I could still picture her sitting on the floor between us three kids, her hands folded in her lap as she watched with pure excitement as we opened our gifts. Sometimes the gifts were more expensive than others, but there was always a look of fear in my mom's eyes when she would glance at my dad to see if he was watching.

It wasn't that he cared about what we got for Christmas. Hell, as long as he didn't have to pay for it, it didn't matter to him. But if he knew that she was working enough hours to be able to spend a lot on our gifts, his temper would flare, and he would beat her for keeping money from him.

I shuddered at the memory of her trying to stifle her screams from the bedroom as he threw her into furniture and called her every name in the book. I would try to distract Natasha, so she didn't have to hear it, though there was never a way to block it out. He was loud enough that the neighbors would hear, and eventually, someone would call the cops, or Mrs. Everly next door would come over and take us kids to her house, where it was safe. Not until I was an adult did I ever question why she didn't do something more to help my mom. She knew what was happening and yet looked the other way while telling herself that she had done a good thing by taking us out of the house.

I was ten the first time I decided to do something to save my mom. My dad had been drinking and had her pinned to the wall with the barrel of his shotgun held against her throat. Seeing her in that position had made my blood boil, and before I could think about it, I picked up one of her frying pans and swung it at his head. Unfortunately, I missed and got the beating of a lifetime that no one could save me from.

It wasn't long after that that I started having blackouts, especially when my dad would get mad. It felt like some sort of coping mechanism to protect myself from what I knew he could do to me. I hated that it made me feel weak and vulnerable because I could never remember what happened when I woke up. Soon my dad had taken a job out of town, and he started coming home less and less until one day, he just stopped.

We didn't hear from him again until after we turned eighteen, and he was no longer responsible for any child support—not that he would have paid it anyway. Then, finally, he came home and handed my mom divorce papers, threatening her life until she signed them. I remember once he left and slammed the door behind him that my mom sat at the kitchen table and cried. I had never seen her openly cry like that in front of us, and when I asked her if she was okay, she simply said, "I'm free. I'm finally free."

I was lost in my thoughts and hadn't heard my phone ding as I entered the last few pages of the report. Once it was done, I clicked save and leaned back in my chair, thankful that I had one big piece out of the way. There was still another week's worth of work to get done, but I had all day and night to work on it.

I pulled out an energy drink from the brown paper bag sitting at the end of my desk. I pulled the tab back and opened it, ready to fuel myself up for another work sprint. I knew that I would crash hard later, but right now, I didn't have anything else to focus on but work. I had texted Elena over an hour ago, and she still hadn't responded.

Not that I expected her to. What was she really going to say? *It's okay that you've been acting like a lunatic and making me think I'm going crazy, I still love you anyway!* Yeah, right.

Regardless, I said what I needed to, and I meant the apology I had given her. While I would have rather given it to her in person, that wasn't really an option. Aside from Max's not-so-subtle warning to stay the fuck away from his sister yesterday, there was still the fact that she had asked me for space and hadn't said that she was ready to see or talk to me again.

I picked up my phone and responded to the text message from my mom, confirming that I would be there for Christmas Eve. This year marked ten years since Natasha's death, and my mom wanted to go see her favorite play that they were putting on at the community center near where we grew up. She was buying tickets and wanted to know whether to get one for Elena.

It killed me to say no, that we wouldn't need a ticket for her. I was barely able to tell myself that it was over between us. I wasn't in any position to break my mom's heart even more right now. So instead, I lied and told her that Elena had to work that night, so she couldn't go. As far as I knew, it wasn't that far off from the truth.

Thirty

Elena

4 Hours Ago

"Thank you, ma, but I don't feel like going anywhere tonight." I balanced the phone between my ear and shoulder while I pulled my hair into a messy knot and secured a hair tie around it.

"Yes, I know that you're making manicotti," I sighed heavily, hoping she would get the hint. "But I'm tired and just want to stay home and relax tonight. I'll see you soon for Christmas."

My mom grumbled on in Italian for a few minutes before accepting that I wasn't coming over for dinner. I knew they were all worried about Trevor and I breaking up—had we really broken up, though? Anyway, I knew they were concerned and cared about me, but I didn't have the mental energy to deal with them tonight. I wanted as much peace and quiet as I could get.

I had spent the afternoon binge-watching *How I Met Your Mother* when I needed a break from the true-crime shows. I was proud of myself for watching as much as I had without having a full-blown panic attack. When I would feel myself slipping into one, I would focus on five things that I could see, four things I could touch, and three things that I could hear. I didn't have to get to the last two before I felt myself calming down, which felt like tremendous progress, though there was quite a bit of a sting every time I imagined that Trevor was here helping me through them.

No matter how hard I tried, I could not get him off my brain today. Hell—that was a lie. It wasn't just today. It was every minute of every hour since the moment he walked out of my door that day. Since then, nothing has felt right, and I wanted nothing more than to talk to him and fix things. Trevor felt like the air, and I didn't want to just take a breath — I needed him to breathe. He was my lifeline, and I felt like I was slowly dying inside without him.

I picked up my phone for the hundredth time and checked for any missed calls or text messages. I hadn't heard anything from him since his message earlier. I knew he was waiting for me to respond, but I didn't know what to say. I typed out different messages and then deleted them because none of them got the words out that I desperately needed him to hear.

You don't have to apologize. This isn't your fault. You don't have to be sorry for being who you are, I love you anyway. I'm not afraid of you—I know who you really are. Trust me, I believe in you. I love you. I need you. I don't want to live without you.

Against my better judgment, I picked up my phone and replied to his text message.

Me: We need to talk in person.

I knew that Max would be pissed off once he found out, but he should know Trevor better than to think that he would ever do anything to hurt me. Even I knew him better than that.

I got up and turned off the TV before heading to my bedroom to lay down for a bit. I put my phone on the nightstand beside my bed and curled up against the pillow as my eyes fluttered shut. Within minutes, I was asleep.

<u>Thirty-One</u>

Trevor

1 hour ago

When Elena's text message came in, I was beside myself. I nearly choked on the water I was drinking when I read it. I had decided to switch to something *without* caffeine when I felt like I had reached the point of smelling colors and hearing numbers.

I responded quicker than I should have and let her know that I would be working late tonight but that I could call her when I got done. I hadn't heard from her since then, which had left me feeling uneasy that maybe she had changed her mind.

I thought about postponing the rest of what I needed to get done so I could rush over to talk to her, but that was what had gotten me into this predicament in the first place. I've never been so unfocused at work and never in a million years would have normally let things get this out of control here. My job was my life most of the time, and I took running my own business very seriously. I was ashamed that I had allowed it to get so out of control but was also grateful that Roman had put me in check before it was too late.

It was already seven, and my stomach was growling, asking for something more than liquid for dinner. I opened a new browser window on my computer and placed an order for delivery since I didn't want to stop and go grab something to eat. The sooner I got done with work, the sooner I could call Elena and see if she still wanted to get together and talk.

Once the order was placed, I minimized the window and returned to the other report that I needed to work on. I was busy entering the data when I heard my phone ding. I picked it up and felt my lips tug up in the corners with a smile when I saw Elena's name on it.

Elena: I just woke up from a nap, so I'm sure I'll be up late tonight. Let me know when you're done.

I let out the breath that I had been holding and shot back a quick confirmation message to her before turning my attention back to my computer. I was so focused on getting caught up on work to get out of there to see Elena that suddenly I wasn't hungry anymore.

"How much longer are you going to keep at this?" Roman asked as he stood by my desk and looked at the pile of paperwork that I had completed, which thankfully was larger than the pile I had yet to get done. I had been so caught up in it that I hadn't noticed him come in.

I pushed back from my desk and stretched. I was stiff and sore from leaning over my desk for so long and knew I needed to get up and move around soon. I looked at the clock on my computer and noticed that it was already after eight, and I hadn't bothered to stop to eat the dinner I had delivered. It was still sitting in the brown paper bag on the edge of my desk.

"I'm tapping out now," I sighed, pushing the papers away from me. "I'll come in tomorrow and finish the rest of it."

"I can do it this week, don't worry about it."

"I appreciate that, but you have enough work on your plate without adding mine. It's my fault that I got so far behind, so I'll make sure to get it done before I leave."

Roman nodded his head and tapped his finger on the stack of files that sat on the edge of my desk.

"How's your mom doing?" he asked.

I scrunched my face and shook my head. I felt bad enough that I hadn't been checking in on her more often than usual, but things had been busy, and she pushed me away every time I had tried. I knew that she was struggling with the holidays but this year felt like it was harder for her than it had been before.

"She confirmed that she got the tickets for the play and was bummed that Elena wasn't going to be there. Other than that, she hasn't said much."

"Have you talked to Elena?"

I felt a smile tug at the corners of my mouth and tried to remind myself that it didn't mean anything. She said she wanted to talk in person, and for all I knew, that was just so she could break up with me face-to-face and watch the agony on my face as my heart shattered around her.

"She texted me earlier and asked if we could talk. I'm supposed to let her know when I'm wrapping up here."

"Well then, I'll get out of here so you can go talk with her. Let me know how things go."

"Will do."

I returned his smile and started clearing my desk before shutting off my computer. I could feel the excitement bubbling inside me from the thought of seeing her again. I knew that Max had warned me to stay away from her, but I couldn't. She was like a forbidden sip of water when you were stranded in the middle of the desert. Sometimes it didn't matter whether you were supposed to have something if it was what you needed.

I picked up my phone and sent her a text message to let her know that I was done and to see if she wanted me to come over so we could talk. A few seconds later, my phone showed the bouncing dots on the screen as she responded.

Elena: Perfect timing. I'll be waiting.

I tucked my phone in my pocket and put on my coat. By the time I left, Roman had already shut down everything up front, so I didn't have to. I checked to make sure no one else was there before I set the alarm and locked the door.

It felt like it was going to take forever to get to Elena's apartment. My excitement to see her overshadowed any lingering doubts that I had that this wasn't going to go the way I was hoping it would. My connection with Elena was stronger than I've ever had with anyone before, so I refused to believe that our love for each other couldn't save what we had. I knew that I had my flaws, but I hoped that she would be able to see past them and remember why she had fallen for me in the first place.

As I sat on the train waiting for my stop, I caught my reflection in the mirror and shuddered when I saw myself. I didn't look like myself. The bags under my eyes, combined with the thinning of my face from skipping who knew how many meals this week, reminded me of my brother right before he died. Granted, he was using drugs at the time, but there wasn't much that differed between us now. I focused on my eyes, wondering if I could see the same evil in them that I had found in his so many times over the years.

The train jerked to a stop, and I got up. My illusions of happily ever after crumbled when my reflection looked back at me one last time, reminding me again why I wasn't good for Elena. It didn't matter how much I loved her; I would never be able to save her from the person who would hurt her and take everything from her.

Me.

Thirty-Two

Elena

I chewed my nail as I clutched my glass of wine to my chest, unable to pry my eyes away from the TV as the woman desperately tried to run after the man who had taken her child. She was determined, but I could already tell that he was faster and stronger than her. That's how it always played out. No matter how strong the woman is, there's always a predator that will overtake her. My stomach soured as I thought back to when I had been kidnapped and held captive. I wasn't sure that I would ever escape; each day that passed made it less likely.

A knock on the door startled me, and I flung my arms in the air, sloshing the wine out of the glass. I gasped and set it down on the coffee table before I got up to grab a towel from the kitchen. I patted my arms and chest dry and then tossed the towel in the sink when there was another knock.

I looked through the peephole, my heart still racing from the movie. Whoever was there had their face turned away from me, keeping me from seeing who they were. I was about to walk away and grab my phone when they turned around, and I finally saw their face. Letting out a shaky breath, I turned the lock and slid the deadbolt to open the door.

"Hey, I thought you had to work late?" I stepped to the side and waited for him to come in. Instead, he lingered at the door with his hands shoved into his pockets, his jaw locked in place.

"Are you okay?" I asked, feeling as if something was wrong.

"Fine."

I pulled my head back slightly and tilted it to the side. Something was *definitely* different about him.

"Have you been drinking?"

"What's it to you if I have been?" His words weren't slurred, but the smell of whiskey was heavy on his breath.

"I'm just a little worried about you. You don't seem like yourself."

"Maybe I'm not."

"Did I do something?" I asked, narrowing my eyes in confusion. This wasn't like him and my skin prickled at the realization.

"I don't know. Did you?"

"What's with the games?" I asked, starting to grow impatient and frustrated. I put my hand on my hip and raised a brow. "If something's wrong, then just tell me. Otherwise, I don't know why you're acting this way." I was acting braver than I felt.

"Does it scare you?"

The icy tone in his voice was more jarring than his actual words.

"No," I said slowly. "You don't scare me."

He paused for a moment, studying me with cold, calculating, dark eyes. Something shifted between us, and I felt the icy chill radiating off him.

"Are you sure?"

Suddenly, my instincts kicked in, and I took a step back, away from him as he stepped toward me. My heart was racing as panic forced its way through my veins, sending me back into the darkness I felt when I was held captive last year.

I grabbed the side of the door, slamming it shut when he reached out and caught it. His hand wrapped tightly around the wood as he held it. His eyes locked onto mine, forcing a wave of fear to crawl up my spine. I took another step back, desperate to get away from him. He was inside my apartment now, the door still open.

"You're breathing fast. Eyes are dilated. I would bet that your palms are sweaty. Fear is coursing through your body right now, and you're trying to decide whether or not to trust *me* or your instincts that are telling you to *run*."

"Why are you doing this?" I whispered. He knew what I had been through; why would he think this was funny?

"So, which is it, *Elena*?" My name rolled off of his tongue in a way I'd never heard before. "Do you trust me, or are you going to run?"

"Stop it!" I demanded, my fists shaking at my sides. "Just go! Get out of my apartment! We're done." I pulled my shoulders back and tilted my chin up as my body trembled.

"Actually," he laughed, shutting the door. "We're just getting started."

I watched in horror as he slid the deadbolt in place, knowing that no one would be able to get in if needed. My head was spinning, and my body screamed for me to get the hell out of there and call for help, but it was too late.

"Trevor, why are you doing this?" I asked, my voice as shaky as my legs.

He took a step forward and worked his jaw back and forth.

"You haven't figured it out, have you?"

I stared at him, waiting for him to clue me in on what I was missing.

"Figured what out?" I asked, taking another step away from him.

"You were right, Elena," he replied, sidestepping my question.

"About what?" I didn't really care at this point; my goal was to keep him talking while I tried to figure out a way to get help. I looked around the room, trying to find something—anything that could be used as a weapon—when I suddenly stopped to focus on the bookshelf where Max had hidden his camera. At the time, I had thought it was funny that we had both picked the same spot to hide a camera, but now I was thankful that I knew where it was. All I had to do was get Trevor to turn around to face the camera so Max would see that he was here. Even if he wasn't actively watching—which it was Max, so he probably was—he would be able to go back and watch this later, and there would be proof that Trevor was there and had been doing everything all along.

"That I'm not acting like myself," he said with a shrug as if this was the most casual conversation to have. "I'm not myself, and you, out of all people, should know that."

I moved around in a semi-circle, putting my back to the bookshelf while I tried to position my body to where it wouldn't cover his. I needed Max to be able to see his face and get a good image of it.

"We all go through changes, Trevor. It's okay," I muttered, not entirely focused on the conversation. If Max was watching this live, I could give him a signal, and he would come save me. It was terrifying to think that I needed to be protected from Trevor, but the way he was acting left me confident that I was right to be afraid of him.

"Just to save you from that weird shuffle dance you're doing over there—the camera isn't there anymore. I took it down right after I disabled the ones in the hallway."

My heart dropped as the color drained from my face.

"You knew about those?" I asked, stalling while I tried to think of a plan B quickly. Of course, he knew; Max had probably told him when they were teaming up, trying to figure out how to protect me from myself. While it was true that I needed protection, I wasn't the threat anymore, and Trevor used that to his advantage to get information from Max that he wouldn't normally give away.

"I know everything, Elena."

There was something about how he kept saying my name that sent chills down my spine.

"Why are you doing this?"

Sweat beaded my brow as my blood pressure skyrocketed.

"Because there is something that I want. Something that I *need*. And unfortunately for you, there's only one way to get it."

"What do you need?" I gulped, afraid to hear the answer.

"Your boyfriend's dead body."

Thirty-Three

Elena

My phone rang for the third time in a row, much to Trevor's frustration. Not that there were many things that *didn't* irritate him right now.

I should have known better than to answer the door. I should have listened to Max's advice and stayed away from him. Instead, I was stupid and had texted him to see if we could talk. There was something about the idea of seeing him in person that felt so comforting to me that I was able to overlook everything else and let him in. Big. Mistake.

It felt like I had been sucked into a tornado, thrown into the thickness of the storm, as I stumbled around and tried to hang on to anything that would keep me from being swallowed into the chaos.

From the moment Trevor got here, he had been overly aggressive and controlling. Not much different than the few times I had seen him like this before, but definitely angrier. I was afraid of saying anything to make him even madder than he was. When he mentioned that he needed my boyfriend's dead body—I knew that he had reached a breaking point and had no idea how to handle it.

No matter how many times I've told him that I wasn't seeing anyone else, he didn't believe me. What was even worse was that he was now on a mission to find and kill this person that didn't exist. At first, I thought it was just jealousy at the idea that there might be someone else, but now I could see that there was something more. Something chilling and deadlier.

Twenty minutes after he forced his way into my apartment, he took my phone and refused to give it back to me. I should have been more concerned about it, but there wasn't anything that he could do that would be harmful at this point. If he thought he was going to text my *other boyfriend,* then he would have a hard time finding someone in my contact list, given that I had very few friends, to begin with. If he messaged one of my cousins, they would immediately alert Max and tell him that I was acting odd. Either way, Max would come to save me. I hoped.

For now, all I was focused on was staying as far away from him as possible and trying not to agitate him further. I didn't know how long I would have to wait this out, but I knew better than to do anything to make things worse.

I sat nervously on the couch, tucked into the corner with a throw pillow folded under my arm. An awkward silence fell over us as he paced back and forth in front of the TV, staring down at my phone.

All of a sudden, there was a knock on my door, startling both of us. My eyes widened at the clenching of his jaw as he stared at the door. Neither of us said anything. The ringing in my ears from the blood pulsing through was loud enough to drown out the sound of my heavy breathing while fear consumed me.

"Elena," Natalie called out from the other side of the door.

"It's Natalie. We need to talk."

I closed my eyes and felt the warm tears glide down my cheeks.

"I've been trying to call you, but you weren't answering, and I got worried."

Trevor turned and glared at me over his shoulder. I looked away, afraid to meet the icy-blue eyes watching my every move.

I stayed quiet, afraid that if I responded to her, it would set him off, and we both would be in danger. While there was a chance that she could run and get help, I wasn't willing to risk her life to try.

"I found your letter at my office today," she continued from the other side of the door. "I really need to see you and make sure you are okay. Please open the door."

The tears continued to trail down my face, burning my skin in their wake. *What letter was she talking about?*

"If you're not going to answer me, I have no other choice but to report this and call for a wellness check. I don't want you to be admitted, Elena. Please let me in. Let me help you."

Trevor rolled his eyes and grunted under his breath before nodding for me to answer the door. Once I got close to him, he yanked me by my arm and pulled me into him as he whispered in my ear, "Tell her you're okay and make her leave. If you say anything else—I will kill you."

I nodded and forced the bile back down as I tried to swallow past the lump in my throat. I quickly wiped the tears away with the backs of my hands and sucked in a deep breath.

I reached for the lock and slid it open when I felt something sharp prick the side of my throat. Carefully, I stepped back to crack open the door, the weight of the knife against my skin a frightening reminder not to let her in.

"Hey," I said as naturally as I could as I angled my face into the narrow opening so she could see me but not the knife. "Sorry, I was sleeping and didn't hear my phone."

Natalie pulled her brows together, concern deeply embedded in her face as she studied me.

"Can I come in?" she asked, tilting her head.

"Now isn't a good time," I said, trying to keep the anxiety out of my voice. "Can I call you later?"

"I would rather talk in person," she pressed. "Your letter has me very concerned."

I shook my head and blinked away the tears prickling my eyes.

"Is he here with you?" she whispered, looking behind me.

I closed my eyes and tried to force myself to be strong.

"Okay, well, I can tell that you're tired, so I'll let you go. Call me later?" Natalie said louder than she had been speaking before. She looked at me with empathy as she turned to walk away.

Before I could react, I was flung to the side, out of the way, as the door flew open. Natalie whipped around, her eyes wide with fear as she took in Trevor with the knife in his hand. In one swift movement, he grabbed her by the waist and threw her into the apartment, slamming the door behind him.

"You really fucked up now, doc."

I covered my mouth with trembling hands as I tried to hold in the scream as he backhanded her across the face with so much force that she stumbled before falling to the ground.

Thirty-Four

Elena

I watched in horror as Trevor tightened the rope around Natalie's hands as he bound her to a chair in the corner. Her mouth had a cut on it, and streaks of mascara had run down her face. I sat beside her, tied to the other chair from my kitchen, useless and unable to help either of us.

When Trevor knocked Natalie out, I lost my mind and went after him. Seeing her lay lifelessly on the floor as blood pooled out of her head was enough to spark the fire that burned deep inside of me. I was only able to get a few punches in before he turned and pinned me to the floor with the knife pressed so hard against my throat that I started to bleed.

I kept my eyes on Trevor as he moved around the apartment, muttering about how he didn't need this fucking problem.

Part of me still hoped that Max would come to the rescue, but as time passed, it felt less and less likely that he would. If Trevor had disconnected the cameras, he wouldn't know what was happening anyway. And if he had assigned the rookie cop to watch me, he would probably assume that all was well unless he heard different. The same guy hanging out outside of my apartment for days was the same guy who suddenly seemed to vanish into thin air.

I tried to think of a way out of this but kept coming up empty-handed. It was impossible to do anything while bound to a chair, but it was even harder to try to negotiate with someone who you didn't know. Someone so full of anger and darkness that you were afraid to breathe the same air as them, just so you didn't risk allowing any of that darkness to seep into your soul.

My neck still stung from where the knife had cut me, but I had no idea how bad it was. I found Natalie's eyes linger on it every now and then, so I imagined that it probably looked bad if she was constantly checking on it. I couldn't feel the warm stickiness from the blood dripping down my chest anymore, so I had prayed that the bleeding had stopped for the most part.

Time seemed to pass by at a painstakingly slow pace as the threat of the unknown loomed over us. Trevor quickly checked the rope on both chairs before heading down the hallway and into the bathroom.

Once he was out of sight, Natalie turned to me as much as she could while being bound.

"I'm so sorry you got dragged into the middle of this," I whispered an apology to her.

She shook her head, and her face softened.

"I found a suicide note from you slipped under my office door. I rushed over as soon as I read it. Something about it didn't feel right, and I knew I had to check on you."

"Suicide note?" I asked. "I didn't write a suicide note."

"I can see that now," she sighed. "I should have seen the signs. I knew something was wrong last night and didn't trust my gut."

"What do you mean? What happened last night?"

"I ran into Trevor outside of my office. He was hanging out against the building and cornered me by the alley. He was different than he had been the day before when he came to see me. Angrier."

"He's been coming to see you?"

"Only once," she said quickly, looking past me to check if he was coming back. We stilled for a moment when we heard the toilet flush.

"I'll make this quick," she rushed out, "I think that Trevor suffers from multiple personalities, and whoever this one is—he plans to kill you."

I was about to respond when I heard footsteps coming down the hall. I snapped my mouth shut and pulled my spine straight, keeping the emotion off of my face.

Natalie closed her eyes and let her head rest lightly on her shoulder as if she had fallen asleep. I tried to take slow and steady breaths, hoping that my energy would somehow have magical powers that would help calm him down. Thankfully he seemed calmer than he had been, so I was hopeful that the *real* Trevor—the one I knew and loved—would be coming back soon.

He walked past and glanced at us before going over to the kitchen counter, where he had left my phone. Even if I had been quick enough to pick up the chair and hobble over to get it while he was in the bathroom, it was pushed so far back against the wall that there was no way to reach it with my hands tied behind my back.

My arms tingled from being restrained for so long, and I wondered if I would eventually start to lose feeling in them. He picked up my phone and started typing something before putting it back down on the counter. Then, seemingly satisfied with whatever he had done, he came over and sat on the edge of the coffee table, across from Natalie and me.

"All of this will be over soon enough," he said as if that was supposed to provide us with some sort of comfort.

"Please let her go," I whispered, nodding to Natalie. "She didn't do anything. Do whatever you want to with me but let her go. Please, Trevor."

"I can't do that." He rubbed his lips together and shook his head. "She already knows more than she needs to."

"I promise you, she won't say anything. She's a licensed therapist—her job is to keep people's secrets and help them find peace. She would never do anything to hurt me, so I *know* that she won't do anything if you let her go."

"It doesn't work that way. You should know that Elena," he laughed and rolled his eyes. "God, did you not learn anything with Adam?"

My heart stopped beating, and my blood turned cold when I heard his name on Trevor's lips.

"What did you just say?"

"Did you really think that you could survive him? You got lucky, Elena. He didn't come after you when you escaped because you weren't the one he wanted. If you were, you wouldn't have made it more than five feet outside of that warehouse. He was distracted and was an idiot who fell in love. Had it not been for Hannah, you would have had a different future. Or lack of one," he snorted.

"Fuck you," I spat out with more hatred than I had ever felt before in my life.

"You already did," he raised his eyebrows. "And honestly, it wasn't that great. You would think that a little choking might get you to put more effort into it; instead, you just lay there like a lifeless, terrified, limp fish. Honestly, sex with a corpse would have been livelier than what you did."

He pushed up off the coffee table and shook his head at me as if I disgusted him. I blinked away the tears and avoided looking at Natalie when I felt her gaze land on me.

A single tear fell from my eye, but this time, I didn't bother to hold it in.

Thirty-Five

Trevor

I felt giddy and overly excited as I got ready. I knew exactly what I wanted to say to Elena and how I wanted to apologize for everything that had happened between us over the past few weeks. There were plenty of things that we needed to talk about and discuss, but none of that mattered until I could see her, hold her, and make sure she knew how much I loved her.

I knew that I didn't deserve her. Elena was the good in a world of evil. She was the light that brightened my darkest days. She was the definition of what love looked like and the reason that I didn't deserve to be loved.

One last moment with her was all that I would give myself. One last touch. One last kiss. One last time hearing her say *I love you* before I walked away and broke both of our hearts forever. To love her was easy. To stay with her could very well kill her.

Thirty-Six

Elena

They say that you know when your time is up because you can feel death as it creeps closer, pulling back the layers that have protected you and made you feel safe. The icy cold that nips at your skin, drawing the warmth out of your body as you start to succumb.

Escaping Adam had been one of the defining moments in my life. It was when I realized that I was stronger than I had ever given myself credit for. I was smart, brave, and I had planned every move with calculated steps. There wasn't any room for error. If I slipped up, I would be dead, and I knew it.

Now with Trevor, things felt different. I couldn't push the feeling of death away from me. It covered me like a wet blanket, suffocating any lingering hope that I might survive this. But it was just a matter of time before I would be put out of my misery and free from the demons that continued to haunt me. Trevor was just one of many.

Natalie and I continued to sit in stunned silence, neither of us willing to try to talk to or negotiate with Trevor. It was clear that any leverage that I thought I might have had was long out of the window. There were a few times when I caught him looking over at me, and I saw a glimpse of the man that I used to know. The man who used to love me and cared about me.

My phone had dinged a couple of times with notifications, but there weren't any more phone calls after Natalie got there. I assumed that the messages were from Max and that he was probably starting to get aggravated that I hadn't answered. I no longer felt the excitement of him realizing that something was happening and rushing over to save me. It just confirmed what I've always known—I'm not the kind of girl who can be saved. *If* he got here, it wouldn't be in time. I already knew that.

I leaned forward and strained my eyes, trying to see the time on the clock on the stove. It was too far, and my eyes already hurt from crying so much that I gave up trying. It didn't matter what time it was, especially if my time on earth was ending soon anyway. I was tied to a chair, so it wasn't like I could go mark off items on a bucket list before I died. I was stuck here, at the mercy of a madman with some secret agenda that had yet to be revealed.

I wiggled my fingers behind my back, trying to get some of the numbness to go away. It was no use. *If* my hands were ever untied, they would just fall limply at my sides at this point. I wouldn't be able to fight back or even pick up my phone to call for help.

Trevor walked around the kitchen, setting things down on the counter, but I couldn't see what they were. Whatever he was doing, it was with purpose and determination as he pulled his brows together and focused intently.

I sighed heavily, allowing my body to relax into the chair as much as possible.

Suddenly, there was a knock on the door. I glanced at Natalie as her head whipped up toward the sound. We both knew that this was it if there was any chance of getting help.

It could be Max, or it could be the kids down the hall who were constantly doing some sort of fundraising for their school. It could also be my elderly neighbor coming by to ask for batteries for her remote that she fussed with a hundred times a day because her TV was never loud enough.

I held my breath and waited anxiously as Trevor walked over to the door, the knife tucked into his pants. He slid the deadbolt over, pulled the door open, and stepped to the side.

I gasped when I saw who was standing on the other side. The world spun around me as I tried to keep myself from toppling over in the chair as everything crashed around me.

Thirty-Seven

Trevor

"Elena?" I asked, confused as I saw her sitting in the chair with her hands behind her back. Before I could question what was happening, I looked to her right and saw Natalie sitting beside her in the same position.

I darted in, rushing over to them when I felt a strong hand pull me back. The door slammed shut, and then I felt the cold metal of a knife blade poke the skin on the back of my neck. I held my hands up in front of me and froze.

Elena looked bewildered as she looked between me and whoever was holding me at knifepoint. She looked like she saw a ghost as the color drained from her face. Natalie's jaw dropped open as she tried to process the same thing Elena was.

"Look, I'm not sure what you're here for—" I started to say before the knife pressed deeper into my neck.

"Shut the fuck up," a low voice growled. But it wasn't just any voice—it was one that curdled my blood and sent ice through my veins.

My body tensed, and my muscles stiffened in response. There was no fucking way.

I wanted to turn around and prove that this was all in my head. It wasn't the first time that I had thought I had seen my brother or heard his voice after his death, but every time it ended up being my mind playing tricks on me.

Just like now. I knew that Hunter was dead. I held my mom as she cried and grieved for another child so shortly after losing my sister. My mind was a dangerous place these days, and if I allowed myself to entertain the idea that it could be my dead brother, I would be climbing a slippery slope that had the promise of taking down everyone around me as I plummeted down it.

I tried to focus on the situation and pulled my thoughts away from the nightmares that haunted me. Unfortunately, now wasn't the time or place for that.

"Just tell me what you want. No one needs to get hurt," I said calmly, my hands still in the air by my head.

"It's a little too late for that," he chuckled.

I looked over at Elena, noticing the bloodstain on her neck for the first time. I had seen the gash on Natalie's head but had been too distracted with everything else to stop and focus on their injuries. *Were there more? What else had happened to them before I got here? How long had they been tied up and held hostage?* There were so many questions that I needed answers to.

"Look," I said, starting to turn around.

"That's enough!" his voice boomed as he shoved me forward.

I stumbled but quickly caught my balance, thankful that I was no longer in his grip. I turned around and held a hand to my neck, feeling the trickle of blood from where the knife had cut me in the scuffle. When I looked up, I felt my breath catch in my throat as my world came crashing down around me.

"No fucking way," I muttered, scrubbing my other hand down my face. I shook my head and took a step back, needing to put some distance between us.

"What's wrong? Afraid you've seen a ghost?" he mocked, waving the blood-stained knife in the air between us.

"You're fucking dead." I stepped even further back, running into the coffee table in the process.

I glanced over at Elena, confirming that I wasn't hallucinating and imagining my dead brother standing in front of me.

She was shaking as she sobbed, her body trembling against the chair.

"What do you want?" I asked, moving to stand in front of her. I hadn't been able to protect her before now, but I sure as hell would die trying from this point on.

"Your dead body."

Thirty-Eight

Elena

No matter how much I wanted to scream, the sound wouldn't come out. I was frozen—paralyzed—with fear. Trevor stood there, staring at his *dead* brother, who wasn't dead after all. I couldn't imagine what he was feeling, but I imagined that it was a combination of shock and disbelief based on the way his jaw tightened as he worked it back and forth.

"What do you want?" he finally asked, folding his arms over his chest.

"I already told you." Trevor cocked his head to the side and narrowed his eyes. "Your dead body."

I felt a small gasp of air escape my lips. Everything made sense now that I was sitting there, watching them together. While they looked identical—because they were—there were so many differences that I noticed now that I was studying them. Trevor's body was usually more relaxed when he wasn't being held hostage by his dead brother, whereas Hunter's body seemed to constantly be rigid and tense. There was a light that shone in Trevor's blue eyes and lit up every time he smiled, which was the complete opposite of the cold, icy color of Hunter's.

"Fine," Trevor said, taking a step in front of Natalie and me. "But you let them go."

"I don't think so," Hunter chuckled menacingly.

"And why the fuck not?" Trevor bellowed, dropping his arms as he balled his fists at his sides.

"Because they're all part of the grand plan."

I wanted to lean around Trevor and see what Hunter was doing when I heard a noise in the kitchen. Trevor moved his body again, shielding my view before looking at me over his shoulder.

"Are you okay?" he asked quietly, looking between Natalie and me.

We both nodded but didn't say anything. He turned back to look at Hunter as he approached.

"Plans change," Trevor said firmly. "You're going to let them go, and then we'll deal with whatever the fuck you think this is."

"Do you really think you can stop me?" Hunter laughed and walked closer to us.

"We both know that you're not a killer, Hunter," Trevor replied calmly. "You wouldn't kill your own brother, so let's just step back and figure this out."

"Why wouldn't I? I killed Natasha."

Trevor flinched at the words, and before I could fully process them, I saw Trevor charge Hunter, tackling him to the ground. He swung hard, his fists repeatedly making contact with Hunter's face before he groaned and rolled over.

I watched in horror as blood puddled around him on the

carpet. He groaned loudly and clutched his hand to his side as Hunter pushed up and held the bloody knife in the air.

"Who's next?" he asked, looking between Natalie and me.

Thirty-Nine

Trevor

"Get the fuck away from them," I yelled, forcing myself up off the floor as I kept pressure on the wound. There was blood everywhere, but I didn't have time to stop and worry about it. Elena was in danger, and there was nothing that I wouldn't do at this point to save her. If Hunter wanted my dead body, he could have it, but I would go to my grave making sure that Elena was safe.

Hunter stood behind them, slowly trailing the knife up and down each of their cheeks, leaving a trail of blood in its path. Elena pinched her eyes closed and cried while Natalie remained stoic. I knew that she had come across plenty of psychopaths in her profession, but I couldn't imagine that she had ever dealt with one in person.

I sat up, taking a slow, deep breath that hurt more than it should. I knew that I needed to find a way to call for help, but as I watched him untie Natalie, I knew there wasn't time. I was the only person who could stop him before it was too late.

"Let her go, Hunter," I commanded, pushing myself to a standing position. "You said you wanted my dead body, so let her go."

"Unfortunately, she's already seen and heard too much," he said with a shrug as he yanked her up from the chair after the ropes had been cut. Elena sobbed loudly beside them, her eyes wide with terror as she watched.

Hunter lifted the knife and held it against her throat as he pulled her hair, forcing her head back. She swallowed hard, and I watched the tears slide down her face.

"I'm so sorry," Elena whispered, rocking her chair to try to get free.

"Hunter, don't!"

I tried to dart over to grab her, but I was too late. The knife plunged into the side of her neck, and within seconds, the color drained from her face as the life slipped out of her body.

I closed my eyes and lowered my head as I heard the thud on the floor where she fell lifelessly in front of Elena.

Elena was crying so hard that no sound was coming out of her. Her body shook violently in the chair as she tried to get free. Before I could get to her, Hunter reached behind her and untied the ropes holding her down.

She jumped up once she was free and rubbed her hands over her wrists where she had been tied up.

Hunter took a few steps toward her as she rushed off to the kitchen. She looked around wildly before picking up a knife from the kitchen counter and pointing it at him.

"Stay the fuck away from me!" she yelled, her voice wavering as it echoed through the small room.

"Don't worry," Hunter assured her. "You're not next."

He stopped and turned to look at me.

"He is."

Forty

Elena

My hand trembled as I tried to hold the knife steady. I forced myself to focus on Hunter and not look at where Natalie was lying on the carpet, dead because of me. Had I not been seeing her, she wouldn't have gotten caught up in all of this.

I knew that I wasn't in any position to stab Hunter, but at the time, it was the first thing that I had seen on the counter where he had lined up a handful of different weapons. Some looked like they were purely there to torture someone, while others looked like they could kill someone if I put enough effort into it. The knife was shorter than the one he had, and I knew that he would stab me with his long before I got close enough to stab him with mine.

There wasn't much time to figure something else out as I watched Trevor clutch his stomach to try to stop the bleeding. He had sat down on the edge of the coffee table, unable to support himself anymore.

"Don't you come another step closer," I warned, shaking the knife at him.

"Why? What are you going to do if I do?" He licked his lips and took another step toward me. "You know that I like it when you're scared."

"Stop it," I hissed, looking from him to Trevor.

I kept walking, allowing my back to glide against the counter as I moved away from him.

"Did you tell him?" he asked, nodding to his brother.

I narrowed my eyes and pulled my brows together. He was trying to distract me, and I knew it, so I ignored his question and kept going, determined to make my way over to Trevor.

"I bet he just loved hearing about how good I fucked you," he prodded. "The way your pussy clenched so tight around my cock as you came. You were so fucking wet, and I knew that you liked being controlled, even if you fought it at first."

I tried to swallow down the bile that was rising in my throat.

I could feel every trigger being pressed as he kept talking.

"He was never very good in bed," Hunter continued. "His girlfriends in high school used to tell me how great I was when I would fuck them the way they wanted to be fucked. Trevor never could meet their expectations, so it doesn't surprise me that he didn't meet them with you either. He was always such a lackluster person in everything he did. Always so afraid to push the limits."

He shook his head and set the knife down on the counter.

I watched him cautiously, wondering why he would voluntarily give up the weapon he was using. I felt more unnerved and suspicious when he didn't reach for anything else.

"He isn't lackluster," I bit out, desperate to stand up for Trevor to his brother. "He's far better than you'll ever be."

Hunter tilted his head back and laughed.

"Maybe." He shrugged. "But the difference is that I take what I want. I don't sit around and wait for people's permission."

"What is it that you want?" I asked, hoping to keep him talking long enough for me to circle back around to get the knife.

"There are a lot of things that I want, but more importantly is what I *need*."

Your boyfriend's dead body.

"I don't understand," I said quietly. "Why do you need his dead body? There has to be another way to get what you want."

"There's not."

His tone was short and clipped, and I knew that the *friendly* Hunter I saw a few minutes ago was gone.

"So you're just going to kill your own brother?! You don't think people will ask questions and figure out that you killed him?"

"Nope," he replied, letting the p pop. "Because as far as anyone knows, he's still alive and well."

I pulled my head back, confused.

"Our father died a few weeks ago," he sighed and reached behind his back, pulling out a gun. "He left behind a substantial, very impressive inheritance. Fortunately for me, he never bothered to marry again or have any more kids, leaving one sole heir. And since I'm technically dead, that means that I need a new body so I can go claim it."

I covered my mouth with my hand and looked at Trevor.

"So you're going to kill your brother and pretend to be him?" I asked in disbelief.

"Exactly. Which means that I need to tie up all of the loose ends."

My heart was pounding so hard in my chest that it felt like it was going to explode.

"Loose ends?"

"I'm thinking a murder-suicide," he said whimsically. "Given the suicide note you left for your therapist and the ones still to be delivered to your family, the police will see that you weren't well and killed those who tried to help you. She was first," he paused and nodded to Natalie's body. "Then, when Trevor got here, you decided to kill him before taking your own life."

I shook my head, forcing the idea out as quickly as it came.

"There's no way you're going to pull that off. You can't make it look like I committed suicide," I argued. "The forensics team will look at the angle of the gun and rule it a homicide. No one would ever believe it."

"That's the funny thing about life, Elena. No one bothers to look that deeply when there's a suicide note. Trust me, I know."

"Natasha," I whispered as I sucked in a deep breath.

"Exactly. I made her death look like a suicide, and no one batted an eye. Of course, it helped that I had spent months tormenting her and accusing Trevor of doing it during his stupid blackouts. Dumb ass never bothered to do any research to see if it was even possible to do the stuff I accused him of while he was passed out on the floor like a total bitch. Add in a mom who is too busy to care about her kids, and I had the perfect situation lined up."

"Why did you kill your own sister?" I asked sadly.

"She was in the way, and she started to catch on to things that she didn't need to know about. I was getting mixed up with the wrong people, so I had to fake my death. I knew it wouldn't be long before she ratted me out and told my mom. I didn't need that kind of attention, and believe it or not, I was trying to protect my family from the people who would eventually come after me. I guess, in a way, I did them all a favor. Now it's time for him to do one for me."

He looked behind him at Trevor, who was barely sitting upright on the coffee table as his face grew paler.

"I think asking your brother to die so you can take over his identity is a bit much of a favor to ask," I bit out angrily.

His face hardened with anger. My pulse quickened as he lifted his hand and pointed the gun at my head.

"Like I said, I take what I want."

He turned and aimed the gun at Trevor. Before I could blink, I heard the sound echo through the apartment as a bullet whipped past me.

Forty-One

Trevor

"Put your hands in the air and drop the gun!" Max yelled as he rushed into the room.

I was lying on the floor, all strength having left my body as I slid off of the coffee table and crumpled into a pile of uselessness.

"Now, Trevor!" His voice bellowed through the room, and I heard Elena scream.

Before I could get up to see what was going on, I heard another gunshot and tried to cover my head. It felt like being in the middle of a war zone as a few more bullets flew by before I heard a loud thud on the floor.

"NO!!" Elena screamed.

I struggled as I propped myself up on my elbow and saw her hovering over a body.

Blood spilled across the carpet, staining the beige a dark crimson in the process.

I looked around, trying to find Hunter when I saw Max lying on the floor in front of Elena. The door was open as the neighbors started poking their heads in to see what was happening.

I heard people screaming and yelling for someone to call 911. My eyes fluttered closed as I let my body fall back to the floor. If Max couldn't save Elena, then there was no way I would be able to.

Forty-Two
Elena

I sat stiffly in the waiting room chair, holding my head in my hands as I waited for an update on Max and Trevor. Last I heard, Max was still in surgery and had suffered severe damage from multiple gunshot wounds. Trevor was in the ICU, in critical condition from losing an extreme amount of blood as well as internal damage that had to be repaired in emergency surgery.

Back at my apartment, I had watched them carry Natalie's body out as a paramedic examined the wound on my neck. I was so numb at that point that nothing could hurt me. When they asked what my pain level was on a scale of one to ten, I had answered one hundred. This was a pain that I wasn't sure I would ever survive, and the only person I could talk to about it had just been brought out in a black bag tied down on a gurney.

My family lined the walls of the ER waiting room and comforted Trevor's mom as she cried in the corner, unable to believe the events that had unfolded. It was three in the morning, and no one was going to get any sleep until we knew that Max and Trevor were okay.

Hannah had taken the seat beside me as soon as she got there and refused to leave other than to use the bathroom or for an occasional drink of water. My mom was obsessed with trying to get me to eat something but the thought of putting anything in my body right now felt like pure torture. How could I eat when the two people I loved most in the world were lying in the hospital, fighting for their lives?

On top of everything that had happened, Hunter had somehow fled after Max shot him. Unfortunately, I didn't get a good view of where he had been shot, but I prayed that he was sitting somewhere in the dark, dying the lonely, painful death he deserved.

I felt like a terrible person for thinking that, but he really did deserve it, given the things he had done.

Roman had stopped by a handful of times with a guy I hadn't seen before. They spoke in hushed tones and scanned the room frequently. I had wondered if maybe he was someone that Roman had served with, but given the corporate-looking dress slacks and crisp button-down shirt he was wearing, he looked more like someone Max would work with.

It was surprisingly slow in the ER, maybe because the people of New York City finished up their violent crimes and murders earlier, or maybe it was just to torture me every time I heard footsteps coming down the hallway. My feet anxiously tapped against the yellow-tinged linoleum as I waited for an update.

"Any news?" Roman asked as he sat down beside me. The other guy stood next to him, arms folded across his chest as he looked around the room like he was guarding it.

I shook my head.

"This is my friend, Mike Sanchez," he said, nodding. "He's

going to help us find Hunter."

"Okay," I snorted. "Well, he better have superpowers if he wants to find him. He faked his death and lived in the shadows for years before he started pretending to be his brother, and no one noticed." I hung my head and closed my eyes. "I didn't even notice," I whispered.

"He doesn't have superpowers, but he does work with the FBI, and this is sort of his *specialty.*"

I looked up, taking in the dark gray eyes and strong jawline dotted with a thin line of trimmed hair. His jet-black hair was cut short and out of his face, giving him a professional look. Now that I looked at him, he had FBI written all over him.

"Nice to meet you," I said, extending my hand. "And good luck. He's going to be hard to find."

He gave me a curt nod before looking away. He didn't bother to reply, probably knowing that I was right. If Hunter had been able to stay under the radar this long, there wasn't much hope that we would be able to find him before he came back to finish what he started with Trevor.

"You know he will come back to kill him, right?" I asked, looking over at Roman.

He had been there when I told the story to the police and my family. It wasn't a secret at this point that Hunter had faked his death and was trying to take Trevor's identity to claim the inheritance their father left behind. While I wanted to believe that he would stop and give up now that his plans had gone sideways, I knew better than to trust a psychopath.

"We're counting on it," Roman confirmed, looking straight ahead of him as he pressed his hands together between his knees.

"While I want Trevor to survive this, it's terrifying to think he's safer if he doesn't. Who knows what extent Hunter will go to. He killed their sister and then had everyone believing that she committed suicide, for God's sake."

Roman sat quietly for a few minutes, thinking about what I said.

"Hunter is strong and determined," he replied quietly. "But even the strongest, most determined person cannot win against someone like Trevor. He has something that Hunter will never have."

"What's that?"

"A thirst for revenge."

Forty-Three

Elena

I sat in the pew as tears ran down my face, staining my face with grief. The priest led us in prayer, but the words never reached my heart. My mom reached over and squeezed my hand reassuringly as the choir began singing Amazing Grace. On the other side, my father handed me another tissue before blotting his eyes with his.

Their voices were beautiful, filling the church's walls as soft sobs echoed around me. Finally, the pallbearers headed to the front and began to carry the casket out. I lowered my head and allowed my body to shake as I cried.

Soon the song was over, and Natalie's body had been placed in the hearse. I knew that today would be challenging, but I hadn't imagined it would be this devastating.

The guilt I carried with me over her death consumed me. I hadn't eaten in the three days since it happened. I had no desire to do anything for Christmas, even though tomorrow was already Christmas Eve. My depression was at an all-time high, and I shot down every suggestion to find another therapist to talk to.

I waited until everyone left the church before making my way out. My parents had asked if I wanted to go to the cemetery, but I declined and knew that I wouldn't be able to handle it. I needed to say goodbye, and that was hard enough.

"Do you want to go home? I can make some risotto?" my mom offered as we walked to the car.

"I'm not hungry," I muttered, climbing in the back seat.

"You have to eat, Elena," she said with a heavy sigh. My dad got in and started the car, not bothering to get in the middle of what would end up being another fight.

I moved in with them a few days ago, in between spending most of my time at the hospital. Both Max and Trevor had yet to be released, and my days were beginning to blend together. It was probably due to the lack of sleep and forgetting to eat lately that kept me in this numb state of not caring.

Roman had provided a few updates from Mike on their efforts to locate Hunter. So far, he hadn't shown up at any of the hospitals or clinics in New York City, and Mike's team was unable to locate him on any of the traffic cameras in and out of the city. Just as he appeared out of thin air, he disappeared the same way.

Forty-five minutes later, we were back at my parent's house as the sun started to set. The neighboring houses were decked out with Christmas lights that seemed to sparkle in the fresh snow that had fallen. Our house was the only one with no lights and no hint of Christmas cheer. My family had been waiting for all of us kids to get together at the same time to decorate, and that never happened.

I ignored my mom's request to make spaghetti or lasagna as I took the stairs two at a time, desperate for some peace and quiet. It wasn't a secret that my mom and I bumped heads more than my siblings, but after being on my own for a few months, it felt like her overprotective mothering was constantly smothering me.

I shrugged out of my coat and gently pushed the door closed with my foot when I looked down on my bed. Lying on top of my pillow was a picture of Natasha that I had never seen before.

<u>Forty-Four</u>

Trevor

"Take a deep breath. Again. Again."

The doctor continued to move the stethoscope across my chest while I struggled to keep up with the quick breaths she was asking for.

Finally, she pulled away and hung it around her neck before picking up my chart beside her. She scribbled something down before looking at me.

"How are you feeling?" she asked.

"Like I've been through hell and back," I replied bitterly. It wasn't her fault that I was in here or that I was cranky. After snapping at my mom and Roman, they left and gave me some space. It was a lot to process and take in, but that didn't make any of it any easier. Between Max still recovering from numerous surgeries and my psycho brother being on the loose, nothing was keeping me calm.

"I can imagine," she said sympathetically. "Your lab results look good, and your incision is healing nicely. We should be able to discharge you tomorrow, if not–Thursday."

"Merry Christmas to me," I joked, not finding any humor in it.

She smiled, but it wasn't as genuine as when she first came

in. After going through a list of what to expect over the next few days, she left, and I was finally alone. I thought about calling Elena, but I had no idea what I would say to her. She had been by earlier, but the room was packed, and we didn't have a chance to talk. Honestly, I was relieved that everyone was here because I wasn't sure that I would be ready to talk to her anytime soon.

I laid my head back against the pillow and closed my eyes. Part of me wanted to give in to the exhaustion that was clinging to me, but part of me knew that rest wouldn't be an option as long as Hunter was still out there. I wouldn't be able to sleep peacefully until I knew where he was—or better yet—until he was dead.

Not even ten minutes later, I heard a knock on my door before it opened, and Roman walked in.

"You up for some company?" he asked, popping his head through the narrow opening.

"Sure," I said, pushing the button to raise the bed back up to a sitting position.

"My friend Mike is with me. Is it okay if he comes in too?"

I nodded and then remembered that this was the friend that he was telling me about, the one in the FBI with sisters.

As they came in and shut the door behind them, I tilted my head and looked at Roman before asking, "Is he the one whose sister you're banging?"

Mike whipped his head around to glare at Roman, who immediately held his hands up in front of him and took a step back.

"What the fuck?" Mike growled, balling his hands into fists at his sides.

"Woah—you know I'm not screwing around with your sister," Roman said before looking past him to glare at me. "My friend Trevor here just has an ongoing death wish."

"Better not be," Mike warned, punching him somewhat playfully in the shoulder before coming in and taking one of the empty chairs beside my bed.

"Thanks a lot, mother fucker," Roman teased as he smacked my foot before taking the other chair.

"Hey, I needed some entertainment," I shrugged.

"Remind me to subscribe you to a porn site," he replied with a chuckle.

"No thanks, I'm good." I laughed, then immediately regretted it as the skin around my stitches pulled tight and made me wince.

"How are you feeling?" Mike asked.

"Good enough. These damn stitches are a pain in the ass, though."

"When do they think they can come out?"

"A few days, at least."

"That sucks," Roman said, leaning back in the chair. "Guess you'll be leaving all of the new clients for me to deal with while you handle all of the paperwork, *desk bunny*."

I closed my eyes and groaned. While I didn't necessarily love all of the new clients that came rolling in on January 1st with little motivation to actually work out, I loved paperwork even less.

"Haven't I done enough paperwork to last a lifetime just last week?" I complained.

"Hey, that was all your fault for messing it up, to begin with," Roman laughed.

"Well, I refuse to be stuck with all of it. Just wait and see—these stitches will be ready to come out in a day or two, and then I'll be healed and ready to go."

"Yeah, I don't think so." Roman shook his head while Mike tried to hide his laugh with a cough.

"Why not?"

"Because you're not Wolverine. You're a basic human who needs rest to recover."

"You sound like the doctor," I muttered, giving him a dirty look.

"Well then, I guess that makes me pretty damn smart." He winked and then propped his feet up on the corner of my bed.

"What do you think you're doing?" I asked, nudging his foot with my leg.

"Getting comfortable."

"For what?"

"You need to rest, and I'm going to hang out here so you can do so without any trouble."

I looked between him and Mike, noticing the gun attached to his hip for the first time.

"You're here to babysit me so I can sleep?" I asked.

Roman plopped his feet onto the floor and leaned forward, resting his elbows on his knees.

"Your brother faked his death then came back and tried to kill you and everyone you love so he could steal your identity to claim your dead father's inheritance," he said in one long breath. "So yeah, call it whatever you want, but we're not leaving until the threat has been handled."

"Threat?" I raised my eyebrows, wondering if they had any leads on where he was.

"As long as you're still alive, he's a threat."

I ran a hand through my hair, feeling the weight of the IV as it tugged under my skin, and pulled at the tape holding it in place.

For a moment, I felt relaxed, knowing that they would be there while I got some sleep. If I was going to face Hunter again, I needed to be at my best, which meant that I needed to build up my strength again. Just as I was getting ready to lay my head back, I felt a chill spread through my veins.

"I'm not the only one who's in danger," I said, closing my eyes. "He's going to go after Elena again."

Forty-Five

Elena

Silent Night played on repeat downstairs as my mom tried her hardest to lure me out of my room. I hadn't bothered to get out of bed despite my family's numerous attempts to feed me or get me to talk.

I hadn't bothered to tell them about the photo of Natasha that was waiting for me when I got home. It was also pointless to warn them of the impending doom heading my way. I knew that Hunter was just playing mind games until he could get me alone; that's why he left the picture of Natasha for me. Trevor was who he wanted, I was just a bonus, and I knew that he would kill me before he killed Trevor, just to make sure he felt every last bit of pain before he died.

It was oddly comforting to accept my fate and stop fighting the inevitable. Knowing Hunter was coming for me didn't scare me the way it should have. Maybe I was just too numb from everything that had happened, or maybe I had just reached the threshold of what any average person could withstand in a lifetime. In one year, I had suffered more loss and trauma than I had in my entire life. Hell, more than most people would in their entire lives.

I rolled over and pulled the pillow tighter into my stomach. It growled, a reminder that it lacked a basic necessity in life, but I didn't care. I had reached for my phone to call Natalie a handful of times, the ache in my heart deepening every time I remembered that she was dead because of me. A tear slid down my cheek, but I didn't bother to wipe it away. My skin was raw and irritated from a combination of the bitter cold and the constant crying I had done.

Hannah had texted me earlier to check in on how I was doing and let me know that they were keeping Max for a few more days. He had developed an infection that they were watching. She assured me that his partner Mindy had their team working with NYPD to find Hunter and bring him in.

I replied with a smiling emoji face and set my phone down. It was too much work to do anything else. Tomorrow was Christmas Eve, and whether I wanted to or not, I would be spending it downstairs with my family. I already had their gifts purchased and wrapped—though they were still at my crime-scene-ridden apartment—but the best gift that I could give them would be one last Christmas shared with each other before I was gone.

I thought about Trevor's mother and how hard the holidays must have been for her after Natasha killed herself—or rather was murdered—on Christmas Eve. The depths of grief and despair surrounding her family were immeasurable, and I would never wish that heartache on anyone.

She had been on my mind for days, and I had reached out several times to check in on her. She promised that she was okay and that her days were busy between spending time at the hospital with Trevor and picking up extra shifts at work to make up the hours she had missed.

My phone vibrated on the nightstand next to me, and I reached for it, not feeling an inkling of excitement until I saw the name on the screen.

Trevor: I'm getting released this afternoon. Maybe I can come see you so we can talk?

My heart started racing as my fingers flew across the screen.

Me: You should go home and rest, you need it. I can come by and see you when you're settled in. Just let me know what time, and I'll head over.

Trevor: I don't want you traveling by yourself.

Me: You're as much at risk as I am.

Trevor: I hate this.

Me: I hate it too.

I clutched my hand around the blanket and held it tighter to my chest as I waited for his next text to come through. I knew that he was worried about me going over there by myself, but I was even more worried about him. I barely suffered a cut to my neck where he had undergone several surgeries and still had stitches. It wasn't ideal for either of us to go anywhere by ourselves, but I also couldn't risk putting my family in danger by asking them to go with me.

Me: I'll be fine, Trevor. Let me know when you get home.

The dots bounced several times on the screen as he typed. I waited impatiently before his text message finally came through.

Trevor: Ok.

Forty-Six

Trevor

"Do you need anything else?" Roman asked as he closed the fridge and joined me in the living room.

"I think I'm good, thanks."

I sat down, thankful that I wasn't as stiff as a few days ago. The stitches were healing quickly, and thanks to Roman and Mike hanging out in my hospital room so I could sleep, I felt better than I had in days.

Roman had escorted me home from the hospital and had groceries delivered, so I didn't have to go out to get them. Hunter was still out there, but no one had seen or heard anything since he fled Elena's apartment. Max's office chased several tips while NYPD went on wild goose chases that led to dead ends. He was playing games and enjoying every second of it while he scattered the resources that I needed to keep Elena safe. I could care less about my safety when I knew that I was the reason that we had to be worried about hers.

"Elena is still coming over?" he asked, leaning against the wall with his arms folded over his chest.

"I told her that I would let her know when I got home. I hate the idea of her coming here by herself."

He nodded and then pushed off of the wall.

"I'll take care of it."

I didn't bother to ask what that meant as he turned and headed out of my apartment, leaving me to peace and quiet.

We had checked the apartment when we got home, making sure that no one was hiding in the closets or under the bed. It felt silly to look in every nook and cranny, but it didn't stop the unnerving feeling that someone was watching me.

Forty-Seven

Elena

"Hey Roman," I said in a sing-song tone as I walked to the subway, throwing a glance over my shoulder. "You know you're not very stealthy. I saw you right away."

He laughed and quickened his pace to walk beside me. His hands were shoved in the pockets of the leather jacket that wrapped tightly around his muscular frame.

"I wasn't trying to hide," he stated with a shrug.

"So you didn't come all the way over to this side of town to follow me to Trevor's apartment?"

"No, I absolutely did that. I just didn't hide it."

I felt the corners of my lips turn up into a smile, and a wave of guilt washed over me. As quickly as it appeared, it disappeared. I turned the corner and kept walking until we got to the platform and waited for the next train to stop.

"It's okay, you know," he said casually as he stared straight ahead.

"What is?"

"To be happy." He turned his head and studied my face as tears pricked my eyes.

"Happiness is overrated," I muttered before the sound of the approaching train cut me off.

We rode in silence, not bothering to make conversation as people packed into the crowded space around us. I saw him scan the group plenty of times as he positioned his body to shield me on one side while my back was firmly planted against the wall, and an old lady sat on the other side.

After five stops, we finally reached ours. We waited for the people around us to move before he guided me out with one hand on my lower back. I let him lead me even though I knew the quickest way to Trevor's apartment. I assumed he was taking the long way to make sure no one was following us.

Once we were a few blocks away, I found Mike hanging out on the street corner, pretending to check something on his phone. I had seen Max do this plenty of times to know that there was nothing on his phone and that there were probably at least ten other undercover agents lined up around us. Roman's hand tightened against my body, and I felt him tense beside me.

Something was wrong.

Mike's jaw clenched as he slowly looked up and scanned the area around us. Suddenly, Roman pushed me to the side with my back against the wall as he stood in front of me and shielded me.

I desperately wanted to know what was happening but couldn't see anything past Roman's big frame. I heard voices around me as people passed by us, unaware of the danger lurking in the shadows.

"Where?" Roman asked, tucking his chin to his shoulder as he spoke. He was wearing a baseball cap that hid the earpiece until he slightly adjusted it so I could see. "Got it."

He slightly turned his head and whispered over his shoulder to me.

"He's here."

Forty-Eight

Trevor

I had been waiting impatiently for Roman to get here with Elena when I heard the fire alarm go off. I jumped up—and instantly regretted it—and rushed to my bedroom, where the sound was blaring from. I waved my arm as I walked into a cloud of smoke.

My phone sat on the nightstand by my bed, plugged into a charger that was now on fire. I darted into the kitchen, grabbed the fire extinguisher from under the kitchen sink, then ran back in and sprayed it. Luckily the fire was out as quickly as it had started.

My heart was racing as I plopped down on the side of my bed, trying to ignore the throbbing headache from the alarm that was still screaming, and looked at the phone charger on the nightstand by the bed. Once the smoke had cleared, I leaned closer and saw the frayed wires that looked just like Elena's charger.

I had put my phone on charge after Elena had texted me that she was on her way but made sure that the volume was turned all the way up so I would hear if she or Roman called or texted. Unfortunately, my battery was almost dead, so I couldn't wait much longer to charge it. Out of everything that we checked when we got there, the charger wasn't on the list.

I knew that this was just the start. Hunter knew that I was home, and this was his way of letting me know that he was coming for me.

Forty-Nine

Elena

"What's going on?" I whispered into Roman's back as sirens blared around us, surrounding Trevor's apartment as we got closer.

"Fire alarm went off," he said stiffly.

"What?!" I gasped, covering my mouth with my hand.

Roman looked at his phone and guided me down the sidewalk, away from the people pushing past us.

"Trevor is okay," he confirmed. "He got out of the apartment and is heading to the gym. We can meet him there."

I exhaled heavily, letting out the breath that I had been holding. The gym was only a few blocks away, which meant that Trevor wouldn't have to go far before we could get to him. I would feel better once we were together, and I could make sure he was okay.

We were outside the gym twenty minutes later, waiting as Roman unlocked the door. He looked around before stepping to the side to let me in.

The lights were all off except for the one in the hallway that led to their office. Roman led the way, his gun drawn as we quietly approached the room. He stepped to the side and blocked the other end of the hallway while letting me slip inside the office. Trevor sat at his desk, his head back with his eyes closed.

I walked over to him, worried until I saw that he was sleeping. The angle he had his head in allowed us to see the cut on his neck. Knowing that it was Trevor, I took a few slow, steady breaths and walked quietly over to him.

Roman went through the rest of the office while I sat on the edge of the desk and studied his perfect face. It wasn't until my eyes traveled down his body that I noticed his hands tied together under the desk. He wasn't sleeping; he had been knocked out.

"You shouldn't be here."

I jumped up off the desk and whipped around as Hunter walked in, carrying a roll of black trash bags, duct tape, and a large knife.

"Stay away from me," I yelled, hoping that Roman would hear me.

"You need to leave."

My eyes felt like they were going to bulge out of my head.

"What the hell are you talking about? I'm not going to leave him here so you can kill him and steal his identity!"

"I don't have time for this, Elena. You need to get out of here and don't come back. Pretend like you don't know me and forget that we ever met."

"Stop it!" I yelled. "You're not going to get away with this, Hunter!"

"I'm not Hunter," he yelled, standing dangerously close to me as the heat radiated off his body. "Now leave and don't come back. I mean it, Elena."

"Don't fucking lie to me," I spat out, my hands trembling beside me. "I saw the cut on his neck, I know that's Trevor." I nodded my head to where he was still tied up.

"You mean this cut?" he asked, setting everything down on the edge of the desk before pulling his hoodie to the side and tilting his neck so I could see the cut. I narrowed my eyes, noticing it looked identical.

"I'm not going to tell you again, Elena—leave and don't come back. You're not safe here."

"I don't believe you," I cried out. "You're Hunter! You're just trying to get me to believe you, so I'll leave, and you can kill the man I love. I'm not going to let that happen!"

He stepped closer to me and locked his eyes on mine.

"If you love him, you'll do as I tell you to."

"Don't listen to him," another voice croaked beside me.

I turned my head to see *Trevor* waking up. He cleared his throat and blinked his eyes a few times.

"That's Hunter. Don't trust anything he tells you," he added.

I looked back and forth between them, unable to tell the difference for the first time. They were both wearing gray joggers and hoodies that matched.

"Shut your fucking mouth," Trevor number one growled in Trevor number two's direction as he squirmed under the desk.

"Enough," I said through gritted teeth. "I don't believe you," I said to Trevor number one as he stepped back from me and gave me some space.

"You don't have to. Just trust your gut Elena, what does it tell you?" he asked.

"It should tell you to run," Trevor number two behind the desk muttered. "I'm sorry I got you caught up in this. I didn't mean for you to get hurt."

I felt my heart pull at the tenderness in his voice. There was pain and sadness in his words which made me believe even more that he was really Trevor and not Hunter.

At that moment, I knew what I had to do.

I rushed over and ducked down beneath the desk, quickly working the rope around Trevor's hands until it was loose enough for him to pull them free.

I watched Trevor number one's jaw clench as he moved it back and forth.

"That was a stupid mistake to make," he growled so loudly that it startled me, and I jumped back.

"Stupid indeed," Trevor number two agreed as he got up from behind the desk and pulled a gun out of the bottom drawer.

He lifted the gun at the same time that Trevor number one lunged for him, tackling him at the waist and knocking the gun out of his hands. It fell to the ground and slid across the floor. I immediately rushed over and picked it up, remembering everything Max had taught me.

I quickly checked to ensure the safety was off before aiming it at them. The problem was that I had no idea who was who. *Where was Roman when I needed him?*

"Enough!" I yelled as they continued to wrestle on the floor. A few hard punches made contact with bone before I fired a warning shot into the window behind them and got them to stop. I wasn't worried about the broken glass or that someone might hear and call the cops.

They shuffled to their feet but not before one of the Trevors—how do you fucking keep them straight at this point—picked up the knife from the edge of the desk. In one swift movement, he grabbed the other Trevor and stood behind him with the blade pressed into his neck.

"Drop the knife now!" I demanded, feeling my hands slightly trembling. I gripped the gun tighter and widened my feet slightly to keep my balance.

"Shoot him, Elena!" Trevor yelled from under the weight of Hunter's arm as he held him in place—or at least that's who I assumed they were.

I looked between them, hoping for some sort of sign that I would know who the real Trevor was.

"Now! Shoot him!"

"That's what he wants, Elena," Hunter said, tightening his grip around Trevor. "He wants you to believe that I'm Hunter, so you'll shoot me, and then he doesn't have to kill me—you'll do it for him."

"No," I cried, realizing that was a possibility too.

"He won't stop until both of us are dead," he continued, holding the knife against his throat. "You know that. You saw it with Adam—*I'll kill a thousand people just to get to you.* Remember?"

Everything stopped around me for a split second as I thought about what he said. He was right; Adam wasn't going to stop until he killed me. He got distracted with Hannah once he had her, but I knew that he wouldn't stop until he brought me back and killed me. His words repeatedly played in my mind, but I had only told one person what he had said: Trevor.

"Don't listen to him!" Trevor cried out from under Hunter's arm. "Shoot him before he gets inside your head and it's too late!"

I closed my eyes for a brief second, praying that I would have some sort of divine intervention and God would help me to make the right decision.

When I opened my eyes, I heard a gunshot behind me and ducked at the last minute to avoid being hit. I whipped around to find Roman standing there, arms raised with his gun steady between his hands.

There was a loud sound as a body fell to the floor. I couldn't bring myself to turn around and see who it was. Instead, I dropped the gun I was holding and fell to my knees, covering my face as I cried.

"It's okay, Elena," Roman said from above me as he picked up the gun and tucked it into the back of his jeans. "He's okay."

"Elena!"

I felt strong arms wrap around and hold me tightly as my body trembled. I leaned into him, feeling the comfort I had only ever felt with Trevor. Roman was on the phone, notifying someone that Hunter had been shot and giving them the location.

I pulled away from Trevor and looked up at Roman as he stood guard at the door, waiting for the police to arrive.

"Where were you?" I asked, peeling his attention away from the hallway. Suddenly the anger that he had left me started to rise inside me.

"I was here the whole time."

"No," I shook my head and stood up. "I was in here by myself. You weren't here. Why weren't you here?" I yelled as I poked a finger into his chest.

He didn't flinch or pull away as I jabbed at him. Instead, he just stood there and let me have the breakdown I needed.

"I heard his voice and knew that he was here," he said calmly. "I work best in the shadows. If he knew that I was here, things would have gone differently."

"So you left me to handle things on my own?" I sobbed shakily.

"No, I just needed a few minutes to watch from afar so I could make a decision and confirm who was who."

I looked over at Trevor sitting at his desk with his shirt lifted as he checked to make sure his incision hadn't been ripped open in the scuffle.

"Part of my training included studying people and learning their mannerisms. You can tell a lot about someone from the way they act and what they do."

"So you knew which one was Trevor from the start?"

He nodded.

"I feel like the worst girlfriend ever," I groaned, blowing my nose into a tissue I swiped from the box on Trevor's desk. "I couldn't even tell them apart."

"I don't think many people would have been able to if they didn't know what to look for." He paused and looked over at Trevor. "For instance, Trevor has a small mole on his left hand, right above a scar he got when he was a kid. I didn't see either when Hunter was holding the knife. Plus, Trevor is left-handed, whereas Hunter felt more comfortable holding the knife with his right."I looked at Trevor's hand, noticing the scar and mole for the first time.

"Those are such small details to base such a life-changing decision on," I admitted.

"I agree," Roman sighed. "But I knew the moment they saw me. Trevor closed his eyes in relief, and Hunter narrowed his in anger. That was all that I needed to confirm what I already knew."

"Well, I'm thankful you were here," I said before we heard voices coming down the hall as the police arrived.

I moved to the side and sat down as they took over. For once, I felt like I could sit back and just relax.

<u>Fifty</u>
Trevor

"We don't have to do this," my mom objected as she lowered onto the plush chair the waiter held out for her, tucking her full-length dress underneath her as she sat down.

Once Elena was situated, I took my seat between them and pulled myself closer to the table. The restaurant was dimly lit with white Christmas lights scattered throughout, adding a soft ambiance to the quaint room. I pulled the linen napkin from the plate in front of me and laid it on my lap before reaching my hand over to rest it gently on Elena's thigh.

We hadn't had a chance to talk after everything happened yesterday, but neither of us seemed in a rush to have the conversations that we needed to have. Maybe we just wanted a peaceful Christmas Eve, or maybe we didn't need to talk out all of the gruesome details. Either way, things felt normal between us, and I wasn't going to do anything to change that.

I looked over at her, admiring how a thin strand of hair had fallen loose from the updo she had it in and framed her face. Her makeup was done in light shades of gray and silver to match the sparkles in the shimmery black dress she was wearing. She looked downright beautiful, and I found it hard to keep from touching her.

"Would you like to hear tonight's specials?" the waiter asked, standing at the head of the table with both hands behind his back.

I nodded but didn't bother listening as I continued to stare at Elena. She tilted her head back and laughed at something he said, and I realized just how much I had missed seeing her smile.

I looked up to find my mom watching me, a warm smile on her face. Once the waiter left, I took a deep breath and let it out. My mom knew what I was planning to do tonight, but it didn't make it any easier.

My fingers fidgeted under the table as I tried to expel some of the nervous energy I was suddenly feeling.

"Do you know what you're getting?" Elena asked my mother, briefly looking up from her menu to look at her.

"Everything looks so good I can't decide," my mom answered, lifting her menu so I couldn't see the shit-eating grin on her face. I was a nervous wreck, and she was loving every second of it.

"What about you? What are you getting?" Elena asked, lowering her menu to the table.

I swallowed hard and tried to think of an answer. Instead, I blurted out, "Will you move in with me?"

She pulled her head back in surprise, caught off guard by my random question.

I knew that there was a good chance that she would say no. She had already said no to my offer plenty of times before everything happened.

"I, um," she hesitated, and my heart sank.

I turned so quickly in my chair that it squeaked on the floor, drawing the attention of those around us. I offered a quick apologetic smile and then ignored them and focused on Elena. I reached for her hands and lined my chair up in front of her as she turned to face me.

"I know that you've said no before, and I get it," I said quickly. "But things are different now, Elena."

"How so?" she asked softly.

"When I first asked you to move in with me, it was because I thought *you* needed it. Now I'm asking you to move in because *I* need it. Because the thought of going a single day without seeing you drives me mad, and the idea of not holding you every night when you fall asleep causes my heart to ache."

She pulled her lower lip between her teeth and chewed it nervously for a few seconds before looking over at my mom and popping it free. When she looked back at me, she was smiling so big that it felt like it lit up the entire room.

"Yes, Trevor. I'll move in with you."

I pumped my fist in the air triumphantly before reaching forward and cupping her face as I pulled her in for a kiss.

"You just made me the happiest man in the world," I said between kisses.

"Congratulations!" Our waiter clapped his hands and squealed excitedly as he approached our table. He lifted a hand in the air, making a quick circular motion with his finger to another server, then took our order. A few minutes later, a bottle of champagne was delivered to our table as a gift from the restaurant to celebrate our recent engagement. We didn't bother to tell them that we weren't engaged as we toasted and shared this milestone in our relationship with my mom.

After he left, my mom leaned over and hugged both of us as tears of happiness filled her eyes.

"I'm so happy for you guys," she said, blotting her eyes with the linen napkin she had pulled from her lap.

"Thank you," Elena replied, gently squeezing her hand.

"It's about time we had something good happen," my mom joked, her face lighting up for the briefest second before falling with sadness. "Sorry, I didn't mean to ruin the moment."

"You didn't," I rushed to assure her. "It's okay to talk about things. A lot has happened in a very short time, and I know your head has to be spinning just as fast as ours."

The waiter came by to deliver our food before rushing off to another table.

"He wasn't always such an evil person," my mom said with her fork lifted in the air. "He was the sweetest boy until he started school. I still remember the day I got a call from his teacher, letting me know he had gotten into a fistfight with another boy and they needed me to come pick him up. I brought him home and sat him down, ready to give him a stern talking to before disciplining him, but your dad was home and took over instead."

She shook her head and let her shoulders fall with a heavy sigh.

"We didn't see eye to eye on much, but that was the first time I had ever stood up to him. Instead of disciplining Hunter for what happened, he gave him pointers on how to do better the next time. Something changed in Hunter that day, a darkness that shadowed the light I used to see in his eyes. After that, he became his dad's best friend and did everything he asked. I should have known then that he was going to be just like him, I just don't think that my heart was ready to handle it, so I pretended like I didn't see it."

"That had to have been so hard," Elena said, setting her fork down to listen.

"From then on, he was constantly getting in trouble at school, constantly fighting with other kids, defacing school property. Stealing," she sighed. "But then he started picking on Natasha, and I knew I had to do something. I tried to get him to go to counseling, but he refused. I tried every single method of discipline that I could think of, but nothing worked. It seemed like there was no way to get through to him. On top of that, I was working three jobs just to make ends meet, and even if I could find the time to help him, I didn't have the energy to do anything. I was constantly tired, and my depression was spiraling out of control."

"I'm so sorry, mom," I whispered, holding her hand. "I wish there was more that I could have done."

"When I got the news about Natasha, do you know what the first thing was that I thought?"

I shook my head but refused to let go of her hand. We had never discussed this before, and I wanted her to feel strong enough to keep going. I needed to know what my mom went through and the silent battles she faced that I couldn't see.

"I was so mad that she beat me to it."

The air left my lungs in such a rush that I felt lightheaded. My hand fell to the table, allowing hers to release from my grip. I looked at her with tears in my eyes, unable to believe what I had heard.

"When I saw how hard you were taking her death, I knew then that it had been Hunter who was tormenting her, not you. I knew that you would never hurt her, and seeing you in so much pain made me remember how much I loved you and how I would do anything to spare you that kind of pain again. If I could take it away, I would have."

She reached over and grabbed my hand again, giving it a tight squeeze.

"YOU are what kept me going, Trevor. You were my reason for living. You are the reason that I continue to get up in the morning and that I look forward to each new day. I miss your sister more than I could ever explain, but I know that she's free from the pain she was suffering as well."

"I had no idea," I said hoarsely, the tears burning my throat. "I knew that Hunter made my life a living hell, but I didn't know that he did the same to everyone else. I just thought it was because we were brothers, and that's what siblings do." I shrugged my shoulders and realized for the first time in my life that my brother was never the person I thought he was.

"I tried to keep as much away from you as possible. You didn't need that kind of negativity in your life. Once you met Max, I was soooo relieved that you had a best friend who would look out for you and protect you from the darkness surrounding Hunter. Shortly before his *death*, I had noticed some guys coming around the house looking for him. I knew then that he was in trouble, I just didn't know how deep he had gotten into it."

"Enough to dump his car in a lake and fake his death," I grunted. "I can't believe that he got away with it for so long."

"Max said that they found a fake ID he had been using. Apparently, he was already living someone else's life and looked similar enough to them that no one questioned it when he moved to a new city and started over. They're still looking for the guy's body he pretended to be before he came back here. The guy was reported missing by his family six months ago," Elena added. Max hadn't been able to say much, but this quickly became a massive investigation that spanned several different agencies and would likely take a while before it was wrapped up.

"Who knows how many other identities he's taken over the years," my mom said sadly.

"Or how many people he's killed along the way to get what he wanted," I said.

My mom and I had gone to the coroner's office this morning to identify his body. I've only ever seen a handful of dead bodies in my life, but the second I saw Hunter, I knew that it was him. Aside from the collection of new tattoos he had, everything else looked the same, including the birthmark on his back.

I leaned back in my chair and listened as Elena and my mom continued the conversation but felt distracted as I wondered if Hunter had gotten some of the tattoos he had because they were tattoos that the other person had before he took their identity. It wouldn't surprise me to see him be that thorough, just like it wouldn't surprise me if he had killed them as well.

Soon the conversation shifted, and we focused on eating our dinner before it got cold. Once we were done, we pushed our plates away and declined the waiter's dessert recommendations when there was nowhere to put anything else. We would be sitting for a few hours at the theater, and the last thing that I wanted was to be uncomfortable from overeating.

We got to the theater a little earlier than expected and took the time to talk to some of the people that my mom knew. We used to come to the theater a lot when we were little—when my mom could afford to bring us—and it became like a second home to me. Everyone was so friendly and took us in as their own when my mom wasn't around.

The lights flickered a few times to let us know the show was about to start. I grabbed Elena's hand and led her to our seats, smiling at my mom, who was already waiting for us. We sat down and enjoyed the show as a family, remembering and honoring my sister for the night.

Fifty-One

Elena

"That one is from me," I said cheerfully, rubbing my hands together excitedly as Max arched a brow and started to unwrap the small box on his lap.

He had been released from the hospital yesterday morning and was determined to make it to my parent's house for Christmas. Trevor and his mom had joined us, and I had never felt so happy before in my life.

I tapped my feet excitedly on the carpet, watching the red balls bounce on the reindeer noses on my socks in the process. Trevor wrapped his arm around my waist and pulled me into his side before planting a kiss on my cheek. I leaned into him, allowing my body to mold against his where it belonged.

Max tore the rest of the wrapping paper off and tossed it to the side as he examined the wooden box. He tilted his head and studied it for a minute, probably wondering if the box itself was the gift. It was a beautiful box, but it wasn't the real gift.

"Open it," I coaxed, waving my hand to encourage him to keep going.

He smiled and lifted the lid. I watched the emotions flash

across his face before he blinked away tears and looked at me as he covered his mouth with his hand.

Everyone waited impatiently for him to show them what was inside and had him so worked up. He wasn't a man who freely showed emotion, so this was a big deal.

He reached in and picked up a silver picture frame with the words *Superhero* written across the top with a picture of Max and me inside.

"Thank you," he said, his voice wavering. "But I'm not a superhero."

"Yes, you are," I protested. "And I'm sorry that I ever said that you weren't. You've been saving me since I was a little girl and have never let me down."

I let the tears slide down my face as we stared at each other and had a moment that only we understood.

"I love it, thank you," he said and gently put it back into the box.

"You're welcome." I smiled and laid my head on Trevor's chest as we watched my parents open their presents. They always went last, too excited to watch us kids open our gifts that they didn't want to miss out by opening theirs.

My mom thanked everyone as she made her way through the giant pile of presents until the only one that was left was from me.

I had struggled with what to get her this year. I put it off until the very last minute, stressing about how no matter what I got her, she wouldn't like it. She had everything she could possibly want or need, which left little room to surprise her with anything special.

Last night Trevor and I had decided to step into a store that was still open after we dropped his mom off for the night. I browsed the aisles, looking at the trinkets and figurines until my eyes landed on one that took my breath away.

I watched closely as she lifted the delicate sculpture out of the box and looked at it. It was a mother and daughter joined together by a heart that they were both holding. I knew the moment I saw it that it was the perfect gift for her and cried when I bought it. Even though we fought more than anyone I knew, it always came from a place of love, and I understood that now.

Her eyes welled up with tears as she held it, moving it around to look at every tiny detail. Finally, she looked up at me and smiled, holding it to her heart as a tear fell from her eye. *I love you,* she mouthed, and for once, everything in my life felt perfect.

Fifty-Two

Trevor

"I still need to give you my gift," I whispered in Elena's ear as I wrapped my arms around her waist and pulled her back tight against my chest.

"Oh yeah?"

"Yup."

"Well, I still need to give you my gift as well. But unfortunately, it's stuck there until Max works his magic so I can get back into my apartment. I'm thankful that I had left most of my gifts here after I went shopping with my sister, but I hate that I didn't have anything to give you today."

"*You're* the best gift that I could ever ask for. But, if you want to go back to my place later, I can give you your gift then," I teased as my hands slipped down into dangerous territory, given that we were still at her parent's house. We had finished dinner, and her mom promptly kicked us out of the kitchen while she and Elena's sisters worked on cleaning up the dishes.

"We can go now," she offered, facing me.

I saw her grin pull across her face as her cheeks turned a slight shade of pink when she felt my erection through my jeans. Her hand drifted down my stomach and grabbed it, making me hiss in response.

"I thought you wanted to stay for pie?" I asked, closing my eyes while I tried to will my erection to go away.

"I have pie you can eat at your place."

"Let's go," I growled, spinning her around and gently pushing her toward the closet where our coats were kept.

She laughed and opened the door, pulling them out and handing mine to me.

"You guys outta here already?" Max asked, coming up behind us with Hannah.

"Yeah, I'm tired," Elena said as she shrugged into her heavy winter coat.

"Me too," I added even though I wasn't.

"You guys?" she asked, turning to face them once it was on.

"Same," Hannah laughed.

"Well, we can all sneak out at once, and then mom can't guilt us into staying. Strength in numbers, right?" Elena joked.

We said our goodbyes before leaving and taking the train back to my apartment. The ride was long as I thought about all of the things that I wanted to do to Elena once we got there. While I really did have a gift for her, it was the never-ending gift that I couldn't wait for her to open. The one where she rode my face until she came undone and cried out my name for all of my neighbors to hear.

As soon as we got inside, I locked the door and slid the deadbolt in place before stripping off my coat and helping her out of hers. Our mouths crashed against each other as we flung pieces of clothing across the apartment and stumbled our way to my bed.

She was naked except for a black lace bra and matching panties. I was wearing nothing but boxer briefs that already felt too tight against my raging hard-on. I hooked my thumbs in the sides and slid them off, allowing it to spring free as she climbed on the bed and looked over her shoulder with her ass in the air for me to admire.

"You're so fucking beautiful," I said as I stalked over to her and slapped her ass.

"Ow!" she giggled, wiggling it for me to spank her again.

I gave her a quick smack before rubbing the red spot, letting my fingers glide along the crack. Her back arched slightly before she spread her legs a little further, allowing me to go where I wanted to.

With one finger, I pushed her panties aside before running it down her slit, feeling the warmth and wetness from her pussy welcoming me. I played with her for a few minutes, teasing her before finally sliding my finger inside her.

She gasped and rocked down against my hand. I wanted to take my time and give her every ounce of pleasure that I could, but the way she was grinding against me told me that she was as ready for this as I was. I laughed as I slipped another finger inside and heard her moan in response.

She tossed her head, flipping her hair over her shoulder as she looked back at me. She chewed her bottom lip and rocked harder as she locked her eyes with mine.

"I want you inside of me," she urged.

"Your wish is my command."

I reluctantly pulled my fingers out and waited for her to get comfortable on the bed. I hooked my fingers in her panties and pulled them down her legs before tossing them to the floor. Before climbing on top of her, I grabbed a condom out of the drawer and put it on.

I soaked up the image of her lying in my bed– hair fanned out around her face with her full breasts pushed up on display in the new bra she was wearing. I glanced down, smiling when I saw the faint outline of the Christmas tree landing strip.

"Ho, ho, ho," I murmured before sliding inside her. "Santa's coming tonight."

She closed her eyes and moaned as I moved, lifting her hips to meet my every move. I trailed kisses along the side of her neck and down her collarbone before pulling the thin fabric down on her bra and taking a tight nipple into my mouth. I sucked hungrily, desperate for the release we desperately needed.

Sex with Elena was always great, but this time, it was different. It wasn't just the way she scratched her nails down my back or tightened her legs around me as I pounded harder inside of her, but the way that she opened her eyes and watched me as we climaxed together.

I had been worried that I had lost Elena forever, and now I was determined to show her every single second of every single day just how much she meant to me and never let her go again.

Fifty-Three

Elena

2 Weeks Later

"How are things going?" Hannah asked before pushing a french fry into her mouth.

I wiped my mouth and took a drink of soda to wash down my bite of pizza before I answered her.

"Good," I shrugged. "Different."

It was busy in the dining hall on campus, with students rushing around to grab a bite to eat before their next class.

"Do you like your classes so far?" She squirted more ketchup onto her plate, then looked at me while I thought about the question. It had only been a few days since I had started college again.

"I do," I said thoughtfully. "I think changing majors really helped."

She laughed and popped another fry in her mouth.

"Yeah, business is a lot different than psychology. But I'm glad that you're enjoying them."

"How are your classes going?" I asked, taking a bite while she talked. Her classes were very different than mine since she was still studying forensics, much to the dislike of my brother.

"They're good. I'm excited to be taking more advanced classes this semester."

We talked for a few minutes about school before she shifted in her seat and took a drink of water. Putting the cap back on the bottle, she looked around at the students scattered at the tables around us before turning back to me.

"How is everything else going?" she asked quietly enough for only me to hear.

I crumpled up my napkin and tossed it onto my empty plate while I finished chewing.

"Things are good. Living with Trevor is easier than I thought it would be. We finally got all of my stuff out of my old apartment and canceled the lease. My mom is just over the moon that Trevor and I are living together, and I think Max is relieved that he doesn't have to worry about me as much now that things are mostly back to normal."

"And you?" she pressed. "How are *you* doing, Elena?"

I knew what she was really asking, which was why I kept skirting around it.

"I don't know," I answered honestly, looking down at the table. "No matter how hard I try, I can't get past the guilt of knowing I'm responsible for Natalie's death."

The words burned my throat as they pushed their way through my mouth. It was something that I had thought about every single day but had never said out loud, but with Hannah, it was different because I knew that out of anyone—she would understand.

She smiled sadly but didn't say anything.

"Does it ever get easier?" I asked.

"No," she answered quickly, not missing a beat. "It's been over a year since Amber died, and I still blame myself for her death. Everyone has tried to tell me that it wasn't my fault, but at the end of the day, the fact remains that if she wasn't there at my apartment that morning, she would still be alive. Being my best friend is what got her killed."

Tears stung my eyes as I felt the pain in her words.

"Natalie came to check on me. She was worried about me because of the fake suicide note that Hunter left for her. If she wasn't my therapist, she would still be alive."

Hannah reached across the table and squeezed my hand.

"I know that it doesn't change anything, Elena, but I'm glad that you found someone that you were comfortable talking with. I hate that Natalie was murdered by a psychopath, but I can tell how much she loved and cared about you. If she didn't, she would have turned that letter over to the police and initiated a wellness check. She wouldn't have gone to see you herself."

"So you're saying that loving me is deadly," I joked, but neither of us found it funny.

"Not at all," she laughed and released me. "Bad things happen to good people all the time. Maybe we've just had our fair share, and now only the good things will happen to us."

She threw our trash in the trashcan next to us before picking her backpack up off the floor and sliding it onto her back.

"Are you heading to your next class?" she asked as I got up and grabbed mine.

"I'm actually done for the day."

My schedule this semester was super light while I tried to decide whether or not this was what I wanted to do—that and the fact that I had lost my scholarship and couldn't afford to pay full-time tuition. Trevor had offered to pay it for me, but I quickly declined his offer.

After NYPD and the FBI wrapped up their investigations and Hunter's real death was made public, Trevor had been contacted by the attorney who was handling his father's estate. He had considered refusing the inheritance, but when he thought about all of the years that his mother had suffered and went without so she could give them the best life possible, he knew that he should take it.

He had planned to pay off her house and deposit some into her savings account when the money came in. It was such a massive amount that he would be able to do everything he had been saving up for at the gym AND still have enough left over to retire. But Trevor was a hard-working man with a drive and determination like no one I had seen before. It meant a lot to him to own his own business, and he wasn't going to let a large sum of cash change that for him. As far as he was concerned, he still worked a forty-hour workweek and paid his dues, just like everyone else.

Hannah and I said goodbye and went our separate ways as she headed to class, and I headed home. *Home.* It felt weird to say that, but I honestly never felt more at home than at Trevor's apartment. From the time we started dating, it was the only place I was comfortable besides my parent's house.

Now that everything had settled down and we didn't have endless interviews with law enforcement, I tried to find my groove again. I stopped by the store on my way home to grab some groceries to make dinner tonight.

When Trevor got home, I had chicken baking in the oven and a spinach salad ready in the fridge. Trevor was always better at eating healthier than me, so I was learning new ways to cook now that I lived with him, but that didn't stop me from saying yes to my mom's invites for a carb-heavy dinner every week. Even Trevor didn't complain about her fresh garlic bread and rigatoni when he joined me last week.

"Honey, I'm home," he teased, shutting and locking the door behind him. He set his keys down and shrugged out of his coat before finding me in the kitchen.

I was standing by the stove wearing nothing but a black apron that barely covered my breasts and was just long enough to hide the black lace thong underneath.

"Fuck. Me." He leaned against the doorframe, rubbing his finger across his jaw while chewing his lower lip.

"Oh, trust me—I plan to."

I winked and turned seductively, popping my ass in the air to give him a full view as I opened the oven and pulled the chicken out. As soon as I had it set down on the trivet, I felt Trevor's hands slide across my ass and pull me to him. I tossed the towel to the counter and allowed his hands to roam over my body.

He pushed my hair to the side and then untied the apron, letting it fall to the floor. I turned around, covering my breasts with my hands as his eyes clouded with lust.

"Dinner's ready," I said innocently.

He growled before pushing me up against the wall and crashing his mouth down over mine. Our tongues danced around each other as his hands worked the zipper on his jeans. I heard the sound as they fell to the floor and knew that he was as eager to fuck me as I was to be fucked.

He lifted me by the waist and pinned me to the wall before pulling his cock out of his briefs and sliding my panties to the side. I arched my back to give him better access as he plunged inside of me, not having any resistance given how wet I was.

I closed my eyes and dug my nails into his back as he plowed deeper inside of me, fucking me as hard as he could against the wall. I opened my mouth to moan, but his mouth captured the sound as he kissed me harder.

I could hear the picture frames rattle as he moved his hips faster and harder, sending me over the edge with each move. His finger slipped down between us and rubbed my clit, giving me the push that I needed as he came inside of me. We both climaxed simultaneously, neither of us bothering to stifle our moans at that point. His neighbors had given up on complaining about how loud we were after they realized that there wouldn't be anything that stopped us from constantly going at it on every surface in his apartment.

Once he was done, he lowered me to the floor and made sure my wobbly legs would hold me before he let go.

The smile on his face was so fucking sexy that I couldn't get enough of it. I wanted to see it all day, every day. And thankfully, that's exactly what I got now that I lived with him, and we were back to humping like rabbits.

Right after Christmas, we had both gone for an annual check-up and decided that we would both get tested for STDs given that I had accidentally slept with his brother— something neither of us would ever talk about again for the rest of our lives. At Hannah's urging, I took a pregnancy test when my period was later than usual. It turned out that mine was late because of stress, and hers was late because my brother couldn't keep his hands off her. I was excited that I was going to be an aunt, even if I wasn't allowed to tell anyone about it yet.

Now that we both had the all-clear from the doctor, we did it every chance we got without bothering to use condoms. Trevor and I both loved the feeling without them, and I was still on birth control until we decided that we were ready for that level of commitment. Moving in together was a big enough change for me right now, so I didn't see any babies in our near future.

We cleaned up, and I threw on some yoga pants and a t-shirt before we sat down to eat. The chicken was still plenty warm after our quickie, which worked out nicely. We sat on the couch and watched TV for a bit before Trevor set his empty plate down on the coffee table and looked at me.

"So, I was thinking," he started nervously.

He rubbed his hands together, and a faint blush crept up his neck.

"About what?" I asked, setting my plate down and trying to keep the panic out of my voice. *Was he already regretting having me move in with him? Had he gotten bored with our sex life and wanted to spice things up?* My mind was going a mile a minute, worrying over the tone he had used while his anxiety spread from his restless legs to mine.

"Roman and I were talking about this guy he's been seeing. He's really good, and Roman likes him a lot—"

My eyes went wide with surprise before he realized what he was saying.

"No, no," he laughed. "For therapy, Elena. Roman has a guy he's been going to for therapy."

"I'm not judging," I laughed, holding my hands up in front of me.

"Very funny," he mocked, laughing with me. "Trust me, Roman has women lined up waiting for him, and he has never had a problem saying no."

I raised my eyebrows, but it didn't surprise me. He was incredibly handsome with a muscular body that women obsessed over.

"Anyway—I was thinking about going to see his therapist."

My heart fluttered, and I put my hand to my chest. This was a huge thing for Trevor, and I felt so honored that he was talking to me about it.

"Yeah? I think that would be great!"

Something that looked like relief washed over him as he leaned back against the couch.

"I was wondering if maybe you'd like to go with me to a few sessions? Like couple's therapy?"

His voice caught again, and now I knew why.

We had talked several times about this, but it was always

about whether I was going to find someone new to see. Natalie's death had jaded me in more ways than one, but the thought of going to therapy and talking about the last therapist that I got killed felt like too much for me. *What if they thought I was bad luck or started to fear me because of what happened to Natalie?*

I swallowed and thought about my words before I said them.

"Hannah and I talked today at lunch," I started. "I asked her if it ever gets easier—dealing with the guilt of knowing that you're responsible for someone's death."

He flinched and closed his eyes.

"She said that she still feels guilty about Amber's death and that it hasn't changed for her a year later." I paused and took a steady breath. "I know that Natalie's death isn't anything that I'm ever going to forget or just *get over*. But I also know that I benefited tremendously by seeing her after everything happened with Adam. She helped me heal in ways that I didn't know how to heal on my own."

He smiled, but his body was tense again as he waited for my answer.

"I think therapy could be great for you, our relationship, and me."

He raised his brows in surprise.

"I think it's time that I find a new therapist as well."

It was something that I had thought about all afternoon after Hannah and I had talked, and I realized that not going to therapy wasn't going to change what happened to Natalie, but it could impact what happened to me. I felt stronger when I was seeing her, and I knew that I could find that strength again if I pushed myself to get the help that I needed. Grief was a brutal beast to handle, but I owed it to myself to try.

Epilogue
Trevor
6 Months Later

"How are you not melting in that?" I asked Max as I tugged at the tie that was way too tight around my neck.

He chuckled and shook his head. The song changed as the wedding party took its place at the front of the church. Tears filled his eyes as Hannah started down the aisle, her white lace dress wrapped tightly around her swollen stomach. I felt a knot in my throat as I watched them, knowing that someday I wanted this for Elena and me.

I leaned forward slightly and caught a glimpse of her wiping her eyes while trying not to drop her bouquet. She was the maid of honor, and I got to be the lucky one who walked her down the aisle since I was the best man. It was hard not to imagine us up here instead, but I knew that she wanted to go slow and for now, moving in together was a big enough step.

"You look beautiful," Max whispered to Hannah as he graciously took her from her mom. She planted a kiss on Hannah's cheek before taking her seat in the front row, next to my parents.

The ceremony was short and sweet–just what the happy

couple had wanted and what I needed so I could get my hands on Elena again. It was summer in New York City, and the short rose-colored dress that she was wearing begged for me to slip my hand underneath it as soon as we had a moment alone.

We had gone six months with condom-free sex and only had two pregnancy scares along the way. Elena was the one who was scared, whereas I was the one who was disappointed with each negative pregnancy test. I hoped that someday she would want to settle down and have my babies, but I also kept reminding myself that while I was thirty, she was barely twenty and still had her prime party years ahead of her.

After smiling until my cheeks ached, the wedding party was finally released so the photographer could get some pictures of just the bride and groom before the reception. I took the first opportunity that I had to sweep Elena away and make our way to an empty staircase.

"I've been waiting to do this all damn day," I growled as I pinned her against the wall and slipped a hand between her thighs. I planted kisses along her jaw and then down her neck, stopping myself before I tugged the top of her strapless dress down to gain access to her nipples.

"We just had sex this morning," she laughed, not bothering to stop me as I slid a finger inside her. She gasped and let her head fall back while a moan escaped her lips.

"I will never get enough of you," I replied, moving another finger in while rubbing her clit with my thumb.

"Good, because I'm kinda addicted to you," she said breathlessly, moving her hips to grind against me.

"Especially with the daily orgasms."

I felt the strain against my trousers as my dick pressed against them, eager to be free and mark her as mine. There wasn't a time or place when I didn't want to fuck Elena, and her newly increased sex drive was working in my favor.

"Right there," she murmured into my shoulder before biting down to stifle her moan.

I rubbed harder, knowing exactly what she needed to get her there. I felt the first spasms a few seconds later as her orgasm ripped through her and her legs trembled against me.

I pulled my hand away and smiled down at the beautiful woman in front of me.

"They're going to start looking for us soon," she laughed, fixing her dress as I stepped away to give her some space.

"We better get back out there and pretend to be the best damn best man and maid of honor they've ever seen," I laughed.

We snuck down the stairs and joined the wedding party right before they were being led into the ballroom for the reception. Given our roles, we were supposed to be in line behind Max and Hannah, so it was painfully obvious we had been missing when they gave us their not-so-subtle glares as we stepped in behind them.

"Where have you two been?" Hannah whispered to Elena as Max's jaw clenched.

"I needed a drink of water," Elena lied, looking away as her face flushed red.

"You still look dehydrated," Max commented. "Your face is

red and splotchy, and your skin looks sweaty. How far did you go to find water? There's a fountain right there." He pointed to the one across the way from us in between the restrooms.

I was about to answer but snapped my jaw shut when the wedding coordinator person—I had already forgotten her official title—snapped her fingers to get everyone's attention before leading us into the room—saved by the bell.

The doors opened, and an upbeat song played that we all danced our way into the room to. It was fun and lively, and I felt the weight of the world lifted from my shoulders as I watched Elena laugh and smile as I twirled her around the dancefloor before leading her to her seat. I took mine next to Max and prayed that he wouldn't pepper me with any more questions about where we had been or what we were doing. If anything, he should know by now not to ask.

The DJ spoke into the microphone with an update on dinner being served when Max leaned over. I felt my phone vibrate in my pocket and pulled it out.

Before he could ask any questions about Elena, he noticed the frown on my face and nodded to my phone.

"What's up?" he asked.

I read the message again, furrowing my brow.

"It's Roman," I said slowly as I reread it. "He needs time off from work."

"What's going on? Is everything okay?" he asked.

"No, I don't think so," I said as I typed out a reply and waited for him to respond.

A few minutes later, I got his text message:

Roman: Quinn and Rosie are missing. I won't stop until I find them.

I looked at Max, a look of concern passing between us when we knew what that really meant. It wasn't just a random kidnapping; it was an innocent five-year-old who had no chance of surviving her captors without some sort of miracle.

AGAINST THE CLOCK

Samantha Baca

Copyright © 2022 by Samantha Baca.

Content Warning:

This book contains language and storylines that may be bothersome for some readers and is intended for a mature audience. Violence and sexual scenes may be shown in detail as well. The reader is encouraged to reach out to the author directly (authorsamanthabaca@gmail.com) if they would like to further discuss the content warning(s) for this book. Warnings for Against The Clock:

Violence

Child loss (mentioned briefly)

Child Abuse (mentioned briefly)

Sexual Assault (mentioned vaguely, not in detail)

Child Trafficking

One
Quinn

The front door swung open, the rain spraying in from the wind that whipped past. I turned my head, knowing that Roman was back from messing with the generator but felt my body stiffen when I saw five figures dressed in all black, wearing ski masks, rush through the door.

I jumped off the couch, startling Rosie as I tried to shield her with my body. I reached behind for my gun, panic crushing over me when I remembered it wasn't there. It was unlike me not to have it on my body, but I had been distracted after I got out of the shower right before Roman went outside to prepare for the storm that was already upon us.

"NO!!" I shouted, shoving against the bodies as they charged us. I felt strong arms grab me and fling me to the side as Rosie screamed from the couch. I got up and swung at the masked figure in front of me, watching as their head shot to the side from the impact of my punch, but it wasn't enough. Someone held me by the waist, ensuring that I couldn't get to Rosie.

Panic flooded through me as I tried to get free. It was useless, and I knew it. We were outnumbered and I was unarmed—biggest fucking mistake of my life.

I could hear Rosie scream and turned my head toward the

sound right as someone picked her up and tossed her over their shoulder. A black pillowcase was shoved over her head as they rushed out the door. I continued to fight against the strong arms holding me in place, desperate to get to my daughter. My pulse raced and my breathing was erratic as adrenaline pumped through me.

I tried to turn to see where they had gone, the front door still wide open. There was a black van parked right outside, and I immediately recognized it. Seconds later, the back door was slammed shut before it sped off, the sound of gravel crunching beneath it.

I tossed my head back, feeling the sharp pain as I made contact with a head, eliciting a loud growl from the recipient. It wasn't enough to knock him out, but it did piss him off to where he tightened his grip around my throat, making it harder to breathe. I brought my hands up and tried to pry his hands away, desperate for air.

Roman will be back any second. He'll come save me. He'll take me to get Rosie back. Then we'll kick ass and take out everyone who's ever tried to hurt my daughter. She's only five years old…

But before Roman could get there, a hand reached up and covered my mouth with a towel. Everything turned black, and the voices around me faded.

Two
Roman
14 Days Ago

I tilted my head back and felt the cold chill as the beer slid down my throat. It was hot and muggy, making the buttoned-down white shirt stick to my body. The music played loudly throughout the backyard as lights lit up the dance floor where a handful of women in super short dresses were dancing.

I didn't have to look at them to know that they were watching me. Each time the song changed, they would glance at me over their shoulder as they rubbed their hands up and down their body and thrust their hips along to the beat. There was so much effort put into each move, and I couldn't find the energy to try to engage any of them.

There was only one woman who had caught my attention tonight, and it fucking sucked because there was no way that I could talk to her. It wasn't like I was shy or didn't know how to talk to women. It was because she was my best friend's little sister, and I knew that he would kill me if he knew the thoughts going through my head every time I looked at her.

Quinn wasn't anything like the other women around us. Her raven black hair was pulled into a loose ponytail, high up on her head, and she looked comfortable in a pair of jeans and a t-shirt. She didn't wear the club outfits, or the heavy makeup that Mike's cousins were wearing—who I was informed weren't off-limits when I tried to get out of having a drink with one of them. She also looked more relaxed than the handful of FBI agents that lined the wall with their water bottles clutched to their chest, leaving wet marks on the silk dress shirts they probably wore every day, even outside of work.

I knew I shouldn't be so judgmental about the people Mike worked with, but it had kept me entertained for the past hour as I studied everyone at his birthday party and decided who was family, who was a coworker, and who was the unfortunate soul lucky to be considered a friend—me.

Mike didn't want a big party for his birthday, but his baby sister, Sonia, decided they needed to have one. His mom gave in, and they put together a big bash in her backyard and told him he had to invite a few friends. Sonia had handled the rest of the guest list—which explained why half of their cousins and other distant relatives were there.

"Why don't you come dance with me, Papi?" one of his cousins—I had no fucking clue what her name was—asked me, breaking me out of my trance as I stared at Quinn while she spoke to her daughter, Rosie.

"Na, I don't dance," I lied, leaning back to avoid being too close to her.

"It's okay, I can teach you," she purred, reaching for me with the longest red nails I had ever seen.

"He doesn't need dance lessons," Mike cut in, stepping around her to take the seat next to me. He handed me a beer and rested his ankle on his knee. "He's the best dancer here."

This made her eyes light up as my eyes narrowed in his direction.

"Go on, Papi," he taunted, nodding toward the dance floor. "Show her what you're working with."

I was about to open my mouth to object when I spotted Quinn being led to the dance floor by Rosie.

"Fine," I muttered, setting my beer bottle down on the table between us. I got up and took her devil claw as she shimmied her hips toward the dance floor.

Once we were on the wooden deck with everyone else, I tried to force a smile as she looked at me over her shoulder while grinding her ass against my groin. Quinn turned in time to see it, her cheeks splitting while she tried to contain her laughter. She pulled her lips together in a thin line and held her hand in the air as she twirled Rosie a few times.

It only took half a turn before she spotted me and released her mom's hand to rush over to me.

"Dance with me?" she asked, putting her hands together in front of her as she begged. I smiled down sweetly at my favorite "niece," thankful that she had just saved the day.

"Sorry, I can't say no," I said to the devil woman and turned to Rosie before she could object. I caught a brief glance of her flicking her long, dark red hair over her shoulder before stomping off in her stripper heels.

"You saved me, kiddo," I said to Rosie as I held her hands and danced with her.

"Yeah, you looked super scared," she giggled. "Mommy says we should always help people when they need it."

"Your mommy is right," I agreed, looking up at Quinn as she watched us.

I spun Rosie around, noticing how much she looked like Quinn with her dark hair and brilliant blue eyes. Quinn's eyes were a light shade of blue that sometimes turned gray, like Mike's, but Rosie had more of her dad's sapphire blue eyes that made them absolutely mesmerizing. I dreaded the day when she was old enough to date, knowing that Mike would have his hands full as an overprotective uncle.

We danced for a few more minutes until the song ended, and Rosie declared that she needed a drink of water. Quinn was about to go with her when her mom held up a hand and waited for Rosie to join her before leading her into the kitchen.

"Do you want to dance?" I asked, holding my hand out and hoping she would take it.

"Sure," she smiled, letting me pull her into me as we moved our hips to the salsa music.

People who really knew me knew that I loved to dance. When we were younger, I was always known as the life of the party because I couldn't sit still. It didn't matter what kind of music it was—I was moving.

Tonight was different, though. Maybe it was the gentle breeze that brushed past us and caressed our hot skin, or maybe it was how Quinn's petite body fit perfectly against mine. Either way, I didn't want to stop or let go. The song changed, and I looked up in time to find Sonia watching us with a mischievous grin as a slow, sexy song started playing.

I felt Quinn's body tense slightly with the way I held her and thought about pulling away some so I didn't make her uncomfortable.

"I can't remember the last time I danced like this," she said nervously, tucking a stray strand of hair behind her ear.

"Me neither," I agreed. But it wasn't because I didn't dance much these days; it was because I had never danced with someone who made me feel what I was feeling while holding Quinn.

"I don't think Justin and I even danced like this at our wedding," she laughed, then looked away. I knew that it was still hard for her to talk about him after he died tragically on the job. Justin was also in the FBI—witness protection, just like Mike, though they rarely worked together.

I didn't know what to say, so I stayed quiet and gently rubbed my thumb soothingly over her back.

Her mom came out of the kitchen a few minutes later without Rosie. I noticed her at the same time that Quinn did. Suddenly, she pulled away from me, her hands still gripping my biceps as her eyes rapidly scanned the backyard.

"Where is Rosie?" she asked, panic heavy in her voice.

She spun around, standing on her tiptoes, trying to get a better view.

"Let's go ask your mom," I offered, gently leading her that way with my hand on her lower back.

The party was still going with people packed into the small backyard. We wedged our way through until we reached Sandra.

"Mom, where's Rosie?" Quinn asked, grabbing her arm to spin her away from the older man she was talking to.

"She's inside using the restroom," her mom answered, her brow furrowed in response to Quinn's tone.

"By herself?" Quinn muttered angrily before rushing inside.

I followed behind her, ready to help with whatever was upsetting her.

She rushed through the kitchen, bumping shoulders with a few people before she started pounding on the bathroom door.

"Rosie! Open the door," she yelled.

A few minutes passed before she pounded again.

"Rosie—" she started but was cut off when Rosie came out of a bedroom with a man behind her.

"I'm right here, Mom," she said.

Quinn's eyes widened as she looked between the two of them.

"What were you doing?" Quinn asked, reaching for her daughter and pulling her out of the man's grip as he rested his hand on her shoulder. She squatted in front of her and held her hands.

"I needed the bathroom, but someone was in it. So then I went to Grandma's, but I couldn't figure out how to get the door to close because it was stuck. Uncle Saul heard me and came to help me."

Quinn stood up and tucked Rosie into her side, facing me instead of the man she was calling Uncle Saul.

"You only have one uncle, Rosie, and that's Uncle Mike. We don't go anywhere with someone we don't know, understand?"

"Yes, ma'am," Rosie replied quietly, tucking her chin.

"It wasn't a big deal," Uncle Saul said. "I didn't want her wandering around by herself, so I popped in to check on her."

"Thank you," Quinn said through clenched teeth. "In the future, she needs to come find me instead."

"Hey, no harm, no foul," he laughed and held his hands up while Quinn shot daggers through her eyes. He walked by and patted Rosie's head before getting lost in the crowd.

"Mom, can I go outside again?" Rosie asked, tugging on her arm. "Uncle Mike is right there."

Quinn turned her head and nodded as Mike gave her a quizzical look. He reached his hand out and waited until Rosie took it before leading her outside.

I stood by Quinn and noticed how her fingers trembled while she closed her eyes and let out the shaky breath she had been holding.

"What's going on, Quinn?" I asked, gently touching her arm.

She crossed her arms tightly over her chest and avoided looking at me.

"Nothing," she lied.

"Bullshit," I hissed out quietly to avoid drawing attention to us.

Her brow raised.

I folded my arms over my chest, matching her, aside from my chest being much broader and more muscular than her feminine one that I was trying hard not to stare at.

"It's my job to read people, and I can tell that you're lying."

When she continued to refuse to answer me, I let out a heavy sigh and tilted my head to look at her.

"Just tell me what's going on, Quinn."

"I can't."

"Why not?"

"Because I can't."

I paused for a moment, trying to figure out the best way to approach this. I knew Quinn well enough to know that once she shuts down on something, there's no coming back from it. Something was going on, and I was determined to find out what it was.

"If the US Government thinks that I'm trustworthy, surely you can too," I offered with the smile that usually got me whatever I wanted.

For a split second, she looked like she was considering telling me before she snapped her jaw shut and pulled her shoulders back.

"It's getting late. I need to get Rosie home."

She didn't look back as she stormed out and found her still with Mike, dancing happily in the grass. I followed after her but kept my distance, watching as they made their way to his mom to say goodbye. She frowned and looked disappointed but could tell by Quinn's face that it wasn't the time to press her to stay.

They slipped out quietly, with Quinn keeping a hand on Rosie's shoulder the entire time, almost like she was afraid to let her out of her sight. I walked over and sat down next to Mike in the same seats we were sitting in earlier. I scanned the crowd noticing it had started to thin out some.

I looked down at my watch. It was barely after ten, but apparently, people our age didn't party as hard as we did twenty-some years ago. I spotted the guy who had been with Rosie in her grandma's bedroom and was about to ask about him when I heard Mike mutter, "who the fuck invited her?" before slouching down in his chair and pulling his Yankees ballcap lower over his face.

"Nice to see you too," the woman said with fake enthusiasm, hitting the side of his arm with her tiny purse. I knew it had an official name, but I could care less what it was.

"To what do I owe this pleasure?" Mike asked, looking her up and down before getting bored and looking away.

Whoever she was, was dressed nicely in a black dress wrapped tightly around her body, showing off some major curves. Her black heels gave her an extra four inches, making her look even taller than she already was.

"I'm here to meet someone," she replied. She looked around as Mike stood up, then seemed to notice me. Not wanting to be rude, I joined them and extended my hand to hers when she said, "I'm Anastasia."

"Roman," I said, biting the inside of my cheek when I

realized exactly who she was. "It's so nice of you to join us for Mike's big birthday bash." I clapped my hand on his shoulder and felt him elbow me in the ribs.

"Well, given that I know how much he would enjoy that, I'm not here for it." She laughed lightly and looked around. "I'm supposed to meet someone here, but I don't see them."

"Meet someone?" Mike asked, head tilted to the side. "Like as a date?"

I watched the blush creep up her neck.

"If you must know, yes, like a date."

"Dressed like that?"

"What's wrong with how I'm dressed?" She planted a hand firmly on her hip.

"Nothing, it's just a little…" Mike threw his hands in the air when he couldn't think of the words he wanted to use.

"Sexy?" she offered with a smug smile.

"There you are," a man interrupted, bumping my shoulder as he squeezed his way between Mike and me to hug her. "Are you ready to go?"

"I sure am," she replied sweetly, almost flinching when he slid his arm around her waist.

"Cool," he said heavily, the smell of beer heavy on his breath. "Happy birthday, man. See you on Monday."

As they left, I felt my stomach knot tighter when I watched Uncle Saul walk out with Mike's archnemesis from work.

"Who is that guy?" I asked, nodding to them as they left.

"Saul, he works with me. So does Satan's mistress."

"I've heard a lot about Anastasia," I laughed. "But you never mentioned that she's fucking hot."

"She's not hot," he scoffed and furrowed his brow. "She's an annoying pain in the ass who gets in my way instead of helping."

"Sounds like you like her," I teased. "Maybe you should ask her out?"

"Over your dead body," he grunted.

"Isn't it supposed to be over your own dead body?" I asked.

"Not with her. She's like a fucking cat, and there's no escaping once she digs her claws in. I'd have to use your dead body as a barrier first."

674

Three

Quinn
14 Days Ago

I sat on the bed, gently rubbing Rosie's head even though she had already fallen asleep. Tonight had been unnerving—to say the least—but then I had to deal with her massive meltdown on the way home from my brother's birthday party because she wasn't ready to leave.

I was used to always being the bad guy; it came with the territory of being a single mother. But it was hard, and some days it wore on me more than others. Today was one of those days.

My head laid against the pillow I had tucked behind me an hour ago when we first came in here, and I got her settled in for the night. She had stopped crying and didn't bother to tell me what a terrible parent she thought I was for making her leave tonight. She didn't have to, I could see it in the sadness in her eyes long after the tears dried.

Mike had texted me shortly after we left to make sure we were okay, and I wondered if Roman had said something to him. They were best friends, so I never knew where I stood in the equation. While Mike was my older brother and would do anything to protect me, Roman was also like a brother to me, and I trusted that he wouldn't say anything to him if he didn't know what was going on. He never struck me as the kind of person to gossip or discuss something he didn't have all of the facts about. It was probably from his time in the Marines, but Roman was one of those people who sat silently until they decided it was time to take action.

I had replayed the night over and over in my head the entire train ride home, and long after Rosie fell asleep. I knew that it would be hard to see some of Mike's coworkers at the party tonight. I hadn't seen most of them since Justin's funeral four years ago. Even though I worked for the FBI, we never crossed paths, and I loved to believe that fate played an important role in that. That maybe after everything life had given me over the years, I was finally going to be one of those people that nice things happened to.

I picked up my phone and found another text message from Mike and one from my mom. Neither of them seemed as worried as Roman, so I felt comfortable knowing that he hadn't said anything to them.

I replied quickly, pretended that I was tired, and lied that I was calling it a night soon. Instead, I kissed Rosie's head and quietly crawled out of her bed, making sure the nightlight was on.

I crept down the hallway, praying that the squeaky floorboards wouldn't wake her up. I ventured into the kitchen and poured myself a glass of wine, stopping halfway when I remembered that I could no longer afford the luxury of being buzzed. I needed to be alert and aware at all times from now on.

With my small glass of wine, I headed into the living room and sat down, tucking my feet beneath me. I grabbed my laptop and got settled in, not sure what I was even looking for.

When I woke up this morning, I expected it to be like any other day—eat a quick breakfast, get Rosie ready for school, spill coffee on myself at least once before I got into the office, and then listen to my boss complain all day about how incompetent women were since I was the only female in our department.

The day had gone almost as expected until I picked Rosie up from school. People were usually scattered in the pickup line on Friday, so I had parked on the street and gone in to get her. While I was waiting for her to finish talking with her friend, one of the teachers approached me and asked if she could speak privately with me.

I had expected to hear something about how Rosie had exceeded their expectations on a project or had gone out of her way to help another student. That was just the wonderful type of girl that she was. Instead, she pulled me into a classroom and exchanged nervous glances with another teacher, who confirmed she would watch Rosie for me.

Once we were by ourselves, she pulled her cell phone out of her pocket and handed it to me. There was a video on the screen, and my stomach sank when she pressed play. I was nervous and anxious to see what it was since she wasn't acting excited or happy about it. At first, it showed kids playing on the playground, then it zoomed in to focus on the man standing across the street, leaning against a black van with dark windows.

He was of average height and build, wearing a baseball cap that hid his face and dark sunglasses covering his eyes. Everything about him looked casual, from the way he crossed his ankle over the other to how he tapped his cigarette against the side of the van and let the ashes fall.

But I knew better.

I swallowed hard before I handed her phone back to her, unable to get any words out.

Someone had been there, casing the playground. A pervert was lurking in the shadows, watching the innocent children as they ran around and played without a care in the world. MY child had been there, unaware of the danger not even fifty feet away from where she was playing.

When I finally found my voice, I asked why they didn't call the cops when they saw the man watching the kids. Her face fell with her shoulders, and she watched the video again.

"At first, we thought that he knew Rosie because she was the only one that he was watching. But when she looked in his direction a few times and didn't seem to recognize him, we knew that wasn't the case. We called the police, but we're still waiting for them to send someone out…."

Her words had gone in one ear and out the other at that point. I was beyond furious, but I couldn't figure out which part had me fuming the most. The fact that someone had been there watching my daughter or the fact that I wasn't there to do anything about it. I had to trust that she was safe at school, and suddenly, it didn't feel like she was safe at all.

Four

Roman

13 Days Ago

"How was Mike's party?" Trevor asked as I pressed the phone against my ear.

"Fun, uneventful," I shrugged even though he couldn't see me. "I just got to his mom's house to help take the tables and chairs back that his sister rented."

"So basically, you ended the night early and were in bed before midnight?" he teased.

"Hey, I'm almost forty. I can't handle the long nights of drinking and partying anymore. I'm not young like you."

Trevor laughed, and we both knew that it was a stretch to say he was still young, given that he was usually in bed before me most nights, and he was barely thirty.

"Did you at least meet any nice girls?" he prodded.

"Now you sound like my mother."

"Well, she has a point. You're not getting any younger. Soon that mythological super sperm you claim to have will be all dried up, and you won't be able to give her any grandbabies."

"You're just as ridiculous as she is," I laughed. "Now, is

there a reason for your call, or did you just want to ruin my Saturday?"

"I was calling to let you know that I won't be in on Monday. Max needs to pick up some stuff for the wedding, but the only store that has it is in New Jersey, so I'm going to go with him to help."

"Not a problem. I'll get one of the new guys to cover the front desk and have Jackson run the floor while I take care of the admin stuff."

"Thanks, brother. I appreciate it."

"Hey, that's what a partner does," I laughed, then hung up and tucked my phone into my pocket.

It was barely eleven in the morning, but the day was already scorching hot. Instead of my usual button-down shirt and jeans, I opted for a t-shirt and shorts this morning, knowing that I would just get sweaty with moving stuff.

I hadn't seen Mike yet, so I headed for the house, assuming he was already there and probably convincing his mom to make biscuits and gravy for him. He was a total mama's boy, and she was a sucker for her only son—a win/win for them most days.

I knocked on the security door before hearing someone yell to come in. I went inside and wiped my shoes on the welcome mat before heading in the direction of the savory sausage I smelled coming from the kitchen.

"Aren't you going to lock the door?"

I whipped around to see Quinn standing behind me. Her brows were pulled together, her hair knotted in a messy bun on top of her head. Without makeup, I could see the faint dark circles under her eyes and wondered if she had had a rough night last night.

"Sorry," I muttered, turning to lock the door. When I looked back at her, her brows were raised while she waited for me to slide the deadbolt in place.

My fingers moved slowly as her eyes followed every movement until the door was securely locked.

"Better?" I asked.

"Thank you." She nodded and tucked her head.

"No problem."

I followed her into the kitchen, smiling when I saw that I was right about Mike conning his mom into cooking for him. She was standing at the stove with a pink paisley apron tied around her waist while she turned sausage in the skillet.

"Good morning, Mama Sanchez," I said as I gave her a quick hug from behind and kissed the top of her head.

"You know you can call me Sandra," she laughed, shaking her head. "Twenty-some years later, and you're still so formal. Even my own kids aren't that formal unless they want—"

She turned around and pointed her spatula at me.

"What do you want?" She narrowed her eyes playfully, trying not to smile as I held an empty plate out to her.

Her resolve finally crumbled when she took the plate and laughed, loading it with a generous serving of scrambled eggs, hash browns, sausage, and gravy from the different pans scattered on the stove. I thanked her before eagerly taking it and finding a place at the table. I hadn't bothered to say hi to anyone before I reached in and grabbed a few biscuits from the pan in the center of the table.

"Good morning to you too," Mike said around a bite of food.

"It's a great morning," I teased, lifting my fork in salute to his mom. "Thank you again, I'm very spoiled this morning."

"Thank you for coming to help clean up from the party and take all of those tables and chairs back," Sandra said with a

sigh. "Sonia has good intentions but lacks in the follow-up part of most things."

"Be sure to chew your bites so you don't choke," Quinn whispered to Rosie before pulling her hair behind her back so it was out of her precious little face.

"I will, Mom," Rosie replied before popping a sausage link in her mouth and chewing it.

Quinn sat down next to her and picked up her coffee, bringing the mug to her lips but not bothering to take a drink. I could tell that she was distracted by something, but I didn't want to ask in front of everyone.

Suddenly her eyes lifted to mine, and she slightly flinched when she found me studying her. She took a drink of coffee and then pulled her phone out of her pocket. With her head down, I couldn't see her face anymore, so I went back to eating my breakfast.

Once we were done, we helped clean up while Sandra sat down with Rosie and ate her breakfast. I washed the dishes while Quinn dried them, not bothering to look at me. Everything about her felt oddly robotic this morning, and I couldn't shake the feeling that something was wrong.

"What do you have going on today?" Mike asked as he put the leftovers in the fridge.

I looked over my shoulder and found him watching Quinn. Her shoulders stiffened before she turned slightly to answer him.

"I have a couple of errands that I need to run."

"Like what?" he pressed.

"Personal stuff."

"Momma is going shopping for new clothes for me," Rosie volunteered, smiling as she took a bite and chewed.

"New clothes? For what?" Sandra asked, joining the conversation.

"School," Quinn said sharply, gripping the plate in her hand so tightly that I worried she might break it.

"I thought she had enough school clothes? Besides, school will be out in a few weeks."

"She just needs new clothes, that's all."

"Did they implement a new dress code?" Sandra wondered aloud. "You would think that they would wait until the new school year starts before they do that. I mean, you can't be expected to buy a new wardrobe for her when she'll be out on summer break soon anyway. Who knows if she'll even fit in the same clothes when she goes back."

I could feel the tension radiating off of Quinn as she

dropped the plate and didn't bother to try to catch it.

"Enough!" she yelled, her fists clenched by her side. "I'm buying her new clothes because I don't want her wearing skirts and dresses to school anymore. It's my choice. My decision. I'm 38 years old; I don't need anyone bossing me around or trying to tell me what to do."

She turned around and met Rosie's eyes that were welling up with tears.

"I can't wear my pretty dresses anymore?" Rosie cried. "Do I have to dress like a boy now?"

"No, sweetie," Sandra said, pulling her against her chest. "We all just need to calm down for a moment and figure things out. Why don't you go clean up and get that syrup off of your face before Charity gets here?"

"Okay, Grandma."

Rosie padded down the hall to the bathroom while the kitchen filled with silence.

"What in the world is going on, Quinn Marie?" Sandra asked, standing up with her hands on her hips.

"It's nothing, Mama," Quinn sighed, leaning against the sink.

"Then why are you not letting her wear dresses and skirts anymore?"

She took a deep breath and ran her hands down her face before answering.

"Her teacher showed me a video yesterday when I went to pick her up. It was of the kids playing during recess, but when she zoomed in, there was a man across the street watching them. He was leaning against a black van with dark windows."

"Oh, for heaven's sake," Sandra whispered and covered her mouth.

"That's not the worst part," Quinn said quietly, looking down the hall to see if Rosie was heading back. "The teacher said that the only kid he was watching was Rosie."

I felt the air rush out of me. Mike was sitting at the table with his jaw clenched and fists tight. I knew the feeling—I wanted to find whoever this bastard was and smash his face as bad as he did.

"I know that this is your job, honey," Sandra said softly, "but making her wear pants isn't going to stop whoever this is from looking at her."

"I know," she whispered. "I feel helpless right now. I don't know what to do or how to protect her, which is really fucking frustrating given that I do this for a fucking living. I work for the FBI in the child exploitation task force—I literally see this stuff every day, yet I don't know what to do."

"It's always different once it hits close to home," I assured her, though I had no idea. I had been a sniper in the Marines, so nothing ever hit too close to home for me.

"We'll figure this out and find a way to protect her," Mike said, pushing away from the table and standing up. "For now, I'm going to go outside and pack up the tables and chairs while I work off some of this newly found anger."

I gave Quinn one last look before going outside to help

Mike. Even though Quinn wasn't a child anymore, that didn't stop me from wanting to protect her the same way I had growing up. She was only a few years younger than me, and I knew she could handle herself. She had been proving that ever since her husband died four years ago. So why did I suddenly have such strong feelings to help her with this?

Five
Quinn
11 Days Ago

The morning had started rougher than I would have liked for a Monday. Rosie had thrown a fit when I presented her with a stack of pants in different prints and shirts that would match them instead of the skirts and dresses that she loved to wear. It was a battle that lasted long enough for her to rush through breakfast and caused us to be late getting her to school.

We hurried through the empty hallways as I swung open the door to her classroom, looking frazzled and out of sorts as her teacher came over to check on us. Rosie rolled her eyes before flinging off her backpack and taking her seat at her desk. The students looked over their shoulders and whispered before the other teacher got their attention and refocused them on whatever they had been working on before we got there.

"I'm so sorry she's late," I said, blowing a strand of hair out of my face. "We had a rough morning. I'll stop by the front desk before I head out."

"It's alright," Miss Gentry said, holding her hands up. "We'll get Rosie caught up, she didn't miss much."

I blew out a heavy breath and looked around at the class

of innocent children who were smiling and laughing at something one of the kids had said.

"We'll keep her safe," she promised, pulling my attention back to her.

"If anything happens, or if you see anyone who looks suspicious, please call me on my cell. I can get back here quickly."

I opened my purse and fished a business card out of my wallet. She took it and smiled, tucking it safely into her back pocket. I turned and slipped out the door, taking one last look at Rosie before it shut behind me.

The front office was polite and made a note of why Rosie was late. I made sure they had my cell phone number, as well as my mom's, just in case they needed to reach me. I thought about giving them Mike and Sonia's numbers, but they already looked annoyed that I was spending so much time obsessing over every little detail in her file that I thought better of it and left.

As I walked out, I scanned the streets around the school, focusing on where the van had been parked in the video. I studied everything around me—trees that would provide a hiding spot in the thickness of their branches, buildings with narrow alleys small enough for someone to stay in the shadows and not be seen, and businesses with storefront windows that created the perfect opportunity to watch the school without being noticed.

I felt uneasy as I made my way to work, wondering how many other dangers were constantly lurking around her school. It was hard enough being a parent and worrying about your children in an ordinary world, but I found that it was even harder when you worked in a field that consistently showed you how cruel the world is and how ready monsters are to take your children from you.

By noon I had checked my phone at least a hundred times, looking for any missed calls or text messages from Rosie's teachers. Her class would be getting out soon, and my mom had confirmed that she would be there to pick her up. Typically I would be the only one to drop her off and pick her up, but my boss had called a mandatory last-minute meeting that just happened to be at the same time that I needed to leave to get Rosie.

I wanted to Facetime my mom and watch to make sure they got home okay, but I couldn't. Not only would that piss my boss off during his meeting, but it would also make my mom even more worried about me and my newest obsession with keeping Rosie safe.

It wasn't just the video that had gotten under my skin— it was this feeling deep inside of my gut that told me something was wrong. I had learned to trust my instincts a long time ago, and they weren't just hinting that something might be wrong—they were screaming that something was very wrong.

I hadn't been able to shake the feeling, which had led to sleepless nights and dark circles under my eyes that didn't hide well even with the heavier makeup I had worn this morning. The meeting was supposed to start in fifteen minutes, so I shoved the rest of my protein bar into my mouth and grabbed a notepad and pen from my desk.

The conference room was already half full, so I took a seat toward the back and pulled my phone out to find a text message from my mom.

The corners of my lips turned up into a smile as I looked at the picture of Rosie and my mom at her house, sitting on the couch in front of the window. The blinds were open, allowing the sunlight to flow in.

"Good afternoon," my boss said as he entered the room and took his place at the head of the table. I was about to put my phone away so I could concentrate, but suddenly I saw something in the picture that sent a chill through my body.

My fingers trembled as they pinched then zoomed in on the photo. Across the street was a black van with dark windows and a person sitting in the driver's seat.

<u>Six</u>

Roman

11 Days Ago

I was thankful that it was slow at work because with Trevor being out of the office and Jackson calling in sick, it left me running around trying to be in multiple places at once. The gym wasn't usually busy on Mondays, which allowed me to work on some of the admin stuff from the front desk. I had a few clients on the schedule, but I had been working with them for so long that they didn't really need a personal trainer anymore. I knew that they would get started with what we had been working on and wait for me to come guide them through the rest.

By the end of the day, I was wiped and ready to crash out. I stopped by the market store on the corner, grabbed a few things for dinner, and headed home. It was just me, and even though I liked to eat healthy, it didn't mean that I was great at keeping groceries in the house. I made note to do some shopping this weekend and stock up so I didn't have to see the barely legal teenage girl in the lowcut shirt and googly eyes that always seemed to be working when I went to the market.

I climbed the three flights of stairs instead of taking the elevator and walked down the hallway to my apartment before stopping short. Standing outside my door were Quinn and Rosie, huddled together as if she was trying to shield her from something. Panic started to rise as I quickened my pace. Something had to be wrong for Quinn to just show up at my apartment.

"Quinn?" I asked stupidly, but I still couldn't believe she was there.

She spun around and looked at me, a protective hand reaching behind her to keep Rosie in place.

"What's going on? Is everything okay?"

"Do you think we could go inside and talk?" she asked nervously.

I nodded and unlocked the door, holding it open for them to enter before I pushed it closed and slid the locks into place. I set the paper bag down on the kitchen counter and put my hands on my hips, unsure of what to do.

"Is it okay if I turn the TV on for her?"

Rosie stood in front of Quinn with Quinn's hands wrapped protectively over her shoulders. Her brows were raised while she waited for me to answer her question.

"Of course." I shook my head to clear some of the fog while I turned on the TV and flipped through the channels until I found something that seemed appropriate for Rosie to watch.

Once she was settled on the couch, I went back to the kitchen to talk to Quinn. It was an open layout, with the kitchen and living room blending into one large room, which allowed us to keep an eye on Rosie.

"Is everything okay?" I asked, arms folded across my chest

and my voice barely above a whisper.

"I don't know," she admitted and let out a shaky breath. "I keep trying to tell myself that all of this is in my head and that I'm freaking out for no reason."

"But?"

"But I don't think that it's nothing. I think someone is actively watching Rosie, and I'm afraid that they're going to take her."

She swallowed the last few words as silence fell between us. I looked over my shoulder at the little girl sitting on my couch with hair as dark as her momma's and a smile that could light up the dimmest room.

"You have to trust your gut," I agreed. "What happened?"

"My mom had to pick her up today because my boss called a mandatory meeting last minute, and I couldn't go get her. I think that my mom knew how stressed out I've been since her teacher showed me that video on Friday, so she sent me a picture of them sitting together on her couch once they got home."

She stopped talking and looked past me to Rosie. Her eyes filled with tears that she tried to blink away before they fell.

"When I zoomed in on the photo, I saw the same black van from Friday parked across the street."

"Fuck," I exhaled and ran a hand over my face. "Have you told anyone about this?"

She shook her head.

"I don't want them to think I'm crazy if I'm wrong about

this."

"And what if you're right?"

"That's what I fear the most. I can't be with her 24/7, and if someone is watching her, they will know my schedule and when I'm not around. They'll know exactly when to take her."

She chewed her bottom lip, popping it free when she caught me watching.

"So, what's the plan?" I asked, desperate for a distraction from her mouth. "How can I help?"

"I really hate to ask," she hesitated. "But do you think we can stay here tonight while I try to figure out what to do? I haven't slept since I found out on Friday, and I don't think

I'll get any sleep tonight knowing that they followed her to my mom's house."

I wanted to say absolutely, you can take my bed, and I'll sleep on the couch—but I knew I couldn't. It wasn't that I didn't want to help Quinn—I would give my life to protect her and Rosie. Hell, I would give a vital organ or two to protect Mike, but this was different. I needed to know that he would be okay with me helping and letting them stay with me because if he found out on his own, it wouldn't go over well.

"You know that I don't mind helping you, Quinn, but why not go to Mike?"

She sighed and let her shoulders fall.

"I knew you would ask that," she laughed.

"He's my best friend," I replied lightly. "I can't imagine that I would be so easygoing if he went behind my back to help my sister and niece if they were in trouble and he didn't tell me."

"That's not fair; you don't even have siblings."

"True," I said, raising a brow. "But if I did, I would want to know what was going on."

We stood there silently for a few minutes while Rosie laughed at something on TV.

"It's not that I don't trust my brother to protect us, but I feel like I need space to think about things. I know that once he really knows what's going on, he'll be obsessive and trying to take over to where I can't think straight. You guys are two totally different people. Yes, he's strong and had training, but not the same as you had in the marines. You both have a different skill set, and if someone's coming for my daughter, I know that you can put a bullet between their eyes before they even see you."

"I'm not a sniper anymore," I countered, feeling my shoulders tighten.

"It's not something that you lose. You and I both know that. I've seen you play darts with Mike, and you don't miss a single one."

I rolled my neck, trying to alleviate some of the tension.

"It's just one night, Roman." She held her hands in front of her. "Please."

Rosie's innocent laughter floated through the air, and I knew what I had to do.

"Fuck," I muttered on a breath, closing my eyes.

"I promise we won't be in the way. You won't even notice us."

I bit the inside of my cheek at the thought of being in the same apartment as Quinn and not noticing her. That was like watching a giant meteor come crashing toward Earth and not understanding how you got knocked out when it hit you.

"Fine," I said sternly. "But I have some conditions that I will not budge on."

"Okay, whatever you want."

Don't fucking go there.

"First—I'm going to order pizza, and you guys are going to eat. Second—you two will sleep in my bed, and I'll take the couch. Third—I will go with you to drop her off at school in the morning." I paused before adding, "and no matter what, you will tell me if anything happens that I need to know about. If you see something, hear something, smell something—anything that feels off—I need to know about it right away. Deal?" I held out my hand and waited for her to take it.

She started chewing her lip again, not bothering to shake my hand.

"Can we compromise on the bed part of it?"

"No."

"Roman," she sighed. "I do not want to put you out and make you sleep on the couch. We'll be fine sleeping in the living room."

"First of all, you're not putting me out. I'm offering it. Second, you're not both going to fit on the couch, and there's no way in hell that I'm letting you sleep on the floor."

"But—"

"No, Quinn. Those are the conditions. Either take them or leave them. If not, I'll call your brother and tell him what's going on."

She narrowed her eyes at me and folded her arms across her chest.

"You wouldn't."

"Try me."

I took a step toward her, encroaching on her space enough to feel the heat radiating off her body. I wanted to reach out and touch her, caress the soft skin on her face and assure her that everything would be okay.

She shook her head and let her arms fall.

"Fine, you've given me no choice. I accept the conditions and thank you again for letting us stay here."

"You're welcome," I replied, ignoring the tingles that rushed through me at the thought of having Quinn stay the night with me.

It took Rosie telling Quinn that she was hungry before we snapped out of the trance that we had fallen into and stepped away from each other.

"How does pizza sound?" I called over to Rosie, taking a breath of Quinn-free air as I tossed the stuff from the paper bag into the fridge. Even if a five-year-old was on board with sushi, I didn't have enough for everyone and still lacked the groceries I would need to make something edible for dinner.

"Can we get extra pepperoni?" she squealed excitedly.

"Is there any other kind of pizza?" I joked, pulling my phone out of my pocket to call in the order.

Seven

Quinn

10 Days Ago

I woke up around three o'clock this morning, unsure of where I was and why the pillow smelled so delicious, like a combination of cedarwood and vanilla. Once I remembered that I was sleeping next to Rosie in Roman's bed, everything from the day before came flooding back to me.

I inched down the hall to use the restroom, hoping not to wake him up, when I found him sitting on the couch with his laptop. He looked like he had tried to go to bed at some point since he was wearing a t-shirt and athletic shorts. I started to worry that maybe we had kept him up or that he couldn't sleep because the couch was too uncomfortable when he turned around and caught me watching him from the hallway.

I tugged at the flimsy shirt that barely covered the length of the booty shorts that I liked to sleep in. I had packed a quick bag of overnight clothes for Rosie and me before we came over and new outfits for the morning, but it was hard to find the right combination of comfortable and appropriate. It was early June and already getting hot and uncomfortable, so I liked to sleep in as thin of layers as possible.

"Everything okay?" he asked, turning his body to take me

in. His voice was gravely, like he had been sleeping.

"Just got up to use the bathroom."

I walked into the living room so he didn't have to strain to see me.

"Sleepless night or uncomfortable couch?" I asked, praying that I wasn't inconveniencing him and causing him not to get sleep tonight. I felt bad enough for coming here, to begin with, but I didn't know what else to do.

"I slept for a few hours and then got up for a drink of water. Something kept bothering me about the picture you sent me, so I got my laptop out to do some research."

That immediately piqued my interest, and I found myself sliding down onto the couch beside him. I tried to make sure I kept my distance so I didn't make him uncomfortable, but it was hard not to touch him since he was sitting in the middle of the couch instead of on one of the ends.

"What did you find?"

"In the picture, the person in the driver's seat of the van is wearing a baseball cap," he said, grabbing his phone and zooming in on the picture. "I knew that I recognized the logo but couldn't figure out why. I searched for the image, and it comes up as the logo for a little league baseball team."

He turned the computer toward me, and I immediately recognized it.

"That's for the Astros. It's the little league team that Rosie played for last year. Mike coached it until she decided to quit."

"It could be a borrowed hat, but I think it's worth looking into to see if it gives us a lead into who's been watching her. Especially if it's the same team she used to play on."

I nodded my head, completely speechless.

"It's going to be okay," he assured me, gently squeezing my hand.

I flinched momentarily at the contact but not because I didn't want him to touch me. Instead, I felt myself leaning in toward him, desperate for more. There was something about the way that my body felt like it was on fire where his fingers touched me that had me longing to feel him elsewhere.

As if reading my mind, he slowly pulled his hand away and closed his laptop.

"I should get back to bed before Rosie wakes up and freaks out that I'm not there," I stuttered, standing up and almost tripping on the rug.

"Okay," he said before I rushed out of the room and to the bathroom. I peed quickly and then climbed back into the bed, thankful that Rosie had stayed asleep.

I rolled onto my side and watched her for a while, memorizing every little detail on her face the same way I had when she was born and again when Justin died. I hadn't realized just how much I had taken for granted being able to look at him when I wanted to or feeling the comfort of his embrace when I needed it. I promised myself that I would never allow that to happen again and that I would try to soak up every single moment, regardless of how little it seemed at the time.

A few hours later, I woke up to the sunlight filtering in through the curtains and rolled over to check the clock on the nightstand beside me. It was just after six, and I needed to get up and shower before I woke Rosie up.

Slowly I rolled out of bed and grabbed the duffle bag from the floor before tiptoeing down to the bathroom. I didn't bother going to the living room to see if Roman was up yet before I opened the bathroom door and went inside. I quietly shut it behind me, not noticing that the light was already on before I turned around and found Roman wearing nothing but a towel wrapped around his waist.

His brown hair was still wet from the shower, and his tanned, muscular body glistened beneath the water beads.

"Oh my God!" I whispered loudly, my heart nearly jumping out of my chest. I covered my eyes with my hand, dropping the duffle bag to the floor. "I'm so sorry! I should have knocked first!"

"It's fine, Quinn," he chuckled. "You can open your eyes. I'm not naked."

"It's okay," I laughed nervously. "I can just go so you can finish up."

I turned to open the door, not bothering to uncover my eyes, and hit my arm on the knob.

"Son of a bitch!" I tried not to yell, so I didn't wake Rosie, hoping that the sound of me whacking the door hadn't already stirred her.

There was shuffling behind me, and then I felt his hand on my shoulder as he pulled my hand from my eyes.

"It's safe," he teased.

I opened my eyes and found him wearing a fitted t-shirt and joggers, which looked ridiculously good on him.

"Is that what you wear to train people?" I blurted out as my eyes traveled over his body again.

"Um, yeah?"

He pulled his lower lip between his teeth, watching me as he waited for my eyes to finally land on his.

"Sorry," I muttered. "I didn't mean to stare."

"Are you sure about that?"

Was I? Because I was pretty sure that had he not busted me checking him out, I would probably be fantasizing about him teaching me how to do some sort of sexy pull-up at the gym.

I lowered my head and looked away as I felt the heat creep up my neck and spread across my chest.

"The shower is all yours," he said, extending his arm in that direction. "There are towels under the sink. Be careful with the water—it gets hot pretty quickly."

He smirked and walked out, closing the door behind him. I couldn't be sure, but I was pretty positive there was some sort of sexual innuendo laced in his comment.

<u>Eight</u>

Roman
10 Days Ago

The morning started differently than I had anticipated. First off, I woke up with a stiff neck from sleeping on the couch. Second, I was overly exhausted from the lack of sleep because my mind was going a mile a minute. And third, I couldn't shake the excitement that I felt when Quinn walked in on me in the bathroom.

Thankfully, I had already showered and was covered when she burst in, but that didn't stop my dick from stirring at the sight of her skin blushing as she tried to look away. Had Rosie not been there, I probably would have entertained dirtier thoughts than I already had.

While Quinn showered and got ready, I started a pot of coffee and searched through my cabinets to find something suitable to make for them for breakfast. I couldn't imagine that many five-year-olds began their day with protein shakes, and I definitely didn't have any sugary cereal or Pop Tarts lying around.

Rosie woke up right before Quinn came out and stumbled into the living room, rubbing her eyes as she tried to wake up.

"What time is it?" she asked sleepily.

"Just after six-thirty," I answered and poured myself a cup of coffee.

"Do I have to go to school today?"

"I can't imagine why you wouldn't."

"I don't want to." She sat down on the barstool beneath the counter and pouted.

"Why not?"

"It's boring, and we don't do anything fun. I would rather stay here with you."

"Well, I don't get to stay home today. I have to go to work."

Speaking of which, I still needed to text Trevor and let him know that I would be late this morning. I hadn't talked to Quinn about it yet, but I was also planning to escort her to work after we dropped Rosie off at school. I knew that Quinn wasn't worried about herself right now because Rosie felt like the only threat, but I wasn't willing to take any chances.

"Will I have to work when I'm an adult?" Rosie asked as I finished my text message and pressed send.

I set my phone down on the counter and smiled as Quinn walked into the room.

"We all have to work," Quinn answered, sliding past me to snatch the other cup of coffee from the counter. "And you need to go brush your teeth so we can get going. I'll grab you breakfast on the way."

"But Mom," she whined.

"But nothing." Quinn brought the mug to her lips, the steam

billowing over the top. Her eyes narrowed as her brows raised. Rosie plopped off the barstool with a loud sigh and shuffled down the hall to the bathroom.

"They say it's supposed to get easier the older they get," Quinn sighed before taking a sip. "I find that hard to believe."

"I can imagine," I laughed. "She's a great kid, just a whole lot of her mama's sass in that little, tiny body."

"Hey," Quinn protested with a chuckle. "That's not all me. Justin contributed some too."

"Yeah, the good stuff. Like doing well in school and listening to anyone but her mom. It reminds me of someone I knew who was an unruly and rebellious teenager."

She groaned and closed her eyes, holding the cup between both hands.

"Oh, God. It's only going to get worse, isn't it?"

We both knew that she was joking, but the realness of her words was enough to shut both of us up.

"Sorry, I was going to make breakfast, but I didn't think she would be on board with a protein shake."

"She probably would have been all for it. I, on the other hand..."

"I can treat this morning," I offered with a smile. "I know this great bakery that's on the way to her school. We should have plenty of time to stop if we get going soon."

"We?"

"We talked about this when you agreed to the conditions,

Quinn. I'm not budging."

"Sorry," she sighed with resignation. "I guess it couldn't hurt to have more eyes on her and the school."

"Exactly why I came up with the idea, to begin with," I winked.

I turned to put my empty cup in the sink at the same time she turned to walk into the living room.

"Sorry," she said as our chests collided, the hot liquid in her cup almost sloshing over.

My hand darted out to grab the cup before it could spill and burn her, but her grip only got tighter and left me holding her hand. Our bodies were touching, the heat between them almost electrifying.

"You okay?" I asked gruffly.

"Mmmhmm," she mumbled, refusing to look up at me but also refusing to pull her hand away.

We stood there for a few seconds, waiting for the other to make the next move when Rosie suddenly returned.

"What are you guys doing?" she asked, pulling her backpack on over the clean t-shirt she had changed into.

"Nothing," Quinn answered, her voice a higher pitch and shakier than normal. She set her cup down on the counter and wiped her hands on her dress slacks. "Let's finish getting ready so we can go."

They went back to the bedroom to gather their stuff while I tried to focus on what I needed before we left. My mind had never been as scattered as when Quinn was around.

The drop-off at school was uneventful, which we had assumed it would be. Quinn fought me on making sure she got to work safely but finally gave in and let me. By the time I got to work, Trevor was studying me like I was some sort of alien, given how late I had gotten there.

"Sorry, I'll make up the hours," I said as I slid into my chair and sat down to get started.

"Don't worry about it. I was late this morning too."

"Everything okay?"

I turned on my computer and waited for it to start so I could check my schedule for the day. Typically I would know my schedule for the entire week, but today, I barely knew my name.

"Yeah, Elena wasn't feeling well."

"Again?" I raised a brow.

"I think she has what Hannah had."

I scrunched my face, remembering how sick he had mentioned she had been.

"I hope she feels better soon," I offered, while also praying that he didn't catch it and bring it to the office with him. The last thing that I wanted or needed right now was to get sick.

I checked my phone a few times, relieved when there weren't any calls or texts that Rosie was in danger, and then got to work. Maybe today could be a productive day after all.

Nine

Quinn
9 Days Ago

"Let's go!" I yelled over my shoulder. It was hump day, and there was nothing that I wanted more than to be humped. Okay—maybe that was a bit dramatic, but I imagined it would put me in a better mood than I had been in.

Yesterday had gone by like any other day after we left Roman's house in the morning—aside from him going with us to drop Rosie off at school and then insisting that he escort me to work. We checked in with each other a few times throughout the day, but there was nothing to report because everything felt back to normal again.

This morning I woke up with a borderline migraine, likely caused by the lack of sleep that I had gotten last night. I hated that the only good sleep I had recently was when I slept in Roman's bed and pretended that it was his body that I was cuddled against instead of the pillow that smelled like his body wash. Not that I had lathered myself up with it in the shower the morning I got ready there.

When there was nothing to report after Rosie got home from school and no vans were seen hiding in the shadows, I told myself that everything was fine and there wasn't a reason for us to stay with Roman again. Sure I had felt safer being there with him, but that didn't mean I needed to inconvenience him more than I already had.

"I can't find my shoe," Rosie called from her bedroom.

"Can you just put on another pair?" I yelled back, feeling bad for losing my patience. I didn't feel like fighting with her this morning, especially over a pair of shoes.

"These are the only ones that don't make my feet look weird in these pants," she whined, coming into my bedroom holding one shoe in her hand.

"Fine," I sighed, getting up from the bed and smoothing down my skirt. I glanced in the mirror to make sure that I had managed to put on matching heels before I followed her into her room to look for the lost shoe.

We got to school thirty minutes late, and this time, the front office wasn't as friendly and welcoming as it had been on Monday.

"I'm so sorry—it won't keep happening. I promise."

The older woman with a pencil sticking out of her bun gave me the stink eye before writing on a piece of paper and sliding it to the side.

"Tardiness has never been a problem for Rosie before," she said with way too much judgment in her voice. "If this continues—"

"It won't," I interrupted, holding my hands up.

I didn't bother sticking around to exchange pleasantries with any of the other office staff, given they all seemed just as grumpy and in need of a mid-week hump day.

By the time I got to work, my boss had given me the same disapproving look before I slipped past his office and hid in mine. I hadn't had time to eat and didn't bother to grab anything on the way since I was already late. It felt like life was more stressful this week, and I hated the feeling of things being out of control.

I grabbed my blue light glasses from my drawer and slipped them on, ready to start the day.

Just then, my phone vibrated with a text message. I let out a heavy sigh as if this was the break I needed from a long, stressful day that hadn't started yet.

Roman: How are things this morning?

Me: Fine. Chaotic. The usual?

I found myself chewing the inside of my lip, unsure of what to say. The last thing I needed was for Roman to worry that I wasn't okay. But was I really okay?

Roman: Do you need anything?

Me: That's a loaded question.

Roman: Anything that your brother wouldn't kill me over?

I brought my fingers to my lips and tried to hide my laugh. Was he flirting with me? Deep down, I really hoped that he was.

Me: I wouldn't worry about Mike. He's just always angry because he should be hooking up with his partner instead of constantly fighting with her.

Roman: Anastasia?

Me: I think so?

Roman: The woman from the party that left with the creep from the bathroom?

I frowned and tried to think of who he was talking about.

Me: Creep from the bathroom?

Roman: Uncle Saul.

Me: Oh, that guy.

God, I hated that guy. I had never felt comfortable around him from the moment I met him. Justin didn't care for him much either, but they worked together, and right before Justin died, they had been assigned to each other as partners.

Me: She left with him?

Roman: Said she had a date. Mike seemed pretty pissed about it.

Me: Because he secretly wants to bang her.

Roman: I don't think I want to hear about your brother banging anyone.

Me: Yeah, I don't think I want to talk about it either.

Roman: How was Rosie this morning? Did she get her donut for getting an A on her spelling test yesterday?

I lowered the phone to my desk and held my head in my hands. Damn it! I knew I had forgotten something this morning. That also explained her sudden hostility toward me on our way to school.

Me: No, there was a shoe incident, and we were late. I totally forgot about it until now.

Roman: I'm sure she'll understand.

Me: Not a chance. Rosie holds grudges more than anyone I know. I worry about her future boyfriends—especially when they cheat on her in her dreams. They're in for a world of hurt.

Roman: Shit.

Me: Right?

Roman: Maybe you can make it up to her and grab them on your way home?

I felt the idea start to blossom inside of me, finally something good that could turn the day around and get me back on Rosie's good side. Before it could last, I heard the ding on my computer and read the email that had just come in from my boss.

Me: Apparently the universe hates me today. My boss just scheduled another mandatory meeting this afternoon.

Roman: Are you going to be able to make it to pick her up?

Me: No. I'm going to call my mom and see if she can help me again.

Roman: I can pick her up if you want. Just call the school and let them know. I'll be sure to check in at the front desk when I get there.

I felt my heart flutter at the offer. How he even knew the procedures were beyond me, but I didn't have time to stop and question it.

Me: Are you sure? I don't want you to have to miss work.

Roman: I'll just take a late lunch. It's no big deal.

Me: Okay, if you're sure?

Roman: Quinn- stop. I got it.

Me: What about work?

Roman: I can just bring her back here if that's okay? Then I can take her home when you get off.

Me: Okay, but let me know if she starts to be any trouble.

Roman: She's five. How much trouble can she be?

I tipped my head back and laughed.

Ten
Roman
9 Days Ago

"Are you sure you don't want anything else?" I asked Rosie as we stood in line with a handful of random snacks. I had no idea what to feed her and didn't want her to go hungry until I dropped her off when Quinn got home from work, so we made a quick stop for reinforcements. Some for her, some for me. I didn't have siblings, so it wasn't like I was used to having kids around me, and to be honest, I was a little nervous being responsible for Rosie for a few hours.

The school didn't give me any problems picking her up, and while I wanted to think that it was because Quinn had already called and informed them, I had a sneaking suspicion that it was because the women in the front office couldn't figure out how to put their tongues back in their mouth long enough to give me any trouble over it. While that was reassuring on some level, it was more irritating given that we were worried someone was watching her, and I hated to think that it would be equally as easy for them to walk in and take her without any questions asked.

"No, thank you." She set her stuff on the counter and smiled at the older woman who started ringing us up.

"Well, aren't you just the prettiest little thing I've seen all day," she cooed, lighting up as she looked from Rosie to me. "You look just like your daddy." She smiled up at me, and I felt my stomach tighten.

"He's not my dad," Rosie replied matter of factly. "My dad died."

"Oh honey, I'm so sorry."

"Can we go now?" Rosie asked, looking up at me with tears in the corner of her eyes.

I nodded and handed the woman my card, not bothering to listen when she gave me the total. I grabbed the bag and led Rosie out, my hand protectively splayed across her back as we headed to the gym.

Trevor had been at lunch when I left to go pick her up but was back in the office when we got back.

"Hello!" she said excitedly as she bounced into the room, shuffling around the back of my desk to climb up into the chair.

"Hi," Trevor replied with a smile that nearly split his cheeks. "How are you, Rosie?"

"You know my name?" She stopped what she was doing as her face dropped in surprise.

"I do," he confirmed. "I also know your uncle Mike, and my buddy Roman was just telling me all kinds of fun stuff about you before he went to pick you up from school."

"Like what?" Her elbows rested on the desk as her head lay in her hands while she waited.

"Hmm, let's see." He tapped his fingers together before

widening his eyes and looking from me to her. "He told me that you love superheroes and that Hulk is your favorite."

She gasped before a smile spread tightly across her face. I opened the bag of snacks and spread them out across my desk before grabbing the two protein bars and tossed one to Trevor. He caught it and gave me a nod.

"Hulk is my favorite, but I also love Captain America. He's sooo dreamy," she sighed.

Trevor and I looked at each other and then turned back to her.

She tilted her head back and laughed.

"That's what Grandma Sandra says when we watch the movies. I think boys are gross, but she says that someday when I'm older, I'll change my mind." She opened the small bag of Doritos and fished one out before popping it into her mouth.

I felt a rush of relief wash over me.

"Boys are gross," a voice said from the hallway.

I looked up to find Mike walking into the room, a look of confusion on his face as he looked between the three of us.

"Why is Rosie here with you? Where's Quinn?" he asked, looking around as if I had her hidden under my desk or something.

"She had a last-minute meeting and needed someone to pick up Rosie, so I volunteered."

I kept my answer simple, but I knew he would see right through it.

"Why didn't she ask my mom? Or me?" He furrowed his brow, then narrowed his eyes. "Since when do you and Quinn talk anyway?"

"I…. Ummm…." I looked nervously at Rosie, not wanting to say anything that would frighten her or upset Quinn, given I didn't know how much she wanted Rosie to know right now.

"Hey, Rosie, I need to go check on the guys in the back. Do you want to come with me?" Trevor asked, pushing away from his desk and waiting for her to join him.

I raised a brow at him, silently telling him to keep an eye on her.

"I've got her, don't worry."

Once they left the room, I let out the breath I was holding.

"What the fuck is going on, Roman?"

I could either lie and hope that it didn't ruin our friendship, or I could tell the truth and pray that it didn't ruin the new one I felt was forming between Quinn and me.

"Just spit it out," he said, noticing that I was struggling.

I tilted my head back and looked at the ceiling.

"Fine. Quinn came to stay with me Monday night, and we've been talking since."

There, that wasn't a lie, and it wasn't overindulging in the little details that I wasn't sure if I should be sharing.

"Are you two—" he pinned me with a look that felt a little too murdery for my liking.

"Really? That's what you think she came over for? Rosie was there, for fucks sake, Mike." I shook my head but didn't know if I was more frustrated that he had asked or if I was still feeling overly guilty because I had entertained the thought of doing exactly that several times while she was there.

"So if my niece weren't there, you would have been banging my sister?"

"Is that something you really want to know?"

"Don't fuck with me, Roman," he warned.

"Or what?"

"She's my baby sister, and she's been through enough already."

"And I'm not looking for a random hook-up. You should know me better than that, Mike. Besides—that's not even what it was about. Believe it or not—there are other things to worry about other than whether or not your best friend is doing your sister."

I knew the moment the words left my mouth that I had said too much. His face softened some, but his shoulders seemed to tense beneath the blue dress shirt he was wearing.

"Tell me what's going on."

"You already heard about the incident at school with the van. On Monday, Quinn had another meeting that came up at the same time that she needed to pick Rosie up. Your mom went to get her instead, and she sent Quinn a picture of them sitting together on the couch at her house. Quinn knew that it was your mom's way of putting her at ease to know that Rosie was safe, but when she zoomed in on the picture, the same van was parked outside with someone inside it."

Mike clenched and unclenched his fists a few times while working his jaw. I could tell he was pissed, and I didn't blame him.

"Why didn't she come to me?"

"I asked her the same thing." I sat on the edge of my desk and crossed my ankles.

"And?"

"She was scared, Mike. Really scared. She hadn't slept in a few nights and thought that she would sleep better if they stayed with me because she knew that no one would get into my apartment without me hearing them first."

"I can protect her too," he countered but lacked the conviction in his tone that said he believed it.

"I know. She knows that too. But we all know that my training was different from you guys."

He sighed and plopped down into an empty chair by the window.

"So what's happening now? Why is Rosie really here?"

"It's true that Quinn had a meeting today. She offered to have your mom pick Rosie up, but I volunteered instead. I felt better knowing that I could keep an eye on her if she were here with me."

"Have you seen the van since Monday? Should we be filing reports or something?"

I stood up and walked around my desk to my computer.

"We haven't seen the van since your mom's house. I went with Quinn to take Rosie to school yesterday morning, and everything looked normal. She hadn't noticed anything unusual, and Rosie's teachers are on high alert. They actually had a talk with the kids today about safety and what to do if someone tries to take them. But no, we can't file any reports because it's not illegal to have a van parked outside of a school. We don't have any proof that someone is watching Rosie and nothing to go on. You know better than anyone that all we can do is watch and be alert right now."

"Were you able to identify the driver?" Mike asked, tapping his foot anxiously.

"No, but I was able to zoom in enough to get a logo off of the baseball cap they were wearing. Come check it out." I stepped back and let him stand in front of me to see the computer. Pulled up was an image of the little league logo.

I handed him my phone, and he played the video a few times, zooming in to see it.

"Unbelievable," he muttered. "That's the logo from Rosie's little league team."

"I know," I sighed. "Quinn told me. We're not sure if it's a parent, a coach, a fan—it could be anyone who happened to find the hat and wear it. Hell—for all we know, it could have been donated, and someone picked it up at a thrift shop. We have no way of knowing where it came from."

Mike handed the phone back to me and shook his head.

"I know exactly where it came from. It's mine."

724

Eleven

Quinn
9 Days Ago

It felt like it took forever to get to Roman's work, probably because I had this terrible feeling of being away from Rosie all afternoon and not knowing if she was okay. I trusted that Roman would keep her safe, but I also knew he had no idea what to expect from a five-year-old. For all I knew, she had tied him to a chair and painted his nails bubble gum pink while trying to style what little hair he had since it was cut so close to his head.

I shuffled through the door and heard laughter in the back of the gym. I knew the sound of her giggles from a mile away and felt the corners of my lips turning up as I gave the kid at the front desk a quick wave and headed toward it.

"Is that all you got?"

I stopped for a moment before I turned the corner and walked into the room. I knew that voice, but why was he here? Had Roman gotten into so much trouble that he felt he needed to call my brother for backup?

I walked in and stopped in my tracks, holding a hand to my heart.

Rosie was bouncing back and forth in front of a boxing

bag, her little hands barely fitting in the gloves that covered them.

"Come on, Rosie, you can do it!"

I looked around, noticing that Roman was standing next to her, coaching her on where to hit next, while Mike proudly stood on the other side, wearing the biggest grin I had ever seen. There were two other guys in the room, but I didn't recognize them.

She pulled her hand back and then punched with all of her might, her small body looking ridiculously tiny compared to the giant bag.

"That's it, Rosie!" Mike yelled.

I walked over and stood next to Roman, folding my arms over my chest.

He turned his head for a split second, noticing I was there, before turning his attention back to Rosie.

"Okay, how about a break," he said nervously, and I knew he was trying to gauge my reaction.

Rosie spun around, a frown on her face that quickly changed when she saw me.

"Mom!" She ran over and wrapped her arms around me, almost knocking me over. "Did you see me?!"

"I did," I laughed, her excitement enough to make me feel silly.

"He was showing some guy how to hit the bag, and I really wanted to try it. He said no, but then I asked Uncle Mike, and he said yes."

I raised my brows at Mike, who just shrugged.

"Then Trevor jumped in and helped me get the gloves on, and his friend Max came by, and he gave me some pointers too."

"It looks like you're a very lucky little girl who has a whole army of superheroes to protect you," I said quietly, pulling her into me for another hug.

"They talked to us at school today about what to do if someone tries to take you, but I think that if anyone ever tried to take me, I would just hit them instead."

My heart skipped a beat, and I could feel the heat of everyone's eyes on me.

"Well, let's hope that never happens. Now, go get ready so we can go home and give Roman a break."

"Can we stay the night with him again?" Rosie asked as she pulled her gloves off.

My eyes flew open as I whipped my head around to Mike. There was no way that this was going to go over well. I had planned on telling him about it soon; there just hadn't been time.

"Relax, I already know," Mike said, holding his hand up to stop the trainwreck of thoughts pulsing through my head.

"You know?" I looked to Roman, begging for more clarity. Did Mike know about us staying there and nothing else, or did he know about everything else?

"We talked, and there's something that you need to know," Roman said, lowering his voice as he stepped closer. Trevor and Max—I guess were their names—helped Rosie put her gloves away before taking her back to Roman's office to get her backpack.

"What's up?" I asked a little too nervously as I looked between Mike and Roman.

"Remember the hat we saw in the photo from your mom's house?" Roman asked.

"Yeah," I said slowly. I had a bad feeling about whatever they were about to drop on me. "What about it?"

"It's mine," Mike said with a tight smile.

I pulled my head back in confusion.

"It's your hat? You've been stalking Rosie?"

"No," he blew out and rolled his eyes. "But my hat used to be in my office, and I haven't been able to find it for almost a week."

"How do you know it was yours?"

"Because there was a stain on the side from Rosie's peanut butter and jelly sandwich. She was so upset about it and didn't want me to find it, so she got the scissors and tried to cut it off."

"Oh my god," I laughed. "I remember that!"

Roman pulled out his phone and zoomed in on the picture.

"See right there," Mike said as he pointed to it. "That's where it was cut."

I squinted my eyes and held the phone closer. Sure enough, there was the missing chunk. Why hadn't I seen that before?

"So someone stole your hat and is wearing it around town

while they watch my daughter?" I asked, flinging my hands in the air. "Why? It doesn't make any sense."

"Someone is targeting her; we know that much for sure," Roman said.

"But Quinn, you're also missing the bigger picture here," Mike added gently. "It's not just someone. It's someone who had access to my office and knows a lot about her already."

My blood ran cold as a chill spread throughout me.

"You think it's someone in the FBI?" I whispered.

Mike flinched but didn't say anything.

Suddenly all of the pieces started falling around me. It wasn't just that it was someone in the FBI; it was that it was someone who worked with my brother in the witness protection program—the same department my husband worked in before he was killed on the job.

"What was the last case that Justin was working on before he died?" I asked, forcing my voice to be stronger than I felt.

"Quinn—you know that I can't—"

"Tell. Me."

Mike's shoulders fell, and he looked down at the floor.

"Ariel Wyland. She was a victim of sex trafficking. The only one who went to court and put her captor behind bars."

"Where is she now?" I asked, knowing that he couldn't tell me since she had gone into witness protection shortly after leaving the courtroom.

"The U.S. Marshal's office confirmed they found her body yesterday."

Twelve

Roman
9 Days Ago

"I don't think it's a good idea for you to go home by yourself," I said, gently holding Quinn's arm so she couldn't leave.

"We'll be fine," she insisted, looking around for Rosie's hair tie that she had lost somewhere in my office.

"Don't be so stubborn," Mike cut in, giving her a pointed look. "You know better than anyone what we're dealing with, and now your daughter is the target. Let us protect you."

"So what do you suggest?" she asked, hand planted firmly on her hip.

"You can come stay with me," he offered.

"I don't think that's the best idea," Max said from the other side of the room. He and Trevor had stuck around for a bit after I pulled him to the side to ask him a few questions about what was going on. If Trevor trusted him, my gut told me that I could as well.

"Why not?" Mike responded, turning to look at him.

"Because you're as much of a target as they are. Whoever

it is—they're making sure it's obvious that they have a connection to you otherwise, they wouldn't have taken your hat and worn it while sitting outside of your mom's house. That wasn't a slip-up; it was very intentional. Someone is trying to make sure you get a message, and if Quinn and Rosie stay with you, you're putting everyone at risk."

"I agree," I said with a sigh. "It's apparent that this person works with Mike and has access to his office. They probably know where he lives and his routine." I paused and then looked him in the eye. "They'll take advantage of you wanting to protect your family. They want you to be distracted, so you let your guard down. You can't keep them safe and do your job at the same time."

"My job has nothing to do with this," he grunted and ran a hand through his hair in frustration.

"It does," I countered. "You need to be focused at work to figure out who it is. That means you need to be as far away from Quinn and Rosie as possible until we know what is happening. We can't afford to have you distracted and making mistakes."

"I don't make mistakes," he bit out.

"It only takes one, and we can't afford that right now." I rested my hand on his shoulder and squeezed. "I've got them. I promise."

"I'll see if I can get a couple of guys to set up some surveillance," Max offered. "And don't worry—they're good at staying hidden. I'll work out the details with Roman and figure out where we want eyes."

"Not the same guy you had to watch Elena?" Trevor said with a laugh.

"No," Max groaned. "That rookie left and never came back. They're former military, and I trust them with my life."

I nodded and patted Mike before going over to my desk to grab my stuff.

"If you need to take a few days off," Trevor offered as he grabbed his things as well.

"Thanks, but I'm good. I think it's best if we keep everything as normal as possible. We don't want to do anything to spook them before we figure out who it is."

"That still doesn't solve the problem of Quinn going home by herself," Mike said. "I don't like her being there alone with Rosie, knowing that someone is watching them."

"They can stay with me tonight," I replied, noticing the faint blush that crept up the side of Quinn's neck.

"Alright, then I guess that's settled." She swung her purse over her shoulder and looked down at Rosie, who was fast asleep in the chair by my desk.

"I'll carry her," I offered before Quinn could pick her up.

"You don't have to; I can get her."

"Like your brother said, quit being so stubborn."

Her brows rose, and her lips puckered into a look I had seen on my mom several times.

"And so it begins," she muttered.

We got back to my apartment a little after eight. I helped her get Rosie in bed and made sure the bathroom light was on before I shut the door and joined Quinn in the kitchen.

"I couldn't find much in your fridge, so I made you a peanut butter and jelly sandwich," she said, handing it to me wrapped in a paper towel.

"Thank you, but you didn't have to fix me anything to eat. I'll be sure to get some groceries tomorrow."

"You don't have to do that," she said before taking a bite of hers. "We're only here for one night."

I chewed and let my facial expressions do the talking.

"Roman, we can't just live with you. What if we don't figure out who this is for a while? Eventually, we'll need to go back to our apartment and get on with our lives."

"You'll stay as long as you need to, Quinn. It's not a big deal, and I actually like the company."

"You do?" The look she gave me said that she was calling my bluff.

"Yeah, it's kinda nice to have someone to talk to at night."

"I guess." She shrugged and pushed the last bite into her mouth. "It's been so long since I've had someone to talk to besides Rosie that I don't know if I even know how to have an adult conversation anymore."

"I'm sure it's been hard."

She walked to the sink and grabbed a glass out of the cabinet before filling it with water. She took a drink and then turned to me, holding the glass to her chest.

"I miss him."

"I'm sorry, I can't imagine losing someone like that."

I finished my sandwich and tossed the paper towel in the trash before grabbing a glass and filling it with water. We stood side by side in front of the sink, drinking our water, when she spoke again.

"I've been thinking about his accident tonight, and there's something that just never sat right with me about it."

"What's that?" I turned my head toward her.

"Justin was with three other agents in the car when they got in the accident, but he was the only one who didn't make it. They said that he had been fumbling with his seat belt and had taken it off for a moment when the car crashed. If he had been wearing it, he would have had some minor injuries, but he would likely still be here."

"Were the other agents injured in the accident?"

"Yeah, but only minor injuries. I think one guy broke his leg, and another had some fractured ribs, but nothing life-threatening. Justin was the only one who wasn't wearing a seat belt and was ejected through the window. He died on impact."

"God, Quinn," I sighed, not knowing what to say.

"What if his death wasn't an accident?" she asked, turning to face me as she set her water on the counter beside her.

"You don't think it was?"

She inhaled slowly and looked around before meeting my eyes.

"No, I think my husband was murdered."

Thirteen

Quinn
8 Days Ago

When I woke up, I felt lost and disoriented as I looked around, wondering why I felt so comfortable where I was. Then I remembered that I had slept at Roman's again and ended up cuddling his pillow most of the night because it smelled like him.

We stayed up talking for a few hours as I launched into my theory about how Justin hadn't just died in a car accident; he had been murdered. There was nothing that I could do to prove it, but it felt good to finally get the thoughts out of my head. Roman was kind enough to sit there and listen, even though I felt like a crazy person when the only thing I could come up with as to why Justin would never have taken his seat belt off in a moving car was because he was too by the rules.

But it was true—Justin never did anything that even slightly deviated into a gray area. He was, by nature, a goody-two-shoes, and everyone knew it. If you were planning to break any rules or skirt outside of what was considered ethical—you made sure he didn't find out about it because he would tell on you.

That was why it had been so weird to me when they told me

that he had been ejected from the car because he had taken his seat belt off when the accident happened. I argued that he would never do that, and his partner had insisted that it was locked and uncomfortable, so he took it off to adjust it. While it was something that I would do—and had done several times—it wasn't something that he would do. Not even if the car was stopped at a red light. He would have waited until the car was safely parked somewhere before taking it off.

Roman had entertained my endless rambling on the subject until I got too tired to continue and called it a night. I hadn't bothered to apologize for intruding on his space again since it had been him who had insisted that we stay. Unfortunately, this time I didn't plan ahead, so I didn't have a change of clothes for Rosie or myself, and there was no way in hell that I was going to be late getting her to school again.

My alarm on my watch went off at five, so I rolled out of bed and shuffled down the hallway, hoping not to wake him. This time, I made sure to peek in the living room to make sure we didn't have another shower incident. I still couldn't get that beautiful sight out of my head—which I wasn't complaining about.

I snuck into the living room and smiled when I saw him still asleep on the couch. I turned and headed to the bathroom, feeling slightly anxious about leaving Rosie by herself until I remembered that Roman was here and no one was going to get into his apartment without him hearing them first.

I closed the bathroom door but didn't lock it in case Rosie woke up and was looking for me. The shower felt wonderful as I stood under the hot water and let it massage my tense muscles. I would love to fill the tub and just soak for a few hours, but I couldn't remember the last time I had done that.

Not wanting to use all of the hot water, I finished up and stepped out, wrapping a towel around my body. I looked for one to dry my hair with but didn't see any, so I tugged the one off of my body and quickly bent over to dry it as best I could so it wasn't soaking wet.

When I stood up, I gasped and tried to clutch the towel to my body before it fell to the floor. Standing before me was Roman, rubbing the sleep from his eyes before they focused on my naked body. He went from half asleep to wide awake in less than a second.

"Shit, I'm so sorry," he murmured, trying to look away. "I didn't think before I came in and didn't hear the shower. I thought you were still sleeping; it's early."

He bent down and handed me the towel while he looked away. I took it and wrapped it around myself as quickly as I could.

"I got up early because I need to swing by my place to get a change of clothes for Rosie and me before school, and she can't be late again."

"I really am sorry for walking in on you," he said, but there was something in his eyes that said he wasn't sorry at all.

"I guess we're almost even given that I walked in on you the other day."

I tried to laugh and make a joke out of it, but instead, it came out as some weird, muffled, strangled cry type of noise that I had never heard before in my life.

He smiled, and I looked away, suddenly feeling more embarrassed about it.

"Maybe not even," I muttered, thinking how I had only seen him from the waist up, whereas he had seen everything.

"Well, we'll try to make a schedule next time to keep this from happening again."

I could hear the laughter in his voice and clutched the towel tighter to my body. He stepped out and pulled the door behind him to give me some privacy to get dressed.

By the time I was done, Rosie was already awake and talking with Roman in the living room. I got our stuff ready while he jumped in the shower, then we ran by my apartment to change before rushing to school. Rosie didn't care about how quickly we had to walk since she had gotten a doughnut for breakfast when I didn't have time to stop for something healthier.

She walked into her classroom just as the final bell had rung. Her teachers gave us a quick wave before closing the door. I sighed a breath of relief that we had made it on time and leaned against the wall next to Roman. Unfortunately, there wasn't much time to linger in the hall and catch my breath if I wanted to get to work on time. If I kept showing up late, I would find myself in my boss's office again, listening to another lecture about punctuality and job responsibilities.

I pushed off the wall, and we started heading down the hallway when I felt Roman's hand brush against mine. The jolt of electricity that passed between us was enough to make my heart skip a beat, and suddenly I found myself anxious for the day to be over so I could go back to Roman's.

Fourteen

Roman

8 Days Ago

I waited until the end of the day to take my lunch so I could go to the grocery store and be back before Quinn and Rosie got there. I had picked Trevor's brain about what kind of foods kids liked to eat, but when neither of us had any idea, we found ourselves on some popular food blog with an abundance of options that looked easy and kid friendly.

I knew that Quinn was already struggling with the thought of staying with me for a while, so I wanted to make it as comfortable for them as possible. I picked up enough food to last us more than a few days and wondered how I was going to fit everything in the fridge, but that was a problem for another day.

Quinn and Rosie got there a little after six while I stirred the boiling pasta on the stove.

"You're cooking?" Quinn asked with a smile as she shut the door behind her. This morning I had given her the spare key even though she fought me on it. I had also volunteered to pick Rosie up and take her back to work with me until Quinn got home. She had refused and said that things needed to be as normal as possible for Rosie right now, which meant that Sandra would pick her up when she got out around one, and then Quinn would get her on her way home.

I hated not being there to watch over Rosie while she was with her grandma, but I also knew Sandra almost my entire life and trusted that she was safe there. Just because Sandra hadn't known about the van last time didn't mean she was incapable of protecting her granddaughter. She had grown up in a life of military and law enforcement officers, so it wasn't like she was clueless about what was going on. Mike had gotten her up to date, and Sandra was fully on board with everything that we were trying to do to protect Rosie.

"I cook," I laughed, grabbing the towel hanging over my shoulder. "Not often, but I still know what I'm doing." I opened the oven door and used the towel to take out the pan of chicken that I had baked. There were two chicken breasts that I had seasoned for Quinn and me, and then a third breast that I had cut into bite-sized pieces and breaded to make chicken nuggets for Rosie.

I set the pan on the back of the stove and turned the oven off. The pasta was done, so I removed it from the heat and drained it before adding it to the bowl of alfredo sauce that I had already warmed up.

"Go wash up while I help with dinner," Quinn said to Rosie, gently tousling her hair as she bounced off toward the bathroom.

A few seconds later, we heard the water turn on, and Rosie started singing Twinkle, Twinkle, Little Star.

"What can I help with?" Quinn asked, standing beside me at the stove.

I tried not to move, afraid that I would get burned if I did. It wasn't the heat from the stove that had me worried—it was the chemistry that was sizzling between us that scared me.

"I'm good," I answered, my voice thick and scratchy.

"You sure?"

She was close—too close—to where I could feel the tingle of goosebumps as her bare arm brushed against mine.

I nodded and muttered an mmmhmm before stepping away to grab the plates from the cabinet. I turned around to set them down when I crashed into her again. This time it was her fingers that grabbed onto my body to hold me steady before they trailed across my ribs.

"Quinn," I breathed, still holding the plates but not bothering to move away from her touch.

"Yeah?" she asked, her fingers still making delicate trails around my abs.

"When you touch me like that…"

She lifted her eyes and looked into mine as a moment passed between us.

"You make it really hard not to throw these plates to the ground and kiss the hell out of you," I murmured, closing my eyes while trying to keep my grip on said plates.

Before she could respond, Rosie was heading down the hallway, singing another song. Quinn yanked her hands away and stepped back, tucking her head as she turned to the stove. I tried to ignore the way my dick was straining against my briefs but was thankful that my shirt and jeans were enough to hide it.

I put the plates on the counter and then grabbed some silverware while Quinn helped bring the food to the table. It wasn't a big table, but there was plenty of room for the three of us to sit and enjoy a meal together.

Rosie's eyes lit up when she saw her chicken nuggets, and I felt relieved that I hadn't screwed it up. I set a bowl of steamed broccoli and cauliflower on the table, assuming it would be for Quinn and myself, but I was pleasantly surprised when Rosie asked for some. I was impressed with how much she ate as she twirled noodles on her fork and giggled every time she made a slurping sound.

Quinn and I talked about random stuff at dinner, in between stories from Rosie about the things that happened at school or while she was with Sandra. Once we were done, Quinn offered to help clean up, but I insisted that she go get Rosie's bath started, and I would take care of it.

In addition to groceries, I had also grabbed a few things for them at the store that they would need here: shampoo, conditioner, toothbrushes, and of course, a bottle of bubble bath with princesses on it that smelled like strawberries. Rosie squealed when she saw it and asked Quinn if she could take the biggest bubble bath ever as she jumped up and down excitedly.

I had cooked extra for dinner, knowing that there would be enough for Quinn to take some to work for lunch. I wasn't sure if she usually packed a lunch, but I hadn't seen her take anything with her the few days I had gone with her to take Rosie to school. She didn't strike me as someone who ate out a lot, so I assumed she had been too busy and was likely skipping lunch while she tried to make up hours.

I didn't worry about leftovers for myself since tomorrow was Friday, and I was having lunch with Trevor and Max to get some updates on the items he was working on. It felt like it had already been a long time since we first talked about it when it had only been a few days. Life was suddenly chaotic, and I was having difficulty getting in the groove with things.

Rosie giggled from the bathroom, and I smiled, thankful to hear how happy and carefree she sounded. I hated that she lived in a world where bad things happened to sweet, innocent children like her, but I was determined to make sure that she never experienced it. Losing her father was tragic enough.

A little while later, Quinn came down the hall and plopped down on the couch beside me.

"I didn't think I was ever going to get her out of that bath," she laughed. "Thank you for picking up the bubble bath for her, that was really nice of you."

"Of course, not a problem. I also grabbed a few other things for you guys and left them on the counter."

"I saw, thank you for those as well. You don't have to keep buying us stuff and feeding us. I'm more than happy to help pay for stuff or bring our own—"

"Quinn, it's okay to let people help you," I said, interrupting her.

She sighed and sank lower on the couch.

"It's hard. I had so much help when Justin first died, which was great, but now I feel like I should be able to handle things on my own. It's been four years. I shouldn't need anyone anymore."

"It doesn't matter how long it's been. It's okay to need help still. That doesn't make you weak or any less of a mother."

"I don't know how single mothers do it with more than one kid," she laughed, resting her head on the cushion. "I only have one, and it feels like I'm always in over my head and drowning."

"They do exactly what you're doing—they just keep pushing forward, one step at a time."

Her phone rang, and she pulled it out of her pocket, smiling as she looked at the caller ID before answering.

"Hey, Mama."

I thought about getting up to give her some privacy for her phone call, but I got a text message from Max before I could.

Max: Is she with you tonight?

Me: Yes, they're both here now.

Max: Keep them there and make sure your doors are locked.

Me: What happened?

Max: Someone broke into her apartment. It'll be a few days before she can go back.

Me: Did they take anything valuable?

Max: It's more so what they left.

Another text message came through, but this time it was a picture of a seat belt lying on Quinn's bed.

I was still staring at my phone when Quinn ended her call and was staring at me.

"Everything okay?" she asked.

"Yeah," I lied, tucking my phone into my pocket. "You?"

"That was my mom asking if she can keep Rosie tomorrow after school for a sleepover since it's Friday and we don't have plans on Saturday."

"That's sweet of her; I'm sure she would enjoy that."

"Do you think it's okay to let her stay?"

"I don't see why not," I shrugged. "But if you're uncomfortable about it, you can always say no."

"I already told her yes, so I would feel bad backing out now. Besides, we don't even know if anyone is still watching her. I haven't noticed anything weird, have you?"

I wanted to tell her about the picture Max had just sent me but decided that it was better to wait until I could talk to him. I pulled my phone back out of my pocket and sent him a quick text, asking if anyone was going to call and tell Quinn about the break-in.

"I haven't noticed anything," I replied, putting my phone on the couch beside me. "But that doesn't mean that we can stop being vigilant. We have to keep our guard up and make sure we know where Rosie is at all times."

She chewed her nail and thought about it. Before she could say anything else, her phone rang again.

"Sorry, it's Mike this time."

She answered, and I knew he was calling to tell her about the apartment.

"Oh my God," she whispered, holding her hand to her chest.

"Okay, yeah, I understand."

I hated the look of fear in her eyes right now.

"I'll see if I can stay with Roman for a few more days," she said as she caught me nodding my head. It wasn't even a question of whether she could stay with me. I would make sure that they did, especially now that someone had been in their apartment.

Rosie came into the living room after getting her pajamas on and her teeth brushed. Quinn finished up with her phone call and seemed flustered.

"What's wrong, Mama?" Rosie asked, curling up beside her on the couch.

"Nothing, sweet girl." She gently brushed her fingers across Rosie's forehead, making her eyes flutter as she tried to stay awake.

"I can go by your apartment to grab some clothes and stuff if you want?" I offered, knowing that it was another thing weighing heavily on her mind.

"It's okay, I can try to go in the morning."

"Quinn."

She rolled her eyes and exhaled.

"You wouldn't know what to pack," she objected.

"You can tell me. I am pretty smart, you know. I ran some pretty intense operations in the Marines; I think I can handle packing up some stuff."

"You really want to go through my personal belongings and pick the bras and panties that I'm going to wear for a few days?"

I knew that she was being sarcastic, but there was actually nothing that I wanted more. Although, the thought of her wearing them for me was even more thrilling. Heat spread quickly throughout my body, adding a touch of color to my naturally tanned cheeks.

"What if you had an escort?" I raised a brow, challenging her while also trying to steer the conversation in another direction.

"An escort?"

I nodded.

"Like Mike?"

"I can't think of anyone better."

She tilted her head back, closed her eyes, and groaned.

"Ugh. Fine."

"Do you want to go tonight or tomorrow morning?"

She thought about it for a minute before picking up her phone and rolling her eyes again.

"I'll see if he can go with me tonight; that way we don't have to rush as much in the morning."

I leaned back and smiled, feeling slightly satisfied that she wasn't fighting me on it.

Fifteen

Roman

7 Days Ago

I spent most of the morning in an upbeat, happy mood as I counted down the hours until Quinn would be off work and heading back to my apartment. I knew that it was foolish to think that anything could—or would—happen between us, but I still couldn't fight the grin that felt plastered to my face since I woke up. Not having Rosie with us tonight would allow us the time to talk and not have to worry about what she might overhear.

By ten, Trevor came bouncing into the office, a smile bigger than mine spread across his cheeks. I pushed away from my desk and swiveled my chair to face him.

"I don't think I've seen you this happy about it being Friday since you had tickets to take Elena to her first Yankees game."

"Well, this is soooo much better than a Yankees game," he said, sliding into the chair behind his desk.

I gasped and held a hand to my heart, pretending to be stunned by this information.

"What could possibly be better than the Yankees?"

"Elena agreed that we can start trying to have a baby after

Max's wedding. She's finally ready!"

"That's awesome, man! Happy humping!"

His grin stretched across his face as our phones dinged at the same time with a text message alert. I had almost expected it to be from Max about lunch today since we both got messages, but mine was from Quinn.

My fingers rushed to open the message to read it.

Quinn: My mom wants to pick Rosie up from school today.

Me: That's nice of her. I'm sure she'll enjoy spending time with your mom.

Quinn: I'm worried someone will be watching them like last time.

Me: That's always a possibility, but it would be with whoever picked her up.

Quinn: Should I pick her up instead?

Me: If it makes you feel better, I don't see why not.

Me: Do you want me to meet you there?

Quinn: You don't have to do that but thank you.

Me: I don't mind.

Quinn: Hold on

I set my phone down and waited for her next message.

I lifted my head and found Trevor staring at his phone, a cheesy grin plastered to his face again. He looked up and saw me watching him with a brow raised.

"Elena is already thinking of baby names," he answered as

his fingers flew across his phone.

"And here you thought she wasn't ready," I laughed.

"Hey, what can I say? I'm not used to good things happening this easily."

"I think you've more than paid your dues, my brother. Only the best things are heading your way from here on out."

I knew how much he wanted to be a father and was glad that things looked like they were finally heading in that direction for him. Elena was young—ten years younger than him—and that had put them on different pages about starting a family for a few months now.

He smiled and let his shoulders relax.

"Thanks, man."

I returned his smile and then picked up my phone to check the new message from Quinn.

Quinn: Mike is going with her to pick Rosie up, which works better since my boss just called another mandatory meeting.

Me: See, everything always works out. She'll be more than safe with Mike and your mom there.

Quinn: Apparently Mike is also staying the night at my mom's house. I think something has him worried.

Me: I don't know any more than you do, but I imagine that the break-in last night has him on heightened alert like it does us.

Quinn: Yeah, I guess. I just feel like there's more that he's not telling me.

Me: I wouldn't worry about it. Mike wouldn't do anything to put you or Rosie in danger.

Quinn: True.

Me: Try not to obsess over it. The weekend will officially be here before you know it.

Quinn: I wanted to talk to you about that.

Me: The weekend?

Quinn: Yes. I don't want you to feel like you have to babysit me tonight while Rosie is at my mom's house. I can find something to do so I'm not in your hair.

Me: I don't have plans, and you're not in my hair.

Quinn: I don't want to impose.

Me: Stop.

Quinn: …….

Me: Whatever you're typing—just delete it.

Me: I need to get back to work but think about what you want for dinner, and I'll pick up something on my way home.

Quinn: You're so bossy.

Me: You like it.

Quinn: ……

Quinn: ……

Quinn: ……

I felt my insides flip as I waited for her to decide on

whatever she was going to send. The dots would appear and then disappear for a few minutes before she finally pressed send.

Quinn: I'll check in with you at 4:30. Have a good day.

Me: You too.

I slid my phone to the side and tried to force myself to focus on work and not the endless thoughts on what Quinn might have been saying before she chickened out. Did she like that I was bossy? Was it off-putting to her? At the end of the day, we would be having our first dinner together by ourselves, and that felt like it meant more than it should.

Sixteen

Quinn
7 Days Ago

"What?" I laughed, pulling the greasy chili cheese dogs out of the to-go bag and setting them on the counter. "This is what I wanted for dinner."

"You never cease to surprise me," Roman laughed, his arm brushing against mine as he set the paper plates down.

"I try to eat healthy with Rosie, but every now and then, I just crave these chili dogs. That's how my butt got so big when I was pregnant with her. I think they actually put my picture on the wall at one point as their top customer because I went there so frequently and spent so much money on chili dogs. Justin never complained, not once. Not even when my ass grew two sizes," I snorted. "It never went away either," I commented, looking over my shoulder at my plump behind.

I watched Roman's eyes as they followed mine, landing on my ass before he sucked in a breath and looked away.

As much as I wanted to deny that things didn't feel different without Rosie here, I couldn't. It was like there was all of this sexual tension between us, crackling like electricity whenever we got close enough to each other for our bodies to touch.

"So, how many do you want?" Roman asked, studying the pile in front of us.

"I'll start with two and some fries."

"Start with? You're not playing, are you?"

"Nope," I replied, letting the p pop.

He smiled and shook his head as he piled two chili cheese dogs and some fries on a plate and handed it to me. We went to the living room and sat down on the couch, leaving the middle cushion empty between us.

We didn't bother with small talk as we ate. The food was too delicious to waste time with anything but eating it.

Roman took his first bite and closed his eyes as he chewed, a small moan escaping his lips. I tried to look away, but there was something so sexy about the way he looked that I couldn't help but imagine him eating something else.

I held the chili dog in front of my mouth, taking bites without paying attention while I continued to watch the show. His eyes were now open, but he still hadn't noticed me staring at him as he took another bite. I pushed the hotdog into my mouth, not realizing how far back I had shoved it until it hit the back of my throat, and I started choking.

I immediately pulled it out and started coughing as he dropped his to his plate and reached over to grab my bottle of water.

"Are you okay?" he asked as he handed it to me.

I nodded and took a drink, trying desperately to stop the coughing. It was so embarrassing, and how was I supposed to explain what happened? I got so turned on watching you eat your chili dog that I tried to deep throat mine.

"I'm okay," I managed to get out before taking another drink. "I was just a little distracted."

He arched a brow and leaned back against the couch, a faint smirk appearing on his face as if he knew exactly what I had been distracted by.

"Wieners do that sometimes," he replied nonchalantly as he stuck his tongue in his cheek.

My cheeks felt like they were on fire as the heat rushed over them.

"I wouldn't know," I said shyly, looking away as I chugged the rest of my water.

A look flashed across his face, but I ignored it as I got up and collected my plate.

"Are you done?" I asked, nodding to his.

"Yeah, I'll take it though."

"I don't mind." I pushed my hand toward him for him to put his plate on mine. Instead, he grabbed my plate from me and stood up, invading my space, and taking up all of the clean air around me.

"I do. Sit down and relax. I'll clean up."

I knew better than to fight him on cleaning up my trash and sat down.

"Do you want another bottle of water? I also have milk, and I think I might have a few beers."

"Water is good, thank you."

He shuffled around in the kitchen as he threw away our plates, then joined me on the couch again.

"Here you go," he said as he handed me the cold bottle of water.

"Thank you."

I debated rubbing it across my body to try to take some of the heat away, then realized that it would be even more sexual than my near-death by wiener a few minutes ago.

"Do you want to watch a movie?" Roman offered, clearing the awkward silence between us.

"Sure." I smiled and felt some of the tension start to dissipate when he smiled back at me.

He scrolled through the channels, trying to find something, but neither of us was that motivated to pick something. Finally, he gave up and left it on Die Hard.

I tried to focus on the movie, but my mind was constantly distracted, wondering how Rosie was doing and whether she was having fun. When I wasn't obsessing over her, I was thinking about my apartment and the seat belt that was left on my bed. Someone was trying to send me a message—that much was clear. I just wish I knew who it was and what they wanted.

I was so lost in thought that I hadn't heard Roman speak. My legs were extended in front of me, taking up the space on the cushion that was supposed to be separating us. Instead, my toes were pressed firmly against his thick thigh, and his hand rested on my ankle.

"I'm sorry, what?" I asked, feeling bad for missing what he said.

"I asked if you wanted another bottle of water," he said softly.

I looked down at the one in my hand, now empty after slowly chugging it without paying attention.

"I'm good, thank you. Soon I'll be swimming around here with all of the water I've drunk."

"I have plenty," he laughed.

I felt my lips curl up into a grin.

"What's on your mind?" he asked as he gently squeezed my foot.

"Everything," I laughed, though it wasn't a lie.

"Wanna talk about it?"

"Not really," I shook my head. "For once, I just want a break where I don't have to think about anything or worry about anyone but myself. I know that's selfish, but I can't remember when the last time was that I was able to just be me. Not a wife. Not a mother. Not an agent. Just me."

I leaned back further into the couch and sighed heavily.

"It's not selfish," he replied quietly, pulling my foot up onto his lap as he massaged it. "It's okay to take time for yourself, and it's also okay to let someone else take care of you."

I eyed him suspiciously, waiting for there to be some sort of but added to it. Moms don't get breaks; that's the job you signed up for. Wives need to learn how to balance work and family life; it's up to them to make those ends meet without anyone noticing their struggle. Women don't ask for help; we make do with what we have.

I shook my head to clear the thoughts that I had allowed my brain to ingrain into my memory over the years. Justin was a good man, but even he had flaws—and those flaws were with how he viewed women and their role in the marriage.

"I honestly wouldn't have any idea what that's like. I moved out the day after I turned eighteen, and I've been on my own since then."

"It's never too late to start."

He kept working my tired, sore feet, rotating between them as his strong hands massaged every inch. Now that Rosie was getting older, I had started taking her for mommy and daughter dates to get pedicures, but even those massages were nothing compared to what Roman was doing.

"How are you still single?" I blurted out, watching him carefully.

He smiled but didn't look up. His fingers pressed against the pad of my foot, putting enough pressure to release some of the tension that had built up.

"I haven't met the right woman."

"Are you looking?"

"I'd like to think that I would know when I found her," he shrugged, gently dropping my foot, and finally looking up at me. "But as we both know, life doesn't always work out that way. Sometimes the things we want are the things that we can't have."

My heart fluttered at his words, and I couldn't help but wonder if he was talking about us. I could see something hidden in his eyes when he said it—an almost sadness.

"What do you want?" I asked bravely.

He swallowed hard, looking around the room before turning back to me.

"You."

<u>Seventeen</u>

Roman
7 Days Ago

My words hung heavily in the air between us. Did I expect to say that to Quinn? No. Did I regret admitting it to her? Also no.

Her body was rigid next to mine, her feet pulled back to her side of the couch, making the distance between us feel like it was more than it was. I missed touching her already but knew that I didn't have the right to, to begin with.

"Are you joking with me?" she asked quietly, barely above a whisper.

I squared my shoulders and rolled my head back on my neck, looking ahead of me instead of at her.

"I would never joke about something like that."

She adjusted on the couch beside me, pulling one of the throw pillows up to her chest as she held it against her.

"But I'm sorry if I made you uncomfortable. That was never my intention, and you have my word that you're safe here with me. Just because I have feelings for you doesn't mean I'll act on them."

I glanced at her and found her watching me as she rubbed

her fingers across her mouth.

Not wanting to make her feel awkward or uneasy, I got up and went into the kitchen. I had no idea what I was going to do in there, but at least it would give me a few minutes to think without having Quinn near me. It was almost like she was a siren, calling to me and luring me into a murky area that I had no business being.

I was working on cleaning the coffee pot out and getting it programmed to run in the morning when I heard Quinn come in. I kept my back to her, too nervous to face her just yet. I knew I had to at some point, but I had put my big foot in my mouth and now had to pay the price for that.

She moved around behind me, doing something at the sink. I turned to grab the coffee from the cabinet when she turned around, and we collided again. I wanted to make a joke about how we couldn't keep meeting this way, but it didn't feel like it was as light as it should be. Maybe there was a reason we kept running into each other. Maybe it was the universe trying to push us together.

"Sorry," she laughed nervously. Her thick lashes fluttered as she kept her eyes down, afraid to look up at me.

My hands instinctively reached out and held onto her hips. She didn't move away and slowly, her hands slid up my arms and held onto me as if she was afraid to let go. Her chest rose and fell heavily, the air between us thick with desire we both felt.

She looked up, her blue eyes gazing into mine.

I knew that I needed to pull away and let her go, but I couldn't.

My fingers dug deeper into her hips, claiming her as mine.

Her lips parted slightly as I leaned toward her, unable to stop myself. My lips gently brushed against hers, the electricity of it enough to permanently brand this moment into my memory forever.

She lifted her hands and wrapped them around my neck, pulling me closer as she kissed me back, teasing my lips with the tip of her tongue as it begged for access.

I groaned and kissed her deeper, our tongues dancing to a song they'd heard a million times. Her nails scratched at my skin as I lifted her by the waist, and she wrapped her legs around me. I walked to the counter and set her on it as our mouths devoured each other with a carnal need I had never felt before.

Quinn pulled away for a split second, completely breathless. Her chest heaved as she swiped a finger across her bottom lip, swollen from my teeth gently nipping at it.

"I'm sorry," I breathed, resting my forehead against hers.

"I'm not," she answered before lifting my chin with her finger.

She looked into my eyes, and I could see that she meant it. She wanted this to happen as much as I did.

"We shouldn't be doing this," I muttered, frustrated with myself for not being able to stop.

"It's wrong," she agreed, lifting my shirt up and over my head. Once it was off, she threw it to the side and leaned in to plant kisses along my chest. "So wrong."

"Quinn," I whispered her name, closing my eyes as I took

in how fucking amazing it felt to have her soft lips pressed against my body. My dick twitched in anticipation, and I almost groaned in response.

"Let's just live in the moment, Roman. Just once."

There were so many things rushing through my brain that I should have been focused on, but the only thing that registered at that moment was the way my name sounded rolling off of her tongue.

"Please," she begged. "I don't want to overthink this. I just want one night where I get to feel like this."

She continued kissing her way across my stomach as her fingers unfastened my belt and started pulling the zipper down.

"Feel like what, Quinn? Tell me."

She lazily trailed her tongue up my body, pausing briefly to give me one-word answers.

"Wanted."

"Sexy."

She flicked my nipple with her tongue before continuing.

"Free."

"Desired."

"You're all of those things, Quinn," I answered as I held the back of her head while she worked her way back down my torso. "You're all of that and so much more."

She pulled my zipper the rest of the way down and gently reached in, rubbing my throbbing cock with the palm of her hand.

"I knew you'd be big," she said, giving it a firm squeeze.

Before I could answer, her phone started ringing.

Her fingers pushed into the opening of my briefs, ready to pull my dick out when it rang again.

"Your phone is ringing," I said through gritted teeth, not wanting this to stop.

Suddenly she stopped and let go, her eyes widening when she realized that it could be someone calling about Rosie. I scooted back and helped her down from the counter as she ran over to grab her phone while I adjusted myself.

"Hey, Mom," she said heavily into the phone.

I stayed in the kitchen, giving her space while I tried to compose myself. Quinn talked to her mom for a few minutes before Rosie got on the line to tell her goodnight. I leaned against the fridge and scrubbed a hand down my face while I thought about what had just happened.

My phone buzzed in my pocket with a text message.

Mike: How's everything going over there?

I swallowed hard, wondering how I would look him in the eye the next time I saw him. He would be pissed if he knew what Quinn and I had done. Thankfully it didn't go any further, but still, I didn't imagine that he would be pleased knowing that his little sister had been rubbing my dick and licking her way across my chest.

Me: We're good.

There—short and simple. That wouldn't give anything away

because our texts to each other were always quick anyway.

Mike: Call if you need anything.

There were plenty of things that I needed but nothing that I would ask him for. Quinn, on the other hand…

Eighteen

Quinn

6 Days Ago

Roman and I had called it a night early last night after almost going at it like horny teenagers on his kitchen counter. I had no idea what had come over me, but something about the chemistry between us was so intoxicating that I couldn't stop myself. I wanted more. Needed more.

I couldn't remember the last time I had been touched like that, and the funny thing was that he barely even touched me. But the way his fingers dug into my hips was such a turn-on, almost as if he was afraid to let me go. And that kiss—man, that kiss had nearly taken my breath away. No one had ever kissed me with so much passion and desire, not even Justin.

We had gone our separate ways—me to the bedroom and him to the couch—but I knew he hadn't gone to sleep until well after midnight, just like I hadn't. Instead, I had sat on the bed, running my fingers over my lips, and remembering the way his had felt against mine. I was daydreaming of the next time I could kiss him when it occurred to me that there might not be a next time.

Roman had admitted that he wanted me, but that didn't

mean anything. He also admitted that he wouldn't act on it, which was why I had initiated everything. But what if he really didn't want anything beyond what we already did? Hell—I wasn't sure if he had even wanted that to happen or if he was just lost in the moment like I was. His rock-hard dick was on board, even if his heart and mind hadn't been made up yet.

I thought about Justin and found myself comparing them, which immediately made me feel guilty. Justin was my husband—the person that I had vowed to spend the rest of my life with—yet here I was, comparing all of his flaws to where Roman already excelled.

Justin had been a lazy lover, never bothering with foreplay unless it was my birthday or a holiday. We didn't have sex as often as I would have liked, and sometimes I wondered how I ever got pregnant with Rosie. I liked to believe that she was the miracle that I needed in my life and that God gave me that sweet baby to help fill some of the void and loneliness that I felt in my marriage.

But Roman—Roman was different. He was caring and attentive, constantly checking to make sure I was okay and doing little things to make life easier for me. From letting us stay with him to buying groceries for us, he had already gone above and beyond to ensure that we had the things we needed. He didn't disregard my feelings or brush me off when I was upset about something. That alone gave me this hope that was blossoming quicker than I could process it. What would it be like to be with a guy like Roman?

I had gotten up before the sun this morning and climbed out of bed, hoping to sneak in a shower without waking him up. From what I could tell, he was still asleep on the couch, so

I cranked up the hot water and stood underneath it for a few minutes, letting it wash away all of the stress that had been building up.

When I was done, I wrapped a towel around my body and quickly dried my hair with the extra one that Rosie had been using. I looked around for my clean clothes, only to realize that I had left them on the bed.

I quietly opened the door and headed for the bedroom when I heard footsteps behind me. I turned around, expecting to see Roman.

Instead, I found Mike with a scowl set hard on his face as he looked me up and down.

"Is that what you're wearing around Roman?" he asked.

"No," I quickly shook my head and pulled the towel tighter around my body. "I forgot my clothes on the bed."

He nodded but didn't say anything.

"Why are you here this early?" I asked, suddenly irritated with him.

Just then, Roman appeared behind him, his face tight with anger.

"What's going on? What happened?" My heart started racing as I waited for them to tell me.

Finally, Mike sighed heavily and then looked me in the eyes.

"Rosie is missing."

Nineteen

Roman
6 Days Ago

"Rosie!" I called, checking the shrubs between Sandra's house and the neighbors. We had been looking for her for over thirty minutes, and no one had any idea where she had gone.

Sandra had woken up shortly after six and went to check on Rosie. When she found that she wasn't in her bed, she went to the living room and expected to find her with Mike, but she wasn't there either. Mike hadn't heard anything, and all of the doors and windows were still locked.

Their sister, Sonia had rushed over to help Sandra look for her while Mike went to my apartment to see if Rosie had gone there looking for Quinn. When she wasn't there, we all went back to Sandra's to continue the search while Sandra called the police to report a missing child. We all knew that they wouldn't do anything this early on, so I had reached out to Trevor and Max and asked for their help as well.

Quinn was walking the neighborhood with me while Mike checked the front and backyard of the house. Sonia and Sandra were searching inside the house, looking into every place that she might be able to hide.

I saw Max and Trevor heading our way and gave them a quick nod before walking up to knock on another neighbor's door. So far, I had been met with a few disgruntled growls for waking people up this early on a Saturday morning, but I couldn't care less. Rosie was missing, and I would stop at nothing to find her.

Quinn finished up at the house she was at, then met me on the street. Trevor and Max joined us a few minutes later.

"Any updates?" Max asked.

I shook my head and glanced at Quinn. Tears filled her eyes, and I could see that she was trying to keep it together and not fall apart.

"We're going to find her, I promise," Max assured her and gently squeezed her shoulder.

She sucked in a shaky deep breath and tried to let it out slowly.

"When was the last time anyone saw her?" Trevor asked, looking between Quinn and me.

"My mom said they went to bed around ten and that she was still in bed when my mom checked on her around midnight when she got up to use the restroom. Mike was up around four and confirmed that she was still in bed. So I guess a little over three hours ago."

Max's jaw clenched, and I knew what he was thinking. If someone took her, they were already long gone by now. Three hours was plenty of time for them to be in a different state, and we had absolutely no idea what direction they went.

"What do we do now?" she asked Max, a look of desperation on her face.

"We need to call this in, but if I know Mike, he already has. I'll check with him, and then we'll go from there. We'll get all hands on deck and move as quickly as possible."

Quinn turned and covered her face as the tears started to fall. I reached out to hug her, noticing the way Trevor was looking at me. I didn't care if he could see how I felt about her, I needed to be there for her and make sure she was okay.

I wrapped her in my arms and pulled her into my chest, allowing her a safe place to cry without everyone seeing. She wrapped my shirt in her hands and trembled as she cried.

I held her for what felt like forever, knowing that every second mattered but not being able to pull away. Max had already found Mike, and they were discussing who had already been contacted when I looked up and saw Rosie running down the street toward us with a woman walking behind her.

"Quinn, she's here," I said, turning her around.

"Rosie!" She took off running and grabbed her, holding her to her chest as tight as possible.

"We found her," I yelled to Max and Mike, who were standing on the porch. In a matter of seconds, everyone was out of the house and rushing out to see her.

"I'm so glad you're safe," Quinn cooed, still holding Rosie against her.

The woman approached us, smiling at the mother and daughter that had been reunited.

Quinn suddenly spotted the woman and set Rosie down, pushing her behind her. I stepped forward and picked Rosie up, ensuring she wasn't going anywhere.

"What the hell are you doing with my daughter?" Quinn spat out through gritted teeth. Her fists were clenched at her sides.

"Woah, woah, woah," Mike said, quickly stepping in and putting some space between Quinn and the woman before she could punch her.

"Move out of the way," Quinn demanded, trying to push past him.

"I'm not here to cause any trouble," the woman said with her hands in the air. "I was simply trying to bring her home."

"Bullshit." Quinn's nostrils flared, and I wondered if I should take Rosie inside so she didn't have to see any of this.

"I know that we've had our issues Quinn, but I really was just trying to help."

"Why don't you tell us what happened and why you had my niece," Mike said, one arm still extended to hold Quinn back.

"I was waiting for the train and spotted her. But, I didn't see Quinn with her and started to worry."

"Who was she with?" I asked.

"I don't know. It looked like a woman, but they had a hoodie covering their face, so I couldn't get a good look." She looked at Rosie and smiled sadly. "I knew that she didn't know them and that I needed to step in and make sure she got home okay."

"Thank you," Mike said softly.

"It's the least I could do given everything that happened." She lowered her head and walked away.

"That's it? You're just going to let her go?" I asked Mike, trying to keep the anger in my voice from startling Rosie.

"Don't worry, I know who she is and where to find her. Let's get Rosie inside and see if we can figure out what happened," he said, reaching for his niece. She wrapped her arms around his neck and let him carry her into the house.

I waited outside with Quinn for a few minutes while she did whatever she needed to do to calm herself down.

"Okay, so who was that woman?" I asked as we headed inside.

"She worked with Justin and was the one driving the car when he was killed."

Twenty

Quinn

6 Days Ago

"Alright, Rosie, can you tell us what happened and why you left grandma's house?" I asked as I sat on the coffee table in front of the couch and studied her.

We had all taken turns looking her over to make sure she didn't have any injuries, but that didn't keep me calm, knowing that she had been away from us for who knows how long, with someone that we didn't know.

"I heard a puppy crying, so I got up and looked out the window. I couldn't see anything, but it kept crying louder. I knew that it needed help, so I went to the kitchen and checked to see if it was stuck in the dog door."

"Was there a dog stuck in it?" I sat up straight and tried to keep the stress from showing on my face.

"No, but I could see a puppy, so I stuck my head in and tried to find where it went. It was still crying, so I climbed through and looked for it in the backyard."

"Then what happened?"

"There was a woman by the street looking for her dog. She said that she was walking it and it got scared and ran away."

"Do you remember what she looked like?"

She shook her head.

"Did she ask you for anything?"

She nodded.

"What did she say?"

"She said that she needed my help finding her dog and that she would make sure we didn't go too far from the house so my grandma didn't get scared if she couldn't find me."

I swallowed hard as I tucked that little nugget of information aside.

"Where did you guys go?"

"We stayed on the street, but then she thought she heard the dog crying further ahead, so we went that way looking for it."

"And then you guys ended up at the subway?"

"Yeah, she thought she saw the dog run down the stairs, so we followed after it."

I closed my eyes and took a moment to compose myself before talking to her about what had happened.

I felt my mom squeeze my knee reassuringly.

"I did something wrong, didn't I?" Rosie asked, looking at me with tears in her eyes.

I was at a loss for words, struggling to explain to her the danger that she was in. I didn't want to traumatize her, but I also knew that she needed to know the truth in order to protect herself.

"You didn't do anything wrong, but we need to talk about what happened," Mike said, sitting down beside me. I scooted over to make room for him.

"I know that you wanted to help that woman find her dog because you are such a helpful little girl, but unfortunately, she was using the lost dog as an excuse to get you to leave the house."

"Why would she do that?"

"Do you remember in school when you guys learned about strangers and how you shouldn't talk to them or go with someone if you don't know them?" I asked, finally feeling the strength to have this conversation with her.

She nodded, and her face fell when she realized what she had done.

"I was worried about the puppy."

"I know, baby."

"Did she want to kidnap me?" Rosie whispered.

I nodded and felt the tears burn my skin as they trickled down my face.

"What was she going to do with me?"

"I don't know, my love. But please promise me that you won't ever go with someone you don't know, ever again."

"I promise, Mama." She jumped up from the couch and landed on my lap with her arms wrapped around my neck.

"I'm sorry, I didn't mean to scare everyone."

"I know," I sighed, holding her tightly against me. "I

promise that I won't ever let anything happen to you. I love you so much."

"I love you too, Mama."

We hugged for a few minutes until she finally pulled away and asked to use the restroom. My mom went with her, all of us afraid to let her out of our sight.

Once they were out of the room, I sat on the couch and pulled a pillow onto my lap.

"You okay?" Roman asked.

I shook my head and let the tears fall, not caring that I was still surrounded by my brother, Trevor, and Max. Sonia was busy working on taking the dog door out, and her boyfriend was on his way over with supplies to help her.

"Why is this happening to her?" I sobbed, wiping my face with the back of my hands.

"I don't know, but we're going to figure it out," Mike assured me.

"I agree—we'll find whoever it is before they get another chance to take her," Max added.

"They almost had her. If Julia hadn't been there this morning, who knows where Rosie would be right now. They got her out of the house without any of us knowing. And even worse—they knew personal details about the house. Like how would they know to lure her to the dog door if they hadn't been here before? Mom hasn't had a dog in two years. And you all heard what Rosie said about the woman knowing she was at her grandma's house." My voice was rising as my panic started to set in.

"The nice thing is that they're consistent," Max said from where he was leaning against the wall. "They want us to know they have a personal connection to you guys. They've left signs along the way. That makes it easier to narrow it down because it's not a random attack."

"What do you think the coincidence is that Julia just happened to be at the right place at the right time?" Trevor asked.

I hadn't even thought of that until now, but he had a good point.

"She also knew to bring her back to my mom's house—not our apartment. We live in the same one that Justin lived in, so it's not like she wouldn't know where it was. Lord knows she was there often enough when they worked together."

"Do you think that she was the one who took Rosie?" Roman inquired from the other side of the couch. "Maybe she was the one who lured her away and then brought her back? It could be a game for her to point out how easy it was to take her in the first place."

"It's possible, but if it was her, why not just take her and run? Why bring her back?" I chewed my nail anxiously.

A few minutes later, Rosie returned with my mom and curled up on the couch with me.

"Hey, Rosie?" I asked.

She tilted her head up and looked at me.

"Was the woman who was looking for her puppy the same woman that brought you back?"

She didn't have to think about it before she confidently

shook her head.

"No, but she was really mad at the lady who lost her dog. They had a fight before she grabbed me and brought me home."

"What was the fight about?" I pushed, hoping she would remember in as much detail as she did about what color socks her best friend wore every day at school.

"I don't know, but they were whispering—but like mad whispers—and she told her, 'it's not time, what are you doing? You're going to mess everything up!' Then she grabbed my arm and brought me home."

I felt all eyes in the room on me and knew that we had a bigger problem than we could have ever imagined.

Twenty-One

Roman
5 Days Ago

"Okay, so where do we go from here?" I asked as I looked around my apartment at Mike, Trevor, and Max. Quinn and Rosie had stayed the night with me last night but left to spend the day at her mom's house while us guys tried to figure out a plan to keep Rosie safe.

"It's hard to say," Mike replied with a hint of frustration in his voice as he ran a hand through his hair.

"We know that it's not just one person that's involved," Max added. "There are several people at play, and that will make it even harder to narrow it down."

"There's also a strong FBI thread," Trevor said with a nod in Mike's direction.

"I know," he muttered. "I fucking hate this. I can't even go to my own team for help because I don't know who I can trust. We know Rosie is the ultimate target, but Quinn and I are also targets."

"Let's start at the beginning." Max stood up and paced the space between the kitchen and living room. "Things started when Rosie's teachers spotted a van across the street. They were the ones who said that she was being targeted. The police were called, but nothing happened because he was gone by the time they got there. After that, Quinn spotted the same van parked outside of her mom's house after she picked Rosie up from school when Quinn had a last-minute meeting at work—right?"

"Yeah, that's correct," I confirmed.

"And the person driving the van was wearing Mike's baseball cap that was stolen from his office?"

"Correct again," Mike said. "Very few people have access to my office, so it leads me to believe that someone in my department took it."

"Do you think that it was the same person wearing it and driving the van?"

Mike shrugged in response to Max's question.

"In addition to that, we know that Justin was killed on the job in a car accident and that he was the only one ejected from the vehicle because he wasn't wearing a seat belt. Were you with him when it happened?"

I looked over at Mike and noticed his jaw clenching as he balled his fists.

"No. I wasn't with him when it happened. We worked on two different cases, so we didn't cross paths much. Given that we were considered family, the department kept us separated and prohibited us from working on the same case."

"Do you know who all was in the car with him?" Max asked, folding his arms over his chest.

"From what I remember, it was Justin, Saul, Frank, and

Julia."

"The woman from this morning," I confirmed. "Quinn told me that she was the one who was driving the car."

"Does she still work in witness protection?" Max turned to Mike.

"Yeah. She's still there."

"So she would have had access to your office?"

Mike nodded.

"And she knew about the car accident."

"You think she's responsible for all of this?" I asked Max, taking some of the pressure off of Mike.

"I think she's definitely involved. Between the seat belt left on Quinn's bed and the situation yesterday with Julia bringing Rosie home, it doesn't sit well with me. She's up to something, but I don't think she's working alone."

I turned to face Mike.

"Didn't you say that the last case that Justin was working on was a child trafficking case?"

"Yeah."

"How soon after the trial ended was Justin's accident?"

Mike closed his eyes and leaned his head back against the cushion.

"It was the same day."

"And the girl that was being protected was recently found dead, right?" I knew there was too much excitement in my voice, but I felt like we were finally cracking through this mystery and getting closer to knowing what was going on.

"About a week ago," Mike confirmed.

"And the guy she put away?" Max asked, sensing where I was going with this.

"There were two," Mike responded, pulling his phone out and typing something in the internet search bar. "A father and son. The father was the ringleader of the operation and got a life sentence."

"But the son?" Trevor asked.

"He was released two weeks ago."

Twenty-Two

Quinn
5 Days Ago

"Elias Salvador, son of Juan Salvador, age thirty-two, served five years for possession and distribution of child pornography."

I sat at the kitchen table at my mom's house and reached for the mugshot that Mike slid across the table to me.

"Before Justin died, he helped Ariel Wyland put the man who tortured and held her captive for ten years behind bars. Not only did they take down the ringleader of the operation, but they also caught his son, Elias as well. Unfortunately, there wasn't enough to hold him longer than five years, and as you already know, he's been granted early release and forced to register as a sex offender."

"You think this is who is watching Rosie?" I asked quietly.

My mom and Rosie were hanging out in my mom's bedroom, watching movies in bed while she rested. I wasn't sure if it was from all of the excitement yesterday morning or if she was coming down with something, but she seemed not to feel well today, which had me concerned. She was away from us long enough for someone to have given her something, even though she insisted no one had.

"Yes, I think he is." Mike pulled the chair out and sat down beside me. "I think several people are involved, and honestly, I'm not sure who we can trust right now. The biggest connection to all of this is Justin."

"Justin?" I asked, my voice catching in my throat.

"He was the only one who pushed her to testify. That wasn't part of the job, Quinn. He was responsible for securing her until she went into witness protection and U.S. Marshals took over. If he hadn't kept pushing her, she might not have testified, and the case would have gone in a different direction."

"So you think someone is trying to take Rosie because her dad put a child sex trafficker behind bars?" I knew that was exactly what he was saying, but it felt better to hear the words out loud instead of rattling around in my brain.

"They're leaving clues directly related to him and the car accident. It's not them being sloppy. It's them sending a message."

I pulled in a shaky breath and held the picture in front of me. Elias Salvador was handsome—not as handsome as Roman—but handsome enough to get what he wanted from women without having to work for it. His dark eyes hid the evil that resided inside and was offset by a smile that could melt a nun's panties. It was unnerving to see a smile offered so freely in a mugshot photo as if he didn't have a care in the world. It wasn't the look that I was used to seeing of people who realized that life as they knew it was over because the rest of it would be spent behind bars.

I hated that he had been let out early and even more that he hadn't been given a long sentence to begin with. But it seemed that his father had been convicted of the majority of the crimes, and he was simply just another measly pawn in the game.

"So, what do we do now?" I asked, lowering the picture to the table, and sliding it back to Mike.

"We stay vigilant. Alert. We don't take our eyes off of Rosie, and we work as a team to protect her."

"Do you think they're coming for her soon?"

He shrugged and folded his arms over his chest.

"There's no way to know. But I don't think they're just going to back off and forget about her."

My stomach soured, and I could taste the bitterness of the bile as it rose up.

"I hate not knowing."

"I know. Me too." He gently squeezed my shoulder. "But we're going to keep her safe. Not to worry."

"Okay," I whispered.

Twenty-Three

Roman
5 Days Ago

"Is that really necessary?" I asked, standing in the living room with my arms folded.

Mike shifted the coffee table in front of the door and stepped back to look at his work.

"If anyone tries to get in, I want to make sure that we hear them."

"It's late. Can we just wrap this up so I can get Rosie to bed?" Quinn asked with her hands on her hips. "It's been a long day, and she has school tomorrow."

"Yeah, I'll be there in a minute. Go ahead and get her situated, you won't even hear me come in."

"Why are you coming to the bedroom?" Her brows pulled together tightly.

"I'm sleeping on the floor."

I rolled my head back on my neck and waited for the fight I knew was coming.

"Look," she said sternly, holding her hand up in front of her. "I know you want to be here to watch over Rosie and keep her safe, but I don't think that entails you sleeping on the floor. I'll be in there with her, and if anyone gets into the apartment, you guys will hear them before we do."

"Unless they come in through the window," he countered.

"What in the world makes you think someone is going to climb four flights of rickety stairs on the fire escape to get in through the window?"

"It happens all the time." He spread his feet, widening his stance as they continued their stare-off.

"When?" I asked, pulling my head back in surprise.

He tilted his head and looked at me. "Max said that Hannah's friend—"

"Was thrown from a window," I corrected, feeling satisfied when I saw the embarrassment flash across his face.

"Oh, yeah. That's right. There was a lot going on, and I didn't hear the full story."

I didn't bother to go into the details of how she was murdered by some psychopath that also kidnapped Max's sister before taking Hannah. Quinn had enough on her plate to worry about without the gruesome details of someone else's tragedy.

"You don't need to sleep on the floor," Quinn insisted.

"Why not? It's not like there's room out here."

"You can sleep in that chair," she said, nodding to the one beside the couch where I would be sleeping.

"I'm six-two, Quinn. How the hell do you think I'm going to fit in that thing to sleep?"

"Maybe you can curl up on the couch with Roman?"

I watched the sparkle that danced in her eyes when she cautiously glanced at me.

"Yeah—like hell he is."

"Why not?" Mike asked with a decent amount of hurt in his tone.

"Because I don't cuddle men, and even if I considered it to keep you from having to sleep in the chair, your snoring is enough to make me reconsider."

Quinn covered her mouth and snorted as a laugh escaped.

Mike's head whipped toward her before he pointed a finger between us.

"That's the real reason you don't want me in there—isn't it?"

Quinn's head fell back, showing off her long neck as her hair tickled her back and the beautiful sound of laughter floated through the air.

"It's sooo loud!"

"You know what—screw both of you," Mike said playfully, pretending to be angry without letting his laughter slip through.

After a few minutes, the laughter subsided and Quinn yawned. It was late, and I didn't want to spend the entire night trying to figure out sleeping arrangements with all of my new roommates. As long as we kept Rosie safe, that was all that mattered.

"You can take the couch tonight," I offered. "I'll sleep in the chair.”

“That chair will hurt your back,” Quinn protested.

“I’ll be fine. Trust me, I’ve slept on worse.”

“You’re welcome to sleep in the room with us,” she offered quietly, almost afraid to let Mike hear her.

He clutched a hand to his heart and acted wounded.

“You’ll let him sleep in the room with you, but not your own brother? I’m appalled!”

“He doesn’t snore like a freight train,” she laughed. “We all need sleep, and that’s the best way for us to get it.”

“Fine,” Mike grumbled and ran his hands through his hair. “But don’t you try anything funny with her….”

He grabbed his duffle bag from the floor and headed to the bathroom, leaving Quinn and me in awkward silence.

Once he was gone and we heard the door close, we both relaxed.

“You don’t have to sleep on the floor,” she said softly. “I’m sure there’s plenty of room for all three of us in the bed.”

“Na, that’s okay. I’ll sleep better if I’m by the door. If anyone comes in through the window they’ll have to break it first, and we’ll hear it.”

She nodded her head and started blinking rapidly to keep her tears away.

I stepped forward and pulled her into me, holding her tightly.

“It’s going to be okay,” I assured her. “Nothing is going to happen to her with all of us here tonight. It's best to get as much rest as possible so you're ready to go tomorrow. She can't afford for you to be exhausted."

"I know," she said, her words muffled against my chest. "I'm so scared."

I didn't say anything because anything that I would have said would have been a lie. I could've told her that there was nothing to be scared of or that we could handle anything that was thrown at us, but that wasn't something that I could guarantee. While I hoped we would be prepared for whatever happened, uncertainty gnawed at me, making me question everything I thought I knew.

Twenty-Four

Quinn

4 Days Ago

I missed the days of getting up and starting my day in peace and quiet while Rosie slept and no one was out trying to kidnap her. Instead, I was at Roman's apartment, waiting for my turn to take a shower while Mike finished his and Roman worked on making breakfast with the few groceries he had left.

It had only been a few days since he had gone grocery shopping, but I don't think he was prepared for how much three people would eat compared to how much food he usually went through. I felt bad that he was spending so much money on things for Rosie and me, but I hated even more that I didn't have any other options right now. My apartment had already been cleared to go back to, and a new door was installed to replace the one that had been kicked down, but it wasn't safe to take Rosie back, so we were staying with Roman for the unforeseeable future.

Once Mike was done in the shower, I jumped in and didn't bother to wash my hair since the water was already cold, and we were running out of time. Luckily I had taken the time at my mom's house yesterday to wash my hair and give Rosie a bath, which saved us a lot of time today. I pulled my hair up into a sleek ponytail and skipped any makeup. One quick check in the mirror confirmed that I had matching shoes, and that was the most I could ask for today.

"But I really want one," Rosie whined from the living room as I came down the hall.

"I don't think your mom does," Mike replied, sitting across from her as they ate their bowls of cereal. Roman was leaning against the counter, holding a cup of coffee with his ankles crossed and a smirk on his face.

"I could keep it at your place," Rosie offered, wiggling her eyebrows excitedly, earning a frown from Mike as he took another bite.

"What are they talking about?" I asked Roman quietly, reaching for a cup and filling it with what was left in the pot.

"She's trying to convince him to get a dog."

I smiled and took a sip, holding the cup with both hands to keep from dropping it.

"Tired?" he questioned, tilting his head, and studying me.

"A little," I lied. The truth was that I was exhausted and couldn't remember the last time I had even an ounce of energy. The days felt like they were starting to blend together, and I was quickly losing track of how much time had passed by.

"Was I snoring?" he asked, wincing as he tucked his head down and took another sip.

"Not as bad as that one," I joked, lifting my mug at Mike, who had stood up and was heading our way.

"You weren't even in the same room," he said, nudging me

with his elbow.

"I still heard you," I objected.

"Me too," Roman added.

Mike opened his mouth to speak but snapped it shut when Rosie got up and carried her empty cereal bowl into the kitchen and set it on the counter.

"You were so loud, I thought there was a bear in here," she said dramatically, widening her eyes.

"Just when I thought you were my favorite niece," he teased.

"I'm your only niece," she giggled as he picked her up and tickled her sides.

I took a long drink of coffee then looked up at the clock on the wall.

"Go get your backpack and put your shoes on," I called to Rosie. "We're going to be late again."

My boss had been on my ass last week about my recent tardiness, and I swore that this week would be better. It was barely Monday morning, and I was already failing on my word.

I tilted my head back and tossed the rest of my coffee back before realizing that I had underestimated how much was left. The warm liquid dripped down my chin and onto my white silk shirt.

"Son of a bitch," I cursed, setting my cup down and pulling the fabric away from my body. "I don't have time for this."

"Go get changed. I can take Rosie to school," Roman

offered.

"It's okay, you don't have to do that."

I continued to blot at my shirt with a napkin, only making it worse.

Roman reached out and grabbed my hand to stop me.

"Quinn—go get changed. We'll make sure she gets to school."

I hung my head in defeat and waited for a few seconds to regain my composure.

"Thank you. I appreciate it."

I headed to the bedroom to change while Mike helped Rosie get her shoes on in the living room. A few minutes later, she hugged me and told me she loved me before heading to school with two of the best bodyguards any little girl could ever ask for.

By six, I had worked through lunch and sat through hours of needless meetings that put me even further behind on my work. My mom had picked Rosie up from school an hour after the guys had dropped her off when she spiked a fever and started throwing up. The nurse made sure to call me before my mom got there to update me on how she was feeling.

After my mom got her home and comfortable, she sent me hourly updates with pictures of Rosie sleeping on the couch. The curtains were closed, which helped keep the room dark for her but increased my anxiety about not knowing whether the van was back again. Thankfully, my sister Sonia had the day off and was hanging out there to help keep an eye on everything. On top of that, Max had gone by to check on things as well. It was nice to feel the level of support we had right now, but it was still unsettling that the threat wasn't over.

I checked in with Roman to see if he was already home or if he wanted to go to my mom's to pick up Rosie with me. He was stuck at work for a little while longer, so I packed up and headed over there to wait for him so we could go home together and grab Rosie on the way.

It was relatively empty when I got to his work. I nodded to the guy at the front desk before making my way back to his office. He was on the phone when I walked in, so I set my stuff down and headed to the workout area to give him some privacy.

There were a handful of guys lifting weights in one room, but no one in the room with the punching bag. I looked around until I found a set of gloves and put them on. It had been a long time since I had hit anything and I felt the sting in my muscles with the first few punches I threw.

The moment my fists made contact with the bag, I felt this immediate sense of satisfaction that increased with each punch. I tucked my head and squared my shoulders, twisting my torso as I rotated hitting with each hand. I pictured Elias Salvador and his disgusting father, Juan, and kept punching. Then I imagined Julia's face and her smug smile when she brought my daughter back and punched even harder. The more I thought about everything that was happening, the faster I hit until I was struggling to catch my breath and felt a set of muscular arms wrap around me from behind and cover my gloved hands so I couldn't hit anymore.

He didn't say anything, just kept his arms wrapped around me in a layer of comfort. My heart was racing, and my body was on fire as I came down from the adrenaline rush I had given myself. I knew that it hadn't solved anything, but for a few minutes, I felt better letting some of my built-up aggression out.

My body trembled as a range of emotions coursed through me. I tried to keep my composure but couldn't stop the tears before they rushed down my face. I didn't want Roman to see me like this and pushed against his arms to get away, but he only held on tighter. The tears burned my cheeks as they stained my face and ran down onto my shirt.

I leaned my head back against his chest and cried until there was nothing left inside. With a shaky breath, I tried to speak, but the words wouldn't come out. I had no idea what to say to him. His arms loosened around me and slid down to my waist, allowing me the freedom to slip the gloves off.

"I'm sorry," I whispered, turning to leave when his arm reached out and held my waist.

"You have nothing to apologize for."

I stopped where I was, letting his hand rest firmly against my stomach, and looked up at him.

His brown eyes clouded with emotion and I couldn't tell what he was thinking. Before I could overthink anything, he dug his fingers into my side and pulled me back to him. I stumbled briefly before he had both hands planted on my hips and his chest braced against mine.

I looked up at him, knowing that he felt the electricity sizzling between us. He muttered a curse word before leaning in and planting his lips on mine.

"You're going to be the death of me," he groaned before sliding his hands down to grab my ass.

I kissed him back and didn't allow myself to worry about anything else for the few minutes we had before we left to pick up Rosie.

Twenty-Five

Roman
4 Days Ago

My lips pressed hungrily against Quinn's, capturing the whispered moans that escaped her mouth. I wasn't lying when I said that she would be the death of me. Either we would finally act on this spark between us and Mike would kill me, or I would die from blue balls. One way or another, I was a goner.

Her fingers ran through my hair, lightly tugging on the short locks as she deepened the kiss.

"Quinn," I moaned, squeezing her ass as I lifted her to my waist and pressed her back to the wall.

"Mmmm," she answered, grinding her hips against my groin, and creating a friction that was sure to start a fire. "I want you, Roman. Now. Please."

I pulled away, breaking the kiss, and rested my forehead against hers while her fingers anxiously dug into the bottom of my shirt, trying to free me of it.

"Are you sure?"

"Yes," she panted.

"I don't want you to do this because you're upset."

"I'm not. I want you to fuck me, Roman. I have since I was sixteen and you spent the summer at our house playing basketball without your shirt on. You've been driving me wild ever since, and now you're like an itch that I desperately want to scratch."

I leaned in and kissed her, feeling my cheeks splitting into a smile.

"You've wanted me that long?" I asked, relieved that she had felt the same way I had.

"And longer since you're hellbent on making me wait more."

Her hands moved down, working my belt and zipper while I held her against the wall.

"Such a feisty little thing, aren't you?"

I heard the thud as my jeans hit the floor and smiled when she hooked her thumbs into the top of my briefs and tugged them down. My erection sprung free, touching my stomach as her hand glided over it.

I adjusted her on my hips and pushed her skirt up her thighs, revealing a black lace thong underneath. I bunched the fabric as high as I could so it was out of the way and then ran my hand across her pussy, feeling the warmth coming from it.

She closed her eyes and moaned as I traced circles with my fingers before pushing the thin material to the side and parting her. A gasp floated past her lips as she arched her back, giving me complete access as my finger slid easily between her folds.

"Fuck, Quinn," I breathed.

"Told you I was ready."

I wanted to keep fingering her, to feel her body spasm as she lost control, but my rock-hard cock was begging for attention, and the way Quinn's nails dug into my back said she felt the same way.

I was about to lower her to the floor so I could grab my wallet when I suddenly realized that I didn't have a condom.

"Fuck!" I cursed, closing my eyes and tossing my head back in frustration.

"What?"

"I don't have a condom."

I shook my head and then opened my eyes to find Quinn studying me while she nervously chewed her bottom lip.

"I'm on the pill," she said cautiously. "And I haven't been with anyone since Justin. I'm clean."

My heart fluttered at the thought of being with her without using protection, wondering what it would feel like.

"I've never been with a woman without using one," I replied gently. "I'm clean too. I get checked every year and haven't been with anyone in at least six months."

She nodded and took a slow, deep breath.

"Then what are we waiting for?" she asked, the sparkle back in her eyes.

A carnal growl escaped my lips before I pressed them to Quinn's and lined myself up at her opening. Her legs parted further, allowing me to slide inside easily. She was so wet that she welcomed my dick without any hesitation.

I pushed deeper inside, feeling her pussy clench around me as a hiss fell through her parted lips. She arched her back and swiveled her hips in circles, grinding against me as I thrust. My fingers dug into her ass cheeks, holding onto her as we rocked into each other.

Thankfully I had already checked that everyone had left before I walked the last few guys out and locked up, so I didn't have to worry about anyone walking in on us.

"I want to fuck you from behind," I moaned in her ear as I kept thrusting. She scratched her nails down my back and panted heavily.

"Okay," she breathed.

Slowly, I pulled out and helped her to her feet before walking her over to one of the weight benches in the other room. I stepped out of my shoes and tossed my clothes to the side before grabbing a clean towel from the closet and laying it on the seat before she bent over and popped her ass in the air. Her pussy glistened in the light and that was all that I needed to dive back in.

Her chest rested on the seat while her hands held onto the sides to keep from falling off. I spread my feet slightly and lined up at her entrance, making sure to ease into her slowly so I didn't knock her over. Once I was inside, she started bucking against me, meeting me thrust for thrust as I reached down and rubbed her clit with my finger.

Watching her tight ass as it bounced against my cock was enough to make me want to come right then and there.

Add in the incredible sensation of feeling her wet pussy clenching around me without a condom, and I was going to embarrass myself with how long I lasted.

"Fuck me harder," she whispered, looking at me over her shoulder.

Our eyes locked and I grabbed onto her hips, plowing into her as hard as I could while she held on for dear life with one hand and reached down to touch herself with the other.

I held my breath and counted to twenty to keep from coming right away, but when she clenched around me as her orgasm ripped through her, I had no choice but to let go and succumb to mine.

My hips jerked rapidly as my cock twitched inside her, my cum shooting through her before I pulled out, and she collapsed on the bench. I ran a hand across her naked ass, the site a beautiful one with her skirt still bunched around her waist and her heels still on.

I grabbed my briefs and jeans, slipping them on before heading to the bathroom. I grabbed a washcloth on the way and ran it under warm water. Quinn was sitting on the bench when I got back, checking her phone.

"Everything okay?" I asked as I sat down next to her.

"Yeah, I was just checking on Rosie. My mom said she's still sleeping so we don't have to rush over there."

I nodded and held up the washcloth. She arched an eyebrow and tilted her head slightly.

"Lay down," I instructed.

"Why?"

"So I can take care of my mess."

"You don't have to do that. I can go to the bathroom and take care of it."

"Quinn."

She sighed heavily and laid down, her body surprisingly rigid, given the orgasm she had a few minutes ago.

I turned my body and gently pushed her legs open, letting my hand skim the inside of her thigh. I chuckled when I realized that we had been so caught up in the moment that I never bothered to take her panties off; we just pushed them to the side. She had since then fixed them, but I could see the evidence of what we had done on them.

I hooked my finger in them and gently slid them off of her.

"What are you doing?" she asked, popping her head up to look at me.

"Trust me, I don't think you want to wear those anymore."

She giggled and laid back down while I gently cleaned her up. Once I was done, I leaned forward and gently kissed her clit, loving the way she smelled right now. I knew that we

had already used more time than we had so I couldn't go down on her like I wanted to.

She squirmed beneath me and held my head between her legs while I took a few seconds to lick her lips and taste her. I worked my way back up to her clit and gave it a quick flick with my tongue, causing her to gasp.

"Soooo sensitive," she murmured.

I laughed and sat up, pulling her hands to help her up.

"We don't have time right now but trust me when I say that I'm going to eat that sweet pussy of yours as soon as I can."

"Is that a threat or a promise?"

"Both."

Twenty-Six

Quinn

3 Days Ago

My body was mind-numbingly sore when I woke up, but I wasn't about to complain when I had one of the most life-altering orgasms of my life last night. I knew that being with Roman would be amazing, but I had no idea it would be that incredible.

We got back to his apartment shortly after nine, and I knew that Mike was suspicious when he was there waiting for us at my mom's house. We both lied so quickly that neither of us could get our stories straight as to why we were late. My mom was more concerned about why I had been crying, which helped pull Mike's attention away from the fact that Roman had a small hickey on his neck where I had let my desire get the best of me before he took me from behind on the weight bench.

Rosie stayed asleep the entire time as Mike carried her to Roman's apartment, refusing to let him help. We got her settled in, and I spent most of the night watching over her to make sure her fever didn't spike again. I cuddled her close to me and let her soft snores help me drift off to sleep around two in the morning.

Roman had offered to sleep on the floor again, but Mike

quickly squashed that idea—as if there was any real threat to having him in the same room with me if Rosie was there. I might have been head over heels obsessed with Roman right now, but I wasn't about to throw my panties at him with my daughter in the same room. Instead, they both slept in the living room and compromised on who would sleep on the floor in the sleeping bag that Mike had brought from my mom's house.

I stretched and rolled out of bed, making sure I didn't disturb Rosie. She had gotten up around five this morning, throwing up again, so I gave her some more Tylenol for her fever and got her back to bed. I snuck down the hall, closing the door behind me, and stopped when I realized that I couldn't go to the living room to call the school without waking Mike and Roman up.

Instead, I snuck into the bathroom and quietly closed the door behind me. I called the school and left a voicemail to let them know that Rosie was sick and wouldn't be in today. Then I sent my mom a quick text message with an update on how she was feeling. I didn't want to miss work, but I was so exhausted and worn down that I decided it was better to be home to take care of Rosie.

Once I had taken care of calling in, I opened the bathroom door and jumped back in surprise when I found Roman on the other side. I held my phone to my chest and tried to get my heart to stop racing.

"Sorry," he said quietly. "Someday, I'm going to get a bigger place with two bathrooms." He grinned, showing me his beautiful dimples.

"I promise we won't be here that much longer."

It was an odd feeling to promise something that I didn't know if it was true.

"You can stay as long as you'd like."

His voice was smooth like honey, and the way he was looking at me had the heat between my thighs starting again.

"Thank you," I said quietly, looking down as my face blushed. "I'm sure you'd like to have your space back and have some privacy again."

"I don't need privacy."

"Oh?" My voice hitched in my throat, the words getting lodged there.

He shook his head and licked his lips.

Before I could say anything more, I heard footsteps right as a hand reached out and clamped down on Roman's shoulder.

"What's going on?" he asked, looking between us.

"I was asking Quinn how Rosie was feeling," Roman answered without missing a beat, his eyes still locked on mine.

I looked away, not trusting myself to look at him while my brother was standing there, looking ready to murder him.

"She's still sick and had a restless night. Her fever wasn't as high this morning, but she's still running one. I called the school and told them that she wouldn't be there today."

"I can miss work to stay with her," Mike offered.

"That's okay, I already called in. I have some PTO that I can use."

"I can stay with her too," Roman said simultaneously, causing Mike to look between us.

"What's going on between you two?" he asked, pointing a finger.

"Nothing," I lied.

I didn't want to lie, but the last thing I needed right now was to deal with my brother and risk a falling out between him and Roman.

Roman rubbed a hand across the back of his neck and looked away.

"Bullshit."

I swallowed hard. This was not how I wanted him to find out.

"Are you two fucki—"

"Mommy, I don't feel well," Rosie said, standing in the doorway rubbing her eyes.

I pushed past Mike and went to her, pulling her into me as I laid my hand on her forehead to check her temperature.

"You're burning up again," I confirmed, tilting my head to see her face. "Let's get you a cold washcloth and some water."

"Did the Tylenol not help?" Roman asked as he and Mike followed us into the living room. Mike hurried in to move the blankets off of the couch so she could sit down.

"It doesn't seem like it. I gave it to her an hour ago."

"What do you need?" Mike asked as we all headed into the

kitchen while Rosie sat on the couch and curled into a ball.

I closed my eyes and tried to force myself to focus. I was exhausted. But I knew that we would need the basics—at minimum—and I didn't have a way to go out to get them. On top of that, we were running low on clean clothes after she got sick again last night. My mom had a pile of clothes at her house that she was planning to wash for me today, but there wasn't a way for me to run over there to get them.

"Um," I said, pinching the bridge of my nose while I thought about it. "I need stuff for Rosie—more children's Tylenol, Gatorade, crackers, and maybe some soup. Unfortunately, I can't think straight, so I have no idea what I'm missing."

I looked between them, feeling loved and supported by how they were watching me.

"I'll go to the store and grab some groceries plus the stuff you listed. Is there anything you want for yourself?" Roman asked.

"I'm fine but thank you."

He furrowed his brow but didn't fight me on it.

"I have some clothes at Mom's that she was washing for me," I said, turning to Mike. "I don't know if you can grab them on your way home tonight or if it's out of the—"

"I'll get them, don't worry about it."

"Thank you. Both of you are tremendously helpful."

Rosie started coughing, which pulled my attention away from the guys while I went to check on her. I grabbed a cold bottle of water from the fridge and offered it to her, hoping to get some fluid into her.

She took slow sips of water and then handed the bottle back to me.

"How are you feeling?" I asked, pressing the back of my hand to her forehead. She still felt warm but not as hot as she was a few minutes ago.

"I'm sleepy."

"Why don't you lay down and get some rest? I'll be right here if you need anything."

"Okay, mommy."

She scooted down on the couch and curled into the pillow, her head barely touching it before her eyes fluttered closed. I snuck to the bathroom and grabbed the thermometer, then carefully scanned her head to get her temperature. 99.2.

I sighed a breath of relief that it had come down some and was no longer sitting in the 100-101 range that it had been most of the night. I prayed that the Tylenol was working and that the rest would give her body what she needed to fight whatever this was.

When I went back to the kitchen, the guys were talking quietly while Roman wrote down whatever Mike was telling him.

"Be sure to get the ones in the red bag," Mike said, pointing to something on the paper.

"What are you doing?" I asked, standing on my tiptoes to look over Roman's shoulder.

"Just making a list," he replied, turning away from me to

keep me from seeing it.

"Anything else?" he asked Mike, completely ignoring me.

"I think that's it. I'll grab the other stuff on my way back."

"Your way back?" My eyebrows raised off my forehead.

"Yeah, I'm working a half-day today."

"Why?"

"So I can help take care of you and Rosie."

"I don't need help, Mike. I'm fine. Really."

"You're exhausted, Quinn," Roman said gently.

"So?"

"How are you supposed to take care of a sick child when you're so worn down? It would be good for you to rest too." Mike added.

"I do it all the time and have since she was a baby." I folded my arms and narrowed my eyes defensively at him.

"That's not what I meant," he blew out, running a hand through his hair. "I know that you've been doing it since she was born—and you do an amazing job. I just meant that this time it's different because… well, you know…."

"Because someone is trying to kidnap my daughter, and I might be too tired to fight them off if they try?"

"Exactly." Roman's voice was hard but not harsh. "We can't take any chances right now, Quinn. So please, just let us help you."

"Fine," I sighed. It wasn't the worst idea in the world; I just hated that Mike would have to miss work because of me. "I guess missing half a day at work isn't too terrible." I smiled at my brother and then added, "thank you."

"Good, well, I'm glad that we got that settled. Roman is going to run to the store to grab some groceries, and then when he gets back, I'll head to the office. After that, I'll run by Mom's and grab the laundry, but she said to let her know if you need it before then, and she can run by here and drop it off."

"Wait," I said, holding my hand up. "What do you mean when Roman gets back?"

"I called in today too."

"You don't have to do that."

"Quinn…." My name was a warning on his lips, and I knew better than to fight it.

"Fine. But make sure to pick up some more coffee while you're out. I have a feeling I'm going to need it."

I yawned and headed over to the other end of the couch and curled up next to Rosie, lifting her legs to rest on my lap so she had enough room. It was warm in the apartment, but suddenly, I felt chilly, so I grabbed a blanket from the floor beside me and covered up.

Roman gave a quick nod before slipping out the door and closing it behind him. Mike poured himself another cup of coffee before getting a phone call that he rushed to the bathroom to answer. Alone in the peace and quiet, I closed my eyes and laid my head against the cushion.

I had no idea how long I had been asleep before Mike gently

shook my shoulder and woke me up.

"Hey, sorry to wake you, but I need to head to the office, and Roman isn't back yet. Will you be okay for a little bit on your own?"

"Yeah, of course. We'll be fine." I looked over at Rosie, sound asleep and gently snoring again.

"Okay. If you need anything, call me on my cell and keep calling until I answer. I mean it, Quinn—anything at all."

"I'll be okay, and I'm sure Roman won't be gone much longer."

He glanced down at his watch and then checked his phone.

"I thought he would be back already, but apparently, it's taking longer than we thought. I sent him a text message, but he hasn't gotten back to me."

"I'll have him reach out as soon as he gets back."

"Okay." He looked at Rosie and me again, seeming to struggle with his decision to leave.

"Go," I coaxed, shooing him away.

Finally, he grabbed his keys from the table and left.

I closed my eyes and willed myself to stay awake, but they felt so heavy. I couldn't remember the last time that I had slept so well, and my body desperately craved it.

I felt numb, like I was floating through the clouds, weightless and without any worries. A long, flowy white dress covered my body, twirling freely as I spun in circles, dancing to a song that only I could hear. Everything felt right as I kept spinning, laughing the faster I went.

Then suddenly, I hit something hard, and it jolted me out of my bliss. I looked around, trying to find what I had crashed into. There was bright light blinding me as I lifted my hand to try to shield it. Suddenly it went away and standing before me was Justin.

There was a cut on his forehead with blood dripping from it. Instinctively I reached up to wipe it away but pulled my hand back when it went right through him. He wasn't really there. I reached for him again, disappointed when the same thing happened. Slowly he started to fade away, being pulled into a darkness that I couldn't see.

"Justin!" I called out, picking up the bottom of my dress to run after him.

My feet hurt from stepping on the shards of broken glass. There were thick trees around me, casting the shadows that hid him.

"Justin!" I cried out again. My heart raced as I tried to run faster, desperate to find him. He needed help. He needed me.

I kept running, tripping over pieces of debris but not realizing what it was until I got to a single tree in the middle of nowhere. I looked around and gasped, covering my mouth as the tears dripped down my face.

A horn blared off in the distance, but I couldn't see it. Instead, my eyes were fixated on the image of Justin hanging from one of the tree branches with a seat belt wrapped around his neck.

I jolted upright, nearly launching myself off the couch as I tried to shake the image out of my head. My palms were sweaty, and my heart was racing so loud that I could hear the blood pulsing through my ears.

I leaned forward, trying to catch my breath when I heard the doorknob turn. Relieved that Roman was home, I got up and started walking to the door, then stopped when I realized that it wasn't Roman.

Twenty-Seven

Quinn

3 Days Ago

I watched the doorknob rattle a few times before I jumped up and pushed the coffee table across the room, forcing it in front of the door. It was heavy enough to stop whoever it was from getting in for a few seconds while I grabbed my gun. I glanced at Rosie, making sure she was still asleep before running down the hall to the bedroom. I stood on my tiptoes and retrieved my gun from the top shelf of Roman's closet where I had been keeping it.

My footsteps were light but quick as I went back to the living room, gun aimed at the door and hands steady in front of me. I waited for a few seconds before I inched closer, wishing that I had brought my bulletproof vest home. There wasn't time to worry about that right now. Someone was still on the other side of the door, trying to pick the lock.

Rosie snored loudly and rolled over, pulling my attention to her for a brief second. When I looked back at the door, it was being forced open as someone rammed their body into it.

A few seconds later, the wood splintered around the body that burst through the door. Whoever it was had a ski mask covering their face and was dressed in all black, making it impossible to see anything.

Instinctively, I moved in front of Rosie, shielding her from them as I kept my gun aimed at their head.

"Don't come one step closer," I commanded.

They tilted their head and looked past me. I moved again, keeping her hidden.

"Get out now," I warned as my fingers tightened around the trigger.

I studied them and tried to lock away as many details in my mind as I could. The way they stood, their height and weight—things that would be easy to identify later.

They moved quickly, darting for the couch. I kept my eyes focused on them as I pulled the trigger.

After three shots, I lowered my gun and watched them sink to the floor, clutching their shoulder. I reached for my phone to call for help when I heard Rosie crying behind me.

I turned around and found her curled into a ball on the couch, crying and shaking as she looked at the body on the ground in front of me.

Quickly, I tucked my gun into my pants and rushed over to her.

"Shhh, honey, it's okay." I grabbed her and clutched her to my chest, holding her tightly as she cried.

I hated that she had to witness this, but I hated even more that I had allowed myself to be distracted for a split second and that it allowed whoever it was to get away. There was a trail of blood that led to the open doorway where Roman now stood, jaw hanging open and grocery bags stacked on both arms.

"What happened?"

Twenty-Eight

Roman
3 Days Ago

"What the hell happened?" I asked again, tossing the bags to the counter before rushing over to Quinn and Rosie.

Rosie was sobbing uncontrollably as Quinn held her. I looked down at the blood smeared on the floor and then up at Quinn, needing answers from her.

"Someone got in," she said quietly.

I raised my brows, asking the question I didn't want Rosie to hear.

She shook her head.

"Three shots to the chest and shoulder."

My head was spinning while I put everything together. Had I been here, none of this would have happened. First of all—no one would have gotten through the door. Second—they wouldn't have left with a gunshot wound.

Quinn held and rocked Rosie, slowly calming her down. I went to the kitchen and put the groceries away, knowing that we wouldn't need them here after all. There was no way that I could keep them safe with splintered wood for a door.

I pulled out my phone and called Mike, waiting for him to

pick up and answer. By the third time, I was starting to get annoyed when he answered and huffed out, "now isn't a good time, man."

"Yeah, same here."

"What do you mean? What happened? Is Rosie okay?" His tone immediately changed, and whatever had him stressed out a few seconds ago was now replaced with another source of worry.

"Someone just broke into my apartment."

"Fuck. Are they okay?"

"Yeah, Quinn handled it."

I didn't want to get into the details about it now, and honestly, I didn't trust Mike's phone not to be bugged, given everything else that was happening. "What's going on with you?"

"Saul Gomez was just rushed to the hospital. He was shot."

"Where?" My throat was tight, and my jaw clenched. This had to be it—we had our guy. I knew that bastard was after Rosie from the moment I laid eyes on him holding her shoulder at Sandra's house when he was supposedly helping her find the bathroom.

"Leg and abdomen. He was grabbing lunch; it was a drive-by shooting."

"Was anyone else with him?"

"Not that I know of. We're still waiting for more information. He's in surgery now."

I chewed the inside of my cheek, frustrated that it was

starting to sound more like a coincidence than anything.

"Any chance he was also shot in the shoulder or chest?" I asked.

"Not that I heard, why?"

"Because someone left my apartment with three bullets that your sister put into them."

Twenty-Nine

Quinn

2 Days Ago

"If I never have to pack again, I'll be forever grateful," I muttered as I tossed a duffle bag of clothes onto the guest bed at Mike's apartment.

"It's only for a little while," he said gently, leaning against the doorframe with his arms folded over his chest. We both knew it was true, given that neither my apartment nor Roman's was safe anymore; he was the last resort on such short notice. But we also knew it wasn't safe for long; whoever it was would find us here too. That was why we didn't go to my mom's house. I wanted to keep her safe, which meant that we needed to avoid her and Sonia at this point. It was too dangerous to get them involved by staying with them.

"That was supposed to be true about Roman too. I was only supposed to stay there for a few nights, and almost two weeks later, we were still there. I just want to go back to my own apartment and go back to normal."

"I know," he sighed. "But unfortunately, that's not an option right now. We have to keep you and Rosie safe."

"Safe?" I snorted, tossing my phone on the bed. "Do you really think that we're going to be safe anywhere? Whoever it is keeps finding us wherever we go, so I don't see why we can't just go back to my apartment and be comfortable. I'm so tired," I said, rubbing my eyes. "I don't want to keep running and looking over my shoulder."

"The only way around that is to relocate you guys."

"Like through witness protection?"

He shrugged.

"The department that my husband worked for and died on the job? The same department that you work for that seems to have a mole?"

"Technically, it wouldn't need to go through us at all. US Marshals handle witness protection. I have a friend who I trust that I could ask for a favor."

"Mike, you and I both know that neither of us can ask for any favors right now without someone getting wind of it. We don't know who we can or can't trust. There's too much at stake right now to risk it."

"So then you're stuck with me for a while?"

"It looks that way," I said with a soft laugh.

We stayed quiet for a few minutes before he pushed off the wall and ran a hand through his hair.

"I'm going to do everything I can to keep her safe, Quinn. I promise you that. No one is leaving you alone in the apartment again."

"So we're all just quitting our jobs and living here together?" My brows rose high on my head.

"It's not forever. Whoever it is, is getting restless. They're making more attempts. We just need to catch them and end this."

I tried to smile, but it disappeared before it hit my lips. Mike's phone rang, pulling him into the hallway to answer it. We were still waiting for an update on Saul—who had been seen at a food truck a few blocks away from the office when he was shot, which ruled him out from being the same person who broke into Roman's apartment.

"Yeah, okay. I'm on my way." Mike hung up and shoved his phone back into his pocket as he came back into the guest room. "I need to go meet Max to discuss a few things. Roman is in the kitchen with Rosie. I'll grab some groceries on my way back, but Mom is headed over with a few casseroles in the meantime."

"Okay," I nodded. "Thank you."

He smiled, then turned and left. I fell back on the bed and laid there for a few minutes, pretending that my life wasn't currently one big dumpster fire.

An hour later, my mom had shown up with my sister Sonia and a week's worth of meals to go in the freezer. On top of that, she had a pan of chicken enchiladas, beans, and rice that were hot and ready to eat. We sat down at the small table in Mike's kitchen and ate dinner together as a family.

Once we were done, my mom took Rosie to give her a bath while I helped Roman clean up. Sonia was helping blow up the air mattress that they brought for Roman to sleep on. It was amazing how much help and support we had, though I hated the reason why we needed it.

"How are you holding up?" Roman asked, gently bumping

my shoulder with his as I rinsed the plate and set it in the dishwasher.

"I've been better, and I've been worse," I said with a shrug. "So, I guess I'm somewhere in between?"

Yesterday had been a long day dealing with multiple agencies over the shooting. While we didn't have to worry about proof that someone had tried to break in and that I fired my gun in self-defense—it sucked that we didn't have anyone in custody nor a suspect to go after.

"Have they heard anything about Saul?" I asked, looking up at him as he handed me another plate.

"Mike said that he was out of surgery but then took a turn for the worse and was rushed back into another one. I haven't heard anything since then."

"It's so crazy," I muttered.

I added the last few dishes to the dishwasher and then started it. My body was sore and tired as I leaned against the counter behind me.

"I just wish all of this was over already. Or better yet—I wish it wasn't happening to begin with."

"Me too. But we'll keep both of you safe." He took a deep breath and then sighed heavily. "I know that probably doesn't mean much given what happened yesterday…." His head dropped as his hand shot through his short, dark hair.

"Hey," I said gently, pulling his hand down. "That wasn't your fault."

He let his hand drop, our fingers entwining in the process. I turned toward him, pressing my chest into his as his hand snaked around my waist and pulled me tighter.

"I should have been there. I hate that I wasn't."

"You didn't know."

"We knew there was a threat—that's all I needed to know. Instead, I was off looking for something and got distracted. I know better than to let myself lose focus."

"What were you looking for?" My curiosity getting the best of me.

He let go of me for a brief moment as he walked over and grabbed his backpack from the hook by the door. A few minutes later, he came back and handed me a bag of gummy worms.

The corners of my lips turned up as I held it, realizing that this was what he and Mike had been talking about yesterday when I overheard them. I didn't eat a lot of sweets, but gummy worms were my weakness, and the ones in the red bag were my favorite.

"They were out at the market that I went to, so I went to a few other places before I finally found them," he explained.

I held them to my chest and looked up at him, trying to blink away the tears.

"You didn't have to do that."

"I wanted to. I mean, it was originally Mike's idea to get them, but I was the one who had asked him what your favorite snack was."

I wrapped my arms around his neck, careful not to scratch him with the bag. My eyes fluttered closed as my lips brushed against his before they parted, and his tongue swiped against mine.

"You're so sweet," I whispered between kisses.

He pulled away and slowly trailed his lips down the side of my neck. "I wanted to do something nice for you." His teeth gently nipped my skin. "You've had so much going on and needed a treat."

"I had a nice treat the other night," I giggled playfully as I scratched my nails up his back under his shirt. "But this is great too."

"Are you saying that sex with me is comparable to gummy worms?" He pulled back and raised a dark brow at me.

"Well," I laughed. "Both are pretty satisfying."

"But has a candy ever made you come before?" he whispered by my ear, the coarse hair on his chin teasing my skin.

"Hmmm," I teased, playfully tapping my finger to my chin. "I'm not going to answer—"

"What the fuck is this?" Mike's voice boomed from the front door before it slammed shut behind him.

I immediately jumped back, putting enough space between us to douse the flame that was starting to build between my legs.

"It's not what it looks like," I lied quietly, lowering my head to avoid his heated gaze. I wasn't afraid of much, but that didn't mean that I wanted to see my brother's disappointment etched on his face. I could still hear Rosie laughing from the bathroom with my mom, so I knew she wasn't headed out here yet.

"It is what it looks like," Roman confirmed, digging his fingers into my hip and pulling me toward him protectively.

"Is it?" Mike questioned, standing in front of us with his feet spread shoulder-width apart and arms crossed. "Because it looks like you're fucking my sister."

"Mike!" I covered my mouth with my hand, not sure if I was more embarrassed that my older brother knew that I was doing his best friend or if it was hearing the words come out of his mouth.

"Like I said," Roman said with a shrug.

"I warned you," Mike bit out, taking a few steps toward us.

"Yeah. And?" Roman quipped, stepping in front of me and putting a hand behind him to keep me in place. "What are you going to do, Mike? Try to kick my ass because I fell for your sister and we acted on impulse like two very consensual adults?"

"Oh, I'm gonna do more than try to kick your ass."

"Let's see what you've got."

I watched as they stood chest to chest, both of them fuming so hot that I was surprised I didn't see smoke coming out of their ears.

"That's enough," I hissed, pushing in between them. "We have enough going on right now; we don't need to add this to the mix."

"I was just going to say the same thing," Mike replied while looking over at me and keeping his eyes on Roman. "Seems like a bad time to start a new relationship, given everything else that's going on. And I know that my best friend wouldn't be using my sister as a fuck buddy—so obviously, there's a relationship that you guys haven't told anyone about."

I could feel the heavy breath from Roman behind me and knew that he was trying to stay calm.

"You don't know shit—"

"I will handle this," I said, lifting my hand to stop him.

I waited for Mike to stop glaring at Roman and look at me before I spoke.

"Mike, I love that you're still my protective big brother after all of these years, but this isn't something that you need to be concerned with."

"But—"

"Nope. You do NOT get a say in any of this. I am a grown woman and know exactly what I'm getting myself into with Roman. You don't need to step in and protect me when you know damn well that he's a good guy. If he's good enough to be your best friend all of these years, then I don't see why you wouldn't think that he was good enough for me. Wouldn't you want someone like him for your sister? Someone that you know and trust?"

I tilted my head and studied him, pinning him with a look. "Or do I not deserve that?"

He pulled his head back and scowled.

"You know you deserve more than that, Quinn. You deserve more than anyone could ever give you."

"So then, are you saying that Roman isn't good enough for me?"

He looked from me to his best friend, his face softening some.

"I didn't say that."

I released a frustrated breath and forced my shoulders down.

"Well, that's what you're insinuating, and it's just as rude to him as it is to me. I know that you love both of us and care about our happiness, but you need to step back and realize that this is none of your business. Whatever happens between Roman and me is for us to handle—not you."

"I don't want to be caught in the middle if things go south between you guys."

"Then don't. No one is forcing you to be in that position. Before this, Roman and I saw each other at random holidays—it's not like we were constantly around each other. I'd like to believe that someday things will return to a somewhat normal state, and God forbid—if something did happen and we couldn't be around each other—we're adults who can act civil and move on with our lives. It's a shame you don't trust us enough to let us try this and see what happens. It could be something really wonderful." I stepped back and leaned into Roman's side as he wrapped an arm around me.

Mike looked between us, watching the way we held each other.

"So," he said with his jaw still clenched. "This is happening?"

We both nodded.

"Fine," he sighed. "But absolutely no sex under my roof."

He turned and walked out of the room, muttering something under his breath as he worked his tie free from his neck.

Thirty

Roman
1 Day Ago

I slept like shit last night, but that was nothing new. Ever since Quinn showed up, asking for my help a few weeks ago, I hadn't relaxed enough to truly rest. I had debated going back to my apartment to handle things but decided to stay at Mike's place after agreeing that it was better to keep Rosie safe by having more eyes on her.

Quinn and Rosie slept in the guest bedroom while Mike stayed awake in his, and I camped out on the couch in the living room. He had gotten a call around five this morning, confirming that Saul had more complications during surgery and didn't make it.

I was in the kitchen, brewing a pot of coffee when there was a knock on Mike's door. Before I could answer it, he came down the hallway, looking at me, confused. I shrugged, not having any clue who was there, and then went back to grabbing some mugs from the hooks above the sink.

"What do you want?" he asked, slowly opening the door but not enough to let in whoever was on the other side.

"I need to talk to you," a quiet female voice answered.

"Now isn't a good time. We can talk at the office."

"You don't understand, Mike—there isn't going to be a good time. This is urgent."

The door pushed open, and the woman from the party that Mike hated appeared. I pushed at the corners of my mind, trying to recall her name, but the lack of sleep had me struggling this morning.

"Anastasia," he groaned, shoving a hand through his hair in frustration.

"Look—I know that you don't like me and hate having to deal with me, but there's something that you need to know."

"What?"

I leaned against the counter, not making any effort to leave as she tossed her honey blonde hair over her shoulder, and her hazel eyes pleaded with him to listen.

"Frank Bestillos was murdered this morning. They found his body when a neighbor called the apartment manager about a noise complaint. The door was kicked open, and his body was left in the kitchen, bullet to the head."

"What the fuck?" Mike muttered, shaking his head in disbelief.

"That's not all," she said nervously. "Julia was taken to the hospital this morning. Someone attacked her on her way to work in an alley. An onlooker intervened and scared them off before they could do anything else."

I pushed off the counter and joined them.

"Are these all the same people who—"

"Were in the car when Justin died." Mike pulled his lips into a thin line.

"So someone's taking out his entire team?"

She nodded as tears filled her eyes.

"Do you think it's Elias Salvador?" I asked. "It seems pretty convenient that suddenly everyone that was working the case that sent him and his father to prison is now being targeted and murdered."

"I don't know what to do," she whispered. "I can't shake the feeling that something terrible is about to happen. I didn't want to bother you by coming here, but since Justin was your brother-in-law, I was worried they might come for you too."

Before he could say anything, I noticed the red dot that quickly moved from her forehead to her chest, then back up again.

"Get down now!" I shouted, diving toward her and pulling her to the floor as a bullet whipped past us. Mike crouched next to me before taking off toward the guest bedroom where Quinn and Rosie were.

"Take cover, Quinn," he yelled while pulling his gun from its holster.

I dropped to the floor, cradling Anastasia in my arms as I watched the blood pool around her.

Thirty-One

Quinn
1 Day Ago

"I know I've missed work all week," I replied into the phone. "Unfortunately, there have been a handful of personal events that have transpired and won't allow me to come in at this time."

I paused to listen to my boss rant and complain on the other end of the line, knowing that he was pissed off that I was being so vague. Was I going to lose my job over this? Who knew. But I couldn't exactly come clean and tell him that I was hiding and trying to keep my daughter safe from whoever was trying to kidnap her and taking out everyone that my dead husband had worked with. If ever my faith was shaken in who I could trust at work, now was that moment.

"I will touch base with you on Monday," I confirmed. "Thank you."

I hung up the phone and set it on the bed next to me. After Anastasia was shot in Mike's apartment this morning, we had agreed that none of us were safe in the city anymore. I repacked the same duffle bag that I had just barely unpacked yesterday, added some first aid stuff, and made sure that I had plenty of medicine if Rosie spiked a fever again. Thankfully, she seemed to be on the mend this morning, which was one less thing to worry about.

Roman had a friend who owned a remote cabin just outside of the city that we could stay at. We made our way this morning, creating enough of a zig-zag pattern with changing trains and taking cabs that no one would be able to follow us without being noticed. We got there around eleven, and Rosie and I settled in while Roman checked the perimeter to make sure everything was safe and secure.

I hated that everything was constantly so stressful that she had missed so much school this week. I could tell that she was feeling the weight of everything by how cranky she was getting. She needed her normal routine that she hadn't had in almost two weeks. I also hated that I didn't have anything with me to keep her entertained. No toys. No movies. Nothing. It wasn't like I could take her outside and let her play just in case someone did find us out here.

We weren't that far from Manhattan, only a few hours away in Carmel Hamlet, but it felt far enough to give us some time to stop and refocus our attention. Whoever was coming for Rosie was sending us a clear message by taking out almost everyone that Justin had worked with. It terrified me that Mike was still back in the city, the only person who had a connection to Justin who hadn't been shot yet. Roman and Mike agreed that there wouldn't be any communication between them while we were out here, just to make sure the calls weren't traced to where we were. On top of that, Roman's friend said that the cell service at the cabin was pretty spotty given the thick trees that surrounded it, so it would be hard to get calls in or out.

I wanted an update on Anastasia and, more importantly, Julia. I didn't believe for one second that she was innocent in this and had been attacked on her way to work. Everyone else had been shot but her. Unfortunately, we fled as quickly as possible so we could find safety and weren't there when the paramedics came for Anastasia. As far as anyone knew, we weren't there when it happened, and that's how it needed to stay.

Rosie sat on the couch, staring at the TV that I hadn't bothered to turn on. I knew that she was miserable, and so was I. I looked around the small room, looking for a board game or something to entertain us for a while. As I scanned the room, I noticed a camera up in the corner pointed directly at the couch where she was sitting.

I casually adjusted my shirt, making sure that my gun was still strapped to me and easily accessible.

"Hey, pumpkin, I'm going to check on Roman for a minute. Are you okay in here for a few?"

She nodded and kept staring at the TV. I turned it on, assuming that the channels would be static since there wasn't cell service but was pleasantly surprised when I found a DVD player sitting on the shelf below the TV. There were a handful of movies on a bookshelf next to the couch, so I scanned them quickly before popping in a kid-friendly option and setting the remote on the wooden coffee table.

I glanced back at her one last time before I opened the door and stepped outside. I walked around, checking for Roman while keeping my attention focused on the house as well as any movement. Finally, I heard footsteps coming from the back of the cabin and saw Roman as he approached with a branch in his hand.

"Everything okay?" he asked, moving the wood over the

tire marks from the Uber that had dropped us off earlier. It was a ten-minute walk to reach a spot where we would have cell service again, so we agreed that it was best not to risk renting a car that could be traced to us and instead would request another Uber when we were ready to leave or if we needed to go somewhere.

"Did you know that there are cameras inside?" I nodded to the cabin, turning to make sure Rosie hadn't ventured outside.

"Rob said that he had a few up. One in the living room aimed at the couch and one in the kitchen at the front door. They're not on, but I can call and ask him to turn them on if we want him to."

"Do we need them on?"

"It's up to you. Rob does surveillance, and it might not hurt to have an extra set of eyes on the cabin while we sleep. He also has the perimeter set up with cameras that are on 24/7, so he would know if someone approached the cabin."

"But there wouldn't be any way to warn us," I muttered with disappointment.

"There's a landline for emergencies. If he saw someone on the cameras, he would call and check to see if we were expecting anyone. Most of the time, they're set off by animals."

I nodded, feeling a little more comfortable with the cameras inside. At least it was limited to the living room and kitchen. It was a small cabin with only one bedroom and one bathroom, both of which had bars on the windows, so I knew there was no need to have any in those rooms.

"All done," he said, tossing the stick behind the wooden bench against the wall by the front door. I turned to go back inside when he snaked a hand around my waist and turned me to face him.

"How are you doing, Quinn?" His eyes searched mine.

"I honestly don't know. This is all just too much. I feel like I should be at work, trying to solve this case, but I can't."

I rested my head against his chest and inhaled, feeling comforted by his scent. It wasn't much, but I would take whatever comfort I could get right now.

Thirty-Two

Roman

1 Day Ago

I checked in with Trevor for what felt like the hundredth time today. I hated missing work, and while I tried to make up some of the time I'd been home with Quinn this week, I knew he already had a lot on his plate with Max's wedding this weekend. He didn't complain about me being gone and assured me that they had everything covered. Jackson was turning out to be quite the lifesaver these past few weeks with all of the unexpected time off Trevor and I had taken.

I sat on the small loveseat across from the sofa that Quinn and Rosie were cuddled on, watching another Disney movie that Quinn had found. It was boring, to say the least, but I was relieved that we were safe for now. I leaned my head back and closed my eyes.

When I opened them again, I saw Quinn and Rosie in the kitchen, snickering when they looked over at me and tried not to laugh. I sat up and felt something wet on the side of my mouth, so I quickly wiped it away with the back of my hand. Apparently, I had fallen asleep and drooled like a freakin' buffoon.

I got up and stretched before heading to see what they were doing in the kitchen that was connected to the small living room.

"What are you two ladies up to?" I asked, leaning over Quinn's shoulder as she kneaded a dough ball on the counter.

"We are making pizza," she said with a huge smile.

I was glad that she had agreed to make a quick stop at the grocery store just outside of town before we got here. I didn't want us to be stuck without food or toiletries, especially since we had Rosie. I could go days without eating, but the thought of letting her go hungry or skip a meal put a vice clamp on my heart and wouldn't let up until I knew that she would be taken care of.

Quinn had browsed the aisles, looking for something specific, while Rosie and I added a few bits of junk food here and there to the cart. I knew that Quinn and Rosie used to make pizzas at home a lot before everything happened, so I assumed this was her way of making things feel normal again for Rosie.

"It smells delicious," I commented. "What can I help with?"

"Do you want to make the salad?" Quinn asked, eyebrows raised.

"Ugh, do we have to eat salad?" Rosie whined with a scrunched face.

"Yes. Veggies are good for you, and we've eaten way too much junk food lately." Quinn pinned her with a look before turning to me and pointing a finger in my direction.

"Hey, I'm not complaining," I laughed with my hands raised.

"Everything is in the fridge. I found a cutting board and knife and set them by the sink."

"Cool," I said with a genuine smile and then winked at Rosie when she made another disgusted face about the salad. "Just wait until you try my salad, you'll love it!"

"Does it have ice cream or cookies in it?" Quinn joked.

I stopped for a moment and pretended to think about it, which made Rosie giggle. I loved that sound and wanted to hear it forever. I tried to push away the hope that fluttered in my chest that someday I would get to have more of these moments with them.

A few seconds later, I made a sad face at Rosie and started pulling the vegetables out of the fridge. I checked with Quinn to see what she wanted in the salad and what was being saved for the pizza, then I got started. We all worked together happily making dinner and not thinking about the cloud of darkness that seemed to be always looming over us.

After we ate, I cleaned up the dishes while Quinn gave Rosie a bath. She took her phone with her, letting me know that she was going to let her play in the water for a while since she had been cooped up inside for so long. I was about to remind her that there wasn't good cell service here when I realized she wasn't used to being away from it. It had become like a safety net, and I didn't want to take it from her.

She held it up and shook it gently as if reading my mind.

"I have a couple of books that I downloaded a while ago and never got around to reading. Figured I'll have some time to get started."

I smiled, and she returned it, the weight on my shoulders always feeling lighter when her beautiful face lit up the world around me.

They gave me a few minutes to use the restroom before they went in and got Rosie situated. I finished cleaning up and sat down on the couch, relaxing for a few minutes. I thought about going outside to check the perimeter to make sure there weren't any new footprints or tire tracks but then remembered that Rob had cameras set up, and if he had seen anything, he would have called.

He had also told me where the monitor was in the cabin that would show the live view of the cameras. I got up and opened the cabinet door, finding it exactly where he said it would be. The screen was large, with eight different cameras currently showing. The living room and kitchen cameras showed offline like he said they would. I looked around at all of the settings, finding where to turn them on if we wanted to. I needed to talk to Quinn before I did that, but in the meantime, I turned up the volume for the notifications; that way, if anything set off the cameras outside, we would hear it.

They stayed in the bathroom for over an hour before they came out and Rosie was in her pajamas with a big towel wrapped around her wet hair.

"Did you have a fun bath?" I asked, smiling at how happy she looked.

She nodded.

"Mama said I look like a raisin," she giggled.

I laughed and smiled up at Quinn as she sat down on the

couch and pulled Rosie over to her. She rubbed the towel around her hair before she took it off and set it to the side.

"You are the cutest raisin I've ever seen," she said before leaning in and kissing Rosie's cheek, making her laugh again.

I watched as Quinn combed through her hair, getting the tangles out before braiding it.

"Thankfully, it's hot enough that her hair will dry quickly, even in a braid. At least this way, we won't have a mess of tangles to comb through in the morning."

I wasn't sure what was going through her mind, but I could hear the hint of uncertainty in her voice about not knowing what to expect. It sucked, always having to be on the lookout and ready to run at any moment.

Rosie curled up on the couch and watched another movie while Quinn hung the towel in the bathroom. As she was heading back, I heard a ding, and my eyes darted to the cabinet with the monitor. I had closed it, so Rosie didn't get curious about it, but the alert meant something had set off one of the cameras. Or better yet—someone.

Thirty-Three

Quinn

11 Hours Ago

I had been restless and fidgety since the alert for the camera went off earlier. Roman and I watched the video over and over, making sure we didn't miss anything as a raccoon scampered by, trotting right in front of the door. While I had hoped to see someone, I knew that we wouldn't. That would be too easy, and my life right now was anything but easy.

There wasn't anything on the video that indicated that someone was out there, but deep down inside, I knew that they were close. I could feel it in my bones.

By three, I still hadn't been able to fall asleep but was glad that Roman was finally getting some rest. Rosie was tucked into the bed with him on one side and me on the other. Thankfully, it was a king-sized bed, and there was plenty of room without us literally being on top of each other.

His soft snores still filled the room as I stayed awake until five. By then, I was exhausted and felt my eyes start to flutter shut when Rosie rolled over and tugged on my hand.

"Hey, baby girl," I said, sounding more tired than I wanted to.

"I have to go to the bathroom," she whispered.

"Okay, let's go." I tried to stifle my groan as I rolled off the bed and waited for her to get up. Roman shuffled and turned over, checking to see what was happening.

"She needs the restroom," I explained quickly, guiding her through the small room with my hand on her lower back. "You can go back to sleep."

I went with her and waited for her to finish as I leaned against the wall and closed my eyes for a minute. The toilet flushed, then she washed her hands and finished up. I hoped that she was still tired and wanted to go back to bed, but when she sat down on the couch, I knew she was up for the day.

I turned the TV on and set the remote on the coffee table before scampering off to the kitchen to start a pot of coffee. A few minutes later, Roman came out of the bedroom, pulling a clean t-shirt over his head, giving me a quick glimpse of his rock-hard abs in the process.

"Hey, I've got Rosie. Why don't you try to get some sleep."

"I'm fine, but thank you," I lied, feeling like my body weighed a thousand pounds as I tossed another scoop of coffee into the filter. At this rate, we were going to run out before tomorrow.

"You haven't slept, Quinn. You need to be alert, and you can't do that if your body doesn't have the rest it needs. I'll make her breakfast, and we can watch a movie together."

"How do you know if I've slept?" I asked with one hand on my hip.

"Because I heard you tossing and turning all night when you weren't up looking out the window or coming out here to check the cameras."

I groaned and covered my eyes with my hand.

"I'm so sorry I kept you up. I thought I was being quiet."

"You were. But I'm a light sleeper and have been trained to be aware of my surroundings at all times—even while I sleep. Now go lay down and rest. I'll come get you if we need anything."

I tried to find a reason to fight him on it—mainly because I wasn't used to anyone taking care of things for me—but I had very little fight left in me. I went to the room and laid down, making sure that the door was open so I could hear if anything happened.

Within minutes of my head hitting the pillow, I was asleep.

Hours later, a loud thud startled me from my sleep, and I jolted out of bed, looking for the source of danger. It took a moment for my head to clear as I looked frantically around the room, trying to remember where I was. Then it occurred to me that I was in the cabin, and Roman was supposed to be watching Rosie.

I bolted out of the room into the living room as I quickly looked for her. The TV was turned off, and there was no sign of them anywhere. The bathroom door was open, so she wasn't in there, and the kitchen was empty as well. I flung open the front door, ready to take off into the woods to find her when I saw them sitting on the bench right outside the door.

My hand flew to my chest as I tried to slow my racing heart. Roman's eyebrows raised in concern as Rosie's head tilted to the side in confusion.

"What's wrong, mommy?"

"I heard a loud thump and couldn't find you guys."

"Sorry, we came outside for a few minutes to get some fresh air."

I nodded, not sure what to say. Part of me was angry that he had taken her outside without asking me, but then I also knew that it was ridiculous to be upset when they weren't even ten feet away from the door and that he could quickly get her inside safely if someone did come.

"I was feeling sad, so Roman thought it would be fun to come look at the clouds and talk to Daddy."

My heart skipped a beat as sadness overwhelmed me. I looked at him without saying anything and wondered what they had been talking about.

"When I lost my grandpa, I used to sit outside and watch the clouds. I knew he was in heaven and that only the clouds separated us, so I would pick my favorite cloud and pretend he was sitting on it as I talked to him."

I smiled and looked down at Rosie, my arms folded over my chest as if to protect my heart from leaping out of my chest.

"Which cloud did you pick?" I asked her.

"That one. It's small, but it's shaped like a heart, and I think Daddy would pick that one to tell us that he loves us."

I nodded, fighting back the tears that threatened to spill over.

"I told Daddy that I was sad because I miss him and that you seem really sad lately too. I know that he can't come back to see us, but I really wish I could hug him again. Your hugs make me feel better, and I bet Daddy's would too."

"His hugs were the best," I said, squatting beside her and holding her hand. I knew that she didn't remember much about her time with him since she was only one year old when he passed. I tried to tell her stories over the years about Justin and showed her the videos I had of him, but it would never be enough to replace her knowing him and having her own relationship with her father.

"I had a dream about Daddy last night," she said quietly, lowering her head and eyes away from me.

"You did? What was it about?" I squeezed her hand reassuringly, hoping it would give her the confidence to tell me about it.

She looked up at Roman, and he nodded. I tried to ignore the pang of jealousy that rushed through me that she had chosen to talk to him about it yet seemed so reluctant to talk to me. Since when did she keep things from me?

"Daddy was with the lady who brought me home the other day from the subway. They were hugging each other, and then they… kissed." She looked up at me with guilt on her face, and it broke my heart. "Then he left with her, and I kept calling to him, asking him to come back, and he wouldn't. I was really mad at him."

I swallowed down the mix of emotions that she had just brought up and tried to focus on how to respond to her.

"I'm sorry, pumpkin. Dreams can be hard to understand sometimes, but I can promise you that Daddy would never walk away from you. You meant everything in the world to him."

She nodded and wiped a tear from her eye as we heard a clap of thunder far off in the distance. Roman looked up at the sky as the clouds moved with the rush of wind and the blue turned an ominous shade of gray.

"We should get inside before the storm hits," he said, standing up and gently placing his hand on Rosie's back to guide her inside.

Once she was inside, he lingered by the door and whispered in my ear, "I wouldn't worry too much about the dream. We all know how wild our imagination can get."

I forced a smile but knew there was more to her dream than he knew.

Thirty-Four

Roman
2 Hours Ago

Quinn seemed to relax a little as the rain pounded on the roof while she curled up and watched a movie with Rosie. This was probably the most I've seen anyone sit and watch movies, but it wasn't like there were any other options. If it was just Quinn and me, there were plenty of ways that I could fill the time without watching TV, but Rosie was here, and that left few options for a five-year-old.

It was a little after two, but it felt like it was so much later since we got up at five. I was glad that Quinn slept for a few hours but wished she would have gotten a solid eight hours of sleep instead of five. But something was better than nothing, and she seemed to be more alert than she was before.

I had fixed Rosie lunch earlier but knew that Quinn hadn't eaten yet today. Restless and desperate for something to do, I got up and went to the kitchen to make something since I hadn't bothered to eat either. My stomach growled as I turned the bacon in the skillet and flipped the pancakes onto a plate. Who said there was a time limit on when you could eat breakfast?

"Hey Rosie, do you want some pancakes?" I called to her

in the living room. Not that I had to yell or shout, given that they were sitting less than twenty feet away from me in the same room. But pulling her attention away from the hundreds of spotted dogs on the TV was another thing.

"No thanks," she replied happily, leaning forward as Quinn got up and joined me in the kitchen.

"I hope you're hungry," I said over my shoulder as she pressed her body against mine and slid a hand up and down my back.

"I'm starving. What can I help with?"

"Nothing, I'm just about done."

"Sorry, I just assumed you were fixing food for yourself, or I would have come in to help."

"You don't need to apologize," I laughed. "I enjoy cooking for you, Quinn. I wouldn't have let you help, even if you tried."

She blushed and glanced at Rosie, who was still focused on the madwoman screeching her tires on the TV as she chased down the puppies in her car.

We sat down at the small kitchen table and ate, not bothering to say anything while checking on Rosie every few minutes. It wasn't that there was any threat of danger, but more out of habit and that there wasn't much else to look at in the small space without having to stare at each other—and I knew that if I kept looking at Quinn, I was going to start thinking about all of the things that I couldn't do to her right now.

Once we were finished, she helped me with the dishes,

despite my constant protests. We were just about done when the phone rang. A chill ran down my spine as we looked at each other, knowing that Rob would only call if something was wrong.

I tossed the towel onto the counter and rushed over to the phone. My grip was tight as I picked up the receiver and brought it to my ear.

"Hello."

"It's Rob. There's a bad storm heading your way."

I looked out the window and saw a bolt of lightning light up the trees as the thunder clapped overhead. It had been slowly coming down for a few hours but was definitely getting worse.

"Yeah, it's already coming down pretty hard."

"The weather can get ugly out there, so if the power goes out, there's a generator in the shed behind the house. Might not be a bad idea to get it set up before it gets too bad. Just wanted to let you know in case I can't get through on this line."

He talked me through where to find everything I needed in the shed and then guided me on where to find resources if we needed them. I didn't have to ask what he meant. We both knew why we were here, and Quinn and I weren't the first to use his makeshift safe house.

I hung up, feeling slightly relieved that nothing was amiss, though I couldn't shake the gnawing feeling that something wasn't right. There were a few things that I needed to take care of before the power went out, so we weren't caught in a bind, but I knew that getting the generator set up was the first priority.

Thirty-Five

Quinn

The front door swung open, the rain spraying in from the wind that whipped past. I turned my head, knowing that Roman was back from messing with the generator but felt my body stiffen when I saw five figures dressed in all black, wearing ski masks, rush through the door.

I jumped off the couch, startling Rosie as I tried to shield her with my body. I reached behind for my gun, panic crushing over me when I remembered it wasn't there. It was unlike me not to have it on my body, but I had been distracted after I got out of the shower right before Roman went outside to prepare for the storm that was already upon us.

"NO!!" I shouted, shoving against the bodies as they charged us. I felt strong arms grab me and fling me to the side as Rosie screamed from the couch. I got up and swung at the masked figure in front of me, watching as their head shot to the side from the impact of my punch, but it wasn't enough. Someone held me by the waist, ensuring I couldn't get to Rosie.

Panic flooded through me as I tried to get free. It was useless, and I knew it. We were outnumbered and I was unarmed—biggest fucking mistake of my life.

I could hear Rosie scream and turned my head toward the sound right as someone picked her up and tossed her over their shoulder. A black pillowcase was shoved over her head as they rushed out the door. I continued to fight against the strong arms holding me in place, desperate to get to my daughter. My pulse raced and my breathing was erratic as adrenaline pumped through me.

I tried to turn to see where they had gone, the front door still wide open. There was a black van parked right outside that I immediately recognized. Seconds later, the back door was slammed shut before it sped off, the sound of gravel crunching beneath it.

I tossed my head back, feeling the sharp pain as I made contact with a head, eliciting a loud growl from the recipient. It wasn't enough to knock him out, but it did piss him off to where he tightened his grip around my throat, making it harder to breathe. I brought my hands up and tried to pry his hands away, desperate for air.

Roman will be back any second. He'll come save me. He'll take me to get Rosie back. Then we'll kick ass and take out everyone who's ever tried to hurt my daughter. She's only five years old…

But before Roman could get there, a hand reached up and covered my mouth with a towel. Everything turned black, and the voices around me faded.

Thirty-Six

Roman

My body felt like it had been electrocuted repeatedly. I laid on the ground, feeling the rain pelt my face as I tried to find the strength to roll over and get up.

I knew better than to come outside unarmed but hadn't expected to be ambushed when I went to turn on the generator. The storm was coming quickly, and Rob had warned me that we would likely lose power; unfortunately, I thought that we had more time than we did.

By the time I got outside to turn on the generator, the lights had already begun flickering in the house. I knew that it would only be a matter of minutes before we completely lost power and had asked Quinn to find the flashlights, candles, and matches that Rob had stored in the cabinet.

I looked around, checking for any signs of movement around me, though I knew they were already long gone. I heard them seconds before the first man approached me but wasn't quick enough before the second tasered and knocked me to the ground. While I had imagined they wanted to shoot me, I knew they didn't want to alert Quinn to their presence with gunfire. They needed the element of surprise on their side.

My body felt shaky as I forced myself to a sitting position. The rain was coming down even harder, making it impossible to see anything around me. With what little strength I had left, I pushed myself up and hustled back to the cabin. I wasn't sure how much time had passed, but I hoped I wasn't too late.

I rounded the corner and found the front door open and tire tracks in front of the door. I scanned the area, noticing another set that appeared bigger than the first. Knowing that they were already gone, I went inside and geared up to go find the two people who now meant more to me than anything in the world.

Once I was in dry clothes, I put on an armored vest and loaded it with extra mags, a flashlight, and a knife before holstering a 9mm to my thigh in addition to the AR15 slung across my back. Out of all of the things that I was thankful for with Rob, it wasn't the safe house that he had offered us but the gear that would allow me to do what I needed to do to get them back.

I had no idea where I would start looking for Quinn and Rosie, but I knew that I couldn't afford to waste another second. Time was of the essence right now, and their lives depended on me finding them before it was too late.

I walked down the road, following the tire tracks until I reached a spot where I had cell service. I knew that it would be a while before I could touch base with anyone, so I pulled out my phone and sent a quick text message to Trevor, letting him know that I would be taking an indefinite amount of time off from work.

A few minutes later, I heard my phone ding and checked it.

Trevor: Not a problem. Is everything okay?

Me: Quinn and Rosie are missing. I won't stop until I find them.

I turned my phone to silent and tucked it back into my pocket as I kept walking, following the tire tracks until they split at the fork in the road and went in two different directions.

AGAINST THE CLOCK

Thirty-Seven

Rosie

"I have to use the bathroom." I squirmed on the seat and pressed my legs together as I hoped someone would take the dark bag off of my head. It was hot and gross inside of it, and I hated that I couldn't see anything. I wanted my mommy. Where was she?

There were voices whispering around me, sounding angry like the teachers when they go into the hallway to complain about the kids when they think no one can hear them. I always heard them, even when they thought they were being quiet. That's why I always tried to be good, so they wouldn't go talk about me.

Suddenly, I felt my body fall to the side before someone reached out to grab me. I had no idea who it was, but they didn't hurt me like the last person did. This time it was softer, like how my mom would hold my hand when we went to crowded places.

I tapped my feet as I tried to think about anything other than peeing. I didn't want to have an accident. Mommy said I was too old to have them and that the other kids would make fun of me if I had one. I wanted to wait until I could get to the restroom, but no one seemed to listen to me.

"I really need to go potty," I insisted to whoever could hear me.

Someone growled, and the sound was deep, like my Uncle Mike when he was fighting with my mom or grandma. But I didn't think it was him because why would he cover my head and not talk to me?

Suddenly, I was picked up and put over what I thought was someone's shoulder. It was difficult to tell, but it was hard and bony, and I could hear their loud breath by my ear.

Don't pee on them! They'll make fun of you and tell your mom that you had an accident. She'll be really mad at you.

I tried to squeeze my legs shut tighter to keep any pee from leaking out of me when I was plopped onto the floor and the bag on my head was ripped off.

I looked around, letting my eyes adjust to the bright light, trying to see where I was and who was with me when I felt a hand force my head in the other direction.

"Make it quick."

His voice was angry as he stormed off and left me in a bathroom with no windows. I was too afraid to look around so I kept my head down and walked over to the toilet.

My hands were shaky as I reached for my shorts and pulled them down. I looked up slightly, not seeing anyone around me before I sat down and went potty.

It was quiet, and I didn't know where the scary man had gone, but I was glad he wasn't there anymore.

I finished wiping, pulled my shorts and underwear back up, and then flushed the toilet. When I walked around the corner, I noticed a woman waiting for me by the sink, blocking the door.

My eyes widened, and a smile spread across my face.

"It's you! Did you find your puppy?" I asked, tilting my head to the side as I looked at my new friend. Then I remembered what my mom had told me. She wasn't my friend. She tried to take me from my grandma's house so she could kidnap me.

She didn't answer me. Come to think of it, she didn't look happy to see me either. Was she upset about her puppy? Maybe she hadn't found it, and now I had made her sad. I turned on the water, squirted soap onto my hands, and started washing them.

"Are you here to help me?" I asked as I turned off the water.

I looked around for a dryer or a paper towel but stopped when I saw the sad smile on her face as she slowly shook her head no.

Thirty-Eight
Quinn

I laid completely still and pretended to be unconscious as the truck turned a corner down the bumpy, unpaved road. One thing that I learned early on was to remember as many details as possible. The FBI had ingrained that into us from the very beginning, and it had stuck with me since. Details could make the difference between solving a case and saving a life.

While I had lost consciousness for a few minutes—maybe longer, who knew—I had kept quiet once I came to and made sure I stayed in the position I was in when they loaded me into the vehicle. I needed every advantage that I could get at this point, and that meant that if I pretended to be unconscious, they would be more likely to slip and say something about where they were taking me or about who had Rosie.

I kept my breathing shallow and slowly lifted my eyes, making sure they were only partly open so I could look around without anyone seeing that I was awake. I was on my side in the backseat with my hands bound in front of me with thick rope. It felt like I was possibly taking up two seats, but I couldn't tell if anyone was on the other seat beside me. It was too risky to look over and check and even riskier to move my body which would alert them that I was either awake or slowly coming to.

First glance showed two men sitting up front with a middle console between them. Based on the size of the vehicle, I imagined it was a truck or SUV, and given the beat-up interior, I would guess that whoever had Rosie wasn't rolling in money. Either that or they hired their goons and didn't bother to outfit them with expensive, bullet-proof vehicles like those in the mafia had.

I tucked my chin to my chest as slowly as possible and held my breath. So far, no one seemed to notice any movement on my end so I tilted my head a fraction of an inch until I could see the seat beside me.

Sure enough, there was a man sitting next to me, wearing all black just like the other two up front, with a ski mask covering his face. I hated that none of them were stupid enough to take the masks off; it would make it a whole lot easier for me if I knew who they were.

I continued to study him as he held onto the handlebar above his window and stared out the window. There was a .45 in his shoulder holster, and I knew it was likely he had other weapons that I couldn't see, as well as the two guys sitting up front. I slowly pulled my head back and rested it on the seat while I waited for us to get wherever we were going. My body had already been through plenty, combined with a lack of sleep, so I needed to preserve energy any way I could.

Given that I had no idea where we were headed, I was desperate to come up with a plan of attack for when we got there. If I wanted to keep Rosie alive, I needed to get to her as soon as possible. However, I also couldn't stop wondering if Roman was okay and whether he had made it back to the cabin. I hadn't heard any gunshots before the intruders burst through the door, but that didn't mean they didn't use a suppressor to cover the sound. With the wind and rain that pelted against the cabin, it wouldn't take much to muffle it. Not knowing anything about either of them weighed too heavily on my mind and I needed to focus, or I wouldn't be of any help to anyone.

I hated that I had no idea how much time had passed, but it was even worse that I was separated from Rosie and didn't know if she was still alive. I prayed that she was, but I just couldn't stop the pain in my heart at the thought that something had happened to her. If Justin weren't already dead, I would kill him for putting us in this situation to begin with.

My breathing was calm and even, not giving it away that I was awake. I felt movement beside me and forced my eyes closed while I held my breath and waited for him to shift his position.

"Boss said to go the back way," a gruff voice said, breaking the silence in the cab.

"Got it."

It felt like the vehicle was slowing down, but I didn't trust that it was safe to open my eyes just yet. Was I supposed to still be knocked out? How much time had passed before they would just assume that I was dead? I had no clue but decided to go along with my instincts and allowed my body to appear lifeless on the seat as the car stopped.

Here we go.

Thirty-Nine

Roman

My head was still pounding as I trekked through the thick forest, trying not to lose sight of the tire tracks on the dirt road. I took a few seconds to decide which way to go once I had come to the fork but didn't have the luxury of taking any longer than that. Thankfully the rain was slowing down, but I knew I had to hurry before they washed away and I was left with nothing.

I had limited cell service as I walked and was thankful that I had been able to get a text message out to Trevor. I wanted to track Quinn's Apple watch, but that would have cost more time while I waited for the signal to be strong enough to find it, and I simply didn't have time to spare.

It irritated me that I didn't know which vehicle Quinn was in compared to which one had Rosie, but I went with my instincts and chose the bigger tracks. Maybe it was because I knew that they would be easier to track and less likely to fade right away with the weather. Or maybe it was simply that I assumed Rosie was in this vehicle. I knew that Quinn had a better chance of protecting herself and that she would fight like hell to get to her daughter. Rosie, on the other hand, was only five years old and needed all of the help she could get.

I pushed harder every time I felt like slowing down and resting. I had no idea how long I'd been walking, but I did know that there wasn't time to stop now. I looked around for any sign of a building or house but didn't see anything. It didn't matter. I would walk a thousand miles with bloody feet and no food to get to her. Nothing was going to stop me now.

Suddenly the rain started pouring with a vengeance while thunder clapped off in the distance. Apparently, this wasn't going to be as easy as I had hoped. Not that any of it was easy—but I didn't really need any additional complications at this point.

I stopped for a second, took a deep breath, and reminded myself that I had survived worse. I had served in the Marines. I was used to hiding in the shadows and taking the lives of those who least expected it. There wasn't anything that I couldn't do.

Memories of years of stakeouts played through my mind as I continued walking, images I had long since tried to erase from my mind. I reminded myself that I wasn't that person anymore. I was different now. I wasn't a heartless killing machine like I thought I was when I first returned from my last tour. And while I wasn't proud of what I had done, I knew that I would do all of it again in a heartbeat because I had helped rid the world of some of the worst scum it had ever seen.

Even though I wasn't in combat and taking orders, I knew that I was doing the world another favor by eliminating whoever had taken Rosie. There were plenty of sick perverts that would continue to lurk in the shadows and prey on innocent children, but I would be damned if they touched her.

I stopped and ducked behind a large, overgrown tree when I spotted an abandoned-looking cabin in the distance. Parked out front was an older, beat-up truck that had seen better days. Fresh mud was splashed up on the doors, so I knew it was the tracks I had been following. That was helpful, given that the rain was really coming down hard now and already starting to erase them.

Keeping myself hidden behind the tree, I scanned the area and took note of how many entrances there were into the building. I was relieved that I hadn't spotted any other vehicles, but there was a detached garage off to the side, which meant there could be more occupants inside.

The paint was peeling on the front door and the windows were boarded up, making it impossible to see inside. I chewed the inside of my cheek in frustration, knowing that I needed to have a calculated plan before I entered. Rosie's safety depended on it.

I looked around, making sure no one was guarding the perimeter, then inched my way closer to the house while staying in the shadows. If I couldn't see in the house, then hopefully, I would be able to hide outside and listen to what was happening inside. I quickly circled around the cabin with my 9mm drawn and aimed in front of me as I made sure no one was out here with me. Once it was clear, I found a spot beside one of the side windows and squatted beside it.

The blood rushed through my ears, making it hard to make out the faint voices from inside. I knew it would take a few minutes for my pulse to return to normal, but I didn't have that much time to wait. I stood up and leaned closer, resting my ear against the brittle wood, and prayed that it was firmly secured so I didn't risk exposing myself.

"How long has she been out?" a man's voice asked.

"Who knows," someone muttered, sounding further away and less interested.

"The order is to deal with her."

"So then do it."

"Have you checked the account? Has the money been posted?" It was hard to tell how many different voices I was hearing, but this one sounded the same as the first man who spoke, the baritone in his voice recognizable compared to the other voice.

"Not yet," another voice answered. Instinctively I pulled away when it sounded like they were on the other side of the wall from me.

"Then she lives until we get paid," the first man stated.

"But that's not the order."

"I don't give a fuck what the order is. They hired us to do a job, and I'm not doing it until we have that money. There's too much at stake to be fucking around with these lunatics. Get an update on when they're transferring the funds. Until then—she stays alive."

<u>Forty</u>
Quinn

I sat in a chair by the window with my hands still tied in front of me. I couldn't pretend to be unconscious anymore, especially after one of them had kicked me in the ribs and I groaned in response. Now that I was awake, they were discussing what to do with me. It was apparent that I wasn't supposed to live long enough for them to bother with tying me to the chair, which was stupid on their part.

To add to their stupidity, all three of the men now had their ski masks off, allowing me to memorize every detail of their hideous faces. From the tattoos that covered the tall one's face to his neck to the one with no teeth and a receding hairline—they weren't anyone that I had seen before in any of the cases that I'd worked. Toss in the fact that they were discussing how to get rid of me, and I knew that they were simply hitmen for hire and not at all associated with whoever had Rosie.

My Rosie. My heart ached at the thought of my sweet girl somewhere alone with these monsters and I prayed that she was okay. Had Roman gotten to her? Was he okay?

I subtly shook my head to clear it and focused on the task at hand.

While they were busy talking, I scanned the room for anything I could use to my advantage. My hands were still tied and I didn't have a weapon on me, which meant that I would have to rely on improvising.

Two of the men wore shoulder holsters but didn't appear to have any armor on. The third guy didn't have armor on, nor did he appear to have a weapon. He was short and stocky with a gut that begged to be punched. I looked between them, searching for anything that would tell me who would be the hardest to take down—that's where I would start.

"I don't care what they said. I want the money, and I want it now," the short guy sneered into the phone.

The guy with the tattoos rolled his head on his neck, closing his eyes briefly while he did. Out of the three of them, he was the largest and most muscular. The other guy had a few missing teeth, but other than that, he wasn't in that bad of shape. If I had to choose between the two of them—and I did—I knew that the one with the tats would be my biggest challenge.

As if lady luck was on my side, the short guy on the phone turned and paced by the boarded-up window next to the front door and continued to tap the screen of his phone. No Teeth Tom, as I decided to name him, took off down the hall after announcing he was taking a piss.

That left Tatted Tim and me. He rolled his neck again, and I took that moment to make my move. Within seconds, I jumped up from the chair, ducked to avoid his hand that reached out to grab me, and slid down as if I was trying to steal home base. As I was mid-slide, I swung my hands up and punched him in the balls. It was difficult with my hands tied, but I knew it was the only way to disable him quickly.

As he hunched over in pain, I spun around and grabbed the .45 from his holster. Without giving it a second thought, I pulled the trigger and sent a bullet straight through his head. His body hit the floor at the same time the short one came rushing over. Before he could reach me, I put a bullet through his chest and then another one in his head, just to be sure.

Now that two out of the three were eliminated, there was one left, and I prayed that he would be talkative after seeing his two buddies. I needed at least one of them to give me information on where Rosie was and who was paying them to kill me. I waited with my hands steady in front of me for him to come back from the bathroom. I didn't imagine he was in any rush, given that he likely assumed those bullets were for me and that the job was done.

A few minutes later, I heard the bathroom door open, and heavy footsteps headed toward me from the hallway. Before they got there, the front door burst open. I spun around, aimed, and fired.

Forty-One

Roman

I jumped to the side as a bullet whipped past me. My heart jumped into my chest when I saw Quinn standing there with a gun aimed at me. I was thankful that I had been able to dodge it but also incredibly impressed with how accurate her aim was in the first place.

After I heard the first gunshot, I knew that I had no choice but to get inside. Little did I know that it was her in here and not Rosie.

"It's me, Quinn," I announced loudly, even though she could clearly see me.

I didn't bother to look at her as I kept my focus on the man walking into the room. His eyes widened as he saw the two bodies bleeding out on the wood floor, then narrowed as he looked between Quinn and me. Before he could reach his hand up to grab his gun, I raised mine and held it steady in front of me.

"Don't even think about it," I said, using my foot to kick the door shut behind me.

Quinn blinked a few times as if she couldn't believe I was there.

"Quinn, step aside," I directed, moving in closer to the guy as I watched his fingers twitch at his sides. I knew he would make a move to grab his gun, and I couldn't afford for Quinn to get caught in the middle.

She moved a few steps away from me and turned her aim to him. I knew she was focused again as I made it the last few feet and stood in front of him.

"Make one move, and I will put a bullet through your brain, just like my girl here did to your friends. Got it?"

He nodded, his glare as cold as ice.

I quickly relieved him of the guns in his shoulder holster before patting him down and removing a knife from his waistband. Once I was confident that he was no longer a threat, I stepped back and aimed the AR15 at his head.

"Go sit on the couch."

He didn't say anything and did as he was told.

Quinn was still standing there, holding her gun steady with both hands bound together. I wanted to cut her free but didn't trust that he wouldn't do something while we were distracted. She seemed comfortable enough, given that she had already killed two men while bound.

He dropped down onto the couch and then looked between us with his brows raised.

"Let's just cut to the chase," I said, widening my feet as I kept my aim. "Who do you work for?"

He rolled his eyes and looked away.

I clenched my teeth and stared him down. If he wanted to

play games and pretend to be a tough guy, that was fine. We would see just how tough he was.

I glanced at Quinn and caught her eye for a brief second, nodding in his direction. She gave a subtle nod and kept her hands steady in front of her.

I returned my attention to him, picked a spot on the wall half an inch above his head, and fired.

He jumped up, his head whipping around to see the hole in the wall.

"That was the only warning shot you're going to get." I adjusted my aim, making sure he knew that it was now focused on the spot right between his eyes. "Start talking."

"I don't know anything," he stammered, looking from me to Quinn as his eyes softened.

"Stop looking at her like that," I snapped. "She's not going to pity you, dumb ass. You helped them kidnap her daughter; there's no way you're getting out of this alive."

"Tell us what you know," she said coldly, lifting her hands slightly as she reminded him that she wasn't interested.

"As I said, I don't know anything. My boss—the guy with the bullets in him," he nodded to the short guy, "he handled everything. We just did what we were told."

"What were you told?" I asked, pulling his attention back to me.

"Take her out, and we would get $50,000."

I raised my brows and glanced at Quinn. She frowned angrily, and I had to bite back a laugh. She was worth more than that, and we both knew it.

"What about the little girl?" I pushed. We didn't care about how much they were getting for killing Quinn. We needed to know where Rosie was and what the price tag was for her.

"I don't know. I wasn't told anything about her."

"Alright, what happens after you complete this job?" Quinn asked.

"We were waiting for the money. Once we had that, we were supposed to take care of the job and send them proof."

"Send who proof?" I yelled, getting frustrated quickly.

"I. Don't. Know." He enunciated each word as if I were stupid and then turned to Quinn. "He doesn't listen for shit, does he?"

She cocked her head to the side and then raised the .45 slightly before putting a hole in the wall next to mine. I smiled proudly at how accurate her shot was. It wasn't the time to think about it, but suddenly I was imagining dates with us at the shooting range, seeing who could beat who.

"Fuckin bitch!" he shouted and jumped up from the couch.

"Sit your ass down before I put a bullet in it," I demanded.

"As you can see, we both have remarkable aims. I would stop fucking around and tell us what we're asking because I can guarantee you that if you don't tell me what I need to know, I will put as many bullets in your body as it takes until I'm no longer pissed off. And right now—I'm fucking furious," Quinn warned.

He sighed and returned to the couch, suddenly looking

defeated.

"I don't know their names. My boss was handling it. If you want info, I would check his phone. He was supposed to send a picture, you know, proof that it was done."

I looked around for the phone, then spotted it a few feet away on the floor, sticking out from under his arm. I nodded to Quinn, suggesting that she be the one to get it. Between both of us, I had no doubt that she could take him out if needed, but since her hands were still bound, I figured she might need the break.

She returned my nod, lowered her gun to the table beside me, then bent down to pick up the phone. I watched her through peripheral vision while I kept my eyes on him.

I could tell that she hadn't dealt with many dead bodies as she nervously tried to figure out a way to retrieve the phone without touching him. Finally, she grabbed the end of it and pulled it out.

"It's locked," she muttered, looking up at me under her thick lashes.

"Does it need a pin or a thumbprint?"

She swiped her fingers across the screen, a look of determination on her face. Then she bent down, lifted the dead guy's thumb, and tried not to gag as she pressed it against the phone.

It took a couple of tries before she got the angle right. Once it was unlocked, she dropped his hand and stood up, scanning the recent call log and text messages.

"There aren't any names in here." She looked helplessly at

me. "It's all code."

"What are the codes?"

"Red," she said and then looked at the guy on the couch. "What does red mean?" She held the phone in the air and shook it at him.

He shrugged and looked away.

Before the phone could lock again, she started looking through it and then gasped. Her eyes filled with tears as she stared at whatever was on the screen.

"What is it, Quinn?"

She turned the phone toward me. On the screen was a photo of Mike.

"Why is there a picture of your brother on his phone?" I asked, furrowing my brow.

Before Quinn could answer, the asshole on the couch decided to speak up.

"Because he's the next assignment. The payout increases the sooner we deliver him."

"We have to stop them," Quinn whispered.

"It's too late for that," he snorted. "They sent a sniper in this morning."

Forty-Two
Rosie

"I don't like bologna," I said as the mean man shoved a sandwich at me. I kept my hands tucked under my butt so I didn't have to take it.

"Then go hungry." His nose flared the same way Uncle Mike's does when he gets mad. I pulled away, afraid that he might hurt me.

"How long before they get here?"

I looked up at the woman who was yelling into her phone. She looked familiar, but I didn't know why. I tried to hide against the wall and make myself as small as possible on the chair so she wouldn't see me. She was mad. Really really mad. I didn't want her to get mad at me again.

"What do you mean that they're gone? Your guys had one job. ONE. JOB."

She stopped walking around and I was thankful because her shoes were really loud and hurt my ears every time they clicked on the floor. Mommy's shoes sounded like that when she wore her high heels, but she didn't do that too much anymore. She said she was too tired to worry about running around in death traps. I didn't know what she meant by it, but I thought maybe they made this lady mad too. Perhaps she could take them off for a while, or someone could loan her a pair of shoes that she liked better? That might make her less angry.

"So what you're telling me is that not only did your team let them get away, but they killed them first, then stole the truck AND Paco's phone?"

The louder she yelled, the more I thought about asking someone to give her different shoes. She started walking again and pinched her nose. Mommy also did that when she had a headache. Maybe something was wrong with her and she needed help. I looked around for a nurse or someone that could help her. Everyone else looked scared or mean, so I didn't want to talk to any of them. I shuffled in my seat and tried to make myself invisible again.

"Well, given that your team botched the first job, you're obviously not getting paid. What's the status of the other assignment?"

The mean guy with the gross sandwich walked by again and looked at me but didn't stop, so I knew I must have finally turned invisible. It was something that I used when I went places with mommy and didn't want people to see me. I didn't know if it really worked until now. I couldn't wait to tell her about it later.

"Well, at least you guys got half of the job done. I want proof sent to me in ten minutes. After that, find the other two and deal with them."

She hung up the phone and turned around to look at me.

I panicked, wondering if my invisibility had worn off or if she had special powers like Mommy and could see me.

I held my breath and grabbed the seat of the chair tightly as she walked over and squatted in front of me.

"When someone offers you food, you should take it. You never know when it might be your last bite to eat."

She stood up, grabbed the sandwich from the mean guy, and shoved it at me. When I didn't take it from her right away, she got really angry and shook it in front of me.

"Take it!" she screamed at me, jerking her head so hard that her red hair looked like fire on top of her head.

I reached up and took the sandwich.

"Good girl." She smiled at me but it didn't make her eyes sparkle like my moms did when she smiled at me.

Forty-Three
Quinn

"There's still no answer," I sighed, listening as Mike's phone went to voicemail.

We were in the truck we stole after killing the last guy in the cabin. Not only did we take the truck, but we also loaded up on weapons and stripped them of anything useful, including the phone they had been using to keep in contact with whoever had Rosie.

As soon as we had a signal, Roman reached out to a friend and had them start tracking the number programmed in the phone under Red. While he drove, I focused on calling Mike and watching the other phone to see if anyone called or texted with an update on the assignments their team was supposed to complete.

"Trevor said that he and Max were headed over to go look for him."

I hated all of the unknown and wished that all of this was over with already.

A text message alert came through on the other phone, and I immediately put in the password I had changed it to and unlocked it.

Roman glanced over to see what it was, but my excitement was quickly replaced with frustration when I opened the message.

"I swear, this guy gets more naked pictures sent to him than anyone I know. And honestly, he's not attractive enough to generate this much attention from women," I complained and exited out of the message.

"Looks has nothing to do with it," Roman laughed. "You know when you have access to drugs and money, women will do anything to get to it."

"I know. But it's still disgusting." I scrunched my face.

"It's true. Some women will do anything for a little taste of that life."

I leaned my head back on the seat and closed my eyes, hoping that some sort of divine intervention would happen and guide me to where Rosie was.

"We're going to find her," Roman assured me for the hundredth time since we'd gotten into the truck.

"It's been hours. Anything could have happened by now."

"Stop thinking like that, Quinn. You have to stay positive."

"I know," I groaned and blew out an irritated breath. I turned and looked out the window.

Roman's phone started ringing and I whipped my head in his direction as he answered it on speaker phone.

"Hey man," he said loudly. "Have you found him?'

There was a loud sigh—the kind you hear when someone's about to give you bad news and they don't want to.

"We have him."

"What does that mean?" I blurted out, needing more information.

"It means no line is secure right now, so I can't say more than that."

"Trevor!" I yelled, turning in my seat to face Roman. I was starting to lose it and there was no stopping me. I had reached a breaking point, and not knowing whether my brother was dead or alive was enough to snap the final straw.

"Thanks for the update," Roman said, eyeing me cautiously while also keeping an eye on the road.

"No problem. I'll be out of town for a bit and won't have constant access to my cell. Service is kinda spotty out there."

"Gotcha. Thank you."

I stared at Roman in disbelief as he ended the call and stared straight ahead.

"What the fuck was that code for?!" I shrieked.

"They have him, Quinn. That's all they're going to tell us right now."

"How can you be so calm about it? We don't know if he's alive or dead or in need of medical attention!"

He reached over and squeezed my hand gently.

"Trevor is going out of town, which means that Mike is alive and they're hiding him. He's with Max, and the two of them know plenty of doctors that will treat Mike without it being on anyone's radar."

"How do you know this?"

He shrugged and looked out the window, avoiding me.

"Roman."

"Look, I can't get into details but trust me when I say that Mike is in good hands. I hate not knowing if he's okay, but I trust Trevor and Max. If he says that they've got him, they've got him. There's nothing more that we can do, Quinn. Right now, we need to trust them to take care of Mike so we can focus on Rosie."

I let my head fall back and closed my eyes.

"You're right. I'm sorry." My shoulders were so tight that they felt permanently attached to my ears.

"You don't need to be sorry. All of this is beyond stressful, and I get it. But we're a team, and that means that we all help each other when needed."

I felt my heart start to slow back down to a normal pace and focused on taking some deep, grounding breaths. I had to get my mind clear if I wanted to figure out where Rosie was.

"Have you found anything else in the phone?" he asked, nodding to it sitting in my lap.

I shook my head and picked it up.

"I haven't been able to figure out the code. Red could mean anything, and other than dirty texts from countless women, there isn't anything about other assignments, so it's not like I can compare them to see if there's a theme of some sort."

"Maybe we should call Red? See if they answer?"

I pulled my mouth to the side as I thought about it.

"It couldn't hurt…."

I unlocked the phone and found the name Red in the contacts, which was fairly easy given there weren't many names, to begin with. I pressed the call button and put it on speakerphone so Roman could hear it.

We waited quietly as it rang. By the fifth ring, I was already feeling disappointed that they wouldn't answer.

"Since I've been informed that the men I hired are all dead and were left abandoned in an empty cabin without their weapons, I'm going to guess this is Quinn."

My stomach dropped as I stared at the phone. Roman nodded for me to answer her.

"Where is my daughter," I demanded, my fingers trembling as I struggled to hold the phone.

"Oh, sweet Rosie? She's fine. She's right here with me, getting to know everyone as we get her settled in. She's quite beautiful, isn't she?"

"You fucking bitch!" I shouted, blinded by anger. "Tell me where my daughter is now!"

"Tsk, tsk. Always such a hot head."

I looked to Roman for help, but his focus was on the road ahead of him as his knuckles turned white from gripping the steering wheel.

"How do you know that I'm a hot head?" I asked, forcing myself to calm down. It wouldn't do any good to sit here and yell at her. I needed to focus on finding Rosie, which meant that I had to get her to tell me where she was.

"I know everything there is to know about you, Quinn. I've been studying you for a long time. And quite frankly, I've always thought that Justin could do better."

My nostrils flared as my face twisted with anger.

"She's just trying to get to you; ignore her," Roman whispered.

"Well, then, you won't mind me stopping by to say hi," I replied as coolly as I could.

"Unfortunately, we aren't up for visitors right now. It seems sweet little Rosie isn't feeling the best, so I need to tend to her. Make sure she's ready. But feel free to come say hi to my guards. They've been searching for you, so this would make their job that much easier."

I glanced over to find Roman on his phone, speaking quietly into it.

"I don't think so," I snorted. "I am coming for my daughter; come hell or high water. As you've already seen—your men don't stand a chance with me. Now tell me where she's at."

"Don't you get it, Quinn? I already have what I want. What I've wanted for years. Now it's just a simple matter of tying up loose ends and cleaning up the mess your husband started."

"What does Justin have to do with this?" I asked, trying to keep her on the phone while Roman talked on his.

"He ruined my life," she shouted, forcing me to pull away. "He. Ruined. Everything. And now it's time to make it right. To fix what he tried to destroy."

Before I could say anything more, the line went dead.

I tossed the phone on the dashboard in frustration and scrubbed my hands down my face.

"Don't worry, I know where they're at," Roman assured me.

I didn't stop to think about what he said because my mind was too busy and distracted trying to place her voice. It was familiar. I had heard it before.

The wheels in my head were turning rapidly when it suddenly clicked into place.

"It's Julia. She has Rosie."

Forty-Four
Roman

"Okay, it should be right over there," I said, nodding to a small clearing in between the thick forest in front of us.

"So, what's the plan?" Quinn asked, already taking her seat belt off.

I parked the truck on the side of the road, hiding it the best I could, given the size of the damn thing. Then, I turned the ignition off and turned to face her.

"We wait a few minutes; make sure it's safe before we head in."

Her brows shot up off her forehead as her eyes bulged out.

"Are you kidding me? You think my daughter is in there, and you want me to wait to make sure it's safe?! Nothing is safe with her in there right now, Roman!" She turned and reached for the handle as my hand darted across to stop her.

"I don't want to wait either, Quinn, but what choice do we have? We have to be smart about this, which means we can't just rush in with guns blazing. This isn't some cheesy action flick. It's real life, and your daughter's life is at stake. I'm not willing to jeopardize that. We have no idea how many people are inside and what we're facing once we get there. I would hate for them to put a bullet through our heads before we even make it to the door. They likely have cameras set up around the property which means they're going to see us long before we see them. We're already at a disadvantage; let's not make things harder than they already are."

She sunk back against the seat and sighed heavily.

"Fine, you're right."

I knew how she felt because I was just as frustrated that we couldn't rush in and get Rosie but serving twelve years in the Marines taught me that you didn't go in unless you knew what was waiting on the other side. Intelligence was vital, and even though we didn't have time to get all of the information we needed, we had to be smart enough to get the basics.

Ten minutes felt like hours as we sat and waited to see if any cars would come or go from the road that we needed to head down. A no trespassing sign was posted at the entrance, so I didn't expect much traffic other than those we needed to avoid.

We got out of the truck and watched our surroundings for any movement as we geared up. Quinn had taken one of the shoulder harnesses from the cabin before we left and now had it loaded with extra ammo in addition to the .45 and 9mm she had swiped from the dead guys. I adjusted the tactical vest and made sure it was in place before leading the way with my AR15 aimed ahead of me.

Quietly, we stalked through the tall grass, making sure to keep off of the road and stay hidden under the thick trees. We had no idea if they had cameras set up or if they had a team stationed outside, but we would soon find out.

I didn't have to glance behind me to make sure Quinn was still there. Her soft footsteps were the steady reminder that I needed to push forward. I knew that she wanted to take off and run to get her daughter and that it was taking everything inside of her not to. Hell, it was taking everything I had not to do it either.

Finally, the road beside us opened into a large gravel driveway in front of a massive house. There were several cars parked outside, but none that I recognized. We stopped and studied the house, looking for any signs of movement around it.

When we knew it was safe, we slowly moved forward, making sure to stay hidden. We approached the side of the house, and I took my spot at the front of the wall while Quinn trailed around to the back, clearing it before she joined me.

There was an open window above us on the second story of the house, but it was small and likely belonged to a bathroom, given the size. I looked around for other points of entry, frustrated that there weren't any windows or doors nearby.

What kind of people build a house without windows or doors? How creepy and depressing is that?

The kind of people who kidnap and traffic children.

I was about to tell Quinn that we should circle around to the other side when we suddenly heard a voice and froze.

"But I don't want to," Rosie said grumpily.

"I don't care if you want to. You will learn to do as you're told."

I felt my blood pressure rise, knowing that Quinn's was too.

"I just want my mommy."

"Well, lucky for you, I'm your mommy now."

Forty-Five

Rosie

My face felt gross after the tears stuck to it. I asked for a tissue, but the mean lady told me that I wasn't allowed to cry and that maybe this would teach me not to do it again.

I didn't like the house we were in. She kept saying it was home, but it didn't feel like it. There were no pictures on the walls. No windows to look outside. There wasn't even a fireplace for Santa to come down. Nothing about it felt like my home.

I missed my mommy. I wanted to see and hug her, but the mean lady got mad whenever I talked about my real mom. She said she's my mom now, but that's not true either. Just like my mom always told me that no one would ever replace my real dad, I knew that the mean lady was lying and that no one would replace my real mom.

She left me alone in a room and told me to get used to it because it would be my new room. There wasn't anything in it other than a bed and a toy box that didn't have any toys. I hated it already.

I sat on the bed and pouted until the door opened.

"Can I come in?"

"No," I muttered. I didn't like this girl either. She lied to me about being my friend and needing my help to find her puppy.

She didn't listen and came in anyway. When she closed the door behind her, I felt scared, but then she smiled, and it didn't feel as scary anymore.

"You have to be very quiet, okay, Rosie? Julia doesn't know I'm in here," she said softly, the way my mom talks to me when she's trying not to be too loud.

I nodded and watched her sit on the edge of the bed.

"We don't have much time before they come looking for me, but I wanted to talk to you about something. Okay?"

I nodded again.

"Has your mommy ever taught you what to do if a stranger tried to hurt you?"

This time I was afraid to nod, so I just sat there quietly on the bed.

"Do you know what to do, Rosie?"

I shrugged my shoulders. Mommy had told me lots of stuff, and then Uncle Mike and Roman had taught me how to fight off the bad guys recently, but they said I shouldn't tell anyone about it.

"If anyone tries to touch you, I want you to do what your mommy told you to do. Okay?"

I chewed my bottom lip and debated on whether I should tell her that I knew how to fight off the bad guys.

"It's okay," she continued. "You can tell me whatever you

want to. I'm not here to hurt you, Rosie."

My breath felt funny in my lungs as I tried to talk.

"Uncle Mike and Roman taught me how to fight, but they told me not to tell anyone because Mommy might get mad." I lowered my head as if I were already in trouble for saying it.

"What did they teach you?"

I leaned forward and showed her some of the punches I had learned.

"Just like that," I said, getting up and standing in front of her to show her the rest.

"That's great, Rosie," she smiled. "I want you to use those moves they taught you, okay? If anyone tries to touch you, you fight them just like your uncles showed you."

I nodded and felt my cheeks burning from the smile that stretched across them.

"I have to go but promise me that you'll use what you showed me. Okay?"

"Okay."

Before she left, I decided to ask her one more question.

"Why did you lie to me about losing your puppy?"

Her face fell into sadness as she thought about it.

"Because it was my job. I was told to do it." She took a deep breath and then let it out. "I didn't have a choice."

"Why didn't you just say no?"

"They don't like it when you say no. That's why I want you to promise me that you'll fight with everything you have inside of you."

"Did you have to fight them too?"

"No," she said quietly as tears formed in her eyes. "No one ever taught me to. My mom wasn't here to help me, and I didn't know what to do. That's how I got stuck here, in this life."

"Do you think I'll ever see my mommy again?" I asked, my lip trembling as I started to cry.

"I don't know. I really hope so."

She opened the door and left me alone in the room that still didn't feel like home.

<u>Forty-Six</u>

Roman

Hearing Rosie's voice was enough to get both of us moving quickly as we circled to the other side of the house. I led the way with my AR15 and was ready to fire.

The trees were thick around the back of the house, allowing us plenty of room to hide if needed. While I knew that we were likely being watched on camera anyway, I knew that a bullet was more likely to be stopped by a thick tree trunk than thin air, so I took comfort in the resources around us.

Quinn followed closely behind me, her steps almost perfectly in time with mine. I pushed out the flashbacks of being a Marine and stayed focused on the present. I wasn't in combat, and this wasn't a team effort. This was me by myself, trying to save the woman I loved and her daughter.

About fifteen feet ahead of us, there was movement by a large, overgrown tree. I quickly raised my hand, signaling Quinn to stop. I held my breath as I listened for more. A twig snapped beneath their weight as they stepped over it, the loud thud of their boots echoing around us.

A few seconds later, a man dressed in black stepped out of the trees and pulled up his zipper as he headed toward the house. As if suddenly sensing our presence, he lowered his hand to his hip and reached for his gun. The moment he found us, it was too late. My bullet had already taken his life as his body slumped to the ground.

We kept walking, slowly inching around the back of the house while listening for others. I knew they were bound to come rushing out as soon as they heard the gunshot. It wasn't like they didn't know we were there—the cameras had been tracking us since we got through the clearing and approached the house. It was only a matter of time before they sent someone for us, and that person would be ready to kill.

I heard a door slam shut ahead of me and waited. But before I could focus on the two heavily armored men heading my way, I heard a commotion behind me. Quinn gasped as a hand clamped around her mouth. The sound was enough to get my attention, and I spun around and fired another shot, missing Quinn's head by a fraction of an inch.

Her eyes widened, but she bit back the scream that was building inside. I could see the fear in her eyes, knowing how close the bullet had been to taking her life if I had missed my mark. Trust wasn't enough when you were faced with something like that. If it had been me, I likely would have pissed myself on the spot.

I didn't have time to ask if she was okay. I knew the other two men would round the corner and be on top of us in seconds. I raised my gun and waited like a hunter stalking their prey. It was us against them, and I was determined to make it out of here alive.

Just as expected, the two men came around the corner with tactical gear on and .45s pointing in our direction. I didn't turn to see what Quinn was shooting at when I heard her discharge her weapon. Instead, I transported myself back to being a sniper and took them out before they got off one shot. Once they were down and I didn't hear anyone else approaching, I spun around to find Quinn staring down at the three bodies lying on the ground less than twenty feet away from her.

"Nice shot," I commented, nodding my approval.

"Thanks. I don't think I've ever fired a gun this many times in my life," she joked. "It's a lot different than going to a stuffy warehouse and shooting at targets on the wall."

I noticed how her eyes clouded with tears and recognized the emotion running through her. The struggle of knowing that you'd taken a life while assuring yourself that if you didn't take theirs, they would have taken yours. It was an ugly feeling that would crawl into your brain and live in the depths of darkness, always waiting to rear its head when you least expected it.

"We need to keep moving," I said, keeping all emotion out of my voice. Now wasn't the time to feel anything. I had a job to do and needed to focus on that. Mission: Rescue Rosie.

"Okay," she whispered and pulled her shoulders back. She lifted her chin and gave me a quick nod, letting me know that she was ready.

We resumed our positions with me leading and her following behind me. As we circled around the house, we heard a few voices inside but nothing outside anymore. That didn't mean that we were truly alone; it just meant that they would find us before we found them.

"Find them and kill them," a woman shouted, her voice floating through an open window upstairs.

There was an order to kill, but I didn't know how many people it was given to. One? Two? Twenty? It was hard to know how big Julia's crew of goons was, but one thing was for sure—it would only be a matter of time before we would be greeted by more gunfire.

"I think we should separate," I whispered over my shoulder. "I'll take care of the goons; you get inside and find Rosie."

"Are you sure that's a good idea?" she asked nervously.

"I'll follow you in and cover you while you take the lead. It's the only way to make sure we get to her before it's too late. If you come across anyone on your way to her, shoot them. Don't spare anyone. I'll handle the rest."

"Okay."

I took a deep breath, steadied my arms, and said a silent prayer before I kicked the door in and stepped aside to avoid the gunfire as it came flying at us.

Forty-Seven

Quinn

I had never seen this much gunfire in my entire life, including the gory, action-packed movies I watched with Justin before Rosie was born. I ducked and held my body against the door frame, glancing at Roman as I waited for his signal.

He stayed perfectly still with his AR15 held tightly against his chest. I wasn't sure if he was waiting for them to run out of ammo or if he was waiting for them to come outside looking for us. Either way, I wouldn't make a move without his direction.

A few minutes later, we heard heavy footsteps as a rush of armed men came flying through the door with guns drawn. Roman lifted his weapon at the perfect moment, jabbing the butt of it into one guy's face while I shot at another. It felt wildly reckless, but I kept an eye on Roman and shot at everyone else.

The bodies started falling around us as Roman continued shooting. He gave me a quick nod, stepped over their bodies, and went into the house. He rushed through and cleared the living room, then went into the kitchen while I took the stairs two at a time with my gun steady in front of me.

I heard a few shots downstairs but forced myself to keep moving toward the voices at the end of the hall. I was desperate to get to Rosie but knew that I couldn't be reckless. I listened carefully as I walked lightly, trying to keep my footsteps from being too heavy.

A floorboard creaked behind me, forcing me to spin around. I was face to face with a large, burly man whose face was covered in tattoos. He gave me a lopsided grin and pulled a knife from behind his back, swiping it at me as I jumped back. I narrowed my eyes and fired a shot, hating how many people I had now killed in one day.

His body swayed toward me as I jumped out of the way. I continued moving down the hallway and focused on the large bedroom at the far end. This was the room we had heard Rosie's voice from outside, so it felt like the first place I should look.

I slowly turned the knob and pushed the door open.

My heart leaped out of my chest into my throat, strangling the scream that threatened to come out when I saw Rosie sitting on a king-sized bed next to a man. Julia was sitting in a chair beside the bed, talking to them when they all looked up at me.

"Mama!" Rosie shrieked, jumping up to get off of the bed.

"Not so fast," the man said, reaching over and putting her down beside him. "You're not going anywhere."

Rosie's face fell, and tears welled in her eyes.

I stared in disbelief at the image before me. The guy looked familiar, but I couldn't figure out why.

"Give me my daughter," I demanded, my voice quieter and weaker than intended. "Now."

"She's not your daughter anymore. I told you that on the phone earlier." Julia tossed her red hair over her shoulder and tilted her head. "She's not going anywhere."

Anger was boiling inside of me as I watched them. My finger itched to pull the trigger and take both of them out, but I didn't want to traumatize Rosie by shooting a bullet into the man sitting beside her. It would be loud, and there would be blood everywhere, which would upset anyone, let alone a five-year-old.

He turned to whisper something to Julia behind his hand, and I noticed a black serpent-looking tattoo on his neck. In an instant, I knew where I had recognized him from. He was Elias Salvador, the son of Juan Salvador, and part of the child trafficking ring Justin had shut down before he was killed.

"If I were you, I'd lower your weapon," Elias said with a heavy accent. "I wouldn't want you to upset my daughter."

"Don't you dare call her that," I bit out, my hands starting to tremble with anger as I kept my gun as steady as possible.

"It's your choice, but my men will be here in a minute to take care of this," he waved his hand in the air as if I were some mess on the street that needed to be cleaned up.

I watched the Rolex slide down his wrist before he lowered his hands into his lap again. He sat there, looking overly relaxed in his white silky button-down shirt and dress slacks that had been freshly pressed. He didn't look like he had a care in the world, and I knew that was all about to change as soon as Roman got there.

"I don't care about your men," I lied. "We've already taken the majority of them out."

"Is that so?" He smirked, and I wanted to punch the smile off his stupid face.

Where was Roman? I could only stall this guy for so long. We needed to get Rosie and get the hell out of there.

"Just give me my daughter, and I'll let you two get back to whatever this is," I said, pointing between him and Julia with my gun.

"Again, Rosie is our daughter, Quinn. Now leave." Julia stood up from the chair and then immediately sat down when he nodded to her and shook his head.

So he was the one in control and calling all of the shots. That was helpful information to have.

"You know damn well that she's not your daughter. You're out of your fucking mind, Julia."

Silence lingered in the air for a few minutes as we stared at each other. Then he whispered something to her and nodded to me.

"Go on, tell her what happened. Explain why this child is owed to us."

I narrowed my eyes at him, then glanced at Rosie to make sure she was still okay. Overall she appeared to be, but that didn't mean anything. I wouldn't trust it until I could hold her in my arms and see for myself.

"Rosie was our daughter. She died six years ago. A car

accident. You might remember it, Quinn."

My heart sank when I started putting the pieces together.

"You shouldn't be driving when you're this upset," I scolded Justin as he got into the car. "Just stay and talk to me about it. Please."

"There's nothing to talk about, Quinn. I love you. I love our life. But I don't know if I can do this. I don't know if I can be a good father."

He pulled the car door shut as I jumped away. Then he reversed out of the driveway, leaving me in a puddle of tears.

I had sat at home that night, waiting for him to return. After I got a call from the hospital, I rushed over and paced anxiously in the emergency room waiting area for an update on Justin.

My mind constantly got the worse of me as I thought about the worst that could happen. I couldn't imagine bringing a baby into this world without him by my side. He was my everything. I needed him.

When the doctors updated me a few hours later, I was relieved to hear he was conscious, stable, and expected to make a full recovery, though he would be going home with a few broken bones. He was going to be held overnight to make sure his vitals stayed stable, but overall, he was okay.

It wasn't until the next morning that he told me the accident had been his fault. He was distracted and hadn't noticed the light turning red. He went through the intersection, t-boning a minivan. He repeatedly apologized for leaving and promised he would never do it again.

When he asked me to get an update on the other people, I went searching for his nurse and asked if they were okay.

"Unfortunately, the mother is still in the ICU. We can't give out more information than that right now."

"The mother?" I asked as my heart beat wildly in my chest.

"Her daughter was in the backseat. She didn't make it."

When I shared the news with Justin, he cried and held his hand against my flat stomach, vowing to be the perfect father to our baby. I knew that he would never be the same after this and my heart shattered knowing that he would never forgive himself for taking an innocent child's life.

I remembered the night very well, and to this day, it still haunted my nightmares.

"Justin wasn't always a play-it-by-the-rules kind of guy," Julia said once she saw the look on my face. "His recklessness took my baby from me. He took the only thing that I ever loved. The only person who mattered to me."

"And now you're trying to take mine."

"No, Quinn. I'm taking back what was owed to me. Justin took my daughter, and now I'm taking his."

"It's not the same, Julia. You know that."

"As a mother, you know what it feels like to see your child hurting. How do you think I felt being pinned in the car, listening as my baby fought for her life? Hearing her gasp as she took her last breath. Not being able to get the words out to say that I loved her because I couldn't believe what was happening. Nothing can prepare you for that, Quinn. Nothing. Justin never had to pay for what happened. The police called it an accident. An unfortunate accident. But that doesn't make it right, and it's about time he paid."

"He's not here anymore. How do you expect him to pay? You're not getting revenge on Justin; you're taking your grief out on his innocent daughter."

"I tried to make it right while he was here!" she yelled, startling me. "I did everything that I could. He was a stubborn ass, and nothing could get through to him."

"Then accept that and move on. Taking his daughter won't fix anything, Julia. You need to see someone and get help."

"Now you sound like him," she scoffed. "You need to go to therapy. This isn't healthy. You're crazy."

Her eyes widened, and she actually looked crazy as she said it.

"You talked to Justin about what happened?"

"He knew who I was as soon as I started working for the FBI. I could tell that he remembered what happened—how could he not? It hadn't been that long since it happened. He said he wished he could take everything back that night, and since he couldn't, he would find a way to make it right."

I tried to keep from rolling my eyes. That was the stupidest thing I had ever heard. There was no way to make it right when you took someone's life—especially a child. Though I imagined that the guilt was constantly eating away at him, I couldn't see what he could possibly do to fix what he had done. It wasn't like he could just give her a baby.

"Elias and I struggled to get pregnant with Rosie. She was a miracle baby, and we cherished every moment we had with her. Unfortunately, I sustained severe injuries in the accident that night, and the doctors confirmed that I wouldn't be able to carry another child. It would be too risky. But we wanted another child…."

Her voice trailed off and sent a chill up my spine.

"So you started kidnapping other people's children?" I bit out sourly.

"It's not really kidnapping when the parent doesn't want them." She shrugged. "There are plenty of parents who want to escape the burden of parenthood, and believe it or not, everyone has a price."

"Yeah, well, my daughter isn't for sale."

"Trust me; everyone has a price. But this isn't about that, now is it? Because we're not paying you for her. We're taking her. Taking what is owed to us."

"How do you figure that she's owed to you? Just because she has the same name as your child doesn't mean she's destined to be yours."

"Don't you get it?" Julia asked, leaning forward, and looking quizzically at me. "She is the perfect daughter for us. She's the same age that our Rosie was when she died. It's like picking up right where we left off."

I felt a whimper escape my throat and blinked rapidly, forcing the tears away from my eyes.

"No," I blurted out. "I'm not letting this happen."

"You don't have much of a choice, now do you? I tried to make it easier for you, Quinn. I tried to give you a heads-up that this was coming so you could be prepared. I figured you would be fine knowing that you still had a chance to start over with that new boyfriend of yours. You guys look so cozy together, don't they?" She turned and looked at Elias, waiting for his answer.

"The coziest."

"But unfortunately, you seem so determined to stop this, and now you know too much, so we're going to have to change plans."

She got up and opened the drawer on the nightstand between them.

"Why now?" I asked, trying to stall for a few more minutes. I knew that Roman was close, I could feel it in my bones. I trusted that he was staying in the shadows for a reason.

"Well, they actually tried to take her a few days ago, but it wasn't the right time," Julia laughed and pulled a gun out. She wiped it off with the bottom of her shirt and inspected it to make sure it shined the way she wanted it to. "I had forgotten the exact date until Elias told me. Everything had to be perfect. That's why we took her today. Today was the day."

"The day for what?"

"It was exactly six years ago today that our sweet Rosie died."

"This is ridiculous!" I shrieked. "You can't just take someone's child because yours died. Life doesn't work that way."

"It's not just that, Quinn. Justin ruined everything for me. Not only did he kill our daughter, he was constantly putting his nose where it didn't belong."

My stomach dropped when I realized where she was going with this.

"Yeah, that's right. After he convinced Ariel to confess, I knew that he was getting close. Too close. I hated him for pushing her so hard. If he would have backed off, we could have taken care of her the same way we take care of anyone who leaves before they're given permission. So many lives could have been saved. Like his."

I didn't want to ask, but the question flew out of my mouth before I could stop it.

"You killed my husband on purpose?"

She shrugged, then slowly, a malicious grin spread across her face.

"He had what was coming to him."

Elias crossed and uncrossed his ankles as his legs extended out in front of me. He sighed heavily as if he was bored with the conversation.

"Anytime now, my love," he replied, raising his brows at her.

I barely had time to see what was happening as Rosie sprung off the bed and charged at Julia. I screamed and watched in horror as her little body leaped into the air, her fists clenched as they swung at Julia before Elias jumped up and grabbed her.

"You killed my dad?!" she screamed furiously as he carried her over his arm across the room.

Fury blinded me as I stared at Julia. Before I could speak, I heard a woman's voice behind me.

"Put the gun down."

Julia narrowed her eyes and moved her aim from me to the girl now standing next to me.

I wasn't sure what was happening, but since they were aimed at each other, I turned and focused mine on Elias.

In a split second, gunfire rang out in the room and I took cover as I heard a bullet whip beside me. I spun around to find Roman in the hallway, rushing into the room.

Julia was on the floor in a puddle of blood, matching the mess Elias had made on the other side of the bed. Rosie was standing there, screaming, as red splattered her hair and face.

"Go get Rosie, Quinn," Roman instructed, rushing in and blocking me from the other woman.

"I'm not here to hurt anyone," she said, lowering her gun and handing it to Roman.

<u>Forty-Eight</u>

Roman

"Julia took me when I was seven. My mom was a drug addict and didn't care what happened to me. She just wanted that next fix. At first, I thought Julia was a godsend until I was old enough to know what they were doing."

"Why didn't you try to leave and get help?" Quinn asked as she held Rosie on her lap.

"I couldn't. Every time I tried, they caught me. By the time I was thirteen, Julia had started showing me the ropes and told me that if I didn't want that kind of life, then I could work for her. I didn't know what she meant at the time, but I knew that I didn't want the men to touch me anymore, so I agreed. She started teaching me how to lure children away and said we made the perfect team because I was someone they would trust."

"That's why I wanted to help Bree when she lost her puppy," Rosie said sadly, tucking her head into Quinn's shoulder.

"I'm sorry about that," Bree sighed. "I didn't want to do it. But I also didn't have a choice. Julia had changed once Elias came back. She wasn't nice to me anymore. I was afraid of what she might do to me after I saw what happened to Ariel. She told me to lead her away from the house, then got upset after I did because Elias reminded her that it wasn't the right day. They had been planning it for a while."

"We'll need you to talk to the police about this," Quinn said softly. "I'm here to help you however I can, but we need to make sure that there are no other victims that we don't know about. Was she working with anyone else?"

"No," Bree shook her head. "She hadn't done much while Elias was locked up. Once he was out, they became obsessed with Rosie and getting revenge on Justin for the accident and then for uncovering their operation. It was too risky for her to start it up again right away, and she didn't have all of the resources she needed. She was told to hire people to take out Justin's team so there were no traces back to her. She even hired people for other stuff, like breaking into your apartments." She looked between us. That explained the random thug that Quinn had shot in my apartment.

"That's why everyone on Justin's team was targeted and murdered," I commented, not letting on to whether Mike was alive or dead. "Except her."

She nodded.

"Yeah, but she was so desperate to stay off the radar that she hired someone to attack her."

That didn't surprise me any, given how crazy and desperate she had been.

"She hated him for what he did. That's all she ever talked about. There were pictures of Rosie on her walls in the other house, and she would talk to them daily. I started to worry that she was going crazy when she started adding new ones," she lowered her voice and nodded at Rosie. "She ended up bringing us to this cabin because she didn't want anyone to find Rosie and have them take her from them again. I don't know how long she was planning to stay here, but my guess is that none of us were ever leaving here again."

"Well, it's all over now," Quinn said. "The police should be here shortly, and then we can all get the hell out of this creepy cabin."

We all nodded and sat quietly at the table in the kitchen, one of the few places that didn't have dead bodies on the floor. Soon, we heard sirens in the distance and knew the police were headed our way.

"Thank you, by the way," Quinn added. "For stepping in earlier. Rosie told me you had talked to her and told her to fight. Thanks for looking out for her."

Bree smiled sadly and looked at Rosie.

"I didn't want this life for her. No one ever fought for me. I wanted to make sure that she had at least one person who would be there to fight for her if you couldn't get here."

Soon, the house was buzzing with activity as OMI worked on securing the crime scene. We stayed long enough for the mandatory interviews and agreed not to leave town. This was a huge investigation that would span across several agencies, so it was going to take some time before the case was closed. We said goodbye to Bree, and Quinn promised to check in on her as soon as she was able to. For now, she would go with child protective services and be placed into foster care until she turns 18.

Since we didn't want to steal another vehicle or be caught in the truck we had taken to get there in the first place, I called Trevor and asked for a ride.

Max's wedding was over a few hours ago, and Trevor had skipped out early to check on Mike for me. Instead of taking us to my apartment or Quinn's, he drove us to another remote cabin and assured me that it was still within the jurisdiction we agreed to stay in.

"How's he feeling?" Quinn asked from the backseat as we ventured down a bumpy, gravel road. Rosie was buckled in the seat next to her, asleep with her head on Quinn's shoulder.

"I'll let you see for yourself," Trevor said, putting the truck in park.

Forty-Nine
Quinn

Mike was asleep by the time Trevor dropped us off at the cabin last night. We quietly headed to the back, where a guest room had been made up for us. The place was much bigger than the last one we had stayed in, with three large rooms and two full bathrooms.

I didn't sleep much that night because I kept rolling over to make sure Rosie was still beside me. Roman slept on the other side of her, making sure she couldn't get away without one of us noticing. While the threat and danger of someone taking her was gone now that Julia had been arrested, it took some time to register that we didn't have to hover and watch her every move.

I rolled over and smiled at the sunlight streaming in through the window. Today was going to be a wonderful day. Roman and I were together. We had Rosie, and no one was going to take her. On top of that, my brother was safe and alive. What more could I have asked for?

"Good morning, Mommy," Rosie's small voice greeted me as she opened her eyes and looked at me.

"Good morning, sweet girl." I brushed a strand of hair off her forehead, trying to be quiet so we didn't wake up Roman.

"Good morning," Rosie said sleepily, smiling at him.

I looked over her to find him smiling at both of us.

"Good morning, Rosie."

"Can I go see Uncle Mike?" she asked, sitting up and whipping the covers off all of us.

I laughed at her excitement and nodded my head. "Just be careful; he's not usually a morning person," I called after her.

"I heard that," he yelled from the living room.

I smiled and climbed out of bed, groaning as I felt the ache and stiffness in my body.

"You okay?" Roman asked as he climbed out of bed, eyeing me suspiciously.

"Yeah," I laughed. "I'm not a spring chicken anymore. I'm more like an old, grumpy pterodactyl. Way too old to be running around like I'm a twenty-something hotshot chasing the bad guys."

My body was sore, and I could definitely use some Ibuprofen, a hot bath, and probably some Icy-Hot at this point.

"I'm feeling it today, too," he said with a smile.

"Sorry," I winced and scrunched my nose.

"Don't be. I would go through heaven and hell to get to you, Quinn. You and Rosie are everything to me, and there's nothing that would ever stop me. Not old age. Not a bad knee. Not even arthritis."

He came around the bed and wrapped me in his arms.

"I haven't had a chance to tell you how much I appreciate what you did—" I started before he lifted a finger to my lips and stopped me.

"You don't need to thank me, Quinn."

His finger fell to the side and gently brushed against my cheek as his lips lowered to mine.

I melted into him, feeling safe in his muscular arms. The kiss was too quick for my liking, but it wasn't like we had total privacy and could trust that Rosie wouldn't walk in on us. The last thing I wanted to do right now was explain my new relationship to her on top of everything else she had going on.

"We don't need to talk about what happened until you're ready," he murmured. "But please don't thank me. I did what I did because I love you, Quinn. More than I ever knew was possible. I love you, and I love Rosie as if she was my own child. It's a weird feeling, one that I wasn't sure I would ever feel, but I promise that I would do anything for that girl."

"I love you too, Roman. We both do. Rosie just adores you," I smiled, looking up into his eyes.

I thought about everything that happened last night and what Julia had confessed. I still had so much anger inside me that I couldn't see straight.

"What's wrong?" Roman asked, lifting my chin with his fingers as he noticed my mood shift.

"Nothing," I lied.

"Quinn…."

I shook my head and inhaled slowly.

"I can't stop thinking about finding Rosie in that room with Julia and Elias. I keep seeing red from the anger that makes me want to rip their heads off and kill them all over again. I know that Rosie is fine, but I can't stop thinking about what would have happened if I hadn't gotten there when I did. This world is a cruel, disgusting place…."

"Look at me," he coaxed, bringing my attention back to him. "Nothing is ever going to happen to her again. Not with two bad-ass old people watching out for her."

I felt my cheeks burn from the stupid smile that stretched across my face at him calling us old. It was true, which only made it even funnier.

"Maybe we should get a logo and start a team of bad-ass old people?" I suggested. "Make it a cool thing."

"Whatever your heart desires," he laughed and kissed my forehead.

<u>Fifty</u>

Roman

"Come on, it can't be that bad," I laughed, watching the scowl etch deeper on Mike's face as he watched Anastasia from across the room.

"She's here ALL. THE. TIME."

"Where else is she supposed to go?"

"I don't know, but I don't see why we have to be stuck in the same room constantly," he growled, shifting his gaze to where she was sitting in the kitchen by the window. "There are multiple rooms in this damn cabin, they could at least put her in another one at night so I don't have to hear her snore."

"Well, given that you both got shot by someone in your own department who tried to take out your entire team, it makes sense that you are both being protected in the same cabin. And since you both need medical attention and there's only one doctor, I imagine that it's a whole lot easier for him to focus when you're both in the same room at night, so he doesn't have to go back and forth throughout the house all night."

"It's not like the wounds are that bad. Her forehead was barely grazed, and the bullet went right through my shoulder. I'll be up and going again in no time."

"Either way, until all agencies have a chance to do their part of the investigation, you guys are stuck here together for a while."

He glared at me and then turned away to watch Rosie play outside.

"How's she doing?" he asked, nodding at her, and effectively changing the subject.

"She seems to be fine," I replied with a shrug. "I don't know that she's really processed what happened. Either that, or she's too young to know what it all means. Quinn's keeping an eye on her, though."

"And how is Quinn doing? She looks tired. Run down."

"She is. She's been through a lot and hearing the things Julia said is going to sit heavily on her mind for a while. But she'll be okay. I'll make sure of it."

He turned and studied me.

"So, this thing with my sister is the real deal?"

I exhaled heavily, my elbows resting on my knees as I thought about the answer. I'd never been a committed relationship kind of guy, and Mike knew that. It wasn't that I didn't want to be that for Quinn, but I didn't know how to talk about it. Mike had been my best friend for as long as I could remember, and this was his sister. It would forever be a line that I would cross as long as Quinn and I were together.

"It's the real deal, man. I love them. I would do anything to protect them."

He leaned back and smiled the first genuine smile I had seen from him in months.

"I'm happy for you," he said. "Just don't break her heart, or I'll break your legs."

"You'd have to catch me first," I joked, knowing neither of us was in any condition to be chasing anyone for a while.

Mike and I sat and talked for a while, bullshitting just like we used to before everything happened. Anastasia was busy with the doctor and stayed out of his way, even though he still groaned and bellyached every time she walked by. He could deny it all he wanted, but Quinn was right—he had a thing for her. The chemistry between them reminded me of what Quinn and I had fought against until we finally gave in.

By dinner, Quinn and Rosie had cooked and made a delicious meal that just happened to be Mike's favorite. I knew that Quinn felt guilty about Mike being shot, even though he told her repeatedly not to. Cooking seemed to be her language of love, which explained the feast before us.

Anastasia had offered to make herself a sandwich and eat outside until Quinn insisted that not only she join us for dinner but that she also sit next to Mike. I knew what she was up to and tried to bite back my laughter when Mike scowled at the suggestion.

"To friends and family," Quinn said, lifting her glass of water in the air. Everyone raised their glasses in response before we dove into the delicious meal in front of us. It felt good to relax and know that there was no longer anything to worry about.

Epilogue
Quinn
4 Weeks Later

"Is all of this stuff going to fit in here?" I asked with my hand on my hip as I looked around at the boxes scattered throughout the room.

"We'll make it," Roman said, slipping his arm around my waist and planting a kiss on my forehead as he walked past me.

I studied all of the boxes, wondering how we had accumulated so much stuff, then remembered that not all of it was ours. Some were Roman's, which made me feel somewhat better. Still, we had a ton of stuff we didn't need, and now was a great time to get rid of it.

"Where do you want us to get started?" my mom asked as she walked through the front door with my sister Sonia.

"You guys didn't have to come help us unpack." I hugged them and looked helplessly at the mess around us.

"I live next door; it's not like I had to go far," my mom laughed. "Plus, we're family, and we help out. Now, where do you want us?"

Roman and I had barely started entertaining the idea of

moving in together when the house next to my mom went up for sale. It was easier than going back and forth between apartments all the time, and Rosie didn't seem to love the constant shuffling about. Not only that, I didn't feel

comfortable in either apartment anymore, and that bothered me more than I was willing to let on.

As soon as my mom mentioned that it was on the market, we didn't waste any time making an offer. Before we knew it, it was ours, and we were moving in. Neither of us had any issues saying goodbye to our apartments and were able to get out of our leases reasonably easily. It was New York City and there were dozens of people looking for a place to live after moving to the big city and chasing after their dreams.

"Well, in that case…." I laughed. "How about the kitchen? All of the boxes are already in there. That way, we have plates to use for dinner tonight."

"We're on it," Sonia assured me with a pat on my back then they disappeared down the hallway to say hello to Rosie, who was busy unpacking her toys. We had already spent the morning getting her room set up so she could have time to play while we did all of the boring stuff.

I started sorting the other boxes into piles based on the rooms they went to. My goal was to set up both bathrooms and the kitchen today, then work on the living room, our bedroom, and the garage tomorrow. Our room had a bed, and that was about it right now, but Roman assured me that we didn't need anything else. He might have also wiggled his eyebrows and hinted at how he couldn't wait to christen the new room once Rosie went over to my mom's for a bit tomorrow so we could work on the final unpacking before going back to work on Monday.

It was wonderful being next to my mom, especially since Rosie was starting summer break this week, and I still had to push my way back into my boss's good graces after missing so much work lately. Luckily, once it was uncovered that Julia had been actively targeting everyone on Justin's team, he eased up some on me. They also found that she had joined the FBI shortly after she met Elias because he wanted someone on the inside to make sure his operation stayed off of the radar. Julia's mom had abandoned her at a young age, and she was easily impressionable, which made it easier for them to pull her into the organization. After her daughter was killed, she went off the deep end and became obsessed with replacing her, no matter the cost.

I had been in therapy for three weeks now, and Rosie was also seeing a therapist twice a week at Roman's encouragement. Even though things had settled down, I found that I had a lot of things that I still needed to process when it came to Justin and the secrets Julia had revealed that I hadn't known about him. Knowing that Rosie would be right next door at my mom's house gave me a sense of security that I hadn't been aware I needed.

The front door opened, and I looked up to find Mike walking in with a shit-eating grin. He had his hands behind his back as he tried to hide something big.

"What are you up to?" I asked, frowning.

"You'll see." He arched a brow and then called for Rosie.

She came bouncing down the hallway a few minutes later, rushing over to him when she stopped and remembered to be gentle with him. His recovery was going well, but he still wasn't 100%.

"Hi, Uncle Mike!" She wrapped her arms around his waist and hugged him.

"Hey, pumpkin butt."

"I don't have a pumpkin butt," she giggled, then looked over her shoulder to check.

He laughed and waited for her to ask what was behind his back. Roman came into the living room and wrapped an arm around my shoulders as my mom and Sonia joined us.

"Why are you standing so funny?" she asked, looking up at him.

"Because I have something special for you," he said, looking from her to me cautiously.

"You do? What is it?"

"Close your eyes."

She did as asked and waited patiently.

Mike brought his hand in front of him and set a small brown dog kennel on the floor.

"Open your eyes," he said.

Her eyes fluttered open, then she looked from him to the floor and jumped back.

"Is that what I think it is?"

Her voice was small and squeaky, eyes wide as she watched him.

"Why don't you check and see?"

Slowly she kneeled down and peered inside. She looked back up at him for approval before turning the lock and opening the door.

A tiny brown and white dog came bouncing out and into her arms. She picked it up and held it against her chest as the puppy excitedly licked her face.

"A puppy?!"

I raised a brow and pretended to be mad at him. The truth was that I wasn't. Roman and I had talked about getting a dog for Rosie since she had wanted one so badly before everything happened. He shrugged and looked sheepishly down at the floor. I knew my brother well enough to know that he was likely beating himself up now and second-guessing whether he had overstepped by getting her a dog without asking us first.

"What are you going to name it?" I asked, looking from Mike down to Rosie.

She pulled it away from her body and looked to see if it was a boy or a girl.

"This is Honey," she said, then lifted the dog to her face and kissed its nose.

"Welcome to the family, Honey," I said, feeling Roman's fingers as they held me a little tighter.

My life had changed a lot in a very short time, but I could finally say that for once, I was happy and exactly where I wanted to be. I had a man who loved me, a daughter who lit up my world, and now a puppy that was peeing on our brand-new rug. Life couldn't get any better than this.

Other Books By Samantha Baca

The Haven Brook Series

(small-town romantic suspense):

'Til Death Do Us Part (Haven Brook Book 1)

https://books2read.com/u/m2RJNR

The Cradle Will Fall (Haven Brook Book 2)

https://books2read.com/u/b6O0QE

The Ties That Bind (Haven Brook Book 3)

https://books2read.com/u/mqgoz8

A Very Haven Christmas (Haven Brook Book 4- Novella)

https://books2read.com/u/mvqGjj

Three Strikes, You're Gone (Haven Brook Book 5)

https://books2read.com/u/mvqL2z

The Dark Shadows Trilogy

(romantic suspense)

Five Steps Ahead (Dark Shadows Book 1)

https://books2read.com/u/38Q0gO

Ten Seconds Too Late (Dark Shadows Book 2)

https://books2read.com/u/3JRgVB

Against The Clock (Dark Shadows Book 3)

https://books2read.com/u/m2YwoR

<u>The Stone Creek Series</u>
<u>(small-town- novellas)</u>

Chocolate Covered Mistletoe (Stone Creek Book 1)

https://books2read.com/u/3LRk9N

Candy Coated Promises (Stone Creek Book 2)

https://books2read.com/u/mldP5Y

Pumpkin Spiced Possibilities (Stone Creek Book 3)

https://books2read.com/u/bojdwV

<u>Beaumont Creek Series</u>

<u>(small town)</u>

Just One Time (Beaumont Creek Book 1)

https://books2read.com/u/3G52zK

Second Chances (Beaumont Creek Book 2)

https://books2read.com/u/4Aj6Z0

Third Time's The Charm (Beaumont Creek Book 3)

https://books2read.com/u/b5lEyG

Four-ever Single (Beaumont Creek Book 4)

https://books2read.com/u/4j5jMX

Fifth Wheel (Beaumont Creek Book 5)

https://books2read.com/u/4XwKwa

Whiskey Mountain Series
(small-town- novellas)

Something To Talk About

https://books2read.com/u/4X62ag

Something To Think About

https://books2read.com/u/3GWAan

Something To Believe In

https://books2read.com/u/3yVzgB

Something To Live For

https://books2read.com/u/mllEOP

Sugarplum Falls Series
(Holiday Novellas- can be read as standalone)

Blame It On The Mistletoe

https://books2read.com/u/bw1rqe

Blame It On The Eggnog

https://books2read.com/u/38PPY6

Blame It On The Candy Canes

https://books2read.com/u/31DNo7

Blame It On The Blizzard

https://books2read.com/u/b6z6XE

<u>Standalone Books</u>

One Last Wish

https://books2read.com/u/mqg7D9

Finding Love In Apartment 2C (novella)

https://books2read.com/u/bze9aZ

Cocky Counsel: A Hero Club Novel

https://books2read.com/u/31Kzkn

All Is Fair In Food And War (novella)

https://books2read.com/u/bp8qjX

<u>Holiday Books</u>
<u>(novellas)</u>

Snow Place To Go

https://books2read.com/u/4A560N

A Christmas Wish

https://books2read.com/u/4EKXpE

Holiday Hijinks

https://books2read.com/u/4DP6Ze

About the Author

Samantha lives in the southwest with her husband and two small children after abandoning her childhood dream of living in a cabin in Colorado when she found that she couldn't afford to live there and was deathly allergic to the woods. When she's not writing, she's usually spouting off sarcastic remarks while drinking wine out of a coffee mug to look like a functional adult while chasing down her toddlers. She enjoys spending time with her family, watching reruns of Friends, and the 24/7 flow of coffee that can be found in her veins. Be sure to follow her on social media for updates on what she's working on.

You can find her here:

Facebook: https://www.facebook.com/AuthorSamanthaBaca

Instagram: https://instagram.com/author_samantha_baca

Goodreads: http://www.goodreads.com/authorsamanthabaca

Facebook Reader Group:
https://www.facebook.com/groups/2945710968775398/

Webpage: https://authorsamanthabaca.wordpress.com

Newsletter: http://eepurl.com/g0NcSj

www.ingramcontent.com/pod-product-compliance
Lightning Source LLC
Chambersburg PA
CBHW061846310726
48972CB00004B/907